THE GREAT ESCAPEE SERIES BOX SET

BOOKS 1-3

BONNIE LACY

FROSTING ON THE CAKE PRODUCTIONS

RELEASED

THE GREAT ESCAPEE SERIES

Thanks:

To God. He is my Inspiration, my Source.

*To my Dearly Beloved for believing in me and
providing for me so I could play.*

*To my precious family for believing in me
and encouraging me.*

*"The Spirit of the Lord is upon me, because the Lord has anointed and
qualified me to preach the Gospel of good tidings to the meek, the poor,
and afflicted; He has sent me to bind up the heal the brokenhearted, to
proclaim liberty to the [physical and spiritual] captives and the
opening of the prison and of the eyes to those who are bound," Isaiah
61:1 Amplified Bible*

*"A curmudgeonly ex-con senior citizen, a little girl named Bea, and
her addict mother. An unlikely trio crosses paths on the road to
redemption from their pasts in small town Nebraska—with a little help
from above. With true-to-life grit and characters you love to love (and
some you love to hate), RELEASED is a fresh slice of hope in a world
of injured souls."*

—Tosca Lee, NYT bestselling author of Progeny

CHAPTER 1

"I ought to sue you! I can, you know!" Clarence Timmelsen screamed at the warden. He stiffened and shuddered. Tears of rage stung his eyes. "You're kicking me out of prison to send me to a nursing home?" He shook his fist and growled, "I'm gonna sue your ass!"

The warden hung his head as the cell door clanged shut behind him. He turned to face Clarence through the bars, buttoning his black suit, his back rigid, emphasizing each word. "I'm sorry you feel that way. I have no control over the matter." Then he added, "It'll be better for you in the long run."

Clarence rushed the cell bars, white-knuckle-gripped them and glared into the warden's eyes. "In the long run? You mean till I die. That's what you mean. You're just kicking me out to get rid of me." His voice broke. "This is my home!"

He jerked away, but not before catching sight of inmates gathered behind the bars of each cell near his, across the commons area, upper and lower level. All staring. "What are you looking at?" Clarence bellowed. His deep gravelly voice ricocheted off the wall of the cell-block canyon.

The warden tapped his foot. "Good-bye, Clarence. I've known you a long time." He checked his watch. "All the wardens before me knew it would come to this." He cleared his throat. "Unfortunately, I'm the one on watch to carry out this final demand set forth in your proceedings by your judge."

Clarence stared at the warden. Ice shards crackled in his veins, just like when he'd heard the word "guilty" sixty years ago. "You mean that bastard judge set this up? Clear back then?" The mental visual of the judge's eyes burning with malice and the sharp rap of the gavel invaded his memory again, just as it had every day of every year since then.

The warden slowly nodded and stepped away from the bars.

Clarence stumbled. He knew his eyes betrayed anguish as he stared at the warden. He gripped the bars, threw his head back and roared like a wounded, trapped lion.

Silence echoed off the entire cell block until someone in the next cell snickered.

Clarence slowly rotated his head, following the sound. His eyes met Barred's. The rookie. Behind the rookie stood Dirk, the huge professional inmate.

Clarence locked eyes with Dirk.

Barred snickered again. "Ooo, the little ol' ladies'll like you." Another snicker. "You're f—"

Dirk rose up behind Barred, drew his fist back and pummeled him. Clarence held his breath. Dirk finally stopped, and the rookie crunched onto the concrete floor.

Three guards raced past the warden, sticks poised.

Keys rattled. Handcuffs clicked.

One guard pushed Dirk past Clarence's cell. The guard shook his head. "Stupid, stupid Dorko."

The inmate towered over the guard. "M'name's Dirk." A toothless grin spread across his face. "I got yur back, Clarence. See ya on the—"

The officer yanked on the cuffs and dragged Dirk past the cell.

Clarence's eyes shifted back to the warden's face. Old people's home. Wheelchairs lined up in rows. Vacant eyes. People forgotten.

The guards dragged an unconscious Barred past—one eye already swollen shut and purple. His slack jaw trailed blood.

Randy Gerald stepped over the trickle of blood and stood before the cell door. "Clarence." He dipped his head in greeting, smoothing a drab brown uniform over his big belly. He picked at a dark spot on his shirt. Looked like chocolate pudding. He lifted his head, his eyes direct. "I'm here to escort you to your new home."

Clarence glowered.

Randy adjusted his pants. Keys jingled from his belt. "We better get a move on. We have a long drive ahead of us."

Clarence braced himself.

"We can make this easy or hard—you choose," Randy said, hand on his gun. He turned toward the central station and waved at the guard. "You can open."

"Sure thing, Sir," blared the overhead speakers.

The lock on the cell door echoed as it unlatched.

Randy entered the cell and tossed a flimsy shopping bag onto the cot.

Clarence stared at him a long time. At the warden even longer.

His thoughts spun in a million directions: stay in prison, die, maim the warden, escape. None landed on the option facing him right now— a nursing home—his final resting place.

Maybe it was his age, or being caught in a new and unexpected situation, or both, but he wanted to bust out bawling. Only once before in his life had he felt this helpless.

He stepped to the lavatory, intending to gather his belongings, but became distracted by the image in the mirror: steel gray hair combed back from his forehead and falling in waves to a black T shirt, a full beard mostly obscuring a deep scar on his right cheek, blue eyes glaring at him, and wrinkles in places he didn't remember. Memories floated between reality in the mirror and the image of a much younger man, his hopes and dreams not yet shattered by life. The memories stirred emotion buried deep. Emotion Clarence long ago had declared not worth the pain and horror of digging up. So it had remained entombed, sealed with a capstone.

Until now.

"You ready to go, Clarence? Chicago traffic will be fierce this time of day."

Clarence swallowed, smoothed his old wool flap hat over his hair and donned his light tan jacket. He carefully pulled on his gloves and picked up the bag, gathering what was left of a toothpaste tube, the rest of his toiletries, his brush.

He scanned the cell one last time. Each cold concrete block, every crack, the stained out-in-the-open facilities, and the blue-white light overhead. It had held the years of his life, since …

Clarence stepped to the cot, reached under the mattress and removed a folder. He stuffed it into the bag.

He turned to exit the cell only to face three beat sticks in his face.

"Really?" His face burned, his chin jutted. "It's been there sixty years, already."

The warden shoved around the guards, holding his hand out, fingers beckoning. "Come on. Hand it over."

Clarence's nostrils flared as he reached into the bag and produced the folder. The warden opened it, revealing paperwork, yellowed newspaper clippings and an old picture of a young woman.

Another growl rose up in Clarence's throat. He wiped perspiration off his upper lip. The warden picked up the picture and studied it a long time. He slowly met Clarence's eyes, eyebrows lifted.

Clarence raised his head, shoulders back. He looked him square in the face.

The warden squinted and pursed his lips, but carefully replaced the picture, closed the folder and held it out to Clarence.

Guards backed down, beat sticks replaced at their belts.

"Let's make our way out of here, shall we?" Randy stood aside to let Clarence through.

Clarence stepped onto the walkway overlooking the cellblock and froze. Inmates stood inside each cell across from his, both upper and lower levels, pounding on cell bars, stomping on the floors. Some saluted as he glanced their way. Inmates, security guards, administrators, and board members lined the way out.

He swallowed, his jaw clenched. His lower lip threatened to quiver.

He squinted down the long line of people, then back at Randy. "Let's make this fast, huh?"

"Yes, Sir." Randy caught hold of his bag and led him down the walkway.

Sir. Had a guard ever called him "sir" before today?

As Clarence followed, an image of the train station sixty years ago assaulted reality. People had lined the boardwalk then, as they now lined the walkway. His white-haired preacher from back then appeared, shaking his head, judging from across time.

Randy glanced over his shoulder and hesitated. "You coming?"

Clarence hung his head and nodded. He waited with Randy at a heavy windowed door while the security officer gave the okay and the lock release buzzed. The door slid open, and as it did, his neighborhood paper boy appeared from the past—*the* edition of the newspaper crumpled in his hand.

Randy stepped aside to let Clarence through the door.

Clarence shuddered. He couldn't help turning to look back into the cellblock. An inmate paced behind the bars of one cell. His hand rapped against the bars, third finger of his other hand raised in salute, eyes burned into Clarence's.

Clarence shivered. A lot of men in this prison owed him legal favors, but not everybody was going to miss him.

Randy checked his watch.

Clarence nodded.

A young woman rushed to his side, still in her dietary uniform, and touched his arm. "Sir, good luck." She swallowed. "With your life." She brought something from behind her back. "I made you this. I hope it's okay. I mean, I hope you can use it." She practically curtsied and pressed a beautiful knitted scarf into his hands, all blues and greens with a scratchy brown fringe.

He stopped once more and bowed his head. Another vision popped before him—his old neighbor lady. Eyes expressed pain she felt for him, what her mouth could never say. Hand extended with a plate of cookies he couldn't take.

Randy pushed through the door.

Clarence sucked in a breath against the chilly air. A van waited at the curb. Brown, barren land stretched behind it.

One last person from his past appeared next to the van: Judge Green glared him down. He had gleefully and vengefully sentenced him here. Clarence spat and yelled, "I hope you're long dead, you old bastard! Rotting in hell!"

He stumbled, braced his hands against the doorway and backed into a guard.

Randy turned. "Hey buddy. Don't. Don't do that. Don't make this hard."

Clarence struggled against the guards surrounding him, growled, punched and pushed away from Randy.

"God, he's strong. Do we cuff him?"

Clarence snarled and spat as they each took a limb and hoisted him off the ground, through the door, down the sidewalk.

"Don't hurt him. He's eighty years old. Careful."

"Are you kidding? He's a wild man."

Clarence struggled until he could fight no longer and shuddered a sob as the van loomed closer.

CHAPTER 2

The drone of the van's engine elevated Clarence's rage to explosion point. His knuckles turned white against the restraints. Kill mode.

The van pulled away from the prison. He yanked at the shackles encasing his wrists and ankles. Even Dirk couldn't have pulled out of these.

He scanned the inside of the van. Clean. Except for his bag. Socks, underwear, a change of clothes—courtesy of the prison. All he had in the world was in that bag.

He winced, remembering the last moments in prison. Tears threatened to break from his eyes as he squeezed them shut. He blew out a deep breath and shook his head.

"Clarence." Randy pulled into a gas station and shut off the engine. "We're gonna fill up."

"Why is it taking so long? We passed three old people's homes just now." Clarence leaned forward. "Where are we going?"

Randy glanced at Clarence in the rearview mirror. "They didn't tell you? Your hometown. Osceola, Nebraska." He pulled a credit card from his wallet. "That's why it's so far. Chicago to Osceola. I thought you knew."

Clarence stopped breathing. He gasped.

Randy hopped out, swiped his card on the pump and started gassing up. He walked around the front of the van.

Clarence bounced back and forth on the bench seat, fingers stretched out. "No! No! Not Osceola!"

The side door opened. "Sorry about the shackles. But man, you're strong. You gave us no choice." Randy reached down to unlock an ankle.

"Not Osceola. I can't go back there."

"Easy." Randy straightened and tilted his head, hand on his thigh. "It's your hometown."

"I can't go back there," Clarence said. "Those people there … they're the reason I got stuck in prison in the first place."

"I'm surprised they didn't tell you." He bent again to undo a buckle.

Clarence tensed. Poised.

Randy hesitated, grimaced and looked up at Clarence. "You're not. Not again. Listen, Clarence, I've known you a long time. Longer than most of the inmates and staff. You can either ride here like an animal— all locked up—or act like a mature … "

Clarence flinched.

Randy flexed his arm muscles, his hands still on the shackles, brown eyes snapping. "Yeah, you're eighty. Act your age. Or at least act like someone … never mind. Nobody in that prison back there acts like they have any brains. Including you." Randy stepped back and slammed the door.

"No. No. Please." Clarence hung his head. He locked eyes with Randy through the window.

Randy crossed his arms across his chest, his eyes piercing. He finally opened the door. "What'd you say?"

"I said please," Clarence whispered.

Randy raised his head, eyes squinted. He slowly climbed in the van. "Just one stupid—"

"There won't be any."

Randy held his stance.

Clarence focused on the shackles. "I mean it. I'm done." He held his breath, braced himself as Randy bent and unlocked one ankle.

Clarence kicked him in the shin. "Not Osceola!"

"Aggh. Fool! You … are not only stupid … but a liar." Randy struggled to grab Clarence's leg. He whipped his stick around, delivered a blow to Clarence's knee and locked him in.

"Ow. Ow. You f-n asshole."

Randy slammed the door so hard it shook the van. He limped to the gas pump and rubbed his shin.

Clarence fumed and cussed. He rocked the van right and left, against the restraints.

Randy kicked the tires and pounded on the van. The gas pump clicked off. He replaced the nozzle and jumped back in. Started up the van and squealed into traffic.

Randy's eyes bored straight ahead, face beet-red. He glanced back at Clarence through the mirror. "You can make this easy, Clarence," Randy yelled, "or make it hard. You decide. Either way, I am delivering you to that nursing home and leaving you there and you don't have a thing to say about it."

Clarence hung his head and could just barely reach his knee with his fingers. "I don't want to go back there."

"What'd you say?"

"Nothin. Nothing at all," he muttered. He stared out the window, then closed his eyes.

Memories flashed.

He sat in the backseat of Sheriff Faeller's 1950 Ford Fairlane patrol car.

Shackles then.

Shackles …

He jolted awake and blinked. Green lawns beautifully manicured in better subdivisions. Church steeples. He closed his eyes again.

"Damn!" Randy cursed and slammed on the brakes. "Sorry, Clarence. Sorry to wake you. Traffic is terrible."

Car dealerships—rows and rows of cars lined the concrete.

Hotels, construction, truck stops.

Then fields. Brown grass, trees whipped bare of leaves that scattered around the corners of farm buildings and houses.

All a blur.

Clarence opened his eyes, feeling the van stop again. He stared at a sign introducing the kingdom of fast food. A statue of a man with red hair and clown costume greeted him with a grand wave. Cars filled the parking lot. Kids bounced in a play area, scooting down a ceiling to floor slide—round and round.

Randy peered into the rear view mirror. "Gonna buy a little food." He shifted into park and stared at Clarence in the mirror. "I'm gonna give you a choice. Shackles or no shackles. You decide."

Clarence growled and straightened, leaned forward.

"I mean it, Clarence." He pointed to the building. "This is a public place. Little kids. Mommies. Real people. If you aren't gonna behave, you can stay in here, and I'll bring you food." Randy looked out the window. "If you have to use the bathroom, then it's shackles."

Clarence glanced outside, then back at Randy. "I'm not a total jerk."

"Prove it."

Clarence's stomach tightened. "I'll behave."

"I didn't hear you."

Clarence cleared his throat. "I said, I'll behave. I'll do whatever you say." He looked into the rearview mirror. "I give you my word."

Randy stared back, one eyebrow cocked for a full minute. He stared into the restaurant until Clarence thought he'd fallen asleep. He slowly opened his door, then the side door and unlocked each shackle, all without a word. Then stood next to the van. "I think you know the procedure. No—"

"I gave you my word." Clarence stared him down.

Randy nodded, then motioned for Clarence to climb out. He held the door open as Clarence slid to the edge of the seat.

"What do you want to eat? Burger, fries, pop? My treat."

Clarence raised his bushy eyebrows.

"No government funds today. I want to buy you lunch."

"Yeah, burger, fries—whatever you said." Clarence shoved out of the van and tested his legs, his hand still on the door handle.

A man and woman squeezed past him between a car and the van.

A little boy about eight years old, followed by a man, bumped into Clarence. "S'cuze me." High-pitched voice with a lisp. Hair sticking up on top. Carrying a small flat device.

Clarence watched him. So little.

People walked into the building as others exited—carrying bags of food and sodas. No prison jumpsuits. No handcuffs. All free.

He led up the sidewalk and into the restaurant.

"Got a little limp there, Clarence?"

"Nah, just need to stretch my legs."

Inside, voices echoed off the walls. Children shrieked and laughed as they romped in the play area. Bright colors startled him. A sickening mix of hamburgers, fries, and old grease combined to make his already agitated stomach lurch.

He rotated, totally overwhelmed, when it hit him—he was free. But free to do what? He scanned his possibilities. Free to go where?

He found the restroom, rushed into a stall, and the power of that thought overwhelmed him. "Oh God, let me die in here."

Trash littering the floor and missed shots on the toilet made him change his mind. "This is worse than prison."

He finished his business and limped into the restaurant.

Randy waited for him in a booth close by. The table was spread with a fast food smorgasbord—giant drinks, boxes of fries, wrapped burgers, and single serve pies.

Clarence stood over the table, clenching his fists, stomach churning.

Randy looked up, a fry dangling out of his mouth. He chewed it in. "What? You gonna run away?" He pushed at Clarence's food. "Sit, Clarence. This'll work out. You'll see."

Clarence stood firm.

Randy patted the table.

Clarence sat, coat still buttoned, new scarf wound around his neck and stared at the food. He raised his eyes to Randy's. "So this is fast food. Kinda like prison food."

Randy choked, covered his mouth with a napkin, then laughed out loud. "Yeah, I guess it is. I should have gotten you the kids meal. You get a toy with that. Kinda makes the food taste better." He jumped up. "I'll get you one." He raced off.

Clarence picked up a fry and took a bite, watching Randy return with the kid's meal. "Thanks for … this."

Randy laughed out loud again. "Guess I should have bought you a steak and all the trimmings, huh. Go ahead. Open it."

Clarence read the games on the box then flipped it open. He looked up at Randy. "There's food in here. Kinda like a lunch box." He drew out a cellophane bag. "This the toy?" He held it up. "What is it?"

Randy grinned. "Well, it's … I don't know. It's a toy."

Clarence set it down and unwrapped the mini-burger. He took a bite. "It does taste better."

"Told you." He smiled and studied Clarence's face for a minute. "I get why you acted out back there, I think. This can't be easy. You've done more than your time. Fifty—what—sixty years?"

"Sixty. Every board turned me down for parole. Every one of those bastards."

"You deserve a chance at some life outside."

"I don't deserve anything." He lifted the little burger to his mouth, but put it down, without taking another bite.

"Still carrying the guilt around?" Randy tapped a fry against the container. "You paid your dues, man. No early parole? And look what you accomplished in prison—getting your law degree and all—hell, that's a lot more than I've done with my life and I've been on the outside. You've helped a lot of people."

Clarence's eyes stung with tears he wouldn't let fall. "If you only knew." He picked up his hamburger and bit into it, squeezing mustard, ketchup and onion bits out onto the wrapper. His vision blurred as he fumbled for his napkin and wiped his chin, but not his eyes.

Not here.

Not anywhere.

Not ever.

He hadn't cried yet. All these years. Not once. And he wouldn't start now.

Randy dripped ketchup onto the front of his uniform. It landed right next to the pudding stain on his mountain of a stomach. He chattered on, oblivious.

As Clarence continued to glare, a mass of reddish-blond ringlets rose just above the back of Randy's booth seat. That's all Clarence could see.

"So, you can understand why … ," Randy continued.

Clarence leaned closer to Randy but let his line of sight drift to the hair. Then to Randy. Clarence nodded and nibbled on his sandwich.

Slowly the curls lifted higher, shadowing clear smooth skin.

Something stirred in Clarence—something he hadn't felt for so long—something like humor, laughter. Joy.

Randy reached for the pies. "Apple or cherry?" He held them out to Clarence.

Clarence shrugged.

"Okay. I'll take cherry." He shoved the apple pie to Clarence. "We should have it figured out by then, but …"

Eyes appeared, shining clear blue and full of mischief. The child hid her face in her arms then peeked up with a shy grin.

Clarence shivered. She reminded him of someone. He looked away, out the window.

Someone long ago.

"You're not eating, Clarence. Finish up and we'll be on our way. We still have a long road to go."

Clarence folded the meal into the wrapper and dumped it onto the tray.

Randy glanced up. "Something I said?"

Clarence slid over to the edge of the bench and pushed himself up.

Randy blinked. "Uh … I guess we're ready. Hey, thanks for listening."

Clarence frowned. "What?"

"Thanks for letting me rant. You've been there. You know how it is. You have a perspective on it that most don't." Randy pushed the table away, gathered up his trash and slid out of the booth. "And now you're free."

Clarence scowled at Randy and turned away. Free? No. He was headed for a nursing home. Just another prison.

"Uh, I'll hit the head." Randy stopped. "You'll be here when I come back."

Clarence watched him walk away and stepped past the child's booth.

No child.

He looked up and down the aisle. He bent and searched under the table. Only a tiny mitten remained.

He stretched to pick it up. As he lifted it to his face, he caught a whiff of something so fresh, so real, it expanded him into another realm. Another dimension. His feet still planted on earthly soil, but for nanoseconds, his mind and emotions were drawn to another place.

Goosebumps.

Until Randy tapped him on the shoulder. He was buttoning a plaid shirt and carrying a satchel.

"Where's your uniform?"

"Figured I'd change shirts before we got to the nursing home." Randy shrugged. "They don't need to know you came from prison."

Fair enough. Clarence stuffed the mitten into his pocket and placed the kids meal toy on the table.

Outside, as they walked to the van, a hawk circled high above, screeched as it hovered, floated down to the next air current, then soared high.

Freedom.

Clarence followed it with his eyes as he slumped against the van, waiting for Randy to unlock. He climbed onto the front passenger seat, the hollow slam of the door adding the final note to the day.

Locked away.

Free for a minute.

Then bound forever.

"Never look back," he whispered. He wound the scarf around his neck, buttoned the top of his coat, then grasped the brim of his hat.

CHAPTER 3

Katty Randolph floated into consciousness, hovering between drunken stupor and awareness of something terribly off.

She groaned. Someone had to be holding her head down. Little men with jackhammers pounded inside, even when she told them to stop in no uncertain words. Exhausted, her head fell back onto hard, packed ground.

Something licked her calf. Sandpaper would have felt better. She kicked at whatever it was. A startled and indignant snarl sent shivers up her body.

Her eyes wouldn't adjust; the visuals that reached her brain made no sense. Blocks of color bounced off the backs of her eyes. Movement tracked back and forth until she slammed them shut, her stomach threatening to hurl.

She floated back to stupor.

Katty opened her eyes again, and sunlight burned into her eyeballs. Her eyes wouldn't stay open. An awful roar assaulted her ears. Her hands flitted from rubbing her forehead to covering her ears, her watering eyes, and back to her ears again.

Waves of dizziness spiked as she raised her throbbing head too fast.

Her stomach revolted, and up came too much pizza and too many rounds, the glory of her Bar Queen status tarnished. She moaned and rolled herself into a ball.

A low growl grew louder, making her skin crawl with goosebumps. She cracked her eyes open again.

A monstrous dog house kingdom, surrounded by a crumpling fence, ruled over by a scarred and dozing dog, one eye open. He appeared more alert each time Katty looked in his direction.

Shuddering, she pulled at grass and weeds—anything—trying to hide. The roar in her ears stopped and the silence was broken by a man's deep laughter. "Hey Harriet. It moved. It's not dead, so we won't have to bury it. And it's naked!"

The last word ripped through her.

She squinted an eye open and peered through her fingers. All she had on were her favorite striped socks.

A sweaty mountain of a man in the next yard grinned. He raised his chain saw high above his head and pulled the cord.

The sound pierced her head, her body. Every nerve jangled in pain. She struggled and inched toward the house, egged on by coarse laughter.

"Lookit. It moved again. Nice socks." His laughter was joined by a guttural phlegmy cackle.

The dog king growled along with the laughter. A chain clinked as the dog stood, stretched and poised. The stretch was by no means relaxed but preparation for battle.

Katty shifted, breathing faster.

The snarling dog made a flying leap toward her, transforming into a huge lion, jaws open, fangs dripping, teeth snapping. It morphed again, yelping, as it jerked to the end of a log chain, inches from her feet.

Katty screamed, crouched. Scrambling toward the house, she slipped in mud.

"It speaks." More cackles. "Oh, no. It got its socks muddy." Raucous laughter.

Sobbing, she made a drunken beeline for the backdoor of the drug house. She covered her chest with one hand and reached up for the door handle, still crouching, her backside to the audience.

Laughter accompanied her escape. "Oh, no. Show's almost over." The saw ripped a final horror into Katty's soul. "But, we could start a new show." The saw revved, sending tremors through her body as she fell head first inside the door.

CHAPTER 4

The moment Clarence walked through the entrance of Hillcrest Homes, he flipped the emotion switch off. After sixty years in prison, he had that mastered.

He shoved pain and guilt deep, buried beneath daily grind.

But memory wouldn't stay down.

His dad, Dawes Timmelsen, had never missed a day of the trial and his carpentry business had suffered. His voice broke the day the sheriff and deputies transported Clarence to prison: "Son, no matter what, I love you. Be strong."

Clarence still felt Dad's fingers digging into his shoulders as deputies pried him from his father's arms. His father's face haunted him, pain carved in every line.

That was the last time he had seen his dad.

His first day in prison had assaulted every sense. Musty, rancid odors. Harsh cleansers unable to mask the smells of evil and hatred. Malodorous sewage smells. Hardened eyes staring him down. The sounds of humanity, of a community galaxies apart from where he grew up, were shocking, foul. But at the same time, complete with its own standards, right or wrong.

All had assaulted the newest arrival, with grief and pain his closest allies.

The nursing home's odor had its own unique qualities. Layers of cooking odors lingered, nearly dead floral arrangements rotted in foul water, and harsh cleaning and medicinal smells twisted into his senses, making his fast food lunch, already churning in his stomach, lurch as he followed Randy into the facility.

Old faces blended into no one.

A housekeeper rested on her mop, a slight smile bending her lips, warmth in her eyes.

Clarence looked away.

The pain then.

The pain now.

Always this brick of torment in his belly.

An abandoned walker stood outside a door, tennis balls protecting its feet. Another reminder that this was the end of the line.

Hydraulic body lifts blocked the hall.

Beds with railings.

Oxygen tanks.

Wheelchairs.

Each time Clarence avoided one visual, his eyes bumped into another. His body temperature boiled.

All logged in his memory to assault him later. All became a constant blur. He was trapped into this next stretch, this last duration of life.

"Hey, Clarence." Randy broke in. "This is cool. They have a pool table." He patted Clarence's arm. "You gotta get your own stick, man. And look. An ice cream machine. We need to get one of those for the pri—"

Clarence jerked around and glared at him.

A tall shapely woman in her fifties walked up behind Randy and leaned around him, waving. "And you are Mr. Timmelsen, I presume."

"Clarence."

"Okay … Clarence." She stepped beside Randy, and extended a

slender hand, fingernails painted bright red. "I'm Miss Henningway, the administrator here at Hillcrest Homes." Her reddish-blond hair was cut in the latest swoop-over-one-eye style, her make-up precisely overdone.

Clarence stared at her hand.

Randy cleared his throat.

When Clarence didn't offer his, Miss Henningway smoothed her hand over her hair, then picked at a nonexistent spot on her tight black skirt.

Clarence smirked. "This the way to my room?"

"Well, uh, I was going to give you the tour." She brightened. "The million dollar tour of our humble home."

"Our humble home. This isn't where you live."

"No ... but—"

"Well, show me around. Let's get this over with."

She began an obviously practiced speech in what had to be her best tour bus voice. "Welcome to Hillcrest Homes! I am Miss Henningway—"

"You said that."

"Well, um ... yes, and ...." She trailed off and mumbled under her breath. "Welcome to ... I am Miss ... oh yes!" She placed her hands on her heart. "We are so glad to have you, Mr. Timmelsen."

"Clarence. Just Clarence." He stared, seeing not only her female torso and hefty chest, but in his imagination she became the enemy, cloaked in a demon suit, with horns, tail, and spear, complete with glasses. Satan would be proud.

"Uh, yes. Clarence. Come with me, both of you. I'll show you around." She hesitated and pointed at him, squinting. "You're a lawyer, aren't you? I read that in your file, I think." She patted her hair. "You could be our benefactor, what with your background and influence." She beamed and fluttered her eyes over designer glasses. "We could sure use your ... expertise, Mr. uh ... Clarence."

He snorted and beamed sarcastically back. "I'm sure you could, especially my influence. I'd be happy to offer it sometime, if I wasn't so busy."

Randy leaned in beside him, hand placed under his arm. "Easy, Cowboy."

Miss Henningway blinked, cleared her throat and slipped a small post-it from her pocket. She scanned it, tucked her arm under Clarence's and began to drag him along. "Okay." She cleared her throat again, poised her feet together and recited, "We are a Christian facility, providing care for all people—all walks of life and abilities. From people who can live on their own, to the elder … uh—"

"Yeah, the old and unwanted," Clarence growled and pulled away from her.

She continued, as if on her own planet. "We provide all forms of care for those patrons and residents who can't take care of themselves." She waved and greeted a man in a wheelchair, as they passed. "People are friendly here."

To Clarence's amusement, the man didn't look up or acknowledge her.

She paused then pushed a door wide open. "We have a state-of-the-art kitchen."

Clarence and Randy stepped inside.

Two dietary employees froze. One—her hand raised above her head, gripped a head of cabbage; the other—crouched low, his hands cupped.

Clarence took the stance and held out his hands. "Here. Throw it here."

Red-faced, they turned their backs, knives chattering, sending cabbage chunks flying into huge bowls and onto the floor.

Miss Henningway twitched her pursed lips back and forth. Veins in her neck pumped. She backed out of the kitchen and began again. "And this is our beautiful dining room." She practically danced, patting Clarence's arm. "Notice our new flooring. It's smooth and trouble free for wheelchair riders." She tapped a foot.

"Wheelchair riders?" Clarence rolled his eyes. He skirted around her.

Randy poked him.

She continued to tap her foot, looking Clarence up and down. "You're tall for your age."

"What?" Clarence stuttered. "Why'd you say that?"

"Well, most men your age have had some loss of height. You are in ama-a-zing shape."

Clarence looked at Randy, then at her. What the hell?

She moved on. "Our living rooms are newly remodeled, also. New sofas, chairs, drapes, carpeting. The works. All the latest home designs." She paused.

"Oh, you want applause?" Clarence obliged with one loud clap.

Miss Henningway frowned. She sucked in a deep breath and blew it out through her teeth. After a short moment, the fake smile reappeared and she turned. "Shall we?" She directed them to a large community room, equipped with tables, chairs and a kitchenette. Residents were gathering in wheelchairs and walkers. A wonderful aroma wafted from the oven.

"We have a baking class once a week. Oh my, the cookies they bake in there." She patted her tummy tires, blushing. "But activities here are not just for women. They're for everyone." She indicated the pool table, leaning on it in a swoon, but slid along the edge into Clarence.

Only he saw it coming and sidestepped her.

Randy jumped to catch her as Clarence turned away, muffling a snort.

"Are you all right?" Randy helped her get her balance. "You must have tripped with those heels." He cleared his throat. "Or something."

Clarence walked on and passed an old man standing in a doorway.

The man was leaning on a walker, chewing on his words. "Another one bites the dust."

Old bastard.

A TV game show host blared behind him, "You have just won a trip to Timbuktu—all expenses paid."

The man raised an eyebrow. His mouth curved at one end.

Clarence glared at him.

"Harold, don't you have somewhere to be?" said Miss Henningway, stepping between them. "Baking perhaps?"

"Nope, I'm stayin' right here." His eyes never left Clarence's.

Standoff.

Still staring at Harold, Clarence shuffled from one foot to the other, his inner furnace boiling, his fists clenched at his sides. Miss Henningway tugged on his sleeve, dragging him along beside her.

Clarence pulled his sleeve away.

She motioned to another door. "Here we have the spa room, warm and cozy. All new tiles and wallpaper border. A wonderful new jacuzzi, complete with water jets and whirlpools—" She swung the door open to reveal a huge walk-in tub, filled to the top with sudsy water, steam curling around an obese woman who sat in the tub scrubbing her red face.

The woman looked up, washcloth in hand, water streaming down her arm. "Eek!" She flopped both arms, sending water flowing over the sides like a stormy sea, splashing onto the tile floor.

A nurse rushed to her with a towel, covering her ample chest, then slammed the door in their faces. But not before giving Miss Henningway a dirty look. "Do you know how to knock?"

Clarence burst out laughing. "Bonus tour."

Miss Henningway stood in place, eyes piercing holes through the door.

Randy coughed. "Mind if we keep this going? I've got to drive all the way back to Chicago tonight."

Miss Henningway puffed out her cheeks, and just as quickly, turned and smiled a last stilted smile. "Well, here we are." Having reached the hall's far end, she marched into a bedroom and swept out her arm, presenting the room as if it were a deluxe suite in a fine hotel, complete with amenities and a view. "You have a window facing … the parking lot so … you can see the comings and goings. And you get wonderful sunshine." She paused for effect and pointed to the wall. "Also, your own picture of our Savior, Jesus Christ the Lord."

Clarence almost flipped the emotion switch to full on anger. "Yay.

Where has He been the last sixty years and now He's Lord over my room?" Clarence took a step toward the picture.

Randy grabbed his arm and snarled next to his ear. "Back down, Clarence. We can do shackles here, too. You can take the picture down later."

Miss Henningway stared. "Not all believe and—"

"You bet your nursing home, I don't believe."

Randy gripped Clarence even harder. "Shackles."

The administrator pursed her lips, her hands pressed together at her mouth.

Randy released Clarence and nodded at Miss Henningway.

"Um … you have a closet, here." She opened the door to a cupboard, revealing a shelf above and a small clothes bar that would hold one suit and a jacket. Maybe a few shirts.

Clarence glanced down at the shopping bag still in Randy's hand.

"Oh, and the best part. Your bed." She bent down and patted the bright blue coverlet spread on a hospital-style bed complete with bars.

Finally she opened the only remaining door, revealing … a man: pants around his ankles, arms hugging his walker, a grimace on his face.

She gasped. "Mr. Thompson. What are you doing?"

He looked up at her, blinking. "What the hell does it look like I'm doing? I'm taking a crap. Now shut the damn door and leave me in peace."

She complied, holding her nose, eyes watering as she staggered back. "Let's go down the hall to the … um … the chapel." She brightened. "Right this way."

Clarence covered his mouth, eyes brimming, and immediately converted his grin to a solemn face. He glanced at Randy.

Randy wiped his eyes, covered his mouth and clapped one hand on Clarence's shoulder.

Clarence slapped Randy on the back as he continued to wipe his eyes.

"Please." Miss Henningway turned and beckoned to them. "Follow me." As they reached a set of double doors, her pager went off. She retrieved it and stepped away.

Clarence strode into the chapel. Whew. Place needed a good airing out. Wrinkling his nose, he eyed the broken blinds hanging in a window and wallpaper border trailing loose.

Miss Henningway glanced at Clarence, bobbed her head up and down several times and replaced the pager on her belt, resuming her air of authority. "I'm sorry about that little interruption. Your room will be put back in order."

Clarence grinned. "You'll kick the son-of-a-bitch out?"

She ignored Clarence and struck a Vanna White pose. Her thick make-up had taken on an oily appearance. Her hair had turned frizzy, no longer in the smooth swoop. She was fuming, all right. "A very nice little chapel. We have some fine services here. Priests and ministers come in, each taking turns, giving people of different faiths a chance to hear their doctrine preached." She resumed her air of authority, nodding and patting her chest. "Why, I've preached here on occasion myself."

"That's nice." Clarence scanned the room. Mismatched chairs and small altar. The final decorating touch: a huge body lift in the middle of the room. "I'm sure everybody gets elevated." He pushed the button on the lift. The swing assembly slowly rose. Amused, he walked off down the hall.

"Wait. Wait. I have good news," she said.

Clarence turned. "I'm going back to Chicago?"

Randy rushed to the lift, fumbled for the off button and cleared his throat.

Clarence took a deep breath, eyes on Randy. "I was told to be nice here." He pointed down the hall. "Kinda tough when there's an old man shitting in my bathroom."

The administrator's face bloomed, from her neck up to her forehead, in a fiery shade of red. Her upper lip twitched to the side, her hands stayed on her hips. The pager went off again and she shook her finger in Clarence's face.

He put his hat on his head, gave the brim a flourish and pulled his gloves on, starting back down the hall.

Randy hurried to catch up, still toting the grocery bag. "Wait, Clarence. Come on. She didn't know that guy'd be in there. It's all a misunderstanding."

Clarence nodded and kept on walking. "I agree. A misunderstanding that I'm supposed to be here. Take me back to your famous fast food restaurant on the way to Chicago." His nostrils flared, his breathing accelerated. He chewed the inside of his cheeks as tears dared to fill the corners of his eyes. He stomped past Harold's open door and shook his head.

Randy caught up. "Clarence, come on. They'll clean your bathroom again." He covered a snicker. "Then you can add your … uh, you can use it like your own. You'll see."

"They kick me out of prison and dump me here," Clarence growled under his breath. "But it looks like I don't belong here either." He stopped and Randy bumped into him. "Nobody cares whether I live or die. I'm an old man with nobody, nothing." He picked up his pace again. "I need to go to the hills by myself and die."

"You're not going anywhere to die. You have a lot of life to live." Randy caught up to Clarence and edged in closer. "Man, I know this isn't great, but what else have you got?"

Clarence stopped.

In front of him, a TV blared at people in wheelchairs arranged in a semi-circle: snoozing, snoring, some staring with mouths gaping, drool dripping on bibs. One resident rocked from side to side against chair restraints. There was an eerie pause in the racket from the television. No one stirred. One man coughed, spittle hitting the carpet in front of him.

Clarence whispered. "Where else can I go?"

CHAPTER 5

Katty hiccuped and lay trembling on the dirty rug, quickly becoming aware of her vulnerability. A sob escaped along with another hiccup as she hugged the tattered fabric beneath her. She lifted her head, and her bleary eyes tried to morph her own kitchen into this one. Neither was that great—doors hung off hinges revealing free or stolen glassware. Once-white cupboards became the new dingy cream. Her past and today flowed into one.

"Phil, why … ?" she muttered. Horror flooded memories every time she spoke or even thought his name. The visual hovered just behind every present day, making her shudder. A silent cry burst from down deep.

She pushed off the floor and slipped, leaving a trail of muddy sock prints. She looked down and froze.

Naked. That wasn't just a psychotic drug-induced dream. She was "in all her glory" naked. Except for the muddy, striped socks.

"Where're my clothes?" Terror crashed in. "I … I gotta get home. Bea's alone. Oh my god. What time is it?" She rushed to the living room only to be stopped short by grunts and snores. And a stench that smelled of every rotten egg, all the feedlots in Nebraska, and garbage trucks dripping week-old waste.

Bodies. Breathing, sleeping bodies. A couple rolled in blankets on the floor, arms draped over each other. A man sat up against the wall, arms limp by his sides, roach clips and beer bottles scattered beside him. A woman snored, her body covering another's head.

The sofa was empty. Some party.

She tiptoed around an overstuffed chair. A man, crumpled upside down over the back of it, appeared dead until he snorted.

Katty covered her chest, then her privates.

She fled into the hallway, but not before an eye cracked open.

"Ohhh. Gotta go. Gotta find my clothes." Near panic, she tiptoed down the matted carpet and peeked into a bedroom. Three guys— snoring so loud the floor vibrated under her feet. Time on the digital clock was 4:48. Good. Time to sleep it off before Bea … wait. Light cracked between the tattered shade and window. Oh no.

She slipped into an end bedroom, snagged a pair of jeans three sizes too big and shoved one foot in before falling. She tried again, then zipped them. She rummaged in one corner and was rewarded with a T-shirt declaring "Peace in Us."

Good enough.

As she yanked it over her head, she spied her own purse on the floor, partly obscured by a body. She bent to retrieve it.

Groans, a punch and a crack came from the living room. She paused and listened, clutching the purse to her chest, still crouched over the man, almost toppling backwards.

Keeping one eye on the hallway, she checked her purse. Empty. Except for dirty Kleenex.

Another muffled noise, closer. A man stumbled out of the living room.

She pushed away too fast, choked and hurled onto a man's back. He never moved.

Kitchen noises.

Every cell in her body screamed fear. Run!

Someone rummaged in a drawer. Something dropped onto the floor. A drawer squeaked shut.

Trembling, she peered into the hallway and gasped as a large knife pierced the air, gripped by a thick hand.

Still in her drunken dream world, she cried, "Phil. Don't. I *want* to have this baby."

Blindly, she stumbled back into the bedroom and frantically scanned the room. A broken window was blocked by a broken-down air conditioner. She stood in the only other escape route.

"I'm gonna find you," a low voice growled. "I'm gonna have what you promised." That voice wasn't Phil's.

A body behind her stirred.

Katty turned to a bleary-eyed woman raised up on an elbow, pointing at her. "That's my shirt … my…" The woman fell back onto the floor.

Katty tried the closet door as Knife Man found his way into the bedroom. One eye was matted shut, bruised and swollen. Blood caked in his beard. The open eye gleamed with a sick evil.

He lunged at her, only to trip and fall over a body, knife spinning in the air. People groaned as he crushed them under his weight. The knife bounced off a woman's back.

Katty scrambled over him leapfrog style but caught her foot on someone's arm and went sprawling.

Someone grabbed her foot.

She shrieked, wriggled out of the slimy sock and crawled onto the kitchen floor.

At the back door she pulled herself up by the doorknob and yanked the door open.

Footsteps pounded behind her.

"Gotta get to Bea."

She never looked back.

CHAPTER 6

Clarence shoved the tray away. His stomach growled, but when he smelled the food, MacDonald's threatened to make a reappearance. He glared at his supper—a cold turkey and cheese sandwich, jello fruit salad, stale potato chips and two cookies. And the ever present coffee. He understood the sandwich. No one had known what time he would arrive. According to the digital clock glowing down at him from atop the kitchen pass-through window, it was now 6:18 PM.

Prison food had been better than this.

His legs throbbed, along with his head. His hands shook in his lap. He stretched his fingers against the table surface, but the tremors continued. He was a fit man, having worked out every day, walked every day, more than the younger inmates. But he didn't feel fit now. He felt one footstep away from his funeral.

Randy had driven away less than an hour ago, but it seemed like ages. Randy's last comment to him: "I'll be back to see you, Clarence. I promise."

Clarence was pretty sure he'd never see Randy again. The trip from Chicago to Osceola was a long one for a man on security guard's pay.

He didn't remember feeling this bad when he was first incarcerated, sixty-two years ago—longer than most people stayed married. He stared at the dining room floor. Whatsername was right. It was new flooring. It gleamed. One of those new laminated fake floors. Easy to get around on if you used a wheelchair or a walker for your getaway vehicle.

His stomach churned. Worse than butterflies. He belched, and spit gathered in his mouth. He half rose in his chair and frantically scanned the area for a bathroom.

Breathe deep. Think of something else. Distractions. The only thing he could think of right now was how to get out of this place and die. Throwing up was just a side effect of the main event.

His hand flew to his mouth as another threatening belch rumbled upwards. He sank back down in the chair.

Ahh. Better. It was going away. Just indigestion. That fast food.

Then up it came. MacDonald's having its way—all over the table. He belched again, grabbed the extra napkins at the adjoining place setting, shook the utensils free and covered his mouth, trying to breathe slowly.

In and out.

He looked at the mess on his tray and almost got sick again, pushed away and faced the other side of the room.

Calm down.

He stirred. The table next to him had been long vacated. Dirty plates removed, table scrubbed. The next table over had a lone coffee cup lingering with a crumpled napkin. No chair. Wheelchair driver.

He raised his head.

Table after table, empty.

No wheelchairs.

No walkers.

No staff.

Just him and his tray of …

A ragged breath bubbled from deep within. A sob stayed just below control. Waiting to roll him over. Waiting to add the capstone to his day.

When he shoved away from the table, the chair legs scraped the floor and bumped the table. Coffee spilled onto the sandwich. He stared as it seeped under the bottom slice of bread, turning it a dingy shade of brown. That cinched it.

He stood. Blood rushed to his head and he faltered. His hands jerked to the table, bracing for a fall that didn't happen. He found his legs, straightened slowly. Head erect. Breathed deeply for a moment.

Okay.

He concentrated on making his feet move, carefully placed them one at a time, focused with every step.

Whew.

Beside the double doors he paused and read the menu for tomorrow. Tuna casserole. What a treat. His stomach rolled. It was probably from the same cookbook that the prison used. He'd have to make sure he wasn't around for that one.

He looked left and right, down both gray-tiled hallways. Which way? Searched for something familiar—a picture or decoration to jog his memory as to which way back to his room. He should have listened better, or taken a pencil and marked the walls.

Didn't matter. He'd find a place to steal away to—somewhere to get lost in—and die. It was either right or left down a doomed hallway. One way or the other. Didn't make any difference.

Funny. A person always knew where he was going in prison. No choice there.

Here, he had all the choices in the world. He could even use someone else's bathroom. He could do anything he wanted, more or less. But he stood crippled with indecision, trapped beside the kitchen door, and the only help he got—the only input he had received—was knowing they were having tuna casserole the next day.

He stared down the left hallway and took a step. Almost every door was propped open. TV's blared, each set on the same channel. He never missed a word as he wandered down the hall, his hand grasping the continuous railing. Vanna White. Wheel of Fortune. He heard the wheel spinning from one room. Pat Sajak's voice, "One thousand dollars." Next room—applause. The contestant's voice guessing, "P." Pat Sajak's voice, "Three P's," from the next TV. Ping, ping, ping. On down the hall he guessed letters along with the contestants, until he came to the corner.

This wasn't right. He didn't remember a therapy room. He turned and groaned as he gazed back down the now-even-longer hallway. He slumped, hands digging into his pockets.

Now TV's shouted, the commercial blared even louder. Motorcycles roared in multi-stereo. Someone yelled, "Woo-hoo!" Howls. "This is why we do this. Freedom. The open road."

Clarence stopped, fists clenched, arms tensed. He had to get out of here, but not tonight. Tomorrow he'd find a way out.

The noise pushed him down the hallway until he saw a head peek out farther down.

What was his name? Henry? Harold. Old buzzard. Nosy old bastard. Old dress shirt untucked over wrinkled outdated dress pants. Dress socks with a hole in one toe.

"Lost aren'tcha." Harold nodded as Clarence passed his doorway.

Clarence glared straight ahead, ignoring the comment.

Deep chuckle. "I did the same thing when I moved here. You'll find your way and the place will get a smaller feel to it."

Clarence chewed on the inside of his cheek, chin jutted out, nostrils flared.

"Okay. Well. Talk when you're ready. I'm not goin' anyplace."

Clarence grunted. Neither was he. He made the turn. Yeah. Past the nurses station. One. Two. Four doors on the left, at the end. Whew.

He stepped into his room and checked the bathroom.

Unoccupied.

He inspected the toilet.

Clean.

He walked to the window and stared into darkness, fist on the glass. He pounded softly. Harder still. The window vibrated with each blow. He calmed as his hands reached to grip bars that weren't there. His forehead dropped against the glass, his mind replaying the day, beginning at prison. His insides lurched, his legs went weak.

He turned away.

His grocery bag still sat on top of the chest of drawers, calling him to unpack, to settle in.

He ignored it and stretched out on the bed fully clothed, comforted by his hand resting on the restraining bar.

His hand tightened around it. He stared at the ceiling. Someone pushed a rattling cart past his doorway. TV voices mixed into indiscernible chatter. Someone called out for a nurse to help her make water. A door slammed.

He closed his eyes.

An alarm went off somewhere, making him jump. Beep, beep, beep.

He closed his eyes again.

First nights.

This first night swam with memories of a first night long ago. He had been terrified. Crippled by grief. Not letting himself cry, he had choked back sobs. Stared at the ceiling and cold concrete walls then. Water-stained, peeling vinyl wallpaper now. Strange bed then. Strange bed now. Unfamiliar sounds. Taunting voices from the next cells, the next rooms.

He rolled to face the wall, gripping the bars with both hands, squeezing his eyes shut.

Whispered threats from the next cell then.

Voices from his own fears, now.

CHAPTER 7

"Bea?" Katty cried as she raced up the trailer home steps. Tripping on overgrown weeds growing through the stair treads, she fell hard, slammed her shoulder against the door and landed spread-eagle on the deck.

She groaned, held her shoulder with one hand and gripped her toe with the other, rocking back and forth in pain. Her mouth spewed what her heart and body felt.

She reached up to open the door and winced. She pulled herself up with her other hand, only to have the doorknob fall off in her hand. She fell back down on the deck and stared at the doorknob, then at the door. Then at the knob.

Chin crumpled. Tears gushed.

"F-n doorknob. F-n day. F-n life."

She heaved the doorknob.

Glass shattered.

She sat up, kicked the glass aside and kicked the door open. She slammed it against the wall inside and crawled in.

"Bea? Beatrice! Where are you?"

Silence.

"Oh, God. Baby Bea?"

Katty struggled to her feet, leaned on the kitchen counter and visually searched the room. The harvest gold kitchen opened to the living room, divided by a dining room of sorts. Only it wasn't used as a dining room. More like a toy room, library, shop, trash bin, storage closet. Reality: kitchen, living room, dining room were all one room— trailer house style.

"Bea?" she called.

Katty slid down the hall against buckled paneling and searched the first bedroom. She shoved under and around boxes cluttering the floor and lost her balance, landed on a stack of magazines, creating a small landslide.

No Bea.

Next room. Bea's

Katty barged in. "Bea. I'm home, sweety. Baby Bea. Mommy's here."

Sugar, sugar, sugar.

The bed hadn't been slept in.

She ripped the blankets from the bed, toys from corners, checked under the desk. She slammed the closet door open and swished her hand back and forth among the clothes and toys.

No Bea.

She stumbled into the bathroom. Empty. Her heart pumped faster. She tore the shower curtain from the bar above the tub. Nobody. She shoved at the bottles on the counter, toppled some onto the floor. Nothing. Nothing except a doll's hairbrush on the counter beside the sink. Bea's doll brush.

Katty grabbed it and ran into her bedroom.

"Bea! Where are you? Mommy's here, Baby," she sobbed.

She tore the bed apart, stripped the covers off. Pillows flew. Bedspread slid onto the floor, catching the bedside lamp with it.

She searched her closet. Slid closet doors back and forth, knocking one off the track.

Finally she heard a hiccup from the corner. She dragged the rocking chair away from the wall and there was her skinny daughter, hair matted against her head. She fit perfectly under the rocker.

"Bea. Why are you hiding?" Katty dragged her out and picked her up.

Bea was trembling, her face wet. A sob escaped her lips. Her brown eyes were swollen and terrified.

"Mommy?" Bea's hoarse voice whispered. "Mommy?"

"You scared me, Bea. I couldn't find you. I looked everywhere and I couldn't find you."

Bea collapsed into Katty's arms. "Mommy. Mommy. Where were you? It got dark and you didn't come back." She sobbed. "You left me alone. Me and Dolly."

Katty crumbled. "I'm so sorry, Bea," she said. "Mommy forgot what time it was and … I'm sorry, Baby. I'll never do it again. I promise."

Morning sun shone through the window curtain. Bea played quietly, brushing Dolly's hair with the hairbrush, softly singing a melody from her heart.

She sat next to Mommy on the bed, wanting to talk to her, but knowing from the way Mommy was stretched out that if she woke her up, she'd get yelled at. Or worse. She'd seen Mommy this way before. Sometimes Mommy became that other Mommy.

Bea's tummy rumbled, but she tried to ignore it. She combed Dolly's hair, then her own. Then Dolly's.

Rumble.

She glanced at sleeping Mommy, then slowly, carefully slipped off the bed and shuffled backwards toward the kitchen, never taking her eyes off Mommy's face. She knew the places on the frayed, carpeted floor that creaked. It became a dance down the dark hall as she lightly hopped and skipped from one safe spot to the next.

She pushed a chair over to the counter, scraping it along the thin linoleum and caught it in a hole. She quickly tip-toed to see if the noise woke Mommy.

Whew.

On the counter next to the bread, Bea found her favorite snack—peanut butter. She was careful with the knife, slowly drawing it across the bread. She pinched off a corner of the bread that was green and threw it away, smothering the rest in more peanut butter. The green didn't look right, but peanut butter made it better.

Bea sang songs to herself and Dolly as she snacked. Sweet little melodies. Softly. Bite the bread. Hum the song. Lick the peanut butter. La-la-la.

Bea looked at Dolly, who had lost interest in the food. Dolly leaned against the empty cupboard and slowly slid onto the floor. Bea sat her upright next to her and dropped a cracker in Dolly's lap.

"You need to eat your supper, so you can play and grow big and strong," Bea whispered. She patted Dolly on the head and stared at her for a long moment. "I promise I won't leave you alone again, Dolly. Ever. Ever."

CHAPTER 8

Head nurse, Carol Neeton stood outside Clarence's door. She raised her hand to knock, then withdrew it. She pushed her hand into her white jacket pocket. Her fingers touched her pen and automatically clicked it several times. She checked the chart again and frowned. No family listed. No references. Sometimes residents had no surviving family, but … nobody to even contact?

She read further, shaking her head. Note to self: review Henningway's notes on Clarence. More than once the administrator had conveniently forgotten to chart vital background information. So maybe the man who drove him here was a contact.

At least Joe had someone. She tapped the chart. Two years since the stroke and he still wasn't responsive. She blew out a breath and blinked. Gotta get there tonight after work—if Henningway didn't rag on her and detain her.

She checked the photo beside Clarence's door. The man was handsome even if he was eighty. Joe would've been that good looking if he hadn't of had the stroke.

Deep sigh. She replaced the chart in the cart and knocked on the door. "Clarence?"

Silence.

She peeked, then tiptoed into his room. "Clarence? Hi, I'm Carol. How're you doing? Just checking in … to see how you're acclimating." Her voice trailed off. "Your nurse told me you've not been out of your room … at all."

No answer.

She stopped just shy of the bed. Clarence lay facing the wall, gripping the restraining bar. Big man. Long wavy gray hair—Henningway would want that cut.

His rumpled clothes looked like he hadn't changed them since he had been admitted—what two days ago? Black T-shirt, khaki-colored chinos. Still wore his socks and joggers.

"Clarence, it's time for dinner." She leaned over his bed but couldn't see his face. She patted his shoulder. "Hamburgers tonight. Brownies for dessert."

No response. Out of habit, she assessed his breathing. Steady, but not deep. Awake.

She cleared her throat. "Clarence, I know you can hear me. You've sequestered yourself in here for two days. If you don't come out, I'll have to request a doctor's order for a feeding tube."

She waited. Shook her head. "And believe me, you don't want that."

Nothing. No response. No movement.

"And the next step is sending you to a psych ward and you don't want that even more."

Barely discernible change in breathing. Slightly faster.

She bent over, speaking close to the back of his head. He hadn't showered or shaved. "Clarence, this has to be the hardest thing you've ever been through, but believe me, it does get better with some effort from you. I have read your blood pressure results myself and I know for sure. You are not dying. You are healthier than I am."

"You'd be healthier if you weren't so fat," Clarence said.

Carol grinned. Before she could think of a comeback, something exploded through the window, pelting them both with glass shards.

Carol uncovered her eyes.

Clarence had sat up in bed. He stared wide-eyed out the window.

"Oh my God ... what is that?" She pointed at the floor. A huge bloody mass of feathers and talons lay partly obscured by the bed.

Clarence crouched next to it.

She backed away, automatically reaching for her pager. "I'm calling maintenance."

"It's a hawk," said Clarence. He looked out the window. "What on earth?" He reached down to touch it. "Still alive, I think."

Carol's pager sputtered. "Jim. Jim. You there? We have ... uh," she turned to Clarence. "You said a hawk?"

Clarence nodded.

"We have a hawk in room 204." She glanced at the window. "Oh ... and a broken window. Can you ... can you come right away?"

The pager sputtered. "What? A stalk? A stalk of what?"

Carol eyed it. Still not moving. "I said a hawk. You know the bird kind?"

"Hawk?"

"Yup. That's what I said. A hawk. It broke through the window." She leaned over to inspect it. "And it's a big one. Clarence thinks it's still alive."

"Through the window?" Jim's voice cracked.

She turned and pointed at the window. "That's what I said ... through the window."

She replaced her pager. "Well, it got you off your butt, Clarence," she said. "Nice bird. Good bird." She leaned over it. "Wow. Big bird."

"Can we keep it?"

"What?" Carol squeaked.

"Can we keep it? In a cage or something." He pushed the bed against the wall to reveal the whole bird. "Rust colored tail. Look at that wingspan."

"It's as big as your bed ... almost. We don't have anything here to ... we need to call the Humane Society ... or the nursing home for birds."

"Its wing is hurt ... bleeding. I don't suppose you'd have any medical supplies here would you?" He turned to face Carol, a glint in his eye, one eyebrow up. "Miss Head Nurse."

Carol scrunched her nose at him, hands on her hips. "Whatever gets you off that bed, Clarence."

She retrieved her pager. "Oh, and Jim? We're gonna need a huge cage. Get all the finches out of the aviary, or something." She crouched to the floor and attached the pager to her belt again. That was one huge bird. Even though it was big, there was something so ethereal about it. "Amazing … something so … powerful … so divine."

"In *my* room. Humph. Coulda killed me if I'd been standing by the window, there."

"But you weren't. You were still on your bed. After two days, Clarence."

He looked up at her, then down at the bird. He started to touch the bloody wing, then pulled his hand back. "Why are you here, old bird? What were you thinking, breaking in my window?"

Carol had questions of her own as she watched Clarence stroke the beautiful hawk.

Gasp. "Clarence, your hands. Let me see."

He hid them behind his back. "No. They're fine."

She pulled one forward. "They're burns. What happened?"

He shoved them into his pockets. "It was a long time ago. Never you mind."

Where did this man come from really, and who was he?

CHAPTER 9

Bea watched Mommy's hips sway to music grinding from her phone.

Mommy stood back and fluttered her eyelids, held her arms out in a ta-da, fingers holding the mascara wand. She wiped at the corner of each eye, patting at smudges. Sipped from the styrofoam cup and sighed, looking in the dresser mirror again.

"Aw, hell," she said and added more liner, smudging even more.

She posed her face, first left, then right.

Bea played on the floor, dressing Dolly and undressing her. She popped her head up every once-in-a-while, watching Mommy make up. When Mommy fluttered her eyelids, Bea fluttered hers. When Mommy smacked her lips together, Bea smacked hers.

Mommy leaned close to the mirror and looked directly into Bea's eyes. "What're you looking at?" Mommy's black eyes glared, reflecting back at Bea.

Something in Mommy's eyes flickered, snapped. Stirred fear in Bea. She shivered.

Mommy stepped back and stared at herself for a long time.

Quiet.

"Mommy? Mommy? Are you going out? Mommy?"

Mommy turned and rushed at Bea. "What?"

Nose to nose.

Mommy's eyes had turned dark. "Mommy—"

"Don't Mommy me."

"Your voice sounds funny." Bea's eyes brimmed with tears. "And your eyes look funny … your eyes … you're that other Mommy." Bea scooted back.

"What?" Mommy hesitated. "What?" she said again, her voice sounding more like Mommy's.

Bea hiccuped, swallowed, her chin quivered. She fought it. Held it in until her eyes spilled over, tears streaming down her cheeks. Her mouth clamped tight, her eyes never leaving Mommy's.

Mommy groaned. "I don't have time for this."

Mommy's eyes changed again.

Bea was only four, but she knew her mommy. And right now, pure evil raged from Mommy's eyes.

Then a flicker of … Mommy sparked through.

Another change. Evil again.

Back came a twinkle … of … Mommy, until Mommy came through. But Bea knew the rage was there, just under the surface.

"Mommy?" Bea whimpered. She swallowed. "Are you going to leave me?"

Mommy gulped. "I'll just be gone for an hour or so." She glanced toward the TV. "I'll set you up with some movies." She smiled, fluttering her eyelids. "And I'll be back before the first movie is over. Okay?" She held out her pinky. "Promise."

Bea stared at Mommy's finger, then up to Mommy's face. What she saw there wasn't comforting, but she decided to play along, hoping against all past experience that Mommy wasn't lying. Again.

Bea hooked her little finger around Mommy's. "Promise." Her eyes searched Mommy's for a sign that this time—this time would be different.

Mommy smiled wide, red lipstick framing her teeth. Her eyes said she really believed she could come home before Bea's bedtime. That whatever she did out there, it wouldn't mean Bea fell asleep alone. Again.

Bea's eyes pleaded that just this once, Mommy could really do it. That she could come home when she said and make Bea feel safe.

"Mommy?" Bea gulped. "Mommy, could you stay home?"

"You don't think I'd put all this make-up on just for you, do you?"

Bea blinked.

Mommy reached for her drink and downed it, licking a last drop off her lips. She walked to her TV and shuffled through DVDs until she found one and set it up, starting the TV.

"There. Now there's only one movie in and you just watch your old mom." She shook her finger. "She'll ... I'll be home before this movie is over. You'll see." She posed herself in the full-length mirror. "Uh-huh. Now, don't I look smashing."

Bea just stood there. Mommy looked beautiful. But she was going away again. Bea was scared to answer. She wanted Mommy to stay home, but Mommy never did. It didn't matter what Bea said, Mommy would still leave.

Mommy swooped down and breathed on Bea. "Don't I look pretty?"

Her mouth had that evil smell again. Bea backed away.

"Don't I?"

"Yes, Mommy. You look pretty."

"That's what I thought."

Mommy blew a kiss and slammed the door on her way out.

The movie blared. The beginning exploded with color and excitement.

But Bea stared at the door.

All alone.

She crawled once again under the rocking chair, pulling her pillow and blanket along with her.

CHAPTER 10

The next morning, Clarence tapped on the chicken wire enclosure of the aviary in the entrance of Hillcrest Homes. "They had to remodel the finches' house for you, didn't they?" The hawk dominated the cage. Its tail feathers caught on the wire floor, curling. Massive. Even though its wings were tucked, they still filled the space. Beady eyes stared at Clarence. Talons gripped a branch too big for finches. "I'm sure those silly birds don't mind loaning it to you for a while."

Miss Henningway walked up to the birdcage beside the aviary. Red, yellow, brown and green finches fluttered around a lone blue and white speckled parakeet. The tiny birds pecked at the larger bird. Their wings flapped against its head and body.

She clucked at them. "Poor little birdies. Sweet things." She studied the aviary, then the birdcage. "Did that big old mean bird take your pretty cage?" Cluck, cluck.

The hawk quaked and suddenly spread its wings, rocking the aviary.

Clarence jumped back. "Your wing! It's … it's—"

"Eek!" Miss Henningway stumbled.

Clarence rushed to keep her upright. She might be the enemy, but he couldn't let her fall.

She swooned against him. Her eyeglasses magnified fluttering eyes.

He shoved her upright, his hands released her arms and he backed away.

"Humph. You are … " She clamped her bright red lips shut and stomped away.

He continued to tap against the aviary. "I know how you feel, old boy. But that's what you get for breaking into my room."

Old Harold Dexter shuffled into view. "Talking to birds now, I see. Next it'll be the dog in the dining room."

"There's a dog in the dining room?"

"Naw. Just wanted to see if you were listening."

Clarence growled. He waited for Harold to mosey on down the hall. "Looks like your wing is healing already. Pretty fast. You ought to be outta here in … I oughta be out of here … in …"

The bird stared.

Clarence stared back. He looked behind him, then back to the hawk. "Me, too." He clicked on the wire with his nail. "Cohorts in crime." Tap, tap. "They'll throw you out, just like the prison threw me out."

Tap, tap, tap. One nurse in the nurses station was busy charting or whatever. Another walked away from him, down the hall. She disappeared into a room. "How are you this morning, Mrs. Albertson?" A very loud voice. The door closed.

That hall was empty. He slowly rotated to another. Quiet. Nobody. A body lift stood at the end of the hall. The exit was so far away. He slipped past the wheelchair rows, all facing the TV. No one moved.

The woman in the nurses station hadn't moved from the desk.

His eyes focused on the exit and he started shuffling toward it.

A door just before the exit opened and a big black woman entered the hallway. She had to weigh three hundred pounds. "Sure your family will be here Saturday. It's yo birthday fo pete's sake."

He stepped closer.

Her hand was on the door jamb, her eyes never left Clarence's face. Someone answered from inside the room, but he couldn't hear what was said. The black woman answered. "They be here this year fo sure. It ain't everyday a person turns ninety. Punch yo call light if you needs me."

Closer. He glanced at the exit. Shuffle. Shuffle.

The woman leaned against the wall, her arms folded across her ample chest. Her hair was tied up in those dread things and gathered in a big bun at the back of her head, only some stuck out. Her bright blue uniform had little yellow ducks all over. She fiddled with a stethoscope hanging around her neck as he walked closer. Her eyes focused on him.

"Hey Mr. Timmelsen. How's it goin'?"

"Name's Clarence. I'm just taking the tour. Getting some exercise." He raised one knee, then the other. "I'm used to a specialized gym workout."

"Uh-huh. You get all settled in didyanow?"

"Sure." He reached the end of the hallway—right next to the exit door. Was she ever going to get back to work?

Her pager went off. "Well, Mr. Clarence, have yoself a good day and let us know if we can be of hep to you." She checked the pager and moseyed on down the hall. Just as Clarence was going to push the door open, she turned. "Goin' to get some air?"

"Uh. Just looking out the window here." He faced the door and tapped against the glass. "You have a nice little garden out back here."

Her pager beeped again. "We sho do. Gotta run. Mrs. Hatly is persistent today."

She turned the corner and Clarence pushed the door open, slipping out into the sunshine. He stood tucked next to the exit, in the space between the door and a window. He hesitated there for a minute, breathing in the fresh air. The birds chattered and squirrels chased up tree trunks.

As soon as the door closed, he hustled to the closest tree. Then to another. He hid behind the sign proclaiming Hillcrest Homes. Across the street and into the park.

Freedom.

An hour later, Clarence stood on the sidewalk outside a grocery store peeping in, shuffling side to side, trying to spy between flyers taped to the inside of the glass. He leaned back and checked out the exterior of the store: white paint peeled from old red bricks, a frayed awning flapped in the wind over the entry door. A sign with faded letters swayed slightly askew overhead—The Olde Towne Market.

He cupped his eyes with his hands and peered inside again, leaning against the glass. Lights on. The radio blared the newest canned music from an outside speaker. Country twang.

A slender woman wearing a white shirt, too-tight jeans and a green-and-white-striped necktie clomped toward the front door. Clarence caught the word Manager on her name tag but couldn't read her name. She stuck a single cigarette in her shirt pocket, her hand on the door.

Oh-oh. She glanced his way. He spun around to avoid being seen.

Wait. No one was onto him here. He was a customer, just like that guy inside the store, pushing a cart full of baby food and diapers.

Clarence stepped close to the glass again, eyed the ads taped haphazardly to the glass and pretended to scan them carefully. "Oh, look. Here's an ad for puppies. Six weeks old, had their shots," he read. "Aww, cute little things." He nodded at a pretty young woman heading up the sidewalk toward the store entrance, and he tapped the glass. She smiled at him. "I should have my shots," he muttered. He pointed to the phone number fringe at the bottom. "I need to get one of those." He tilted his head. "402-572-1224. Gotta call or they'll be gone."

The woman entered the store, glancing at him, letting the door close behind her.

He stretched to read another ad higher up, letting his eyes fall toward the manager inside again. Now she stood pointing toward him, jaws jabberwalking to another white-shirted employee, a tall young male. He tied a green apron low on his hips.

Clarence rotated a quarter turn, toward the cars in the parking lot, jingling coins in his pocket. He turned to the store again.

Out of the corner of his eye, he spied the manager and employee walking toward the back of the store. They stopped, pointing to a leaning display, then pointed to the front, the back, then another aisle. Standing face to face in disagreement. The manager tucked her cigarette over her ear, reached out and shook the display, knocking several cans to the floor.

Now was his chance.

He put on *the* smile, eyes twinkling. He opened the door and found the puppy ad. "I need one of those." He tore one strip off. "402-572-1224. I'll call this number as soon as I get back home." He strode to a cash register.

"Hello, Sir. What'd you say?" A tubby girl, sixteen or so, stood next to the cash register. She cocked her head at him, revealing an obnoxious red stripe running throughout her mouse brown hair.

He didn't answer.

"Uh … how're ya doin' today? Lookin' for some puppies?" She yanked at the plastic shopping bags on a stand, separating them, pulling the end one open. Her fake gold name tag said MINDY ASHTON.

Clarence stopped and watched everything she did. "I see you're really busy today. Got your bags all ready, do you? Ready for that rush?" He smirked and pushed his fist into the air with the old one-two. "Where're you from anyways? Nebraska? Shelby? Chicaaaa-go?"

"Sir, I'm from here." She pointed to the floor. "Osceola, Nebraska. This is where it's at, Dude." She grinned, braces gleaming, and crossed her brown eyes above her glasses. Red pockmarks scarred her light skin. Doughnut rolls circled her middle.

"Dude?" He cleared his throat. "Why in my day—"

"In your day, you didn't have pop, TV, cell phones, or internet." The tall, gangly employee had returned, carrying a roll of trash bags. JOHN POTTER, according to his name tag. He glanced toward Mindy and smacked his forehead. "Oh, yeah. You had internet. But back then, it was called Pony Express."

Grrr. "Where're you from? The devil?" Clarence stomped past the registers and found himself face-to-face with the manager, arms across her chest, one pierced eyebrow raised.

"Sir." She greeted him and tapped her foot. "Or should I call you, Osceola?"

"I'm not from here."

She grinned. "Okay. But you're here now. So where are you from?" She tapped his chest. "You're new in these here parts, right?"

He looked down at her finger touching his shirt, at her name tag—TANDY LARKIN—then up to her face. "Did you know that your clerk up there, whatshername, is doing nothing? Absolutely nothing?" He looked back at Mindy and pointed. "See? She's just hangin' out."

Mindy grinned at him, waving with one hand, twining a lock of her hair with the other.

"If she was busier, she lose some of that baby fat. She's never going to find a boyfriend with all that hanging on her."

Mindy's face fell, smile vanished.

John stepped in front of her, pushed his black-rimmed glasses up on his pointy nose and slicked back his dark shaggy hair. Placed his hands on his hips.

"Oh. Oh, I get it. She does have a boyfriend. It's that loser. The one from the devil." Back to the manager. "Where's he from?"

John adjusted his apron and boomed out. "Omaha."

Clarence swung back to John. "Oh. Omaha. That explains it." He sauntered past Tandy.

"Sir, what's your name? I don't believe the customer's always right with you around. That was just plain mean. We try to be nice—"

"Nice." He planted his feet in the middle of the aisle. "If you were *nice*, you'd get me outta that place up there on the hill." He shook his head. "It's nasty up there. The place stinks. The people stink. They shit in any bathroom they want."

John crept up beside Clarence. "Oh, so you're from … up there." He pointed, a mock villainous expression on his face. "Then it's a good fit, huh. Nasty, stinky place for a nasty, stinky man. High five, Osceola?" He held his hand well above Clarence's head. "No, wait. You can't reach." He looked way up at his hand, on the end of his long skinny arm, then down at Clarence.

"John, get to work." Tandy eyed Clarence. "And for you Mr. Osceola, you'd better get your little tooshie up front and apologize to Mindy."

Mindy smiled and picked up a bulging trash bag, spun it around and fastened it. "That's all right. Sticks and stones will hurt my bones, but words will never hurt me." She carried the trash bag past them, bumping it against her leg with each step.

Clarence stepped in behind Mindy and swaggered in her footsteps.

"Osceola, stop. That's enough." John held his hand out traffic-cop-style in front of Clarence.

Mindy sighed. "It's really okay. He reminds me of Grandpa—sorta. He was mean … uh, he had a streak in him, too."

Tandy started toward the back of the store. "Okay, kids. I have work to do." She retrieved the cigarette from her ear. "I hope that in my absence you can all behave yourselves, get your work done, and be nice." She slowed and turned toward Clarence, waving the cigarette in his face. "Extra nice." She stopped. "Oh, and by the way, the nursing home called. They are looking for one Clarence Timmelsen." She pointed at him. "That'd be you, Mr. Osceola?"

A buzzer went off at the check stand. They all swirled to see who had set it off.

Clarence made a bee-line for the back room but got wedged between the manager and a shelf of cereal boxes.

"Let me go," he puffed. "I have to find some … sardines and crackers." He tried again. "I need to use the bathroom."

Glass crashed up front. Tandy immediately forgot Clarence and ran in the direction of the noise.

"Oh, no. I hope it's not pickles again."

"Bring the broom."

"Grab the mop and paper towels."

"Mop emergency in aisle … by the check stands," It sounded like John's voice over the loudspeaker. "Whew. Pickles."

Clarence edged to the back room and bolted for the door. "Saved by the buzzer," he whispered. He looked over his shoulder. "And pickles." Quietly he opened the back door. Immediately the wind caught it, throwing it open, and slammed it against the building. He glimpsed a hawk, just like the one that had broken through his window, rising with the wind current. He stepped into the sunshine, shielding his eyes. The bird circled the building as he shut the door behind him.

"Where're you going, beautiful bird? What are you circling?"

Clarence rotated with the hawk, following its lead. Around and around he followed the bird in a rhythmic dance—the bird in the air, Clarence on the ground. The hawk rose, glided, dove, then soared again on the wind current. A bandage appeared partly torn off one wing.

He squinted into the sun. They let it loose already? Maybe it wasn't hurt as bad as they thought. Or maybe that demon lady, Henningway, claimed the aviary back for those little fake birds.

Silence.

The hawk hovered, wings dipped up and down. Then the powerful bird lifted, banked, and dove right for Clarence.

He ducked and lost his balance.

As he flailed, the bird screeched, piercing his eardrums, sending shivers up his spine.

He tumbled on the concrete, to his hands and knees, and the bird flew around behind him. "Are you hunting me?" He tried to track it, but the sun blinded him. "I helped you," he shouted. "If I had a gun I'd shoot you right now, I would, you old buzzard. I'd shoot you dead."

Clarence grappled for a handhold. He staggered to his feet, to the building wall and leaned against it, catching his breath. He brushed his jeans off and examined the palms of his hands. Old, tough ropy scars lined them, traveling up the inside of one arm. One little finger curved inward, like a claw.

Immediately, he transported back in time, back to when he was a small boy wearing a plaid hat with earflaps and a light jacket. His mother had just died of polio. He had blindly run away into the cold night and bumped into a seasoned hobo, warming beans over a fire. The old man showed him how to warm his hands, but before he could stop Clarence, the boy stuck his hands into the flames. Clarence was so cold, he kept reaching out and touching the fire, terribly burning the palms of his hands. Grief-numbed, he had hardly felt the pain.

Smoke cleared.

Clarence stumbled backward along the wall of the grocery store. His foot kicked an old lead pipe, and he bent to pick it up. He looked up to the sky and shook the pipe at the hawk. "You coulda gotten me killed, old bird."

The hawk circled and screeched, dove directly at Clarence, and pulled up, just missing him again.

Clarence's hand pounded his chest as he gasped for breath.

CHAPTER 11

Bea's little fingers braided Dolly's hair over and over. Braided, then combed out. Braided, then combed. The doll's hair broke off easily from age, but also from being brushed again and again. Braided again and again. Ever since Mommy had taught Bea to braid.

She smoothed her own hair. Then Dolly's. Then hers again.

Comfy in her car seat, Bea hummed and swayed her head with the melody. The car was quiet and warm, a window partway open. Licking her thumb, she washed Dolly's dirty face, just as Mommy did her own. One doll eye stuck open, the other eye blinked. Bea held up the doll to admire and smiled. Then she hugged Dolly, sighed, and settled in to wait for Mommy. Almost asleep—

Screech!

Bea jumped and looked at Dolly, then at the store front. No Mommy. She closed her eyes again and relaxed.

Screech!

This time she struggled out of her car seat. She checked the entry door of the store.

No Mommy.

She dropped Dolly to the floor, bending to peek under the seat, the floor, around her car seat.

There it came again, that awful piercing sound. She watched goose-bumps grow on her arms and she shivered, rubbing them. She picked up Dolly and hugged her tight as she looked out the car windows, left and right.

Stop.

There.

She pressed her face against the window, eyes wide. An old man. And a bird. A big bird. The bird flapped its wings, flew higher, then dove for the man.

Mommy opened the car door and tossed a sack onto the seat. Glass clinked in the bag. "F-n store. F-n people. F-n headache." She rubbed her temples.

Screech!

"What the … what's that sound?" Mommy turned behind her. Her hands covered her ears. "God that hurts." She gasped. "That bird is going to kill him." She turned to look at Bea. "Wha?"

Bea lifted her eyebrows and shoulders.

"Stay here, Bea." Mommy slammed the door and started running.

Katty dashed to the old man, who stood pounding his chest, gasping. The hawk flew off, flapping its huge wings.

The man turned away as she rushed toward him. "I'm all right. Leave an old man alone."

"That's exactly why I won't leave you alone. Because you're old."

He turned and glared. "Yeah, I'm old, but I'm not dead."

"I didn't say you were, old man." She bent to brush his pants off.

He slapped her hand away. "Stop. I'm okay."

"Old fool. Old man. Where's your family, old man?"

"I don't have any family," he yelled. "Just me. Nobody else."

"Why? You chase them off, didja?"

He clenched his fists. "None of your damn business." He looked behind her. "You can't even take care of the family you have." He pointed toward her Nova station wagon.

She swung around and looked. Bea was crawling out the open car door. Katty yelled. "Bea. Get the f- back in the car seat." She charged back toward the car. "You know better than that. Get. Back. In there."

Bea stopped short of stepping onto the concrete. She whimpered, her eyes focused behind Katty.

"Baby, I know I kept you waiting a long time, but I'm sick. And I broke a jar of pickles in the store and made a mess." She smelled her hands. "Stinky."

Bea wrinkled her nose.

Katty picked her up tossed her into the car seat. "Stay there. We don't have far to go. Just sit still in your car seat."

Katty dragged herself into the car, slammed the door and turned over the engine, then she glanced out at the old man. The bird still circled above the parking lot. "Stupid old man. He's gonna get hurt by a stupid bird." Gunning the car, she backed out only to slam on the brakes as another car swerved into the parking space beside her. "Damn! Why don't people look where they're going?"

She reached behind her. "You okay baby?" She pushed Bea back onto her car seat, then gunned the car again, only this time—

Scream.

Thud.

"Oh, God. Oh God. I hit something." Katty gripped the steering wheel, then slowly turned in her seat. "Or someone. Oh God. What'd I do?"

She shifted into park, slowly opened the car door and stepped outside. One foot in front of the other. Until she reached the back of the car.

"Oh no."

A woman pushed herself off the ground, brushed her clothes off and picked up her purse and groceries. "You hit me! I thought you saw me. What were you thinking?"

Katty leaned over to help pick up the woman's groceries, and the world started spinning. She reached out to steady herself on the car.

"You are drunk. You shouldn't even be driving. And you have a child with you." She grabbed a can of peaches from Katty. "Of all the nerve. You should be arrested."

"Oh no. Please Ma'am. I just got over the … flu … and I had to come out to get my baby some milk. It's not what you think."

"Liar. You're just lucky I'm not hurt. By the looks of you, I'd never get a dime out of you anyway." She shoved Katty away, limping on the way to another car.

"Ma'am, everything okay?"

Katty spun around. "Wha?"

A young officer—black haired, skinny—tipped his hat to Katty. "I was driving by when the department got a call from the store here. Are you all right?"

Katty slowly put her hand on the bumper of her car. Deep breath. Hopefully the pickle stink covered up her breath. "We're fine. Just a little shaken up." She pointed to the woman walking away. "She said she's fine too. This parking lot is dangherous."

"Oh, there's someone with you?" He walked to the side of the car. "This your daughter? She isn't buckled in."

Katty jumped. "Oh! Did she get out again? She is getting good at that."

He smiled down at Bea. "Hey there, Little Houdini. Cute." Hand on his pistol, he turned to Katty. "I don't think I know you … uh, I'm new in … "

Her lips curved into a seductive smile. "Thesh parts?"

The officer nodded. "Yeah. Um, I didn't catch your name."

"That's because I didn't throw it at you." She grinned and shrugged her shoulders. Good line. "Why do I feel like we're in a movie?"

He smiled and hesitated. "I just to need to see your driver's license before I let you get back to your daughter." He nodded at Katty, then waited.

Katty stopped breathing. "Uh, yeah. Sure." She didn't move.

"Is there a problem, Ma'am?"

"No. No. I'll just scoot by you to get my purse." She stepped slowly around the officer, taking her time with each step, touching her car where she could for support. "It's right here."

She sat in the driver's seat and rummaged in her purse. "Yeah … "
She opened the glove box and dug around. "It's here somewhere." She
attempted a laugh, then staunched it. Back to her purse. "It's here … "
She panicked. Turned and flashed a smile. "It must be in my other
purse. I'm so sorry."

He shoved his hat off his forehead and reached inside his jacket. He
clicked a pen as he opened the ticket pad. "I'm going to have to give
you a warning. Driving without a license." He scribbled then tore off a
sheet. "Here you go. You need to be sure you have it with you at all
times."

Katty folded it and stuffed it in her jeans pocket. "Yes. I'll go right
home and get that purse." She snapped her fingers at Bea. "Bea, don't
let me forget to do that."

He pointed at Bea. "You might have to tie her *and* buckle her in the
car seat."

Deep slow breath. She attempted a laugh. "Thanks, uh, Officer for
stopping. Nice to know you'll be around … uh … you're around when
I need you … when we have problems." Katty fluttered her eyelids.
She stood slowly, opened Bea's passenger door and climbed in. "Let
me buckle you in again, Sweetie. I don't know how you get out."

She leaned into the car, her face inches from Bea's. "Now let's
pretend these straps aren't all twisted and," she dug under the liner, "all
caught and I'm buckling you in, okay, Sweetie?"

Bea nodded; they played the game well. "Okay Mommy. I'll sit
still while you buckle me in again."

Katty smiled and rubbed noses with Bea as she made a clicking
sound between her teeth. "There. You're all safe again." She ruffled
Bea's hair. "Now don't unbuckle yourself again, ya hear?"

Katty stood slowly, gaze following the young officer to his squad
car. Her stomach churned. Her head was spinning.

Breathe.

Bea gripped the sides of her seat and stretched to see the old man.

As Mommy slowly backed the car out, something happened. She stared at his eyes; he stared into hers. Bea didn't understand, but she knew she couldn't look anywhere else but his blue, blue eyes.

CHAPTER 12

Carol glanced at the chart. More med changes? What was Miss Henningway thinking? Residents were already nodding off in their mashed potatoes.

She searched the dining hall again. Each empty chair should have a definite reason for being vacant. Mrs Samuelson was still at physical therapy. Andy had checked out to spend time with family. Mr. Butress's empty chair hadn't found a replacement resident.

Carol rotated.

Clarence's chair was empty. Bib draped over the back, table set for lunch. Water in the glass. Coffee cooling in the cup.

"Where is that man?" she muttered. Her inner alarm went off. AWOL. She wasn't sure if she'd rather have him depressed in his bed or … gone.

She replaced the chart in her med cart and spun slowly on her heels. Scanned again. Maybe he'd sat in the wrong chair. Eyes on each person. Staff feeding residents, carrying serving trays.

Mrs. Samuelson tottered in, slowly placing her walker in front of her and walking into it. Each step careful and measured. Determination on Mrs. Samuelson's face—never to fall again. Stepped over and over until she reached her table and sat down.

Staff hurried to serve her the meal, leaning into her good ear, yelling, "It's baked chicken breasts, mashed potatoes with gravy, corn and cole slaw today, Mrs. Samuelson." The aide shook out her bib and attached it around her neck. "Then for dessert, we have apple crisp."

"Oh, that all sounds good, dear." Mrs. Samuelson fussed with her bib and patted her tummy. "I'm hungry today."

Carol continued around the dining room.

Mrs. Getty's head nodded into her food. Carol gently lifted it and squeezed her shoulders, wiping cole slaw off her nose with her bib.

She kept scanning the room.

Harold's eyes caught hers, and he smiled. His open suit jacket—the lapel sporting an American flag pin, dress shirt and snagged dress pants—looked out of place among the usual flannel shirts and sweat pants the men usually wore. Always the detective on the job. "He's gone, I bet."

Carol grinned back. "You read minds, don't you, Harold?"

He grinned. "Naw, just goin' on past experience."

She nodded and adjusted his bib and napkin. "Sorry you have to wear this, but—"

"Regulations," he finished her sentence. "It's okay. Somedays I don't spill a drop. Others?" He rolled his eyes, then lifted the bib to reveal several smudges of pink yogurt from breakfast, smudged on his shirt pocket. "I missed."

"Uh-huh. I know. Me too." She opened her white nurses jacket and licked a finger, sampling an imaginary spot on her shirt. "Yup—mmmm. Me, too. I had chocolate yogurt. What flavor's yours?"

He laughed. "Strawberry."

She patted his bib. "I'd better go check his room. See you later." She passed him, backed up beside him again and rubbed his shoulder. "You're a good man, Harold."

He bowed his head, then lifted his eyes to Carol's and whispered. "You're a good woman and nurse, Carol. You listen to our words … but you listen to our hearts."

She hugged him. "I only hear what God gives me, but thanks." She straightened and extended her imaginary sword. "Now, onward. On to be the vigilante, the detective." She glanced at him. "The warrior, to search out this nursing home kingdom for Sir Clarence."

He burst out laughing, cupping his bib to his mouth. He coughed and swallowed. Cleared his throat and sputtered.

"You okay, Harold?" She knelt beside him. "Sorry. Didn't mean to make you choke. That's kinda frowned upon here. I don't want to have to chart you up."

"Naw. You made me laugh. That's always good for spitting food." He wiped his mouth. "I'm fine. Hope you find your missing kid."

"Yup." Carol nodded as she stepped away. "Me too." She waved as she headed down the hall, past residents wheeling and walking back to their rooms.

She walked by the nurse's station. "April, have you seen Clarence?"

The aide looked up from charting on the handheld computer, glasses slipped down her nose, squinting. She rubbed her temples. "What?"

"Ha. You'll catch on to that monster machine. If I can do it, you can." Carol drummed on the desk beside her. "Clarence. Have you seen him?"

"I got him another plate of eggs this morning. He seemed extra hungry for some reason. But that's the last time I remember seeing him."

"Okay. Could you help search the place? Then let me know what you find and we'll put it out on the pagers. Just a hunch."

"K." She rose, pocketed her computer and followed Carol.

Carol took one direction. April went the opposite.

Carol surveyed the common living room right outside the nurse's station. It was already filling with wheelchairs, occupied with sleeping viewers. Only one little lady intently watched TV—the only one sitting in a straight back chair. She glanced up and reached out her hand as Carol passed her.

"You'll find him."

Carol stopped in her tracks. "Who, Mrs. Hatly?"

"Why Clarence, of course." She smiled sweetly. Chin-length, gray hair curled around a pink ribbon. A flowered dress and matching sweater hid bony flesh. Skinny sup-hose-clad legs dangled from the chair. "He seems to be a nice man. When I first moved in here, I wanted to run away, too." She patted the arm of the chair. "But something kept me from doing just that."

Carol hugged Mrs. Hatly's thin shoulders and kept on maneuvering and squeezing between each chair and wheelchair, making a note to herself: spend more time with Mrs. Hatly. Such wisdom tucked in there. She always felt good after talking to her.

Last chair.

No Clarence.

Down another hall.

She opened the laundry room door and walked in, pushing hanging sheets aside. Washers and driers chugging away in some kind of Indian drum cadence made her want to dance along. She pushed aside one last damp sheet to see Rosita—one of the newest employees—folding towels at a large table. Rosita's face was flushed. Sweat beaded on her upper lip and dripped from her forehead, her hair wet in ringlets.

"Do you always hang sheets to dry?" Carol asked, still grasping a sheet.

"Sí. The dryers can't keep up."

"It's hot in here." Carol fanned her jacket out and in, shaking her head. "Is it always this hot?"

Rosita wiped at her forehead with a tissue. "Yes. And this is late winter." She nodded toward the open window, a snow bank right outside. "Snow air cooled."

Carol could feel the breeze where she stood. "Don't catch cold, Rosita."

"I sweat so much, no germ could live in here." She patted her chest. "Besides I pray."

Carol stopped short, her hand on the table. "What?"

Rosita stopped folding. "I said, I pray." She eyed Carol and added the towel to the pile.

Carol stared.

Wow. "Me, too."

Rosita smiled. "Now, what'd you come into my little office for, Miss Head Nurse Carol?"

Back on task. "I … oh, I can't find Clarence. You know, the new guy from Chicago? Have you seen him?"

"Naw. The lady reses sometime come in to help fold, but a man has never come in."

"Yeah. Okay." Carol laughed and stepped through the open doorway and paused. "Thanks, Rosita." She started to close the door, but opened it again. "Keep on doing that praying stuff, okay?"

"Sí, Miss Director, Ma'am."

Carol paused outside the closed door and made another note to herself: go fold clothes with Rosita on breaks. She could rub against that stuff all day.

She knocked on Clarence's open door. "Clarence, it's me, Carol." She shook her head. Nobody. She checked every corner of the room and bathroom, then poked into his closet. His jacket hung on the hook, and his flap hat sat on the shelf.

She punched the button on the pager. "Hello all. Keep an eye out for Clarence. He isn't in his room or bathroom and his jacket and hat are still here. Check all halls, gardens, conference rooms—all rooms. Chapel. Report back ASAP. I do not want to call the Sheriff on a resident, again. We all know what happened last time."

Various voices echoed from the speaker.

"Right on."

"Okay. On it."

CHAPTER 13

Bea kicked the back of Mommy's seat as she watched the old man and his bird. Mommy steered the car into the street, and Bea squirmed to keep him in sight.

"Bea! Quit kicking!" Mommy tore open a pack of cigarettes and tossed the wrapper toward the floor on the passenger side, only to have the clear wrapper stick to her fingers. She shook her hand hard but it wouldn't let go.

Bea giggled, but stopped when Mommy glared at her in the rear view mirror.

Mommy flicked harder and the wrapper floated off her hand. She tapped the end of the pack, popped a cigarette out and reached for the lighter. She hit the radio instead, which blared loud music. Mommy groaned, glancing in the rear view mirror.

Bea squirmed in her car seat but couldn't quit watching Mommy. Something was happening. Mommy was different. She was changing.

Mommy lit the cigarette and sucked in on it, her cheeks pulled in, eyes closed. Head dropped back against the headrest as she slowed for the red light. She held her breath, then blew the smoke out.

Cars screeched to a halt on both sides of their station wagon. Horns honked. But their car floated through the intersection.

Mommy opened her eyes but drifted away into her world—her world of smoky cigarettes.

Traffic swerved.

Someone honked in the car behind.

"Mommy?" Bea whispered.

Mommy squinted one eye open and shivered. She sat up and held the cigarette daintily between her pointer finger and middle finger, letting it stick up like a beam from a little flashlight.

Bea looked down at her own fingers, mimicking Mommy's.

More horns honked.

Bea stared as the smoke from the cigarette lazily curled up to the ceiling of the car, swirling along every crevice and opening. When it drifted into the back seat, it made her cough and cough. "Mommy?"

"Oh, sorry baby. I'll open my window." She pushed the window button, but it didn't work. "Damn." She pounded on it but it didn't open. She cracked her door open. The smoke floated toward the opening. "That better?"

The car zigzagged.

Bea grabbed the arms of her car seat. "Mommy, why do you smoke? It stinks. It makes my eyes burn. Don't your eyes burn?"

Mommy slammed on the brakes, flipped around in her seat, face to face with Bea, eyes wide. Another horn blared.

Bea pressed back into her car seat, hugging Dolly.

"I smoke … because I like it." Her voice became louder with each word. "Okay? That's all you need to know." She turned back toward the front of the car and pounded the steering wheel. The car lurched forward.

"Mommy?"

The car swerved into a parking lot, just missing a delivery van.

"Mommy?" Bea coughed. "Mommy, could you buckle me in?"

"Not now!" Mommy snickered. "I've never strapped you in and I don't need to start now!" Mommy kicked the car door open wider, pushed out of the car, and slammed the door behind her.

Bea blinked. Her chin quivered as she wound Dolly's hair around one finger.

Mommy paced back and forth, puffing on the cigarette. She glanced at Bea, shook her head, then quickly looked away. Glanced again and stomped her foot. She sucked on the cigarette. Her eyes squinted through the smoke. Then she stood still, staring away, and flicked cigarette ashes to the pavement. One more suck on the cigarette and she dropped it to the concrete and ground it with her boot. She slowly put her hand on the car door handle but didn't open the door.

Bea hugged Dolly tighter and whispered, "Mommy?" A tear slid down her cheek.

Finally the car door clicked and Mommy climbed in. Fresh air rushed in until she shut the door.

She looked down at the steering wheel. "I need them. Cigarettes. I need them, okay?" She stopped. "I have to do it." She stuck her jaw out and sniffed, nostrils flaring. "I'm not proud of it. Not any more. I used to think it was cool." She fingered the cigarette pack. "But now, I don't. I hate it." She threw the pack against the passenger door window. "I hate it."

Mommy stared at Bea in the rear view mirror, then looked away.

"I can't stop, Baby Bea. I'm … addicted to it. Do you know what that means?"

Bea shook her head, hiding behind Dolly.

"It means I have to have it. I can't go a minute without thinking about it."

Silence.

Mommy stared at Bea in the rear view mirror and started to cry.

Bea cried, too.

Mommy picked up the cigarette pack, messed with it and popped another cigarette out. She looked back at Bea. "I get sick when I try not to smoke. It's like a demon inside of me. Like it's controlling me. I can't help it."

Bea's stared at the cigarette in her mommy's hand. "Mommy—"

"I know. That's icky, but it's true." She stopped. "I don't know why I am telling you all this, but I am. I'm sorry Mommy smokes, Baby Bea. I'm sorry I can't stop. It's like a demon inside of me, chasing me, picking at me. Telling me I have to have another cigarette. Getting me all sick and … mean." She sputtered out a cough. "Making me cough." She turned and stared at Bea. "Making you cough." She rustled on the front seat, then held a kleenex to her mouth and coughed.

Bea stared again at the cigarette, then at her mommy, then at the smoke still filling the car and jumped down onto the floor—right behind Mommy. "Mommy, don't get sick. I love you, Mommy. Don't get sick. Please just throw them away. Throw them out the window. Flush them down the toilet. I saw you do that once. You flushed them and some pills down the toilet. Do it, Mommy. Do it again."

Mommy whipped around in her seat and faced Bea, nose to nose, her eyes wide. "You saw me do that? Pills too?" She turned red. She gunned the car engine again and again. "Well, you can just get sick then. Just get sick for all I care. You deserve it for spying on me."

Frightened, Bea hugged Dolly tight against her chest. She jumped onto her car seat and squeezed her eyes shut, kissing Dolly's head. She whispered, "Dolly, I won't ever smoke. I won't make you smell that smoke. I won't ever do that to you. I love you Dolly." A tear slid down her cheek and dripped onto Dolly's head.

Mommy looked into the rear view mirror and choked, gave Bea a mean look and coughed a rattly cough. She grabbed the cigarette and lit up, took a drag on it, then swerved out onto the street. A lone tear streamed down her cheek. She sucked on the cigarette, opened the window and threw it out into the street. She grabbed the pack of cigarettes and threw them, too.

She yanked open the glove box and dug around, the car weaving into the other lane.

A car drove right at them. It blared its horn, and Mommy drove the car back on her own side, the car rocking back and forth. "There!" Mommy yelled. She grabbed one more pack of cigarettes and threw it out the window.

Mommy caught Bea's eyes in the rear view mirror. "No more," she yelled. "Okay?" Then she lowered her voice. "No more cigarettes, Baby Bea." Sobs broke from her throat and her eyes filled with tears. The car swerved back and forth.

Bea held on tight to her car seat and coughed again, eyes scrunched closed.

CHAPTER 14

Carol kicked at a piece of rock strayed from the rose bed in front of Hillcrest as Sheriff Dennison radioed the dispatcher. She had hated calling the police about Clarence's disappearance, but now he'd missed supper too. She couldn't let him think he could leave any time without checking out. If she let him get away with it once, he'd do it again and again.

She crossed her arms across her chest and paced, glancing at the sun slicing lower in the sky. The birds had begun evening twitterings and lullabies.

No family to call. No one to reinforce the dangers. No one to back her up.

No one to care whether he lived or died.

Sheriff Dennison put down the radio and turned toward her. He raked his fingers through his already tousled sandy hair. No pot belly on him. But those dark eyelashes. "Well, they spotted him at the grocery store down on Central Street. He was fine—ornery, but fine. Not involved in the hit-and-run."

Relieved, she shrugged. "He seems like he doesn't care, but there is something deeper about him. I haven't quite figured him out yet."

"You care too much. He's just an old man that doesn't want to be here. They're all that way at first, right?"

Carol nodded. "Some." She nodded again and bit her lips inside her mouth. "Most."

"Hey, don't take it so hard. I'm sure he's all right. The grocery store manager said he was, anyways." Sheriff Dennison chuckled. "In fact, she said he was pretty stalwart, I think was the word. Or, maybe she said stubborn. I'm not sure."

Carol smiled. "Okay. Well, keep in touch. I'm sure he'll come back. I hate calling you, but with him, his physical status is so good, he could go to the next county and back. Or … not back."

He nodded. "Maybe he will. More power to him."

Carol raised an eyebrow. "You, sir, don't have to answer to the state or the home office about why one of your residents has run away."

He shrugged. "Tell them he's a community mediator between the nursing home and the town." He grinned. "Besides, it happens from time to time. And I'm sure you're not the only facility to go through this." He raised his eyebrows. "Right?"

Carol nodded and turned to go inside. She looked over her shoulder. "Thanks, Denny. Thanks for caring."

He saluted. "Sure thing, Carol. Sure thing." Down at his belt, his radio started squawking. "Hey." He picked it up. "You took great care of Mom. And you probably will of me, too." He grinned. "That's scary. Gotta go." He spoke into the radio, "Dennison here. Still at the grocery store? Okay. Thanks."

Carol slowly nodded and took her time walking back up the sidewalk.

"Hey Carol. How's your husband doing? I mean, has he gotten to come home yet?"

Facing the building, she shook her head.

"Is he any better?"

"No. He still can't talk. Sometimes I think he knows me."

Silence.

Footsteps scattered gravel behind her. Denny walked around in front of her and spoke softly. "We could go for ice cream sometime. You and me. It wouldn't hurt anything." He shrugged. "Just friends."

Carol looked deep into his green eyes framed with *those lashes*. She hadn't forgotten staring longingly into them many years ago.

Deep sigh.

And a smile.

"Thanks, Denny." She studied the sidewalk, hands in her jacket pockets. Then back into those eyes. "Really. Thanks."

"But … no."

"You know I can't." *Breathe*. "Won't."

He nodded. "I know. I had to ask. You're a godly woman that any man would be proud to be married to." He nodded again. "And I know that deep down your husband still knows that."

Carol held her breath. Joe was just fifty years old. They'd had twenty wonderful years together before the stroke took him down. "I hope so."

They gazed at each other for a full moment.

The radio sputtered. "Sheriff—checking in. These stories don't quite check out. Might need to talk to you."

Denny smiled. "Gotta go." He bowed low, hand on his heart.

Carol giggled and curtsied. "I do too. I really hope no one's looking out the windows right now."

"Ahh, the gossip begins."

Carol smiled as he jogged back to his car.

She started up the walk again, but stopped outside the entrance and turned to look toward the town. Sigh. "Where are you, Clarence?" She hoped he came back before she had to let the home office know he was gone. Shading her eyes, she grimaced. On the other hand, she'd lied to the home office before on the residents' behalf. Why stop now?

She glanced at the trees, the rose garden, the view of the town. Beautiful. Peaceful. She could live here. Somebody cooks for you. Somebody bathes you, cleans for you. Rosita does your laundry. No responsibility at all.

She sighed. No, when the time came she'd probably resist living here, too.

She pushed in her access code and the door swung open. She walked through, her arms outstretched. Her subjects awaited … like a queen, she entered her domain.

Lisha Hall, a very heavy dark-skinned woman with long dreads tied on top of her head, met her in the lobby, carrying … were those pipes? An armload of old plumbing—different lengths and sizes. She kicked at the trail of rust and dirt.

"Lisha, what are you doing? Where'd you find those?" Carol caught one as it fell. "You been dumpster diving again?"

"No, silly. Guess."

"Pft. How would I know?"

Lisha's head bobbed up and down as she chopped the air with a pipe. "In the bottom of Clarence's closet. Along with the picture of Jesus."

CHAPTER 15

Clarence picked a path through the debris in the alley behind the grocery store, sidestepping the occasional dog pile, puddle and tire rut. Arms extended on either side balancing, he felt like a tightrope walker minus the pole. He stopped and rested every once in a while, stooping to pick up an object that drew his attention from among the weeds.

Key? No. Just junk. He tossed it down and took another step. He tripped as he spied something, then leaned over for what turned out to be a gum wrapper. Wrigley's. He threw it to the wind.

Something else sparkled in the sun—a bright something. He stumbled, tripped, then balanced, only to find another candy wrapper. "Willy Wonka." He turned it over. "They've done pretty well through the years."

Half burned trash and papers littered the alley and lot. Rusty pipes, bent this way and that. Overgrown weeds and brush.

Another shiny object gleamed through the refuse. He groaned as he bent to pick it up, turning it over in his hand. It was a dime store ring, a cheap plastic thing. He flung it away and gasped as a scene from his past unfolded before him.

A much younger Clarence squatted easily and sifted through the tall grass to fish out the gleaming diamond ring, dazzling and blinding as it reflected the sun's rays. He knelt on the hard gravel and stared at the beauty of the facets. He turned it this way and that, admiring the cut, the brilliance, the colors emanating from deep within.

Stunning.

"And I will not marry you in a hundred million years," Sally wailed. "Not ever. Ever."

Clarence glanced at her, then stared as the young woman slowly morphed into a tree standing in the distance, his mind still in the past, his body stuck in the present.

Deep rattly breath.

A train whistle startled him.

As mind and body reconnected, he shook as he searched in the weeds, parting the grass, combing through the debris. Where had it gone? He cut his finger on a rusty can. Damn. That nurse Carol would make him get a tetanus shot. Or take some kind of antibiotics. Or both. He sucked on the cut.

The nursing home van drove up the hill. Large green letters on the side read *Hillcrest Home, "Home of God's Most Beloved."*

Cringing, he ducked behind the corner of the grocery store, then peered out. He hated that slogan. If he were God's Beloved, he certainly wouldn't be living there.

He'd be back in prison.

Or dead.

The van turned into the parking lot, then circled back out. Jim the maintenance man was driving, and Bill his assistant hung out the passenger window, squirming in his seat, craning his neck.

"Buzzards," Clarence muttered. "Flying around looking for dead stuff." He pulled his head back behind the brick wall, scanning the alley, feeling more alive than he had in years. He could barely make out the silhouette of a hawk in the tree, against the darkening sky. "Ha, old bird. Trying to sneak up on me, huh. You thought you had me."

Clarence pondered the bird as it cocked its head. Stare-down, man against bird. Bird against man. Neither one giving in. Both stubborn. Both toughened against life.

Clarence held up a fist. "What have you got in you, old bird? What are you made of?" He stopped to listen and dropped his fist against his leg. "You are made of feathers and that's all. Feathers. You hear me, old bird? Just bones and feathers."

The hawk screeched. Clarence jumped and covered his ears. The bird majestically rose into the air, wings spread wide and glided over Clarence. Damn, that wingspread had to be over four feet.

Something small dropped out of the sky. Clarence ducked, covering his head with his arms. It bounced off his shoulder and pinged off a rock, into the rubble below.

He sighted in on the landing place, crawled over to it, and picked up the dime store ring.

"Argh." He sat in the dirt and held it up. The cheap metal and rhinestone barely reflected the remaining sun light. "This again."

He searched the sky for the hawk.

Gone.

CHAPTER 16

Carol peeked through the front window of the grocery store, shuffled to her right, then left, scoping out the store's front end. She didn't see Clarence anywhere, and she hoped calling Denny didn't create a disaster.

Hand on door pull. Smile on face. Hold her breath. Blow it out. Walk in.

Ding. The door alarm rang out announcing her entrance.

A young clerk—Carol recognized Mindy—peeked from around the end of a shelf. "Hi. Can I help you find anything?"

"Well, it's not an anything I need to find. It's an anyone. Like in a person."

Mindy rounded the end cap and stood at the register, straightening her green apron. "Yeah? Who, anyone?" She grinned.

Carol dug into her jacket pocket and pulled out the admissions picture. She held it for Mindy to see. "His name is Clarence … "

Mindy grabbed the picture. "Oh, I know Clarence." She tapped the picture. "He was just here today. He's … uh … well, let's put it this way—"

"He's rude, mean, loud, and insulting." A tall, male employee walked up beside Mindy. "And that's just the beginning. He's—"

Mindy poked him. "That's enough, John. I think she gets the idea, don't you, Ma'am."

Carol grimaced. "Sounds like you've met Clarence, all right. Can you tell me when, where? What'd he do that was so bad?"

John glanced over at Mindy and she glanced back. Oh-oh. Carol braced herself.

"Well … he was here a little while ago."

"What time?"

He checked his watch. "An hour ago? You know, give or take."

"Did he say where he was headed?"

"Wait a minute. Is he in trouble? I mean, like in danger? Because, well, I did see him head out back," Mindy said, her hands in her apron pocket. "He was being, well—"

"Mean. He was being mean." John interrupted her.

Mindy squirmed and retied her apron. "Yes. I said that Clarence is so much like my old grandpa. Clarence is better looking, but Grampa was always outa sorts."

"Your grandpa was mean, Mindy." John touched her shoulder. "You've told me about stuff he did. Burning your little doll. And other stuff."

Carol grimaced and stared at Mindy.

Mindy nodded. "Yeah. He was mean." She rubbed her arm and seemed distracted for a minute. "And Clarence … well, I felt like I used to feel when Grandpa was around."

Carol sighed. "I'm so sorry he hurt you. I wish I knew more about his past. He has no family—no wife, no kids. He grew up around here, but as far as I know, he moved away soon after he grew up." She looked left, then right. "I shouldn't have told you that, but if you know more about him, maybe you can understand him. Maybe you can help us find him. He moved back here because he had nowhere else to go. He couldn't live on his own, but no one would take him in."

"Sounds just like Grandpa, but we took him in."

"So, he lived with you?" Carol shook her head. "Must have been tough."

Mindy sighed and rearranged the newspapers. "Yeah. But he's gone now." She bowed her head. "I only hope—"

"Do you think you could show me where you saw Clarence heading? It might be a place to start." She checked her watch. "He's getting past med time. He already missed lunch. And supper."

"Sure. I need to tell my boss, though."

"That's fine." Carol said. "I'll wait for you."

Mindy returned a few minutes later. She and Carol walked out behind the store among the weeds and trash.

"It was right after he left the store. I think he hung around. I opened the door to bring a bag of trash out," she pointed to the dumpster, "and that's when I saw him again."

"What was he doing?"

"Well, at first I thought he was hiding, or looked like it. But when I opened the dumpster, I looked up and saw him bending down over here someplace. I almost said something to him, but my boss hollered at me to come help her. It's truck day today, so there's lots to do. Groceries to put away and stuff."

"I understand." Carol stepped to the spot. "He was maybe about here?"

"Yeah."

Carol bent over, looking onto the ground. Maybe he had dropped something and bent down to retrieve it. She brushed her hand over the tall weeds, trying to see the ground.

Mindy closed the dumpster lid. "Why doesn't he have any family? Even Grandpa had us. We weren't much. At least he didn't think so, but we helped him when he needed it. Fed him. Took care of him and stuff. A place to sleep." Mindy shook her head. "That's tough. And lonely."

Carol straightened and searched Mindy's face. "Yes, Mindy. Lonely, it is." Joe in a nursing home thirty miles away. Joe staring at her with vacant eyes. Only once in the last three years had he greeted her with a flicker of recognition. Lonely it is. The back door opened and John pushed a cart loaded with trash outside. Carol turned back to Mindy. "Are you okay?"

"Yeah, it's just that, well, I feel bad. Grandpa had us. Clarence has nobody." She shifted her weight. "And, well, we like kinda talked back to him."

John flipped the dumpster lid open and tossed in the trash bags. "No, Mindy. You didn't talk back to him." He slammed the lid shut. "I did. He was saying stuff about you and he can't do that. Not on my watch."

Carol half smiled.

Mindy blushed.

John stretched taller.

"That's okay, John." Carol said. "Sometimes I find I get along better with him when I stand up to him. But I'm still getting to know him. He just got here." She shrugged. "I've already told you way too much for that privacy act." She pointed along the brick building that led to the alley. "Did he go down that way?"

"I hope not. That's not safe." Mindy pointed down the alley. "He might have gone over there. Maybe."

An older woman wearing a long green-and-white striped necktie appeared at the store's back door. "Mindy? John?" she called. "You still work here?" Her head turned toward Carol. "Oh, I'm sorry. I thought you left." She approached the threesome. "Are you getting what you need?"

Carol nodded. "Well, it's a start. I appreciate your help, Mindy." She shook her hand, then John's. "And yours, John." She glanced at the older woman—obviously the manager—and back to the kids. "Please, with your boss's permission, if you see him or hear anything, could you call me at this number?" She handed Mindy a business card.

"Sure."

"Thanks, you two. Have a good night." She shook hands with the manager. "They're good kids. Thanks for giving me their time."

"Sure. Hope you find him. Let us know if we can do anything else."

Carol turned to go, but not before she caught sight of a huge bird perched in the tree above them. Was that? Couldn't be the same hawk. "Do you see that?"

John rotated his head, looking at all the branches. "Where? Oh, the hawk? He lives here."

"Like he's your neighborhood hawk?" Carol chuckled. "They must be all over. We had one break into the home, through a window." Her eyes opened wide. "Clarence's window, as a matter of fact."

John folded his arms across his chest. "Really."

"I wish he could tell us what he sees day in and day out." Carol cooed to the bird. "Wait, wrong bird. What sound does a hawk make?"

As if in answer, the hawk lifted off the tree branch and swooped down toward them, screeching.

Carol ran toward her car, covering her ears. She turned to see where it went. Huge. Loud.

The others appeared from behind the dumpster.

"That's what they sound like," John said.

Carol hurried to them. "I'll know next time." She adjusted her jacket. "It's like it heard me ask."

The manager brushed off dirt from her shirt and re-clipped her tie as the bird flew back up to the branch in the tree. "I'm calling the Sheriff's Office or a wildlife association to come pick him up. He's dangerous."

"Please don't," John piped up. "I'm out here every day, doing the trash, running the compactor. He's never done that before and believe me, I've teased him so he should have." He grinned sheepishly. Then held up his hands. "Really. I feel something from him."

The manager cut in. "Fe-e-el something?"

John's head dropped to his chest. "I know it's weird. Sounds creepy. But I think he serves a purpose somehow. I don't know how to say it, but really he has never done this before. Please give him another chance."

"If he does it again, he's gone. We can't have him dive bombing customers. We won't destroy him, but the guys can catch him and take him into the country somewhere, where we'll all be safe. Us and him."

John nodded his head and kicked at the gravel. "Fair enough."

"Nature boy." Mindy squeezed John's hand.

"I don't know, John. What purpose could a bird have? But, hear me bird." Mrs. Larkin spoke loudly and distinctly. "I'm putting you on notice. You dive at anybody again, and you're a gonner." She pointed at the hawk. "Ya hear?"

The hawk stared down at them.

John half chuckled, half breathed out. "See what I mean? He's got some … purpose."

"Then tell us where Clarence is, Mr. Hawk." Carol waved as she walked to her car. "Please."

CHAPTER 17

Clarence hid behind a tree and watched Miss Henningway drive away from Hillcrest Homes. Having a room on the parking lot side had its advantages. She didn't look happy … but then she never looked happy unless she was bragging about nursing home awards she had achieved.

Clarence also watched the side entrance door. No one coming or going. He needed a spotter inside. He made a run for it as fast as his old legs could carry him and crouched beside the tan brick building. Almost home. The windows beside him opened onto resident rooms, his included. Eyes were upon him. He reached the door, pushed the automatic door opener and peeked in. One hallway was clear. He couldn't see down the other. TV's blared. Someone dropped a bedpan. The sound echoed over background voices and TV chatter.

He slipped inside and tiptoed straight to his room. Nice and handy at the end of the hall, almost next to the exit.

He hustled to the bathroom door but froze as he felt a hand on his shoulder. He swung around to see a dark-skinned woman, huge in stature and in girth, grinning at him. Lots of big teeth. Dreads sticking out from the back of her head.

He pointed. "Uh, I gotta go in here. It's been too long."

She never stopped grinning, even as she spoke. "Uh-huh. It has been too long. You go somewhere, Clarence? Did you have a date?"

"You are mean. I gotta go." He slid into the bathroom and slammed the door against the visual of her. "She better think twice about pushing me around."

"What you say, Clarence?" She cracked the door open. "Sorry, couldn't hear."

All he could see was teeth.

"What'd you say again?"

He grabbed the doorknob and slammed the door, shutting her name tag lanyard in the door jamb. He could read her name on it as he relieved himself. Lisha. He chuckled. A visual of her hanging by a cord to his bathroom door made him burst out in laughter. He opened the door.

"Oh, you think that's funny, Mr. Clarence?" She tucked her lanyard under her white uniform jacket, cupped his shoulder, and steered him in front of her—eye to eye with him. Black eyes. An inch from his. Freckles. And large pores on her nose.

"Yeah. I thought that was funny. Didn't you?" He laughed his best fake laugh, then stopped abruptly and sneered his best fake smile.

She scowled back. "You are in so much trouble Mr. Clarence. We might get to chain you to your chair. Or at least to your bed. Maybe torture you with, I don't know, drops of water or sumthin'."

Clarence raised his eyebrows. "Oh, yeah?" He squinted. "Iss on."

Her right eyebrow quivered. She slowly released his shoulder. "You missed din-ner. I 'spose you're spectin' dessert? Are you all washed up?" She headed down the hall, laughing.

She had to be at the dining room, she sounded so far away.

Ha. Ha.

Leaving the door open, he walked to his window and stared at the trees waving in the wind. Even the leaves seemed to be taunting him. He sighed and shook his head, hands slipped in his pockets, and muttered, "Bastard judge. Had this all figured out, huh." He jingled his coins, then patted his back pockets. "What the f-?" He patted his shirt pockets. "Where is … my f-n wallet?"

"Clarence." A female voice spoke behind him. "How did you get back in here and where did you go and why do you put me through all this and … and … and … you are in so much trouble."

He turned to face Carol, red-faced and out of breath, huffing and puffing.

Clarence started in. "You need to lose weight," he snapped. "You're out of shape and breathless. You can't even walk down the hall without overexerting yourself."

Carol stomped her foot. "Stop. Shame on you, Clarence. Shame on you, for putting me through … no, for putting all of us through this. You've been gone all day! We were worried sick."

He swallowed. "You were just worried because you would have to call the Sheriff in. You were just worried about your record with the home office. Your point system or whatever it is." He grimaced as he patted his back pocket where his wallet should have been. "You weren't worried about me. Just your job. Your accreditation. That's what you were worried about."

Carol stopped. "Yes, I was worried about all that. Of course. It's my job to be on top of all that. That's what I do." She took a step toward him. "But I was also worried about you, Clarence." She poked his chest and backed him to the window. "Because I care about you. I care about each and every resident. So when you pull a stunt like you did today, I worry. Are you all right? Did you get hurt? Did you fall?"

"And can't get up?" Clarence smirked.

Silence.

Her brown eyes inches from his face. "That's not my job, Clarence. That's my heart."

He stared at her. "You still need to lose weight. All of you do. You eat too much here. And where the hell is—" On second thought, she didn't need to know about his wallet. He'd find it—without her or anybody else's help.

"Where's what?"

"Never you mind."

Carol's chest rose and fell. She squinted and her chin quivered. She quietly left the room.

Clarence turned to the window, hands in his pockets, as a tear started down his cheek. He quickly wiped it away.

"So you're back. You're in so much trouble." Yet another voice from the open door.

Clarence turned and slammed the door in Harold's face, but not before he heard Harold say, "Hey, you're crying. I'm sorry. You okay?"

He leaned against the door and choked back the tears.

CHAPTER 18

Bea sat at the kitchen table, stirring her cereal as she chewed, singing softly—sweetly—swinging her legs in time.

Slam! Mommy dropped the washer lid.

Bea jumped.

"I wish he'd call." Mommy checked the clock, then turned the washer dial. Water rushed into the machine, splashing loudly. "Bea! Can you stop that singing already?" Mommy's voice got louder, along with the clicking of her long black polished nails on the metal lid. She turned and glared at Bea. "Really. Can't you stop?"

Bea sucked in a breath and choked, eyes wide, the spoon frozen in the air, dripping milk onto the table and floor. Her face turned hot as she coughed up cereal chunks. The spoon clattered to the floor.

"Bea! You're dripping milk all over, Baby Bea." Mommy said her name in a hard, angry voice and rushed to the table. "You're making a mess. Why can't you eat right, like everybody else?" She slammed her hand onto the table beside Bea's cereal. Everything jumped, including Bea. "Look, you spilled on your shirt. Now you'll have to change before school."

Mommy grabbed the spoon and threw it into the sink. "Get yourself cleaned up. Now!" She pointed toward the bathroom. "And don't forget to brush your teeth."

Bea cleared her throat. Her lower lip quivered, and she felt tears in her eyes. "I'm not done eating." She was still hungry.

"I'm not done eating," Mommy mimicked back in a high, scary voice. She grabbed the cereal bowl, spilling more milk on Bea's shirt.

Bea scooted off the chair and ran down the hall. When she shut the bathroom door, she made sure the latch was silent. She let go of the knob, one turn at a time, until it stopped. She stepped onto the stool in front of the sink.

As she looked into the mirror, she let the tears flow down her cheeks. No sound. Not a sob. Just tears streaming from her eyes, dripping onto the counter, into the sink.

The pretty brown eyes in the mirror watched the hurt and pain drip down. The little girl in the mirror helped her calm down, helped the tears stop. Told her to be strong.

Bea sighed a deep ragged breath, changed into a clean T-shirt and picked up her toothbrush and toothpaste. She turned on the water, squirted toothpaste onto the brush, and screwed the cap on straight. A quiet melody stirred in her heart and she began to hum as she brushed her teeth.

"Do I hear water running?" Mommy's loud voice broke in. Loud raps on the door echoed into the bathroom, into her song, into her heart.

Bea turned the water off quickly.

"You know better than to let the water run while you brush." Mommy pounded on the door again. Bea jumped and dropped her toothbrush. It bounced down her shirt, trailing toothpaste all the way down.

Bea took one look and let out a wail.

The door burst open. Mommy stepped into the room. Her face didn't look like Mommy. Dark glinted in her eyes, forehead scrunched, lips stretched over her teeth.

This was somebody else.

Bea cried harder and harder as Mommy crept closer.

Mommy leaned over her. She shook her head and crouched low, face to face with Bea.

Bea stepped back. Almost falling off the stool, she gripped the sink.

Mommy stepped closer and grabbed Bea's wrist, slapping her hard on the cheek.

Bea shrieked.

Suddenly something changed in Mommy. Her face looked different. Her eyes were soft again. She sucked in a deep breath and shook all over.

She grabbed Bea again, but Bea tried to pull away.

"I'm sorry Baby," Mommy said. Her voice sounded softer, sad. "I'm sorry. I don't know what got into me. I … I'm sorry." She started to cry.

Bea struggled, but Mommy held on tighter, saying over and over and over, "I'm sorry. I'm so sorry." She opened her eyes, inches from Bea's. "Baby, I would never hurt you." Her eyes fluttered up. "I … oh." Cupping Bea's burning cheek with her hand, she buried her head against Bea's chest and cried again.

Bea's cheek stung as Mommy stroked it. She slowly circled Mommy's neck with her arms and smelled Mommy's hair. Her own sobs spilled out all at once, and she crumpled onto the floor in Mommy's arms.

CHAPTER 19

Clarence found his jacket and stretched one arm into a sleeve. Then stopped.

He couldn't wear this. They would know.

He pulled it off and hung it back in his closet.

His hat, too, must be left behind. Slowly he closed the squeaky closet door and checked his watch. Meds, check. Lunch, done. He should have till supper.

He glanced over at his bed. He had arranged pillows, then tucked in the bedspread to make the "legs" bend right. He straightened, jingling coins in his pockets. Out of habit, he patted his back pocket. No wallet. Grrr.

He walked to the window overlooking his escape route. Where was that wallet? It had … money, yes, but also his only picture of her in this world. He let his fingers lightly skim over the pipes he'd hung there. Nice wind chime. Deep sigh. Sixty years in a cell produced crazy habits.

Clarence moved to the door and listened for movement, then stepped into the hallway. Prison Break 101: just one more skill he'd learned as an inmate in that other prison.

He lifted his head. Stuck out his chest.

No. Head down. Hands in pockets. Sour look on face—well that part wasn't hard. Shuffle feet.

"Hi Clarence." A cheerful voice stopped him.

He looked up. The dietician.

"Uh … hi." Head back down. Shuffle. Shuffle. Hand out of pocket to wipe his cheek. That'd get her. Deep sigh.

Shuffle on past.

"Hey Clarence. You gonna come into the activity room to help make cookies?"

"Naw. Gonna move around a bit, then take a nap." That'd fit perfectly with the bed arrangement—all those plumped up pillows. He should have been a criminal. No wait. He was one. He had studied with the best of them.

Besides, he had never baked in his life. Even cooked for that matter. Mess call. Line up. March to the mess room. Stand in line to pick up food tray. Place tray on table. Stand behind chair until released. Sit. Eat. That was it for his cooking experience.

He reached the end of the hallway. He looked out the window, sad, sad.

About face.

Shuffle. Shuffle. Shuffle.

"Excuse me, please. Can you help me?" Mrs. Hatly held her hand out to him from her doorway.

He started to make excuses. He glanced at her disheveled hair, glasses askew, and quickly looked away.

Naked. Her hands shook as they gripped the walker.

He looked to his escape route—and back to Mrs. Hatly. Eyes cast down.

"Mrs. Hatly, you must be cold. Let me get your robe and," he searched her room, "warm you up."

A pink and white robe lay rumpled on the floor beside her bed. He snapped it up, gently wrapping it around her. He buttoned the top button and searched her face.

She looked up at him, and apparently something clicked.

No more confusion there.

"Was I?" She checked herself. "Was I … " She grimaced and looked away.

"As a jailbird." He nodded. "But it's okay. Nobody saw."

A tiny tear slipped from under her glasses and dripped to her robe. "I was a teacher. High school physics. I had a *mind*."

Clarence reached to wipe her cheek, then caught himself and stuck his hand in his pocket.

"I do that sometimes." She shook her head. "I get confused and don't know where I'm at." She closed her eyes, her head bent low. "And … well … you know."

"It's okay, Mrs. Hatly. I didn't see a thing. I'm just glad you're back."

"You're a liar and a gentleman." She peered up at him over her glasses and offered a sweet smile.

He chuckled. "Well, you got the first part right." He looked behind him. "Hey, I'd better let you go. I'm on a mission."

"I know," she whispered. "Be safe."

Clarence stopped. He cocked his head. Then leaned forward and gave her a light peck on her cheek.

She gasped. Her fingers touched the spot.

Clarence stumbled and backed away. "I'm sorry. I didn't mean to do that." He pushed his hands at her. "Sorry." He took a step backward and bumped into the doorway, then turned and rushed down the hall, peeking behind him.

She watched him from her door.

Smiling.

He made his way to the exit door. His hand rested on the door handle.

Looked both ways. Back to Mrs. Hatly, who stood where he left her, her hand still on her cheek, still faintly smiling.

Exit. Easy.

Oops. Carol.

Back inside.
Shuffle to other doorway. Head down.
Coast clear.
Open door.
Jailbreak.

CHAPTER 20

Bea bounced onto the sofa, picked up Dolly and hugged her tight. "You're such a good dolly," she whispered, kissing her. She smoothed the doll's hair, then began to undress it, carefully unbuttoning the tiny jacket and removed it, sleeve by sleeve. She unsnapped the onesie and checked the doll's diaper and groaned. "Oh, gross. You're poopy. Now I'll have to change you and clean you a-l-l-l up."

Bea hesitated and looked into the doll's eyes. "Oh, that's okay, Dolly. It's okay. You can't help it." She snuggled the doll's face. Kiss. Kiss. Kiss. "You're just a baby. I'll take care of you."

"There are no new messages." The answering machine played in the kitchen.

"Damn him. Why doesn't he call?"

Mommy peeked around the corner and smiled a shy smile.

Bea hid her face in doll clothes.

"Whatcha doing, Baby Bea?" Mommy asked softly from the kitchen. She played with some papers on the counter and patted her shirt pocket. She walked to Bea and leaned over her.

Bea peeked up into Mommy's face, checking her eyes.

Mommy was back. Real Mommy.

She turned her face away. "I'm playing," Bea said. She held Dolly up for Mommy to see. "Dolly's got dirty pants and I have to change her." She gathered up different clothes and play wipes, then looked away. Her other hand brushed her sore cheek.

Mommy sat on the edge of the sofa. "Baby, I'm sorry about earlier." She wiped her eyes. "That wasn't me. That's not the way I treat you. I'm struggling with not smoking. It's really hard."

Bea looked up at Mommy's face.

"Okay. Drugs too. I really want a cigarette. Bad." Mommy rubbed her arm. "I've got to do this. For you. I've got to do it for you."

Bea took a deep breath. "No you don't, Mommy."

Mommy stiffened beside Bea. "What?"

"You don't do it for me, Mommy. Do it for," Bea pointed at Mommy's chest, "you, Mommy." She patted Dolly's back.

Mommy grasped Bea's finger with her own. She drew their hands to her mouth and kissed Bea's fingers. Then rubbed her face against Bea's hand.

"How did I get so lucky to have you for my little girl?" She put their hands in her lap. "If all the little girls in this big world were lined up, I'd always choose you, Bea."

Bea searched Mommy's face and then stretched out her arms.

Mommy pulled Bea onto her lap and tucked her head under her chin. She always fit just right.

A deep breath filled Bea's chest, and she blew it out.

"I'm so sorry for the way I treated you Bea. Please forgive me."

"I forgive you Mommy."

"Please say a little prayer for me to get over the cig ... all of it. It's harder than I ever knew. I think about them, dream about them. When I'm in the grocery store, I walk by them five times." She shook.

"I do pray for you Mommy. And I'll help you. When you want a cigarette, come to me and we can play dolls. Or read a book. We could go to the park." Bea felt like her chest would burst as ideas came into her mind.

Mommy laughed. "Oh I get it. When I need a cigarette, you'll help me by letting me do something you want to do, right?"

Bea covered her mouth.

"Sounds good to me."

Bea gasped in a giggle. "Mean it, Mommy?"

"Well, for you. An-n-nd, for me, too. It'll be fun, if we make it fun." She turned her head to the side. "Sounds like what my dad used to say, sort of. He always said that life was what you made of it. If you made it shi … well, crappy, then it'd be crappy. But if you chose to make it good, then—"

Bea piped up. "Then it'll be good."

CHAPTER 21

Clarence stumbled along the alley behind Hillcrest. He glanced behind him. Scanned the row of trees as best he could. They grew close together, almost hiding the houses on the other side.

Good cover. No one was tailing him, so far as he could tell. Good to get outside again. He suffocated in that place.

He scanned the sky. No wind. It was chilly, but the sun beamed through the tangle of branches and warmed his head and back. A good spring day.

He checked his perimeters and straightened, on alert. With sixty years of being incarcerated, moving in and out of solitary, of frequent pat-downs and spread-eagle searches, and threats from other inmates, he had never relaxed. Never trusted. He barely breathed without permission.

Now, he breathed deeply of the fresh clean air. No stale nursing home air for him.

Birds twittered brightly. They called back and forth, answering each other.

Clarence listened to the different songs. "Even the birds have friends."

He stumbled, arms out to keep his balance.

"You'd walk better if you watched where you are going."

Clarence froze. He slowly u-turned in search of the voice, to see Harold sitting in his wheelchair, partially hidden by a tree. His beady eyes stared through the branches, the sun glinting off the always-there flag pin on his lapel.

"Didn't you ever join Boy Scouts? They always taught you to walk without making a sound."

Clarence stomped toward Harold. "What are you doing out here? Did they send you to spy on me?" He gripped Harold's jacket sleeve, wobbling the wheelchair. "Come on, did they?"

Harold grabbed the arms of the wheelchair, "No! I knew you'd be out here. I saw you the last time you ran away. You're not pulling anything over on me, Clarence." He grunted. "And honestly, you're not fooling anybody else, either. I've been following people all my life and you aren't the slickest escapee I've ever tracked."

Clarence squinted, then spit on the ground in front of Harold. "I don't care. You can't hurt me. You're in a wheelchair. By the time you get inside to tattle on me, I'm long gone."

"Oh yea, right. You'll get as far as the grocery store again, then get tired and turn around and come home. Or you'll get hungry and need supper. You ain't pullin' the wool over my eyes, buddy."

"Buddy." Clarence clinched his fists. "Buddy. Why, I ought to—"

"Ought to what, Clarence?" Harold's head jerked up. "Come on, buddy. Buddy, Buddy, Buddy. Lay it on me. You'd do what?" He straightened in his wheelchair, arms braced on the wheels.

"You shouldn't have come out here. You shouldn't have followed me." Clarence kicked the wheelchair, knocking it onto one wheel. "How're you gonna get back inside, huh?" He kicked it again, toppling it into a tree.

Harold struggled to regain balance. He pushed against the tree. "You don't scare me, Clarence." He righted the wheelchair, steadied it. "You can't do anything more to me than what's already been done."

"Oh, yeah? You're the one stuck out here. Did you bring your girl-friend with you? What's her name?" Clarence made a play of searching the trees. "I don't see her."

Harold coughed, his hand on his chest. "You're mean." He coughed again. "You must be really unhappy inside to be that cruel," he sputtered.

Clarence turned his back on Harold and mimicked him in a high, sing-songy voice. "You must be so unhappy to be that cruel." He growled as he kicked stones onto the road ahead of him. "Yeah, I'm mean. Been called that and worse all my life. Mean. Bad. Ugly." He turned back to Harold and kicked rocks at him, one narrowly missing his head. "All my life, people hated me, kicked me when I was down." His eyes swam. "But I decided one day, that no one would ever hurt me again. No one, you hear?"

He turned, fists at his side and stomped through the trees, then across the street into the park behind the community building. Litter from picnics long past gathered in mini mountains: gum and candy bar wrappers, dried leaves, cigarette butts. He kicked them all into the air. A wind current whipped the trash into a funnel twisting and slapping into Clarence. He covered his eyes until it died down. Damn leaves. Damn trash. Damn life!

From tree to tree he walked and hid, walked and hid, until he crossed the railroad tracks, finding his way out of the park.

Across the highway.

Then up the hill to the store.

He turned and searched his winding path. No one followed. The glint of the sun on a wheelchair could just barely be seen through the trees.

"Miss Carol? I need you in Clarence's room right away," said Lisha Hall into her pager. "You're not gonna believe this." She walked toward the window, hands on her generously padded hips. "I don't believe this. What's wrong wit this man?"

Hanging from the top of the window were pipes and rods—all kinds and sizes—rusted ones, shiny and polished ones, skinny ones. Connected with old shoe laces and cord.

Head Nurse Carol pushed the door open all the way and gasped. "What is all this?" She stopped at the entrance, and her eyes slowly scanned the window. "What are those ... are those the pipes you found?"

She opened the closet door and peeked in.

She looked back at the window.

"Well, I'll be. Did he make wind chimes?" Carol folded her arms across her chest.

Lisha tapped one, knocking it into another. "Thas not wind chimes, fer sure. Sounds like sh—" Lisha tapped one with her fingernail. "Nuthin."

"Maybe he doesn't want another hawk breaking in." Carol walked to the window and grasped a pipe in each hand as she faced the window. "Feels like I'm in a prison cell."

"Or ... I'm tryin here ... sun reflectors? What are they? Sun catchers?"

Carol turned to Lisha, exasperated. "With lead pipes?"

CHAPTER 22

"My Dolly is so beautiful," Bea sang softly. She tickled Dolly's neck, kissed her on the forehead and picked up the brush beside her, singing as she brushed the doll's hair. A car horn startled her and she jumped, looked out at the street flying by, then back at her doll.

Her legs swung up and down with each stroke of the brush. Up and down went the brush. Up and down went her legs. Like a side-ways pendulum. Singing as she brushed. Singing as she kicked. Up and down. Up and down.

Mommy cussed and stomped on the brakes. Bea braced herself and gripped the car seat and Dolly flew to the floor. The car started moving again as Bea jumped down and picked up the doll. She scrambled into her car seat, watching Mommy in the rear view mirror.

"Can't you see, you damn jerk?" Mommy slammed on the brakes again. Bea slid forward in her seat, dropping Dolly again.

Mommy's cell phone rang. "Grrr. Not now." She grabbed her purse and dug in it, eyes on her purse. "What're all these cars doing in this dinky town?"

The car zigzagged.

Mommy cussed.

She found the phone. "Whatdya want? Oh, hi. How are you?" Her voice changed. This voice was sweet, like honey on Bea's peanut butter. Mommy slammed on the brakes. "I'm fine. It's so good to hear your voice."

A car honked, and Mommy turned the steering wheel fast.

Bea scooted herself back as the car jerked, sending her flat against the seat. For a split second, she glanced out the car window as the street whizzed by. She spied the old man.

He looked at her.

She saw his blue eyes. Something stirred inside her. She leaned in her car seat as they passed, straining to keep him in sight.

"Well, let me see. Friday? I think so. Sure." Mommy looked back. "Bea, sit back."

Bea scooted back, then lifted off her seat and faced the rear of the car.

The man turned his head. He stopped walking and watched as they drove past.

"Bea Baby, you need to sit down or I'll have to buckle you in." Mommy always said that, but never buckled her in. "I mean it." To the phone. "I'm sure we can work out some sort of babysitter."

Bea looked behind her at the rear view mirror and saw a stern look on Mommy's face. With the way Mommy had been lately, she knew she'd better turn around. She sat down, holding Dolly by the hair. But the brush slid down to the floor.

"Ohhh," Bea said. She looked at Mommy's face in the rear view mirror.

Mommy chattered into the phone.

Bea peeked down at the floor, then back up at Mommy. Mommy's face was set forward, eyes on the street ahead.

"What do you want to do?"

Floor.

Mommy.

Floor.

"Okay, that sounds fun. Party on!" She looked at the rear view mirror. "Hold on to your cookies, Bea." said Mommy.

The car swerved to the left, throwing her and Dolly right. The brush slid and bumped across the floor of the car and stopped against the other car door.

She hung her head, staring at the brush. Back to Mommy. Down to the brush.

She slipped out of her seat, making each movement like a kitty on attack. Eyes on target. Feet stretched toward the floor. Stop. Toes touched the floor. Stop. Sliding shoes along the floor. Stop. Hold. Mommy glanced back and smiled, still on the phone.

Bea smiled back, straining to hold her place.

Hold it.

Hold it.

Mommy's eyes focused on the road ahead. "Well, I miss you, too."

Move. Scramble to the brush. Back to her seat. Climb up, knee in the seat. Slowly turn around and sit down.

Mommy glanced in the mirror. "We're almost there Baby." She cocked her head to the side. "You okay? You look funny."

Bea nodded her head, hair bouncing with each bump. Eyes wide, looking ahead through the windshield.

Mommy's eyes fastened to the street again. "Okay. Well, I gotta go. See ya then." She threw the phone onto the passenger seat.

Whew.

"You're sure being quiet back there. You're usually singing." Mommy stretched to see all of Bea. "You sure you're okay? Is Dolly okay?"

Bea nodded her head, kicked her feet with each nod and held up Dolly so Mommy could see her. She smiled a sweet smile, then looked down at her dolly. Her hand gripped the doll's hair. Her fingers wrapped around the brush. She blew out a breath, glanced out the window and began brushing the doll's hair again.

Quick glance to Mommy in the rear view mirror. Back down to the doll. Out the window again.

She remembered the old man's eyes as she smoothed Dolly's hair again. Blue eyes. And long, wavy gray hair. "My Dolly is so beautiful," she sang again, swinging her feet, kicking the back of the driver's seat. "My Dolly is so sweet."

Mommy chimed in. "My Bea is so beautiful. She is so sweet. But quit kicking my seat."

Bea laughed and sang along until Mommy's phone rang again.

CHAPTER 23

Clarence turned up the hill into the grocery store parking lot. He really shouldn't be here. They'd turn him in one of these times.

But not today … he hoped.

He peeked between the tattered fliers taped to the inside, then checked the side parking lot to see who was working. Mindy's ancient Chevy sat there sporting a pink stripe across the door. The beat up Toyota pick up was John's.

Smiling, Clarence crossed his arms across his chest. After all, what was the worst they could do? Send him back to prison? Not a problem.

He pulled on the door handle and peeked in.

From inside. "Boom. Boom."

Clarence jumped back out and let the door close in his face. He searched the interior of the store through the glass. John stood peeking around the nearest aisle end cap, grinning, waving an invisible gun.

Clarence shook his head. Jerk! The kid should be in a mental hospital. He turned to walk away, but Mindy pushed the other door open from the inside.

"Don't let John get to you, Clarence. He's a bug. He's harmless. He doesn't even hurt small children. So he won't hurt you." She stuck out her tongue at John. "I'll make sure of that." She held out her hand. "Come on in. Boss Lady isn't even here, so you're safe."

Clarence hesitated then entered the store. "I'm not afraid of him. I'm afraid of what I will do to him, given half a chance."

John guffawed and walked from behind the shelves. "Oh you would hurt me?" He posed, fists up, feet in a fighter's stance, beckoning with one finger. "Bring it on, Dude."

Clarence busted out laughing. "Okay—Dude." Fists up, he pranced back and forth. His mind blinked to a few sparring lessons in prison. "I may be eighty, but I can handle you. I've done a little fighting in my day." He threw a right jab into John's face but missed.

"Ha! You can't reach me. You're too short." He started to punch Clarence, but Mindy stepped between them and pushed her hand into John's chest.

John stretched his long arms around her and punched at Clarence, grazing Clarence's cheek.

"Stop. You have to respect your elders, John."

"Yeah, John. Respect your elders." Clarence punched John hard in the shoulder. "I haven't lost my touch. I used to win some trophies in my day." Another memory blinked in—the trophy of a black eye.

"Ouch! Respect? For the way he talks to you? Why are you being so nice to him, anyways?" John took another swing, his jaw jutted. "He's been nothing but mean to you and you know it."

Mindy ducked John's right hook. "I know, but it says we're supposed to turn the other cheek, if I remember right." She looked at Clarence. "Doesn't it?"

Clarence turned his other cheek.

John reached around Mindy and slugged Clarence in the jaw.

Clarence staggered back. "Ow." He held his cheek then lunged at John but hit Mindy instead.

Mindy stumbled, blinking.

"Mindy, you okay?" John grabbed her shoulders and peered into her eyes.

She stuttered—stunned for a minute. "Uh … yeah. I'm fine. I have brothers, remember?" She turned to face Clarence rubbing her cheek. "You hit me!"

"Look at him." John shielded Mindy with his body, leaving plenty of her visible on either side of him, and pointed at Clarence. "He doesn't respect you. Besides, if you turn the other cheek with him he'll spit on that one too. Don't open yourself up to him. He'll just bite you in the butt."

Clarence stopped and cleared his throat, fists still in the air. "First of all, I would never bite a woman in the butt. It's just not sanitary."

Mindy opened her eyes wide, took one look at John and burst out laughing.

"And secondly, I've been sued more times than I can count and I always win. Put that in your pipe or bong or whatever you use, and smoke it."

"Your what?" John said.

Mindy stopped and turned to Clarence. "Wait a minute. What did you do in your life? I mean, what was your job?"

Clarence looked at her, then at John. "Never mind. None of your damn business. You wouldn't care anyway." He shifted his weight and noticed the display of candy bars behind John. "Toss me one of those candy bars and I'll be on my way exploring this inspiring burg of a town. I won't bother you two again."

John reached in, pulled out a large candy bar and flung it at Clarence. "Might as well get him for all he's got. Ring it up, Mindy."

"John, you have no respect. You need—"

"It's okay, Mindy. I'm used to that kind of treatment." Clarence shoved his hand in his pants pocket. "Doesn't bother me anymore, if it ever did. He's just like one of the peons that I used to put in prison."

Mindy raised her eyebrows.

John took a step toward Clarence.

"John. Down. Settle."

John didn't seem to hear. He pushed toward Clarence, bumping into Mindy. Hands out of his pockets in fists, eyes squinting, lips pursed.

"Not again." Clarence rubbed his cheek.

"John you can't do that, he's elderly." She looked over at Clarence. "Sorry Clarence, but you … are. Kinda."

Clarence smirked at John, threw two dollars from his pocket onto the check stand and pushed out the door. "Thank you for your hospitality, Mindy, John. It's been a real interesting experience. Have a terrible day. Both of you."

Footsteps thudded behind Clarence. He turned in time to see Mindy rush John.

John reached out to punch Clarence but hit her instead.

"Ow. Ow." She shoved him back. "Again?"

"Mindy! Why did you do that? Are you okay?"

"I'm fine." She rubbed her cheek.

Clarence popped his head back in. "Good thing your girlfriend is hefty. She can keep you in line better."

"You Muther @#$%^*%!" John came at him, hands raised, Mindy right behind him. "I oughta punch your lights out, old man. Show you what a real man is made of."

Clarence stood outside the door, hands against the glass, one finger beckoning, then walked away. He tore open the candy bar and threw the wrapper onto the concrete.

John pounded on the door. His cussing filtered though the glass.

Clarence smiled, relishing what he'd stirred up. Mmmm. Candy bar —good. Battle with John—score.

He rubbed his jaw as he walked up the hill. A demolition zone ahead, surrounded by yellow barricade tape, drew him.

He shoved the last bit of candy in his mouth, brushing his hands together.

The yellow tape stopped him and he scanned the site. The insides of adjoining walls were visible; old wallpaper peeled from crumbling plaster. There were holes in the walls where demolition equipment had cut in. Downstairs, the walls still displayed a variety of wallpaper and paint in blues, greens, browns and roses, each telling layers of history. A pile of dirt remained in the middle. No floor, just dirt. The far wall was totally gone, revealing old bricks from the adjacent building.

Clarence scanned the whole site—walls, bricks, dirt. What used to be here? He jingled coins in his pockets. His fingers caught on the tiny dime-store ring in his pocket, and his heart stopped. He staggered a step back from the tape, gasping and coughing. His other hand pounded his chest.

"The bank. Oh my God. The old First National Bank of Osceola." He gasped again and sucked in a deep breath, hand on his chest.

The building grew before him out of the debris to stand in its former grandeur. New rose-brown bricks. The entrance opened on the diagonal of the front corner with a beautiful overhead portico, columns and entrance lights. Windows beside the entrance framed the loan department office. He remembered it well. He and Dad always made appointments there, to ask or beg for a loan to keep the woodworking business going. It was a big bank and had three teller windows. Rich, striped wallpaper covered the walls, creating a backdrop for the modern lighting.

He remembered the woodwork especially. He and his dad had handcrafted it all. Measured, sawed, pieced, hammered, sanded. When they were done, it was more than functional. It was beautiful. His dad had innovated corner pieces and trim, making useful and beautiful additions, all because it was his passion to give more.

That was Dad.

Clarence pictured his dad leaning over a section of board, sanding back and forth. He would stop to examine it with his fingers, testing to see if it was glass-smooth, as Dad used to say. He'd blow the sawdust away, then begin again. He never tiring of making a piece as beautiful as he could. Dad had fit the pieces together in this bank—a giant jigsaw puzzle of offices, paneling, teller booths. Stained each piece to perfection, rubbed the finish to a smooth glossy sheen.

Clarence toyed with the coins in his pockets, fingers coming to rest on the tiny ring, exploring it. He withdrew it from his pocket and flipped it over and over. Cheap little thing. Probably some little girl's heartthrob gave it to her as a grade school promise. The band had tarnished. The rhinestone was loose, ready to fall out.

He let it drop to the ground without thinking and reverted again, back in time, to that moment when another ring had fallen to the ground.

He looked up at the bank building to see Sally, his fiancé, screaming at him from the top step. Her lips moved, her forehead shone damp, her face beet red. Anger revealed her true character, hidden under surface beauty. Natural curls circled her head, mocking him as she shook, stomping her foot on the step.

He could hear the words once again. "You slime. I never want to see you again. I can kiss who I want to kiss. You were never good enough for me." And the bomb that blew the depths of his heart. "I never loved you anyway."

Clarence remembered looking down at the ground as he did now, only back then, the beautiful diamond had sparkled in betrayal, mocking him.

He bent down, picked up the dime-store ring and examined it in the bright sunlight.

He glanced around to see if anyone watched him.

No one.

But who had witnessed the scene on that day long ago?

The whole town.

He looked over the building in his memory, shaking his head. What had been a monument to his dad's fine workmanship was now Clarence's empty tomb of tortured pain.

Until he remembered one more thing.

He had started to turn away from the bank that day, but not before he glimpsed a different young woman—her sympathetic eyes gazing at him from a back window. He still felt the tug on his heart.

He had tossed the diamond up in the air and caught it, to the tune of Sally still screaming obscenities and stomping her foot. The farther he walked away, the lighter he felt.

Oh Annie ....

CHAPTER 24

Carol closed the chart. "I wish I had family to call. Someone who cared about him." She glanced around the conference table, at the staff members listening and taking notes on her shift report.

Lisha interrupted. "I wish I had someone to call, too. I'd give 'em a piece of my mind." She built up steam and let it empower her words. "That Clarence is a pain in the a—"

"Enough, Lisha." Carol slapped her hands on the table. "We don't talk like that here. You took an oath when you completed the classes. No foul language. And more than that, you agreed to care for these residents, to honor them, and to support them."

"I didn't agree to get bossed around and cussed out to my face." Her jowls bounced as she shook her face back and forth. "I didn't agree to that." She folded her arms across her ample chest. "What's it say in the Bi-i-i-ble? Do unto others as they do to you."

Carol laughed out loud. "That is not what it says and you know it. You are twisting the Word of God. He'll getcha for that."

"Whatever. That man is mean to the core. He has no respect for anybody or anything. I'll be nice to him to save my job, but that's it. Otherwise, iss on."

Miss Henningway burst into the room, a picture in her hand. She shoved it in front of Carol. "This has to go. Today!"

Carol took the picture from her. "Clarence? Clarence has to go?"

"All right!" Lisha nodded.

Miss Henningway shook her head and grabbed the picture back. "No! His hair. His hair has to go." She folded her arms across her chest. "Today."

"But—"

"It looks awful. It's greasy. He probably has head lice. It has to go. So inform his nurse that she must send him to the barber today."

"Well, he needs to be consulted—"

"No! It has to be done. Today." She tapped her shoes together and left the room, the picture floating to the table. Her heels thudded down the carpeted hall.

Carol picked it up.

"He's not gonna like—"

"He's gonna be so pissed. Glad you're his nurse, Lisha."

Carol hesitated. She looked at the picture. "All right." Carol stared at her notes, shaking her head and biting her lips. "I just want you all to know," she said, choosing her words carefully, scanning each face at the conference table, checking the door, "that when you are under my watch, you will be respectful, helpful, loving, and honorable to each and every resident. Is that clear?"

Quiet.

"Is that clear?" Carol repeated louder, her head bobbing forward with each word.

Staff eyed each other. Heads nodded.

Carol met eyes with Lisha, who was not moving an inch.

Carol's voice softened but rose in authority and firmness. "Is that clear?"

Lisha stared back.

Carol held her ground.

Lisha cleared her throat.

Carol didn't move a muscle. She never broke eye contact.

Lisha squirmed in her chair. "Okay. I give. But only because of you. He is a mean man. I've had too many of those kind in my life. Lording over me and crushing what I want, who I am." A breath caught in her throat and she glanced around the table. "I'll do it for you. Because I respect you, Miss Carol." Her eyes diverted to the door Miss Henningway had exited through and back to Carol. "Only for you." She leaned back.

Carol still held her ground, but she gave Lisha a nod. "Thank you. I appreciate that you respect me. I also challenge you to give others respect no matter what you get in return. Maybe you can't do that right away. But day by day, I want you to become that kind of person, because you are that kind of woman."

Lisha sighed and mimicked. "Day by day."

Carol patted her notes and charts. "Are we all good?" She paused. "The elderly have been through so much, and given so much. We can learn from their wisdom. They still have a lot to give and it's up to us to make their last years blessed."

"All Clarence gives out is—"

"Lisha."

Lisha stopped and bowed her head.

"Okay. Let's get at it. Does everyone understand Mrs. Gelt's new treatment and how to ambulate her?"

Heads nodded, including Lisha's.

Carol rose and pushed in her chair. "Any questions? Revisions?"

Carol headed for the door.

Behind her, Lisha's voice: "Well, maybe."

Carol stopped at the door and looked over her shoulder. "Yes?"

Lisha had stood. All head had turned toward her. She cleared her throat. "You're a nice lady, Miss Carol, don't get me wrong, or nuthin'. But, uh, you haven't had a hard life like some of us here. You jes don't understand how hard it is."

Carol pursed her lips and stared back. Just last night she had held Joe's hand and prayed for God to take him, so he wouldn't suffer anymore—but also so she would be free from this burden. "You have no idea, do you?" she snapped. "You only think about yourself and your life. You don't stop to think … "

Silence.

She scanned the room before her. Each one looked down, fidgeted, held her breath, pretended to read her notes.

Carol turned and left the room.

CHAPTER 25

Clarence half raised his hand as the car sped by again—at the little girl perched in the back seat. She stretched around to see him.

She remembered him … she remembered him from the other day. He shoved his hands into his pockets, jingled his change and kicked at some rocks in the street.

He'd remember her anywhere. He glanced behind him toward the car. A mental picture flashed into his mind of that kid in MacDonald's, on that terrible day.

Jingle. Jingle.

He paused and felt the tiny glove in his pocket, squeezed the thumb, memorized the itchy feel of the wool.

Heedless of cracks in the concrete, he plodded along the sidewalk. Until he bumped into a rebar stake driven into the ground.

Yellow caution tape was woven around another property here. This lot was empty—as in no-building empty—but demolition debris scattered it: chunks of concrete, broken bricks, plaster. A gaping hole revealed part of a red-bricked stairway heading underground.

He backed away and pivoted to get his bearings.

What building once stood here?

He couldn't think. It'd been too long.

He pointed next door, to the building still standing. "That used to be ... and next to that was ...."

He counted back down the street and shook his head. Dress shop—Mrs. Gordon. New facade, new windows, but still the same old building. He just ... couldn't remember the next one. Shaking his head, he stepped along. Each building held stories from his past—just with the last sixty years layered in.

One solid brick building reminded him of the day Dad bought Clarence his own gun. It had felt like graduation day. That was the day he put all the toy guns away. The blanky, the train set that choo-chooed "They'll be Comin' Round the Mountain," dump trucks. The only toys he'd kept out were a teddy bear his mother made and the toy carpenter set.

He rotated toward a newer building—the hardware store, where Dad had sent him on a regular basis. He stepped to the glass and cupped his hands around his eyes, peering inside.

A haze parted, and he was inside the old hardware store, as a boy. He reached into the nail bins lined up against the counter and gathered the cold nails in his hand—cold, even in summer. They clinked, as one by one, they slid from his hand into the bin.

Tools appeared in rows along one wall. Hammers, screwdrivers, lathes, saws, levels. He slid his hand over the new wood in the hammer handles and saws. The smell of new wood, new tools, always made his skin tingle. He ran his finger along a saw blade, hearing his father reprimand him, telling him he would cut himself. He always cut his fingers. Always.

Deep sigh.

The past began to clear. Inside the building a man stood scowling. The man's mouth moved. His hand pointed to a woman sitting at a desk.

Clarence couldn't pull away from his memories, every screw, each piece of hardware. He was only aware of himself and his dad, moseying through the old hardware store, examining everything.

"Oh, I miss those days," he whispered and gulped. "I miss my dad. Wish I could see him again."

"Hey mister."

Clarence jumped away from the window, hands raised. "What the—"

"Mister, move along. You can't just stand out here. You're gawking —you're loitering. You're supposed to come in and spend your money. If you're not gonna do that, then buzz off." The man waved him on.

"Says who? Who do you think you are?" Clarence squinted at the man. Tan skin—player—either on a golf course or on a boat. Short blond hair and by the looks of him, it should be gray. Button-down plaid shirt and dress pants.

"I'm Pete Malovitch, that's who. And this is my business. My building." Pete's hands circled his hips, chin jutted out. "Quit staring in people's windows, old man."

Clarence looked into the store, really seeing the inside this time. A desk and a counter. Signs on the wall advertised insurance deals. Books lined shelves along one wall. A young woman smiled from behind the desk, ear piece wrapping itself around her jaw. She moved her lips, writing, and waving at him, all at the same time.

Clarence started to wave, then caught himself, his hand dangled at his side. Anybody working with this guy was of the devil.

He shook his head, let it fall to his chest and shuffled on.

Pete. Pete Malovitch, selling gambling, er insurance policies where that wonderful hardware store used to stand.

Criminal.

CHAPTER 26

Bea held out her hand to Mommy and jumped out of the car. Mommy picked her up and twirled her around and around. Squealing and giggling, Bea looked up at trees spinning, the sun sparkling through branches, leaves dancing.

When Mommy released her, Bea walked away in dizzy drunkard footsteps, still giggling, arms outstretched for balance. She stopped and turned to Mommy. "Mommy, Dolly wants to come with. She loves the slide."

"No, Baby Bea. Dolly has to stay in the car. When you get tired, then you shove her off on me. Got it?"

Bea stopped and looked into Mommy's face. "Are you okay, Mommy? Do we need to talk? Play dolls?"

Mommy made an angry face. "Why do you think we're at the park? I am slipping. I want a puff. Just one puff of a cigarette." She clasped her hands together then roughly put them behind Bea's head and pulled her close. Then whispered, "Or something else."

Bea's heart lurched, but she let herself be pulled in.

Mommy began to tickle her, making her giggle, her mouth closed. She tickled her in her tummy, her armpits until she laughed out loud.

"Mommy, stop."

Mommy didn't stop but kept on tickling, pinching Bea.

"Ow, Mommy, stop it. You're hurting me."

Scary mommy was back.

"Mommy stop. That hurts. It's not fun anymore." Bea tried to push Mommy away, but she was strong and Bea was not. "Help me Mommy."

Mommy didn't stop. Bea pushed at Mommy's hands, her fingers. She pinched at Mommy to make her quit, but couldn't find a hold. She fell to the grass and kicked for all a four year old was worth.

Bea was crying now. "Mommy. Mommy."

Big hands grabbed Bea from the ground and snatched her from Mommy, lifting her away.

Bea looked up into the old man's blue eyes and threw her arms around his neck, sobbing. She huddled into his chest. The gray whiskers on his face scratched her tender skin, but she didn't care.

He spoke softly. "Hey. Hey. You're holding on so tight, I can hardly breathe. It's okay now, little one. You can relax. I won't let her hurt you." He pulled her arms from his shoulders. "See, she's walking away now. It's okay. She's not hurting you any more."

Bea's shoulders shook with each hiccup, as she watched Mommy walking away. "Mommy." The man set her down. She escaped from his arms and ran, crying. "Mommy."

Mommy fell to the ground, sobbing, just as Bea reached her.

"Bea Baby. I need help. I can't do this alone anymore. I hurt you." She uncovered her eyes and searched Bea's arms, her legs. She pointed. "See? I hurt you. I scratched you. Oh, God, you're even bleeding." She erupted into sobs, hands covered her eyes and she fell to the ground.

"Mommy. It's okay. I'm okay. It doesn't hurt anymore. See?" She wiped at the blood, but only succeeded in rubbing it around and making a mess on her shirt. Her lower lip quivered.

Gentle hands lifted her again.

The blue-eyed old man sat down on a park bench and snuggled Bea onto his lap. He wasn't scary at all. He snuggled Bea, her head tucked under his chin, but she could still see Mommy as he smoothed her hair with his fingers. "Shhh, Little One. Shhh. It's okay now. It's okay."

Bea relaxed, catching a whiff of something like Mommy's perfume, only cleaner, like outside smelled sometimes. His whiskers caught her hair. His warmth made her feel better, drowsy.

Mommy pushed herself off the ground, brushing leaves and dirt from her jeans. "I'm an awful Mom. I hurt my own child." She looked up into the man's eyes. "I need help. I can't do this alone."

Bea put her hands on either side of the man's scratchy cheeks and turned his face toward hers. "Mommy doesn't smoke anymore. She threw her cigarettes out the window yesterday. She is a good Mommy, isn't she? She loves me." Bea burst into tears. "She's a good mommy, isn't she?" The last words broke into a wail.

The man patted her head and rocked side to side. "Yes. She is a good mommy because she threw her cigarettes away. She just needs some … help. Someone to help her through the rough spots. That's all." He rubbed Bea's cheek with his thumb. "She's a good mommy, Little One."

Bea nodded and slumped against his chest, patting his arm. She coughed and closed her eyes, curving into his chest.

Clarence continued to comb through the little girl's fine curly hair, kissing the top of her head. He closed his eyes. His arms felt so full, his heart so satisfied. Was this what it was like to have his own … ? As she relaxed against him, he focused on the young woman. "Um … do you … do you have anyone around here to help you?"

The young woman opened her eyes. "Who me? I don't need help. I'm fine." She glared at him, stumbled, reached out her hand to steady herself against the bench.

"You're full of shit and you know it." Clarence hesitated as he stroked the child's hair. He gathered steam again. "You hurt your daughter. She is precious. And you can't pull the wool over my eyes. I have dealt with every kind of evil there is." He covered Bea's free ear. "What if I hadn't come along when I did. Would you have stopped?"

She straightened, her chin jutting out. "Yes. I wouldn't hurt my own child."

Clarence smoothed the girl's hair from his stubble, pushed her sleeve up revealing bloody scratches and gave the woman a stern eye until she turned away.

The girl watched her mother walk away, but stiffened as she pivoted back to them.

Tears filled the woman's mascara-smudged eyes. "Oh, God. Oh, God." She slumped onto the bench beside Clarence. "I don't have anybody. No one. It's just her and me." She hugged herself. "I don't know what to do." She shivered. "I become someone else. I go from me to … that other mommy. She is mean. She is … violent." She gasped. "I'm afraid of her too."

Clarence didn't soften his tone, just his volume."Will you let me help you?" He looked down at the child. "And her?" He hugged the little girl into his chest. "Before you really hurt her."

The woman jumped, startled. Her jaw jutted. Her eyes squinted. "Who are you and why would you want to help us?"

Why indeed? "I asked you a question first. Will you let me help you and her? I can find people to help."

"Why? What's in it for you? What are you going to get out of it?" She jerked her head around, eyes close to his. "Are you a cop? Who put you up to this? Huh?"

Clarence didn't flinch, but gazed into her eyes, then looked down at the child. "Nobody puts me up to anything. I was a lawyer in my day, and a damn good one."

The woman jerked upright, as if someone had pulled on her marionette strings. "A lawyer? We don't need a lawyer. I can't pay a lawyer." She jumped up and grabbed at the girl. "Come on Bea. Let's go home."

Bea. The little girl's name was Bea. Bea clung to Clarence's neck. Tears stung his eyes as he embraced her even harder.

The woman stopped and searched Bea's face. "Bea, I'm your Mommy. We have to go. There are things—"

"No Mommy. He can help us. He can. I know he can." She locked her fingers behind Clarence's neck.

"But … " The woman stomped away, hugging herself, head down, kicking at rocks on the pathway, glancing behind her. Then stopped and slumped.

She walked back to them, stared into Clarence's eyes for a moment. She held out her hand. "I'm Katty."

"I'm Clarence." He shook hers.

Katty crouched down in front of Bea. "Honey. Baby Bea," she started then glanced away, fidgeting with Bea's shoelaces. Clearing her throat, she looked back at Bea. "I haven't been a very nice Mommy today." She swallowed. "Not a very nice person." She looked away again for a long time. Finally she spoke again. "Bea, Mommy did some things that if we let this man help us, I could go to jail." She quickly looked up at Clarence. "I should go to jail. It's more than the cigarettes, Baby Bea. Much more."

CHAPTER 27

Mindy leaned over, slid the old metal container out of the checkout stand and gathered the corners of the trash bag. She shook the trash together and pulled the bag out of the can. It stuck. She yanked again. "Dang. It's caught …"

She pulled harder just as a hand slipped around her chubby waist.

"What are you doing, Mindy?" John's voice was so deep.

She jumped. Her head bumped up and met with a bony chin. Hard. "Ouch. Dude."

The bag caught on the container, tore and spilled smelly contents all over the floor. Moldy, runny tomatoes. Black bananas. Cigarette butts. Old wet store ads.

"Oh man. Look what you made me do now." She reached up to smack John's cheek, just as he grabbed her hand and kissed the back of it.

"Not here."

"You say that no matter where we are. Can we anywhere?"

Mindy laughed and hugged his waist. "You are so funny." She pointed to the security cameras. "She can see us, you know. We're gonna hear about this." She pulled a new trash bag out of the box. "Look at this mess. Stinky, stinky."

"I'll help. I made you do it."

She pointed at the camera again and raised her voice. "Did you hear that? Darn right, he made me do it."

A voice blared over the intercom. "Devil made ya do it! I saw it all!"

Mindy poked John. "See?"

"Grrr!" He bent to hold the trash bag while Mindy tossed the garbage in.

"Hey, look," she said. "A wallet. How did it get in the trash?" She wiped her hands on her apron, retrieved it from the mess and opened it up. "Huh. No credit cards." She looked at John. "Who doesn't have credit cards today? No driver's license. Here's an ID … kinda strange. And … woowoo. Mo-ney." She picked through it and straightened. "Lots of mo-ney. Whoever owns this one is rich."

John leaned over her shoulder and counted as she flitted through it. "One million, two million—"

"Stop." She slapped it closed. "But there is a lot in there." She looked up at John, eyes wide, braces flashing. "If you hadn't a tried to kiss me, and I hadn't of jumped and torn the bag, we wouldn't have found this wallet in the trash. Amazing."

"Yeah, so, can we try it again?" He moved closer, his lips puckered. "The kiss thing, I mean. See what else happens."

Mindy laughed and shoved him out of the way. "I've gotta get this to Boss Lady." She glanced at the camera. "I mean, Mrs. Larkin. Sorry. I'll be coming right there to give this to you." She waved the wallet at the camera.

The entrance door buzzed, and in walked Clarence wearing a slight smile.

"Hi Clarence. You're looking chipper today. It's a great day outside, isn't it?"

"How would you know?"

Mindy smiled. "Well, I drove to work with my window down. That's how I know. It's beautiful out."

"What would you know about beautiful? You are fat and have braces and pimples."

Mindy took a step back. Just like Grandpa. Mean.

John stepped in front of her.

"It's okay, John. Sticks and stones, remember? Although that was extremely harsh." She slipped in front of John and took a deep breath. "What can we help you with today, Clarence? A candy bar? The food probably isn't that great at Hillcrest, is it?"

Clarence stood still for a long time and stared at Mindy.

She grew uncomfortable. "I … is something wrong, Clarence?"

He combed his fingers through his shoulder-length gray hair. His blue eyes were set deep—even deeper now. For being old, his skin didn't look very wrinkled. "Why are you so nice to me? When I am so mean to you."

Oh that. "You're trying to be nice right now, aren't you, Clarence? It's just as easy to be nice to people as it is to be mean."

Clarence kept staring at her. "That's the stupidest thing I've ever heard. And I've heard every remark and every excuse."

"Oh, have you, Clarence." Mrs. Larkin walked up behind him. "Does the nursing home know where you are? Or should I let them know?"

He shook his head. "No, you shouldn't let them know because they know where I am. So there. And yes I've heard it all."

"Well, then, I bet you've heard this one, too. Go home. Go back to the nursing home and stay there. You cause trouble and hurt feelings everywhere you go." She folded her arms across her chest. "Go home."

"Mrs. Larkin, um, he wanted to buy a candy bar. Didn't you, Clarence?" Mindy walked to the candy end cap. "What kind? Baby Ruth? Snickers? We've got 'em all."

Clarence walked up beside her and checked out the display and assortment. "What's this one?" He picked one up.

"Twix."

"That's the one on TV. On the commercials." He dropped it back into the box. "I don't want it. I used to really like … I don't see it. What kind do you like, Fatty?"

Seeing her reflection in the metal sign, she hugged her middle. "Well, I like 'em all, but I really like Baby Ruth, Gramps."

He glared at her. "Don't you call me that."

John piped up. "Then don't call her ... uh ..."

"Fatty?" He turned from John to Mindy. "I can call you Fatty, can't I?"

Mindy leaned into Clarence's face. "Sure. If I can call you Gramps, Gramps."

Clarence turned red. His nostrils flared.

"Caught at your own tricks, huh Clarence." John stuffed his hands in his apron pockets and rocked on his heels.

"You'd better be nice to these kids, Clarence." Mrs. Larkin pointed to Mindy and John and held out her hand. "The wallet, please."

Mindy dropped it into her hand.

Clarence leaned toward Mrs. Larkin and tried to swipe it.

She turned away and opened it, exposing the money. She flipped through it and checked the ID and frowned. She looked at the document, then at Clarence. Quiet. "No one touched your money. No one here stole from you. And you have your wallet back. I want it said about us here at Olde Towne Store that we are honest and upstanding. You owe John and Mindy a big thank you for finding this. You hear me?"

He held out his hand and she slapped the wallet onto his palm.

"Don't you ever insult Mindy and John again. They are the good kids."

Mindy wanted to burst. Nobody had ever said that about her before. Not Dad. Never Gramps. And never Mrs. Larkin. Everybody always called her trash.

"Well if they are the good ones, I gotta see the bad ones."

Mrs. Larkin put both fists on her hips. "I ought to call the cops on you. As a matter of fact, I—"

Mindy rested a hand on Mrs. Larkin's arm. "Please don't. He's just an angry old man. Just like my Grandpa."

Clarence was already out the door, but his last words found their way inside. "You bet, I'm angry. I got my wallet back, but my whole life's been stolen from me."

CHAPTER 28

Still parked near the playground, Katty pounded the steering wheel and pressed her fingers to her eyes. "Oh God. Oh God. Oh God." Her breath came in ragged gasps, as the old man walked away. Sweat ran down her back and under her arms. "He knows." She cringed. "Someone knows."

"Mommy?"

"Not now, Bea." She shuddered involuntarily.

"You cold, Mommy?"

"Bea!"

Kick. Kick.

"Bea. Stop kicking the back of my seat!" She whipped around, swinging her hand toward Bea.

Bea's eyes widened, terror changing her sweet demeanor into a terrified, vulnerable child. She ducked.

For the first time, Katty saw the change before she hit. She stared at Bea, terrified herself. Terrified of who she had become. Terrified of what she might do.

Time slowed. Light specks floated and sparked between Katty and Bea—flowed back and forth in front of Bea.

Katty sat mesmerized, seeing Bea's face through the fragments, the terror softening.

Bea seemed transfixed too. The light specks became elongated and wrapped around her. She put her hands out, and whatever-it-was touched her hands in such a real way that Bea's hands moved—clapped. The expression on Bea's face was not fear but awe.

"Patty-cake." Bea kicked. Her hands moved again. "Patty-cake, Mommy. Patty-cake." She giggled and kicked. Her eyes followed the light flashes. She looked up at Katty.

Katty wiped her wet cheeks and stared into Bea's brown eyes as Bea stared back.

Bea jumped when her hands moved again. One shot way up above her head and jerked back. It jerked again. Bea laughed. "High-five." She kicked her feet into Katty's seat.

Katty ignored the kicking, spellbound. She held her breath as Bea laughed again—so melodic—like a wren on a spring morning.

The light disappeared as quickly as it had appeared. Katty searched the interior of the car but saw nothing unusual. Whatever it had been, it was gone.

Deep sigh.

Was it a flashback from drugs?

Bea looked at Katty and started to say something but closed her mouth.

"What, Bea?"

"What was that, Mommy?"

No, not a flashback. Bea saw it too. Bea played with it. "I don't know, Honey, but I feel so good right now. So peaceful." A tear rolled down her cheek, her fist at her chest. "Somehow, everything's gonna be okay. I don't know how or when, but I just know."

CHAPTER 29

The next morning, Clarence stood, hiding behind the office door, waiting for his chance. The office lady was on break. No one could see him, or so he hoped. The buttons on his dark shirt scraped against the door. *Damn!* He sucked in his stomach and held his breath.

Silence.

With the morning he'd already had, he wasn't sure he'd ever come back. Miss Henningway had knocked loudly on his door, waking him, and announced he was getting a haircut today—no more greasy, long hair for him. She had rounded up Lisha and two maintenance men to hold him down. No amount of hollering on his part made them back away. He had hollered about his rights as a resident, a citizen of the United States. And he was a lawyer—he could sue them. He cussed until they were done and were sweeping up his hair. Damn them all to hell!

He raked his fingers through the inch-long hair on his scalp and peered through the gap between the door and doorjamb. He pushed aside thoughts of finding his file to steal. He needed to get out of here —one way or another.

He could barely see the branches of an overgrown plant across the hall, almost covering the main entrance door. A pedestal stood beside the plant, topped by an already spent floral arrangement.

The automatic door opened, making Clarence jump. A motorized wheelchair occupied by an elderly gentleman wearing huge dark glasses drove in, turning down the left hallway. The automatic door paused open long enough for him to hear a car door slam, an engine rev, and gravel crunch on concrete as a car left the parking lot. Light reflections traveled across the walls until the door closed.

He blew out a breath.

Voices chattered past his hiding place. Footsteps clomped on the carpet. "We need to call the police."

"I know, but you heard Carol."

"Maybe we should just do it ourselves. Call the Sheriff's office. You and me. Call it in."

"No. You can. I'm not doing it. You do it. I'm already in enough trouble as it is."

"Wait a minute, I thought you were just agreeing with me that we should call. Weren't you?"

Quiet.

"Well?"

"I don't know. It seems kind of mean, don't you think? He's so old and stuff. He doesn't ever hurt anybody." Slurp on a straw. "If I lived here, I'd run away too."

"You are so talking out of both sides of your mouth ...." The conversation trailed off as the door closed behind them.

Clarence peeked out.

Gone.

He peered into the reception area. Empty. The only movement was the plant leaves next to the door, blowing up and down in the breeze from the door closing.

Now or never.

He edged from behind the door just as Mrs. Hatly walked into the room.

Her face lit up when she saw him. "Clarence." She clapped her hands. "Just who I wanted to see." She stopped. "You got a haircut."

He cringed, raking his fingers through his hair. "Yeah. They had to hold me down to cut it."

She nodded. "I heard you. It … you look nice."

He held his finger to his lips. "Shhh. I've got to go out. Don't tell, okay?"

She giggled and nodded. "Okay." She put her finger to her lips too. "Okay. Shh."

Loud voices approached.

"Did you check her chart?"

"No."

"It gives explicit instructions on how the doctor wants the treatment done."

Lisha and another aide marched into the room, holding hand-held computers side-by-side. Lisha pointed to hers. The aide nodded. They were on a mission.

"Oh." Lisha looked from Clarence to Mrs. Hatly. Back to Clarence. "What are you two up to? Going for coffee in the dining room? Gonna go to baking?" She grinned. Those big teeth. "Good to see you here, Clarence."

He tried not to smirk. "Good to see you, too."

"No. That's not what I meant. I meant—"

The other aide grabbed her arm. "Better not. 'Member what Carol told us."

Clarence looked from Lisha to the other aide. "What'd Carol tell you?"

Mrs. Hatly stepped up and lightly put her hand on his arm. It hovered just above his sleeve.

Lisha sighed and stepped away. "Oh she tells us a lot of things, huh. And I am being nice to you today, Clarence. I made the choice." She widened her grin. "Always a kind word to you." She nodded to Mrs. Hatly. "And you too, Mrs. Hatly."

Mrs. Hatly giggled, hand still on Clarence's arm.

A buzzer went off somewhere down the hall.

Lisha checked her watch. "It's almost time for that treatment. Let's go." She saluted them. "See ya around." She looked back. "Oh, and nice haircut, Clarence."

He growled and hung his head. He watched, leaning into the hallway with Mrs. Hatly, to see both aides disappear into a room down the hall, door slamming. He turned toward her and paused, their hands still clasped.

"Ohhh." She removed her hand to cover her mouth. "Your hands." She gently turned them over. "Oh, my, How did you ... what happened?"

"Burned 'em. I was just a kid." He squeezed hers and gently slid his hands from her grasp. "Gotta go."

Her brown eyes twinkled, as if she enjoyed being part of the conspiracy to undermine the regime.

Clarence tipped a nonexistent hat and walked to the door, waving.

Her gnarled and swollen fingers fluttered. "Bye, Clarence. Bye bye."

He turned and pushed the door, letting automation open it the rest of the way. Stepping through, he paused to look behind him. He put his finger to his mouth, winked, and walked down the sidewalk to the parking area.

He surveyed the building, noting each window, each shadow. Checked for security, or to be exact, Lisha.

Made it. Made it out again. He breathed deeply, patting his chest. It had been too long.

Still, he scanned the rows of windows again. There. Harold. Shaking his finger. Clarence shook his backside at Harold and gave the old prison salute, sticking his tongue out for good measure. "You old buzzard. Don't you tell." He wagged his finger with each word. "Don't. You. Tell."

Harold gave Clarence two thumbs up.

Mrs. Hatly appeared behind Harold and tried to give thumbs up too, only hers turned sideways. Thumbing for a ride.

Clarence jumped, startled. A half smile crossed his lips.

He walked away with a light step. The sun was shining. The birds chirped. What a day.

Miss Henningway hid behind the designer drapes in her plush office as she watched Clarence walk down the sidewalk. He almost skipped like a giddy kid going to the movies.

She'd make sure he slowed down.

She opened his file. Flipped a few pages until she found his former address. Bet he'd had a killer house, him being a lawyer.

She typed the address into a Google search and hit enter. Pictures began to load. She checked the address. The right address. Somebody sure made a typo.

She typed in the address again. Pictures of a prison loaded on the desktop of her monitor.

Ahhh, downtown. He turned and looked behind him. He didn't remember walking through the park, past the grocery store or the flower shop.

He trudged on down the sidewalk.

A door slammed behind him. Footsteps. He nodded at a passerby. Voices greeted voices. One seemed familiar … he turned to see. Pete Malovitch—the insurance man selling gambling policies.

"That man ought to have a permanent residence in the cemetery."

Clarence stiffened. He plodded on, his hands balled into fists, as a door opened and shut behind him and the voices faded. He stopped in front of another building, but not before looking behind him, making sure Pete wasn't watching.

No Pete. He slipped to the window glass and peered inside.

Shocked, he jumped inside a restaurant—and back sixty years. And not just any restaurant, but The Dinnerbell—the most popular place in town. People traveled from miles around to taste the roast beef dinner and apple pie Mrs. Darcy prepared. She had grown up cooking for her brothers and sisters and now happily prepared food for the community.

Clarence sat at a table by the windows. He had no idea what he wanted to eat, much less what the menu said. He couldn't take his eyes off Annie—that beautiful reddish-blond haired girl who had watched with such sympathy from the bank, when Sally had flung back the diamond ring.

She scanned the menu across from him, then handed it to the waitress. "I'll have the hot beef sandwich." She reached for her glass and brought it to her lips.

"And for you, Clarence?" The waitress poised her pencil above the pad.

"What?" He fumbled with the menu, then closed it. "I'll have your special, whatever it is."

"Sure thing, Clarence. Coming right up. Beef Stew for Two?"

Annie raised both eyebrows, a sweet, teasing smile on her lips. Her shoulder length hair curled around her neck and ringlets escaped her barrettes. Her brown eyes and smile made the sun shine in his heart.

And to think she was the judge's daughter.

"Uhhh, no. J-Just a cheeseburger."

"Okay. Any fries?"

"Uhhh, yeah. Fries." He continued to feast on Annie's every feature that was above her neck.

She blushed, cleared her throat and sipped her water again.

Clarence watched her—everything about her. Her smile. Her eyes. Her hair haloed about her head. Her teeth. Her—

"You're staring at me."

He slowly nodded, then leaned forward and clasped his hands together, elbows on the table. He reached across to her and held out his hand.

"It's okay," Clarence whispered.

She searched the restaurant, her eyes wide, and slid her hand toward his. Their fingertips barely touched.

He whispered again. "No one's watching."

She placed her hand in his. He closed his fingers around hers.

A slow smile spread across her face, and he relished the warmth.

The waitress brought their meal and they ate one-handed. When their dirty dishes were cleared away, they still held hands. Dessert came and went. The check came, and Clarence paid it.

Still they clasped hands.

"I have to go, Clarence."

"I know."

Moments later. "I really need to go."

Annie looked down at their hands … and winced. "What did you do to your hands?" She opened them and gently fingered broad, ropey scars. "What happened?"

He shrugged. "It happened when I was a kid. It's nothing."

She shook her head. "Nothing? Those are burns, are they not?"

He nodded. "Yeah. When I was little … it was right after Mom died." He sat still then sucked in a breath. "I was … I ran away and found myself by an old hobo's fire."

She gasped.

"Oh, he didn't do it. It was me. It was cold out, and I stuck my hands in the flame. I couldn't even feel it. He yelled at me to pull them out, but I 'spose I was hurting so bad missing Mom I didn't care."

Annie stared at his face, then at his hands. She pulled them to her lips and closed her eyes.

And prayed.

Clarence could still feel his hands in hers, her lips on his fingers, this many years later. Goosebumps skittered across his arms; chills made him tremble, just as he had back then. He leaned against the window, hand against his chest. His eyes filled with tears.

He examined both hands, still scarred—changed some with age and time, but still disfigured.

Only then did he see reality inside the store. Boards piled along one wall, stacks of old flooring. An electric table saw commanded the center of the room, whining as a man pushed wood toward the blade. Sawdust covered the floor around the man's feet. The smell of fresh sawn wood wafted through the open screen door. Next to the saw was a worktable littered with scraps of crumpled sandpaper and a half-finished cradle. Boards of different shapes and sizes were propped up around it. Cans and jars of varnish and stain lined open shelving.

A deep breath escaped his chest. He wiped at his eyes.

The whine of the saw paused, and the man waved.

Clarence half-waved and pretended to turn away.

The man dipped his head, gesturing for Clarence to come inside. When Clarence didn't budge, the man walked to the door and opened it. "Come on in."

Clarence backed away, hands held up in protest. "No. I have places to go."

The man laughed and reached for Clarence's hand, dragging him inside. "Me, too. But what is more important than playing in sawdust?" He wiped his hand on a rag and then held it out in greeting. "I'm Michael. This is my woodworking shop. And you are … "

Clarence stared at Michael's rough, outstretched hand—a long fresh wound running up his right arm, then his own scarred hands. He shifted his gaze to the interior of the store, taking it all in.

"Your name, sir?"

Clarence rubbed his hand on his shirt and offered it. "Uh, Clarence. My name's Clarence."

"Welcome, Clarence. Good to meet you." Michael spread his arm wide. He was unusually tall and muscular, dark tight curls covered his head and trailed down the nape of his neck. "Welcome to my humble," he kicked aside wood scraps on the floor, "wood shop. Are you a woodworker?"

"I … uh … used to be. Long time ago." His eyes followed Michael's arm around the shop, then back to his saw-dusty face. "Way before you were born. Way."

Michael chuckled. "I bet some of it's still the same. I used to only use old tools. No electricity." He pointed to a wall display. "But I gave up when I couldn't meet customer deadlines."

Clarence found himself across the room, gazing at the antique tools. He reached up to touch, to feel the old wood and metal, and immediately transported back to his dad's workshop. As he touched each smooth surface, each blade, he saw his dad using it, working with it. Clarence caressed them one by one, shuffling along the wall. Michael's presence was ignored, his whereabouts forgotten.

Clarence stopped, turned and half smiled, letting his head drop to his chest. "I … I'm sorry. I don't know where I went just now."

"You know where you went, Clarence. Where?"

Clarence turned to the wall of tools for another feast, wiped his eyes, then faced Michael. "I guess … I went to my dad's workshop. He owned all these tools, or ones like them, and I worked with him every minute I could." He tipped his head. "Or should I say, I hindered him as he worked." He swallowed. "I'd forgotten how much I loved working with wood, but … working with him."

"Don't be embarrassed, Clarence. I have the same memories of my dad." He patted the table saw. "Only with power tools instead of those." He motioned toward the wall. "I can't imagine getting to create usable furniture or even a house with those."

"Yeah. It's sure different now." Clarence, hands in his pockets, wandered to the workbench where Michael stood. "May I?"

"You bet. Help yourself." Michael continued to sand the wood, holding pieces and fitting them together. He lined them up, forming the rest of the cradle.

Clarence watched him, then picked one up that had already been sanded and rubbed his fingers across the edges and flat areas. "There is nothing like that smooth edge. Nothing like it."

Michael tossed him a piece of sandpaper, his eyebrows raised.

Clarence stared at the paper, then to Michael's face, before he grasped it in his hand. He scraped his nail along it, letting his fingertips feel the rough surface. Slowly he picked up a piece of wood from the table, and he watched Michael as he rubbed the paper along the edge of the wood. He sanded for just a few seconds then abruptly dropped the wood down along with the sandpaper and turned to leave.

"Clarence. You don't have to go." Michael stopped sanding and walked around the table. "I enjoy having someone to talk to, to share time with. Kinda like old times with our dads. Please stay."

Clarence stopped mid stride, breathing faster, then pushed his hand at Michael and walked out.

Michael followed him to the door. "Come back, Clarence. Sometime."

CHAPTER 30

That old buzzard was loose again.

Pete Malovitch thumped his finger against the window frame in his insurance office. It had been a long day already, and now he had to put on his doctor's hat and fill out bogus claims. Dad had taught him well; the extra income came in handy when he needed to shut up his wife and kids.

Was the old man ever actually inside Hillcrest? Pete was willing to bet he didn't even go to the bathroom there anymore. How could he, when he was always downtown?

Pete watched the old man walk down the street and anger ignited inside and boiled over. He clicked his fingernail on the metal frame repeatedly … and paused.

Something swirled in his head as he hesitated. Memories. Pictures mixed with voices. Images of his dad reading the newspaper at the kitchen table.

His little boy eyes watched Dad's thick fingers rub the newsprint until ink blackened his thumb and fingertips. The weakened paper crumpled even more when Dad cussed. His little boy senses blistered with the profanity.

"Tess, look what's in the obits. Old man Timmelsen died."

Pete's mom rushed to the table, grabbing her purse and jacket, ready for work. "What? That old—"

"Who's old man Timmelsen, Dad?" Pete peered over the table.

"He's just about the biggest … "

He only heard tidbits of the rest, because his mother cupped her hands over his ears. But he could guess what came next. It always did. Never failed. His dad read the newspaper and cussed his way through until the weather. He cussed that too, only not as bad. Pete loved to watch him read the comics. His belly shook so. Dad even read some to Pete. Real father-son time.

Pete whistled through his teeth as he continued to spy on Clarence. "I wonder … "

He rushed to his desk, turned the computer monitor toward him and typed in *Dawes Timmelsen*. He glanced to the window. He couldn't remember the son's name. He was pretty sure Dawes had done a bunch of work for Dad.

He clicked enter. Timmelsen had been a good carpenter, as he remem …

Dawes Timmelsen. As he scrolled down, he read aloud, "died Tuesday of complications." So how old was the article? "June 6, 1989."

He stopped scanning mid-page, where it read, "Timmelsen will be remembered for crafting some of the most well-known buildings in Osceola, Nebraska, appreciated for remodeling and erecting most people's homes and barns." Pete nodded. Timmelsen had built this very building.

Outside a loud truck roared past, but inside, silence. Pete read on. Time stopped and switched directions. He reached the article's final words: "Mr. Dawes Timmelsen was the father of Clarence Timmelsen, who was incarcerated for … "

The son went to prison? For killing his wife?

"Woah." Pete rolled his chair away from the desk, hands in the air.

He jumped up and rushed to the window, sliding left and right. "Where is he?" He pounded the window, accompanied by his father's choice words. "Where'd he go? That's what we have living here amongst our wives and children?" Not that he honestly cared, but he'd heard the phrase his whole life. Adding the word 'amongst' gave his fury real Biblical clarity. Clout.

He tapped the glass again.

"Sarah?" He raced to his secretary's adjoining office. "Sarah?"

Sarah stood at her desk, brushing crumbs from her short red skirt. Her black blouse gapped at the buttons and if she turned just right, which she did frequently, her black lace bra showed. She rushed to the door. Tall and beautiful, her spiked hair added three inches to her eight. "Pete. What's wrong?"

"See if we have anything in our archives about Dawes Timmelsen —Clarence Timmelsen, too. Both of them." He marched to the wall of files and ran his finger down the labels. "T. T, where're the Ts?"

"Let me." Sarah shoved him to the side, lingering next to him, and pulled open a drawer marked inactive. Her polished fingernails clicked down each file until she pulled one out. "Dawes Timmelsen." She pulled another. "Clarence." She served them with a wink. "Anything else?"

Pete blew out a breath. "No. Not for now. But hold that thought for later."

He rushed to his office and slammed the door behind him. Tossing the files on his already cluttered desk, he filled his coffee cup and sat, sloshing coffee onto the files.

He muttered as he read, pulled at a tissue and soaked up the spilled coffee.

An hour later, Sarah knocked on the door and opened it. "You still reading those old files?" She shook her head. "Hey, I'm going out to grab a bite to eat. Want me to get you anything?"

Pete shook his head. "No, but when you get back, cancel this afternoon. We have work to do."

She wrinkled her nose and sighed. "Okay. But, no overtime tonight. My son—"

"I know. He has a game. This won't take long." Pete looked up at her. "I promise."

Sarah opened her mouth, then clamped it shut, eyebrows arched.

"Oh, and you have someone," she looked behind her, "that is insistent on seeing you—now."

A woman pushed past Sarah, extending her hand. "I'm Miss Henningway, the administrator at Hillcrest Homes. I'm here to see you about insurance."

Pete glanced at the file open in front of him on Clarence Timmelsen. Hillcrest Homes, huh.

He closed the file and waved her to a chair. "Come on in. No problem. We have a clear afternoon."

Hours later, Miss Henningway left and Pete couldn't believe his good luck. She had literally opened a door—two doors—for Pete to strut through. One: she had presented, in her subtle but sly way, a business venture he could not refuse. Two: she had provided a way into the very guts of Hillcrest—a backdoor way of getting back at Timmelsen.

Pete fingered a newspaper photo of a young Clarence Timmelsen, ink staining his fingers. Lucky day. Lucky chance meeting with Miss Henningway. It seemed they both had it in for Mr. Clarence Timmelsen.

He let the picture float to the desk, grabbed his phone, and dialed a number.

"Hello, Sheriff?"

CHAPTER 31

Clarence stumbled along the worn path behind the old library. He pictured people—mainly kids—who must have cut through here, from the back alley to the front door of the library. They must have begun at each individual home, into the street, onto the path, converging at the library.

Paint peeled off the old sign and the wood had faded, but words were still readable: Public Library ~ Hours: 10-5 p.m., Monday through Friday. 1-5 p.m., Saturday. Open to the public. "Books are the answer to questions." by Mabel Linger.

He'd helped Dad put that sign up.

Leaves swirled around his feet. They skittered off the sidewalk and gathered in bunches in midair, obscuring the library sign. When they cleared, he himself emerged—a young boy dressed in denim overalls over a plaid shirt, hands deep in his pockets, brain deep in thought.

At home, seated at their table, Dad pored over library plans. Clarence perched close by and leaned over his shoulder, firing out question after question. What is that room? Where do we check out books? And the most important one: where are the bathrooms?

The building took shape, and he and Dad climbed up and down ladders, nailed the window trim in place, painted the boards, waved at passersby, whistled as they carried boxes of donated books. He remembered every step of the creation, even Dad painting the words and times on the new wooden sign.

The building rose before Clarence's eyes. Original wood, new paint, brick laid in an impressive diamond pattern at the top, glass sparkling, reflecting Clarence and Dad. A shiny brass doorknob beckoned.

Dad sat back on his heels, inspecting the paint job. "Did I spell it all right, son? Is it straight and even?"

Clarence leaned against his dad. Then he stood, scanning the sign with the building as background. "It's all good, Dad."

Leaves scattered again.

Cars gathered in the parking lot.

Clarence walked up the sidewalk, pulled the door open—no more brass doorknob—and stuck his head inside. People sat on chairs circled around a central speaker at a podium. Mostly older women, but some men of various ages were in attendance. The woman at the podium looked up and smiled at him.

"Come on in and join us. There are some chairs available yet." She motioned for him to enter.

He nodded and slipped into a chair in the back row next to a young man, maybe in his thirties. They exchanged a nod and looked back to the front.

"As I was saying—"

Clarence's mind strayed again—to the building dedication, when Annie, his future wife, gave the welcome. As a clean-cut young man in a long-sleeved plaid shirt, typical of his age group and working class, he rubbed his palms down the sides of his new jeans and hid his hat under the chair.

Annie cleared her throat and began. "I'd like to welcome you all to the Polk County Library Dedication. The building is now complete, well constructed by Mr. Dawes Timmelsen and his crew." She continued, "I'm sure townspeople and the whole community will gain enjoyment and education in this building as it is used throughout the coming years. Please ... "

Clarence didn't hear much else. He noticed Annie's brown eyes so beautiful, framed with dark lashes. Her mouth was sweet as it moved around her words. Her hair was done up in a formal bun with tendrils escaping around her face. Her neck was pure and white above her blouse, and that was thankfully all he could see above the podium. Otherwise, his mind might have wandered where it ought not to go.

"It's time for refreshments. Son, would you like a cup of punch?"

Clarence didn't respond.

"Son?" Dawes shook his son by the shoulder. He shook harder and spoke directly in Clarence's ear. "Son."

Clarence jumped and kicked the chair in front of him over, causing a domino effect with folding chairs in front of it, clattering and crashing. He tried to catch them too late; he shook his head at the pile in front of him.

"Son, where were you? Why didn't you answer me?"

Clarence picked up a chair and righted it. Then another and another.

"Help me Dad. Hurry," Clarence whispered, eyes pleading for help.

Dawes looked at Clarence. Then looked at Annie. A big grin spread across his face.

Clarence's face burned hot.

"Well, well, well. Son, I suspect there is a story to tell here." He continued to pass looks between Clarence and Annie.

Clarence righted the last chair and stood facing his father. "What, sir? What was that you said just now?" He wiped his face with his hands and stood straight, as if in front of a firing squad.

His father brushed off Clarence's shirt. "Nothing. I just finally figured things out."

"Things, sir?"

"Yes, things. I just figured out the rest of the story." He looked up at the podium, where Annie stood visiting with the local dignitaries. He turned to Clarence and nodded his head to the front. "That, or rather, she is the rest of the story."

Clarence's eyes followed his father's direction. He punched his hands in his pockets, jingling change, his neck heating up all over again. "Sir?"

Dawes clapped his son on the shoulder and laughed. "It's okay, son. I'm sure this will all play out soon enough." He paused. "You want some punch? You might want to offer Miss Annie some while you're at it." Dawes smiled a gentle teasing smile and slapped him on the back. "While you're at it, get me some too. I'm a little thirsty."

Clarence half smiled at his dad, then peeked up front, meeting Annie's eyes.

Dawes doubled over in laughter. "So," he gasped, "it's mutual. That's the best kind."

Clarence hurried to the refreshment table and knocked over a stack of glass cups, breaking two and catching four. He set the rescued cups on the table, brushed up the crumbs of broken glass into his scar-protected hands. He carried them out the door, down the sidewalk, hearing his father's laughter in the background.

As he walked to his house and shop, a mile away, he muttered to himself the whole way. He'd never felt so stupid. Or so embarrassed. Annie was so pretty. She'd never talk to him again. He'd have to pay for those glass cups. Dad was going to either kill him or tease him to death, one or the other. Or both.

Once he arrived at the shop, he dumped the glass into the trash barrel, brushed the shards off and wiped his hands on the slop cloth, pressing one shard into his flesh. He jumped. He felt that. "You might know it. I knocked over chairs, broke some glasses, and cut myself in all of this. This is not a good day. I wished I drank because I'd be heading there right now." He stomped to the house, changed clothes and called in his dad's horse, Leather. "Come on, boy, we're going for a ride and I hope you are up to a wild one, because I think that's what I need, to blow off this afternoon."

They rode away to the hills behind the house and didn't come back until sundown.

By that time, Clarence had simmered down a bit. He'd worn himself and the horse out by running and galloping as far and as fast as they could.

He pulled the saddle off, hung it and brushed down the horse, talking a mile a minute. "She is the prettiest thing I've ever seen. She's like ... like the brightest star in heaven. She's prettier than the prettiest flower on this earth. Leather, you hearing me? She is so smart, because they don't call just any body to lead a dedication celebration."

Someone cleared their throat.

Clarence jumped, spun around and knocked over the grain bucket Leather was eating from.

His father grinned and walked over, picked up the bucket and scraped the grain back into it, righting it for Leather to finish eating. "It's okay son. I was the same way the first time I laid eyes on your mother. And I said all those things you were saying just now to my horse. And I've kicked over some things and almost died of embarrassment just like I think you must have today. Your mom still loved me and even married me, after I had the stickers removed from my back side."

Clarence looked at his dad. "What? Stickers? What did you do, Dad?"

Dawes hung his head then looked his son in the eye. "I ... was showing off for her, swinging by a rope into the river and instead of landing in the water, I landed in a patch of stickers."

Clarence grimaced. "Oh Dad."

"Uh-huh. I know. It was real bad, I'll admit. And she was the one that helped Doc pull them out." This time Dad blushed. "Yeah. Way to meet each other. She was Doc's nurse for a time. You think I was embarrassed? Damn right, I was. My bare bottom up side while your mom held a light over me, so Doc could see better. You bet I was embarrassed. I cried into my pillow."

Clarence gasped, wide eyed, then burst out in laughter so hard he fell against the fence.

Dad grabbed Clarence and pounded his back, laughing himself.

Clarence wiped his eyes and laughed again at the visual. "I never knew, Dad. Is that why she was always snapping you on the behind with a towel? A not so gentle reminder?"

His dad wiped his eyes. "Well, that's another way to think of it."

He looked out over the hills behind the place. "You remember more than I thought. I miss your mom so much. It feels like forever since she passed." He rubbed Clarence's neck. "I wish you could have known her better, Clarence. She so loved you, the little time she had with you. Planned for you. Sewed little … things for you. She just beamed when she carried you. And when you sang in that Christmas program at church, she cried."

He shook his head. "My, my. I didn't mean to go all over that. But it's kind of good to talk about her."

"Dad … um … do you think Annie is a good match for me?" Clarence studied the cut on his hand. "Is she the one?"

"Son, only you will know that. Only you and her and … um …." He pointed to the sky. "Him."

Clarence had never heard his dad speak of God in any way.

They stood together and watched the evening sky change from blues, then pinks, purples, oranges, yellows and rich dark blues. Silently they walked to the house.

"Sir?"

Clarence jumped. "Wha? What did you say, Dad?"

He looked into the face of the young man sitting beside him.

"Dad? Sorry, sir, but I'm not your dad. Were you dreaming? Are you okay?"

Clarence stared at him then looked around. The woman still stood at the podium in front, now smiling and writing in a book while someone waited and chatted with her. A refreshment table was set up complete with a coffee urn, cups, and sugar cubes and creamer. People gathered around a small plate of cookies, dropping crumbs onto the table and floor as they munched and chatted.

The man addressed him. "Would you like something to drink, sir? They have coffee and maybe punch."

Clarence nodded. "Oh, yes. Yes. I'm sorry, I was remembering this library back when it was first built, and I guess I was more there than here."

"So-o-o, coffee or punch?"

"Coffee sounds good."

"I'll be right back."

Clarence searched the faces of those standing around the room. Could any one here be a descendant of people he once knew? Like Annie's family? A niece? Clarence thought back. A sister? He remembered a sister working at the hardware store. Annie had been so proud of her because she was a woman before her time. Annie had talked about her with respect and admiration, even written stories about her. Annie had been a wonderful writer—so full of promise.

Annie's dad was another story. Jackass.

"Here you go, sir. Here's your coffee. I assumed you wanted black —no sugar or cream?"

"Black is fine. Thank you."

"So-o-o, you said you knew this building back when it was built? Did I hear you right?"

"Don't I know you from someplace? Do you work at the nursing home?"

"No." The man snapped his fingers. "I remember you. You stopped in at my shop yesterday."

"Your shop?"

"My woodworking shop. I was building a cradle."

"Oh sure." Clarence tapped his temple. "I don't remember your name."

"Michael." He reached over and held out his hand. "And you are … Clarence?"

"Right." Clarence grasped Michael's hand and shook it. Michael's jacket sleeve slid up on his arm, revealing a wound, deep and long, obviously still healing by the fiery red color.

Clarence pointed. "That's quite a scar." Something clicked. "I remember you. Your scar." He glanced at his own scars.

Michael pulled his sleeve down. "Yeah. So you knew this building back then."

"Yup. My dad built it."

"Did he? Who was your dad?"

"Dawes Timmelsen. He was a carpenter, builder, fixer upper, father, banker, farmer. Well, you get the idea. Jack of all trades. He could fix anything, but being a carpenter was his golden job. He created beautiful buildings in this town for people."

Michael leaned over to sip from his styrofoam cup. "Sounds like you have first hand experience with his work. Did you work with him?"

"As much as he'd let me. I learned a lot from that man."

Michael leaned nearer. His eyes were a deep blue, bluer than Clarence's. His skin was as smooth as a baby's. "And he learned a lot from you, too."

Clarence raised his head and looked directly into Michael's eyes for a few seconds. "What on earth do you mean by that—he learned from me, too?" Another second. "And how would you know anything about him—or me?"

"Just from what I've heard from you … and … seeing his work." Michael averted his eyes and stammered. "He seems like the kind of man that was humble, kind, teachable." He looked at Clarence. "Am I right?"

"Well, yeah. Sure." Clarence gazed out the window. "He was upstanding. A kind man to all." Clarence met Michael's eyes. "But how could he have learned anything from me? I was … I was—"

Michael leaned into Clarence. "You were a young man hit hard by circumstances, by life, and your dad watched you go through some of the same things he had gone through—only worse."

Clarence flinched and spilled his coffee onto his pants. He jumped again at the heat.

Michael scrambled for napkins. He rushed to Clarence, sat and blotted at the stain.

Clarence pushed his hands away. "No. No. It's … I'm just clumsy." He sat back and stared at Michael, his voice soft. "How'd you know all that?"

CHAPTER 32

Bea happily swung her feet back and forth and munched on chicken strips, one in each hand. She traded one for a French fry, singing, "French fry first. Chicken bite next. French fry first—"

"Bea! Shush. You're driving me crazy." Mommy sipped her drink. "Just eat."

Bea hummed the same melody, switching the fries and chicken bites back and forth. She glanced at the front window of the Tasty View Dive-Inn and spied the old man walking by outside. She kicked her feet faster.

Bea watched the entrance door.

No old man.

Back at the window, she stretched her neck and saw his back as he walked past the building. Catching sight of his funny, short gray hair ruffled by the breeze, she jumped on the bench beside her booster seat and bumped her plate, dumping chicken bites and fries all over the table and onto Mommy's plate.

"Bea! What are you doing?" Mommy lurched forward, corralling the food before it hit the floor.

Bea was so intent on seeing where he went that she didn't answer.

"Bea, sit down on your seat right now, or we'll go home."

She looked down at her now empty plate, food all over the table, then over to Mommy's full plate, then up to Mommy's face.

"Hurry up and sit down. Now!" Mommy pointed to the bench, a mean frown on her face.

Bea stretched to see if she could see him.

Gone.

"Sit!"

She slumped and sat down but missed her booster seat, landing next to it on the bench. Her lips trembled, but one look at Mommy's face and she straightened up. She righted herself, feet on either side of the booster, and sat carefully. A french fry was on the bench beside her and she popped it in her mouth.

Mommy picked up Bea's food and dumped it back onto her plate. "What were you thinking?" Mommy looked out the window. "What was so interesting out there, that you had to upset the apple cart?"

"What?" Bea picked up a chicken strip and took a bite. "Apples, Mommy? Where?"

Mommy sighed. "I shouldn't use those words with you. You always take me literally." Mommy berated herself. "You are too smart for … no, not going there. You are so smart." She tapped her drink cup. "If you eat all your food," she hesitated, "you can have ice cream."

Bea jumped again, knocking herself slightly off the booster, but righting again. "I can?" She proceeded to cram every French fry into her mouth.

"Not so fast." Mommy gasped. "Don't swallow your food whole. Take time to chew."

———

Katty shook her head, sucked on her soda. Empty. She popped her cup on the table and scanned the restaurant.

A man's eyes smiled at her over his coffee cup. She read the cup: Lacy's Plumbing — 1-800-Big-Drip.

She froze. She knew those eyes. Goosebumps skittered up the nape of her neck, sending shivers across her back.

He put the cup down and checked his watch.

Whew. Not who she thought.

She inspected him without looking too interested. Kind of good looking in a rough sort of way. Nice leather jacket. But those eyes. Reminded her of … but seeing the whole face, she couldn't get a fix on who he looked like.

She could get used to those eyes looking at her over—

Bea choked on her fries.

Katty jumped. "Bea, are you okay?" She moved over beside Bea and patted her back, grabbed for napkins. "Here. Spit it out."

Bea spit the food into the paper napkins, and Katty wiped her mouth.

"Can I help you?" A deep male voice vibrated behind Katty. She turned.

Those eyes again.

"Is she okay? I noticed you jumped up and then … " He smiled at Bea. "Are you okay, little girl?" He reached his finger out to tuck under her chin.

Bea hugged into Katty's side.

His voice sucked Katty in. She struggled to pull away. "Uh, I think she's okay. She choked on her food." Katty wiped Bea's mouth again and stood. "She just got excited about ice cream and started to cram food into her mouth and she choked."

"Ice cream." The man smiled. "I get excited about ice cream. Let me buy."

"Oh, no. It's okay. I was just waiting for her to finish her food and she choked. I can get it."

He reached into his wallet. "I feel bad she choked." He pulled out a couple of twenties from a full wallet and laid them on the table.

Katty stared at the money. She slowly picked it up and handed it back to the man. "Take it. I can get the ice cream."

"You sure? I'd love to get it for her and for you." He blinked down at her.

Agh. Those eyes.

Katty held out the money and pressed it into his hand, feeling vibrations underneath the money. "Thanks anyway. Please take your money. We're fine. Aren't we Bea?"

Bea's eyes bounced back and forth between Mommy and the man.

He said something and Mommy stared at him—at his face.

Mommy talked to him, and Bea watched her face move and change.

His bright blue eyes looked hard, like marbles. He looked down at her. She shivered and hugged her middle. She didn't like those eyes.

"Are you cold, Baby Bea?" Mommy reached down and ran her fingers along Bea's arms. "You've got goosebumps all over."

Bea shook her head, her eyes never leaving the man's face. "Let's go, Mommy. I'm tired." She climbed into Mommy's arms. "Please? Let's go home."

"You haven't had your ice cream yet." Mommy searched Bea's eyes, then shook her head. "Let's have your ice cream and then we can go." She picked up the pieces of chicken and dropped them on Bea's plate and sat down beside her. "Would you like to join us?"

He smiled and bowed. "Don't mind if I do. Thank you." He sat across from them and cocked his head. "If I join you for ice cream, I can treat, right?"

"Okay. I 'spose," said Mommy. "Just this once."

He looked a long time into Mommy's eyes.

Bea followed back and forth, from Mommy to the man and back again. The man raised his hand, his eyes never leaving Mommy's, and snapped his fingers.

A waitress, clearing the table next to them, jerked her head up. "Yeah? Whatdaya want?"

The man slowly lowered his arm and locked directly onto the waitress' eyes. He still smiled, but he changed. His face changed. His eyes turned black.

The waitress popped over to their table. "Yes, sir?"

"We would like some ice cream, please," he said. He looked over at Bea. "What kind would you like, little one?"

Bea hid under Mommy's arm.

"Bea? Tell him." Deep sigh. "She likes vanilla please."

"And for you?"

"I'll take chocolate."

The man raised his voice. "That'll be one vanilla and two chocolates in a dish. Thank you."

"Yes, sir."

Bea peeked from under Mommy's arm and watched the waitress scurry from their table, casting backward glances at them. The waitress bumped into another waitress who was carrying three filled plates spread across her arm. The dishes wobbled but none fell. Both waitresses breathed a sigh of relief. So did Bea.

The man cleared his throat and smiled at Mommy. "Now, where were we?"

"Um, I'd like to start with names. What's yours?" Mommy blinked her eyes and smiled.

"Oh, of course. I'm sorry. My name is Lex. Lex Forgé." He leaned into the table. "And who might this young lady be?"

Mommy turned to Bea. "Tell him your name, honey." Mommy nudged Bea.

Bea hugged closer under Mommy's arm, peeking at the man.

"Sorry. She's kind of shy sometimes. This is Bea." Mommy nodded toward him. "Bea, say hello to Lex."

Bea peeked out and mouthed hello, and closed her eyes.

He burst out laughing. "How cute. And who might you be, Ma'am?

The waitress cleared her throat and set down bowls of ice cream. "I think she had the vanilla and that leaves chocolate for the both of you, right?" She stood back, hands clasped in front of her.

He nodded to her. "Right. Thank you." He waved her away.

Mommy slid the bowl closer to Bea and handed her a spoon.

"And yours?"

"My what?" Mommy picked up her spoon.

"Your name. What's your name? We told ours. Now it's your turn."

Bea peeked out, watching him and he watched her back.

"My name is Katty. Katelyn Randolph."

He held out his hand. "Pleased to make your acquaintance."

Mommy reached over the ice cream and shook his hand.

They held hands like that, arms stretched over the ice cream, for a long time. She dropped her spoon onto the floor, the clatter breaking the spell.

"Oh, Bea. Now we have to get you a clean one." Katty looked up for the waitress, but she already stood beside the table with a spoon in her hand, holding it out to Bea.

"Why … thank you. You're so speedy."

Lex smiled as he stuck his spoon into his ice cream. He pulled out a huge bite, and let it drip back into the bowl.

Mommy fed Bea a bite—or tried to, but Bea pursed her lips, closing her mouth. "You don't want any right now? That's okay. Take a bite if you feel like it."

Mommy shook her head and slid her spoon into the bowl, playing with the melting dessert. Mommy watched the man, and he watched Mommy. She stirred the ice cream then loaded her spoon with a bite, bringing it to her mouth. Opened her mouth, closed her eyes. Then licked her spoon.

"Mmmm. Haven't had ice cream this good in a long time." She looked at his. "Aren't you eating yours? It's yummy."

"I'm enjoying you eating yours. Even if little Bea can't eat hers." He twirled the spoon in his bowl then locked eyes with Bea. As she watched, his blue eyes turned cold again, dark, black. Hard like marbles again.

Scary.

Bea fidgeted. "Mommy, I have to go potty."

"Really? I'm right in the middle of my ice cream. Can't you wait?"

Lex stared at Bea. She shivered and hid under Mommy's arm. "Mommy. I have to go now. I can't wait."

"She can go by herself, can't she?" His voice rumbled across the table.

Mommy hesitated. "Uh, no. No. She's too little." She turned to

Bea. "Why are you hiding? You were fine before. Listen, let me finish mine and then we can go potty, okay?"

Bea slid under Mommy's arm again, peeking out.

Mommy dipped into the bowl and scooped up another bite. "Eat yours, Lex. It's melting. You don't want to waste it."

He stirred it and dipped the spoon for a bite, brought it to his lips and licked a taste. "It is good."

"There. You took a bite. Makes me feel like a pig when you don't eat. I'm gobbling mine down." She eyed Bea's. "You sure you don't want yours Bea? It's going to melt."

Bea shook her head under Mommy's arm.

"Okay." Mommy sighed. She replaced the empty bowl with Bea's full one. "Somebody's got to eat this. Kind of melted though." She drizzled the ice cream from the spoon inches above the bowl. "Not gonna work."

Bea jerked on Mommy's sleeve. "Mommy, I have to go. Please? I have to go potty." She looked over at Lex. Terrified.

"I'd better take her. Sorry. We'll be right back." She scooted out of the booth and reached for Bea behind her.

Lex smiled up at Mommy, then looked at Bea. "It was nice to share ice cream with you, Bea."

Bea stared at his full bowl, climbed out of the booth and scrambled in front of Mommy. She pulled Mommy along, away from the table and away from him.

CHAPTER 33

Clarence peered through the window of the old restaurant. Empty. Ceiling tiles littered the floor. Wallpaper peeled and trailed from the plaster. Litter and dirt obscured anything of merit.

A screech high above startled him and he jumped, head tilted back, searching the sky. That old bird.

Clarence shook his fist at it, then realized it was circling: first, a huge swoop and back around, then a smaller circle and a smaller one. Smaller and smaller until it hovered right above him.

Clarence shook his head in wonder. "How can you do that? What do you want old bird? Why are you here?"

The hawk screeched again. The sound bounced off the buildings, making Clarence jump again. He relaxed as the bird flew away.

It flew north over the huge courthouse, circled twice, then out into the country. Probably had a mate somewhere. Funny old bird.

He looked back to the building. It had once been regal and solid. The brickwork testified to the gift of a true craftsman: fancy diamond patterns above the windows crisscrossed in an overlapping grid, ornate tiles installed alternately, added the artistic touch. Light trails streaming between a gap in the neighboring buildings revealed dust particles floating in the air, creating squares of sunlight on old wooden floors.

Clarence snapped his fingers, remembering: this used to be the law office. He couldn't remember the names of the lawyers, but they were good folk. Dad had called on them more than once.

He checked the street for people or cars then rattled the doorknob. Locked tight. He walked around the block to the back alley, figured out which was the old law building and found the back door.

He gripped the old metal doorknob, but it fell off in his hand. "Oh-oh," he whispered. He tried to tap it into place—but it fell off again. Shrugging, he let it lie on the ground where it had fallen. He pulled on the handle above. The door opened.

He looked both ways and then slipped inside.

It was pitch dark. He stretched his arms out in front of him and stumbled against something metal, then bumped into what felt like a chair. Sliding his feet, he felt his way back to the door and pushed it open a bit to let in more light. As his eyes adjusted to the darkness, he stood stock still, listening. Short breaths echoed in his ears.

Soon he could make out old shelves on one wall and a hallway leading to the front of the building.

He studied the floor, determined not to fall. Instantly the interior lit up, as if someone had flipped the power on. Sconces lining the hall illuminated beautiful wood wainscoting, flocked wallpaper above. Oriental rugs covered oak floors.

Clarence followed the rugs into the front office where the receptionist sat, writing longhand onto a document. She looked up at him and smiled. "Did you find everything okay?"

Clarence held his hat by his side and bowed slightly, his head down. "Yes ma'am. I did."

She pointed to a row of carved chairs along the far wall. "Have a seat. They should be done soon."

"Thank you, Ma'am." Clarence shuffled over to the chairs but stood looking down at the deep velvet upholstery.

"You won't get it dirty." She pointed again. "Go ahead and make yourself at home, young man."

"Uh, I'll just stand here and ... " His eyes found a bookcase. "I'll just have a look at these books instead. If that's okay."

"Sure it's okay. Suit yourself, son."

"Thanks." Clarence read each title, tilting his head to the side. His fingers walked across the spine of each book.

"You can take one down and look at it."

He looked over his shoulder at the receptionist. "Thank you ma'am. I just might have to do that." He reached over and pulled one from the shelf. Smelled it.

"Take it to that table there and read it."

Behind him stood a beautifully carved table with massive legs. Papers and file folders were stacked on one corner and a map took up most of the space, but he found room at one end.

He reverently opened the book one page at a time and scanned the words. Real cases. A case about a fire. A whole family of kids burned to death along with the father when he tried to rescue them, as the mother watched. Clarence shook his head.

Voices rose in volume, and a door opened from somewhere in the back of the office. Clarence turned to see his dad shake hands with Mr. Clynder. "Thanks Ted. I appreciate your time and anything you can do."

"Sure Dawes. I'll be getting back in touch with you in a few days. Will that work?"

"You bet."

He patted Dawes on the back. "I like what you're planning."

They nodded and turned to the front of the office—eyes on Clarence.

"You reading law books, son?" Mr. Clynder pounded him on the shoulder. "Good way to start in the business, if I do say so myself." He grinned at Dawes. "Is he going to be a woodpecker like you, or a lawyer like me?" He hung his thumb in his vest pocket and grinned. "What case are you on, son?"

"Well, sir, this here fire case. Sounds real tough. Real bad."

Ted nodded and paused. "Yes, that was bad. They tried to make it the mother's fault, but—"

"Yes sir." Clarence pointed to the book. "They proved it was the father's fault. Excuse me, sir, for interrupting. The mother was going to have another child, the book said."

"You seem to have a penchant for cases." He winked at Dawes. "If your dad can't keep you busy, come on over and I'll use you."

Clarence's head popped up. "Really? Dad? Could I do that? I'd like helping people out."

The men laughed.

"We'll see, son. We'll … "

Clarence closed the book, and a dust cloud obscured the table. Dust danced in the sunlight streaming in through the front windows. Beautiful wallpaper no longer covered the walls but could still be seen hiding under layers of peeling paint. Old bookshelves stood on the opposite wall, as before. But there was no desk. No receptionist. No table. No book. No case to study.

Paper fragments and newspaper clippings floated into the sunbeam, catching his eye. Clarence chased them as they flitted and floated and caught one mid-air. He walked closer to the windows, holding it up to the sunlight. It was a newspaper clipping of a little girl with a sweet smile and bouncy curls.

She looked vaguely familiar. He shoved a hand into his pocket, stirring the coins and fingering the toy ring. "Huh." As he shook his head, his stomach growled. Where could he have seen her? He held it closer to his face in the direct light, and his heart lurched. He pressed it to his chest, his hand covered his mouth. He brought it back into the light to study once again and cupped it in the palm of both hands.

"Oh, my darling, my darling."

CHAPTER 34

"Mommy, I want to go home. I don't like that man. He can't have ice cream with us. Mommy, I want to go home."

Bea kept trying to explain things to Mommy while she used the bathroom. She finished and pulled up her panties and smoothed her dress down. "Mommy, I don't want to stay. I don't want to see him any more." Why wouldn't Mommy understand?

"Settle down, Bea. What is so awful about him?" Mommy held Bea up to the sink to wash her hands then used the toilet herself. "He's a nice man. He bought us ice cream. Or rather, he bought me some. I've never seen you not eat ice cream before. And I know you're shy sometimes but not deathly afraid of anyone."

She finished and washed her hands, checking herself in the mirror above the sink, tilting her head from side to side, then closer in, checking her eye make-up. She pulled paper towels from the dispenser and dried her hands, still looking in the mirror, smacking her lips together. Touching up her hair, she smiled.

Bea watched Mommy the whole time, eyes moving from the real Mommy to the Mommy reflected in the mirror.

Her face was changing again. Into someone different. Somebody scary. Bea stared without answering Mommy, watching the change. Part of her was fascinated. Part terrified.

Soon Mommy stopped messing with her hair and face and looked down at Bea through the mirror. "What? What are you looking at? What's wrong? And why haven't you answered me?" Mommy whipped around. "Why aren't you answering me, Baby Bea?" She leaned down closer.

Bea backed away, eyes wide, mouth open.

Mommy stopped herself with a gasp. "You're afraid of me," she whispered and stooped down in front of Bea. "You're afraid of me, Bea. Aren't you. Right now."

Bea nodded slowly, eyes never leaving Mommy's.

Mommy looked at the bathroom door, then back. "It's because of that man, isn't it."

Bea swallowed.

Mommy kept looking at the door. "He makes you scared, doesn't he." She sat back on her shoes, still staring at the door. "You changed when he came over. You hid behind me the whole time and wouldn't eat ice cream."

Bea spoke for the first time. "You changed too, Mommy." She pointed at Mommy's heart.

"I didn't change."

Bea took a deep breath. "Yes you did, Mommy."

Mommy looked at Bea. Her breathing got faster. "Naw. Did I?"

Bea nodded. "You changed then. Now Mommy's back."

Mommy shook her head amazed, touching her hair. "Why? How?"

Bea started to cry.

"Honey. Baby Bea." Mommy gathered Bea into her arms and held her. "There's something about that man. That Lex man. How can he change people? How did he change me?" She held Bea away. "Why didn't he change you?" She put her fingers under Bea's chin and lifted her head. "Why didn't he change you, my little one?"

Bea looked back at Mommy. Real Mommy. Bea didn't move. She couldn't say anything. She couldn't take her eyes off Mommy. Just breathe.

"Wow. This is crazy. How can he have that kind of power over people? Over me?" Mommy stood up and checked her zipper. "We better go."

Bea flinched and shook her head.

"No, Bea. We won't go back to our table. We'll just leave. God give me strength to not look into those eyes." She laughed. Then stopped. "Those eyes." She stared at Bea. "Something's going on, huh."

Someone pounded on the door. "You done in there, yet?"

Mommy opened the door and looked out toward their table. "He's not there."

She grabbed Bea's hand and pulled her past the ladies waiting in line. She gathered their jackets from the booth as the waitress wandered over.

"Your man had to leave. He said to tell you to take the money. That you might need it someday." She chewed her gum on one side of her mouth and stared at the two twenty dollar bills lying on the table under the silverware.

Mommy stared at them too. She picked them up and shoved the money into the waitress's apron pocket. "He's not my man. And it's yours." She closed the pocket and held her hand there.

The waitress gasped. "Really?" She patted the pocket. "I can have it? That's forty bucks."

"I said you could, didn't I?" Mommy helped Bea on with her jacket, zipped it up and slipped her own on. "Thanks for the service. You did a good job."

"Thanks." The waitress stopped chewing as her hand clenched her pocket. "Uh … really. Thanks."

CHAPTER 35

"I own this building, and he broke in." Pete Malovitch bent down and grasped the old doorknob. His property rights had been trampled—by someone no better than a homeless man. "Look, Sheriff. Look at this. Broken. It's obvious he broke in."

Sheriff Dennison knelt beside Pete and examined the doorframe. "Pete, this door is so old a squirrel could get in." He tapped on the old wood. "And they probably do." He brushed the dirt with his fingers and held up a screw. "How do you even know that doorknob came from this building?" He stood, hands on his hips. He looked left and right along the alley. "There's so much garbage along here, how can you tell what came from where? How do you know it was him?"

Pete stood and faced Sheriff, eye to eye. "Because, I watched him break in, that's how."

"You what?" Sheriff stepped away and shook his head. "From where?"

Pete pointed to his car parked behind the insurance building. "I saw him from my office window, came out back and hid behind my car." Pete shrugged. "I saw the whole thing."

Sheriff shrugged. "All right, let's go in and see what we can find."

Pete pulled the door open and they entered the dark backroom.

"Pete, this guy is harmless. He's just an old—"

"Harmless? What about that?" Pete pointed his flashlight at trunks lined up along one wall. He walked to them. "Looks like they've been moved. See the trail?" He shined the light along dust tracks. He lifted a lock. "And the lock has been hacked on this one."

Sheriff followed along, shining his own light on the drag marks. Then the lock. "It's been sawed all right, but where would he get a hacksaw? He lives at the nursing home. The nurse there said he was admitted with almost nothing to his name."

"Well, there ya go. He's looking for something. His kind don't have anything and they want everybody else's stuff." Finally getting somewhere. Pete opened the trunk. "Look. See? These are old insurance cases I've gone to court on. Some legal cases here too. I'll bet he's lookin' for information—you know—to use against me. Didn't I hear he's a lawyer?"

"Pete. He's eighty years old. What would he have against you? And he just moved here. It seems contrived, somehow."

Pete drew up tall. "You callin' me a liar, Sheriff? You sayin' I rigged this? I've been here all my life, just like you. And yeah, he just moved here." He dug deeper under paperwork. "Look here. Here's the file on old cases. Looks like they've been tampered with."

He opened a file and stepped back to shine more light on the folder. "Well, looky here. It's an old case file. What's that old guy's name? Cal?"

Sheriff stepped closer. "Clarence. Clarence Timmelsen."

Pete handed the open file to Sheriff and tapped on a picture. "Isn't that him? Isn't that our guy? A few years younger, but I'll bet that's him."

Sheriff scanned the top newspaper article then sifted through the rest of the file. "Yes. This is Clarence. Look. Here's a picture of his dad back then. Looks just like Clarence now." He handed it back to Pete. "What's this doing here? Where'd you get all this?"

Satisfied, Pete shuffled the papers back in order. "All part of my dad's business before I took over. He was a lawyer *and* insurance agent. This is what that old man was after. Trying to cover stuff up."

He pointed to the file. "This is the kind of man we have around our women and children, Sheriff. And if he's breaking into buildings, private property now, what's he going to do next, huh? I've seen him with that little girl and her mom in the park. Look on your database. Is he a child molester? Where'd he come from? Yeah, he grew up here, but where's he been the last sixty years? He was incarcerated—he's been in prison, for heaven sake." Pete stepped back.

Sheriff expelled a deep sigh. "Number one, I can't believe he'd hurt anyone. Yes, the file speaks for itself. But, he served his time. Number two, maybe he did break in here, but what did he hurt?" He faced Pete. "He's just an old man in a nursing … " He trailed off.

Pete grimaced. "Caught yourself, didn't ya? You thought of it before I did." He ramped it up. "Sheriff, what if he does something at the old people's home? What if he hurts someone there? I'd hate to think … " He tapped the file, stirring up more dust. "You see what he did back then. What if he's been progressing all this time—getting deeper and deeper into crime to where nothing is sacred. No one is safe from someone like that. They stop at nothing." Pete looked out the front windows. "And he's right here. In this town. Right in our midst." He paused and pointed to the street. "Among our women and children."

"Okay. Enough drama, Pete. I'm going to need to check those files." Sheriff motioned to the room. "And access this building for investigation."

Drama? No. Justice. "You bet. I'm all about helping the law do their job." Pete handed over the files. "And feel free to check the rest of the trunk. I'm not sure what's in there, but my business is your business, Sheriff."

"Thanks, Pete. I appreciate your help in this."

"All in a days work." Pete shined his flashlight beam for Sheriff to see his way out.

Sheriff stepped into the bright alley and closed the door.

Silence and darkness filled the space.

Pete stepped to a trunk he had shoved into a dark corner and opened it. He picked up a folder he had stashed there. Walking to the window, he checked the street, then flipped it open and re-read a journal entry written in his dad's own hand.

"Sunday ~ Today sealed the deal. Judge and I made sure, since Timmelsen was knocked out in the accident, he would never know the truth—that Annie was thrown from the car, not shoved. The 'evidence' against him stuck, plus the testimony of a well paid jury. Judge set it all up. Timmelsen will go to prison for life. Even if he goes before parole board for good behavior, he'll never be free. Judge also passed down a decision that Clarence will be sent to Osceola nursing home. Serves him right. I should have married Annie."

Pete slapped the folder shut. "All in a days work."

CHAPTER 36

Sitting in his car, Lex tapped a starred contact on his phone, then held it to his ear. "Hey, Phil baby. I found your kid."

"Oh, yeah?" Phil Daynton answered. "Is she pretty?"

"She looks just like you, man … uh … not to say you're pretty or anything." He clicked the blinker on and off. "She kept hiding under Mommy's arm. You think she's onto me?"

"Ha! You are scary."

"So Phil. What's the big deal about finding her?" He reached to turn down the volume on the police scanner. "I have two or three kids that don't know where I am—they don't even know I exist. Why is this one so important?"

"None of your f-n business. This is a deal—a business deal—nothing else. The less you know, the better."

The inside of the Dive-Inn was visible from Lex's car. He had been careful to park where he couldn't be seen—behind a combine at the neighboring implement dealership. Katty led little Bea back to their booth. They were talking to the waitress. "Naw, man," Lex said, "I'm invested. Spill it."

Phil coughed on the other end. "No, you don't understand. Just do the job you were hired for."

Lex started the car. "Screw you. I'm outa here. You can do this on your own."

"Okay. Don't run." Phil growled. "Long story, but the short version is that this little girl is the only kid I didn't eject. Katty got knocked up if I just looked at her, so I had 'em taken care of, know what I mean? She hid one from me, but I caught on and ended it myself."

"Eww. God, you're a demon." Lex smirked.

"But Katty started looking a little … ragged, ya know? The drugs did their thing on her." Sound of a pop-top and a couple slurps. "Anyway, I left. But she musta been pregnant because the timing fits. She had our kid. I didn't even know until her supplier told me."

"What are you gonna do once you get here?"

"What any self-respecting father would do. That's my kid, man. She's mine and I'm gonna raise her … like any soft, fresh baby girl should be raised." He sucked another drink. "Got the picture?"

"Yeah, I get it. You are evil. Pure evil." Lex changed ears. "What about the mom? Where is she in this family picture?"

"That'll work itself out, if you know what I mean."

Lex eyed the gun on the floorboards. "Yeah. I think I know what you mean."

CHAPTER 37

Clarence stood in the entry of the old town hall, up on tiptoes, peering through the little glass window in the door. He drummed his fingers against a door panel. Paint peeled from the wood, its crunchy texture under his fingers. He brushed some paint chips from his shirt and leaned in again to peer through the window.

There wasn't any real furniture or seating—all he could see was trash.

A hand clasped his shoulder. He jumped.

"I was afraid you'd jump if I spoke. You jumped anyway."

"You're the guy from the library meeting … uh … Michael?" Clarence reached out his hand.

Michael shook Clarence's hand firmly and grasped his other elbow at the same time.

"So, did your dad build this building too?" Michael looked up at the old town hall.

Clarence tapped the old wood. "Yeah. The town fathers or council, I guess they called themselves back then, used to meet in each other's homes before Dad built this. This was pretty impressive back then. Now?" He nodded and picked at the paint. "Pretty sad."

"I have keys. You want to go inside and look around?" Michael jangled a key ring in front of Clarence's face.

Clarence backed up a step. "You have keys? You mean it?" He looked up at the window. "I'd love to get in there and look around. See if it holds any memories for me."

"Done deal." Michael inserted a key into the lock and it clicked.

"How did you happen to have the key? That's amazing."

"Oh, just a small thing. See," Michael looked down again at Clarence, "I happen to own this building and several around town. I can do what ever I want with them." He pushed the door open wide. "Including letting my friends see the place. Cool, huh."

Clarence barely heard Michael as he walked through the doorway. His natural eyes saw the dust, his natural foot kicked a board, his natural nose smelled old musty odors, but his spirit and memories experienced totally different scenes.

The swirling of dust particles stirred up around Clarence's knees sparked memories of the new building back then.

That day. The day he and Annie married.

She looked extraordinary. Her hair was pulled back and up, but the ever-present ringlets trailed down around her neck and ears. Her brown eyes twinkled with excitement as she looked into his. Tiny pert nose, beautiful full lips, tiny earrings sparkled from her ear lobes. Her neck appeared smooth and flawless, and as he let his eyes roam over the rest of her, he let out a deep breath as tears sprang to his eyes.

Her gown was white. That's all he remembered.

They married in the town hall and not a church, because her father was the judge and they wanted to be married by him—in *his* church, so to speak.

The hall was decorated with streamers draped all about. Very simple, but their every dream came true.

His dad was his best man and Clara's sister, Hattie, the maid of honor. She was beautiful, but her appearance had stirred up chuckles. Hattie would rather be in pants, but for her sister's wedding she'd do anything—even wear a dress in public.

There was no procession, no band or organ. Annie's mother had hummed the wedding march, and they all joined in.

Clarence faced Annie, and the only words he really heard after the I do's were, "You may kiss your bride." The memory of that first kiss lasted forever.

The guests were few, but they made it a festive evening. Music had been provided by Clarence's dad and a neighbor man on the fiddle and guitar. Clara's mother had baked and decorated a beautiful cake. Those moments with his bride, his new wife, were sweeter than that cake by far.

When they caught each other's eyes, Clarence was moved to tears and Annie laughed for joy. Then she cried and he hugged her without thinking and instantly withdrew from her, aware of the judge's eyes on them.

As they prepared to depart for their wedding night, his dad drew Clarence aside in the coatroom and hugged him. "Son, you're a man now, and I'm so proud of you as a son, but as a man too." He choked. "I know you got as fine a woman as your mother was, and I know she's in heaven cheering you both on." He grabbed Clarence and hugged him tight, slapping him on the back.

They parted and shook hands as the judge and Annie walked in. "Well, are we ready to consummate this marriage?" The judge held his arm around his embarrassed daughter, his other thumb hooking his black suspender.

Clarence stole a look at Annie. She glanced at him, and they both looked away.

"Come, come. You'll never give Dawes and me any grandchildren if you stay that shy." He slapped Clarence's dad on the back. "Huh, Dawes."

"I reckon they'll get to that in their own time, sir," Dad said, his hand rubbing his son's shoulder. He spoke volumes with his touch, more than the judge did with his harsh words.

Clarence took a deep breath and held out his hand to Annie. She left her father's side, and the moment she dropped her hand into Clarence's, the dust swirled, leaving him once again in the dimly lit old town hall, tiny particles following the light from windows to floor. Goosebumps.

Michael stood beside him.

"Woah, Michael, I'm sorry. I went back … in … time. I … it all began here." He turned away and wiped his eyes. Faked a cough.

"Hey, Clarence, you okay? The dust and dirt getting to you, man? Maybe we should go," Michael said. "What if we get something cold to drink?" He checked his watch. "The Dive Inn is open and it's almost time for supper."

Clarence looked up at Michael. "You are so tall. Were your parents really tall?" He hadn't really noticed before.

"Yeah. Everybody in my family is really tall. Some more than others." Michael held out his hands. "So, how about it? Supper?"

"Could we just look around a little longer? Are there any lights or has the electricity been turned off?"

"Oh, I think it's on. Let me go and fiddle around. I'll be right back. Could be just a matter of needing a few light bulbs."

He left the room. Clarence spun around in a circle. "I sense you here, Annie. And when I'm here I feel like a young man. I feel like I did on that day, my Annie." He danced along the sunbeams, and dust sparkled in the sunlight as he held her tightly. "I love you so much and miss you so. We were robbed of our long life, many children filling a house and lives with laughter." Another sob escaped his lips as the lights flashed on, blinding him for a minute.

Michael walked back into the room, smiling. "I hope this doesn't dim or tarnish your memories, seeing it like it is now with all the dust and dirt," he said. "I hope to get started on this little project soon."

Clarence sneezed and coughed again, facing Michael. "What are your plans?"

Michael scanned the room. "I love old buildings. They have so much history and memories." He paused. "I want to make it like new, and maybe use it for my home, or offer it up for sale as an office. I'm not sure." He stopped in front of Clarence. "Any ideas?"

Clarence nodded his head. "Does this town have a community place or fellowship hall?" People don't get together any more."

"Great idea, Clarence."

Clarence cleared his throat again. "Or a wedding chapel. Someplace where other couples could begin their lives together." He cleared his throat, suddenly embarrassed. "Pretty silly, huh."

"No, Clarence. Now that you say that, I can see it." Michael walked to a wall close to where he was standing and rubbed at the wood. "And since your dad built this, it's got good bones, a good foundation. I'm sure cleaning it and fixing it won't be a problem. Bring it back to its original beauty."

"Um ... I could help."

Michael whipped around and looked squarely at Clarence. "You'd do that? Really? With all your past experience of working with your dad?" He smiled. "I'd love that. But will you ... will it be—"

"You mean the nursing home?" He shook his head. "I run away from there all the time."

"I don't want you to get in trouble."

"I'm already in trouble with them." Clarence thought a minute. "Except one nurse. I think Carol truly cares. She is a gem if I've ever seen one." He held up a finger. "And I've seen one before her."

"If you are sure, because I'd love to have you teach me." Michael stopped and cocked his head. "Did you help him build this one too?"

"I sure did." Clarence surveyed the room. "If I remember right, I put up the wood around the doors and windows. Plus, the staining and painting."

"There you go, then. Let's get at the plans." Michael checked the calendar on his phone. "Tomorrow? After lunch?"

Clarence offered his hand. "Deal."

CHAPTER 38

The next day, Bea sat in her car seat playing with Dolly. She murmured while she dressed Dolly in the same dress she had just taken off, caressing her broken brittle hair. "You're such a good dolly baby. I love my little baby. Your hair is so pretty. You look nice today in your new dress."

Bea held her close, closed her own eyes and hummed a tune that Mommy sang to her when she was a baby. She opened her eyes when she remembered Mommy singing that song to her again—just last night. She smiled and rocked back and forth.

A large white van pulled up beside their car with lots of letters on it.

Bea eyed the letters. She already knew some of them. "H! Two h's." She pointed at the letters and counted. "One, two. Letters and numbers. One, two, three." She looked at the sides and windows. "People riding in a car with lots of letters and numbers."

The van door slid open, and a leg stuck out.

Bea pretended to not stare and hugged Dolly, playing with her clothes. She snuck a peek at the leg coming out. "One leg, two legs. Two legs coming out."

Only there was just one leg.

The driver smiled at Bea as he lifted a wheelchair out of the back of the van and opened it.

Bea tried not to watch, but her eyes were drawn to an elderly woman with short gray curls and big eyeglasses. She stretched out and grasped the arms of the wheelchair and stood.

Bea still only saw one leg. "One leg, two legs."

The lady swiveled on her one leg and sat down in the wheelchair.

The driver adjusted the footrest.

Bea couldn't resist and stared—still waiting for the other leg to follow out of the van.

No leg.

She looked down at her own kicking legs. "One leg, two legs."

She looked over at the lady as the driver wheeled her backwards to the curb. "One leg."

The lady looked up and grinned, waving.

Bea leaned into the back of her seat and looked the other way but peeked out of the corner of her eye.

The woman smiled.

Bea half smiled, squirmed and kicked her feet but looked away again.

A door slammed from the other side of the van and other people walked to the sidewalk.

The woman looked back at Bea and waved. The driver backed her up onto the sidewalk.

Bea stretched to see her as she was wheeled away and began to sing and murmur to Dolly. "One leg, no leg."

Mommy burst out of the store with her grocery bags and stepped off the sidewalk to let the woman be wheeled past. She ran back to the entrance door and held it open for them, smiling back at Bea.

Bea watched Mommy holding the door and smiled. "One leg, one Mommy. One leg, one Dolly. One leg, one Bea." She pointed to herself.

Mommy walked on the sidewalk back to their car and stood aside to let the other people through. She smiled and nodded. Then she walked to the driver's side door and opened it, tossing the bags onto the passenger seat. She peeked around to Bea and reached behind the seat to tickle her feet. "Hi Baby Bea. You okay?"

Bea nodded and giggled as she tried to kick away Mommy's tickling fingers.

Mommy sat down and started the car and backed out.

Bea sang her new song. "One leg, one Mommy. One leg, one Dolly. One leg, one Bea."

"One Bea. Baby," Mommy added as she backed out of her parking place.

Bea sang with Mommy as she kicked in her seat, glancing out the car window.

She stopped singing and bent forward in her car seat. The man with the bird.

Mommy looked back in her rear view mirror. "Baby, sit back in your seat. Don't get me in trouble, now. Okay?"

"Okay." She kicked the back of Mommy's seat with her feet. "Mommy, that's the man."

"What man, baby?" Mommy looked around the parking lot. "Quit kicking my seat. What man?"

"The man in the park."

"Where is he?"

"There." Bea pointed to the blue-eyed old man going to the grocery store.

He turned as he opened the door and looked back, like he knew they were talking about him. His eyes caught Bea's. He raised his eyebrows and winked.

She kicked her legs and grinned.

He looked up at the sky, and he seemed to be watching something.

Bea looked to the sky too, trying to see whatever he saw.

"There Mommy. There's the bird he had with him that other day." Bea squirmed in the car seat, leaned into the window and caught sight of the hawk circling high above them, going up, up without flapping its wings. A screech made her flinch as it lifted higher and higher, still circling. Bea pressed her hands against the glass. The bird swooped between trees and the building and then up, up again out of sight. When it dove back into sight again, it made her jump.

The man stopped and stared at the bird.

Bea looked up again, then back at the man.

He was staring right at her. A smile broke across his face.

Bea kicked the back of Mommy's seat, swinging her legs.

"Bea! Quit kicking my seat." Mommy sighed then started the car. "Let's go home and eat. Ready?"

Bea shoved herself back in the car seat and raised her hand to the man.

He waved back at her.

Mommy waved and backed out, gunned the car to the exit.

At home, Bea followed Mommy to the trailer, dragging a bag of apples along the sidewalk, her dolly tucked under one arm.

Mommy inserted the key into the lock. "Huh. I'm sure I locked it." She let Bea in. "Bea. Really? Apples do not belong on the ground. Pick them up. I bought those for a treat and now they're gonna be bruised."

Bea lifted them as high as she could, but the bag still touched the ground.

"Here. Let me have them. You go in and help put stuff away."

Bea entered the trailer house, but stopped short. There was a man sitting on the couch.

Mommy bumped into Bea, carrying too many bulging bags. "Bea. Come on. Move it. I gotta …."

Bea backed onto Mommy's foot.

"Ow. Bea!" Mommy dropped the groceries. "Oh God." She scooped Bea into her arms, crushing her close, cheek to cheek.

Mommy's eyes looked dark. This wasn't Mommy. But this Mommy wasn't mean or hurting Bea.

This Mommy was terrified.

A deep voice boomed from within the trailer. "Well, hello, Katelyn. You're lookin' … good."

The man stood up. "And who have we here?"

CHAPTER 39

That afternoon, Michael stopped at Hillcrest Homes. Visual layers of angels and demons overlapped the physical building: walls, trees, resident rooms, lamps, beds, bulletin boards, plants. Many beings towered above the roof and trees—some heads obscured by clouds. Angels surrounded the nursing home in lines except for a couple gaps. One or two angels nodded as he walked into the building; all the demons glared.

Michael stuck his head into the open office door and knocked on the counter. The angel behind the receptionist leaned down and nodded, his arm across his chest.

Michael nodded slightly in return.

Photos of smiling, toothless children, strung together by blue and pink ribbons, hung on the partial wall of the cubicle. Sparkly streamers drooped with a deflated ballon; the message on the ballon, "Happy Birthday, Grandma," was still visible, only in a contorted font.

The receptionist didn't look up from her computer, but answered. "Yeah? Whadiya want?" A small cross hung from her necklace hovering above a too-low blouse. Dark circles emphasized bags beneath her eyes she had unsuccessfully tried to hide with make-up. Tiny lines traced her eyes and mouth, her forehead.

"I'm here for Clarence Timmelsen. Is he here?" Father's heart began to reveal the roots of the receptionist's pain. Michael glanced at the guardian behind her. His eyes revealed the rest.

She smirked. "Lemme check. Maybe. Maybe not. He might be in the park or downtown. Or … at the grocery store. Or even in the police station. It's hard telling where he will be … these days." She glanced up at Michael, then right back down to her work. She flinched and slowly, her eyes inched up to Michael's full height, eyes wide, her mouth dropping open. Breathless, she sputtered, "What … can I help you with, Mr. … Mr. … may I have your … name?"

He flashed his grin. The angel behind the receptionist sputtered. "Sure. My name is Michael, and I'm here for Clarence Timmelsen."

The receptionist didn't respond. Her mouth gaped open. Her face went blank.

The angel behind her placed his hands on her shoulders.

Michael leaned in. "Ma'am? Excuse me, ma'am. Are you all right?" He waved his hand in front of her face. The smile might have been too much.

A nurse scooted around the corner and into the doorway of the office. "Jane? I need you to call a family for me."

No answer.

"Jane? Are you … " She noticed Michael and stopped. "Whoo-wee!" Elbow on the counter, her chin on her hand, she stared into his eyes. "Um, who do we have here, Jane?"

Jane didn't answer.

Another nurse rounded the doorway at top speed. "Jane, where are those files we talked about? I need … "

Michael stepped back. The room was getting crowded with humans and angels and—

"Hello." The nurse looked from Michael to Jane. To Michael. "I'm Carol. Can I help you?"

Michael nodded to three huge angels surrounding Carol. One was an angel that spent time closest to the Throne.

"I'm Michael." He held out his hand to her. "I'm here to pick up Clarence. Clarence Timmelsen? He agreed to give me some of his valuable time." He glanced at the nurse and Jane, still standing like pillars of salt.

Carol shook his hand. "Girls. Um, girls?" She clapped her hands in front of the women.

"Oh. Oh, yes." Jane stretched.

The nurse removed her elbows from the counter. "I was just in here … um. I know I came down here for something." She pointed and nodded, her ponytail bouncing. "I'll just go back to the nurse's station and … " She waved to Michael. "It was nice … meeting you, sir. You look nice … uh … you're a nice … man."

He bowed his head and she backed out of the office.

Carol raised her eyebrows. "Sorry about that. I don't know what got into her. She must need to go on break. Sugar low. Or high."

She turned to Michael. "I'll show you Clarence's room. If he is going to work with you, you'll need to know what room he's in."

"Sure." He paused, looking down at Jane. "Have a great day. Thanks for the help." He waited for a response.

No response. Her angel snapped his fingers.

Carol snapped her fingers too, and Jane jumped. "Oh my," Jane said. "I'm sorry Carol. I didn't see you."

"It's okay. I've got it covered." Carol started down the hall. "You seem to have made quite an impression with the office staff and nursing staff to boot. I'm sure you are worthy of their worship, but … " She closed a door to a resident room as they walked past, muffling the loud TV. "How is Clarence going to help you?"

"I purchased a building downtown, and Clarence happened to wander in the other day." He stepped aside for a horribly stooped man with a walker. The demon leaning on the man's back glared and positioned itself between the man and Michael. Michael continued, following Carol, "We started talking and I learned he and his dad—especially his dad—had built it, so I asked if he'd be willing to help with the renovations. He agreed and that's why I'm here." He hesitated. "And no, I am not worthy of their worship."

"Sure. It was just a comment. Not intended for truth." Carol pointed to a picture of Clarence beside a door as she knocked.

Two angels, positioned one on each side of the door, genuflected as Michael approached. He nodded and they stood again. They were old friends and he barely contained himself from roughhousing with them, pounding them on the back, wrestling. He distracted himself by studying Clarence's picture. His chest almost burst at seeing the angels posted there. He toned down a grin.

"Clarence?" Michael reached out his hand and clasped Clarence's, pumping it up and down nodding at two more angels—one in each corner of the room. One had full weapons: a glowing sword sheathed to its hilt, and a carved shield bearing the marks of his rank. They both bowed to Michael as he entered. He nodded, his eyes on Clarence. "How are you, Buddy? Ready to go?"

Clarence combed through his hair with his fingers then turned to Carol. "Did I tell you I got a job? I'm going out with Michael. We're working on his building."

"Okay." She cleared her throat. "At least you didn't sneak out. And at least you're supervised. That's more than I can say for the last week." She patted Clarence on the arm. "I think this man is a good influence on you, Clarence, so it's fine with me."

Michael's face grew hot. Inhabiting a human body was tough. He never knew whether he would perspire, cry, or belch. Just being around them grew harder each day. Energy surged through him with encouragement from Father. He focused on the angels and the Word. He had known this assignment would be lengthy and difficult.

Clarence grabbed his jacket from the closet and closed the door behind him. He winked at Michael. "Ready?"

"I am if you are. Good to have you with me today." Michael winked back, eyes alerting the angels on post. Clarence's eyes twinkled today. Interesting day.

Carol checked her watch. "Are you going to be gone for supper?"

Michael looked down at Clarence. "We don't know yet. Is that okay?"

"Sure. I don't have a problem with that. Just make sure he gets fed and sits down once in a while. That's all I ask."

"Oh, I'll be okay." Clarence took off down the hall.

Michael nodded. "So, you're saying you want me to boss Clarence? Sure thing, ma'am." He laughed. "I'd better catch up with him." He high fived angels lining the hall as he passed. A demon ducked into a room, hissing and spitting. An angel quickly brandished two swords, crossing them in front of the demon.

A tiny lady stopped Clarence in the hall. When Michael caught up to him, she was showing Clarence her mail.

Clarence reached for the papers. "This is your insurance?"

She looked way up at Michael. Even though she looked astounded, she didn't smile. Her eyes were red and swollen.

"Oh, Mrs. Hatly, this is Michael. Michael, this is Mrs. Hatly."

She barely nodded, her attention right back to Clarence. "I hoped since you're a lawyer, you might be able to figure this out. My insurance has always paid." She pointed to the document. "And now they refused." Her eyes filled with tears. "I don't know what to do. If they don't pay, I can't stay here." Her chin quivered.

Clarence put his arm around her. "Can I hang onto these so I can figure this out?"

She nodded and wiped her eyes.

"I'm sure it's just a mistake somehow." He looked up at Michael. "I'm going to help Michael out today. Then I'll come back and sort this out."

She patted Clarence's arm. "Thank you. You're such a gentleman."

He smiled and gently hugged her.

"You have a good day." She reached her hand to Michael and swallowed. "Take care of my friend."

Michael leaned his head down, her tiny hand in his. "I will, Mrs. Hatly. If anyone can figure this out, Clarence can."

Outside, Michael slammed the door to his old red pickup and waited to start the truck until Clarence shut his. An angel riding in the bed of the truck pounded on the top of the cab, giving the all clear.

Carol and Jane waved from the entrance door. Their angels crowded behind, imitating them. Michael clamped his lips shut and looked away from Clarence until he could talk without laughing. The nursing home was going to be interesting.

"They really like you, Michael. Those women." Clarence pointed.

Michael laughed, but tried to fake a coughing fit.

"You okay, Michael?" Clarence reached over to pat him on the back.

Michael nodded, engrossed in clearing his throat.

"No, they really thought you were hot stuff in there. I saw how they looked at you. You had better look out, 'cause they'll be after you."

Michael rolled his eyes. "Naw. I'm not looking. They'd get tired of trying and not getting any response. Besides, they like you better."

"Ha. Like me better?" Clarence snorted. "No." He tapped his fingertips together, fidgeted in his seat. "Y-you should know right now so you can dump me out if you want." He sucked in a deep breath. "I'm an ex-con." He turned to Michael. "I spent the last sixty years in prison." He stared at his hands in his lap. "So if you can't handle that … well … tell me now and I'll get out of your truck."

Michael looked out the windshield, the trees waved and fanned. "I know about you being in prison."

"You checked me out then."

Michael shrugged and nodded slowly. "You could say that."

Clarence nodded. "Okay. Just as long as we're on the same page. I don't want any surprises for you."

"No surprises." Michael started the truck and backed out. "You were in prison how many years?"

"Sixty."

Michael whistled. He turned out of the parking lot. "How'd you make it that long? I mean, didn't you want to break out a few times?" He thought of some of his former angel comrades now in chains.

Clarence huffed. "You bet I did." He glanced at Michael. "The first few years … I guess I was … in denial." He rubbed his thumbs together. "My wife was dead. I couldn't believe I'd … I can't even remember the day she died," he blurted. "I guess I got knocked out." Silence. "So … I just … tried to stay out of trouble."

"But couldn't you get parole?" Michael shifted gears. Grinding. How did humans shift, listen, talk at the same time? No wonder they lost focus with the Commander.

"I tried, but hit wall after wall." Clarence turned away from Michael. "When I left prison a week ago—feels like forever now—the warden said the judge back then set it up to send me here to the nursing home."

"The judge, meaning your wife's father?" They passed the grocery store as they drove up the steep hill. Downshift. Downshift. Should have gotten an automatic.

"One and the same. If he set that up, I guess he made it so I'd never get paroled." He pounded his knee. "Damn, I got angry. Still am. I decided that nobody would ever run my life again. So I studied and got my law degree, but I'm not sure even that helped, because here I am." He waved his hands. "Enough about me. You have family? Anyone?" Clarence adjusted the seat belt.

"I do, but in a different way than most. I have lots of family." A visual flashed in front of him, superimposed over the layout of the street: the host of heaven. He smiled. "Just not in the usual way." He turned a corner. "I'm just a loner. It seems strange I'm sure, to you. But I just stick by myself."

Clarence looked away. Michael glanced at him. "You got quiet, Clarence. Did I say something wrong?"

Clarence shook his head. "No. You sound like me. I consider myself a loner too. It's not an easy life, but it's just how it is. I would have loved to have had someone, but … it didn't … work out."

Michael paused. "Is this going to be too hard for you Clarence? I mean working on the building where you were married? Too many memories?"

Clarence shot Michael a sharp look.

Oh-oh. Said too much. Did he tell me he'd been married at the town hall or—

Clarence shook his head vehemently and visibly relaxed. "No, I feel close to Annie … when I'm there." He fiddled with the zipper on his jacket. "I feel so alive there, with all the memories. Even the memories of her father— the old bastard."

Michael chuckled. "I take it he wasn't an easy man to get along with." He parked in front of the building. Angels surrounded it. Each angel was unique in dress, looks and weaponry. Each angel recognized Michael and nodded, or bowed or knelt. Angels lined the inside. Their anticipation, their excitement was growing.

Clarence shook his head again. "No. I took his precious little girl away from him," he whispered.

There was pain in Clarence's voice. After sixty years. "Well, here we are." Michael said. "Time to work."

Clarence stubbed his foot on the way through the door. He pointed. "First thing is to fix that."

"I'll add it to my growing list."

Clarence turned away, then immediately turned back toward Michael, wiping his eyes. "Where's the broom man?"

Michael laughed. "Here's all the cleaning supplies, tools, and building materials. Feel free to organize." He rummaged in the closet, knocked over a bucket of old nails and tarnished hardware, and handed Clarence a broom, dustpan and brush. "Here you go. Knock yourself out." He ignored the laughing angel. Felt like his first time out out heaven.

Clarence set the dustpan and brush down in a corner and set to work. Swirls of dust particles danced in the sunlight as Michael opened windows.

"Too much air?"

Clarence looked up and stopped sweeping, bouncing the broom on the floor. "Nope. It's okay. It's musty. Needs fresh air." His eyes flitted around the building. "I wish you could have seen this place when it was all new. I can almost smell the fresh sawdust." He resumed sweeping. "I love that smell."

Michael began wiping down walls and dusting cobwebs off the ceiling. "Did your dad do the electricity too?" He caught his finger on a rough corner. The pain from that splinter jolted him. Blood distracted him for a minute.

Clarence nodded. "Yup. Back then, you didn't subcontract out. You did it all yourself. Some guys were better at it than others. Dad was better than most, at all of it." He stopped sweeping. "Was this anything after being the town hall? I mean did any other businesses occupy it?"

Michael wiped his finger on his jeans. "I don't think so. Odd, isn't it. That such a sturdy, well made building, was never used for anything else." He adjusted his ball cap. "Who owned it back then?"

"My father-in-law did. He owned half the town." Clarence looked up from the dust pan. "Literally—half the town. He always joked in a cocky way, that he'd get the rest someday. I think he died doing just that." Clarence looked away. "Just stuff I'd hear in Chicago. I never came back. Until now."

Michael replaced a light bulb.

"You don't even need a ladder for that, you're so tall." Clarence tapped the broom again. "You know where I grew up." He spread his arms wide. "Here. Where'd you grow up?"

Michael opened a box of new light bulbs. "Well, I grew up around … Idaho. Lots of places. I don't remember much of my childhood. You're really lucky you remember so much. You remember your dad. You remember building this … building." He grinned.

"Yeah, and some of what I do remember, I don't want to remember." Clarence continued sweeping toward the back room. "But one thing is for sure."

Oh-oh. "What's that?"

"I don't remember this place being so dirty." He sneezed.

"God bless you!" Michael laughed. Two angels flew away, apparently on assignment. Michael bid them safety.

Clarence shuffled in and around the old junk, sweeping under and moving chairs and tables. For a moment, it seemed like Clarence was interacting with something or someone. Almost dancing as he swept the floorboards, there was such grace to his movements. Clarence closed his eyes every once in a while and moved with the broom like he was holding someone in his arms.

Michael averted his eyes and smiled. His heart wanted to burst for Clarence as he traveled back in time to dance with his beloved wife. Those precious feelings between and man and a woman, something Michael knew nothing about.

Michael quietly went about some tasks: changing light bulbs, cleaning bathrooms, wiping down wood paneled walls. He paused at a window and stood for a time, relishing in the moment for Clarence.

The broom clunked to the floor.

Michael jumped and turned.

Clarence was nowhere in the room. The entrance door swung open.

"Clarence!" Michael followed him out the door. "Clarence!" He rushed around the corner. No Clarence. The guy was old but fast.

The hawk flew directly above, circling. It mounted ever so much higher on wind currents then dove to where Michael stood. The bird fluttered, inches away from his face, screeching. The wind from its powerful wings stirred the invisible domain. Ripples encircled them. The power of the Father poured through time.

Then it spread its wings wide—eyes focused—and soared above the trees surrounding the old building.

Clarence was the target.

The bird flew higher.

Higher.

Michael nodded at the bird. *Soon, old friend, soon.*

CHAPTER 40

Sheriff Denny Dennison shoved paperwork across the desk to Todd, his deputy, who frowned and said, "Sheriff, this doesn't seem right. He's just an old man. What did he do to deserve this?" He put his hat on, pushed it back, scratched, then pulled it down tight. "He's already in a kind of jail, isn't he? Isn't that enough? I mean, what can he do from a nursing home?"

"I know." Denny rested his elbows on the desk. "But the background evidence is certainly there. He spent his last sixty years in prison … for killing his wife."

Todd's eyes popped. "He what?" Eyebrows arched as he whistled through his teeth. He shoved his ball hat up on his forehead. "He killed his wife? Like back then, when they were young?" He shook his head. "For real?"

"According to all the files from Pete, and the police database—for real." Denny shuffled papers. "I even called the prison. It all checks out. And now with him breaking and entering, well … we just have to bring him in." He slowly stood up, groaning. Some days, he wasn't so fond of his job. "We have no choice. I don't like it any better than you, but we have to do what's right."

Todd nodded and pulled his hat down. "Okay. Where do I find

him?" He picked up the papers and tapped them against the counter as he walked past.

"Start at Hillcrest. Ask Carol—if she's there." He sighed. "Then start searching the town. He wasn't at Pete's buildings. Pete saw him at the park once. He's been at the grocery store. He's definitely leaving a trail."

"Okay, sir. I'm on it."

As Todd pushed out the door and headed to the squad car, Denny reached for the phone.

He'd better call Carol.

CHAPTER 41

Katty eased in front of Bea, moved just inches with each step, every breath a gasp. Prickles of fear rose on her skin. Bea's arms tightened around her neck.

"I said. Who do we have here?" Phil leaned forward on the old green recliner.

The room turned cold. Katty's gut wrenched. "Phil. You're b-back." She slid one foot inches from the door.

Stop.

"Yeah, I'm back."

God he looked evil. Or she'd changed. She slid the other foot toward the kitchen, kicking a grocery bag.

Coughing to cover her silence, she edged toward the counter, carrying Bea. The knife she had used to split an orange at breakfast still lay in the sink. She let her arm dangle there, slid the knife along her skin under her sleeve and hid it behind her back, wincing.

"Whatcha thinkin, little darlin?" he whispered in her ear, his hand on her shoulder.

Katty jumped. "I—I didn't hear you get up." She choked, his scent still raw in her memory. She shivered at his breath on her skin.

He slid his hand down her shoulder, to her elbow. "Who is this little filly? Introduce us."

Bea scrambled in Katty's arms, climbing away from him.

Katty struggled to hold her, shifted her to the other hip. A rare surge of adrenaline spiked in Katty, a Mama Bear's rush to protect her young. Phil had to die before she would let him have her daughter!

Phil followed Bea. "Peek-a-boo!" He bent to look at her. He snapped up to Katty's face, eye to eye with her. "She looks a lot like … us." He grinned, his breath putrid, his voice syrupy. His eyes radiated all the vivid, horrendous memories of their past together: his brutal touch, cruel words, sadistic acts of violence. "I'm glad I couldn't find you … I would have … she wouldn't be here. What we couldn't do with *her*." One eyebrow quivered. He cocked his head.

Katty hooked her arm around Bea's middle, got her balance, and bolted toward the door.

Phil sprang and grabbed her elbow. "Oh, no. Don't go. I want to get to know my … daughter." Phil swung her to face him, gripping her shoulders. "Oh-h-h. You're trembling."

Slivers of terror ran up Catty's back. His touch made her want to retch.

He ran his fingers up Bea's arm. "So soft and fresh." He looked directly into Bea's face. She had scrunched her eyes shut. "Oh, she's shaking, too. Like a little leaf." He reached under Bea's arms with both of his hands. "Come to Papa."

Katty flicked the knife from her sleeve into his gut and twisted it. Blood gushed from the wound and swirled. The room morphed into their past bedroom. Phil was backing away from her, a bloody knife in his hand.

She screamed from then to now.

She tore loose from him. Ran for the door, clutching Bea to her chest.

"Bitch! Bitch! Where do you think you're gonna go, huh?" he roared. "I found you this time. I can find you again."

CHAPTER 42

Clarence found himself outside the old town hall, hours after he had run out on Michael.

"Michael, you here? I want so much to believe. I want you here. You make me feel like a good person again." He tried the doorknob.

Open.

He pushed the door, wiping his face with his shirt sleeve. What he saw amazed and scared him at the same time.

The room he entered was perfect. Just like when he and his dad had finished it. The wood paneling appeared new and smooth, clean and rich. He rubbed it up and down with his old weathered hand and shook his head.

He heard a slight rustle behind him and turned to find one person in the room with him.

Annie.

He gasped, putting his hands to his face, and shuddered. His skin felt different. Soft. Smooth. He held his hands out in front of his face. His hands appeared to be the hands of a young man. Strong, filled out, well muscled. No age spots. No wrinkles or thin skin with scattered bruises. Just the familiar burn scars.

He lowered his hands and beheld his bride. She stood before him, as lovely as on their wedding day, but this time dressed differently. She wore a skirt with a tucked-in blouse and an apron, blotched with white. He looked closer at her face. She had white powder on one cheek. And the sweetest smile he had ever seen. Satisfied. Happy.

A small child peeked out from behind her skirts and shyly smiled up at him.

Clarence dropped to his knees. He looked up at Annie. "Who is this? Is she … ours?"

Annie smiled and nodded. She patted the little girl's head and gave her a gentle push.

He opened his arms and she tip-toed a step to him, a shy smile on her lips.

Annie gave her another pat toward Clarence.

The little girl came face to face with him. Blue eyes to blue eyes. They examined each other, then she leaned into Clarence's shoulder as he enveloped her in his arms. "Oh, my sweetie. Oh, my God." He cradled her, smoothed her unruly hair, then cupped her chin. " You are so beautiful. You look just like your mamma. And you remind me of … someone I've seen before." He looked up at Annie, then at the child. He laughed as he brushed the white powder from her cheek. "It's flour," he said. "Are you and Mommy baking?"

The child nodded, eyes twinkling.

There was a noise at the door, and the child ran behind Annie's skirts.

No one there.

Clarence turned back into the room. Annie was gone. So was their child. He rushed to the spot where he had last seen them and fell to the floor. "No. No. No." He struggled, trying to embrace them, to make them come back to him. Sobbing, he patted the floor all around, tears mixed with dust and dirt. He looked up at the room. Old. Dirt swept into the corner where he himself had swept it. One new lightbulb replaced.

He sat back on his haunches, hands on his legs. There was the broom he had left in the corner.

"But you were here. Annie, where did you go? My darling. My

Annie. And our child. Where did you go?" he cried. "Please come back. I'll change. I'll treat you well. I won't be mean any more. Annie … oh my Annie."

Silence.

Emptiness permeated Clarence as he sat on the dirty floor.

"Michael is even gone," he choked.

He sat there on the floor for many minutes, in the dust and the silence.

A horn from outside made him jump, and he realized he must have sat there quite some time. The rays of sun were lengthening.

He tried to stand, but only made it to his hands and knees, and pushed himself up from there. He stumbled and leaned against the wall, getting his balance.

He crumpled from grief and fear, bending to his knees again. "How can I go on?" He looked to where she had stood. "How can I go on without you, Annie?" He reached his hand in the air to where she had stood.

He straightened slowly, every cell of his body screaming. Just a moment ago, he had felt so young and alive. Now he felt every minute of his age. Heaviness overwhelmed him. He stumbled and shuffled across the room to the door, looking back again to where she had stood. "I lost her again."

As he stepped out onto the stoop, he heard the familiar cry of the hawk and looked up. The bird circled higher and higher, then tucked its wings and dove right for where Clarence stood.

CHAPTER 43

Katty shoved Bea into the back seat.

"Mommy!" Bea screamed and pointed. "He's coming!"

"Bea. Get in your car seat! NOW!" Katty jumped into the car and slammed her foot in the driver's-side door. "Ow! Ow! My God!"

One look at Phil stumbling from the threshold, holding his bleeding stomach, made her suck it up and slam the car door. She found the keys but dropped them as he tripped down the steps and landed on the ground next to the car.

"Mommy! He's coming! Mommy go go!" Bea shrieked in her ear.

"Bea, get in your seat! Now!"

She fumbled along the floor, found the keys and managed to shove them into the ignition and crank it over. The engine sputtered to life. As she slammed it into reverse, Phil grabbed the door handle. She screamed. "Hold on Bea!" She roared out of the driveway, catching sight of him rolling and getting pummeled as the tires threw up loose gravel. The car swerved until she reached asphalt. Then the tires caught, spinning and squealing. They raced away.

Bea thudded across the back seat, wailing. "Mommy, Mommy, Mommy!"

"Oh my god! Oh my God!" Katty tore around the corner.

Behind her, Bea bumped something again. She sobbed and sobbed.

"Bea! Into the car seat!" Katty flew around another corner. "I'm not slowing down, Baby! Gotta get away from that man. Don't ever want to see him again." She glanced into the rear view mirror. "He'll never get his filthy hands on my little girl."

Bea climbed into the car seat again and buckled. "Mommy."

She tore around another corner. "He's never going to get you Bea. Never. Never going to use you like he used Mommy."

"Mommy, I buckled—"

A siren pierced the terror.

"No!" Katty gunned the engine. Tires screeched. She checked her rear-view mirror as the car swerved wildly.

Blam!

Katty slammed into the steering wheel.

Bea cried from the back seat.

Gravel and sand pelted Katty through the side window.

"Mommy!"

Katty opened her eyes. The windshield was buckled. Bricks and rocks tumbled on the hood. Steam hissed from the front of the car. The hood had crumpled against a brick-fortified mailbox.

"Oh. My. God." Katty lifted her head from the steering wheel. Her head throbbed and blood seeped from her nose. She blotted it with her sleeve and blinked, shaking her head.

"Oh my God! Bea!" She stretched, looking into the rear view mirror.

Bea sat in the car seat sobbing, stretching her arms toward Katty.

"Bea! Bea! You all right?" Tears mixed with blood. "Baby?" She jumped out and onto the backseat, grabbing at the car seat straps, face to face with her little girl. "You're strapped in? Oh my God! You're strapped in!"

Katty unbuckled Bea and crushed her to her chest.

CHAPTER 44

Lex shifted his weight closer to the driver's side door. He was parked behind the implement company, near a row of green combines. From where he sat, he could see the highway traffic, the park, the drive-inn. And if he craned his neck, he could see the employee parking spaces at the grocery store.

He tapped his trigger finger against his loaded gun, half listening to the police scanner on the seat beside him, half listening to the intercom from the implement company. Some bitch was always asking for help in the sales department. She must be helpless. Spring planting time, he guessed.

An employee, dressed in the typical button-down work shirt and pants opened the back door again. The guy had come out two other times: once to empty trash into the dumpster nearby, another time to get something from his pickup. Each time, he had noticed Lex sitting there and had waved the first time. The third time, he just came out and busied himself with some old machinery parts lying against the building, rearranged them a couple of times and looked directly at Lex.

Hurry up Phil. Get your kid and let's get outta here.

Lex wasn't sure if he wanted a kid hanging around. And he was pretty sure Phil wasn't going to get Father of the Year. More like—

Static crackled from the scanner. Lex turned up the volume. "Caucasian male transported to ER. Life-threatening stab wound to the abdomen. Mega loss of blood." Time spent as an orderly a few years back would come in handy after all.

Lex leaned forward. "Phil? What did you do? You let a puny woman get to you?"

He started the car and backed away from the farm equipment, flipping the employee off, but at the last minute thought better of it. Might need this little hide-away again. He waved and held up his beer, grinning.

The man laughed and waved back.

This town was A-okay.

CHAPTER 45

Clarence balked. He strained against the handcuffs. The deputy pushed him toward the open cell door.

"It's just until we figure this all out sir … uh, Mr. Timmelsen."

Clarence barely heard the words. Didn't move. Stared at the bars.

"Sir?" Todd stepped around in front of Clarence and pulled him along.

Clarence stumbled. His eyes darted from the bars in the cell to the bars on the windows. He shuddered.

"It won't be for long, sir. Just until Sheriff can find answers."

Clarence couldn't move. His feet planted themselves just outside the cell door. "No." His legs crumpled.

The deputy caught him before he fell and heaved him to the cot.

He sank down as the deputy unlocked the cuffs and closed the cell door. The lock clicked, and Clarence jumped. Bars were everywhere—in front of him, in back of him. He stared as the deputy walked down the hall behind an overlay of bars.

Clarence shivered, stared down at his hands and rubbed where the cuffs had pinched.

Handcuffs.

Bars.
Again.

CHAPTER 46

Lex hid behind the entrance door in the ER hallway, waiting for his chance. That buffoon deputy, guarding the door to where they had Phil, needed to be gone. Somehow. He squeezed his arm against the gun holster inside his jacket.

The deputy spoke into a radio. "Sheriff? Todd here. They're examining him now." He pointed behind him to the closed door he was guarding.

Lex squinted. What a dweeb. Dork thought he'd contained Phil Daynton?

"Good. Stay with him. Don't leave his side." The radio sputtered. "I don't care what you have to see in that ER, ya hear me?"

"Yes, sir." The Dep pushed the door open and hesitated just inside. A nurse pushed past him, carrying bloody linens. She threw them in a laundry hamper, just outside the room.

Dork swallowed and paled.

She turned to go back in the emergency room and grinned, holding up an emesis basin. "Need this? You are the fastest case of green I've ever seen."

Lex eased behind the hamper. Easy does it.

Dork shuffled past the gurney to Phil Daynton's head. He was as white as the hospital sheets. Love to see him spill his guts.

Medical personnel rushed around the room. A doctor entered and assessed the patient. He began chirping out orders. Staff rushed accordingly, grabbing suture kits, meds, towels.

"No pulse. Shockers. Get the shockers." The doctor was firing orders as fast as he could talk. "Start the IV. He's loosing blood fast."

Beep, beep, beep. Buzz. Whirr. People shifted fast.

Lex poised himself. He'd broken Phil out of worse places.

"Watch the levels, people. Okay. Looks like surgery. Gotta go in and patch him up. Prep him."

"No way he's going to make it through this. He's lost too much blood."

"He's shutting down. Get him to surgery, STAT!"

Lex peeked around the hamper. Looked like the dork was gonna hurl. His shirt was wet under the arms and down his back. His eyes watered and crossed and bam! He swooned, his head slammed against a counter and he was on the floor. Good boy.

All personnel, just for a minute, hustled the deputy out a side door and onto a gurney.

Go now!

He skimmed around the hamper, hand on his gun, and scooped Phil up. "God, you've gained weight."

Phil's eyes popped open. A grin spread across his face.

CHAPTER 47

Clarence shivered, though fully dressed and covered with a blanket.

He stared through a window far above. More bars. Trees, twisting and taunting in the wind, partly obscured the streetlight, splaying patterns and shadows groping toward him over the cold concrete floor.

His sparse room at the nursing home now seemed like luxury. This cell had concrete block walls, just like prison. Nicer facilities, at least. It struck him that this cell should have felt familiar—like home. He had lived his whole adult life in a cell. Even though these walls were devoid of his years of artwork, scratches and hash marks, it was still a cell with bars and concrete.

But it all felt strange.

He covered his head with the blanket. He didn't belong here. The thought shook him. If Hillcrest was not his home, he was truly homeless.

Off to his left, the office door scraped open. A crack of light beamed toward him.

He tensed, barely making out a silhouette. The shadows shifted, and a person walked to Clarence's cell, hands resting on the bars.

"Clarence?"

Clarence held his breath.

"Clarence? You asleep?"

He raised up on his elbow. "Who is it?" He shielded his eyes against the light. "Who's there?"

"It's Sheriff Dennison." He jingled his keys. "I need to talk to you. I'm going to unlock your cell and come in. Is that okay?"

Clarence nodded. "Yeah. Sure. You're the sheriff. You can—"

Keys jingled, and once more, there was the click of a lock.

Clarence struggled to get up, but the sheriff gently pushed him back down.

"Please, don't. I'll sit on the floor." Sheriff Dennison eased himself to the concrete. "I need to talk to you. I got called in on an accident and we're done working it, but I can't go back home without talking to you."

Clarence rose up again. "Sheriff, you don't have to. I know what I am. I know—"

"Shhh." Sheriff shook his head. "I didn't want to bring you in. You've done your time." He whistled under his breath. "Sixty years. Damn." The shaft of light from the streetlight outside the window played across Sheriff's face, reflecting off his eyes, his badge.

"And I want you to know I'll do everything I can to protect you and your rights."

"Rights." Clarence choked on a laugh. "I have no rights. You said it yourself. Sixty years in prison and now I've been shipped off to a nursing home. What rights do I have?"

Sheriff Dennison stared at the floor. His jaw worked back and forth. After a long moment, he looked Clarence in the eye. "If I read the law correctly, you start over as a new, totally cleared citizen." He cocked his head. "But hey, one thing? I did get to read in your file— you're a lawyer? You studied while you were in prison? That ought to help establish you as a cleared citizen. Ree-habilitated."

Clarence stared at the bars. "People don't see me that way. All they see is ex-con."

"I'm the sheriff, not them. They can have an opinion, but ulti- mately, it's up to me and the court. And right now, I'm going to let you sleep, then in the morning, we'll transfer you back to Hillcrest."

Clarence closed his eyes. "Yeah. From prison to the old people's home, to here, back to the old people's home. I have never had any say over my own life since I was … back … a kid of twenty. Sixty years. Dad tried to visit me, but that bastard judge disallowed even that."

"Who was the judge? I haven't had a chance to go that far in your records."

"Percy Green." Clarence wished he could forget his father-in-law. "I can still see his face—jaw set with revenge." But could he blame the man, after what Clarence had done to sweet Annie? Sweet, sweet Annie. Clarence rolled away from the sheriff. "I wish he'd shot me instead. All this'd be over. I'd be dead." He covered his face with the blanket. Jaw tight. Hands clenched.

The cot shifted as the sheriff stood. Then the faint click of the door. Just one click, the latch. No cell door lock.

He pulled the blanket tighter around his head and squeezed his eyes shut.

CHAPTER 48

Denny Dennison glanced up from his desk and looked out through the office windows as Todd, his head bandaged, escorted a bedraggled brown-haired woman and a female toddler from the squad car. The woman appeared to be in her late twenties—hard to tell. Tough looking.

Once indoors, the woman shook Todd's hand from her arm. Blood streaked from her nose to her chin. One sleeve was bloody from elbow to wrist. "I don't need to be here. I can't—"

Todd gave her a gentle shove toward the desk. "Ma'am, you just drove into a brick mailbox. You don't have a choice."

The woman limped to the counter, carrying the child. The toddler was bleeding too, from a cut on her arm. The side of her face might be bruised.

Denny hustled to the door of his office. "Todd. Hospital?" He pointed to them.

"No hospital," the woman demanded, shaking her head. "No way!"

Denny walked to her. "This your daughter?" He looked her over, then the child. "Ma'am, your daughter is bleeding and needs to be looked at. You, too."

"No." Her head high. "No hospital. Please, just let us stay here." The woman stumbled. Drunk?

He frowned at Todd. "Did you test her? Is she … "

He shook his head. "Just traumatized. Been babbling about some guy that came back. Keeps saying he can't have her daughter." He shook his head. "She wasn't even going to let me drive her here until I got another deputy to follow us in her car. It's beat up, but drivable."

Denny exhaled. "Sit here and let us get a report. What's your name, Ma'am?"

She stood stiffly beside the chair. "Randolph," she said. "Katelyn Randolph. This is Beatrice."

Denny reached for a box of tissue, placed it beside her and reached across to check her nose. "That might be broken, Ma'am. Katelyn."

"Katty." The woman started weeping and sat down, squeezing the child against her. Beatrice shuddered but stared, eyeing first Denny and then Todd.

"Oh." Denny picked up a document on his desk and handed it to Todd. "You okay to transport this prisoner back home? I'll cover this."

"I'm fine." Todd picked up the page and looked it over. "Right away." He disappeared through the back door, toward the cell block.

Denny pulled several tissues from the box and thrust them into Katty's hand. "Katty. Tell me what happened."

She gulped, swallowed, gently blew her nose and began. "He's evil. He used to … " She looked at Denny, over at the dispatcher seated close by, and then back at Denny.

She blew a breath out, raised her chin and said, "I think I killed him. Just now. I think I killed him."

Denny straightened. Serious domestic violence. He grabbed a scratch pad and pen. "Where, Ma'am? What's your address?"

"212 Frederick Street."

Trailer court. He faced the dispatcher. "Sally, get a cruiser down there, STAT." He pulled an empty chair closer to Katty and Beatrice and sat.

"What if I killed him? You can't take my baby from me. She's all I have."

Denny shook his head. "Slow down, Katty. We don't know anything about him, yet. And we won't let anything happen to your daughter. She looks like she's been through enough."

Beatrice hugged into her mommy, pulling away from him, but not before he had touched her cheek. Poor child.

The cell block door opened. Todd stepped through first, his hand at the old man's elbow.

The little girl raised her head as Clarence walked into the room. His hands cuffed behind his back, head down. He didn't look left or right, just at his feet as he stumbled past them.

"Mommy!" Little Beatrice peeked from under her mommy's arm. "Mommy. That's him."

Denny flinched. Had he been wrong about Clarence? "That's him?" He leaned down. "Little one, who? Who are you talking about?"

The girl hid behind her mommy, but a tiny finger pointed toward Clarence as he shuffled by.

"Clarence?"

Clarence stopped.

Denny said it again. "Clarence?"

"What?" Clarence lifted his head.

"Wait a minute, Clarence." Denny stood, holding up a finger. "Child, you know Clarence?"

The girl wiped her nose on Katty's shirt. She nodded and quickly ducked under her mommy's arm.

"Clarence, you know this little girl?" Denny pointed at the rough-looking child.

Clarence looked at Denny. Then at Katty.

The child peeked out.

Clarence's eyes softened. "What happened to you, little one?"

Katty Randolph perked up at last. "Bea, he's the man with the hawk. Isn't he? And at the park."

"Are you okay, little one?" Clarence almost whispered.

Beatrice—Bea—nodded and rotated in her mommy's lap, facing Clarence. Fearlessly. No, more than that. Eagerly. Gladly.

"Well, I'll be." Denny whistled. "Clarence, how did you meet these two?"

He opened his mouth to speak, cleared his throat and started again in his raspy voice. "We didn't—officially. We … just … happen to see each other some days." He looked at Bea. "Don't we, sweetheart. You're the best thing in my day."

She nodded and almost relaxed against her mommy's shoulder. She hopped onto the floor and touched Clarence's handcuffs, looking at Denny.

Denny folded his arms across his chest. "Uh, Todd. I think we can do without those."

Todd unlocked them and clicked them back onto his belt. Clarence rubbed his wrists, gazing at Katty, then Bea, then at Denny. "Are they," he cleared his throat, eyes on the sheriff. "Are they okay?"

"Boy, we are totally messing with the Privacy Act here." Denny shook his head. "We haven't been able to get a statement from them, uh, her." He shook his head again then folded his arms across his chest. "Um, Clarence. With your law degree, do you think you might be able to help me out once in a while?"

Clarence stared at Denny. His expression changed and he blinked. "Um, you mean … if you think that's okay." He nodded.

The dispatcher's radio started squawking. "Sheriff. The guy is still on the run." She turned to Denny.

Denny glanced at Katty.

Katty shivered. "He's still alive?" She pulled Bea onto her lap.

"Tell Jim to stay on it. Bring him in." Denny turned to Clarence again. "Well, Clarence? Ready to reopen your law books?"

CHAPTER 49

Lisha tucked the hand-crocheted afghan around Mrs. Hatly's knees. "There you are. Take a snuggle nap." She checked the call light and clipped it to the blanket, then pushed the chair around so she could monitor the hall activity. "Anything else?"

"There he goes. He's back. Was he really in jail?" Mrs. Hatly pointed down the hall.

Lisha turned just in time to see Clarence, escorted by a deputy, turn the corner down another hall. "Well, the lost is found. Or the dead has a'risen. And … I'm not supposed to say he was in jail, Mrs. Hatly." Lisha folded her arms across her chest. "You said it. I didn't." Still, she leaned into the hall to catch a glimpse of them.

"I hope he's all right." Mrs. Hatly pulled the afghan up on her chest. "He's such a nice man, that Clarence. He dressed me one day. I was naked as a jailbird, uh, a jaybird, in one of my spells," she chuckled, "and he walked up to me, covered me up with my robe and kissed me on the cheek." She shivered. "He's exciting."

Lisha's eyes popped. She edged out the door as Mrs. Hatly's head drooped to her chest with a quiet snore, a sweet smile on her face.

Lisha fanned her own face as she strode off down the hall. Harold stood guard at his door, hands braced on his walker. "A bad penny always comes back."

"Harold. That's not nice."

"Probably better than what you're saying right now." Harold stared her down.

"I … like … him. Clarence, I mean." She backed up face-to-face with him.

He shook his head at her. "I've seen you walking behind him, doing your little act."

Lisha bounced, eyes squinted, shoulders shrugged. "Whatchu mean, my little act?"

Harold chuckled. "Busted aren't you? You mimic him—how he talks down to you, how he points his fingers, his tone of voice. I'm surprised he hasn't heard you, much less Carol or another nurse." He rolled his shoulders and hips, imitating her perfectly.

Lisha pursed her lips, eyebrows arched high. She slowly brought her hands to her hips, one hip bumped to a new high. "You don't miss nuthin' do ya, Mr. Harold?"

He smirked and puffed out a satisfied breath. "It's my job."

She sauntered to the living room and helped two residents untangle their wheelchairs. "You two been racin' again?"

One chuckled. The other snored.

Two ladies sat side-by-side on the sofa, chattering loudly. "There's that man." One pointed at Clarence. "I told the nurse, he has to go back to jail or prison or wherever he came from."

The other leaned forward, her fingers cupping her ear. "What's that?"

"I said," she yelled, "I told the nurse that man has to go back to prison."

"You're so right. We don't need his kind here in our home." She peered at her friend over large round glasses, and leaned in closer, talking just as loud. "He might rape one of us."

The other woman gasped, hand over her mouth, shuddering.

Lisha stared then pivoted to see Clarence stop abruptly. He dropped his head, shaking it. His hands balled into fists.

The deputy said something to him Lisha couldn't hear, patted his back and moved him forward.

Carol crossed her line of vision farther down the hall.

Lisha snapped out of her trance and raced after her into the Nurses station. "Carol."

She glanced up. "Lisha, I'm busy. This whole place is in a turmoil right now."

"Thas what I wants to talk to you about." She placed her hands on her wide hips. "Our jailbird."

Carol snapped her head up, glanced over the counter at the residents, then stared into Lisha's eyes. "Our jailbird?"

"Oh-oh."

"Lisha, I don't ever want to hear that come out of your mouth again."

"Yes, Ma'am." Lisha ducked.

"Now. Was there something important you wanted to talk to me about?"

"Yes." Lisha straightened. "There is." She leaned in closer. "The little old ladies are afraid he's gonna … you know. And the men want to shoot him, or have him castrated. It's awful for someone to have spent their life in prison, only to be sent to this heavenly home for … the elderly."

Carol smirked. "Did I just hear angels singing?"

Silence.

"I'm sorry, Lisha. I'm—"

The deputy clicked past the nurse's station and tipped his ball hat. "Ladies." He stopped and leaned over the counter, checking his surroundings. Lisha spotted his name badge: Todd Cochran. Bandage on his temple. "He's harmless. He may wander the town a bit, but he wouldn't hurt a flea, or little old lady." Todd glanced down the hall.

Lisha acted surprised. "Oh, we weren't talking about him. We were just—"

"Talking about him." Carol finished Lisha's sentence. "Thanks, Todd. We both needed a little reminder," she turned toward Lisha, "that we, as staff, treat all our residents, and each other, as guests. And that they deserve the utmost," she straightened, "respect."

Lisha, her shoulders back, tried to look convinced.

"Good. Glad to hear. He's been through hell and back. So he could use some kindness."

"But, I heard he was a lawyer. If he was in prison all this time, he couldn't be a lawyer." Lisha shrugged.

"He is a full-fledged attorney—passed the bar exam and every-thing. He went to college while in prison and got his law degree."

Lisha glanced at Carol.

"Wow," Carol whispered.

"In prison?" said Lisha.

Todd dipped his head. "Yeah I know. If I made half as good a use of my time on this earth." He adjusted his cap. "Well, speaking of time, I'd best be going back to work—saving lives and all that stuff." Then he walked away.

Lisha stood next to Carol for a full minute then turned to face her. She didn't speak.

Neither did Carol.

Lisha chewed on the inside of her cheek as she chewed on what Todd had just told them. "Well, at least he didn't just watch the boob tube and make drug deals while he was in the slammer."

Carol pretended to smack Lisha. "You goof." She sighed, looking down the hall toward Clarence's room. "I'm surprised, too." She frowned. "I guess I better … go down there … see how he is." She scratched her head as she looked back at Lisha. "What do you say to a—"

"Jailbird?"

CHAPTER 50

"Shut-up. You need to shut-up so nobody will hear you." Lex parked behind the combines and grabbed a bag from beside him. He jumped into the back seat beside Phil. "God, she really got you."

The wound was gapping and maybe three stitches had been started at one end. "You are one lucky son-of-a-bitch that I used to work at a hospital."

Phil coughed. "So like you're … a doctor … now?" He coughed again, and the wound opened more.

"Hell, yeah." Lex opened the bag and pulled out a bottle of medicinal whiskey and some peroxide. "Used to clean up the ER with this stuff."

Phil opened his eyes. "Whiskey?"

Lex laughed. "Peroxide on the counters. Whiskey for my health."

Phil broke out laughing, ended up coughing. Blood seeped.

Lex opened the whiskey, lifted Phil's head and poured a sip into his mouth. Phil coughed, but swallowed it down.

"Burnin' Baby." Phil dropped his head onto the seat. "Come on heal me, Lex Baby."

"God, you're burning up." He wiped his hand on his jeans and braced himself. He poured from the peroxide bottle into the wound.

Phil jumped and groaned. He pushed it away and began to writhe.

"Hold still." Lex slugged him and all was quiet.

Except for a gasp from outside the car.

Lex jumped out and there stood the John Deere employee gaping at Phil.

"Dude. Just in time." Lex reached into the car and pulled out a couple beers sitting next to the gun. "Let's just be honest here, son. You didn't see a thing." He handed him a beer, tipped his own, glanced behind him at the gun. "Agreed?"

The employee looked at the gun, at Phil, then at Lex and nodded slightly. He popped the top and sucked the beer down. Then turned and walked away, tossing the empty can into the weeds.

"Smart man." Lex dug in the sack and pulled out bandages and proceeded to patch Phil up.

CHAPTER 51

Carol knocked on Clarence's door. "Clarence, you in there? You ready for breakfast?" Fake happy voice.

She slowly pushed the door open.

Clarence was lying on his bed, fully clothed, facing the wall.

"I know you're not asleep, Clarence." She closed the door. "We have to talk." She tiptoed to the bed and stopped.

No movement.

"Please let me help you."

His shoulders twitched.

"If we play it your way, I have no recourse but to call the home office. And they won't deal with you like I'd like to." She gathered steam. "I'd like to treat you with respect—to honor you—to honor what you have done and given in your life. But the home office? They'll send you to a psych ward."

She edged around the end of his bed to see more of his face. "You're a lawyer and you've been in prison. You know what lockdown is. You might never have been inside a psych ward, but you've heard the key turn in a lock. Then you're alone with your demons. You know what's involved, don't you Clarence?"

He shifted on the bed, shoes tapping against each other.

"I'm not trying to scare you," Carol said. "I realize you don't scare very easily, but I'm trying to get you to realize what I'm up against. At a certain point, it will be out of my hands."

Clarence's shoulders started shaking. He gasped. He broke out in sobs, his fist at his mouth.

A knock came at the door. Lisha stuck her head in. "They're serving. Is he …?"

Carol shook her head. The door closed.

A deep ragged sigh arose from the bed, and Clarence wiped his eyes. He peeked at Carol and sobbed again. He rolled to his back, exhaled deeply and sat up on the edge of his bed, elbows on his knees and face in the palms of his hands.

Carol looked everywhere but at him. Nothing on the walls—only a calendar offered by the nursing home. Nothing on the table, except the utilitarian lamp provided by Hillcrest Homes. No cozy afghan draped over the chair. No decorative pillows or knickknacks. The only decoration on the front of his door was his nameplate and picture taken upon admittance. Oh, and that scarf with uneven fringe. Even Carol knew a dropped stitch—like someone had hurried to get it done. Somebody made it for him.

What had happened to his family, if he ever had any? No friends came or called, except for that tall guy, Michael Whatshisname.

She couldn't think about anything but Clarence. Helping him find his way back home. Back to the place where he could live in peace, instead of insanity and unforgiveness. Helping him come to grips with his past and find peace for his future—whatever that was and how ever long that was.

He glanced at her and shook his head. A last tear tracked down that wrinkled cheek.

Carol walked over and sat in the chair and looked out the repaired window, then peeked back at Clarence.

He looked out the window, too. His breathing settled. Leaves outside danced in the breeze, twirling about each other. Birds twittered in the morning light.

At last Carol checked her watch and rose. "Just a warning—Miss Henningway has you on her schedule."

He wiped his face.

With her hand on the door, she thought of Joe. She couldn't help Joe, but could she help Clarence?

CHAPTER 52

The next morning, Clarence slapped his hand over his mouth. Laughing in Pete's face would not go well.

"You son-of-a—" Pete Malovitch jumped out of the chair.

Miss Henningway rushed to shut the door to her office at Hillcrest Homes. "Pete sit down and shut up. People will hear you."

Pete leaned over the insurance adjuster sitting between him and Clarence, poking his finger in Clarence's chest. "You are such a bastard. You need to get your f-n nose out of other people's business."

"Now Mr. Malovitch. Let's keep this civil." The adjuster pushed back his Brylcreem hair. "There has just been some sort of mistake. I'm not sure where the claim payments went, but I'm so thankful Mr. Timmelsen here, found the mistake."

"Someone just checked the wrong box or something. I wonder where the money went?" Clarence wiped the grin away and folded his arms across his chest.

"He *and* Mrs. Hatly will have their payments reinstated. And there are others … " He opened his briefcase, removing several documents. "A Mr. Adams. Mr. Otto. A Mrs. Walters." He glanced at Miss Henningway. "May I meet with them today? I'd like to get this settled."

Clarence snickered. "I'm afraid you'll have to go two blocks east to find them."

Pete growled.

Miss Henningway drilled Clarence with her eyes.

"Ahh. They're on an outing? I'll wait. It's good for the elderly to get fresh air."

Clarence snorted. "They are getting fresh air, that's for sure." He leaned forward, ready to push out of the chair. "They're dead."

The adjuster gasped. He chattered as he spilled the contents of a file folder on the floor. "D-dead?" He bumped his head on the desk as he tried to retrieve them.

Miss Henningway groaned. "No. They live here. Just down that hall." She pointed.

Exasperated, the adjuster turned toward Clarence.

"How do you know this?"

"Googled it."

"What?" Pete's voice cracked.

Clarence looked at Miss Henningway. "I just borrowed one of your computers—they're pretty cool." He stood. "One of your nurses helped me do it." He picked up a pile of papers he'd been sitting on. "Oh, and Harold. He lives here. He's a detective and a pretty good one. He helped me get the files … " He handed them to the adjuster. "It's all there. The dead people and Mrs. Hatly and me."

He eased behind his chair. "Now if you'll excuse me, I'm sure you can take it from here. I have to get to breakfast before they shut it down." He ran for the door and down the hall. *Pete's gonna kill someone.*

Dining room. He could hide behind all the wheelchairs.

"Where is that son-on-a … ?" Pete burst into the dining hall, trying to shake off two aides and Jan, the office receptionist. "Take your hands off me! Where is that bastard Timmelsen?"

Clarence hid behind Mrs. Bernadine, who was in a leaning wheel-chair, getting fed. Oatmeal drooled out of one side of her mouth. He patted her arm. She chewed and eyed him. "It's okay, Mrs. Bernadine."

He had never really talked to her, but the way her eyes looked, she was all there. She got it. She just couldn't move.

"Sir, you will not disturb our residents." Jane hooked Pete's arm with hers and started back down the hall.

He swung her around and slammed her into the wall, knocking over a cart loaded with plastic water glasses.

A resident screamed. Several aides backed wheelchairs away. A dietary aide carrying a tray loaded with fruit bowls stepped on a rolling glass and tumbled to the floor, applesauce flying.

Clarence pushed his chair back and stood. He walked toward Pete, his fists clenched. "What do you mean coming in here and scaring these good people?"

"How'd you get out of jail?" Pete stomped toward Clarence. "I had you put away."

"What?" Clarence's voice broke. "That was you?"

Jane, still sitting on the floor, spoke into her phone. "Hillcrest." She nodded. "Pete Malovitch." She tapped the screen. "Cops are on the way."

"Good. They can put you back in jail, Timmelsen."

"What do you have against me? I did my time."

"You have no right poking your nose in other people's business." Pete roared. "You ... you ruined my life!" Pete rushed Clarence, his fist drawn back.

Someone shoved a walker in front of Pete and he fell flat into the applesauce.

Harold.

Tottering, he grinned, his bib still around his neck. Baggy sweat pants stained from his breakfast. He leaned on the walker like a world-class Samurai warrior having just finished battle.

Pete scrambled back to his feet, wiping his hands on his shirt, just as two deputies skidded beside him.

Pete pointed at Clarence. "Deputies. Put that man in jail!"

Jane pointed at Pete. "No! This is the man. Get him out of here!"

Pete ran toward Clarence but Mrs. Hatly appeared out of nowhere and rammed him with her wheelchair. She pushed her glasses up on her nose, her eyes twinkling.

Clarence jumped to see another arm reach in and push Pete down.

A deputy clicked handcuffs on Pete and dragged him to stand.

"You can't get away with this. I have evidence. Sheriff Dennison knows all about it." Pete jerked at the handcuffs. "Timmelsen's a liar and a cheat." He pointed at Clarence with both hands.

The deputies dragged him out. He was still yelling.

Clarence walked past Mrs. Bernadine, patted her arm, and pushed out the door.

Movement to his right made him turn his head. The cops were locking Pete in the squad car, but behind them, at the other end of the parking lot, Miss Henningway was scurrying to her vehicle, a bulging bag in her hand. Purse slung over her shoulder. Making a run for it, eh?

The hawk screeched in the distance. One other thing he had to do. This was not going to end well.

CHAPTER 53

Mindy burst into laughter again. "Oh, you so can't hurt me anymore, Clarence. You are a funny man and I love you."

Silence. Mindy swallowed. Said too much again.

Clarence's eyes bugged out. He coughed, leaning on the counter.

Mindy giggled and said it again. "I love you, Clarence. You are like my Grandpa. Mean and wild."

Clarence threw the money down, picked up his candy bar and walked out.

A lady paid for milk and Mindy gave her change back. John bagged it and walked to the door.

Clarence slipped in and waited in the corner, sidestepping away from John.

John pushed the door open. "You come back to insult Mindy again? You need another candy bar to push in her face?"

Clarence didn't say a word, but waited inside the door.

The woman followed John outside.

Mindy watched them through the window, Clarence visible in her peripheral.

Clarence cleared his throat.

Mindy glanced up. "Nice lady."

Clarence coughed a fake cough. He stepped forward and cleared his throat again.

John opened the door and walked inside.

Mindy looked at Clarence directly. "Is there something you need, Clarence?"

"I'm sorry." He turned, bumped into John and pushed the door open so fast, his candy bar slipped from his fingers. He burst through the doorway and never turned around.

She picked up the candy and pushed the door open. "Clarence. Your candy bar."

He kept on walking, pushing his hand at her.

Mindy crumbled. She looked up at John then back at Clarence hurrying away.

CHAPTER 54

"I really appreciate your hospitality, Deputy. Your little cop car world is fascinating. All the gadgets and everything. What little kid wouldn't want to be a cop nowadays?" Pete held out his hands to get the handcuffs unlocked.

The deputy hesitated, but unlocked them.

"Here's a little something for your trouble. And I'm sorry I cut loose back at the nursing home in front of all those sweet elderly people." He counted out two hundred dollars and pulled the cash from his wallet. All those fake policies were coming in handy today.

"You can find your own way home, Pete." The deputy slammed the squad car door. He patted his pocket. "And we won't tell anyone about our little deal. Sheriff frowns on—"

"Bribery?" Pete piped up. "It's not so much a bribe, but a donation to the stalwart defenders of our little burg." He shoved his wallet back into his pocket.

The police radio broke in. "Sheriff, this guy's crazy. I had him, I swear. He bleeds all over like he's dying and the next minute he kicks me in the gut and gets away."

Sheriff let loose an unusual string of words over the radio.

"An escapee?" Pete brushed off his shirt and adjusted his belt.

"Oh." The deputy looked up and down the street. "Some guy was after the gal inside."

Pete followed his gaze. A younger woman stood talking to Sheriff. Timmelsen's friend and her kid from the park. She and Timmelsen had seemed pretty tight. She looked beat up. Pete folded his arms across his chest and yawned. "Yeah?"

"Well, evidently they have some history, because she knifed him and got away."

"What does he want with that bitch?" Pete tipped his head toward the building. "She looks like somebody you'd run like hell from."

The deputy laughed and stepped closer to Pete, his face cocked away from the building. "It's his kid. Bet he wants the little girl."

Pete pounded his open hand on his chest. "No. She's so innocent. I've seen her. Very pretty."

The deputy glanced at the building, then quickly away. "I hear tell Sheriff's got the old man helping—you know the one from prison. He's helping get her free of all past charges."

Pete nodded. "Oh, he's slick, that's for sure." His blood wanted to boil at how slick Timmelsen was. Pete took a step away. "Well, won't keep you anymore. I can walk to my agency. It's only a block away."

The radio sputtered again. "He's got an accomplice. Guy's driving a 1991 Buick LaSabre, white."

The deputy waved and jumped into the car. "Duty calls."

Pete saluted him and started a slow jog through the alley and hit the backdoor of his building. Probably should keep the place locked up. He opened a safe, pulled out his 9mm Ruger. Always kept it loaded. He shoved it inside the front of his pants and pulled his shirt out over it.

Maybe he and that runaway guy should join forces.

Get his little girl for him.

And put Timmelsen back where he belonged.

CHAPTER 55

Carol scanned the horizon above the car, punching the unlock button, looking in the direction of the grocery store, then to the park. "God where is he? Help."

She hopped onto the seat of the car and fished for her keys under the mat. Turning onto the street, she rolled down her car window and heard the screech. She slammed on her brakes, stuck her head out of the window and searched the sky.

There.

Screech!

Her heart lifted as she saw the hawk far above, gliding so sure, so powerfully. He seemed to be circling above the park, so she gunned the car forward.

She reached the entrance and slowed down to a crawl. She drove through, looking into the picnic shelter, at the campground area. She stretched to see the creek. Looked behind the large entrance stone markers, at each tree. Driving on, she checked every park bench, even the playground equipment.

She drove to the pool area, now empty of people and cars. Stopping the car, she got out. She walked around the pool enclosure and shook the chain link fence.

She peered into the pool, accumulated rainwater only inches deep. She wandered around the pool house, but it was locked up. She rattled the padlocks.

She turned and surveyed the rest of the park. From the restrooms and picnic shelter, the trees, the parking lot, the bushes, the bridge. "Clarence, where are you?"

A huge, ancient slide stood apart from the rest of the playground. Yellow caution tape enclosed overgrown weeds and vines winding around the railings to the top. A sign hung across the ladder. Keep off. Must be the only piece of equipment left of the old playground. A plaque attached to it read, "Donated to the City of Osceola, Nebraska by Judge Percy Green."

She got back in her car and drove to the restrooms and got out. She knocked on the men's restroom door and listened.

Quiet.

Pushing the door open, she peeked in and gagged. The smell seeped through her fingers and choked her.

She backed out of the room and caught her breath. Her eyes teared up, and she coughed again.

She knocked on the women's restroom door. No response. She gulped fresh air and pushed. Same mess all over. Same nasty smell.

She walked back to her car, gasping.

Screech!

She jumped. She shielded her eyes from the sun and stretched her neck, glimpsing the bird right above her, flying in a tight circle. She watched it for a minute, drawn to go to her car. She opened the car door, reached for her phone and dialed. Tears pooled in her eyes as she tapped the door with her fingers.

"Sheriff's Department. How can I help you?"

Sigh. "This is Carol Neeton from Hillcrest Nursing Home. I'd like to call in a missing person." She wiped her eyes. "Yes. Clarence Timmelsen. Yes. There was a scuffle and he ran off."

"Okay. We'll take it from here."

She covered her face with her hands, then slowly lifted her eyes. "God show me. Hawk show me where he is."

CHAPTER 56

Katty shifted the car into drive. The deputy had said it'd be okay. What a mess. Gotta get out of town. If Phil found them again …

"You okay back there, Baby Bea?"

Bea kicked the back of Katty's seat.

"I don't even care if you kick my seat anymore, Bea." Katty pulled away from the stop sign. "I don't know where to go. We can't go to the trailer." She blew out a deep breath. "I don't even … I don't know." She wiped her cheek.

"Mommy?"

"What Baby?"

"Mommy, I see those little lights again. The sparkly ones. They're all around me."

"Bea? Are you all right? You hit your head when I slammed into the mailbox."

"No, Mommy. I'm fine. The Lights are back."

Katty pulled over and parked. She turned in time to see Bea's face surrounded by light specks, reflected in Bea's brown eyes.

Bea kicked her feet. "Mommy, it tickles." She looked all around the car. "Mommy, they're around you, too."

Katty jumped. One flew close to her face. She began to quietly weep. She slowly reached out her hand and one sat just above her fingers. She swallowed. Another gently landed on her head.

Bea giggled.

Katty looked back at Bea. The lights filled the back seat, framing Bea's face.

Bea looked at her. "Mommy." She kicked. "That other Mommy's gone."

"What?"

"That … mean Mommy is gone." Bea wiped her eyes. "All I see is you, Mommy."

CHAPTER 57

Pete faked a swagger as he cut across the alley behind his agency, waving at a man bent over, working on a tractor. "Nice day, huh."

The man nodded. "Yeah. Nice day." Jeans and one of those newer form-fitting T-shirts. Farming had come a long way from overalls.

"Are you done spring planting?"

The man jerked his head up, a scowl on his face. "We're just starting."

"Oh. Yeah. Right." Oops. It was only April. "Well, see ya around."

Pete jumped into his black late-model pickup. It was a stand in for the luxury car he kept hidden in his garage at home just for out-of-town trips.

He put the truck in drive. He didn't even know names. But he knew the vehicle—a white Buick. There were only maybe twenty of those in town, mostly driven by little old ladies. He'd written the insurance policies.

He drove down the alley, crossed the street and into the next alley. Cars parked there were awaiting miracle work of the body shop. Town had three body shops which meant claims, which meant opportunity. He had deals with two of the owners to split the claim money three ways: the client, the body shop owner and him. Business was good.

Wait. Was that them? He drove closer. Gah! Mrs. Mason.

He turned behind the lumberyard. There. Behind the implement dealership. Damn. He backed up and turned the other way. The stupid road didn't go through there. F-n small towns.

He pulled his gun out and slowly drove close to the back of the car, blocking it in between his pickup and a row of overgrown cedar trees. He'd hidden here himself a couple of times, to get out of the office when he needed a little nip.

If he could just get to the driver side without them noticing.

He opened his door and the buzzer sounded. Damn!

A man sat up in the front seat of the car. He had a gun.

Pete rushed to the door and pushed his Ruger in the man's face. "Hold it. Put your gun down. I have a deal in mind you won't want to miss."

The driver didn't put his gun down. The guy on the back seat looked unconscious. Maybe this wasn't such a good deal. He was in bad shape. His eyes opened and an unnatural gleam shone from them.

The guy leaned up with a groan. "What kind a deal? Who are you?"

"I want Timmelsen out of town. Or dead." Pete cocked his gun and pointed it at the man. "And I hear you want the little girl and her mom."

"Just the girl." The guy grimaced. "What's in it for you?"

"Revenge. Pure revenge."

CHAPTER 58

Clarence glanced up as the screech became louder. "Where are you, old bird?" He strained to get a good look at the sky. "Too many trees."

He rolled out from under the huge old spruce. "Ouch, I'll be picking needles out of my butt for a long time." The tree pointed to the sky, and from Clarence's vantage point, the sky went up forever.

The hawk circled the top of the tree. "Hey, bird. What are you doing old fellow?"

The hawk screeched and circled, flying higher and higher, then dove, floating on the wind currents, wings gracefully outstretched, curving up at each tip.

"You are magnificent. You old bird."

"And so are you, Clarence."

He rolled over on his hands and knees and looked up into Carol's face.

"What are you doing here?" He pushed himself off the ground, brushing his knees and hands, scattering spruce needles. "How did you find me?"

Carol chuckled at Clarence, then pointed to the sky, following the hawk in his flight pattern. "Your old bird told me. Right over the tree. I looked everywhere, but it wasn't until I heard him screech that I took notice. He was right over your tree, if I can call it yours." She pointed skyward. "He showed me."

Clarence watched the bird float freely in the air. "What are you saying, old bird? What are you trying to tell me?" He looked down at Carol. "Us. What are you trying to tell us?"

A squad car followed the winding road through the park and pulled in beside them. "Excuse me. Have you seen a wounded man, about six foot tall, reddish brown hair come through here?"

Carol looked at Clarence and shook her head. "No. Nobody here but us. Oh, and I found Clarence Timmelsen." She pointed.

"Okay. Thanks." The car drove away.

Carol scanned the park. "There. Let's sit awhile, shall we?"

"What? Before I stand in front on the firing squad?" Head down, shoulders slumped, he followed her to a bench and sat. "A little reprieve before I die?"

She plopped down. "Stop. I'm exhausted from trying to keep up with you. Where do you get your energy to run away? I know it's not the food. You taking vitamins?"

"You ought to know. You give me my pills. Everyday."

"Huh. You mean every day that you haven't already run away. When you're not there, I have to chart that you refused your meds. Or that you were unavailable. How is a resident unavailable in a nursing home?"

"I see your dilemma."

"No, you don't. You have no clue. We are in so much trouble with the home office." She sat back and sighed. "I see why you come here." She pointed. "That old slide is huge. They don't build them like that anymore." She craned her neck. "It's quiet. You can smell the outdoors and not … well, you know what we smell in the nursing home. The sounds here are wonderful, especially your old bird." She shifted on the bench. "Except this bench is hard."

He pointed to the tree and grinned. "It's pretty soft under that tree where you found me. Except the needles poke though."

Carol chuckled. "You deserve to get poked."

Clarence sighed. "I suppose I do." He looked over at Carol. "I know I haven't been easy to get along with."

"No. You haven't."

He picked at the flaking paint on the bench. He cleared his throat. "I … " He coughed. "I'm … sorry."

"You mean that, don't you?" She faced him. "You really mean that."

"The other day in my room, when you just sat with me? I uh … well … " He picked at a leaf that had floated its way down. "You are a good woman, Carol. You remind me of someone I once knew. She was a beautiful wonderful woman, so full of promise, so ready to burst into life."

He stopped and clamped his mouth shut. He chewed on his inner cheek. "You remind me of her. She was my—"

A rustle in the tree above, distracted him for a moment, then the hawk broke free of a branch.

Goosebumps.

It flew low to the ground, picking up speed, tucking wings close to its body as it dodged trees, banking left and right.

"Wow," Carol gasped. "There is something … divine about it. Like it knows more than we do. I've never seen anything like it."

Clarence swallowed, his leg twitching. "I know. When I first came here, he would hang out outside my window and peck at the glass. I've never heard of a hawk doing that either." He chuckled. "That was before he broke in. I began to be able to feel when he was out there. He would wait until I came to the window."

The bird soared upwards, catching the air current and lifted up even higher until it flew seemingly into the sun.

"It always seems to be drawing me somewhere." He whispered and shielded his eyes.

"I am feeling drawn too. I don't know what it means for me." Carol looked at Clarence. "Do you know what it means for you?"

He nodded.

Carol stood and checked her watch. "I have to get back. You coming?"

He reached out and clasped her hand. "I'm not sure." He looked at the hawk. "I think I need to find a little girl and her mommy."

CHAPTER 59

Katty pushed Bea in the grocery cart. Her heart was pounding. A headache was coming on. "We need things to snack on. Quick. Easy." She grabbed two bags of potato chips, one bonus bag of pretzels. Internal jitters told her to run. "What do you want, Bea? Cereal?"

At the word, *cereal*, Bea's head popped up. "Please, Mommy? Please? Cheerios? Honey Nut Cheerios? Please?" Bea kicked her feet. "And roni and cheese, Mommy." She pointed. "That one!"

Katty rubbed her temples and shook her head. "No, I think we'd better have liver or … " She looked around then whispered to Bea, nose to nose. "We have to buy stuff we can eat in the car, okay? Not sure we can go … back. For awhile." She backed away, looking into Bea's eyes. "Remember?"

Bea nodded her head up and down, a solemn expression in her eyes. "Yeah, Mommy. Okay."

"How about … chicken in the can? Wish we could get soup," Katty said, then stared ahead. "Could we do soup? Nah." She focused on the shelf. "Beans." She tossed in a couple cans. "Baby hot dogs. What's it say? Vienna sausages. Whatever." She cleared the shelf, two cans at a time. "Protein." She handed one to Bea.

"One." Bea looked into the cart. "Two. Three. Lots."

Katty pushed the cart to the end of the aisle and Phil jumped out in front of them.

Katty froze.

Bea looked behind her. "Mommy?" Bea grabbed at Katty's shirt, literally climbing and pawing. But Katty had buckled her in.

"Well, hello ladies," Phil said. His skin was wet. His eyes looked glassy. "I love to see the females get excited when I'm around." He grinned as his eyes traveled over both Katty and Bea. "What brings you out today?" He brushed Bea's hair out of her face, and she tried to shrink away from him. He held out both hands to her. "Come to Daddy."

Bea frantically clawed at Katty. Goosebumps covered her arms.

Katty fumbled at the safety buckle. Her hands shook. It wouldn't come apart. She tried to steer the cart away from him, but Phil grabbed it and held tight.

She'd never seen his eyes so black. His pale face glistened. "I just want to say hello. I don't want to *hurt* you or anything." He opened his jacket, glowering.

Katty gaped at the bloody mess; the belly wound was only half stitched. She stumbled a step and then shoved the cart into his midsection.

He doubled over.

She wrenched the cart back again, almost tipping it over, Bea still aboard. Bea screamed and clutched at her.

His hands gripped the cart, like vise grips. He straightened slowly. Growling. Grinning.

Katty hugged Bea's head into her chest, taking another step back.

He followed, only the cart between them.

"I just want to be *friendly*." Phil rammed the cart into Katty with such force she flew backwards—feet in the air—into a tall display, knocking over cans of soup.

Still buckled in, Bea shrieked and kicked.

Phil yanked the cart toward him and leaned over it, stroking Bea's hair. "You are so pretty, little one."

Katty clutched at the rolling cans, trying to right herself.

"You look an awful lot like someone I know very well." His feet shifted. "An awful lot." He leaned toward a glass freezer door. "Well, I'll be." He bent toward Bea. "You look like me!" He screamed the last word.

Katty struggled to get up. She kicked the cans aside and lunged for Bea.

Clarence ran around the end of the aisle and jumped Phil.

"Clarence!" Katty yelled. "Help!"

Lex decked Clarence, wrenching his arms behind him.

Bea! Clarence had to get to Bea. "Let me go, you bastard." He kicked behind him, trying to trip whoever gripped his arms.

Katty's attacker turned toward him, inches away. He looked dead, smelled worse. His eyes—nothing in prison could have prepared Clarence for those eyes. Black circles ringed glassy eyeballs and something ghastly flitted in their depths.

Terror crawled up the back of Clarence's neck.

"Old man." The man growled and looked at Bea, then back at Clarence. "Oh. Isn't that sweet? Is this Grandpa?" He patted the top of Clarence's head. "Every little girl needs a grandpa." He punched Clarence hard in the cheek.

"Phil! No!" Katty yelled.

Clarence flinched and struggled against his captor, but he never looked away. That, he had learned in prison. Stay focused. But in his peripherals, Katty quickly unbuckled Bea, grabbed her out of the shopping cart and started down the aisle.

Good girl.

Phil swiveled a look at Katty and Bea. "Little Bitch. Bitch," he roared. "You can't get away. I'll always find you." He tripped on a rolling can, but found his footing and started after Katty.

Clarence stomped his heel hard into his captor's foot. He pulled a hand loose and shoved it into the guy's face, grabbed his nose and twisted it. Stabbed his fingers into eye sockets. The guy let loose Clarence's other arm, growling in pain. Clarence dove after Phil and tackled him. They both landed on rolling cans. Phil kicked, but Clarence held onto Phil's belt.

Something hard and cold shoved into the back of his neck.

He held on, a death grip. He would not let go, even if Phil dragged him to hell. He would not let go.

"Thought you could outsmart me, huh, Clarence Timmelsen." That voice. Still sprawled and clutching Phil's belt, Clarence cranked his head far enough around to see …

Pete Malovitch!

He held a black Ruger. Deadly. He cocked it. "Let him go." He popped Clarence on the head with the butt.

Clarence jumped at the pain, releasing Phil.

"Go get your bitch, Phil." Pete's voice was low and deadly. "I'll be right with you, after I take care of this jailbird." Pete turned Clarence, gripping his ear hard. "Pretty tough for an old man, aren't you. I never should have underestimated you son-of-a-bitch." He rapped Clarence's head again.

Clarence's eyes watered. The room spun.

"*You* should have died in that a crash long ago, you bastard. Not Annie. Dad was supposed to marry *her,* instead of my stupid mom. He and Judge had it all set up. Brakes in those old cars were always going out. Judge paid a lot of people. Paid a jury. But she was killed, so he set you up!" He pounded Clarence's head again and laughed in his ear. "Sixty years, for a crime you didn't even do."

Clarence shivered and choked. Pete's words sounded as if he were in a tin can. The words were there, but slowed down, each syllable dragging.

"And now you die for it, bastard." He aimed the gun at Clarence's ear. "Now you d—"

Blam!

Clarence gasped. His ears rang. The grip on his arm went limp. Pete fell over cans, landing hard. Blood spattered Clarence's cheek.

Terrified, he felt his head. Nothing hurt but his ears. And his head. His breath came in gasps.

Confused, he looked up.

Sheriff Dennison held a gun pointed at the ceiling. Two Deputies ran up the aisle and trained their guns on Pete.

Clarence crawled to his feet and stumbled up the aisle. "Bea."

CHAPTER 60

At the end of the aisle Clarence turned the corner to a scene he would never forget. Katty lay unconscious, a nasty bruise on her right temple. Still breathing.

But Bea was nowhere.

Mindy and John sat back to back, tied up behind the check stand, silver tape covering their mouths. They motioned with their heads to the door, making sounds through the tape.

Had to find Bea. Drops of blood led him.

As he stepped outside, the hawk screeched. He felt it vibrate in every cell. It must have been circling until he came outside. The clouds were ignited by the waning sun, purples and blues the backdrop.

"Lead me on, old friend. Where is she?"

The bird circled, screeching louder. Clarence struggled to follow. His eyes blurred.

He started to cross the highway. A semi blasted its horn, roaring past. He stumbled on the train tracks. Hand railings on the bridge pulled him along, over the creek.

"Old bird, where are you?" His eyes watered. It was futile to look under every tree and bush. He could hardly go on. He rubbed the back of his head. Wet. Blood on his fingers.

Movement. There. Just a flicker, like a reflection from the traffic on the highway or the sun reflecting off a pop can. It seemed to hover in midair.

The hawk flew in tighter circles until it floated right above the flicker.

Then he saw her and ran.

Perched at the top of the huge old metal slide was tiny Bea, shaking in terror. Her mouth was taped with duct tape. Her arms were outstretched, hands taped to the metal sides of the uppermost deck. She couldn't move. She was staring at him, pleading with her swollen eyes, screaming in spite of the tape.

The hawk dove at him, knocking him off his feet. "You dumb bird!" Until he saw.

Phil crouched below the slide, almost hidden by dead bushes and vines trailing up the slide supports. He had gathered kindling and trash and had started a fire directly below Bea. His eyes blazed. "If I can't have her, she'll be a burned up sacrifice by the time you get to her," he yelled.

Bea bounced up and down, wailing.

Gunshot.

Clarence turned. Three squad cars sped across the highway toward them. Sheriff Dennison leaned out his window, his gun pointed up.

The hawk screeched from above.

Something flashed into Clarence's mind from way back—a moment of clarity from his childhood. His mother's voice piped into his hearing. "My Father." She had always called Him "My Father," like He was only hers.

He closed his eyes, squeezing tears onto his cheeks. "My Father." He'd almost reached the slide.

The fire crackled up the vines on the slide supports.

Phil took off running.

Clarence stumbled. A Keep Off sign lay crumpled on the ground. He put his foot on the ladder's lowest rung.

Bea's face was wet and red. She pulled and struggled against the tape, squeaking his name.

He gripped the metal railings and managed another step up. The railings were already hot—hot through his scars. He plodded up the ladder between burning vines. A small flame started on his left sleeve. He batted at it and kept climbing.

"Which art in Heaven." Another rung. "Hallowed be Thy name." One more. The railings were burning his hands now. "Thy kingdom come. Thy will be done, on earth, as it is in heaven." His eyes stung with heat and smoke, but they never left Bea's. It was almost like she was in a different world. He could see her screaming, crying, jumping, but all he could hear was his mother's voice. "Give us this day our daily bread. And forgive us our trespasses as we forgive those who trespass against us." His foot slipped on a rung. His shoes must be melting. "And lead us not into temptation, but deliver us from evil."

Bea. He ripped melting tape from the slide deck. She hugged his neck and clung to him. He pushed through the opening, onto the slide itself. It's wooden side railings were starting to burn. Shutting his eyes and enfolding Bea in his arms, he launched.

His feet hit ground. Strong arms and Sheriff Dennison's voice: "Gotcha, Clarence." A siren wailed, and red lights flashed through his eyelids.

Hands lowered him onto a soft surface, but he clung to Bea. "For Thine is the Kingdom, and the Power, and the Glory."

In his arms—on top of him now—Bea finished with him. Her tiny, hoarse voice with his ragged voice: "Amen."

CHAPTER 61

Clarence opened his eyes.

Blinding light.

He wiped his cheeks. Tape. Or bandages.

Whispering voices.

Beeping.

Beeping.

BEEPING!

Clarence shuddered. "Stop that noise!"

Silence.

A bird screeched.

"Clarence?" That voice. "Oh, he's loosing consciousness—"

Screech.

Clarence ducked as the bird swooped again, heading straight for him. He braced himself, arms and hands covering his head. The flap of powerful wings and rustle of feathers was nothing compared to the screech that drilled his senses. The sound raged through his veins, vibrating to his core.

He straightened and shook his fist. "What are you doing, old bird? Why are you trying to kill me?"

The bird circled higher and higher, then dove for him again.

Clarence ran across the street to an old house. A woman, getting out of a car in the garage, yelled and dropped her bag of groceries.

He skirted around the house to the alley behind and stumbled through the backyard. Prickly fear traveled up the back of his neck. He tripped in a tire rut and tumbled.

Another screech sent chills down his spine. He pushed himself up.

He shuffled to the next street and stopped to find his bearings.

Nothing. He recognized nothing.

Lost.

The hawk circled, screeched again, and dove, driving him across the street and farther. Concrete turned to gravel. He shuffled and stumbled over the sidewalk, across that street, into another yard, through a fence, driven by the hawk.

Until he found himself outside of town. Open road. Shelter belt of trees in the distance.

He rotated in the middle of the dirt road. Trees along fence lines, fields of crops, old abandoned buildings. Nothing he recognized. He looked back at town. More than a mile away.

He hollered at the sky, shaking his fist, wishing he could reach the hawk and knock it to the ground. "You dumb bird. I am going to be in so much trouble. Carol will call the cops herself, this time. They'll put me in lockdown or the psych ward."

The bird circled back and dove again, driving Clarence even farther from town. Stumbling, exhausted, he fell to his knees and gasped for breath.

Then he saw it.

An old, old car rumbled toward him, stirring up dust. He could hear the rough, uneven sound of the engine—an old engine. Dusky streams of purple, orange and dark blue broke up the western sky. Dad had always said this was a dangerous time of day to drive. Hard to see animals out hunting. Hard to see people walking along the road.

Like he was now.

He scrambled up off his knees and tripped into the ditch, careful to keep sight of the car.

Out of the corner of his eye, he spied a deer sprinting across the field, running toward the road.

Clarence yelled, "Look out!" He pointed to the deer.

The driver couldn't see the animal. He was laughing with the passenger, a young woman.

Clarence froze.

He knew this place.

He knew the car.

He knew the driver.

"No. No! Please look up." Clarence pointed again and waved his arms. "Oh, no. It was the deer. Oh my God. It was a deer and not … Oh God."

Clarence crumpled to his knees and watched in horror as the car plowed into the deer. It swerved out of control, off the road, throwing the passenger—his Annie—into the ditch. The car rolled over her with a sickening thud.

Clarence screamed and screamed, pounding at the air. "Oh God, not again. Not … this … again."

He tried to stand, but fell to the ground and lay sobbing. "It wasn't me. It was a deer. We hit a deer. Oh my Annie, you knew I would never hurt you. Oh my Annie forgive me."

He lay in the ditch for what might have been minutes—to him, eternity. Sobbing.

Until he felt a hand on his shoulder. He started and jumped. Raised his head.

Michael. In full-dress angel costume. Wings and all.

"Michael. You … " Clarence pushed up on both elbows looking toward the car … and Annie's body.

There was only a ditch. Filled with weeds and debris, trash. A plum thicket.

No car.

No Annie.

He sobbed into his hands once more as Michael hovered behind him, hand still on Clarence's shoulder.

Clarence wiped his face on his sleeves. "So, you're back, huh? I thought you'd left me." He could barely look Michael in the eye.

Michael smiled, but didn't answer.

Clarence stared for a long time into the sunset. Sighed deeply. "I didn't kill her." He searched Michael's eyes this time. "Annie. I didn't kill her."

Michael shook his head.

"She was pregnant, wasn't she? At the time of the accident. There was a baby." Clarence wiped his face.

Michael slowly, gently nodded. "Yes, my friend. She's a precious little one."

Clarence looked from Michael to the fading sky. A ragged breath escaped. So many questions answered.

CHAPTER 62

Blinding light.

Beeping.

Clarence felt his face. Bandages covered his eyes.

Hard plastic over his nose and mouth. He ripped it off.

"Uh-uh, Jailbird. Not on my watch."

Raspy voice again.

Someone pulled something over his head and pressed plastic over his nose and mouth.

He ripped it off and tossed it. Landed somewhere with a splot.

Giggles.

Someone grabbed his wrist. "Just taking your pulse."

He groaned. Phew! What was that smell?

"Is he in pain?" A soft voice. Who?

"Naw. He's just mad about the oxygen mask and that I'm messing with him." The nurse leaned close. "You are one lucky son-of—"

Bea! He grabbed at her. "Where's Bea?"

He ripped the bandages from his eyes.

He blinked and rubbed them. Flowers lined a high shelf and window ledge. Flowers?

Sunlight streamed through the blinds at the window.

He blinked again.

Michael.

"Michael. You're here."

The mask came back on.

Clarence patted his face. He yanked it off over his head and tried to sit up.

"Oh no you don't, mister. Down. And this stays on until I say so." The nurse pushed him down. "Who is Michael?"

"He's my friend." Clarence coughed and pointed. "Michael, you fraud. You're an angel."

Michael smiled.

"Put the mask back on, Jailbird." She adjusted the side elastic bands tightly.

Clarence pushed up the mask. "You called me Jailbird."

"Well, that's what you are, aren't you?" Her hands on her hips. "You spent time in prison, escape from the nursing home regularly, I hear. Then visit the jail. The name fits." She pushed him down on the bed again.

The top of a little head appeared above the edge of the bed.

"Is this who you're looking for?" The nurse lifted little Bea onto the bed. Her eyes were watering. A bandage covered one wrist. She wore a hospital gown and some of her hair frizzled to the side of her head.

But she was smiling.

"Bea." He raised an arm, and she crawled onto his chest, her head next to his. "Bea," he cried, and patted her with his hands. "Oh, oh. Ow." Bandages on his own hands. He held one up and looked at the nurse again.

She frowned. "Burned. Both of them. Burns on top of burns. Hopefully they will heal … in time … with treatment."

He swallowed the lump in his throat.

"Need a drink of water? You need to keep up your fluids. And … " She almost chuckled, but cleared her throat instead. "And your backside is burned a little too."

Ohhh.

Bea raised her head. "What's a backside?"

Katty leaned in. "It's your butt." She patted Bea's. "This." Her face softened. Her eyes lingered in his. "You. You saved my baby daughter." She continued to pat Bea. Her face crumpled. "How can I ... ?" Her chin quivered. She choked and leaned over Bea, hugging them both, crying.

He gulped. His cheeks were wet. His tears and hers.

She stood, wiping her eyes. "I got you wet." Laughing, she grabbed a tissue and blotted his cheeks.

Clarence breathed out one contented sigh.

"My Father," Bea said.

He lifted his head. "Where did you learn that?"

"From you." She tapped his chest. "Who art in shaven." She raised her head. "Does God shave? Are you my grandpa?"

The nurse leaned in with a tall plastic lidded cup, a straw pointed straight at him. "Drink up, Jailbird."

He watched Bea as he drank. Ahhh. Cold water.

The longer he looked at her, the stronger something rose in him: visions of Annie kissing his fingers and praying over his hands, so long ago, and ... and her love for him. He hadn't experienced that kind of love since ... then.

Until now.

"Where's your bird?" Bea's eyelashes fluttered.

"Sweetie. Its ... uh outside." Laughter bubbled up in Clarence. "My bird's outside flying high." He reached for her hand.

Someone knocked at the door.

"Where's that Clarence? I gots to find him for Mrs. Hatly, here. Is there room for a wheelchair?"

Lisha. In all her ... glory. Big teeth and all. Still in her uniform. What a woman. He caught himself smiling at her.

Mrs. Hatly. Oh, she was cute. She stood from her wheelchair and barely came up to the level of the bed. But those twinkling eyes. She patted his arm and kissed his cheek. And Bea's. Wiped her eyes and his.

He blinked.

The distinct creak of a walker. Harold. "Had to see my buddy." He reached over Bea and patted Clarence's shoulder. He clasped Clarence's arm.

Carol stepped from behind Harold. Tears in her eyes. She leaned over Bea and hugged him. "I'm so proud of you, Clarence."

Clarence's throat constricted. His vision blurred. "You're my special angel, Carol." He looked at Michael and nodded.

Lisha piped up. "Hey whatever happened to your friend." She grinned. Damn she had teeth. "You know. Tall, dark and gorgeous."

Clarence chuckled and looked at Michael. "Oh, he's around."

Michael nodded back and winked.

Someone touched Clarence's arm.

Clarence jumped. A huge bouquet of flowers was quivering in front of him. Stunning. A head peaked from behind it.

"Randy." Clarence tried to sit up.

"Down boy." Randy gripped his arm. "I told you I'd come back to see you. Never thought it'd be so soon." He put the bouquet on the shelf and brought something from behind his back. "Brought you a treat. We all know how hospital food can be."

A kid's meal from MacDonald's.

Clarence laughed.

Bea jumped. "A Happy Meal!"

"Want some Bea?" Clarence nodded toward it.

"Yeah." She sat up and opened the box and popped a chicken nugget in his mouth. And one in hers.

Harold reached around and pulled out a French fry for him and Mrs. Hatly. Bea handed a nugget to Mommy. The nurse moved to the other side of the bed so she could keep making Clarence drink.

Out of the corner of Clarence's eye, Michael bowed his head. Clarence paused and bowed his, one eye open.

Michael's head slowly lifted, his eyes directed to heaven. Powerful wings slowly appeared and unfurled. He raised his arms up and blinding light seemed to meet him, pulling him to full stature.

Clarence started to weep.

Bea dropped her nugget into the box and snuggled back down onto Clarence's chest. "He's so pretty."

Lisha made a joke and the room erupted in laughter. All seemed unaware of the miracle taking place.

"Can you see him, too?" Clarence whispered and watched where Bea's eyes traveled, his arm holding her close.

"Your angel? Yup." She watched until her eyes slowly closed. She quickly opened them, looked at Michael, smiled at Clarence and her eyes closed again.

Harold sputtered, forgetting the punch line to a joke. More laughter.

Clarence pressed his stubbled cheek against Bea's head. He softly wept as Michael disappeared.

Ahhh. Family.

Author Notes

When I first wrote Released, I was preparing to write it in NaNoWriMo (National Novel Writing Month). It's a great way to puke out a rough draft, 50,000 words in the month of November, every November. I made the 50,000 words that year and several after.

I always plan to start preparing at least in September but especially in October. Yeah. I freaked when it hit October 28 and I was putting the Halloween candy out. Panic. So I took the easy way out: setting—Osceola, Nebraska—where I live, main character's name—Clarence, my dad's name. Whew! That's done! (I don't think he will care—he's in heaven!)

Our local nursing home is NOT Hillcrest Homes! The sights and smells I wrote about aren't in any way reflected in our own nursing home. The people—staff or residents in the book—are NOT in any way like the REAL, precious people actually living and working in our local nursing home!

Any resemblance to local people is purely coincidental. I love our town and people.

This book is mostly written from an ex-con's point of view. Clarence sees EVERYTHING in a negative manner, from the tattered wallpaper in his room to the smells. Nothing is going to please him because he'd rather be dead!

Oh … and Clarence is me.

Gasp.

Anger? Yup. Bitterness? Yup. Stubbornness? Whew. Yes. I was imprisoned by my own emotions, but now I'm free because of the saving Grace of Jesus Christ. Is anybody reading this still imprisoned by emotions? Let"s talk. Contact page on my website. I'll answer.

Things I learned during this process?

---

1) You can print a whole manuscript after the little x appears above the PGBK cartridge telling you to replace the cartridge. There's a whole lotta ink still in there! Just a little trivia. *Smiling*

---

2) Never give up. The enemy, the voices, procrastination will hammer you. They'll tell you the story is stupid. Or people will laugh. Or the worst: people will never read it. It'll lie like a lump somewhere in a digital backyard. But the more you dig in, the stronger you get. I use 2 Corinthians 10:5. I speak it out loud to those voices. "I bring THAT thought captive to surrender to the obedience of Jesus." Maybe even stomp my foot. It helps.

Then I sit down (because I stand up and shout at the voices sometimes) and write. Grinning. It's kinda fun to be crazy.

I use that verse like a thought filter. Think coffee maker. Put the filter in, the coffee in. Pour the water in and hit start. What comes out is hot, smellin' good. Tastes good.

Stay with me—I bring that thought to Jesus and let Him put it through HIS thought filter. In other words, it has to pass through HIM. When it comes out, it is pure, hot and strong.

Just like good coffee.

"Jesus said to him, I am the Way and the Truth and the Life; no one comes to the Father except by (through) Me." John 14:6 Amplified Version

ACKNOWLEDGMENTS

Writing a book becomes a family/community endeavor. Like a building, the foundation has to come first—otherwise it will all collapse. My thanks goes to NaNoWriMo. Without you, I never would have gotten a rough draft finished! (Plus other rough drafts, to be published down the road a bit.)

Thanks to my Prayer Warriors. When hit by fear or frustration, I'd send an email. Peace would roll over me. I could hear God and make decisions. I still made mistakes, but because of your encouragement, I got back up. You are a Lifeline.

Thanks to Kathy Tyers Gillin, my editor. Because of you I can publish with a smile. (Grinning at what was. Smiling at what it.) You took my mess and made it readable—hopefully something powerful in people's lives. I enjoyed every email, every comment. Even "Eek!"

Thanks to Jane Dixon-Smith, my book designer, who designed the inside and outside. I love this cover! From the first email you sent, I could tell it would be fun to work with you. You are patient to put up with my insecurities. Very talented and gracious.

My critique group. We have jumped from one place to another and will continue to do so as our lives evolve! One thing always stays the same: we shred each other's manuscripts with love! Red pens allowed!

Thank you Layne Gissler. I had no idea what I was doing in writing about prisons or ex-cons or … well, thanks for letting me pick your brain and for setting me straight on things. I appreciate the job you do.

Thank you Marla for being my Deputy consultant. Thanks for all you do that we don't see.

I am blessed to have a family photographer who is a professional!

Lori, thank you for always accommodating me and finding just the right pose to hide a few things and enhance a few! Plus, it's fun!

My beta readers: Jan, Sheila, Pastor Al, Layne, Lori, Jo and Cassie. Some are family, all are friends. Thanks for the time you gave to this project. I asked you to be brutal. Some of you were. Ahem! (Grinning.) Thank you!

Judy Krysl, thank you for getting me on the road with the cover design. We both believe that God's timing is perfect! I enjoyed working with you. And THANK YOU for naming the book! (In the first sample of the book cover, Judy threw up a name to hold the title place. "Released." God brought that word everywhere to confirm that this was the title of my book.) Thank you. Thank you!

I'm a novice at writing all these inside-the-book pages, but I feel thanks goes to McDonald's as a setting in an early chapter. Using your restaurant made my job easier as everyone has been to McDonald's! http://www.mcdonalds.com/us/en/home.html.

There were several scenes where I used TV commercials and Progressive fit super well. I love those commercials! https://www.progressive.com. And the game show, Wheel of Fortune helped me find a comical and solid way to get Clarence down a hall to his room. http://www.wheeloffortune.com.

I also want to thank the many authors who have gone before me in this incredible journey of indie publishing. All have been helpful and open about what has worked for them. It is an amazing journey and with the many opportunities available today, both digitally and print-on-demand (POD), it is an exciting time to write!

Yay, God!

THANK YOU READER

Thank for reading Released. I identified with Clarence. I hope you did too, because there are more books about him coming soon!

Look for other titles, short stories, novels, kids' books in the future. You can keep updated by email if you go to: www.bonnielacy.com **Fill in the window and sign up for free stories or backstory chapters. I have a whole slew of them! I send you news on upcoming books, projects and my writing life. I won't blow up your inbox!**

If you like *Released* or any future works by me, please take time to leave an honest review where you bought the book. It helps me sell my work! **Thank you so much!**

RESCUED

THE GREAT ESCAPEE SERIES

To Jan
My sister by blood
My sister in crime
My sister in Jesus Christ
The Boss

Colossians 2:12 - Message - "Going under the water was a burial of your old life; coming up out of it was a resurrection, God raising you from the dead as he did Christ."

ONE

June 11, 1937 ~ Osceola, Nebraska ~ Journal of Dr. Walter Stevens, Professor of Agriculture ~ University of Nebraska ~ Assistant Henry Green on my personal payroll. Found a new pool today—really a cave. Drove camper through Nebraska on Highway 92. Great new road west from Omaha and my '35 Ford pickup pulled just fine. Stopped in Osceola—Henry's hometown—for early lunch at Thelma's Eatery and Diner. Home-cooked food. Pie! Even had new candy bar—"3 Musketeers." Package of three little bars. Henry got two and I ate one—too full of roast beef and pie to eat more. Up and coming little community. Decided to stretch our legs and walk our meal off. Left camper parked at Thelma's.

Railroad tracks and the highway divide the town. Fine Court House. Businesses seem to be on the South side of the tracks. There's a street named Gospel Ridge on the North side. No wrong side of the tracks here.

Beautiful June day. Low humidity, though the sun was brilliant. Drawn to the park. Heard water gurgling from somewhere. Everywhere else is dry. Our ongoing studies show horrible devastation. Found a pool under RR bridge, right at the East edge of the city park. Impossible. The creek bed is cracked and flaking. How could there be a pool?

Measured about nine by twelve feet of surface, very clear water. No visible bottom. Signs posted: "Keep Out," and "Witch hole." Frayed red plaid shirt tied to one—warning flag. Henry found a branch about ten feet long. Drove it into the pool several places. Couldn't touch bottom. The last time, the branch just disappeared. So many questions.

Present Day ~ "Here it is. Want to show this to Michael." Clarence Timmelsen tucked the faded newspaper article into his black T-shirt pocket. Oh-oh. The pocket had torn away from the shirt, leaving a small hole at the seam.

He could wear it today and toss it tonight. Great way to do laundry —shirt gets dirty and full of holes—throw it away. Rosita, the laundry lady at Hillcrest Nursing Homes, would like that. She was always commenting on how little laundry he had. Probably because he hadn't started wetting the bed … yet.

Michael should be here by now. Clarence checked his watch. Probably should stick around and set up his law office, but he needed to escape again. Looked like a beautiful day.

He walked into the office from his bedroom. Kind of a nice commute.

Two rooms—bedroom and office. It felt like a high-end hotel compared to one cell in prison.

Carol had helped frame his law diplomas and certificates so he could hang them. The top left row was …

He rummaged in the closet for the tool box, found a tape measure and measured from the ceiling … yup … off.

The maintenance guy would come running if he heard a hammer pounding. Any other day, Clarence might feel like antagonizing him— but not today. That's why he would leave the hammer in the tool box.

He'd had his breakfast of eggs and toast. Coffee with Mrs. Hatly and Harold. Always good to start the day with friends.

He'd been at Hillcrest Homes for six weeks, but he could still hear the mess-hall in prison—it had imprinted on his brain. The sound of trays clattering bounced off walls, feet shuffled—or stomped, and underneath it all, a legion of male voices rumbled. You never knew when, not if, a fight would break out. Clarence had usually sat by himself to keep out of trouble. Only stainless-steel trays and spoons in his part of prison—probably because they still thought he'd killed his wife. Annie.

At Hillcrest, he had knives, forks *and* spoons. And dinnerware. Napkins. Even music to eat by—sometimes a lady brought her keyboard and serenaded them. And he had the company of sweet little Mrs. Hatly. And Harold. Well, Harold was Harold. Him and his always-upside-down American flag pin on his lapel.

Breakfast was Clarence's favorite meal. The rest of the food was edible. What he wouldn't do for a big juicy steak once-in-a-while instead of casseroles all the time. At least he didn't have to cook or clean up.

Hard to believe it had only been, he checked the complementary Hillcrest calendar, six weeks since he had been kicked out of prison. So much had happened since then. He stared out the window, and a visual of memories growing up in Osceola played over his mind: building the library with Dad, going to the Clynder law offices—that might have been where law started for him, and Annie—in the library, in the restaurant, at their wedding.

All had crashed to a halt at the accident. He blinked, tapping against the glass, emotion building. Even now. He tapped harder. Sixty years later.

He moved his hand, or hammering a nail in a wall wouldn't be the only thing the maintenance guy would have to fix.

The required law documents were hung. Almost impressive. The complimentary picture of Jesus was still in the bottom of his closet. He'd come a long way from the jerk he'd been in prison, even in six weeks, but he still wasn't ready to build a shrine to Him.

The cleaning woman, Mrs. Gustafson, alerted him when he needed to bring Jesus out of hiding on inspection days. She was a gem. Always brought him goodies from home. Her home baked cinnamon rolls were the best. If she slipped him one, he quietly closed the door to his room and locked it. He didn't unlock until he had licked all the frosting from his fingertips.

Annie smiled at him from a faded photograph in an antique frame Carol had scrounged up for him. She was his inspiration to keep on living. She would have wanted him to live a life that mattered.

He was still working on that.

The frame with bright balloons bouncing all over it held his Little One, Bea, and her mommy, Katty.

Katty had gone through rehab and was almost finished with an online school to be his assistant. He was so proud of her. She was a top student.

He opened his fists and studied the scars on the palms of his hands. Angry-looking burns. Still tender. All worth it to save Bea.

He kissed his fingertip and planted it on Bea's cheek.

Family.

His reflection in the mirror satisfied him for a workday. Shoulder length gray hair slicked behind his ears—it had grown fast since the last administrator of the home demanded he cut it. Couldn't do much about bushy eyebrows, but his bright blue eyes surprised even him today. Sky blue.

He flicked off the ceiling light.

"You got important places to be, Mr. Timmelsen?"

Clarence jumped and turned toward the gritty voice speaking from near the closet. "Who's there?" He cleared his throat. His voice was husky but never that husky. "What do you think you're doing here?"

"Moved in last night. Next door."

Clarence flipped on the light again.

A man stepped from the corner of his room. Deep wrinkles on dark skin. White spiky hair. Black piercing eyes. Strange black suit—no collar on the black shirt.

"Well, you didn't move into *my* room. Go back to yours." Clarence stiffened. "Who gave you the right to be in here, anyway?"

The man smiled. "You did."

"What?" Clarence pounded his chest. "*I* did?" He pointed in the man's face. "You can't just walk into someone's private room."

Sinister smile again.

Who the hell was this guy? Some evil relative of Phil Daynton? Probably somebody from the loins of that bastard, Judge Green. "Who are you—the devil? You must be a long-lost relative of John's from the grocery store. He's from the devil, too."

The man grinned. "I'm from everywhere. I'm from next door. I'm from the next town over." Teeth flashed white against his mottled skin. "I'm from your heart. I'm from the same country you are, Mr. Timmelsen."

Clarence's inner furnace boiled over. A vise grip tightened around his head, making it throb. "Well, Mr. Everywhere," yelled Clarence, pointing, "get the hell out of my room!"

Carol Neeton, the Director of Nursing, rushed into the room. "What is all the yelling about?"

Aide Lisha Hall, followed her, stethoscope trailing from her pocket, pounding her ample chest like a racer who had just finished a sprint. Only she wasn't a sprinter.

"It's him! He's in my room!" Clarence pointed at the man. Only … he wasn't there. He twisted left and right. "Where'd he go?" He opened the door to his bathroom. "He's gone." He tore at his bedcovers, pillows flying. "He was just here!"

Carol looked at Lisha.

"Damn it! I'm not crazy. This guy just appeared in the corner there. He has white hair, dark skin and it's all wrinkled." He looked from Lisha to Carol. "I'm not kidding. He said he moved in last night, and that he's my neighbor."

"We did have a guy move in just next door, but he's limited to bed rest." Carol shook her head. "I don't think he's your man. He won't be wandering the halls, huh, Lisha?"

"Not in this life, Mr. Clarence." Lisha flipped the stethoscope around her neck. "You can peek in his room and see if it's him."

"Yeah. Reminds me of that old man that was shitting in my bathroom the day I checked in. What was his name? Thompson? He dead yet?"

"Clarence, that's not the way we speak about the deceased." Carol held the door for him and walked into the hall.

Clarence followed her into the room next door.

The room, Room 202, was pretty much like his. Walk in the door. Bathroom to the left with built-in closet. Window on the opposite wall. Bed this side of the window. Even the night stand and chest of drawers were of nursing home issue—just like his.

Except Clarence had two rooms. One, his bedroom, Room 206. The other, Room 204, was his office with a desk, some chairs and a bookcase. Even his office had another bathroom. He guessed for those emergency moments when a guest needed to go at the same time he needed to.

The man on the bed didn't stir. He didn't blink. He stared at the wall above the dresser—at the calendar maybe.

"Man, his room is emptier than mine. He just has a calendar. Not even a picture of Jesus."

Lisha's nostrils flared. "Oh, yeah. Been meaning to talk to you about that. It don't count hangin' it in the back of yer closet, right Miss Carol?"

Carol leaned over the bed. "Mr. Wainwright? It's your nurse, Carol. How are you doing today?" She checked each tube and the oxygen meter.

No sign of life except open eyes. And a pointer finger, with an oxygen monitor clipped to it, tapped up and down on the blanket. Dark skin all right. White hair. Seemed like the same man, but—

"So you can see, Clarence, Mr. Wainwright is not capable of moving more than that finger. Seeing him in your room is impossible. Not sure what or who you saw, but it can't be this man. He did move in last night." She turned to face him. "You must have heard them. Or dreamt it. That I give you."

The guy was a vegetable. Skin and bone. Still … something about those eyes.

Clarence stepped closer to the bed and leaned toward Carol. "What's his name?"

"Mr. Wainwright."

"Mr. Wainwright. Sorry about the mistake. But I swear you were in my room just now. I don't know how …. " He shook his head, jingled change in his pockct and faced Carol. "In prison something like this happened. Old man died and left behind his demons. Bet this guy's demons got loose and came in my room." He leaned over the bed. "Better keep your old demons to yourself, buddy. I got enough of my own."

"Clarence!"

"Just bein' honest, Carol." Clarence blinked and wiped his eyes. Hand over his mouth. He gagged. "Damn, he stinks. Smells dead."

"Shh. Come on. Time to go. Give him his peace."

As they stepped to the door, Clarence glanced over his shoulder. "Creepy old man."

Mr. Wainwright's eyes were no longer burning a hole in the wall, but staring straight at Clarence, with a wicked, rheumy look.

Clarence grabbed Carol and Lisha. "Look. He moved his eyes."

Carol turned. "He did. Wow."

Lisha stepped back into the room. "Hi Mr. Wainwright. You feelin' better? Had a little comp'ny?" She patted his arm. "Dang. This guy got no meat on him at all."

Clarence muffled his mouth. "You should give him some of—"

"Shush, Clarence. Is he okay?" Carol reached into her jacket pocket and pulled out a pen. "Check his vitals. I'm sure with moving and all, he's probably disoriented and uncomfortable." She walked to the door. "I'll check his chart to see what's on order for him."

Lisha wrapped the blood pressure cuff around his bony arm and proceeded to pump it up, holding the stethoscope in place on his arm. She let the air out slowly, but pumped it up again. This time she took even more time to release the air. "Huh. I can't get a reading."

She cocked her head toward Clarence. "Could you get Miss Carol for me?"

"Sure." He had started to leave the room when Carol whipped in with a clear plastic med cup, filled with bright pink liquid.

"I'm not sure he can swallow, but at least it's liquid." She lifted it to his mouth. "Mr. Wainwright, I have some Tylenol here for you." She hesitated. "Wow he's cold." Back to the man. "You seem uncomfortable, and this might help you relax. It's tough changing homes and beds and all." She started to part his lips with the cup and spoke to Lisha. "You get his temp yet?"

Mr. Wainwright's eyes shifted again. They turned black. His body became even more rigid. His eyes focused on something behind them.

Clarence took a step back as Michael appeared behind them at the door. "Michael. Hi."

A thick guttural growl came from the direction of Mr. Wainwright's bed.

Clarence jumped.

Pink medication splattered from the medicine cup onto Carol's hand and his gown. "Mr. Wainwright. You need to calm yourself."

The man shuddered and hissed. His eyes seemed to spark as Michael stepped into the room.

Clarence slowly stopped to look at Michael again. Then back to the body on the bed, still hissing and spitting. Back at Michael. Shivers skittered up his spine like a flea race in a circus. The room grew colder.

Michael seemed to grow taller the longer Clarence looked his way. Oh-oh. Angel costume. Wings started to sprout.

Lisha finally found her tongue. "Michael … uh, he don't like you." The whites of her eyes were visible surrounding the brown. Goosebumps lined her usually smooth brown skin.

Carol yelled close to his ear. "Mr. Wainwright? Mr. Wainwright!" She patted his cheek. " Snap out of it!"

Clarence shivered.

This was no man.

TWO

June 11, 1937 ~ Journal of Dr. Walter Stevens ~ Henry had dinner tonight at his brother's in Osceola. He came back to the camper drunk and angry. Seems his brother reneged on some promise to make him law partner. He stood by the pool a few minutes, then stripped down. I teased him—the women of Osceola wouldn't like a man that smelled like fish. Argued with him. Even wrestled him down, but Henry knocked me back. Slammed me against the rock wall. Stubborn. Stupid. Had him by the ear—before he went under. He gasped and seemed to shudder, sucked in water, and shoved me away.

He never came back up.

Present Day ~ Noell Carpenter stretched to her tiptoes on the concrete step and peeked through the diamond-shaped window in the front door.

Sigh. *God, how does Gamma live in this?*

She closed her eyes.

Breathe.

The familiar terror rose in her chest. She swallowed it down and checked through the window again. The front porch had been enclosed years ago—originally planned for a sun room. But as Gam had walked back and forth, in and out, things had piled up. Until the new room was packed. A narrow path trailed through the mess—from the entrance to the door leading into the living room.

Piles of clothing. Boxes stacked high. Full shopping bags, cardboard. It had maybe started out fairly organized—with flattened cardboard boxes, labeled totes of clothing, old games—all categorized. An old duck from a grocery store bath soap display crowned one pile. It was a wonder it hadn't slid off the pile of magazines it reigned over.

Another item caught her eye. Always did. Every time she peeked in the front door, or when she tiptoed past the piles into the house, it stood out from the rest of the hoard.

It was an antique coffee cup with a business name on it—an advertisement giveaway back then, she guessed. She could read it from outside the door. "Osceola Times ~ Your favorite Paper with Up-To-Date News." There was a chip out of the bottom rim. Noell liked to imagine the newspaper editor slamming it down on his desk, declaring the newest article to be the best of the century. Someday she would ask Gam if she could have it.

She opened the screen door, propped it with her foot and pushed the wood inner door, careful to ease it against the ceiling-high stack of newspapers behind it. Didn't want to start an avalanche. She might be the one buried.

Gamma called from inside. "You there, Sweetie?"

Sigh.

"Yeah, Gam. Give me a minute." She slipped her backpack off her shoulders. "Or two."

Now to unzip her backpack. One zipper ran over the top to the sides. One zipped across the front. Another at the bottom. She pulled a sheet of paper towel out and carefully unfolded it, laying it on the front step beside her feet and set the backpack on it, making sure the backpack didn't overlap the paper.

Step one: done.

Next, she shook a plastic shopping bag, crackling in the breeze. Standing flamingo-style, she slipped her foot out of her thrift store boot and pulled a new white bedroom slipper from the backpack. Her feet went on auto-pilot: into the slipper and into the house with that foot. The boot went inside the plastic shopping bag.

Only the other boot was stuck. A strategically placed brick beside the doorway became her boot puller. The boot came loose, fell on the step and bounced onto the sidewalk below.

Sigh. Some days it was so easy.

Not today.

A tear plopped onto the canvas backpack, darkening the blue fabric.

Deep breath.

She pulled the other slipper on, stepped down and retrieved the wayward boot.

She had been tired before, but now …

She stepped inside the porch. The sight of the piles of boxes—some leaning, one exploding across the side of the only path through—always made her gasp.

She had seen it all before. She peeked inside before entering everyday—ever since she had grown tall enough to see through the little window in the front door.

She stood just inside and waited, her eyes pinched shut. Her breathing became short gasps.

She knew what was coming. It happened every time she entered the house. Somedays were just worse than others.

First one pile of magazines appeared to slide her way. Then the stack of boxes marked "Clothing" she had tried to stabilize the day before, toppled. Putrid piles of hoarded junk floated toward her, opening up her forever nightmare. Everywhere she glanced—the clutter, the boxes, the clothing—morphed into water crashing into her.

Something grabbed her foot; the slipper floated away. She choked and struggled to breathe. The more she thrashed and kicked, the more she was pulled under—under the water and trash.

Even though the water appeared murky and cloudy, yellow eyes glared at her; an evil grin taunted her—daring her to break free. She tried to pry her foot loose, but grimy fingers grabbed her hand.

She kicked with her other foot and the hand transformed into Mommy's hand, the face changed into Mommy's—eyes terrified, mouth open in a muffled scream. The face disappeared, the water receded. Boxes and clutter on the porch once again.

She coughed and sputtered. "Oh God! Oh God! Take away that nightmare!" Couldn't let Gam see. She wiped at the water on her face. Water. Always water.

It was just a … dream, right?

The only memory she had of her mom was always a terrifying dream. If she told Gam, Gam would cry. Every time she woke from that dream—from the first time till now, she prayed, "Jesus make me strong. Jesus, take away the dream. Jesus, please take away the scaredy-cat in me."

She did it now. "Jesus please take away my fears and take away that dream."

Whew.

The slipper had landed on top of the magazines.

How did that happen, if it was just a dream? She shook her head, her chin jutted out. She would not cry—at least not now.

She hopped over to the slipper, shoved her foot in and slung the backpack over her shoulder, reading the antique mug as she walked by.

Something didn't smell right. Gam always insisted that no critter could find its way in. The house was tight. Noell wasn't so sure. Something smelled … dead.

She opened the door to the living room.

"My baby's home!" Gam sang it out and shuffled to her, using a walker. Step into it. Pick it up. Move it forward and start over. Almost a dance. Almost.

"Gam." Noell hugged her and dripped on her plaid shirt.

"I didn't know it was raining." Gamma tipped her head to look out the window. "You're all wet."

"I know. Sprinklers." No sense freaking Gamma out. Noel was already there herself. No sense in having them both terrified.

Some days she could feel Gam shrinking. Today was one of those days. But the smaller she seemed to grow, more love poured from this woman who had taken her in years ago.

"How was the job hunt, dear?" Gamma gravitated back to her spot —the only clear spot on the sofa. That piece of furniture was her pride and joy. She had paid cash for a $3,000 Italian leather sofa way back when. And now magazines, newspapers, documents obscured the beautiful red upholstery. The clutter probably protected the leather.

"Not great. I have some prospects, I think. The hospital was interested. The newspaper office didn't have any openings, but she said I would be perfect for their office." She shrugged. "I'm not sure what that means."

"They like you and see that you are smart. That's what that means." Soft gray curls fell away from her face. Gam was the oldest grandma that looked the youngest, in spite of the walker. Her hair was longer, naturally curly, her eyes were snappy behind glasses and her mouth was snappy, too. She was a pretty lady in spite of her age of seventy-eight. She even dressed younger. She lived in jeans.

And she was fun to talk to—share a girl joke or two, but no place to sit. Not a place for anyone to enjoy Gamma's company.

After the nightmare Noell had just experienced, she needed some Gamma.

"How about the city office? Any openings there? I used to love working there. And I'm sure you would be welcome on my recommendations." She straightened. "I won awards there and bonuses." She pointed to Noell. "You could too."

"Well, I'll put my application in there, too, so we'll see." She shrugged. She moved to the stairway. "Need anything before I go upstairs, Gam? More water? A snack?"

"No. No, I'm fine. I just had a cookie." She popped her head up. "Made some fresh today. Help yourself. Take them upstairs with you."

Noell headed to the kitchen, opened the refrigerator door, counted to five, and scooped up two cookies. It was okay. They were fresh. Besides. Gam made them. She waved at Gam as she took the stairway, two steps at a time, and opened the door to her bedroom.

Ahhh. Breathe. She stepped inside and silently closed the door behind her.

She leaned against the back of the door and surveyed her room. Pristine. Sparse was a better word. Only two mementos sat out on her desk: the only thing reminding her of Mom—a baby bracelet. And Gam's Bible. That antique cup would look good next to the Bible.

She slid her backpack off her shoulders and kicked off her slippers. There was only one place she ever felt okay about doing that, and it was here in her room. The bed was made. Neat freak. No clutter. Closet door was closed.

She changed clothes and plopped down on her bed. What a day. Somebody had to hire her. She had to get out of here and find a place of her own. She dreamed of where she would live. Something with a little space. It would take money. She had saved ever since she was old enough to sweep Gamma's floors before all the hoarding had begun. Paper routes. Babysitting. Scooping snow. Lawn mowing.

She had even worked for Mr. Hardesty in his body shop. At first, she answered the phone and did minimal bookwork, but as he got to know her and she stuck around, she learned how to repair dents, touch-ups, detailing. She figured how to take apart an inside door panel one day when Mr. Hardesty was away. The customer had been in a hurry, and Noell tinkered until she fixed the door handle. Pretty proud of that one.

She should call him and see if he needed any help. He'd had to replace her when he needed more help and she was still in school. They'd both been bummed.

Her phone buzzed. She kept the ringer off so Gam wouldn't worry or get startled. Gam still had the landline going, so she was okay with Noell having her own cell phone. Besides, Noell paid for it herself. All good.

"Hello?"

"Yes, is this Noell Carpenter?"

"Yes. This is she."

"This is Dottie at Osceola Community Hospital. I'd like to let you know you have a job here if it still works for you."

Noell sat up. "Cool. That's great."

"You'll need to come in for training tomorrow, okay?"

"Yeah, sure … I mean, yes, of course." She slid to the edge of the bed. "What time do you want me there? What should I wear? Do I need to bring anything?"

Dottie laughed on the other end. "How about nine tomorrow morning? Just wear casual and we'll get you set up with a uniform, depending on what department you end up in. We have several opportunities open, so we'll see where you fit. Okay?"

"Yeah. Yes. Sure."

"And we'll do some lab testing, blood work and urine testing. Drug testing. It's just routine. We do it on everybody, even the doctors."

Pictures of blood smears and needles spun in front of Noell's face. Her mouth went dry. Sweat seeped under her shirt. She cleared her throat. "Um, what opportunities are open, if I may ask?"

"Oh … what we call the bedpan brigade and housekeeping. Nothing too strenuous, although you do need a car to drive back and forth. Or a bike. Whatever it takes to get around, back and forth."

"I can ride a bike. But, bedpans? What will I do with bedpans?"

Laughter. "People poop and pee in bedpans, so you'll be helping patients use them and when they are done, you dispose of the poop and pee."

"Dispose of it? Um … where? How?"

"Into the toilet. We have nifty sprayers hooked into the toilet so you don't have to use your hands to clean it out. Just spray away. Sometimes you need to wipe the bedpan out if it's especially … gooey, but not usually."

Noell belched and fell back onto her bed, her phone slid onto the floor.

"Really easy. Well, I'll see you tomorrow … you there? Still interested? Noell? Are you still there?"

Noell covered her mouth and gagged. She scrambled for the phone, but the bathroom called her first.

"Noell? Noell?"

She leaned over the sparkling clean toilet in her private bathroom and threw up. Gah. Dottie said good-bye. The phone buzzed.

Guess the hospital won't work out.

THREE

June 12, 1937 ~ Journal of Dr. Stevens ~ Thelma gave me a mug from the diner. Nice lady. Probably felt sorry for me. Emotion is surprising me—hadn't known Henry all that long.

He had been a good assistant. Some problems had become apparent, but everybody has problems. There was a child somewhere he'd never gotten to raise. He had leaned toward the eccentric but …

I slept by a pool last night.

Why did I ever let Henry go in *any* pool?

In Arizona, Henry had helped make a major discovery—one upper pool connected to another below—at the bottom of the hill. He swam all that way underwater, but as he reached the lower pool opening, he became entangled in vines and almost drowned.

Chilly last night in Osceola. Heard raindrops on the trees for a time, but it never hit the ground. Just a tease. Called a dry thunderstorm.

I slept by the pool instead of the camper, in hopes Henry would show up—somehow. Hope beyond all hope.

Can't believe Henry's balding head and ornery grin won't appear below the surface of this pool.

I can't believe he's gone.

Present Day ~ Clarence read out loud from a yellowed newspaper clipping as Michael backed away from the parking place at Hillcrest Homes. "Says here, 'Famed and notorious professor of agriculture and self-avowed archeologist, Dr. Walter Stevens's assistant drowned yesterday in a freak accident in Osceola, Nebraska.'" He flicked the paper back and forth with his finger. "Seems his assistant, Henry Green, fell into a pool in a cave they were studying near the Gospel Ridge. Wonder where Gospel Ridge is now?"

Michael shrugged. His hand gripped the gearshift on the column, but he was obviously struggling to find first gear. Either the truck was growling or Michael was. Maybe both.

"Yuck—what a way to go. Listen." Clarence read further. "'He sucked in the putrid waters from the pool as he succumbed to the pool's clutches. When interviewed, Dr. Stevens said he reached for Mr. Green, and had hold of his hand, when Mr. Green pushed away. Dr. Stevens warns all: "Don't go near that pool. You won't come back."'" Ugh."

Clarence folded the clipping. "Wow. Wonder if that pool is still here." He straightened. "We should check it out." Michael wasn't listening. His dark blue shirt appeared even darker at his upper back and underarms. Surely angels didn't sweat.

"What is all that notorious and self-avowed stuff?" Michael finally found first gear. "Where'd you get that clipping?"

"Good shift, Michael. You're getting it. I 'spose angels don't get to drive old trucks too much."

Michael grinned. He was such a muscular stud. For not being able to put in a personal request about what kind of an angel he'd want, Clarence considered himself pretty lucky. God did good. Six weeks ago, he'd never even thought about … having his own angel. Had Michael been with him in prison too?

"Michael—"

The big guy started to shift into second. Grinding. He sighed and shoved the shifter back into neutral. Clutch in. Shifter to second. Sweat dripped from dark ringlets at his temples.

"Just wiggle it. It'll go in."

Grind.

Back to first. Clutch. Speed up. Into second slowly.

Perfect.

Whew.

Michael blew out a breath and flashed a huge grin.

Clarence laughed. "High five, man!" He held his hand high, forgetting Michael's stretch and hit his elbow. Laughed again when Michael adjusted so they could slap hands.

"Hey. Wasn't that the weirdest thing you ever saw, in that guy's room just now?"

"What guy?" Michael must have been concentrating on his driving. Even angels frowned.

"You know. My neighbor at the nursing home."

Michael looked at Clarence out of the corner of his eyes. "Oh. Yeah." Then eyes straight ahead. "What about him?"

"That was just weird. Even scary." Clarence straightened and leaned forward. "I thought you were going to do the angel costume thing in there."

Michael shook his head.

"What? Tell me there wasn't something going on there. Seemed like when he saw you, he started spitting and hissing. How would he know you? He doesn't seem like the angel sort." He hesitated and chuckled. "I know. I'm not the angel sort either."

Michael appeared to be biting his lips. When Michael decided to clam up, he clammed it up and no amount of pushing would make him talk.

"Okay." Back to the clipping. "I found it in one of my old journals —you know—all those boxes from prison. Yeah, this guy Stevens sounds like a character." Clarence waved the clipping back and forth. "From the University of Nebraska, huh? Sounds more like a movie character." He folded the newspaper clipping. "Can we skip work for a while today and look around? Work on the Town Hall can wait, right?

See if we can find what this guy," he opened the clipping, "Dr. Stevens might have found?"

"Sure." Michael's voice boomed, even when he answered softly. "We have time. Some of the wood we ordered for that wall, isn't in yet anyway."

Clarence read the article again. "Gospel Ridge." He rotated in the seat. "That's just North from the park and the nursing home, I think." He craned his neck. "Just up the street. See any street signs?"

Michael shifted into third. The truck lurched.

"Grinding, Michael."

Michael shook his head, muttering.

"What?" Clarence leaned toward him.

"Nothing."

"Did you cuss, Michael?"

"No. I was just telling Father if I was meant to drive a stick shift that He should have built me with a gear shift knob for a hand and a clutch for a foot." His voice trailed off as he turned into the park.

Clarence burst out laughing. "That's okay, Michael." Clarence looked up at the sky, wiping his eyes. "I don't see any lightning coming your way."

Boom!

"What the … "

Michael shook his head and got out. "I … uh, hit the guard rail."

Clarence laughed—a shake your belly kind of laugh. "I thought it was That Old God swinging a two-by-four at you!" He climbed out, wiping his cheeks and walked to the front of the truck. "It's not too bad." He scanned the rest of the truck. "Looks like it's happened a time or two, right?"

Michael blushed as red as the truck, stepped in front of it and pushed it a couple feet away from the guard rail. Licking his finger, he wiped at the bumper. "A little scrape." He checked the guard rail. "Oh-oh. Red paint." He straightened. "Think they'll arrest me?"

"Did you just push the truck? By yourself?" Clarence shoved against it. "It doesn't even budge when I do that." He straightened, eyeing Michael. "Are all angels that strong? Can you lift the truck?"

"Naw. I mean angels are strong, but I don't want to lift it." He brushed his hands together. "It's dirty."

"You mean you could, but you don't want to." Clarence chuckled. "You're something else, Michael." He turned toward the park. "Let's explore a little."

He stuffed the newspaper article in his T-shirt pocket. The first thing he saw when he stepped from the parking lot was the huge old playground slide. He shivered. The palms of his hands tingled. He clenched them to make it stop. "I … I, uh." He couldn't finish.

Michael stepped beside him. "Little Bea is alive because of you, Clarence." He reached for Clarence's hands and pried his fingers open. The palms and insides of both arms looked like he wore red braces. Only he didn't. Thick burns ran from his palms to halfway up the inside of his arms.

"Was that only six weeks ago?" Clarence stared at his hands, but saw that day. Running till his lungs would burst. Searching to find little Bea and the shock of seeing her at the top of that old slide, hands duct taped to the bars, mouth taped shut. But her eyes. He'd never forget her terrified eyes. "Uh, let's, um … walk to the swimming pool." He wiped his face and took off.

"Nice little playground area." He pointed. "Swimming lessons are on." He glanced at Michael. "You know how to swim?"

Michael blinked.

"Swim. You know." Clarence moved his arms in his best version of a breast stroke. "Like that. Come on."

Michael followed Clarence on up the hill.

"When I was a kid, the pool was in the same place." He chuckled, rubbing his hands together. "Only we didn't have the huge frog spouting water." He rotated toward the nursing home. "I can see the park from where my rooms are now."

The kids were noisy—singing, yelling, jumping, splashing. A few parents sat visiting or reading. A radio blared from the building speakers. Sun sparkled off the water.

Lifeguards, sitting on their elevated thrones, blew their whistles.

Rest break.

Kids slogged out of the pool at the edges or up the ladders and huddled, wrapped in their towels.

"Look! There's the guy from prison."

"He killed a lady."

"Hey mister! Go back where you belong!"

Clarence swallowed. Nostrils flared. "L-let's look over here, Michael." He tugged on Michael's shirt.

"Look. Look. What's he doing?"

"He's crazy."

"Go away! You need to go away and die!"

The whistles blew again and the kids forgot all about Clarence and jumped into the pool.

All except two little kids—a dark-haired girl and a freckle-faced boy.

Oh, no.

Clarence wasn't sticking around for more name-calling.

The boy pointed his tiny finger through the chain-link fence. "Look at that big guy." He wiped his face with a green and yellow striped towel. His wet reddish-blond hair plastered against light skin.

"Yeah. He comes into my room at night and sings to me when I'm scared."

"Sometimes he has wings."

"Yeah. He's nice."

No one seemed to hear except Clarence and Michael.

Michael slowly turned, facing them and smiled.

"Hi, Mr. Angel Man." She waved. "Mommy says you dance with me in my dreams." Wide blue eyes pulled them in. Her innocent smile displayed missing teeth.

Michael nodded.

A woman came up behind the two and shushed them, pulling her cover-up together around her shoulders. "Don't talk to strangers, kids. Be nice." She glanced up. "We're praying for you, Sir." She scooted the kids back to the baby pool.

"Bye, Mr. Angel Man. See you tonight in my dreams."

Clarence stumbled almost to his knees. "P-praying for me." He blinked.

Michael reached for him, supporting his weight, one arm around his shoulders. "I got you, Clarence."

"She said she's praying for me." He shook his head. "I don't think I've ever heard anyone say that before." He glanced behind him as they walked away.

The woman was watching them. Smiling and nodding, as she towel-dried her hair.

The little girl waved.

Clarence wiped his face. "I'm okay. I … I just …." Deep breath.

"Where do you want to go now?"

"You sing with those kids at night?" Clarence grinned. "I thought you were with me at night."

"How do you know where I am? You're snoring."

"Got that right." One more glance back. "Well. Here's the old Boy Scout cabin." He stretched his hand. "This was built around the time I was born, if I remember right." He peeked in a window. "Used to have Scout meetings here."

The door knob rattled.

Clarence looked down to see Michael's hand on it, wiggling it. Clarence peeked in a window, but the Boy Scout flags and tables there didn't bring the expected interest. He scanned the room again. Something …

"Locked." Michael cupped his hands around his eyes, peering through the glass. "Locked up tight. Maybe they don't meet here anymore." He checked the siding. "Pretty dilapidated." He rubbed his hand over it. "We should fix up this building." He picked at peeling brown paint and caulking around the window, then started down the hill, stooped to pick up an empty pop can and hooked a shot into the trash can.

Michael detoured to push kids on the swings. The swings screeched as the children pumped back and forth. Then he jogged to join Clarence on the road that circled the play area.

Clarence sidestepped a pile of dog poop. "Watch out." Weren't there dog laws nowadays? "The clipping said a pool in a cave. Where could a cave be around here?"

"Maybe the city bulldozed it." Michael stepped over the poop. "The city wouldn't just let a cave be open in town. Kids would fall in or get lost, somehow."

"That's how some drowned back then, I guess." Clarence stumbled as he checked the article. "A kid and a woman both drowned sometime before the assistant did." He stopped to read. "Hmm." He pointed to the article, then surveyed his surroundings. "A pool in the park." A foot bridge, below the Scout cabin, crossed the creek to another picnic shed to the right, closer to the railroad tracks. A monstrous cottonwood tree waved it's leaves, sparkling in the sunlight, down below to the left edge of the park—right down by the railroad tracks and the creek. And another bridge. "Let's head down there."

Michael followed Clarence to the tree, then the bridge. He ducked under it. "What about here?" He kicked at some footings, and dirt gave way.

Clarence side-stepped down. "I can't believe kids wouldn't explore under here. If I was a kid, I'd be down here everyday."

"Me, too. I love to explore." Michael stretched his arms wide. "Father's laboratory for you humans to enjoy."

Clarence skidded on some gravel, almost falling.

"You shouldn't be down here. What if you fall?"

"I'm okay Michael. Besides, I've got you." Clarence grabbed hold of a small tree growing from underneath the bridge as he climbed farther under. "Wouldn't it be something if we found that doctor's cave right here? First time out?"

Michael reached through some brush, yanking it out. A few dead branches trailed along, revealing a small opening.

"Could that be it?"

"Let me see." Michael took a branch, broke it to a foot long and began digging. "Seems pretty soft. Easy to dig."

Chunks of dirt and rocks fell in.

Clarence picked up a stick and helped Michael. The hole expanded to almost three feet across.

"Cool!"

Clarence almost jumped out of his skin and turned around, facing a boy about eight years old. "What do you want, kid?"

"What are you doing here?"

"We are doing a ... scientific experiment."

"Cool!"

Damn. Wrong thing to say to a kid to scare him away.

"We are trying not to disturb a thousand year old piece of dirt. We are scientists, researchers who are studying ... the life cycle of the boring, hard to see carbon ... hopper."

"Carbon hopper? Cool."

"No, son." Clarence turned, waving the kid away. "You don't realize what it means. It's dangerous. We can't have anyone else around here, or the c-carbon hopper might run away." He ushered the kid up out of the creek bed and to the playground area. "Stay up here kid, if you know what's good for you."

The kid pointed. "You. You're that man from prison. Aren't you." He cocked his head and stared Clarence down.

"Well, yes ... I am." Clarence put on his mean face and the kid jumped back a few steps. "That's me and don't you ever forget it. Hear?"

The kid ran away, looking back at Michael. He glanced at Clarence only once after Clarence gave him a last growl send off.

"That'll keep him away. I didn't think about kids following us here."

Michael watched the boy run to a house adjacent to the park. "That was mean."

Clarence turned around and faced Michael. "How would you have done it?"

Michael gently picked Clarence up by the collar and lifted him over to the park bench and sat him down. "That's what I would have done."

Clarence gasped and tried to catch his breath, holding his chest, his eyes popping. "Wha? What? What was that?"

"That's how I would have done it. It scares them, but doesn't hurt their feelings at all." Michael crossed his arms across his massive chest. "And they think I'm pretty cool after they recover, too."

Clarence growled at him. "You scared the waddin' right out of me. I can hardly breathe." He pounded his chest as his breathing slowly returned to normal. "I might have peed my pants."

There had been many a time in prison …

Michael smiled and hopped into the creek bed.

Clarence followed, a little slower, stepping carefully around rocks and clumps of weeds. Not even a trickle of water flowed through the cattails and grass. Dried hoof prints trailed the creek out of town.

Michael bent down under the bridge and looked into the hole. "We could almost crawl through." He stuck his head in. "Really dark. We'll need some kind of light." He turned to Clarence. "Got a flashlight?"

"No. You?"

"No. They say one should always carry a flashlight in their vehicle. I have one back at the Town Hall for when we work there."

Clarence poked his stick in farther. "Maybe we can just open it up more and that will—"

Michael did the same with another stick, until they had an opening about the size a man could fit through. Or a couple of dare devil kids.

Clarence stood and looked to where he had seen the kid run home. Sure enough, there were two now, standing outside the house watching Clarence and Michael. He slowly put his hand on Michael's arm. "We gotta do this when no one is around."

"What? Why?"

Clarence nodded his head toward the boys.

"Oh-oh."

"We'll have to come back when they are in school." Clarence said. "Wait, it's summer." He wiped his hands on his pants and crawled up the creek bank.

A rumbling of falling rock and dirt stopped him. He jerked around to see Michael push through the hole and disappear. All that was visible were his shoes.

Clarence climbed back under the bridge and cautiously patted

Michael's feet. "Hey buddy. I thought we were coming back when no kids were around. We don't—"

"It's cool in here." Michael's head and face appeared, dirt in his hair and on his cheek. "And I found your pool."

"Wow." Clarence crouched down. "Let me see." He scrambled for a stick to dig with, making the hole larger, but it broke and he lost his balance. He fell into the hole, tumbling farther in. "Oh. Ow!" He grabbed at a rock. A tree sapling. Tuck and roll, like a football player— an old football player. Except, when he stopped rolling, his foot was wedged, oddly, into some kind of crevice, and his shoulder jammed against rock.

"Clarence! You okay?" Michael's body filled the hole, blocking the light. Sounds of him scrambling against the hard-packed dirt, the old timber support, roots.

For a moment, it was black. Clarence could barely see his hand, then something reflected. Just for a minute. Smelled like a dank basement, only fresher.

Water?

Something sprinkled onto Clarence's skin. Dirt he guessed. From the fall. Something cracked. Rocks tumbled and hit his feet.

Finally Michael pushed through the hole and light hit the surface of … a pool.

Clarence's gut lurched. How far down did it go?

Water sparkled when rocks plunked into the water surface. Circles expanded and flowed out to the edges.

Clarence coughed, holding his leg. "Yup. I think we found our pool."

FOUR

June 12, 1937 ~ Journal of Dr. Walter Stevens. Moved camper to Osceola Park, near the pool. Sat in open doorway of camper, drinking coffee, staring at the pool. A dove cooed. Couldn't find it in the huge trees. Pretty little area. Nice slope down to the creek. It'd be prettier if it was green rather than dried up. Nebraska humidity hasn't stifled fresh, clean air yet.

Question: why did water fill the pool, when the creek bed is cracked and flaked?

Question: what was so terrible that Henry was willing to give up life?

I must be tired. Last night, I unrolled my sleeping bag beside the pool. Was hoping … didn't sleep at all. Feeling disjointed. Need to write all this down while it's still clear.

Present Day ~ Michael bent over, bumped his head against the ceiling of the cave, knocking what seemed to be mineral deposits loose onto his shoulders and hair, stinging into his eyes. He brushed his shirt off and blinked. Felt like when he'd gotten sawdust in his eyes at the shop. He wiped the tears as he stepped toward Clarence's voice, feeling his way with his hand against the hard rock wall. When he touched the wall, his fingers stuck, freezing against the cold stone.

Strange. Underground rock wouldn't do that in winter, much less in early summer—especially in a cave. Painful cold. It would take more than blowing hot breath on his fingers to thaw them out. At least for human flesh.

He blew on them anyway. Warmth thawed his hand. White mist flowed and illuminated the space in front of him. The mist froze into slivers that hung in the air, until he swung his arm through them and they scattered onto the waters surface. This felt suspiciously like—

"Hey Michael. Help an old man up." Clarence's voice reached Michael's ears from somewhere deeper in the cave, layering with an unearthly sound …

Buzzing. Different from the nurses' phones at Hillcrest.

Michael checked behind him, through the hole they had broken open, to the park. Maybe a mower or chainsaw. The truck was where they had left it.

It buzzed again, now more like a hiss. Like a tomcat hissing. Between a hiss and a growl. Like a herd of tomcats hissing and growling.

Time retracted into timelessness.

A brownish murk swirled above the water enveloping more white mist of Michael's breath hitting the cold air.

Strange sensation. The evil presence in the cave grazed Michael's human skin. He shivered as little bumps appeared across his arms, even in the dim light. Same feeling on the back of his neck. Interesting— residing inside two realms: the invisible realm and earthly realm. He knew what to expect in the invisible realm—comrades in the heavenly host, duties in the court of heaven, worship in the throne room. Oh, and demons. But the earthly realm was so unpredictable. He never knew what these humans would do.

"Michael?" Clarence's voice took on a growl, too.

As Michael's eyes became accustomed to the faint light, tiny specks could be seen hovering over the surface of the pool. He stepped toward Clarence.

Must be a breeding pool for mosquitoes. Or some other bugs. Was this earthly or …

Goosebumps again. He touched the wall. Freezing.

Putrid, sulfurous air choked him. He wiped his eyes.

Yup.

Demons. Demons masquerading as pretty fireflies.

They hovered above the surface of the water, like tiny mosquitoes —buzzing. Their minuscule wings reflected the limited light, flitting up and down. They swarmed together, layering with what Michael saw in the spirit realm—sick yellow eyes. They looked like bird swarms that rose and fell, gathering again into bubble shapes, morphing into one giant bird-like creature, hovering over the surface. The longer he studied them, talons became visible and grew, until razor-like edges appeared to cut the thickened air. Then they scattered again, into tiny beings.

Clarence, crumpled against the wall, slapped at one on his arm. "Damn mosquitoes." He flicked it away, wiping a trail of blood from where it had bitten him. He slapped again.

If Clarence only knew what he was hitting. The price of bug spray would be at an all-time high.

Michael slid on some gravel as he worked his way to where Clarence was sitting. "You okay Clarence?" He chuckled. "At least you're not a scaredy-cat." He'd heard that term somewhere—probably from Clarence.

Clarence held out his hand. "Is that a nice way of saying I should look before I leap? Or, am I just plain stupid compulsive?" He groaned as Michael pulled him up.

Michael brushed at Clarence's pants. "Did you hurt yourself? Break anything?"

Clarence slapped his hands away. "I'm okay. Uh … sorry." He toned his voice down. "I'm okay … thanks." He licked his finger and wiped away the blood on his arm. "This is the only blood I see. And it's mine."

Michael wrinkled his face. Maybe not all Clarence's blood—might be other blood mixed in. "Clarence? Maybe we should get out of here." This park and this cave especially, seemed to be a thin place—like a portal that demons and angels accessed. Probably part of the reason he and Clarence had been sent to Osceola. He glanced toward the cave opening. "Might be almost lunch time, you think?"

"A little blood isn't gonna get to *me*. You queasy, Michael? Do angels get nauseous?"

Michael tamped down the surge of anger. Images looped through his mind—images of bloody sacrifices in the temple, battlefields from the beginning of time, blood streaming down a cross. He closed his eyes, wincing, swallowed and drew in a deep breath.

"Okay. Now that we're down here, what do you want to do?"

"Explore!" Clarence took a step, but instantly his legs buckled and his hand shot out to the rock wall.

Michael caught him before he fell. "Clarence, you're hurt."

"No. I'm okay." He pushed Michael away and jumped as he touched the rock wall again. "Wow! That's cold!" He turned to Michael. "See? Looks like frost on the walls. But … it's summer." He flapped his arms against his side. "It's really cold in here." As he flapped, demon spirits stirred, swarming in and out through the cave opening, some disappearing into the park.

Good-bye demons. Michael stretched to see the playground equipment just as the swarm enveloped a young mother and two kids. She evidently had seen them coming and had her bug spray out. She jumped up from the park bench and emptied the can into them. She cussed. Sprayed. Then cussed some more.

One by one, tiny creatures fell to the ground like dead flies. A putrid smell way worse than bug spray reached Michael's nose as a dirty orange vapor rose from the ground.

When the haze began to lift, the bug-like demons rolled together into one large demon—each tiny one molding together to form the scales, the extremities, the massive head. It jumped up on its legs, arms out in front, shaking—but plainly not from fear.

It shook its fists at Michael, then at the lady who had sprayed them.

Language even Michael couldn't understand spewed from its mouth, along with greenish-brown spit. It shrieked and headed in the direction of the lady and kids.

Michael flinched. "Comrades! Up in arms!" He pointed toward the demon.

Two trees just up from the creek, shuddered. Branches, one on either side of the trunk, grew in girth. Limbs and leaves morphed into feathers on massive wings. A head appeared at the top of the trunk and all in one swoop, two angels charged the demon, swords flashing.

It never saw them coming.

"Michael what on earth are you waving at? More mosquitoes out there?"

Michael nodded. "You could say that." He turned to Clarence. "Ready to explore more of the cave?"

Clarence collapsed to the cave floor, scattering rocks as he landed. He looked up at Michael. "I think I broke my leg."

FIVE

June 12, 1937 ~ Journal of Dr. Walter Stevens ~ Thelma's Diner. I sat alone in a booth at Thelma's Diner, waiting for breakfast. Trying to capture all I can recall from yesterday and last night. And all that happened and was said at the diner earlier. Documenting everything. Just the researcher in me, I guess.

Also eavesdropping. Apparently Henry's disappearance stirred up ugly memories of that pool.

The town fathers asked me to stay and delve into the pool mystery, but plainly, the townspeople want me gone.

Present Day ~ The backpack was heavier than usual, but not as heavy as Noell's heart. An iron skillet inside her backpack bounced against her in rhythm as she walked. Several copies of an herbal magazine cushioned mismatched dishes. Her face burned as she thought of what Gamma would say if she knew. She had no idea how long it would take to clear out Gamma's house if she packed out say, ten items, each time she left the house. Part of her knew she was stealing from Gamma. But part of her wanted to believe she was helping clear out what the years had dragged in.

The thrift store loved what she donated and the little ladies there promised to never tell. It was for a good cause—the hospital, right? She was helping Gamma clean, right?

She loved the old smell of the thrift store. Loved digging through the books and even found one or two—usually fantasy or just a good story—a distraction from life.

Every once in a while, she found a treasure like the cup she was going to claim at Gam's. Another find had been a painting of a pool in a secluded area of a forest. Not a picture of water crashing and destroying lives, but of a serene, peaceful little lake. The trees almost hid the tiny pool, branches hanging low, protecting its secrets. She bought it and immediately hung it in her room beside her bed. Just enough below the lamp so it made a small vignette. Nice.

On the way to the thrift store, she passed right by the roads utility building. Huh. Wouldn't hurt to apply there. See what they had available, if anything. Wouldn't hurt. Besides, dirt she could handle—real dirt anyway.

The Roads Department building was pretty plain on the front. The only way you could identify it, was by the hard hat on the pole and the word "Roads." That was it.

She pulled the door open with her hand tucked in her hoodie sleeve. Her thumb slipped out and made contact with the metal handle.

Oh no.

She braced, knowing the chattering would begin.

Millions of voices raced through her mind, layer upon layer, like the season opener of the Husker football team. Deep voices. Women's. A child whimpering.

I hope they can repair that spot in the road. What kind of car is that? I think he likes me. I hate my life. Mommy, Mommy, you're hurting me.

Every conversation, every thought. Every comment, fear, joy, gripe of every person who had grasped that door handle transferred to Noell. Flooded her mind, her emotions.

Not now.

Not here.

Noell backed out of the open door and tore down the steps. She skirted around the corner of the building and crouched on the ground.

Other people's germs. Gah.

Every person who had touched the door handle left cells or germs or finger prints. Those zillions of molecules sucked through Noell's skin and traveled to her thoughts.

Faces populated her consciousness before she could grab sanitizer out of her backpack. She even recognized a few: the lady who worked at the drive-inn—the one who always took the money, a guy she had seen driving by Gam's house the other day—why she remembered him, she couldn't guess, a young woman half dragging a tiny whimpering girl. And Gamma? At the Roads Department?

Sanitizer. Sanitizer. She squirted some onto the palm of one hand and rubbed them briskly together. Whew. Voices slowed. Faces blurred and faded.

She still saw Gam.

Okay. Settle down. Go back in there. They might have a job opening for office clerk or something like that. She could run a copy machine.

She sucked in a deep breath and stood, checking the street and drive. She peeked around the corner.

Uh-oh.

Mr. Grimes, a neighbor from two houses down from Gamma's. At the Road's Department? Creepy old man.

Noell could see his kitchen window from her room upstairs at Gamma's. Some nights he would stand at his sink, washing dishes or getting a drink and look out his window at her. She knew he was. She could feel his eyes on her.

He walked stiffly with a walker too, like Gamma. No way she wanted to open the door after him. She knew what he was into.

One day, when she was younger, he had asked her to help with something in his house. "Come on into my house, little one. You can climb to reach something in my kitchen. I'll make it worth your while." He had lifted his walker, pointing it in the direction of his house. "I have ice cream and cookies for your reward." He held the door open and she walked in past him. She got halfway through his entryway when she smelled it. Barely at first, but with each step, his scent became stronger. Eww! Stinky eggs.

She had spun around and bumped into him. As she scrambled under the walker and between his feet, his shoes gave off a dusty, reddish brown mist. Gramps had taken Gamma and Noell to Arizona one year and the dirt was that same color.

She pushed off from his shoes and tore out the door. Why she had turned to face him again, she didn't know: maybe to see if he would actually drop his walker and race after her, or maybe to figure out what that red mist was.

Either way, a reddish-brown light began to glow from his body, faint at first, then more visible—just as the stench grew unbearable. An outline of something grew around him, rose above him.

Chills skittered up her arms.

A head formed, then a torso and long arms. Long legs.

She tried to look away as her heart pounded harder. She didn't want to look. She would have more bad dreams. She crouched—tried to look at the floor. Oh, for Gamma's arms around her.

Her feet had grown heavy as if someone was hanging from them. She used to sit on Grampa's foot and wrap her arms and feet around his leg, riding on his foot with each step, until he could no longer move.

Locked down to the spot.

The eyes. Terrifying. Something moved in those yellow eyes.

The being and Mr. Grimes stepped toward her.

Mr. Grimes had forgotten to use his walker when he charged after her. He yelled naughty things, threatened her and Gamma, to make her come back.

The creature stretched its arms after her.

She tried to scream, but only a gasp came out. Something unlocked her feet, and she fled. She made sure she never put her big toe in his yard again.

His scent had made her brain go crazy. It spiked pictures she didn't want to ever see again. Over the top sensations until she threw up and had to shower to wash it all off.

After Gamma had promised she would kill Mr. Grimes if he ever came after her again, she had wrapped Noell in a big blanket and rocked her until she finally quit shaking and fell asleep.

Creepy old man. Dirty old man.

She turned toward the building entrance. Hurry up, Mr. Grimes.

When she peeked around the corner, he was doing his walker shuffle down the ramp. The last couple feet, he picked up the walker and stepped to his car trunk. He opened it and threw the walker into the trunk, slamming the lid. He hopped into his car and drove off.

Not. Going. In. Especially after him.

She'd rather work at the hospital emptying bedpans than go in after he'd been inside. Well … maybe not.

Maybe they needed help at the thrift store.

She carefully wrapped her sleeve around her hand and opened the door. No voices. No faces. Whew. No bell dinged either. No one was in the office. Smelled like cigarette smoke. Ugh. Maybe this wouldn't work.

"Hello?" she called.

No one came to the counter. Papers fluttered on the counter, as the door closed behind her. A bulletin board against the rear wall proclaimed safety precautions. Someone's coffee cup had tipped over, draining the residue onto official-looking paperwork. Clear vinyl protected a calendar on the counter in front of her and if she cocked her head just right, she could read day-off requests that had been inked in red. One name was especially repetitive—Rat. What kind of a name was that?

She turned to leave when a truck skidded in and parked in front. A utility truck. Maybe this would work out.

The man walked in, talking on his cell phone. "Yeah, yeah. He escapes from there all the time. They say he grew up around here." He didn't even see her until he got to his desk, sat down, righted his coffee cup—wiping at the mess and happened to look up.

He jumped. "Oh, hello. I'm sorry." To the person on the phone he said, "Hey, I gotta go. There's a young woman … yeah, and I gotta go." He turned away from Noell. "Yeah that's what I said. Gotta go. I'll call you later."

He tapped it off and stood. "Uh … sorry about that. We don't get many people in here." He gave her a sheepish grin. "May I help you?"

Noell cleared her throat and swallowed. "Yes. I … uh, am here to see about a job. Do you have any openings … for … anything? Outside?" She hesitated. "Even inside?"

"Not at the moment. We did have an opening, but filled it last week. It usually takes a day to see if a guy," he cleared his throat, "or gal, will work out. He seems to be good, so far."

"Okay, well if you have anything could you let me know?"

"Why don't you fill out an application so I have your info and all? Then if we have anything open up, like I said, we just hired a guy, but if anything comes around, we can give you a call." He walked to the desk and rummaged through a drawer, pulled out a sheet of paper and grabbed a pen. "Here you go. Why don't you come around here and sit at the desk and fill it out?"

"Okay. Sure." She followed him to the desk and sat in the office chair, scooting forward. Sliding her backpack off her shoulders, she forgot about the extra weight. It hit the concrete floor harder than planned and something broke. Oh no. Now she felt even worse about stealing Gamma's stuff.

She shook her head and settled in the space. A framed photo of a little old lady was displayed to the right of the coffee mess. Shoulder-length gray hair held back with a pink head band, brown eyes twinkled behind wire rimmed glasses, a joyful smile. Head held high—like a queen.

Noell smiled back.

He stared for a minute, seemed to realize it and went to the other side of the office, found a copy of the Polk County News and unfolded it.

Noell concentrated on the questions in the application. They were the usual: name, address, phone number. She pulled out her phone and tapped to the information she needed.

A question had her stumped. What experience did she have? Roads. She had never … plowed or cleared a road in her life. She mowed. She put that down. And weeded. She kept Gam's yard and flower gardens and vegetable gardens up very well. In fact, the neighbors always commented on how nice they looked, which earned them free flowers and tomatoes.

She filled in the rest of the information with the date she could start being … tomorrow.

"Um, I'm finished. What do you want me to do with it?" She clicked the pen shut.

"I'll take a look and see if I can read it." His eyes twinkled when he smiled. He looked it over, pointing at each answer, reading out loud. "Looks good, Noell. Hey, I'm Mr. Ivertson, but you can call me Steve." He reached out his hand. Thick hand and fingers.

Uh … no.

He waited.

Awkward.

She placed her hand in his. Strong grip. She liked him. Whew.

"Thanks Mr. … Steve. Thanks for your time."

"I'll look things over and if we think we can use you, I'll call."

The radio squawked alive. "Hey, Steve. We have a problem, man. New guy's down. He sprained his foot walking on a sidewalk, the klutz. We're taking him to the hospital now. Wanna get out the paperwork so's we can fill out the report when we get back?"

Steve rushed to the intercom. "Sure thing."

"Hey, we're gonna need to fill that position. This time of year, there's too much outside work for the road crews to do it all and you can't always help, with running the office. Just a thought. Might call the newspaper and put in an ad."

Steve looked over at Noell. "I don't think we need to get in a rush about it. We might have it covered."

"Hey Steve? What about your grandson … Brian. He's a brute."

Steve shook his head. "No. He found a job in Columbus."

"Okay. Well, if you have someone in your back pocket, go for it. But we had to wait long enough for this loser."

"Things have a way of working out, Bud." Steve leaned into the mike again. "Take care of the kid."

He nodded to Noell. "Ready to get to work? You're going to need work clothes, boots. We got the hard hat."

Noell stared. "Yeah. Yes. I'm ready. What time and where?"

He grinned. "Here, at 8 o'clock sharp."

"I'll be here." She started to wave. "Thanks. Bye."

"Thank *you*." He saluted.

As she closed the door behind her, she paused. He had saluted her. Like Grampa used to.

Later at home, Noell pawed through a pile of boxes on the old back porch. She slid one off the top of the pile and opened it only to find piles of folded fabric—all cotton plaid. She labeled the box: Plaid Farmer Shirt Fabric.

The next box held more of the same. She lifted off another box. A mouse scampered farther under the line of boxes, making her jump. Her skin crawled, fingers trembled. Blowing out a deep breath, she made herself open the next box. T-shirts. Orange. All new, but … old. One after another—all the same shirt. She unfolded the top one. Orange was the right color—but with black lettering: X Marks the Spot. What was Gam doing with a whole box of orange shirts from … X? What was X? Where on earth did she get these? Probably wasn't any use asking Gam because she wouldn't remember.

She pulled three out and held them up to her chest. Big, which was okay. The smell wafting from the one she held reminded her to wash them before she wore them. She tossed four toward the kitchen doorway. Might as well make use of Gam's plethora of supplies.

Another box off the pile. She'd never done this; she'd never *gone through* any of Gam's stuff. Probably okay to do it now when she needed it for work. Gam always told her to help herself. So she was. More fabric—all corduroy—all black. Too bad it wasn't Halloween. Bet the school could use this. The magic marker squeaked as she labeled the box: Black Halloween Corduroy for schools. Might as well save time and label it now. You never knew.

The bottom box had printing on it. Men's work boots. Oh, if only.

She ripped it open.

Boots all right. Steel toed. All leather. These had to have been expensive. But, the fact that they all had bright pink leather ankle inserts probably explained why they sat in a bottom box in Gam's hoarder house. She pulled out a pair and checked the size. Nine. The next pair was even bigger. Oh, please. The last pair—size eight. Yes!

Shirts. Boots. Now all she needed were jeans. She pushed at another stack of boxes … annnnd boom! The stack came down around her, contents spilling, a muffled sound of glass breaking.

Oh-oh.

"Hon? You okay out there?" Gam's voice quavered from the living room. "Noell? You okay?"

"Yeah, Gam. Sorry I disturbed you. Just finding things for work and knocked over a stack of boxes." She whispered. "And maybe broke something."

Gam appeared at the door with her walker. She yawned.

"Oh, Gam. I'm sorry. I woke you."

"It's okay, Hon. I needed to wake up." She checked her watch. "Been napping for an hour. If I don't get up, I'll never sleep tonight." She ventured into the porch. "Did you find something you can use?"

Noell held up the boots. "Score!" She showed Gam. "See? These are just my size!"

"Pink, too, I see."

Noell laughed. "Well, I don't really care if they're pink, or purple or brown. But they are free." She glanced up at Gam. "I mean—"

"I have told you that anything in these boxes, or my house for that matter, is yours. I'm just glad you can use them."

Noell grabbed a shirt from the box. "And these shirts are just right."

"Kinda big, aren't they?" Gam tipped her head. "You don't have to look like a boy, do you?"

"They're fine, Gam. Works better for me if I do look like a boy. I'll be working with a bunch of men." She pushed the boxes into the narrow aisle and opened one. "Aww. Cute. Gam look. Little tiny cups and saucers." She held a set up. "What are they for? Tea parties?"

Gam frowned. "I don't remember." She reached for one. "They are cute. Is that what's in the whole box?"

Noell held up boxes of four more sets—all different colors. "Pretty much." One set matched a dish she still had in her backpack. Her face felt hot. Such a turmoil: she was sneaking things to the thrift store, and at the same time, Gamma said she could have anything here. She swallowed and carefully replaced the sets. "I'm glad they didn't break when I knocked everything over. I think something did, but not these."

"It's okay." Gam surveyed the whole porch. "I just don't know how this all happened. I can't remember half—more than half—the stuff in my house." She shrugged and looked up at Noell. "It's a sickness, I'm convinced."

"Maybe." Noell raised her eyebrows in sympathy. "Is it any worse that I am so germaphobic?" She pulled open another box. "Overalls?" She unfolded one and held it up. "Huge." She held another pair in front of her. "It'd be too weird if you had my size in here." She dug deeper, piling them on the floor. "Yeah! Here's one." She tugged it from the box. "And another."

"Throw 'em here and we can wash them."

Noell tossed them to land on Gam's walker.

"Nice shot," Gamma said.

"Is it okay if I—"

"You can have anything here you want. Make use of it." Gamma shrugged. "I keep saying it needs to be cleaned out. Maybe this is what will get me going on it." She sighed. "I don't know when all this happened. Your Grampa loved auctions, couldn't resist a sale." She dipped her head. "And then after he died, I guess I kept right on buying." She folded the overalls over the walker bar. "An auction here. Hardware store downtown had a going-out-of-business sale, and I'd go." She looked around the porch. "It's all useful ... or ... it was. To somebody."

Noell stepped over the piles and hugged Gam. "It's okay Gam. Look how it's helping me." She glanced over her shoulder. "I don't need the extra large ones, but this is really saving me money." She hugged her again. "Thanks Gam. I'll help too. Okay? We'll do this together."

"Maybe guys at your work could use some of this."

Noell looked at the box of pink boots. "Well … some of it." She laughed. "We could start a new fad with those boots." She pulled at another box and laughed. "Gam, did you know I would work for the roads department?" She held up an orange work vest with stripes of reflective tape running up and down the vest. "Gam? A boxful!"

"I didn't know." She shook her head, a smug look on her face. "Maybe."

SIX

June 12, 1937 ~ Journal of Dr. Walter Stevens ~ Thelma's Diner. The door bell—literally a bell—keeps ringing, as people keep coming in. A man across the aisle keeps repeating that the pool was of the devil. Over and over. Each time, someone shushes him. But he says it again. "The city needs to fill in that pool."

I'm not sure dirt will keep demons in.

A young boy, who appears to be about eight, in the next booth, keeps staring.

Terrifying.

The kid never blinks.

Present Day ~ Clarence leaned against the nursing home wall in the reception area, letting one crutch rest against his body. "I don't know how I get myself into these predicaments." Tears threatened but he wiped his whole face.

Deep breath. Push on.

Michael came in the door, carrying the hospital release bag of orders and meds.

Lisha walked up beside Clarence. "You want a wheelchair, Mr. Clarence?" She pointed down the hall. "Iss a long way to your room."

"Naw. Naw. I got this." It *was* a long hall.

Something bumped behind his knees.

Carol. Wheelchair.

He sat. Never thought a wheelchair would feel so good.

Lisha propped his leg on the footrest, picked up his crutches and joined Michael, grabbing the bag. "This all they sent, Mr. Michael? No ropes to tie him in his bed? Keep him out of caves 'n stuff."

"Lisha!" Carol shook her head. "Give him some sympathy."

"Well, iss true. Need to lash him to his bed or his chair. Then he won't—"

"Enough!" Carol patted Clarence's shoulder.

"She's right." Clarence's chin jutted and his eyes burned. "Stupid old man. Stupid ideas."

"Aw, Clarence." Lisha stepped alongside the wheelchair. "I didn't mean nothin' by it. Just kidding."

He worked his jaw side-to-side. "No. You're right. Stupid to think I can go into pools and caves. I just need to stay in my room and die." He stared straight ahead, nostrils flaring, eyes burning. He was barely able to lock in emotions.

An elderly, blue-haired woman squealed from her room. "Oh, Mr. Timmelsen! What did you do?"

Damn! He covered his eyes. If only he could disappear. Where was that time-travel stuff when a guy needed it? He motioned to Carol to keep moving, but she stopped.

He pulled himself up in the chair and gave a half-smile. "Hello Mrs. Martin." He patted his leg. "It's not broken. It's nothing serious. Just a splint." Damn it hurt. Sedative from the procedure must be wearing off. He wanted to kick himself. "I'll be all right."

Mrs. Martin mouthed an O in sympathy, as Carol pushed the wheelchair on by. "Uh, I'll tell Mrs. Hatly." She waved her frail hand. "She'll want to know."

Clarence ducked down. The gossip had begun.

He counted the rooms as they flew past, until his own. Mr. Wainwright's door was closed. Good. Good riddance.

At his room, someone had taped a "Get Well Soon" sign to his door. He grabbed at it, but missed as they turned into his room. Balloons hung from his mirror, and a lone cupcake sat on a Happy Birthday party plate. No candle. No party.

As they crossed the threshold, a strange foreboding invaded Clarence. He had partly been kidding about wanting to die—just wanted sympathy. But … something felt off in his room. A darkness settled over him, fear maybe, or maybe his leg hurt, but his rooms felt different. He hadn't even been gone a day.

"Looks like someone set up a welcome home party." Carol parked the wheelchair next to the bed and locked the brakes. "Staff must have closed up your room when they cleaned this morning." She opened the blinds and the window. "Needs some fresh air and sunlight."

Sunlight helped brighten the room up a bit, but still, there was something wrong in Hillcrest room 204.

Carol leaned in. "And you aren't going to die. It's not even that bad of an injury, as injuries go." She checked his pulse and blood pressure. "Good as new." She brushed his shirt off and checked his arms. "I want you to take a shower."

Clarence Timmelsen burst out laughing. "You want me to what? I just get back from the emergency room and you say I need a shower? They washed my face *and* my leg in the hospital." Clarence slumped. "I'm gonna die, anyway. I won't need a shower when they shove me in the ground."

Carol backed out the door.

"No. No!" Clarence fumbled with the wheelchair. "Damn! Damn, damn." He stretched his hand to Carol. "Don't leave me with her!"

"Oh, wah." Lisha Hall crossed her arms across her ample chest, a glint in her dark brown eyes. Her ever-moving hips circled to the tune of "I'm in charge here, and I don't care what you have to say about it!"

He found the wheelchair brakes and released one. "I don't need a bath. Go get Mr. … uh, who was the guy that was shitting in my toilet when I first got here? Go get him. He probably still stinks."

"He died last week." She reached up and yanked at his hair, grown longer over the month. "Hair's greasy. An, watch your mouth! This ain't no prison!" She pinched a brown nose with her fingers, her pinky waving. "There is a smell in here that is worse than your favorite cheese."

He glanced at a table in the corner of the room and scrunched his face. The paper plate of leftover cheese and crackers had only been sitting out for a few days. "It's the cheese, I swear. Michael didn't finish it up."

"That cheese don't smell like BO!" She shook her head. "You gettin' baptized! I get to legally drown you!" She pointed toward the door. "You're comin' with me!"

"Isn't there some kind of nursing home policy that states that this is my home and I don't have to do anything I damn well don't want to?" He stuck his face in hers.

Her mouth twitched back and forth. "Ya know, you don't look like you're eighty, but I could hep you get there." Dreadlocks tied at the back of her head, shook like a limp Raggedy Ann doll.

He twisted his lips to the side. Not gonna laugh. Not gonna. Tears threatened as he eyed her size twenty-something aide uniform, pink elephants frolicking all over it as she bumped her other hip up for emphasis.

"Dontchu laugh, Mr. Clarence."

He snorted.

"Dontchu even. I'll have to wrap my stethoscope around your neck and tie it tight."

He covered his mouth. Oh, he loved this goofy woman. But if she ever found out, he was dead, like in stink dead.

He turned to look one more time—maybe she'd quietly left the room. She stuck her tongue out and grinned that toothy big-mouth grin. He lost it. "I'll go. Just gather my stuff, okay?" He poked his finger at her. "When I get back, you can help me put my journals and stuff away." He glanced at the stack of boxes.

She looked at his leg. "I'll help. Now, let's go!"

She gathered soap and towel and washcloth from the bathroom, clean underwear and socks from his chest of drawers and dumped it all on his lap.

She steered him into the hall and almost ran into Harold Dexter. She grabbed him just in time, before he toppled over his walker.

"How are you doing, ole buddy? She round you up for a shower, too?" His hair dripped onto the shoulders of his plaid shirt, his little upside-down American flag pin sparkled. He sniffed the air. "You don't stink. Much." He raised his hand high in the air. "Hey, sorry to hear about your leg."

Clarence slapped Harold's hand above his head as he passed him. "It's okay. Hey. Come over later."

"I can do that." Harold fumbled with the flag. "Maybe then we can shoot a round of pool?"

Clarence glanced at his leg. "Sure. We'll see how it goes."

Lisha prodded Clarence from behind. "No pool for you if you don't get a shower."

Harold pushed his walker ahead. "She gonna drown you, Clarence?"

"She thinks she is. She doesn't know it, but when I get in there, I turn the faucet on and just sit on the stool and watch the water run down the drain. Then I splash a little on me." He grinned. "She never knows."

Harold laughed. "You slick dude, you. Then rub in some soap behind your ears and you're good."

Clarence high-fived Harold again. "You got it buddy. That's my cologne."

Lisha sniffed the air. "Huh. Must be why Harold here, always smells better than you do with his after-shave. What's it called Mr. Harold? Wet Dog? Cain't 'member."

"Ouch! I'll remember you when it's time for Christmas gifts."

"You'll forget all about it come Christmas. With your mind, the way it's goin'."

Lisha opened the door to the shower and pulled a trash bag out of her pocket. "Git your pants off and I'll wrap your leg. Gotta keep it dry." She turned her back and counted, "One-Mississippi, two-Mississippi. Ya done yet?"

He stripped and wrapped a towel around himself. "I'm done. Let's get this over with."

She wrapped the plastic around his leg and taped it.

Just before he closed the door, he stuck his tongue out at her. Then he closed it and locked it.

The doorknob rattled.

"I can git a key, Mr. Clarence. You old ..."

He started the shower and got undressed. Ahh, quiet. She could yell but not loud enough to be heard over the running water. He started to push out of the chair, then remembered the brakes. He pulled himself up by the grab bars and stood under the hot water. He *was* dirty. This was so much better than those open showers at the prison. You could never relax there. You never knew who was going to sneak up and ....

He worked his jaw back and forth, teeth grinding. His stomach clenched.

He gripped the bar of soap so hard it slipped out of his hand and hit the shower wall.

Slow down, Clarence. Breathe. You're not in prison anymore.

He held onto the grip bar, picked up the soap in the washcloth and got wet. It hadn't been so bad toward the end, but when he first got to prison—the memories almost brought him to his knees—even now, sixty years later. God, he shouldn't be alive today.

That was when he had learned to keep to himself. Never trust anyone. Even the guards. Well, some guards. Lester had been the one guard who would somehow always show up when Clarence was in trouble.

Clarence would find himself surrounded by huge, evil inmates.

Threatened.

Terrified.

And Lester would appear, beat stick in hand, eyes darting from face to face.

Clarence could never quite figure out why the inmates backed off. Lester was stocky but a full head shorter than most.

If they didn't back off right away, Lester would side-step the biggest inmate to the nearest wall and press the beat stick against the man's neck until he relinquished. Pipsqueak, the squealer of the gang, would always scream in a high-pitched voice, "Call off your angels, Lester. They be choking me!"

Angels? Michael was an angel, but … Clarence had never seen him do the stuff Pipsqueak had screamed about.

He lathered up. White soapsuds slid away from the palms of his hands, revealing ropy scars. He'd been burned bad twice. Once right after his mom had died. Then again just a few weeks ago. They were still tender.

Strange. He'd been so completely focused on saving little Bea he had hardly felt the slide poles burning his hands. Seemed like a lifetime ago. That little girl and her mommy had claimed a huge piece of his heart.

He turned off the water and toweled dry. Patted his belly as he dressed. He needed to get a treadmill. Or walk more. He looked at his plastic-wrapped leg—when it was better. They'd never had desserts at prison like they did here. Brownies. Angel food cake with glaze. Apple crisp—his favorite.

How could Pipsqueak see Lester's angels? Why could Clarence see Michael? Not everyone could. Well, the nurses and women sometimes seemed to—called him irresistible.

Little Bea could see him—angel costume and all.

She was just sweet. That had to be why.

But Pipsqueak? He was not.

Michael half-smiled.

Clarence had no clue.

Michael had parked the truck and taken him into Hillcrest. Poor guy. Michael had never broken or sprained legs, arms, anything as a human, but from what he could see, it hurt. Clarence was in pain. He never even noticed when Michael left.

Of course, that was no fault of Clarence's. Most people never thought about the supernatural, or the invisible realm.

Maybe someday, he'd let him in on the … secret.

He chuckled to himself.

No secret, except to those who didn't believe.

The one's who did wouldn't be surprised. Well, maybe some would be and maybe a little.

Free of that grinding little vehicle. He didn't want to complain, but he wasn't used to limitations or restrictions on his movement.

The only restriction he relished in was following the Father's love. Wherever Father moved, he would go too.

He stood a minute, closing his eyes.

Yeshua. Firstborn of all creation. Prince of Peace. Creator of mankind.

He lingered, wings unfurling, soaking in the Father's wealth of love. His spirit soared, lifting him into the atmosphere. The rush of exhilaration caught him off guard today. Probably because he had been in human form almost past his tolerance. Just about outside of his province of Father's protection.

Deep sigh.

He floated back to the ground, and his wings faded.

A wide-eyed kid stared as he walked by, following a woman. She stopped at a doorway, and he bumped into her. Michael chuckled at the stories he would tell his mom. Poor kid.

It happened a lot. Some kids were still so pure that the other realm was very visible to them. They hadn't been abused or so affected by the world—yet.

Michael connected on a regular basis with a couple of kids. Their sweet spirit was refreshing and a joy.

He laughed just thinking about one little girl who, whenever she saw him, broke out in dance. Swirling and kicking and jumping. Sometimes she got into trouble, because of course Mommy or Daddy didn't see him. Or it happened in a place where she shouldn't be dancing, according to the *rules*.

Time was short. People didn't know.

But *she* did. She knew to dance while dancing was still allowed.

Michael didn't know the future—it wasn't for angels to know.

But.

He could see that the earth was becoming even darker. Everyday it grew darker and darker. People became more corrupt. Cruelty abounded.

Just thinking about what he saw people do to each other, no matter what culture, nationality, or faith, made Michael cringe and tear up.

Nation against nation. Father against son. Son against father. Neighbor against neighbor and friend against friend.

How Father's heart grieved.

SEVEN

June 12, 1937 ~ Dr. Steven's Journal ~ Breakfast at Thelma's Diner. Every seat is occupied. Overalls and jeans. Suits. House dresses. Every walk of life. All seated in protest to my presence. I came unglued. "What are you looking at?" I startled even myself. I leaned over my plate of eggs and bacon, poured syrup over all of it, making a lake to dip my toast in.

At that point I'd had enough of the stares and whispers. Felt like I was back in the classroom when students were thinking about the weekend binge and their college plunderings, instead of the lecture I'd worked hard to prepare.

My stomach growled and so did I. I cut my eggs, dipped the bite in syrup and just about got it to my mouth. But the staring and loudly whispered comments pressed at me. I dropped the fork on my plate. The clatter brought everyone to attention.

Huh. I should use that in the classroom. Drop a fork on a plate.

"Okay." Really loud. Louder than in a lecture.

A woman somewhere shushed me.

"These people don't care if I yell." I stood up and walked the aisle between my booth table and the counter. "You people are nosy and want to know what I am finding, so I'll tell you."

Present Day ~ Noell opened a couple cans of vegetable beef soup, dumped the contents into a sauce pan and turned up the heat under the pan. Had she eaten lunch?

Gams sat at the kitchen table, flitting through grocery ads. "Man, the cost of bottled water has gone up. I might have to start filling my own."

Noell rolled her eyes. "Gam—"

"Now don't start. I know it costs less if I fill my own."

"You can just drink out of a glass."

"Listen to you, Miss Picky Face."

Noell looked down at her new white slippers.

Gam cleared her throat and flipped pages.

Noell glanced around the kitchen. Coupon boxes were piled next to the stove. They didn't hold coupons, they held money. Cookbooks were stacked floor to ceiling—all along the outside wall—not just one stack, but lining the whole wall. Gam said it added insulation. She said she'd get around to reading them … someday.

She and Gramps had had a good time going through them and trying recipes. Probably that was the main reason she hoarded them—because she couldn't have *him*.

There were days when those walls pushed in on Noell.

Today was one.

Gotta get her own place.

And not argue with Gamma.

She sprinkled salt and pepper over the soup in the pan and added a handful of shredded cheese to melt as she stirred. She opened the cupboard door and chose two bowls. Funny, the insides of the cupboards were clean and orderly. "Oh, I saw Mr. Grimes at the Roads Department. He is so creepy."

Gam stirred. "He didn't come on to you or anything, did he?"

"I didn't even talk to him. I hid when I saw him and didn't go in until he left, but—"

"If he ever touches you, I'll kill him." She pointed to the 22 rifle propped in the corner behind the back door.

"Gam, you—"

Gam looked at Noell, a determined look on her face. "I'm serious. I can shoot that thing. At least I used to. I used to be a crack shot. Just ask your grandpa ... "

"Oh, Gam." Noell hugged her and kissed her forehead. "You still miss him."

"Terribly. Seems like yesterday he ... we were cooking. Laughing." She sighed and turned the page on the flyer she was reading. "When he was here, we did everything together." A tear slipped down her cheek. "I hope and pray you find a man just like Grandpa."

Noell smiled and stirred the soup. "Me too."

"Say, could you hand me that list above you there? The one with the pink hippo on it?"

Noell reached above the stove and picked through the papers, coupons, and general clutter on a small shelf. Old mail, used stamps, old lists. "Where? I don't see a hippo on anything." As she moved things on the shelf, she knocked an old pencil stub into the soup pan. "Agh. No! That's nasty."

"Honey, just fish it out and it'll be fine. We can still eat the soup."

She removed it with a slotted spoon. "No. I'll have to start over. That's nasty."

"It's okay. Just turn up the burner. The heat will burn out the ... germs."

Noell shuddered. "Seriously?" She choked, dropped the spoon. Ran into the bathroom and slammed the door. She knew she was loud and Gamma heard, but she couldn't handle the fact that she might be ingesting germs and eraser crumbs. You couldn't wash that off—or out. The thought made her retch even more. Her eyes watered, her mouth watered. She grabbed a clean washcloth from the linen closet, rinsed it in warm water and wiped her eyes, her face. She breathed deeply as she looked at herself in the mirror above the sink. Busy geometric wallpaper surrounding the mirror made her dizzy. Her eyes crossed and she gasped as her legs crumpled. She fell to the floor, knowing she was going down, arms flailing to prevent a fall against the hard porcelain toilet, sink or bathtub.

"Noell? Noell honey? Are you okay?"

Gram's voice became fainter, then louder.

She opened her eyes and saw huge beings behind Gam—all smiling down at her, long flowing hair, so she almost couldn't see their features, their eyes gleaming.

She wanted to dance as she looked at them but she blinked and they were gone. "Gam, did I hit my head?"

"No dear, thank God." She patted her chest. "You could have so easily, in that tiny bathroom."

Noell looked around her. She sat on Gam's favorite furniture—the Italian leather sofa. "How did I get in here?" She tried to sit up, but Gam pushed her down. "Did you carry me all the way in here? Gam?"

Gam laughed. "Oh, my sakes no. The paper boy came by just at the right time. He heard me scream and ran in. He carried you in here. He's," she turned in her chair, "where did you go, son? Well, for Pete's sake, where did he go?"

A guy peeked into the living room from the front porch. "Uh … here Ma'am. Didn't want to interrupt."

"Come on in, and you're not interrupting anything." Gam ushered him in with her arm. "Meet my granddaughter. She's awake and can't believe you carried her in here."

Noell lifted her head slightly. "Hi. Thanks for helping me. I'm surprised you could," she really looked at him—trim, fit, muscled out, "lift … me. You're a paper boy? You look more like …" She checked Gam. "Well, thanks."

He was blushing. "Glad to help. Just happened along at the right time, I guess."

"Would you like something to drink … or … " She sat up, making both him and Gam jump.

"Don't you think you should rest, honey? Just lay back and rest while we get *you* something to drink." Gam pushed out of her chair and sank back down. Second try, she stood and was able to stay standing, arranging her jeans and shirt. "What can I get you?"

"Water would be fine, Gam." She rushed ahead. "But, could it be—"

"I know. One of my store-bought water bottles. Sure baby." She sat her walker down in the direction of the kitchen. "Anything for you, sir?"

He shrugged. "Sure. I'll take a water. Please."

Gam shuffled out to the kitchen.

Noell glanced at him.

He cleared his throat. "My name is Fletch, Fletch Anderson. What's yours?"

"Noell Carpenter. Nice to meet you."

His eyes flitted about the room, bouncing on every pile, each stack of boxes. They rushed back to hers like a scared puppy first meeting the neighbor's Rottweiler.

Her neck was on fire. Her stomach clenched. "I'm sorry … for this … " She swallowed. "It's … well … it's kinda messy."

He waved the apology away. "It's okay. It's easy to see that your grandma isn't able to do it all herself. It's a lot to take care of, a house is."

She gathered her courage. "Where do you live? Close by?"

"I do. I live on the other side of Mr. Grimes." He smiled.

Cute. Blond hair trimmed up front and sides, longer in the back. Filled out his T-shirt.

"The old house with the black front brick. Black brick is kinda unusual, so you probably remember seeing it." He blushed again.

Even cuter.

"I do remember it. Nice old house."

He nodded. "I like it. Uh—"

"Here we are. Sorry it took so long, but I remembered the cookies I baked." Gam pushed the walker ahead. A bag dangled from it that held the water bottles. She offered one to Noell and one to Fletch.

"Thank you, Mrs. … Um, I'm sorry Ma'am. I didn't get your name."

"Oh, people just call me Gam." She sat down with a grunt. "I'm Gwendolyn Randolph Carpenter." She wrinkled her nose. "Gam is just fine." She jumped. "Oh, the cookies." She reached into the walker basket, retrieved a plastic lidded container and opened it.

"I'm hungry." Noell jumped. "Gam! The stove! The soup!"

Fletch waved her back down. "It's okay. I turned it off. Nothing burned."

"Whew! Thank you, Fletch." She hesitated. "You want to stay for supper? We're having … soup." She eyed Gamma. "Maybe."

He smiled. "I really should be getting back to my paper route. People get mad if their paper isn't on time." He stood and held up the water bottle. "Thanks for the water."

"Wait! Here're some cookies for the road!" Gam held out the container.

He grabbed a couple. "Thanks. Gotta run." He held the container for Noell to reach into, and hesitated. "Sometime maybe we could … go for a walk, or take in a movie … sometime."

Noell took a cookie and tapped it against the container. "Sure. Sometime. A walk would be fun … fine … sometime."

Fletch smiled and took a bite. He looked for a place to set the container down, then handed it to Gamma. "See ya then." To Gam. "Thanks for the cookies." He mumbled through crumbs. "They're great. We don't … bake … cookies." He held the water bottle high. "And the water."

"You're sure welcome. Come back anytime—even when you don't have to deliver papers."

"Thanks. I will." He left by way of the front porch and stumbled into a stack of cardboard boxes.

"He's nice. A nice young man. And he rescued you." Gam raised her eyebrows.

"Shhh. Gam, he can hear you." She half stood, stretched. "He isn't even out the door yet."

The front door squeaked as it closed.

Noell blew out a breath. She'd hardly talked to guys she knew in school, much less a total stranger. "Can we just have cookies for supper? I feel like the whole day is upside down now. How can everything go crazy all of a sudden?"

EIGHT

June 12, 1937 ~ Dr. Steven's Journal ~ Thelma's. Stood up for myself. Made a woman cry. Never a good day when you make a woman cry.

I turned to the packed diner, hands on my hips. "I was just traveling through town with my assistant—with Henry. We were exploring your little demonic cave when he drowned there. I have no idea what is in your pool that would make three people disappear. I'd like to know, too."

I brushed crumbs out of my beard. "What your town fathers failed to research was that the one they now called on to check this all out—me—is in fact, just a professor of agriculture at the University of Nebraska in Lincoln." I growled again—felt good. "I'm not even a hydrologist. He studies water." I pounded my chest—a little dramatic, I admit. "I study ... dirt!"

One man snickered.

I pointed directly at the man. "Exactly. I study dirt and how to make things grow." I took my wallet from my back pocket and slipped a card out. "Here are my credentials." I even waved the card in front of Snicker man's face and a few others, including the waitress as she poured coffee. "See? What's it say on this University Staff card?"

The waitress leaned in to read the card, dripping steaming coffee onto a huge man in open-air overalls; the sides flapped open to reveal his fat belly. "Professor of Agriculture," she said.

"Hey! That's hot!" The man rubbed his hand. "Watch it!"

Either she was oblivious to burning a customer or didn't care. She nodded to the people in the diner. "That's what it says, all right."

"So in your estimation, does a Professor of Agriculture—meaning a guy who teaches about dirt and seeds?" I hesitated and thought a minute. "Crops and growing things." I took a breath, hoping to gain the sympathy of a few farmers. "Does what I do have anything to do with a pool that magically swallows people and doesn't let us find them to bury them?"

"Yes. Yes, it does." A woman, sharing a booth with a simply dressed man, spoke up. "It does." She swallowed, never made eye contact and never stopped stirring her coffee. "We have enough goin' on here with farmin' so bad." She looked around the diner, then her eyes pierced mine. "Have you ever been in a dust storm, Mr. Professor? You ever been in dust so thick you can't breathe?" Her eyes welled up. "And Mr. Professor … why, with this drought, would a pool be filled with water?" She jumped from the booth and pushed past me, her hands covering her mouth. Sobbing.

Present Day ~ Michael hovered between Clarence in the shower and Mr. Wainwright's room.

The demon in Mr. Wainwright was stirring. It must sense that the body it inhabited was not the best choice for taking over Hillcrest … or the world, if it got that far. The old, wrinkled and badly aged body was close to shutting down. And look out Hillcrest when that happened.

That was a tough moment for an angel.

If humans only knew.

Clarence turned off the water in the shower, unaware of Michael's presence.

Michael chuckled as Clarence spewed a few choice words. Must be tough to dry off, dress, and stay standing—all with an injured leg.

Clarence was very sturdy, normally, and had kept strong and active in prison, shaming younger men when he ran on the treadmill or outside in the enclosed courtyard.

Lisha stopped by the door and listened. She shook her head and chuckled when Clarence erupted with a few more words. "Musta dropped his sock." She tried the doorknob, then knocked. "You okay in there, Mr. Clarence?"

"How the hell do you think I am? My leg hurts. I'm in a nursing home." Pause. "And I dropped my sock in the water."

Michael smiled. Goofy man. Goofy, goofy man. Been through some stuff, that's for sure. Only Father knew the outcome of this man's life.

Michael always had known kids and animals could see him. But why Clarence? This guy was not pure in heart. Not anymore.

"Well, pick up your sock then, Mr. Clarence." Lisha faked a sob and rattled the doorknob. "I can't hep you if you don't unlock this door."

"You don't care," Clarence said. "I just hurt my leg."

She patted her hefty chest. "Oh, be still my heart. I'm cryin for you. It's not broken—you're just saying that to get sym-path-y." She pounded on the door. "Now open this door, or I can't hep you!" She reached in her pocket and drew out a key just as the door opened.

Clarence stood in the doorway, hair plastered against his head, his favorite Led Zeppelin T-shirt on backwards. The plastic bag from his leg was on the wet floor beside the wheelchair.

A young high school med aide, Tandy, walked by carrying a glass of juice.

"If that's fo Mr. Wainwright, you're gonna need a straw." Lisha took the damp towels from Clarence.

Tandy smirked and drew a straw from her pocket. "Oh. One of these?"

Lisha squinted. "Little Miss Smarty Pants."

"Well, at least I'm little." Tandy bumped up her hip in imitation of Lisha.

Clarence chuckled. "Wonder where she learned that." He bumped up his hip, holding onto the grab bar to keep his balance.

Lisha backed up. Her eyes popped so big there was white all around the iris.

Clarence sat in his wheelchair. "Michael. Here it comes." He covered his face. "Thar she blows!"

Michael couldn't help himself. Laughter bubbled up from his gut and burst out his mouth.

"I've never heard you laugh before, Michael." Clarence chuckled. "You should do it more often."

Michael laughed again. "I'd just get you in trouble."

"Who's Michael?" Tandy swiveled on her heel. "Who laughed just now?" Goosebumps dotted her arms. The straw sailed to the floor.

"Aw. Are you scared Little Miss Smarty Pants?" Lisha patted her back with an extra push toward Mr. Wainwright's room.

Tandy stumbled, but righted herself. "I'm going to report you Lisha. You'll be sorry you pushed me." She picked up the straw.

"Oh, I'm scared o you." She turned to Clarence. "Come on Mr. Clarence. Let's get you to your room, so's you can lay down."

Michael stood in the hall between Clarence's door and Mr. Wainwright's. He watched Lisha help Clarence to his bed and at the same time he could see Tandy drop the straw into the juice and hold it to Mr. Wainwright's mouth.

Keys jingled from down the hall. The maintenance guy stopped and checked his clipboard. He circled something on the paper and entered Mr. Wainwright's room. "Here to check the blinds."

Tandy glanced up and grinned. "Really? He has been complaining that they're broken."

The maintenance guy shook his head. "Ha. Ha."

She focused on Mr. Wainwright. "Here Mr. Wainwright. Take a sip of juice." She sighed. "So sad." She dripped some onto his lips. "Bet he can't even taste this."

"Bet he can't even hear you." The maintenance guy tapped the window, pulled the blinds up and down. "Seem okay to me." He checked it off his list. "You're Tandy, aren't you?"

"That's what the name tag says." She stuck her tongue out. She read his, wrinkling her nose. "Carl. Somebody must have hated you to name you Carl."

"Hey! I like my name." He checked the chest of drawers and pulled the top drawer open, digging through the contents with his pen. He hooked a gold pocket watch and pulled it out, the chain entangling with a string. "Jackpot." He slipped it into his pocket.

Mr. Wainwright's eyes moved as Michael drew near the door to his room. He began gurgling and spitting the instant he saw Michael.

Carl pulled the watch out. "Think he knows?"

Tandy shook her head. "Naw. He'll never know. He's almost dead anyway. I heard the nurses talking about him. They can't figure out what's keeping him alive."

Carl dropped the watch back into his pocket and fished around in the drawer again.

Michael entered the room.

Carl looked up. "You feel something? Something just changed in here."

"Well yeah, stupid." Tandy wiped her hand on a tissue. "I just felt something. He just spit on my hand."

"What's going on with that guy?" Carl tried to follow where Mr. Wainwright's eyes went. "It's like he can see something." He flopped the clipboard against his hip. "There's nothing there."

Michael stood next to the bed.

The demon rose up from the upper part of the body and glared at Michael. "You leave them alone. They're my new recruits and you can't have them. They have a flair for the boss's ways."

Michael stood his ground. "Father has a claim on them and no matter what you do, they are His."

Tandy froze. "What did you say?" She stepped away from the bed.

"Nothing. I didn't say anything." Carl patted his shirt pocket.

"They are mine!" The demon roared. Mr. Wainwright's body heaved several inches off the bed with the force.

Michael slowly shook his head.

"Mine!"

Carl shuddered. "What? What's going on here?"

Tandy shivered and dropped the juice. "Did … did you see that?" The glass bounced off the vinyl flooring, and juice splattered against the wall. She ran from the room.

Carl followed her.

Lisha rushed to the hall. "What's going on here? What's all the ruckus?"

"He's … he's possessed." Tandy threw the straw and ran.

Michael calmly walked from the room and stood beside Lisha.

She took a deep breath and entered Clarence's room, hung up the towel and checked her list. "I don't know why, Mr. Clarence, but when I'm with you I want to smack you on the forehead, but then I want to hug you."

"Don't you smack *me*. I'll smack you right back." He glanced at Michael. "Besides, Michael is here, and he'll get you if you hurt me. Right Michael?" Clarence crossed his arms.

"Oh, really. Well, you tell your Michael that I'll smack whoever I wanna smack." She poked the air, unknowingly stabbing Michael in the ribs.

"Tell him yourself. You're tickling him right now," Clarence said.

She poked Michael again. "Ha. Ha."

Michael laughed.

Taking a step back, Lisha's eyes grew huge. "You weren't laughing." She checked the room, patting her chest. "And I wasn't, either." Poking Michael again. "Then who was? There's nobody here but you and me."

Michael patted her shoulder. "You're doing a great job, Lisha, taking care of these people. Especially Mr. Clarence."

Lisha teared up and listened. "Did you … ?" She sucked in a ragged breath. "Right now I feel like I did when my big brother was alive and he told me I was bein' a good girl. Atta girl time. How?"

Clarence glanced from Lisha to Michael.

Michael nodded.

Back to Lisha. "Well. Maybe you did get an atta girl. But from M-Michael."

NINE

June 12, 1937 ~ Dr. Steven's Journal ~ I watched the woman through the window as she ran to a pickup truck. She hopped inside, and slammed the door.

Oh no.

"Was that? Was she family of one of the … ?"

The man who had been sitting with her slowly stood and turned to face me. He towered over me and I'm very tall and lanky. He walked right up to me and stopped, his chin at the top of my head.

"Our son drowned in that pool." His Adam's apple bobbed up and down. His jaw flexed. He stabbed me in the chest with his skinny finger.

I stepped back with each stab, until I was backed into a table.

"And I don't care if you deliver babies, I want you to find my boy … er … find out what happened to him down there." His feet were planted at fighting stance as he talked. His fists clenched. Then he pointed to the truck outside. The woman must have been hiding on the seat, but she could still be heard.

I swallowed and straightened—pulled myself up to as much height as I could muster—still only eyeball to buttons on the man's shirt. I glanced at the truck, then up at the man in front of me.

One-by-one, I met eyes with each person now standing, surrounding the man. Every eye was upon me. This was one community I didn't want to disappoint. The atmosphere was sparking. Emotions stabbed little arrows toward me from each person in the diner, making goosebumps rise on my skin.

I couldn't blame them.

I grabbed my straw hat from the bench seat. "I'll try to find the boy. But just so we're clear on one thing—I don't know anything about doing this and I can't promise anything. I can't promise I'll find his … him. I can't promise anything." I adjusted the toothpick in my hat band. "Are we clear?"

The man relaxed and lowered his fists, nodding. "Clear."

The people gathering behind him all nodded.

"Clear."

"Agreed."

A small-boned woman waved her hand from in back of the crowd. They parted. She was standing on a bench seat. "Just one thing, sir. If I may."

I nodded. "Yes, Ma'am."

She stepped onto the floor and walked toward me. "My sister drowned in that pool, too." She blinked away tears. "Could you find her too?"

I blew out a breath and stared at her, then glanced outside toward the truck. I slowly nodded with each word. "I'll do my best." I breathed deeply. "I just may die trying, but I'll … I'll do … we'll do what we can."

Present Day ~ Clarence woke. Prison didn't allow naps unless an inmate was sick. He was in trouble … but wait. This wasn't prison. This was the old people's home. There was his calendar proclaiming Hillcrest Homes. Must have been sleeping hard, because he felt like he was trapped inside a prison cell. Time to get … he groaned. Leg. Ow.

Stupid to hurt it. Stupid to go in that cave. What had he been thinking? He was not a sixty-year-old man anymore.

He would stay in his room. Stay in bed.

Die.

He slowly rolled over, away from the wall, pulling on the restraining bars. "I hope this heals fast. They should have cut off the damn leg." He rubbed his eyes.

"Hello, Clarence." A raspy voice greeted him from across the room.

Clarence's eyes popped open. Heat burned up his torso. He shuddered as every nerve in his body screamed "run."

Mr. Wainwright stared back at him from the love seat. Grinning. Black eyes snapping. He tossed out a candy bar. "Three Musketeer? It'll help get your mind off your poor leg. Sorry you hurt it, but you need to learn to keep your nose … and your leg … out of other people's business."

"C-Carol?" Clarence raised up and tried to swing his leg around to the floor, but got nowhere. "Ow! Carol!" He focused on the man dressed in all black across from him. "Get out! Get out of my room!"

Carol rushed in. "What? What on earth is the matter? Why are you yelling?"

"Get this bastard out of my … " Only Mr. Wainwright wasn't there. "He's … Mr. Wainwright was just here. Check the bathroom. Probably shitting in my … or my closet."

"Clarence, you've been through a trauma and you're getting all mixed up."

"I am not! Look. Look! He left a candy bar. Three Musketeers. He asked if I wanted one. And he threw it at me."

Carol teased him. "Mr. Wainwright can't blink an eye by himself, so how could he come into your room and leave you a candy bar?"

He tried to sit up. "Oh. Ow."

She helped him roll to a sitting position. "I've got a pain pill for you."

"No. I don't want one." He rubbed his head, his fingers through his hair. "I swear he was here. Just like before." He looked her in the eye. "You don't believe me, do you."

She chuckled. "Well. It's hard when he *is* right in the next room, pretty much comatose. He hasn't spoken or moved on his own since he was admitted."

"He moved his eyes and spit at Michael."

"He did spit … at Michael. He got his pink Tylenol all over my hand. I give you that." She eased onto the love seat. "But Clarence, it's impossible for him to be in your room."

"He sat, right where you are right now." Clarence searched the bed for the candy. "Here." He held up the candy bar. "Here we go. Evidence that he was here. Where would I get a candy bar?"

"The candy machine down at the nurses station." Carol shook her head. "Clarence." She frowned. "Ever since you were admitted, I knew we would be friends. Do I like all the residents? Of course. Some … more than others. But I knew you and I would be friends."

"We *are* friends." Clarence flipped the candy over and over. "And I know this is weird. Crazy. But … why would I make this up?"

Silence.

She pressed her lips together. "I don't know." Shook her head. "I don't know. Let's just go on from here. Deal with what's in front of us." She pointed. "Like your leg. I was on my way with a pain pill, when I heard you yell my name."

"I don't want any pills."

"It'll help you this first few days so you can relax instead of tensing up. It's hurts more when you're tense." She dumped a pill into the palm of his hand. "Hey. The burn scars on your hands aren't as red. Getting better."

He tossed the pill in his mouth and gulped down water. "No more after this. I'll see how I am without it."

"You're just like Joe. He never wanted to take any meds. This is just to get you through the next few days." She nodded. "Okay?"

"Just a couple days." He dropped the candy bar onto the bedside table. "How is husband Joe doing?"

"Same. The same." She fiddled with the paper med cup in her hand, then looked up at Clarence.

"Rough, huh." He nodded.

Her eyes welled up and she nodded.

She perked up. "Remember when the hawk broke into your room?" She looked out the window. "You were holing up then, too. I don't think you're supposed to stay in your room. You need to get out of here everyday, or hawks … and neighbors break in." She smiled.

He chuckled and nodded. "That was some big bird. Wish we could have kept him."

Mrs. Hatly toddled by the open doorway with her walker and winked. Oh she's cute. A sparkly pin accented her white blouse and a pink ribbon headband, matching her sweater, held back her shoulder-length gray hair. But her brown eyes. Always twinkly. "Is this a good time to visit?"

Carol jumped up. "Of course it is."

Lisha followed Mrs. Hatly carrying a tray of cookies and coffee. She placed it on the side table and pulled it closer to the bed.

Oh-oh. He'd been railroaded. By three ladies. What a way to go.

Carol excused herself and Lisha served them with finesse, her little brown pinkie at attention.

Mrs. Hatly giggled when Lisha handed her a cup of coffee.

Clarence's face burned. He picked up a cookie and nibbled it.

Mrs. Hatly broke hers and ate the bite.

He stole a look at her.

She giggled and closed her eyes.

She was a much better guest than Mr. Wainwright. She made him feel all gooey inside, but Mr. Wainwright made him downright terrified.

Clarence didn't say a word—just ate his cookies and dipped into his coffee. And peeked at her.

Every time he looked at her, she had her eyes closed and was smiling. Every once-in-a-while, she moved her lips, then took a bite of cookie.

Prettiest lady on the planet.

Later, Lisha peeked in. "Uh, sorry to break this up but time to get ready for bed." She helped Mrs. Hatly stand and gathered their dishes.

"Thank you, Lisha, for the coffee and cookies. Delicious."

"You're welcome, Mrs. Hatly. Want help going back to your room?"

"I can make it."

Clarence perked up. "I'd help you, but … "

"That's okay. I hope your leg gets better. You have a good night, Clarence. God willing, I'll see you in the morning."

"What do you mean, God willing?" He tossed the candy bar to the trash.

"Good shot." She pushed back her head band. "Well, some night one of us might slip into heaven." She pushed up her sleeves and started out the door. "Good night, Mr. Timmelsen."

He sat up straight. "Good night, Mrs. Hatly. I hope to see you tomorrow."

And she left.

What if she died over night?

That would break his heart.

TEN

June 15, 1937 ~ Dr. Steven's Journal ~ Poolside samples of water and soil. I dipped the glass test tube in the pool and waited for water to bubble in. This would be the sixth sample. Before I carefully placed it in the holder with the other five test tubes, I tapped it with a fingernail. There was something different about this water—almost luminescent. Beautiful rainbow of blues and greens. I glanced back at the pool.

Incredibly clear.

———

Present Day ~ Katty Randolph hit *enter*. Her fingers fumbled at the computer. How long would it take before she didn't want a fix?

She shivered. Would she ever?

Coffee didn't help. She was addicted to that, too.

Cartoons blasted from the TV.

"Bea! Turn that down!"

She stood too fast, and her chair caught on the torn vinyl. Crappy trailer house. The chair landed hard behind her, making her jump. Every cell shattered. Her skin crawled.

Bea didn't even hear it.

Katty stomped to the TV and turned it off. "You have been in front of this TV for hours. Go outside and play." Too loud. Louder than she meant.

Oh God.

Clarence had said this would be tougher than getting Bea away from her rotten dad.

"Mommy."

"I can do this. I can do this." Katty turned away and wiped her eyes.

"Are you crying, Mommy?" Bea's tiny fingers caressed Katty's leg —made her skin crawl.

The month in rehab had been terrible. No Bea. No drugs. No booze. But this: back to life, going to school, helping Clarence set up his legal firm.

God.

The trailer was a disaster. Toys. Too many toys.

She picked up a broken Barbie. Pieces of the latest fast food toy giveaway scattered under the sofa. Torn books. Food bits from when the neighbor kid—The Terror—had been over.

Trying to be the model mom. Play dates. Healthy treats. Not too much TV.

She flopped onto the couch, and odors of too many spilled drinks floated to her nostrils. Juice. Booze.

The couch wasn't the only thing that stunk.

Her life stunk.

How had she let Clarence talk her into this? Be his legal assistant?

Little fingers folded between her own. Dirty fingernails. Tiny fingers rubbed hers. Big brown eyes searched her own.

Precious. Precious.

Katty had never loved Bea more than when the effects of the drugs mostly wore off. For the first time she really saw her little girl. How could she have done all … treated her like …

She choked and drew Bea to her, onto her lap and breathed. This little piece of her. Yeah, of nasty Phil, too. Conceived in abuse and birthed alone.

But now Katty could see. Turn that horrible beginning for this child into something real and … meaningful.

God help me give her the love she deserves.

A tiny tear dropped onto their entwined fingers.

Bea looked up. "Mommy, you're crying again."

"I just love you so much." Katty wiped her face and snuggled deeper into Bea. "We're gonna make it. We're gonna be okay."

Bea gasped. "Mommy, the lights."

Katty raised her head. Tiny lights floated around them, dancing between them, on Bea's head.

Bea giggled. "There's one on your head. Two. Three. One's on your nose." She leaned away, staring into Katty's eyes. "They're in your eyes. Sparkles in your eyes."

Katty blinked. Don't move. Don't miss this. Were they … Clarence called them angels … had they been here all along? Had she just been too drunk to see?

Oh, precious, precious.

Bea snuggled into her and held out her hand. A bigger one lit there, shining, sparkling, soothing.

"Oh, God. Dear God. These lights are too beautiful to be from anywhere but You. I don't get it. I don't know if I'm going crazy … " She brushed back Bea's tangled hair. "But if you can see them, Baby Bea, then it's not a flashback or … withdrawal."

She leaned into the sofa and pulled the tattered quilt around them. "Homework can wait. That para-crap will wait."

"Mommy. Where's Clarence?" Bea pulled the quilt up under her chin.

"I don't know, Baby." She sighed. "At the nursing home, I guess. He doesn't run away from there so much anymore."

"We need to go see him."

"What? Right now?"

Bea looked out the window. "Yeah. Right now."

Katty snuggled Bea close. "Baby Bea. He's busy. And it's late. We can't just go." She pulled the quilt up under Bea's chin. "Why? What are you … thinking?"

The tiny lights reflected in Bea's deep brown eyes, flitting, stirring all around her head. She seemed unaware of their presence right now.

"Mommy. I see water. Clarence in water." She looked into Katty's eyes. "Is he swimming?"

ELEVEN

June 16, 1937 ~ Dr. Steven's Journal ~ The cave wasn't the most convenient place to complete my research, so I picked up the pan and climbed up the hill to the campsite. I had spent yesterday setting up a table, chair, and journals right outside the camper. Didn't have to worry about rain. I made my own equipment to suit my use and the test tube holder is one of many. A round pan with a flat lid was just deep enough to cover the test tubes in a wire rack. Just right for when I do field work.

Like at the devil pool.

Present day ~ Stop sign.

Oh. No.

Michael downshifted. Why could he not anticipate these stops until he was almost too late?

He came to a full stop and shifted down again. He should ask Father or another angel about stick shift trucks. He never could get the sequencing down. Clutch in. Brake on. Then shift. Oh wait. Wasn't it shift, then clutch?

Guess not.

Grinding.

Sigh. He was going to ruin this truck.

It wouldn't be so bad, except Clarence snickered every time he would grind the gears.

Like now.

Clarence had his hand over his mouth, but Michael knew he was laughing.

"Did you ever drive a stick shift?"

Silence.

"Well, did you?"

"I'm not saying." Clarence reached over and patted Michael's shoulder. "You're doing a great job grinding them gears ... for an angel." Clarence turned toward him. "Hey, isn't there some kind of magic you could use to help you find the gears?"

He had his hand over his mouth, but Michael could see him grinning. Good to get Clarence out again and see him laughing, even if it was at Michael's expense. Clarence tended to get depressed and shut everyone out, so when Michael had suggested they take a drive, using the excuse to look for pools, Clarence was ready to go.

Clarence wiped it away. "I mean. Well, not magic, that would be ... well, what if you prayed?"

Michael stuck his tongue out. Why humans? Why not dogs or cats. Or rabbits. Why humans?

Clutch.

Shift into second.

"Smooth." Clarence applauded. "That was smooth."

Face was getting hot. In the human world, that meant he was blushing. His face must be red. He glanced in the rear view mirror.

Yup.

Wait.

He looked in the mirror again.

Angels. A whole host of them.

One sitting between them.

What was that low rumble?

Michael sought Father.

The angel put out his hand and sword to stop.

Michael slowed and stopped.

Killed it.

"What?" Clarence straightened. "Why are we stopping in the middle of the road?" He had his finger following along each mile line. "Why did you stop?"

Michael ignored Clarence as he let himself seek Father's face.

Stop. Don't go any farther. Get out of the truck and back the way you came.

Michael opened his door. "Get out. Go back the way we came."

"Well, I don't see—"

"Now!" Michael stepped out. The angels surrounded him as he stepped backwards away from the truck. He looked over at Clarence, who was just getting out.

An angel swooped in beside Clarence, grabbed him and sent him flying past the truck's tail end, cane nowhere in sight. At the same instant, the front of the truck jerked down and forward, the ground sucking it down.

Michael scanned the area.

Tiny mice scattered in terror. One ran under the truck. Another skittered toward the hole. Wrong way.

Angels already on it.

A farmer sat on a tractor to the right of the road, just over the fence. It looked like he was backing to a long trailer stacked with irrigation pipe.

Michael had been so involved with grinding the gears, he had lost connection with the invisible world.

Always stay focused. He wanted to kick himself.

Too late now.

The truck shuddered as the ground opened in front of it.

An angel grabbed Clarence again and flew him farther back on the road. Clarence was screaming above the roar of the shifting ground.

Angels escorted Michael to the same place.

Dust settled and debris clattered to the ground. It seemed like hours, then it was quiet.

Clarence stopped coughing and pounded his chest.

Michael reached over to pat his back.

That wasn't Clarence.

Michael looked up to see a large man right beside him. Red in the face, sweat poured from under his ball hat, which read "If You Ate breakfast, Thank a Farmer."

The man hadn't seen Michael or Clarence. His eyes were glued to a spot just ahead, to the right of the truck.

Michael followed the man's gaze and gasped.

The tractor's exhaust pipe was sticking out above the surface of the ground. Nothing else was visible. No engine. No big tires. Just the exhaust pipe.

"Look at that." Clarence limped toward it.

Michael grabbed his arm. "Clarence, listen."

He stopped. "What is that? That rumble?"

The farmer's hand flew to his mouth. "My tractor!"

The ground roared and shook.

The tractor shifted. The exhaust pipe disappeared.

The farmer screamed. "My tractor! I just got it yesterday." He sobbed and shuddered. He started toward the hole.

Michael tackled him. "Sir, you could have been down that hole with it. You are alive."

Clarence was trembling. "Right. You could be dead! You can get another tractor."

"A hole swallowed it." He moaned. "I don't have insurance for a hole! For some monster that swallows tractors!"

Both Clarence and Michael patted his huge shoulders. "Sir, you are going to be okay."

The man's stomach growled. "My lunch! My lunch was in that tractor. My lunch was eaten by a hole!" He fell down in a fit. He pounded the ground.

Michael watched as his own truck shook and shuddered. In a way, he wouldn't mind if …

Silence.

Pop!

The whole section of ground gave way, sending his truck to the same grave as the tractor. Right under his own sinking feet—

Angels swooped in, scooped up the farmer and Clarence.

Michael jumped into one angel's arms, grinning. They landed on level ground. Michael's angel dusted him off, making a show of it. "You okay, Sir? You shouldn't get dirty." Hard slap on the back.

Michael coughed and leaned over, hands on his knees.

"You okay, Michael?" Clarence hollered.

Michael waved. "Yeah. I'm fine." Head back down and speaking so only the angel could hear. "I just need to wrestle down a pigheaded angel, that's all." He kicked behind him, tripping the angel, who flew out of the earth's atmosphere.

Another angel butted him from behind, sending Michael headlong into the dirt.

"Michael!" Clarence started up the incline. "You okay? Did you hit your head?"

Michael wiped the grin off his face. "Naw. I'm fine. I'll be right there."

As soon as Clarence walked over and peered in the hole, Michael turned and slammed his fist into another angel's chest, sending him flying into the physical realm, visible to anyone human. His laughter echoed between the hills.

Clarence turned again. "Was that you laughing?"

Michael started toward him. "Naw. I think it was a bird or something. Some scared animal. Must have been startled by the sink hole."

The angel rushed Michael from behind and pinned his arms across his chest, so it looked like Michael was just standing, his arms crossed. He was able to hold his ground, tottering to a standstill.

"Hey, sorry about your truck, Michael." Clarence glanced behind him at the hole.

"It's okay. It might be okay, if we can just get it out somehow." Michael broke free, sending another angel tumbling through the atmosphere. His deep laugh rumbled across both dimensions.

Clarence jumped and grabbed the farmer's shoulder for balance. "Whoa! Watch out. Here comes another landslide!"

An alert resounded through the invisible realm, and the host of angels saluted Michael. "Got to go. Good to rumble with you Brother. God keep you." The angel sped off, along with others. A trail of lightning sparks followed them.

"Michael, did you hear that?" Clarence shielded his eyes from the sun. "Such a strange day. Thunder. And not a cloud in the sky. Weird stuff."

Michael picked his way to where Clarence and the farmer stood. "Yeah. Was that lightning just now? Maybe the sink holes are caused by lightning strikes. Or thunder. I didn't hear any, though." He patted the farmer's back. "Sorry about your tractor, Mr. … "

The farmer seemed in a daze. "Mr. … Gustafson. Merle Gustafson." He fished his cell phone out of his pocket and stepped away. "Hello, Mabel? Call our insurance … "

An angel flew over, slowed and gently placed Clarence's cane on the ground in front of him.

"Michael!" Clarence pointed at it. "Did you see that? My cane just appeared."

Michael grinned as he bent to pick it up. "Well, miracles do happen."

Clarence took the cane, examined it. "I got my cane back, but I'm afraid your truck is a goner. It bashed into the tractor." Clarence shook his head. "I'm not sure what kind of a crane could ever pull them out." He patted Michael. "Sorry."

Michael tried to feel disappointed. "Well, I'll just have to start looking for another one, I guess." He nodded at the farmer.

This time it would be an automatic.

TWELVE

June 17, 1937—The Osceola Times: "Famed and notorious Archeologist and Professor of Agriculture, Dr. Walter Stevens' assistant drowned yesterday in a freak accident. It seems his assistant Henry Green, fell into a pool in a cave they were studying near the Gospel Ridge Road. He sucked in the putrid waters from the pool as he succumbed to the pool's clutches. Upon interviewing Dr. Stevens, he said he reached for Mr. Green, and had hold of his hand, when Mr. Green pushed away. Dr. Stevens warns all, "Don't go near that pool. You won't come back." Mr. Green's head went under again and Dr. Stevens grabbed for his hair and his ear. According to Dr. Stevens, "It was the strangest thing. I had hold of him. But he pushed my hand away. Maybe it was just a fish." Since there is no body to bury, members of the community will hold a bar-side service next Thursday, the 24th of June, for Mr. Henry Green at 6 p.m., giving all attendees time to celebrate his life thereafter."

I let the article flutter to the table and shook my head. My stomach growled, reminding me I hadn't eaten in two days. How can someone forget to eat?

Back to the article. Nice of the community. Seemed a nice reason to throw a drinking binge. Henry would have liked that.

I wanted to run, or drive, as far away from Osceola as I could get, but I knew I couldn't. Either I find Henry or the secret to this pool.

Or both.

Present Day ~ Noell clicked her nails on the washer as water poured down on her *new* clothes. That was always funny to her: they had to be years old, not just months, but had never been worn. New. Old.

She chuckled as she slammed the lid and checked the settings. They were just overalls and T-shirts, so normal setting should work.

She glanced at the boots sitting on the side chair. Pink. That made her chuckle. Oh, she'd get teased. She didn't even know the other employees, but she had a feeling they'd laugh.

She examined one. They were really well made boots. Worth a couple of hundred dollars, at least. Smelled new—a musty sort of new. Stitching was perfect. The sole had never touched ground. No dirt. No dust. No dog poop!

No skin cells from someone else's foot to make her go crazy with voices and pictures of that person's demented life. It had taken repeated sprays with cleanser and rubbing with a towel to clean the boots she wore now. The only voice she heard when she put them on was hers. Which wasn't all that great either.

She shook off her slipper and gingerly pushed her foot inside the boot. Felt okay. She wiggled her toes. Plenty of room, even if she had on thicker socks for winter.

Huh. She started to flip off her other slipper when Gamma cried out from the porch.

Crash!

"Gam?"

She stopped and listened.

Louder this time. "Gamma?"

She dropped the other boot and ran. Clunk in the boot. Slide in the slipper.

Clunk. Slide.

She pushed open the porch door.

"Gamma! Gam? Where are you?"

Boxes were scattered all over one end of the room, in the aisle. Everything was in a shambles. The only thing she could see of Gamma was her walker and it was up-side-down.

"Gam!" Noel screamed and tried to dig herself toward the walker. One box fell on top of her and broke open, puking out fabrics in a rainbow of pastel colors. She tried to push it to the side but there was no place to put it.

"Gam?" Noell dug deeper. "Gam, are you okay?" She reached between two boxes, trying to fish for Gam's hair, her sweatshirt.

Hair. Gam's hair. Soft hair.

Noell was weeping now. "Gam? Answer if you can."

She somehow found the strength to leverage between two boxes and push one off, then lift the other.

She knelt. "Gam. I'm here."

She watched her chest.

"But you're not." Sob. "You're already gone."

Gamma's glasses were askew—half on and half off.

Noell took them and wiped the lenses on her T-shirt. Then eased them onto Gamma's face, careful around her ears and nose. She stroked Gam's cheek. A tear was there.

She checked Gam's chest again.

Gone.

Wiping her own face, she scanned the boxes broken open around them, until she saw fabric in Gamma's hand.

She gently pulled it from her fingers—still watching for signs of life.

None.

What was this fabric from? It was a dress. Just about her size now.

She tried to see what box it had come from.

They were all too tossed around.

She smelled the dress.

Oh God! Shouldn't have done that!

No. She had to stay with Gam.

No!

Gam's smells first. There was love, joy, then fear and grief.

Oh, Gam.

What was this dress from?

The smells took her deeper.

Deeper.

No.

The dream.

Mommy.

Mommy's hand reached out to her from the water. The dress fabric floated and billowed around Mommy's body.

Her eyes gleamed with a love that Noell had never seen in previous dreams.

Then Mommy drifted away. Her eyes never closed. Her hand always reached toward Noell.

"Mommy." Noell stretched her hand out. "Mommy, don't leave me."

Sobbing, Noell felt hands lift her from the water.

She turned to see Grampa, his eyes full of tears. "Grampa. Mommy."

She looked down at Mommy, only it was Gamma.

She looked up at Grampa.

But it was Fletch. He had tears in his eyes, too.

His hands gripped her arms, pulling her from the mess.

She stared into his wide eyes, until …

"Gam." She broke. "Gam's dead."

THIRTEEN

June 19, 1937 ~ Dr. Steven's Journal ~ The Pool. Good thing it was summer, because it was still chilly in the cave.

My heart was pounding. I am a good swimmer, but so was Henry. And maybe the woman who drowned was a swimmer also.

I sit and start to untie my leather boots.

I checked the knots in the heavy rope tied around my waist and followed it to where it stopped in the hands of the heavy-set man wearing the open-air overalls. The man nodded.

He had just shown up with the rope draped over his arms.

I nodded back and sucked in a deep breath. And blew it out. Sucked in another. And out. One more look at the man and I drew in a breath and stepped into the pool. There was no choice but to go in.

.

Present Day ~ Noell hesitated at the door.

Hillcrest Homes. Room number 204. That was the correct number. The name was right.

She glanced at the page from the phone book. The right address. A nursing home?

She glanced back down the hall. Wheelchairs. People snoozing. Walkers. Nurses.

A dark-skinned aide passed her. "Hey suga." She stopped. "You need somebody?" She checked the door. "Oh, you muss be at the wrong place." She turned full-on.

There was a lot of her.

"Um." Noell held up the page and pointed to the entry. "Clarence Timmelsen? A lawyer?" She shoved it into her purse and started down the hall. "I must be really messed up."

"No. That's him." The aide knocked on the door. "You might a messed up, but this is where he lives and laws." She pushed at the door. "Mr. Clarence. Someone to see you."

Only no one was in the room.

The woman knocked again. "Mr. Clarence? Where you at?" She checked the rooms. "Nobody home. Huh." She dropped her pen and notepad into her pocket. "I'll go chase him down. Be right back." She waved Noell into the room. "Jus go on in and sit a spell."

"It's okay?"

The woman's dreads bounced as she walked. "Sure. Go on in and sit down."

Noell almost chuckled. This woman chasing anybody down would be almost funny. She bit her lips so as not to laugh out loud as the woman barreled down the hall.

"Clarence?" The woman peeked into every room as she passed them. "You hiding, Mr. Clarence?"

Noell could still hear her, as she stepped into the room. It looked like an office. She turned and compared it with the bedroom across the hall. Definitely a bedroom. Back to his rooms—definitely an office with framed documents adding the credibility she needed to see. Probably could fake those, too.

Cute little girl in the balloon photo. The woman with her looked familiar. Must have seen her around town.

A yellowed newspaper clipping had been slipped in along the edge of the frame of one of the documents. She slung her backpack over her shoulder and skimmed the article. Huh.

Noell read it in a whisper. "It seems his assistant Henry Green, fell into a pool in a cave they were studying near the Gospel Ridge Road." A pool in Osceola? Who was Henry Green? Dr. Stevens seemed famous—for back then. 1937?

Katty gathered Bea into her arms. "I don't know if Clarence even knows how to swim." She breathed in Bea. So sweet. Even if she did need a bath. Something so fresh about her. "Shall we go see him? I'm sick of studying."

"I'm sick of studying too, Mommy. Let's go!" Bea jumped down and found her shoes. "Put my shoes on, Mommy."

Katty laughed. "Uh-uh. You can do it." She slipped on her sandals and grabbed her purse. She checked her face in the mirror. Fine wrinkles around her eyes and mouth—she was only twenty-four. Oh well. No make-up—they were just going to the nursing home. Most people there couldn't see.

Bea pulled on one boot and then the other.

Wrong feet.

"Do you really think you need boots Bea? It's summer." She pulled them off and found Bea's sandals and strapped them on. "Ready?"

Bea raced to the door, then back to her drawings. "I need to take this to Clarence. He needs a new drawing."

Katty smiled. "He sure does." There were only five hanging on his wall, right now.

She closed the door and locked it. Felt so secure with the new lock. Clarence had made sure it was safe. The new deck looked good, too. The planter dressed it up even more. She'd never had flowers before. She'd never had the money … before. Gulp. It had always gone for booze or cigarettes or … drugs.

"Mommy, come on. Clarence needs us."

Katty bent to pick a leaf of lavender. She pinched it and breathed it in. Best smell ever. She tucked the leaf into her pocket.

Bea jumped up the steps. "Mommy. I want one."

"Don't pull the plant out. Just take your thumbnail and cut one leaf off … like this." She showed Bea how.

Bea walked to the car sniffing it.

Noell read more of the article, until a man cleared his throat from the hall.

His loud voice made her jump. "Lisha, that you? Who wants to see me? I have an appointment … now."

The woman lumbered back to the doorway. "Where you been? I've been looking all over for you." She pointed to Noell. "Your appointment is here, and I ain't yo sec-re-tary."

"I was outside having a smoke."

Noell raised her eyebrows. This might not work.

The woman flicked his ear. "You don smoke, 'member?"

The door opened all the way, and a tall, rough-looking man stood before Noell in jeans and a black T-shirt with a yellow-plaid necktie, a splint on his leg. Graying hair slicked behind his ears and curled to his shoulders. A full beard was clipped close to his face. Bushy eyebrows arched above clear blue eyes. His skin wasn't even all that wrinkled.

"Are you Noell?" He held out his hand.

"Uh, yes." She dropped her sweater.

He limped and stooped to pick it up.

She reached for it, but he swung it into the room in welcome.

"Well," said the aide, "ya found Mr. Lawyer Man, and I have to give somebody a bath."

Noell hesitated.

"He's okay. He just looks scary. He's really a pussycat—right Mr. Clarence?" The aide chuckled and patted Noell on the shoulder.

Sanitizer. Sanitizer.

She held her breath.

The aide must have just washed her hands. Sometimes the vibes didn't flow through clothes. Whew.

"If he gets scary, or sum-thin, I'll be down the hall."

"Thanks … uh, Lisha." She automatically read the upside down name tag. Gamma always thought that was astounding.

Before Noell caught herself, she righted it.

She braced herself for voices or trembling.

Nothing. Huh.

"Oh, yeah. I caught it on a bed when I was tuckin' in the sheets." Lisha patted her chest. "Thanks."

"Come on in and … " Again, he waved her sweater into the room. "It's nothing fancy, but it's my little office. Sorry to make you wait."

She stared at the shirt and the tie. Then at him. Was she still in the wrong place?

His eyes followed hers to his tie. "Oh. Pardon me. A friend and I were just teasing about the fact that I should dress more professionally." He pulled the tie from his neck and wound it around the doorknob. "May I help you?"

She stared at his shirt. Led Zeppelin? "Are you Mr. Timmelsen? Clarence Timmelsen?" She glanced at the wall again. All of the certificates proclaimed "Clarence Timmelsen," so he had to be legitimate.

The sun was shining. Birds were pooping on Katty's car, so she guessed the bird kingdom was okay. The wind wasn't even blowing today. Beautiful day.

She buckled Bea into the car seat Clarence had bought for them. He really felt like a grandfather. She didn't even want to know if she had a real one or not. He'd probably be mean, just like her mom and dad had been. Why hadn't she seen before, how precious this little one was and that she was following exactly in the same path as her parents had— cruelty, abuse, addictions, rape, incest? She blinked back tears so Bea wouldn't see. The drugs and alcohol had masked her wounded soul. Now, though it was painful, she was determined to bust through and face it all. No masks.

Even Clarence was gruff sometimes because of what he had been through, but he melted when Bea walked into his rooms.

The parking lot at Hillcrest was full. She had to park farther away. Sometimes resident families needed to be closer to the door. There had been a day that she wouldn't have thought about that. About what other people needed.

So much had changed since she had become sober.

What hadn't changed was that Bea could unbuckle her car seat in two seconds flat. She always beat. Car seats were supposed to be child-proof. Little Houdini.

"Bea. Wait! Don't get out. You are so short, other people can't see you and if you run out—"

She ran out.

"Bea! Stop!"

Bea finally did stop but not before a small pickup had to slam on the brakes to avoid hitting her.

"Bea!" Katty grabbed her hand and yanked her back. "You almost got hit!" Her hand was at Bea's backside, ready to …

Bea's face crumpled and she shrank from Katty. "I'm sorry, Mommy. I just want to see Clarence."

"I know. But you wouldn't see him if you were dead, right?" Some days with this child about did her in. It didn't help that today of all days, she woke with a splitting headache. When would this be better? She wanted a fix so bad. Just one drink.

A med aide walked past on her way to her car. "Gonna have to tie that kid up. She's always running ahead, huh."

Bea clung to Katty.

"No, not tie her up. Just make her mind." Katty picked up Bea and marched across the parking lot to the entrance and put her down. "I won't tie you up, but I will make sure you mind. You are so fast! That truck could have hit you!"

Bea snuggled into Katty's neck. "I'm sorry Mommy." She placed her little hands against Katty's cheeks and turned her head. Face to face. Nose to nose. "I'm sorry Mommy." She looked deep into Katty's eyes.

They forgot about the world or anyone else around them and connected. Katty had never let anyone look into her soul that deeply.

But here was her own four-year-old daughter doing just that. Deep sigh.

"Excuse me." A lady toting two beautiful bouquets, pressed the automatic door plate with her elbow.

Katty jumped and stepped aside. "Oh, sorry. We were just … I'm sorry."

"Don't stop that huggy-huggy stuff for me." She grinned at them on the other side of the now-closed-door and made a face at Bea—her eyes crossed and mouth wide.

"Yes. Please come in." Clarence pulled a chair closer to the desk and sat in the other one, propping his leg up on an open desk drawer. "Have a seat. Um, would you like something to drink? We have pop, coffee—"

"No thanks." The seat appeared worn, but not dirty. She sat, hugging the folder to her chest. What was she doing here? She should have gone downtown to another law office. She didn't have a clue. That's what yellow pages were for.

He sat back in his chair. "You were reading my wall of frames. I hope it all looks satisfactory to you."

Noell looked at the wall again. "Yes, it does. Cute little girl." The newspaper clipping fanned in the airflow, catching her eye again. "Interesting article."

His eyes roamed over the frames. "Article?" Found it. "Oh, yes. Quite a perplexing thing. Poor Henry Green. I wish we had more information, but I'm just beginning to search it out." He patted his leg. "That's how I hurt my leg."

She cringed. "Is it going to be okay?"

"Oh, sure. It's better everyday." He folded his hands in his lap. "Well, what brings you here today, Noell?"

Tears threatened again. No. He'd offer some old dirty handkerchief, or Kleenex from a dusty box. She couldn't cry here. She swallowed. "My name is Noell Carpenter."

He held out his hand. Thick fingers. Spiky white hairs grew from between each knuckle. Long fingernails. Like Grampa's.

Gah. Her insides turned to jelly.

She stared, then slowly placed hers in his.

Breathe.

Her vision exploded with pictures of hammers, saws and sawdust. Old cars drove on somewhat familiar streets. Signs on buildings looked like ones from the antique shop. A younger version of the man before her embracing a beautiful young woman. An awful car crash. Pictures of a prison—lines of inmates dressed alike in orange and a terrified Mr. Timmelsen backed against a wall. She cringed, and just as she was about to run out the door, she saw him walk into the town as it was now.

She jerked her hand from his and scooted away.

"Are you okay? You look like you just saw a ghost. I know I'm old and scary, but usually people just want to slap me or kick me, not shy away."

Words wouldn't come out. She started to stand to leave, but saw her sweater hanging on the back of his chair. "It's just me. I … uh … "

"It's okay. Is there something I can help you with?"

Lisha barged into the room. "You can hep me wit this plate o cookies and milk, thas what. And I want to slap you almost everyday." She balanced a tray with a plate of cookies and two tall glasses of milk. "Sometimes every minute." She stopped. "Lookit your messy desk. Now, how am I s'posed to set this down?"

Clarence pushed the boxes to the opposite edge of the desk. He brushed what appeared to be crumbs to the floor.

"Thas better." Lisha carefully placed the tray and gave Noell a napkin, patting it onto her lap, then offered the cookies.

Her stomach began to churn. "Um, no thank you."

"What?" Lisha stepped away, her hand on her hip. "What? You don't like cookies?" She looked down her nose at Clarence. "What is wrong with this gal, Mr. Clarence?" She carefully picked one up, holding her pinky in a salute, and placed it on the napkin on Noell's lap. "There. And here's your milk, so's you can reach it, in case you're a dipper." She backed away, hands on both hips.

Clarence held out a hand.

"Oh, you can git your own." She sauntered out the door.

"See how she is?" Clarence reached for the napkins and a cookie. He dipped his in a glass of milk and slurped a bite down. "Mmm." He looked over at Noell. "Aren't you going to eat yours? She'll be back and will make sure you do, so you might as well do it in peace."

Lisha's voice rang from the hallway. "I heard dat." A cart rattled past the open door.

He stood, limped to the door, using the wall for balance and shut it. "There. We might have some peace."

Noell stared at the glass of milk, then the cookie still on her lap.

Clarence licked a drip of milk from his finger.

She picked up her cookie and licked sweat from her upper lip.

He seemed to be taking a long time eating his.

She finally stowed her file behind her on the chair, scooted closer to the desk and picked up the glass. The cookie just fit. She dipped and took a nibble. Not bad. Another tiny bite. Chocolate chip. Her favorite. Gam's too.

A tear escaped her eye. She knew he was watching her. No pressure.

At the last bite, she almost regretted it was gone. She drank the cold milk, even sucked up cookie chunks and set the glass back on the desk, licking her lips. She folded the napkin and wiped her mouth.

"Better?"

She shrugged and half-smiled. Nodded. "Thanks."

Bea giggled as Katty set her down.

"Push the button, Bea." Katty made sure she had hold of Bea's other hand, before she ran into the building, possibly knocking a resident over. "Let's go see Clarence."

They pushed the automatic door button, Katty's mind still on the visual of that pickup almost hitting Bea. "Just remember. You are gonna stay in the car seat until I get you out from now on. No running ahead. Got it?"

Bea was distracted by the ice cream machine. "Mommy. Can I have some ice cream?"

Katty bent down to Bea, eye-to-eye. "Did you hear me? You have to stay buckled in until I unbuckle you. And no running ahead." Katty turned Bea's face toward hers. "Got it?"

"Got it." Bea danced beside the counter, almost bumping into Mrs. Hatley with her walker.

"Bea! Look out. You're going to knock her over."

Mrs. Hatley wasn't much bigger than Bea. She almost didn't need to bend to talk to Bea. "How are you sweetheart?" She touched Bea's cheek with her withered hand.

"Good." Bea's eyes never left the ice cream machine.

Mrs. Hatly giggled. "She wants ice cream." She looked up at Katty. "Can she?"

Katty shrugged. "I guess. She lives for it."

"Me too. And I live here. You'd think I'd be tired of it." Mrs. Hatly reached for a cone with a white wrapper and filled it expertly. "Here you go Little Bea."

Bea said thank you at the same time Katty said, "What do you say, Bea?"

"Are you having one Mrs. Hatly?" Katty took hers and licked.

"I've had mine for today. Goes great with breakfast." She patted Bea's head. "Heading to see Clarence?"

Bea started to dance. "Mommy can I go?"

Katty took her arm. "Slow down or you'll spill your ice cream cone. And walk." Down the hall were several residents in wheelchairs and walkers. Using canes or holding onto the railing. "No running. Got it?"

"Got it." Bea skipped until Katty caught up with her. She stopped and jumped up and rotated. "Bye, Mrs. Hatly. Thanks for the ice cream."

Mrs. Hatly laughed and waved. "Bye, Dear."

Bea stuck her head in Harold's door and ran to him, almost dumping the ice cream cone down his shirt.

"Whoa Little Bea!" He hugged her. "Can I have a lick?"

She held it to his mouth. "Sure. Here."

He laughed. "No. I just had one. You eat it. I was just kidding." He set her on the floor again. "Beside I can have one anytime I want." He patted his gut. "And I don't really need anymore."

Katty rounded up Bea. "See ya Harold."

He waved. "Bye, you two."

"By Harad." Bea blew him a kiss.

He caught it with his hand and blew her one back.

Katty sighed. People here had Bea so spoiled. Guess it wasn't a bad thing. She looked down the hall behind them. Every person who could see her, were all watching Bea. And every one of them had a huge grin on their face.

She looked ahead of her at Bea, skipping and dripping ice cream on the newly replaced carpet. Touching everyone. She was chatting with one woman who had no idea who *anyone* was, much less this tiny munchkin, who made even *her* smile a toothless grin.

Something so rich came over Katty at that moment.

What if Clarence hadn't shown up in the park that day? What if his big hands hadn't picked Bea up and away from Katty? Katty had already scratched and clawed Bea by then. What if he hadn't intervened and sat Katty down on that park bench and firmly gotten in her face about her addictions and parenting habits?

Her eyes filled with tears as she watched Bea jabber to the staff. She knew no stranger.

"So tell me why you're here, Noell." He took out a small yellow legal pad and clicked his pen open.

She sat, drew in a deep breath and opened the file. "This is my grandma's." She hesitated. Sobs threatened. Another tear slid down her cheek.

A Kleenex box slid into view under her chin. There was Grandpa's hand again, only attached to Clarence's arm instead. She followed the hand up the arm and the arm to the face.

There was gentleness there. And heart. For her.

He might be rough looking, but …

The tears gushed. Sobs. She pulled one Kleenex after another, until the sobs dwindled and there was a pile of smashed, balled-up tissues on the floor.

"Oh, I'm sorry. I'll get—"

He already had the trash can beside her, picking the mess up.

"Oh, God. Let me. That's nasty." Sobs erupted again. "I'm so sorry."

He tucked the Kleenex box beside her on the chair and positioned the trash can beside her.

"You-you picked up my snotty … " Hiccup.

He looked at his hands and nodded.

Ropy scars lined the insides of both hands.

"Your hands." Before she thought, she gently touched them. "Oh my." Aware of how close she was to him, she pulled back. But not before he clasped her hand in his.

Flashes of a tiny girl. He was holding a tiny girl in his arms with such love and completeness.

Oh, this was not going to work. This was too much. How could she sit here and every other minute want to burst into tears?

He held out his other hand for the file and released her hand.

Biting her lips together, she handed it over.

He opened the file, flipped through the contents—death certificate, funeral cost estimates, the deed to the house. Thank God for that lockbox—Gamma had kept everything she might ever need in a heartbeat, in there. She hoped it was all there, because going through the whole house to find one small document would take at least three years.

"So, this was your grandma, Gwendolyn Randolph Carpenter?"

Noell nodded. "Excuse me." She skirted into the bathroom with the Kleenex box under her arm and blew her nose. Yuck. She washed her hands and sat back down. "Yes."

"And she just passed away I see … five days ago. You've had the service?"

She shook her head. "Tomorrow." People talked about closure when they had a service for their loved ones. There would be no closure. Some lady she didn't know would sing a song. A preacher would preach about someone he had never known. They'd had to put it off till now to give her a chance to find all the right documents.

"What was the cause of death? Says here on the coroner's report she fell?"

Noell fidgeted with the box of tissues. Deep breath. "She did, but she was knocked down by falling boxes." She looked up at Clarence. "Lots of boxes. That's why if there is something else you need, I might never find it."

He shot her a rueful smile. "Kind of a hoarder, was she?"

"Yes. Not kind-of."

"I see." He clicked on his computer and started a search. "Looks like she owned the house and property free and clear. I'll need to go to the courthouse and take care of all the proceedings, but I think it looks pretty easy to transfer it all to you. Do you have an ID with you?"

Noell fished it out of her purse.

Looks good. It all looks good, Noell. I think it should be pretty easy. There are no other siblings or relatives that would have a right to this property?"

"None that I know of."

"Okay, well, I'll get on it. I'm assuming you just want to put the property into your name so you can live there and assume rightful ownership?"

"I guess. I'm not sure I want to live there, though." Actually, she wasn't sure she could bear it at all. "It's … well, pretty full of stuff." Including memories—thousands per square inch.

"Maybe at a certain point you might want to have a sale."

She cocked her head. "Maybe. I just don't know yet. I don't know how to do this."

He turned to her. "You need to give yourself some time to figure things out. Don't jump into anything too fast. You need to let yourself

... grieve, too." He seemed to drift away when he said that. "We all need to let things take their course in these matters."

"Okay."

Clarence closed the file and tapped it on the desk. "Do you want to check back in a day or two and I can let you know what I've come up with? Do you need any help at the house? I have a very large friend who is as trustworthy as God, who could help."

"Trustworthy as God?"

Clarence grinned. "Yes. As God. His name is Michael." He hesitated. "But, somedays, he seems ... to be busy, so we can't find him."

Odd. "Well, I guess I'm going to need the help if he isn't too expensive. And what does this cost?" She waved her hand over the file.

"Nothing."

She started to open her mouth but closed it. She shook her head. "Grandpa always said if it's free there's something wrong with it. Or something like that."

"I know. There's a saying like that." He leaned his elbows on his knees. "I'm just going to be honest with you." He glanced up at her then back to the floor. "I spent some time in prison. No, I spent sixty years in prison."

Bea laid her ice cream cone on a nearby counter. She hesitated beside a reclining wheelchair where a woman, sound asleep, snored with her mouth open.

Katty jumped. She could almost read Bea's mind. That stinker was going to climb on. She was torn between rescuing the poor woman or wiping up the ice cream—until a nurse held up her just-a-minute finger.

"She's okay. Let her be." The nurse watched from a foot or more away as Bea slowly climbed on up.

Bea kept a constant soft-voiced chatter to the woman as she settled on her lap. "It's okay, lady. I won't hurt you. You are okay. I only kill bad guys. I don't kill ladies. I'm a lady too, so I don't kill ladies." She sat ever so gently on the woman's lap.

The woman's eyes fluttered open and the first thing she saw was Bea's precious face.

Katty held her breath and stepped closer. Bea's face glowed. Her eyes were round and soft as she looked at the woman. Her hair curled around her head like a halo. Bea's whole head glowed.

Katty rotated. Where was that light coming from? There wasn't even a skylight above. She cupped her hand over her mouth.

The nurse still motioned for Katty not to interrupt, wiping her own eyes.

The old woman raised a fluttering hand and caressed Bea's cheek.

Bea leaned into it, placing her own hand against the woman's. "It's okay, lady. You're gonna see Jesus soon."

The woman's eyes grew large. A tear slipped down her cheek. She started babbling to Bea.

"I know. I know." Bea gently touched the woman's cheek with her other hand. "He's coming for you." She looked down at the wheelchair. "You won't need this in heaven." Bea's head popped up. "Can I have it? This looks like fun."

The woman bubbled with giggles. Spittle drooled out one corner of her mouth.

The nurse jumped to wipe it away but Bea beat her to it and wiped her hand on her shorts.

The woman cooed. In her own world she seemed to made sense.

Made sense to Bea too. Because Bea answered back in the same language.

By this time, two other staff members had gathered beside the nurse.

One was weeping.

The other took her phone out of her pocket and took a picture.

Holy moment.

Katty sighed. Oh if only Bea had that with Katty's own parents. She didn't even know where they were and that was fine. This was much better. This was pure.

And miraculous.

"What is going on here? Why is that child on my mother's lap?"

A stern, loud voice made them all jump.

A slender woman stomped up to the nurse. "What is she doing to her?" The woman was dressed in designer jeans and a soft black leather jacket, a leather purse slung over one shoulder.

The nurse jumped and gently lifted Bea off the woman.

The old woman protested. "No. No. No. NO!" She reached for Bea with her good arm. Her wrinkled face contorted in anguish. "No. No!"

"She shouldn't have been on her at all!" The woman started to slap Bea.

Katty jumped but the nurse moved faster.

The nurse lifted Bea to the other side of the woman's wheelchair, away from the daughter and let Bea kiss the old woman.

The woman hugged her, patted her back and kissed her. A toothless kiss was never so pure and lovely.

Bea patted her and spoke back to the woman, soothing her.

The woman babbled back, softer now.

Katty stepped beside the nurse and lifted Bea from her, careful to avoid the daughter.

The daughter seethed. "Children should never be allowed in here in the first place. Same thing for hospitals. No children allowed." She roughly caressed her mother's hand, avoiding her face. "That little girl needs a spanking."

"No. She deserves a medal. An award for reaching your mother, when none of us could ever get her to respond. She deserves a hug at least." The nurse stepped to Katty and hugged little Bea. "Thanks little one." She tucked a finger under Bea's chin. "You can come here anytime." She looked at the daughter. "Kid's are welcome here."

A cat strolled up and rubbed against the daughter's leg and meowed.

Bea scrambled from Katty's arms to pet it.

The daughter kicked at it—missed, and got Bea.

"Ow! She kicked me!" Bea bounced to the carpet, rubbed her arm and wailed.

The cat hissed and bit the daughter.

"Ow!" The daughter kicked at it again.

The nurse had anticipated the second kick and picked up the kitty, handing it to the aide next to her. She grabbed Bea and handed her to Katty. "Are you okay, sweetheart?"

"I'm going to talk to the board about this!" The woman turned the wheelchair around. "Maybe this nursing home doesn't need my dollars anymore." She stormed down the hall.

The old lady continued babbling and stretching to see Bea.

Bea started to cry as she was wheeled away.

"Stop!" The nurse grabbed Bea and caught up with the daughter. "Stop."

The old woman calmed down.

Bea stopped crying.

The nurse leaned Bea over so she could lay her head on the old woman's chest.

The old woman patted Bea's head, babbling and sobbing. "Love. Love. You."

Bea lifted her head. "I love you, too."

The daughter snarled. "Well, I never got that from her."

"Hmph." The nurse started back to Katty, Bea still in her arms. "Makes sense." She stood in front of Katty and started to hand over Bea.

Bea clung to her neck, hugging the nurse.

The nurse patted her back and kissed her cheek. "Thank you, Little Bea. You made Old Gloria's day. You made her life, just now." She set her down in front of Katty. "And you can come here anytime." She kissed her again.

Katty scooped up Bea and hugged her. "Baby Bea, I've never seen you do that before."

"It's because of Jesus and the little lights."

Noell froze. The pictures in her mind had been right. She shivered. Except for Mr. Grimes, it was the first time her visions had been confirmed.

Clarence checked her face. "I know. You're wondering if you should even be here in this room with me right now. Am I right?"

She couldn't move.

"Yup. Prison." He sat back. "And if I … well, things happened there." He swallowed. "Bad things. I was just a kid when I went in." He seemed to forget about her and disappeared into his memories. "Fights broke out." He jingled change in his pocket. "I killed a man."

She hugged her backpack on her lap. Held her breath.

"They kicked me out of prison to this nursing home. I was … no I still am, angry. At what life stole from me. Ask Sheriff Dennison— he'll tell you I was innocent." He rubbed his beard and clasped his hands together. "But since coming here, I have met some of the greatest people in the whole world. I haven't told anyone else this, but I know I'm here for a reason."

He shook his head. "I'm not religious, but there's something going on here and I have to do everything I can to find out what it is." He turned to her. "Make sense?"

She bit her lips again. And slowly shook her head.

He chuckled. "I know. It doesn't make sense. But even that black lady that brought us the cookies and milk?" He shook his head. "Ornery as she is, I know even she is helping me replace all I lost all those years. I'm not your regular lawyer either." He spread his hands across the front of his T-shirt. "Led Zeppelin."

Something like happiness connected her heart with her lips. He was kind of likable. In a weathered, hard sort-of-way.

"So … free." He tipped his head and faced her. "I don't know how long I have left on this earth, but there are things I still want to do. And one is help other people. No, keep others from having to go through what I went through. You're young. You have your whole life ahead of you. If I can somehow help you get where you need to be in life, even if it's just helping you with your grandma's estate, then why not?"

She locked eyes with him. Sincerity? Honesty? "Okay. Thanks. Thank you."

He stood and proceeded to wrap the rest of the cookies in a napkin. "You'd better take these, so Lisha doesn't hang us both for not eating them. Okay?" He held them out to her.

"They were really good."

"Especially in cold milk."

She nodded as she stuffed them in her purse, just as a knock came at the door.

Lisha popped in. "You two done wit my tray? You ate them all?"

"Yup! Thanks Lisha." Clarence held out his arm to Noell. "This is Noell and she will be coming here once in a while."

"Hi." Noell half-nodded.

Lisha laughed. "Yeah, I know I'm scary." She pointed at Clarence. "But he's the scary one. Never, I say, never take him seriously. He's all hot air."

Clarence shoved her out the door. "And to think I thought she was the enemy when I first moved here." He closed the door after her. "I was right."

Through the door: "I heard that."

Noell picked up her purse. She hesitated. "Um … who is the little girl?"

"Little girl?" He squinted.

Noell had never, ever pursued her visions, her pictures that opened up when people touched her, or when she touched a doorknob or their belongings. Ever.

Until now.

"When you shook my hand … before. When you touched mine, I saw … or I got a picture of a little girl in your arms. She had big brown eyes and kind of thin hair." Deep breath. She blinked. "She must love you very much, because she snuggled into your arms."

To her surprise, he teared up too. He shook his head, chin quivering. "That's my Little One. My Bea." He stepped to the wall with rows of frames and photographs. "Here she is with her mommy, Katty."

Noell stepped closer. Sweet. "She's so tiny. Really pretty. So's her mom. Where are they? Do they live here?"

"They do. Katty is in fact, going to school to be a paralegal, to work here with me." He grinned.

For the first time ever, she was glad she hadn't run out. "Wow. I hope I get to meet them someday."

"I'm sure you will, Noell."

Katty walked down the hall to Clarence's room, Bea's arms tight around her neck. "What? I can kind of understand Jesus. But the little lights?"

"Clarence!" Bea struggled to get down and ran to Clarence.

"Little One!" His deep voice rumbled as he reached out his arms and gathered her close. He smothered her in kisses, breathing deeply. "Oh I've missed you!"

"We were just here yesterday!"

"Oh, I know, but I need you everyday!" He held her away to look at her. "I need my Bea fix everyday! Did you grow?"

Bea giggled and went for the tape dispenser on his desk.

Katty shifted. "I need a fix everyday, but it's not exactly … "

He tilted his head and looked at her. "Tough day, Katty?"

"Everyday is tough." She shook her head. "Does it get any easier?"

"I admit I haven't had withdrawals, but I experienced them first-hand with many cell-mates over the years." He stood in front of her. Slowly he pulled her close, her head at his chest.

His after shave smelled like outside in the morning—fresh and restoring. She shuddered as she breathed him in. Her arms found their way around him, holding on tight. Before Clarence, she'd never had a hug that didn't require something in return.

"It's gonna be okay, Katty. You'll see. It always works out."

She nodded into his neck. Another deep breath. And another.

He slowly released her and held her at arms length.

Those eyes. So blue. The sky was the same color through the window behind him. She wiped her tears from his neck.

A young blond woman was standing behind the door.

Katty jumped. "Oh! I'm sorry. I didn't see you there. Sorry Clarence, we butted in on an appointment. I-I'll be all right."

"I know you will. But I needed that hug just as much as you did." He laughed. "Maybe more." He turned to the young woman and held his arm wide. "This is Noell. We've just been talking about what to do with her Gamma's things and how to settle her estate."

He put his arm around Katty's shoulders and faced Noell. "And this is Katty, my … assistant, my friend, my … daughter? Granddaughter?" He chuckled and reached for Bea. "And this is Bea, my little," he looked at Katty. "My little great-granddaughter." He put his arm around Katty. "This is my new family."

Wow.

Bea hugged him then stopped. "Were you in water? Did you take a bath?"

He chuckled. "Well, I took a shower." He sniffed his armpits. "Why, do I stink?"

"She came to me a little while ago and said you were swimming. Talked about water." Katty raised her eyebrows. "Demanded to come see you."

Clarence looked Bea in the eyes. "Hmm. Well I don't know. Was it a shower or a pool you saw me in, Little One?"

Bea put her hands on each side of his face. "You were underwater. There wasn't any ladder to get out. You were swimming underwater and couldn't get out."

Clarence looked at Katty, his eyebrows raised.

Katty shrugged her shoulders and looked back at him. "Maybe it was the Frosted Flakes she had for breakfast?"

Bea pointed to Noell. "You were there, too."

Clarence turned to Noell. "Noell. Are you all right?"

Noell still stood behind the door. Her face had turned pale. Her eyes were wide.

"Maybe Noell knows what it means." Katty pointed at her.

They all turned to Noell.

"Are you okay, Noell? You look terrified." Clarence put Bea down.

Noell stood "I-I need to go." She had gathered her things.

Clarence held out his arms to her.

Noell blinked her eyes. Her cheeks were wet. "I'm sorry." And she ran.

"Noell, don't go." Katty stepped to the hall, then back to Clarence. "We ran her off. I'm sorry."

Noell rushed down the hall, past the nurses station, and disappeared around the corner.

Clarence hobbled to the door. "No. We were done, but her Gamma just died and she is pretty tender."

"She's really pretty." The memory of her own reflection in the mirror earlier—fine lines and all—flashed in her mind.

Clarence patted her shoulder and hugged her. "And so are you." He turned into the room. "And so are you, Bea." He choked on his words.

Bea had taped her drawings to the wall below Clarence's framed certificates, but the tape was stuck in her hair and on her shirt and to one picture. She looked up, grinning as Clarence pulled it off her shirt.

"What happened?" Katty followed him.

"Look." He laughed. "We might need to buy more tape." He leaned over Bea. "And you *are* pretty, too."

"Oh, Bea." Katty shook her head. "How on earth did you do that?"

From making an old lady smile, to getting all taped up. There was no end to Bea's talents.

FOURTEEN

June 19, 1937 ~ Dr. Steven's Journal ~ Today is the day. The pool beckons. I have never been so terrified. I stand by my outdoor lab, arms crossed over my chest, staring into it. Mumbling.

I know I need to go in. There is no way I'll ever find out what's in that pool if I don't.

I wiggled my toes in the dirt beside the pool. I don't know how Henry did it—how he jumped in. What had he been thinking? I knew what *I* was thinking—that this was the last place I wanted to be. The water was cool and refreshing as I stepped in, but one moment I was just up to my knees and the next, I was underwater. I glimpsed the Open-Air Overalls Man before I plunged in—he saluted. Not a good sign.

Present Day ~ Michael sighed. There were days when people saw Michael and things of the Kingdom, and then there were days when everyone in the world were so engrossed with phones, business, life, that they didn't see what was right in front of them.

Today was one of those days.

He walked down the hall in Hillcrest, passed several residents and staff and was only greeted by one angel—Chrioni, who had a long-time assignment over Mrs. Hatly. Lucky angel.

Michael passed her, smiled and waved. She always saw him. He always felt her prayers.

He passed by Mr. Wainwright's room on the way to Clarence's. The man, or rather, the demon, hissed and gurgled through its host, Mr. Wainwright.

Michael shook his head.

Sad.

Mr. Wainwright's body didn't stand a chance of survival with a demon of that rank trying to operate through him.

As Michael stood at the doorway, Mr. Wainwright shuddered. His eyes bulged and his upper body left the bed as he pushed a hand at Michael.

The man began to shriek, drawing Lisha, then Carol. They tried to restrain him, but the demon was strong and the body of Mr. Wainwright was not.

Mr. Wainwright shuddered again and dropped back on his bed.

A fragile voice behind Michael spoke, "God help that man. Don't let him die without You."

Mrs. Hatly shook her fist and Chrioni grinned behind her.

Michael turned to see Carol close Mr. Wainwright's eyes.

There was a pause.

A life was gone from the earth, but a much more sinister being was released to roam.

The first thing the demon saw as it slithered out of Mr. Wainwright was Michael.

Chrioni and Michael joined swords above Mrs. Hatly as the demon rushed from the room.

Michael followed the demon on down the hall. It must be looking for another host. They were always wild-eyed when they came out of a body, but this one was unusual. It was a higher rank than most, because the other demons growled and grudgingly bowed as it passed them. It was not the biggest Michael had seen, but something about this creature was different.

It flitted down the hall, in and out of rooms, until it entered the reception area and bumped into a man entering the building.

The guy had a black suit on, black-rimmed glasses and pure white hair.

The receptionist stood and held out her hand. "Mr. Zee?"

The man shook her hand, looking her up and down. "Yes, I am. Are you the greeter for my new kingdom?"

She half-smiled. "My name is Loretta. I'm the Office Manager here at Hillcrest. I could give you the penny tour."

He nodded. "I'd like that."

Michael edged around the man and so did the demon. It must smell something—an attractive aroma—to hover like it was. Or it sensed an assignment. Either way, Michael was on alert. He couldn't do anything unless the receptionist took authority with her words.

As she showed Mr. Zee around, the demon followed, seemed to be listening. Noting possibilities.

When Loretta entered the administrator's office, Mr. Zee slapped the nameplate on the door and informed her that the first job she needed to complete was correcting it to Mr. Zee, Administrator, not Miss Henningway.

He strutted around the desk to the chair and settled in.

Michael realized that the demon recognized Pride and Arrogance in the man. It took seconds for it to make itself at home in Mr. Zee.

The body that the demon now inhabited was strong and fit, unlike Mr. Wainwright. The demon had chosen well. Very strategic and cunning.

This demon. Michael had seen it before but not for a long time. It was the same one to inhabit Henry Green—hence the candy bars from its host. Good thing Clarence had thrown that one away. The demon could have owned the town by now if Henry hadn't given up.

Mr. Zee's eyes fluttered—a download.

Michael couldn't read his mind or the mind of the demon, but he could guess at the assignment: conquer the receptionist, then Hillcrest Homes.

Then the town of Osceola. It'd try to get back what could have been his through Henry, long ago.

A shaky voice penetrated Michael's thoughts. "Father, keep us safe. Protect us and our angels. Shed Your Light … give us wisdom."

Mrs. Hatly.

Michael soared. An answer. A Hider. The demon was a Hider and that meant that Michael would have to be extra diligent and gather in more of the host, for a Hider could go undetected for centuries, just as this one had—at least since Henry. It was a high-ranking demon—a principality.

Thanks to Mrs. Hatly's prayer, Michael had the answer to centuries of questions.

FIFTEEN

June 22, 1937 ~ Dr. Steven's Journal ~ The Pool. I'd heard of people seeing their lives pass before them like cinema as they drowned. I'd rather have Les Misérables play in my mind than my past. Back up for air. Overall Man was still there. Still saluting.

Under water. Beautiful water. Instead of reflecting light, it seemed to *be* light somehow. Not like a flashlight beam, but it radiated light, like a warm brick gives off heat. I adjusted my goggles—there seemed to be shadows of fish? Too big.

Present Day ~ Clarence buttoned his suit jacket around his Led Zeppelin T-shirt.

Well, it wasn't *his* suit jacket. He'd borrowed the jacket from Harold. It was a little snug. He tapped the American flag pin to make sure it was upright.

He leaned against Michael's truck. "Nice service, huh Michael?" Probably should have used his crutches—his leg was starting to throb.

The church was the usual white churchy building with a tall

steeple. Steps led up to the sanctuary where they had just come from. He guessed that for a church it was okay.

Michael seemed distracted. They had been inside listening to the preacher drone on about the Bible, kind of. At least he was speaking eloquently about God stuff. And about Noell's grandma without even knowing her.

The angel should have felt right at home.

"Um, Michael, you okay?"

No answer.

Clarence gave him a shove.

"What?" Michael pulled out of his stupor and looked down at Clarence.

"I just made a comment and you ignored me. I said, nice service."

Michael barely nodded, glanced back to the church building, then at Clarence. Then at the church roof. His eyes were focused, his body tense. He seemed to grow taller, more filled out. His fists clenched, but Clarence couldn't see why. A couple of birds flew off, but that was all.

Angels were really strange sometimes.

One old man appeared from inside the church and started down the steps, followed by an elderly lady dressed to the nines. It was summer, but she even had a fur stole on. Her hair was done up in a swirl or a bun or some such style. Heels. Oh my. Kind of pretty for an old lady.

Mrs. Hatly had her beat, though.

Where was Noell?

There she came—

No, it was the preacher. He turned and held out his arm to someone behind him.

Clarence counted up: the soloist, preacher, four servers, organist. There had been more people helping with the service than attendees. Oh, and the little boy helping the preacher.

And Noell. Here she came.

Clarence buttoned his suit jacket and stood tall when she stepped outside, but unbuttoned the jacket right away, to breathe. He needed to get his own suit if he was going to lawyer in this town. More funerals —maybe weddings. The Led Zeppelin shirt would stay, somehow.

Noell shook the preacher's hand and made her way down the steps. Her long blond hair was tied back with a white ribbon. She'd honored her Gamma by wearing a white summer dress.

"She's a really pretty young woman, huh, Michael."

No reply.

"Michael!" Clarence jabbed Michael in the arm.

He was still watching the roof. Maybe Clarence needed to get his eyes checked, but he didn't see a thing. A loose shingle or two. But nothing that would distract him to that extent.

She reached the bottom of the steps and stopped, looking lonely and abandoned. The expression on her face broke Clarence's heart. She looked like she wanted to … well, her Gamma had just died, and from her story the other day, she was completely alone.

Huh. Just like him.

He looked up at the giant next to him. Well, at least blood ties were all gone.

She slowly walked in their direction. Her eyes were swollen and red. She clutched a couple of programs to her chest. The closer she got, the more her chin quivered.

Clarence opened his arms. What was it about these nice young women? He was an ex-con, but somehow, they were drawn to him. It wasn't even creepy, just … nice. He used to be nice before prison, but now, most of the ladies at Hillcrest thought he was a bastard. Called him names to his face. Sometimes he probably deserved it.

But Katty and little Bea and now Noell seemed to be drawn to him. He guessed he had something they needed. Felt good to be needed.

And they … they reminded him of Annie. His Dearly Beloved, even after all these years. He'd never forget her. Her love. The way she had looked at him, as if he was the only man on this earth.

Noell hesitated, then took a step closer. Then another. And soon she walked into his hug.

The tears poured out. Sobbed. She was just a kid. All alone.

Clarence felt Michael stiffen beside him. He looked above Noell's head.

The preacher walked toward them.

Weren't angels supposed to like preachers?

He held out his hand to Clarence, ignoring Michael.

"Hello." Clarence extended his hand too.

Noell started and turned around, leaning into Clarence when she saw who it was. She tried to smile.

Clarence shook his hand and released. "Nice service, Rev."

"Uh, thank you." He turned to Noell and handed her a paper. "I forgot to give this to you." He smiled a suggestive smile. "I hope you'll call me if there is ever anything I can help you with."

What did he mean by that?

She nodded, taking the paper, tucking into Clarence all the more.

She opened it as the man walked up the steps to the church.

He turned at the door and saluted them.

Noell gasped. "This is his bill."

"For services rendered?"

Michael jabbed him.

"Sorry. That just came out." He cleared his throat. "He could have waited and sent it next week."

She scanned the bill and wiped her eyes. Hiccuped.

"It's okay, Noell. From what I saw yesterday in your grandma's file, she left you with more than enough to live on, plus take care of this."

She looked to where the pastor had rushed to and shook her head. "He did the job, but I'm not sure Gamma would have liked him. He was creepy." She looked up at Michael. "Sorry."

Michael smiled at her and took her hand. He bowed deeply.

She blushed.

Clarence stared at Noell when she shook Michael's hand and blinked when Michael kissed hers. "Noell! You can see Michael?" The preacher obviously hadn't seen Michael, but Noell could. A nice warning about the preacher.

She chuckled. "Of course I can see him. Why wouldn't I?" Her eyes flitted between them.

Clarence slumped. "Well, most people ... " He looked up at Michael and sighed.

Noell wiped her face and yawned. "I better get to work."

"Looks like you better take a nap first." Clarence touched her shoulder. "I'm sure the Roads Department could do without you for one day." He straightened. "We should go have lunch at the Tasty View." He checked with Michael. "Right?"

No response.

Back to Noell. "My treat," Clarence said. "Besides, don't churches usually have a lunch after a funeral?"

Noell shrugged. "The preacher told me that since it would be such a small service, it would be too expensive to feed just a few." She shrugged. "I guess he's right."

Clarence stared at the door where he'd last seen the preacher. "Damn bast … " He shook his head. "Sorry."

A wind began to stir up leaves and twigs in a small whirlwind in the street right next to them. Each leaf and piece of trash collected into a vortex and rose up in a pillar. Taller and taller.

Chirping and screeching of birds became louder as they gathered, making conversation difficult. There couldn't be that many birds in this small town. There appeared to be hundreds—maybe thousands— rolling and swarming, up and around and heading right for Clarence, Noell and Michael.

Michael pushed into Clarence and Noell. "Run, humans." He herded them toward the huge church sign and hid them behind it.

Leaves and birds splattered against the big sign.

Clarence crouched against Noell.

Michael seemed to grow again, rising tall, hovering over them.

Debris hit Noell's legs making her flinch.

"Watch out. Here it comes again!" Michael ducked into Noell and Clarence, his huge arms around them. He seemed to stretch, covering them with his body, like a spiritual tent.

Michael moved. He shifted. Tensed.

Clarence looked up to see Michael pointing into the wind. Plainly, Michael was tall enough—or could stretch enough—to see over the sign. Clarence scrunched under Michael and tried to look around him, but he couldn't see anything other than leaves and trash slapping against the sign and Michael.

He seemed to be directing something. Or commanding … that was it.

Who was this guy, anyway?

Michael could see something that Clarence couldn't. Or was there a layer of this human world under a layer of Michael's angel world. Like two different realms superimposed over each other.

Michael released them and backed away, his eyes still intense. His body still engaged.

Clarence backed up. "Noell, we're crushing you. Are you okay?"

Her hair had come undone, the ribbon on the ground. She covered her mouth with both hands and collapsed at their feet.

"Noell. It's okay. It's over now." Clarence looked up at Michael. "Right, Michael? It's gone, right?" He helped her stand, picking leaves from her hair. "What was that?" Clarence put his arm around Noell's shoulders. "What can you see that I can't—we can't see? Were those demons and not just birds?"

Noell began to tremble. "No, wait. Demons?" She stared at Clarence, then Michael.

Clarence let go of Noell and pressed closer to Michael. "Michael." He lowered his voice. "Michael. Y-you've told me you can … you know, really … with your eyes." He stretched his arms wide. "That there is activity here, things going on that we normally aren't aware of, right? Sounds we can't hear, either. Right?"

Michael visibly sighed. He stared at the church building. Seemed to be thinking.

"Yes. There is a realm." He scanned the church yard. "A realm where … angels and demons operate. And, there is something," he cleared his throat. "Something is brewing."

Clarence shook his head. "I thought the invisible realm was like when computers send messages. Like radio waves. The computer makes a little airplane message and flies it to another computer. Right?"

Michael chuckled. "Kind of."

Clarence stomped his foot. "Don't humor me, Michael." Clarence scanned the property. "In prison, I could feel it, almost sense something. A wave or," he searched his memory, "a presence? I'd be in my cell and something would pass through me. I couldn't see anything, but it gave me chills."

"I can feel something right now." Noell nodded and wiped her face. "My skin is crawling. My head wants to explode."

Clarence looked up at Michael. "How can she feel it and I can't?" He pointed at Michael. "And how can she see you?"

"Wait a minute." She touched Michael's arm. "Why wouldn't I see you?"

Michael leaned down to her. "You have a pure heart. You're not without troubles or problems, but your heart remains with Him."

She frowned, shaking her head. "But … I don't go to church."

"That's not it. A good church is great, although …" He paused. "It's about Him." Michael pointed to the sky.

Clarence jingled the change in his pocket. "You mean, God?"

Noell blew out a breath. "Wait? Are you an angel?" Shaking her head, she began to weep.

Michael smiled.

Clarence stood as tall as he could."Yup. He's an angel."

SIXTEEN

June 23, 1937 ~ Dr. Steven's Journal ~ The Pool. I held my hands together in the form of praying hands and stopped, still holding my breath. Prayer. Yes Lord. I get so busy. I ask for your protection for us all—especially the man who is holding the other end of this rope.

Up for air. Back down. As I pushed my hands together the water became thick. Or some sort of pressure pushed my hands apart. The more I am in this water, the more it baffles me. It's beautiful, but mysterious. I studied slide after slide under the microscope and saw the same bacteria, algae, and amoeba.

Nothing dangerous here.

***

Present Day ~ Noell knew she was as conspicuous as a purple lion in the jungles of Africa, this first day at the Roads Department. Or as a white woman in an all-Spanish church.

Pink work boots. Orange shirt. The blue overalls weren't bad. Just baggy. No skinny jeans for this job. A new-old lunchbox that touted Mickey Rooney from Gam's stash. She should take it to the antique store and see if she could sell it. Mickey Rooney was from like in the fifties, wasn't he? Wonder what it was like to be famous on a lunch box.

Most people wanted fame and fortune. He got a lunch box. Who was this Mickey Rooney, anyway? Bet Gam would know.

Wait. Gam. Tears threatened. Not here.

Maybe the lady that ran the antique store would know.

Whew. Her jacket was too warm, but she wanted it along. Her always-present backpack hung from one shoulder, complete with a red bandana that Gam had tied there.

Did everything have to make her think of Gamma?

Getting a lawyer to help her take care of Gam's stuff, like her will and the house? God, that had been hard. It had been tough enough to call the funeral home, much less the lawyer.

The Roads building was in sight, a couple blocks away. Oatmeal she'd eaten for breakfast felt like a brick now.

This was a job she'd never done.

But she was excited, too. She was ready. Would she be driving one of the rocking trucks that she saw around town? Or doing office work? It'd be terrible if she got there today and they stuck her on the copy machine—1000 copies an hour. Ugh.

Would she be raking leaves? Driving one of those huge maintainers? She had't even thought of that until now. How did you drive one of those things?

Or would she be mowing the sides of the roads, the ditches? She'd seen a woman doing that in another county. So much to think about, and she hadn't even started.

She reached the building. It was a typical roads building, made of red concrete blocks and metal siding. A sloped roof with plenty of wires going in and out. She'd heard that they broadcast road conditions to places like the sheriff's department and the schools. Five or six towers reached for heaven from the roof and around the building, making her look up too. As she opened the entrance door, a whoosh of air followed her. Leaves fluttered inside with her.

That would probably be her first job here. Sweeping up those leaves.

She walked to the counter. No one was here. The clock on the wall said 7:52, so she was a little early, but the place was unlocked.

She should have eaten something different. Her stomach had to be filled with those little fruit flies fluttering around inside. The ones that hovered over the bowl of too-ripe peaches. She wished she could swat at the ones in her stomach.

Steve Hatly was the office guy's name. Or the manager. Or the boss. He had seemed nice when he hired her. Hopefully he was always nice.

A truck drove up behind the building. Half a minute later, the back door of the building opened and Steve popped in. "I knew you'd be on time. You hit me as the kind of person that would either be early or right on time."

She waved shyly. "Hi."

He motioned her on back to the break room. "Hey. Sorry about your grandma." He cleared his throat. "Thanks for letting me know. I saw her name on the Funeral Home sign—Gwendolyn Randolph Carpenter? I'm really sorry Noell. Do you need more time off?"

She fidgeted with her backpack strap, head bowed. "That was Gamma." Her chin wouldn't stop quivering. "But, I'm all right. There's stuff to do at home, but I needed to—"

"Get away? I know. I'm not very good at that kind of stuff." He nodded, lifted his hard hat and scratched his head. "But if you need—"

"No, I'm okay. I need the money. A funeral costs … "

Silence.

"Uh, yeah. Tough for a young girl your age to deal with. If there's anything I can do … "

Awkward silence.

"Well, Come on in and I'll show you around." He pointed to lockers along one wall. "Here's where you can stash your stuff." He looked over at Noell. "You travel light for a girl. My wife would have brought a suitcase to stay all day."

She smiled. Lockers would be nice. "Can we lock our locker?"

"Sure. We even have some combo locks, so just let me know if you want one." He waved toward the restrooms. "There's the bathrooms.

We have a men's and women's, so's you have one all to yourself. The guys all have to share and you will be liking not having to share with them. Us." He chuckled, pointed to himself.

"Here's all kinds of vending machines. The last boss loved candy, so he installed three snack machines and two drink machines. Kinda nice. I'm not sure we'd get the city to do that now." He opened a refrigerator door and showed her a space for her food. "Everybody is pretty respectful of each other's food."

He opened the microwave door and closed it fast. "Gross. It's a full kitchen. Microwave, stove, cupboards. You can claim a cupboard if you like. It comes in handy if we are here overnight." He looked at Noell. "That doesn't happen very often, but when it does, like in an ice storm, or disaster, or snow storm, it's nice to have a place to warm up some soup."

He reached into a cupboard drawer and handed Noell a combination lock. "You okay with remembering numbers and stuff? Like your own combination?"

She nodded.

"Some of the guys aren't … well, every once in a while, somebody has to hack a lock because they can't remember the combination numbers."

"No, I can remember stuff like that."

Steve stepped back and surveyed Noell. "I'll bet you're a pretty smart girl. We can sure use somebody like you here."

She smiled. "Hope it works out." She was beginning to sound like Steve. Which wasn't a bad thing. She was gonna like this guy.

The entrance door slammed.

"Hey, I found it first."

"Naw, it's my pop. Hands off!"

Voices got louder the closer they got.

"You are not my boss. And I found it first!"

"Well," Steve said, "the kids—er the others are here. Let's go meet them. It's as good a time as any. I'll show you what I want you to do in a bit."

She stashed her lunch box in her locker along with her jacket and backpack and locked it. She yanked on it. Seemed secure. She ripped off the tape with the combination written on it and pressed it on the inside of her hard hat.

Deep breath. Meet the guys. She was no more eager or good at meeting new people than she was eating someone else's cooking.

She turned to go into the next room when she heard one of the guys. "Really? A girl? To replace Ned. You are kidding, right?"

Another voice. "A girl can't do what he did."

"Besides, he's coming back sometime."

"Guys, she is in the next room. And we need the help now. I'm sure she will fit in fine. She seems to have a lot more on the ball than you did, Ken. We had to teach you how to run the coffee maker. Remember?"

Noell slipped into the main room, wishing she was invisible.

"Here she is." Steve swept his arm toward Noell in the main room of the Roads Department. "Here's our new hire."

Noell wanted to slink past them all and slide out the entrance door, like an invisible ninja. Instead she nodded at the row of guys and swallowed. Her face and neck burned. She'd never measure up to these guys—to this job.

There was a line of five guys, including Steve. All were of the male gender, but as one or two ogled her, their place on the status quo slipped to bottom feeders. She may be a hard core germaphobe, but she also had built-in radar where men were concerned. She was proud of it. She lived by it.

Steve introduced them all. One man seemed older—his name was Bill. Gray and brown hair barely visible under the hard hat. Lines around his dark eyes and mouth— bet he smiled a lot. He tipped his hard hat at her.

She tipped her head.

Another had unruly curly hair stuffed under his hard hat, but a nice smile. He also filled out his work shirt the best of them all. "Hi." His name was Rat, for whatever reason.

She turned to the last two. One seemed Spanish descent, but sometimes it was hard to tell until they talked. His name was Miguel. The other guy, Ken, was maybe nearer her age and well … cute by a high school girl's standards, but Noell could see right through him. He wouldn't look at her though. At least the Spanish guy smiled a friendly smile, even though he looked tired this early in the morning.

Steve held out his hand. "Guys, this is Noell Carpenter. Ned's replacement."

Someone, Noell couldn't detect who, snickered.

"You mean Ned's temp replacement."

"Remember." Steve commanded respect. "We all started as novices when we got here. Well, except for Miguel here." Steve scratched the stubble on his chin. "I think today, since we are starting over kind of, with Ned gone and Noell new, we should start with the typical shove-it."

Groans all around.

Noell looked at each man, then Steve.

Steve grinned at her. "It'll be a good way for us all to get to know you and learn to work together. I'll show you where you need to be and help you today. We are all helping each other."

Ken blew out an exasperated breath. "I feel like I'm in Kindergarten."

"Huh. You act like it too." Rat shoved him to the door.

They filed out to the trucks. Rat walked beside Noell. "Nice boots. Where'd you get the pink?"

She smiled. "My Gam … er, Grandma had them. Thanks." She got in the truck up front with Steve, avoiding the men in the other truck for now. They slammed doors, and Steve revved the truck. "The shove-it," he explained, "is filling pot holes. It's a fill-the-day-up task, but has to be done in a rotation because the roads get so much traffic these days." He nodded her direction. "You'll direct traffic around where we are filling holes. Your sign has STOP on one side and SLOW on the other. Just watch the traffic and let them flow as we work. We don't work in a long stretch of road when we do this, like in big time construction, so if you run into trouble, I'm right there. It helps us to get to know each other and you. Okay?"

She nodded. "Okay."

They drove about five miles outside of town and all got out. It was a long stretch of asphalt road, but she could see places that needed to be filled. The guys in the other truck were unloading equipment, tar, and buckets.

Steve showed Noell her sign and where to stand. He turned it one way, then the other. That was it. Pretty easy. STOP. SLOW.

The guys got set up on the road, and Noell took her place. Just her and the sign. She looked both ways. And again. No cars. No trucks. Not even a bicycle. This could get boring. She thought back to the hospital and bedpans. Hands down. This was better.

She could smell the fresh air, even though it was laced with tar. She could see and hear birds chirping. Way better than … well, what bedpans had in them.

Wait. A car. Or a truck. Hard to see from this distance.

It turned off before it got to where they were working.

After a while, the guys started bickering about something. They had to clean out the hole, blow away any debris, and fill it with hot smelly tar. Yuck. Rat and Miguel were the only two who seemed to know what they were doing. Ken didn't know didly; *she* didn't know didly, but could tell already Ken knew nothing about the job. Or didn't care. Both. Rat was right in there as was Miguel. Steve, as foreman, had to stand and watch and make sure it was done right. And Bill seemed to be able to do anything because he probably cared.

Oh, another car. Or truck. Too far to see again.

As it drove closer, she saw it was a newer red pickup truck. Two men were in it. She looked behind her at the gang, to see if the truck needed to stop or slow. She caught Steve's eye. He shrugged. He was no help.

She turned to the pickup and checked the road both ways and how much space they were taking up.

Ken's leg was over the line.

She turned the sign to STOP and held it up for the pickup to see. It was still far away, so she had time to change it, but she felt they should stop. Out of the corner of her eye, she saw Steve nod. Whew.

This couldn't be hard, but it was her first day, her first time doing this. And for the safety of the guys, she had to do it right. Plus, she wanted to keep this job. For some reason, she felt this was falling into some sort of a plan. Maybe. She had never dreamed of working construction.

She truly wanted to make a difference, but how?

Today? She could make a difference for the men in the red truck driving toward her, to keep them safe, no matter how they felt about her making them stop.

Today. She could make a difference in the Roads guys' lives by keeping traffic away, so they wouldn't get hurt.

The red pick up stopped. She glanced down at the work in progress and at Steve, who had become very interested in making sure Ken cleaned the debris out of the hole. She glanced behind her. A car was coming up fast from the other direction. She had to make the pickup stay put. Dust and the glare made it hard to see if the occupants were paying attention. She tapped the pole onto the asphalt—STOP!

The other side of her sign read SLOW, but if the car was doing anything, it was speeding up.

"Steve?" she shouted.

Steve stepped beside her on the center line, a kind of shield from the dust and dirt but also the car.

The car came up on them quickly, but at the moment it might have passed them and possibly hurt Steve, it came to a halt, sending gravel and dust flying. The driver at the wheel lurched forward in his seat. Not hurt, but startled. Had he even seen them until now?

"Woah! That driver is crazy." Rat growled as he tamped tar down with his shovel. "What was he thinking?"

The guy looked as baffled as she felt. She turned around to make sure the pickup was still stopped, and it was. They were put. They were not edging forward. Just waiting.

Steve pointed to the sign. SLOW. And motioned for the car to go. The guy must have been very startled by stopping so fast, because he just inched by as he drove around them.

"Did you see that guy?" Rat stood behind her. "He was terrified for some reason."

"Well, he stopped crazy fast, but didn't hit the windshield. Just shook him up, that's all." Ken bounced the shovel on the surface of the road. "I've stopped fast before and didn't know how I did it. We may never know," he finished in a soft, sing-songy voice.

The guys laughed—all except Steve. "Okay. He's around. You can … you know what to do, Noell." He nodded. "Good job."

Good job? She grinned, teeth and all. She never smiled that big. But she never heard "good job" from anyone but Gam.

She flipped the sign to SLOW and nodded to the men in the red pickup.

They started up and drove around them and stopped beside Noell. "Hey. What's a road crew doing out here?"

Noell smiled and showed them the holes. "Just fixing the road."

The old man leaned over the younger one. "It's a great day to be out here, huh. Beautiful sunshine, birds twittering."

"Hey!" She pointed. "Mr. Timmelsen! Right?" Those blue eyes. She'd know them anywhere. "And Michael! Hi!"

Clarence squinted and held up his hand to block the glare.

She lifted her hard hat.

"Noell? What are you doing out here?" Clarence chuckled. "Well, dumb question on my part. You're working for the Roads Department. Good job!"

She grinned again.

"And, yes, it is a beautiful day!" She checked the road, both directions.

"Say, have any of you guys," Clarence shook his head, "and Noell. Have you seen any caves around here? You're out and about, working the roads all over. Have you seen any caves?"

Noell looked at Steve and back to Clarence. "I haven't, but … I just started working on the Roads crew today." She motioned for Steve to join her. "Steve? Mr. Timmelsen, here, wants to know about caves."

Since the whole crew heard the question, they all stood up like she had addressed all of them, instead of just Steve.

Steve walked over to the red pickup. "Nice truck. What year is this?" He surveyed the back bed of the truck and walked around to the front.

Noell froze. Could Steve see an angel? How could some people see Michael sometimes and people couldn't other times? Did the angel get to choose? Angels could have some fun with that—a red truck without a driver.

Michael cleared his throat. "Uh … it's a 19. Well, I'm not sure. I'm not really—"

Clarence leaned over again. "It's an 2006 Ford." He nodded. "A Ranger, right, Michael? Pretty neat, huh. He just got it, right, Michael?" He looked over at Michael. "Where did you get this anyway?"

The big man blushed. "Well, … uh … Father gave it to me. I didn't get to pick it out, but I love it. It runs good and gets me—us—where we need to go."

Clarence looked at Michael. "You got it from … your Father? Woah." He patted the dash in front of him. "Takes this little truck up a whole new level."

Noell raised her eyebrows and blew out a breath. "Your Father?"

Michael gripped the steering wheel and peered up at her, a half-smile on his lips. His eyes twinkled, challenging her—no daring her, to believe.

She, in her hard hat, dusty in her orange X shirt, hesitated, but rose to the dare and smiled. Full teeth grin. Inside her, something solidified. Something went down so deep in her that she knew. She just knew.

Michael patted the steering wheel. "It's an automatic." He grinned.

Clarence sputtered and raised his eyebrows. "Uh, yeah. Back to the caves. Are there any around here? Seems like this area is pretty flat and wouldn't be prone to caves."

Steve looked back at the crew. "Hey guys. You can still work while we talk, okay?"

Noell checked for cars both ways. Nothing.

Steve tapped his hard hat. "You know, just the other day—"

"Hey Steve." Rat moved the bucket. "Want to check this?"

Steve nodded and turned to Bill. "Bill. You remember anything about a cave or an underground spring? You've been on the crew longer. Anything?" He walked over to the crew.

Bill pushed his hard hat off his forehead and scratched. "You know, I do remember something. It was a while ago, though." He put the hat back on. "It might have been on the old Gustafson place—you know—about a mile," he turned around in a circle, "south from here. That way." He pointed in the direction the red truck was headed. He looked over his shoulder. "But that might have been dug up and leveled years ago. You know how they change the lay of the land for their pivots. *Gustafson* sure rings a bell though."

Clarence and Michael exchanged a look.

Steve perked up. "Yeah. Just the other day—"

"We." Clarence paused. "We know where that's at, huh Michael."

Michael's eyes widened and nodded.

Noell checked for cars again. "What-what happened?"

Michael began tapping the steering wheel. "My other truck, the grinding truck, fell down a sink-hole at Merle Gustafson's place."

Noell leaned down.

Clarence's eyes were wide too.

Steve slapped his hard hat. "That was you guys?" He looked back at Bill. "His other truck is the one at Merle Gustafson's farm." His hand made a dive motion as he whistled. "Along with Merle's new tractor."

The whole crew stopped working and chatter began.

"We heard about that."

"Can you get it out?"

Miguel leaned on his shovel. "Insurance pay for that?"

Clarence glanced at Michael. "Well, we don't think so ... we don't know yet, right Michael?"

Michael shrugged.

"Well, we better be off. Thanks." Clarence leaned over and reached out his hand. "Clarence Timmelsen. I live at Hillcrest Homes. This here's Michael, my ... right hand man." He looked at Michael. "Or am I *your* right hand man?" He laughed. "Anyway, get in touch with us if you think of anything or find any caves around here."

Noell checked the road and flipped her sign to SLOW.

Steve turned back to the crew. "We'll keep you in mind if we find anything."

"Okay. Thanks!"

The red truck drove off, leaving them in its dust. Even though it drove off slowly, there was an awful lot of dust. They all stood coughing until Noell realized that a big semi had pulled up beside them. She hadn't even had time to switch the sign to STOP. The dust had prevented her from seeing it.

A big man with hairy arms leaned out the driver's side window. A dog barked on the passenger seat. "You want me to stop or slow? You decide, because you're the one with the sign, little lady."

Her face burned. She looked over at the gang. "I guess you can go." She tapped the sign on the road.

The driver shifted and drove forward, shifting the whole way down the road, until she couldn't see the truck anymore.

Bill's head popped up. "Hey, you know? There used to be a cave in town."

"In town?" Steve pointed to another car coming close in. "A cave in town? That's crazy. I think your rememberer is done remembering."

"No. Really. Something about … drownings, too." He lifted his hardhat and scratched. Wiped his face. "Seems like it was close to where the nursing home was built."

Noell flipped her sign. "Hillcrest Homes?"

"Yeah. Maybe I should give that guy a call, huh?"

"Okay, guys. I think we're done here. Looks good." Steve picked up a shovel. "We'll go back to town and break for lunch. Then we'll have a go at the downtown curb access. We still need to break down the last one on the East side. Main and Hawkeye. That's where we left off." He patted Bill on the shoulder. "Remember that corner, Bill?"

Bill pulled his hardhat down over his face. "Main and Hawkeye," he mumbled into the hat. "It's because I drove the truck into the street signs and they will be forever in my line of vision."

Rat laughed. "You drove the truck into the sign?" He picked up a bucket and walked to the truck. "Knock it over did ya?"

Bill dropped his chin to his chest and followed the guys, dragging his shovel on the dirt.

They slammed the truck doors closed on the rest of the conversation.

Noell picked up her sign and walked it to the truck. What an easy morning. Other than meeting the guys and dealing with people who don't follow the signs, it was an easy morning. And she got paid for it.

The moment with Michael. Worth it all.

Never had she dreamed she would be comfortable with five guys on a dirt road. Huh.

Steve pounded on the outside of the door. "Okay. Let's go."

Noell smiled to herself. She was going to like this job. She might even let herself like Rat. He needed to change his name though—gave her the creeps.

SEVENTEEN

June 24, 1937 ~ Dr. Steven's Journal ~ Bar-side Service. Three people attended. I was one. Plus the guy sitting at the bar.

"Let us pray."

I removed my straw hat and bowed my head when the Reverend began to pray. First time attending a funeral service inside a bar. A distinct odor of alcohol could be perceived with each word that was prayed.

Never mind. It didn't matter.

Henry's own brother hadn't even shown up. His own brother.

I guess that didn't matter either. I just hope Henry is in a better place—heaven.

The preacher cleared his throat.

The man next to me removed his hat.

Preacher cleared his throat again and the men placed their beers on the table.

"We are all gathered here to remember … what was his name?"

Where had they found this guy? I need to write as much as I can remember—no one would ever believe this funeral. "Henry. Henry Green."

"Yeah. He lived a long life and will be remembered. Amen."

"Amen!" The others raised their beers. "To Henry Green!"

Henry deserved better.

Present Day ~ New day. Clarence dressed and shuffled to the window in his bedroom. Looked like a beautiful day. The park had just been mowed. He could smell it even through the glass. Trees swayed with the breeze, like ballet dancers with their branches held high in graceful form. If he leaned to his left, he could see the bridge where the pool was from his window.

He hobbled to his office. Four walls. A hurt leg. Even though he had been out with Michael for the funeral, he couldn't shake feeling trapped. When he first moved in, he escaped regularly. Explored the town. Now, when he couldn't, he needed to.

At least he had two rooms. Clarence Timmelsen, Law Office. Rooms 202 and 204, Hillcrest Homes in Osceola, Nebraska—a nursing home.

At first when Carol had broached the idea to him, he balked. Would anyone hire a lawyer in a nursing home? Plenty had hired him when his shingle hung in prison. Inmates thinking he could get them free— when they were guilty.

He had no idea who would hire him here, but now that he was getting organized, it made sense. He counted on his fingers—Carol had asked for help for her husband Joe, Mrs. Hatly's insurance company had been skipping out on payments, and now Noell with her Gamma's estate. Sweet girl.

He glanced out the office window. He didn't have to mow. He didn't have to plan dinner and definitely didn't need to cook or clean up, although he was friends with the guy who did. Nice guy.

He didn't even have to clean his room, although he did once in a while to help out.

Living in a nursing home made perfect sense to an eighty-year-old man who had spent the last sixty years in prison. He hadn't always felt that way. Six weeks ago, he had either wanted to die or go back to prison.

When he let himself be honest, getting shipped back to the town where it all started was the best thing that could have happened—most days.

Carol knocked. "Clarence you need anything?" She nodded toward his leg. "How's the pain?"

He shook his head. "It's a low roar."

"If it's roaring, then you need something." She opened the chart in her hand, flipping pages.

"No." He shook his head. "Not."

She pursed her lips. "You sure?"

"Yup."

She wrote in his chart, reading it out loud, "Resident refuses pain meds," and stuck her tongue out at him. Putting the file in the cart, she mumbled something about him being a stubborn man.

He smiled as she left and scanned his rooms. The boxes loaded with books could wait. He closed the cardboard flaps.

He peeked into another box close by. Old law books. It had taken him a long time to even decide to be a lawyer. He had done it all for the wrong reason—revenge.

He kicked at a box. That hurt—still couldn't get used to the pain in his leg. He could go through the rest tomorrow.

Right now? Coffee with Mrs. Hatly, the cutest lady and his best friend in all of Hillcrest Homes. Maybe the world. Next to Carol and Harold, his detective buddy.

Somebody kicked his door open, banging it into the shelving unit behind.

"You Clarence Timmelsen?"

"Yeah. Who wants to know?"

In stumbled a beautiful young woman. Well, she looked young in comparison to the residents. A kid with braces and pimples followed her in, like a toddler chasing candy, tongue practically drooling. They each lugged heavy cardboard boxes.

She slammed hers down on the desk and stood, straightening her gapping blouse. Too short a skirt. Spike heels.

"How do you even walk in those things? They look dangerous." Clarence followed her to the desk and lifted the flaps of the box. "What's all this? What'd you say your name was?"

"I didn't." She caught her breath. "I'm Pete's secretary." When she didn't get a response from Clarence, she continued. "Pete Malovitch? Remember him? You killed him, if I remember right?"

Clarence froze and shoved his hands at her. "I had nothing to do with that. Sheriff shot him." Pieces of the Pete puzzle began to fit together. This woman and Pete … . He checked her left hand. They were—

She slapped a document down on the desk. "Sign here for boxes delivered. I don't want the likes of you coming after me, saying I didn't deliver your stuff."

"*My* stuff? Why would Pete have had my stuff?" He flipped the box flap open again. "This isn't mine, it's … ." The top document. Dad's name. "Dawes Timmelsen?" He tensed and coughed, choked. "How'd you get my dad's stuff?"

"Pete had it in his old building next to ours … uh, his." She sniffed. "He bought the building from the Clynder family." She pointed a long red fingernail at the space on the release form. "Sign." She grabbed a pen from his desk and shoved it at him. "I've been left with clearing out the buildings, so I'm clearing this out to you. If you don't want it, throw it out. Burn it. I don't care, but don't you ever give it back to me. Hear?"

"I hear." Clarence signed her release, then opened the flaps, taking the top documents out. "Thanks, I think."

She stomped out, bumping into the kid. "Drop it down anywhere. And make it fast. We have lots left to do."

The kid dropped his box next to the desk, and ran smack-dab into Carol, knocking her against the wall.

"Excuse me." Carol pulled her white nursing jacket closer to her body, flapping one front over the other.

The kid skirted around her and followed the woman.

Carol leaned into Clarence, whispering. "Who was that?"

"You don't know? It's Pete Malovitch's bi … uh, secretary." He pointed to the boxes. "She was neighborly enough to drop these off. And I have no idea whose they are, except this top paper has my dad's name on it." He sighed and rubbed his neck, tossed the papers back into the box.

"And the kid?"

"No idea! Her love puppy?"

"Clarence!" She popped him on the shoulder. Turning into the room, she scanned the framed certificates on the wall. "I haven't had time to look at these."

He checked the wall too, a half-smile on his lips. Never got to hang those in prison. "Like it?"

"Yes. Very impressive. Looks like a law office." She inspected Annie's picture and the one of Bea and Katty. "Annie was a very pretty woman. Little Bea could be her child."

Clarence looked closer. "You're right. Something about the eyes." He crossed his arms, lingering at the photographs. "Sweet kid, that's all I know. We were drawn together by serendipity or whatever."

Carol laughed. "Maybe God?"

That God stuff. He shook his head. "Maybe not?"

She punched him again. "What if I were to tell you that I believe that Joe and I were drawn together by God? Joe believed it too."

Oh-oh. She was setting him up again.

He removed some papers from one of the boxes and pretended to read one. "Well, if that's what you and Joe want to believe. That's your business." He checked her expression. "How is old Joe, anyway? Doing better?"

"Well." She swallowed. "That's really why I came in." She glanced at the hall. "Could we—"

"Shut the door?" He shoved it closed. "Let me get all official here." He pushed the box to the other side of the desk and offered her a side chair. "Welcome to my law office." He waved at the wall full of frames. "I'm open for business, thanks to this really kind … and cute lady who works here."

She blushed.

He took a seat. "How can I help you, Ma'am?"

She half-smiled. She bit her lips into her mouth and sat. Took a deep breath.

He reached for her hand and squeezed it. "What is it? Joe?"

She nodded.

"Is he worse?"

She nodded again. A tear slipped down one cheek.

His own eyes burned. He had grown to love Carol in these short weeks since arriving at the nursing home. She had such a big heart. She had almost let him keep the hawk.

Carol swallowed again and took a deep breath. "He's worse, and the doctor is counseling me to take him off all support. He said last night that I need a lawyer." She crumpled. "And you're the only one I know." She wiped her face. "Will you help me?"

"Of course I'll help you." He softened his voice. "You let me know what specifically you need, and I'll—"

"Medical power of attorney. That's what the doctor said." She searched his face. "Am I giving up if I do this?"

He shook his head and patted her hand. "No, Carol. You are planning for whatever happens. What if he lives? What if he … this is just a protection for you and him."

"And if he dies? What does it do?"

He pointed toward her. "It gives you direction—the doctor direction. You don't have to think about what to do. It's already set forth. As long as we are assured that Joe understands—that he can sign … even if he can only sign an X." He cocked his head. "Make sense?"

She nodded. "Okay. Well. Let's do this." She looked down at her lanyard, fingered the keys together. "I know he would want me to do the right thing." She stood and opened the door, deep breath. "The other thing?" She bowed her head. "I feel God telling me to forgive Joe."

"What?" Clarence shook his head. "Forgive Joe? For what?"

She held up her hands. "I know. It's not his fault, but I might be holding this illness and what it's done to our life, against him. Kinda. It *is* the right thing, isn't it?"

He walked around the desk and hugged her. "When Annie died, there were a lot of stupid things going on—like her dad, the judge. The town." He jutted his chin out, tears welled in his eyes. It still got to him. "Well … I knew after a while that I had to move on. That's when I got the idea to be a lawyer. At first, I wanted to take Judge Green down for putting me away, so I figured I could get back at him somehow if I was a lawyer. But after a while, people started coming to me—even guards—for help." He shrugged. "I kind of felt Annie giving me that, so I could make something good out of my life—even there in prison."

She took a deep breath.

He hugged her again. "And you will too … make something good out of this."

She let out a sob, but swallowed it. Deep sigh again. She peeked up at him. "Thanks Clarence." She hugged him back. "I'm so glad you moved here."

He laughed. "I didn't have much to say about it." He had wanted to kill that old bastard judge—he *still* wanted to kill him. Judge Green was the reason he was in this nursing home. His blood began to boil, but he squelched it. Stuff it down. Deep breath. "But." He glanced out the window, then back at her. "I'm glad too." He paused. "Maybe. Just maybe that was your God getting me out of prison and … here."

What a precious lady Carol was.

Michael leaned against the wall of the office as Carol and Clarence talked.

Neither seemed to see him.

It didn't matter. He must be available. Be ready for a time when the humans rose to who they could be.

So he was patient.

Of the people he had served throughout time, *most* didn't understand that.

One elderly lady had understood. Harriet. She had taught a Bible study in another town. Before Clarence was born, she had been Michael's charge. Angels had swarmed around her when she yelled out Scripture, and then they flew out on assignment. She had it figured out.

When the Word had gone forth from her mouth, angels had dropped jewels from heaven onto her lap. She'd ask Father where they were needed, and He'd point out the person.

Probably helped the popularity of her Bible study. But, once people —mostly women—heard her teach, they were hooked by her words from Father's heart, more than seeking any gems.

Harriet had seen him every time. From the time she was a tiny girl, she had been able to see him. She never forgot how.

She was one of few.

He hoped that someday Clarence would be able to see him all the time.

The woman with a youth carrying boxes had just left.

An angel had followed each one and they had bowed in greeting— the woman's angel carrying an open book and pen, scribbling what she said as he walked. He barely had time to acknowledge Michael.

Michael'd had some humans like that. Constantly talking.

The woman had slammed her box down on the desk, her face red and flushed. Her black eyes darted from Clarence, to the boxes and around the room. What she didn't realize was a demon about the size of a moth perched on top of her head, grinning at Michael. It had seemed to hold two strands of her hair like reins, turning her head this way and that.

From where Michael stood, she had appeared terrified. Whatever was in her heart must be painful.

Clarence had stopped short when she accused him of killing Pete. A dark thread had flown around Clarence's neck, and a spider-like demon crawled up his right shoulder. It cinched the thread up tight, making it harder for Clarence to breathe, much less swallow. Fear choked out any truth that Clarence might have spoken.

Another spirit had climbed out of her blouse, which was already stretching at the buttons, revealing black lace.

The poor kid with her.

Michael had to restrain himself. Unless the kid told her she needed to fix her blouse, or something like that, Michael couldn't interfere.

When Clarence had scanned the top document, the demon pulled the thread tighter.

A mist rose up from behind the woman—above her, gathering into the shape of a brown-skinned creature that hovered above her. It reeked, and pus oozed from sores on its skin. Probably what stunk.

The woman's voice had gotten louder. "I don't care, but don't you ever give it back to me! Hear?" The big demon crossed its arms across a bulbous chest. It had glared condescendingly at the angels—until it spied Michael. Then it shivered and more sores broke out, the mist becoming thicker.

When she had stomped out and Carol came in, the whole atmosphere changed. Her angel, Jehoel, had bowed low, one shoulder down—football offense style—to Michael and grinned.

No time for a wrestling match.

Michael had skimmed his hand along the thread that by now had made a deep, dark crease along Clarence's neck. When he had released it, it fluttered to the floor.

Clarence let go of a deep breath and swallowed. Rubbed his neck.

Jehoel edged closer. He was a seasoned warrior, like Carol. They made a good pair. He swiftly rotated, sword instantly out.

Something hissed from the direction of the hallway.

Carol visibly shivered.

Mr. Wainwright. More hissing. Stronger. Louder.

Growling. Deep guttural noises.

Michael bowed his head as she and Clarence hugged.

Jehoel did too.

Precious friendships among humans. Almost like angels.

Jehoel's presence grew stronger, his glow brighter. "Rise up, Michael." He drew his sword. "Incoming!"

Michael drew his and they crossed them over Carol and Clarence.

Two demons slammed into the swords and vanished. A putrid brown mist curled around them, hanging in the air.

Carol had peeked up at Clarence. "Thanks Clarence." She had hugged him back. "I'm so glad you moved here."

Clarence had talked about the Lord—Michael held his hand high.

Jehoel clasped Michael's hand. "Lord rules!"

"Always!"

Michael still gripped Jehoel's hand high above his head and prayed. "Father, help us hear your heartbeat. Help us do Your will. Keep us strong."

"I'm glad your charge moved here, Bro. It's been a long time since you and I have been together on assignment."

"Agreed."

More growls.

"I hope you enjoyed your last vacation, Jehoel, because this run is going to tax you plenty. Stay alert. This demon is full of surprises."

"Vacation? That family had numerous children and several grandparents still living. That's a vacation?"

Michael smiled. "The destiny of those children is powerful in the Kingdom."

Little Bea, too.

Carol waved at Clarence as she left the room.

Jehoel saluted Michael and stayed at Carol's side.

Clarence sat at his desk and scanned the paper in front of him. "Dawes Timmelsen. Huh."

Michael leaned against the wall, his head above the roofline, scanning the realm around Hillcrest—watching, waiting.

EIGHTEEN

June 25, 1937 ~ Dr. Steven's Journal ~ The Pool. Open-Air Overalls Man introduced himself today—his name is Paul. Named after the Apostle Paul, he said. "That is the only resemblance." He brought his grandson, who wears overalls too—open air. His name is Ralph. Spitting image of his grandad. Can't wait to meet the rest of the family.

Back in the pool today. I have tested the water at length. Jars line up on shelves and wooden boxes I built against the camper. Each jar holds two inches of pool water and has been tested for buoyancy, by putting a different object into it—a ball, leaf, pen, pebble. Interesting thing—doesn't matter how heavy or light an object is, everything sinks. A leaf sinks. A rock sinks. The pool pulls it under. Is there an undertow? Is there another pool deeper that draws objects deeper? Why would gravity work only on the objects and not the water? Why did it seem that it was the water with the force of gravity? At the deepest the rope would allow me to go, I felt like I would turn inside out. I don't know how else to describe it, but almost like when a person hits a cold spot in a lake or river, I hit a place where I could almost see inside myself. I feel less and less a researcher/scientist and more a guinea pig, but who is doing the research on *me*?

Present Day ~ Noell stood at the copy machine. Fifty copies of this. Fifty copies of that.

She looked around the Roads Department office. How did she go from mowing for Gam, to a flag girl? And now inside making copies.

She really did do a great job as sign girl. Steve even said so the day before yesterday. When she checked the calendar on the counter, she had already been a week on the job. Almost payday!

She tapped the copies on the counter and counted piles. One. Two. Three. Ten piles of fifty copies each. She felt like she was doing stuff that didn't need to be done. Like busy work just to keep her … busy. A waste of her time. A waste of company money.

She looked at the clock. Lunch. She didn't know where the guys were, but it was noon and she was going to have lunch.

She gathered up all the copies and put them in their slots, like Steve had asked her to. There had been no phone calls, so no phone messages. No deliveries. No one had stopped in for anything. Gah. Boring morning.

She walked into the break room, opened her locker and took out her backpack. Her stomach growled as she fished out her lunch and water bottle. She started to set it on the table, but someone had spilled soda or something again. It was sticky—made her cringe. She had washed off the table earlier, just like she always did because the guys came in every day and slammed their junk on the table. They always left it with dirt and crumbs. She was sure they liked having a maid to clean up after them.

The radio sputtered to life. "Hey Noell, we need you out here. Steve just cut himself bad."

Since it had been quiet all morning so this made her jump. She ran for the radio. "Hey Ken. What do you want me to do?" She looked out the window at the company truck.

"Get the first aid kit and drive it out here. We are three miles south on the Stovepipe Road."

"St-stovepipe road?"

"The black top that connects with the street you are on. Just get the kit and jump in the truck. Then drive straight south three miles. You can't miss us. We have the crane."

"Okay. I'll be right out." She grabbed her sandwiches and drink and put them away. She gathered up bottled water too, just in case, and ran for the door. "Got keys. The first aid kit."

She slammed the door, but came back in right away. "Do I lock the door? I don't have a key so I guess not." She went back outside. "But I can't leave it unlocked. They have cash in here. There is equipment in here—"

The radio buzzed from inside. "Hey, Noell, if you're still there, just slam the door. It usually is hard to open so people just think it's locked. Steve has the key in case you did lock it. Come on! We need that kit."

Did they have cameras over the door? She slammed the door so hard she felt like the glass would break. Note to self. See that all vehicles have first aid kits. Not that she wasn't glad to help, but what if it was bad and she didn't get there in time? That made her kick it in gear. She jumped into the truck, tossing the water bottles on the seat. Ahh. Stick shift. Bill had taught her how, but never by herself.

She started it up and killed it right off. Okay. Clutch. Brake. Start it and let the clutch off slowly. Killed it.

She tried again. It roared to life. Yay. She backed out and killed it again. Started it again. Forward.

Three miles. Two. One. She saw the crane up ahead. What were they doing with a crane?

She pulled into a farm drive off the road, close to where the guys were, and killed the engine. Dang! Humbling. Embarrassing.

She shifted into park and got out, retrieved the emergency kit and the water and ran to the group. Steve was down on the ground, groaning. She couldn't see what had happened. But once she saw his hand she understood. He had told her almost every day, even when she was working inside, to never hang onto a cable or it would cut your hand. Oh my.

"I just … I just," Steve looked down at the loader.

It sat at an unusual angle in a deep hole. If a feather landed on it, it would slide down deeper.

A bird lit on the seat.

A low growl became a roar. Noell jumped and shielded Steve as the loader slid deeper into the hole. Dust and mud splattered them all. A terrible choking, flushing sound could be heard from the depths of the hole, taking the loader deeper until only the shovel could be seen above ground.

"I was on that. I was sitting right there. It started to slide and I grabbed the closest thing."

Noell cringed. "A guide wire?"

He nodded and wiped his face. He looked a lot older than he was, lying there with a bloody hand. She had never notice the gray in his hair, until now.

Bill knelt beside Steve. "You could have been in that hole with the loader if you hadn't'a grabbed the wire."

The three of them stared toward the hole.

Noell came to first. "Okay. We have to get your hand fixed up." She knelt beside him and opened the emergency kit. "Anybody know first aid?"

Everybody backed away.

"Big help you guys are." She fished into the kit and found bandages and tape and set to work. "Anybody have any honey in their lunch box?"

"Honey? Are you crazy?" Ken said.

Bill leaned in. "No, I think she's onto something here." He held out his hand to them all. "Anybody?"

Miguel fished in his lunch box and pulled out three little samples. "Si?"

"Bueno, buddy." Bill patted him on the shoulder and gathered them for Noell.

She squeezed one out over Steve's hand and immediately wrapped it in a bandage and taped it up to keep it clean and to keep the honey in place on the wound. "Okay. Let's get him to the hospital."

Steve jumped. "No. No hospital. The last time I was there—"

"Take him to the hospital." Noell replaced the bandages in the kit. "There are pieces of the metal in his flesh and he has to get them taken out. Now."

They all jumped.

Noell didn't know where that came from, but they figured out real fast she meant business.

Steve was still whining about going to the hospital as they helped him to his feet. Finally Rat and Bill, one on either side, lifted him off his feet and got him into the truck. They drove away.

Noell cleaned up the emergency kit and put it away. Ken started to sit down and take out a smoke. Miguel stood, a confused look on his face. He looked at the cable and the crane, like he should be doing something. He kept stepping away from the hole, toward the other truck.

"Well, what *were* you doing?" Noell asked. "We should just keep working so Steve can relax. You know once he's bandaged up, he'll come right back out here."

Ken piped up from the ground. "Aww, he won't come back. They'll put him on some kind of antibiotics and pain meds and he'll have to sleep it off." He threw his cigarette on the ground.

Noell walked over and stomped the cigarette butt out. "We are going back to work." She looked at Miguel. "Okay?"

He nodded. "Si." He walked to the motor and started it up. He pointed to where he needed Ken. Noell followed to see if she could help. They were clearing the way to put a new culvert in, hence the crane.

She put her safety glasses and her hard hat on. Luckily hers were still in the truck. Gloves on. Glad she hadn't dressed just for office work today, like she had wanted to.

Ken walked over to the hole, but not as close as the others had been. "Why would that happen? What would make that fall down in there?" He pointed. "It's a sink hole thing."

Noell crossed her arms over her chest. "Seems to be happening a lot. The Gustafson place, too." Interesting.

She became the gopher as they continued to work. Moved rocks away, handed them a tool, ran to the truck to retrieve something. She gave them all water, even gave lazy Ken a bottle.

When Steve got back they were done with the job, with Ken looking like he'd worked all afternoon.

The hospital had saved Steve's hand and commented on Noell's honey dressing. It had acted as an antibiotic, reducing the chance of infection.

They cleaned up and went back to the office. Steve was still trying to stay at work, so he just sent them all out back to clean up the yard, while his wife brought him lunch. Weeds had taken over the old equipment there, and he wanted it all cleaned out. The city had been getting on him at every monthly meeting.

Noell put her hard hat on and her gloves and headed out with Bill and Miguel.

It was almost a field. Of weeds.

Rat was already on the mower. Noell raked clippings into piles. Miguel used the weed-eater, and that helped things go faster. Soon they were almost to the back lot line. Trees around and up through old equipment. Tall grass had woven itself in and out of the fence, making it almost impossible to clear. They could hardly tell what was out there.

Bill used a chain saw to cut the trees away … and there stood a little camper trailer. He was the first to get to it and try the door. Locked. He walked around the outside. "Looks kinda old and forgotten, but its all here. Kinda cute. Pretty small, but could be fixed up real easy. Anybody need a camper?"

Noell raised her hand immediately. "I do."

Four guys asked "why" at the same time.

It was tiny. Smaller than her room at Gam's house. She peeked in a window. Too dirty to see inside. But the outside looked okay. Dirty, but how long had it been sitting there?

"Well." She hadn't known she needed a camper until she raised her hand, but already she felt totally sure. "I need this camper." She picked up steam. "I am fixing and cleaning on Gam's house, and I could use it to stay in." She hardly stopped for a breath in case one of the guys would protest. "And a place … uh to put some of my stuff while I fix up the house. She'd been meaning to fix it up for a long time and now I have to do it." She had convinced them and herself. "I need this camper."

She'd laid the 'poor Noell' on thick.

Bill pushed up his hard hat and scratched his head. Rat and Miguel were inspecting the windows and siding—seemed to be contemplating how they would use it themselves. She could almost see the wheels turning in their heads. Ken appeared to be … mad, as usual.

Bill wiped his face and replaced his hard hat. "Well, better go ask Steve. I think he'd just give it to you and we can help you pull it home."

She knew the perfect spot. Down by the garden, behind Gamma's house. Just up from the little creek that became a bigger creek when it rained. Perfect.

She almost cried.

She ran to the main building, passing Ken on the way back. Where had he been? He still looked mad. "Steve!" She burst into the office.

He jumped. "Oh no. Don't tell me somebody else got hurt?" One hand was bandaged and in the other, he held a sandwich, meat and cheese stuffed between two slices of bread.

"No. No. Can I buy that camper out back?"

He slowly stood to his feet. "What camper?"

"It's out by the old road."

"You're already out there? You guys have cleaned up all the rest?" He leaned into the window. "Wow. I guess you have."

"About the camper."

"Oh, I see it. Yeah. That's been out there for years … since way before I took over the Roads." He shook his head.

Noell's heart sank. She didn't even know why she wanted it. She just knew she did.

"I don't want anything for it. Just take it. What do you want with it anyway?"

If the story worked once, it might work again. "Well, I am fixing up Gam's house—cleaning it out and stuff, and I need a place to stay until it's all done. Or a place to store some things, too. How much?"

"I said, I don't want anything for it. We'll even help you get it home if you want. Get it out of there!" He turned and smiled at her.

Noell kissed his cheek before she thought. "Thanks Steve." Never in her life had she kissed anyone—other than Gamma or Grandpa. Ever. Deep breath. "I'll make it up to you, I promise."

"Hey, I heard you did a great job after they took me to the hospital. You are a great addition to this motley band of workers."

Her cheeks got hot. She quickly turned away, pretending to fiddle with the elastic sticking out from her hard hat and rushed for the door. She rotated. "Thanks Steve. No one has ever … I mean ever … told me I did a great job. Except Gam." Deep breath. "Thanks."

That made two times Steve had told her that.

NINETEEN

June 27, 1937 ~ Dr. Steven's Journal ~ Church. One of the ladies I met at Thelma's invited me to the Lutheran church and I went. Figured it would appease the townsfolk. There are still many who don't want me in town. I could be walking down one side of the street, with someone heading right for me. They might look up and see me and cross to the other side.

Today at church, one man and his wife were shuffling into the pew where I was sitting, saw me and shuffled right out. I didn't see where they ended up.

During the sermon, the preacher seemed to be preaching right to me. And he was.

Why did she even invite me?

Present Day ~ "Attention!" Lisha opened Clarence's door at Hillcrest wide, banging it against the wall.

"What?" Sounded like prison again. The guards woke the inmates every morning with shouts through a microphone of, "Attention! All inmates who want breakfast—that means everybody—rise and shine." Started his day off wrong every time.

"I mean it Clarence." Lisha glanced behind her, down the hall. "We have the new administrator here today, and he is inspecting everything." The whites of her brown eyes were visible.

"New administrator? Why wasn't I told about this?"

"You mean like in ask yo permission to hire him?" She tapped against the door. "Me too. Why wasn't I told about this?" She busted one hip up. "Because we aren't in charge here." She thumbed down the hall behind her. "They are. Now git up."

He struggled to come out of his dreams. "Well, he ain't inspecting everything. Not like in prison, if you know what I mean. Not gonna happen today or ever again."

Lisha raised her eyebrows. "Well, he checked under Mrs. Hatly's nightgown—if you know what I mean. Seems he gots the idee that the residents are druggies."

Clarence half rose from his bed. "He checked Mrs. Hatly's ... " Tears sprang to his eyes. Not her. Not even the Oust Clarence Brigade ladies. And they'd been after him since they found out he'd been in prison.

Lisha nodded, her chin jutting. Same tears in her eyes.

"I'll get dressed." He threw his sheet off and stepped into slippers beside the bed.

"Hurry. He's in a rampage. Not sure how this'll end." She headed down the hall. "I wish today was my day off."

He selected a shirt and jeans out of his closet and moved to the bathroom, grabbed a washcloth and turned on the water. "Mrs. Hatly." Reached for his toothbrush and toothpaste with his free hand. He looked into the mirror, his blue eyes wide. The water was still running. "What do I say to ... ?" He wiped his face. "Oh my God! She is so pure."

He looked down at the water. Both hands were full so he hung the washcloth back up and brushed his teeth, dropping the toothpaste cap on the floor. He tapped his toothbrush on the sink, harder than usual. He pulled on his clothes, then tossed his pajamas at the door hook.

Who did this guy think he was?

His heart pounded in his chest, and his breathing accelerated. Every time he picked up his phone, he almost threw it. He walked to the window and threaded his belt through the loops.

The spirea bushes lined the parking lot, with full blooms that waved in the breeze.

A visual overlayed the scene outside. A face he hadn't remembered until now. Or he hadn't allowed himself to see.

Mom.

She had been sick and bedridden for a long time. He had been maybe six, so he knew all the hiding places. He'd hidden behind the door until the doctor and Dad went outside to talk. They were only out there for a little bit.

Clarence had seen his chance and tiptoed into her room. He hadn't been prepared for how sick she looked. He hadn't been allowed to see her for a couple days.

He must have kicked something or stumbled, because she opened her eyes and upon seeing him, she smiled. He crawled onto the bed with her and snuggled next to her. She smelled different. He didn't like that smell.

Her hair was strewn around on the pillow. She usually brushed it and tied it back with a ribbon.

Her skin didn't look right—it was white—but sticky-like. She had always worked outside in her garden, the sun bronzing her skin. Freckles even popped out.

He leaned over and kissed her as a tear ran down her cheek. Snuggling in, her watched her chest rise and fall. When her chest didn't rise right away, he'd lift his head to check her face.

She tried to clear her throat. He looked up. She barely shook her head, but the look in her eyes told him what she couldn't physically say.

The moment came when her chest didn't rise again. And she was gone.

Soon after, Dad came in and caught him. He was surprised but not mad. He understood a boy's need for his mother.

He checked her and broke down.

"Daddy." Clarence choked. "Is she … is she in heaven right now? Because she's not breathing. So is she—"

Dad nodded, eyes dripping.

Clarence picked up her hand, but she didn't move. He touched her face. Her eyes didn't open. "Mommy? Mommy?" Something broke in his chest and he let out a long wail. "Mommy! Come back. Mommy—"

Daddy grabbed him and held him, his tears spilled onto Clarence's face. They rocked side to side until sobs slowed. Until they were quiet.

Clarence had taken a long look at her face. The longer he watched, the more peaceful her face became.

And that was the picture that morphed over the spirea bushes outside his window.

Her face.

Michael bowed his head, listened to Lisha get Clarence out of bed to meet Mr. Zee.

Today looked to be a struggle from a human point of view.

Clarence was visibly shaken by what she said. He kept putting his foot in the wrong pant leg.

"Michael, have you seen the guy? The new administrator?"

Michael nodded. "He doesn't sound like a very nice man."

"Got that right." Clarence stood by the window, putting his belt on and seemed to lose track of time. Back to his memories, Michael guessed.

He stared out the window along with Clarence.

Residents were being rousted out of bed. Groans, as old bones didn't want to move after a whole night of being stationary. Someone dropped a cup or something that sounded plastic. It bounced. Lisha's voice was clear—like nobody else.

He smiled. She was a tough lady. But Father saw her heart. Father knew what no other human knew about her. Her wounds. Her pain. Her joys. Although Clarence was getting close.

———

Knock. Knock.

"Mr. Timmelsen, I presume."

Clarence wiped his cheeks and turned to see a man handing a chart back to Carol.

"Clarence. Just Clarence."

"Okay … Clarence." The man cleared his throat. "I'm your new Administrator, Mr. Zee." He held out his hand.

Dark wrinkled skin. Thick white spiky hair. Weird black eyes behind black-rimmed glasses. Suit looked like something from another country—Chinese collar—that Nehru guy. Indian. Whatever his name was. Reminded him of somebody else he'd seen recently.

Clarence stared at the dark hand and thoughts of Mrs. Hatly passed through his mind. He shook his head. Not on *his* watch. Not shaking hands with a guy that treated women that way. Especially Mrs. Hatly.

Carol didn't come into his room, but stayed in the hall, her back to them. That was not like Carol.

Mr. Zee pressed his lips together. Something in those black eyes made Clarence freeze. He had seen eyes like that before—guys in prison who were full of murder. Even his own eyes in the mirror most days. The man seemed intent on an agenda, clearly bursting with his authority.

Mr. Zee glanced around the room and settled back on Clarence. "I see you're dressed and ready for your day. We need to do a little inspection." He pulled on latex gloves.

Clarence looked at Carol.

She had turned around and her face told it all. Eyes were red and swollen. Chin jutted out. But she was in there—that spunkiness was still there. Fighter. Warrior.

Clarence's shoulders and neck tensed. Where was Michael?

"Not on my watch, Mr. Zee. I'm afraid you've got the wrong guy."

"Oh, right." He tapped the chart in Carol's hands. "You're the one from prison. I remember you now." He skimmed his hand over the top of the chest of drawers and nodded to Carol. "No dust." He continued. "I read in your chart you've been incarcerated for murder."

Clarence froze.

Carol stuttered. "B-but he wasn't guilty."

"That's what they all say. Says in your chart you killed your wife— set her up in vehicular homicide."

What had that administrator, Miss Henningway, written in his chart? Little bitch.

Michael nodded to Carol's angel. The new administrator had brought his entourage, and Carol.

Demons on either side of Mr. Zee spit when they saw Michael. Puny little things. Ugly, too. Scars and cuts.

Michael stood at attention. Please, Clarence, just give the word.

"Not on my watch, Mr. Zee. I'm afraid you've got the wrong guy."

Atta boy Clarence. Now just speak the words.

Clarence's fists clenched. Come on Clarence. We could end this before it even begins.

Michael could feel Clarence's blood boiling. One more level of heat and he could possibly explode.

Sounds of snarling and spitting could be heard from the hallway. Michael stood, feet apart. Standing strong.

Mr. Zee strutted past Clarence's desk. He seemed very interested in papers there.

Clarence gathered them into a pile and flipped them into the top file folder.

Mr. Zee paused, seemed about to comment, his eyes still on the folder, but for some reason restrained himself. "The records tell me you served sixty years. I'd say that's guilty."

Sweat beaded on Clarence's upper lip. He jingled the change in his pocket. Terror he hadn't felt in years crept up his spine and gripped his stomach. This bastard was serious. "Even … " He cleared his throat, sucked in a deep breath, and pushed back his shoulders, head erect. "Even if it were true, I served my time. And how do you remember me? I've never met you."

"Oh, I have your file from Miss Henningway. She left some revealing and refreshing information about you."

Clarence's fists clenched. "Oh she did, did she?" He wished he'd bought a gun since moving. His whole body tensed.

"Well, I have many residents to visit today, so better get on with this … inspection."

"And what *inspection* might that be?" Clarence crossed his arms across his chest.

"We check everywhere. I'm sure you're used to that kind of thing, since you were in prison."

"You can check my teeth, Mr. Zee, but anywhere else is off limits to you and anyone else."

"We check teeth, too. Plus anywhere else you might think to hide illegal substances. You don't have anything to say about it." Mr. Zee smiled a sick smile and opened the closet door, parting the shirts. "Your friend, Mrs. Hatly succumbed, shall we say?"

Two men appeared in the hallway behind him and Carol. Tough sons of bitches. Stout, too. Like professional wrestlers.

He glanced at Carol, but she was keeping her eyes down. She seemed scared to death. This guy must have done something to intimidate her. Was Joe okay?

First Mrs. Hatly and now Carol. His whole body became rigid. Not on his watch.

Mr. Zee opened the door to the bathroom. "Seems pretty clean … Clarence. You keep a simple house."

Crazy thoughts zinged into Clarence's head—some he'd had before, but some didn't make sense. Prison memories swirled.

Thoughts, yes about cavity inspections, but about Mrs. Hatly and Harold. Fears of not having enough money to stay at Hillcrest. What if whatever money Clarence had stashed somewhere would be found and confiscated? What if Carol's Joe died? Stupid, stupid, stupid.

His whole life, someone always had taken control. Clarence had never, ever been able to live his own life. Dad was his dad but still had controlled him. Judge Green. Prison warden and guards.

And now Mr. Zee.

Thoughts spun around and around, until he was almost dizzy.

A headache started to pound.

He pointed at Mr. Zee. "You didn't really check Mrs. Hatly in her private—"

Mr. Zee turned and laughed. "Oh, you thought we did that kind of cavity check?" He laughed again, looked behind him at his two stooges and laughed with them.

Ha ha. Funny dorks.

"Oh my, Clarence. We're just not that kind of administration. Maybe Miss Henningway was, but we are not."

Clarence glanced at Carol and met eyes. Her face told a different story. If not down and dirty cavity search, then what? Because she had obviously been crying.

Mr. Zee tapped the desk beside the file folder, scattering papers. "Have a good day Mr. Timmelsen." He started to walk out, but stopped, pulled a candy bar from his suit pocket and pointed to the framed diplomas and certificates on the wall. "Oh, and by the way, you will have to shut down this lawyer crap." He tore the candy open—red letters visible on a 3 Musketeers bar—and chomped a bite. Swallowed. "This is no place for criminals and drug-heads to gather—among innocent elderly men and women."

Clarence blinked as the man walked out, the candy wrapper fluttering to the floor.

Carol met his eyes.

Mr. Zee didn't really know Mr. Timmelsen—yet.

The demons escorting the two men spit at Michael. Low growling alerted him to spirits tucked at each man's feet. They were almost like stick men—like kids drew. But they were real and fiery. Spitting. Claws grew out from their feet and hands. Eyes narrowed when Michael looked at them. Almost covered with a shield or visor.

The men were meant to intimidate. Michael had seen them before and they were cruel.

The stick spirits stepped to Clarence, loaded tiny dart guns and began firing on Clarence. Almost laughable if they weren't so effective.

One after another, darts pierced Clarence's head.

Michael stood his ground. Prayers were coming from somewhere. Two more angels landed.

Carol had her eyes closed.

Now, Clarence. They had the enemy in their hands. A prayer warrior was covering this. Give. The. Word.

Clarence opened his mouth.

About time.

He pointed at Mr. Zee. "You didn't really check Mrs. Hatly in her private—"

More stick arrows flew at Clarence, stinging his cheek, his ear, his mouth and head. Clarence agreed with one enemy thought and three more stick spirits flew in and sent darts flying at that same spot. Michael could see Clarence caving in.

Mr. Zee turned and laughed. "Oh, you thought we did that kind of cavity check?" He laughed again, looked behind him at his two stooges and laughed with them.

"Oh my, Clarence. We're just not that kind of administration. Maybe Miss Henningway was, but we are not."

Michael shook his head as the candy wrapper fluttered to the floor.

Father, give the word. Teach Clarence the ways of Your Kingdom, Lord.

TWENTY

June 28, 1937 ~ Dr. Steven's Journal ~ The Pool. Paul was huffing by the time he pulled me to the surface and he is a big man. There were several more people gathered today. It's humbling being towed out of the water, spitting and gagging, throwing up at their feet. They came for a show and they're getting one—might not be what they expected. Word must have gotten out about the strange phenomenon. Even little Ralph is doing tests alongside mine. Doesn't make sense to him, either.

Present day ~ Today.

At work.

Noell stood taller. The confidence that seemed to bloom from within surely showed to everyone else.

All from a glance from an angel?

She chuckled. And a new, or old, camper? She'd done something so close to the edge, for her, that her whole being, her attitude, every hope and desire seemed attainable—even if she didn't yet know what they were.

Exploring the camper made her feel like a queen.

She smiled.

"Hey! No private jokes." Rat grinned as he loaded a shovel and pick-ax.

Noell smiled.

"Well? What gives? You win the lottery?" He opened a pack of gum and offered her one, unwrapping one for himself.

"Don't mind if I do. Thanks!" The gum smelled good. When had she smelled anything so intoxicating? Strawberry? No. Raspberry. She opened the piece and popped it into her mouth. Mmmm.

"Well, did you?" Rat faced Noell, hands on his hips. "Did you win anything?"

"Wha … what?"

"Did you win any money?"

"Money?" She frowned. "What did I say?"

He leaned on the truck. "Kidding."

Blank. "Thought so." Just trying to confuse her. It had worked.

He laughed. "Do you like to fish?" Tinkering with the latch on the utility truck compartment, he cocked his head. "Would you like to go sometime?"

"Go?"

"Yeah. Fishing. Like a fishing pole, line, and hooks."

"Um. I don't … ." Wait. Gamma's boxes. She might have a pole somewhere. She had everything else. There were life vests somewhere. Noell had run into those when she had been looking for work clothes. Gam's hoarding was becoming more and more useful. Not that Noell loved the mess and boxes everywhere. There was no room to move anymore.

"Well, I think I can find an extra pole somewhere. Let's go soon before it gets too hot."

Noell shrugged. "Okay." She just got asked for a date. And she had accepted. Fishing was better than a lot of things he could have invited her to.

Steve pounded the truck door. "Head out!"

Rat climbed in beside her, making her slide closer to Steve. The other utility truck followed behind with the rest of the crew.

"Where are we headed today?" Rat rolled down the window part-way. "The old bridge again?"

"Yup. Could possibly get 'er done today. We need to make sure we get all the flashers up and road blocks out." He chuckled. "Wouldn't want someone to go flying over that at night! Look Ma! No bridge!"

Noell gasped. "Has that happened?"

"Not specifically. Kids will always be kids." Steve gave a sidelong glance at Rat. "Seem to remember something."

Inside the truck grew quiet.

Rat seemed to squirm. "Well, yeah." He chuckled. "I do remember that." He leaned over Noell and pointed at Steve. "But, I took the worst part of that one."

Noell pressed back in the seat. "What happened?"

"It was late and I … was drinking." He shook his head. "Woke up to cows mooing and I was parked in their shit pond." He sniffed. "I can still smell it."

She wrinkled her nose. "Did you get hurt?"

"Nope. Too drunk."

Steve stopped the truck just short of the old bridge.

"Why are we taking the bridge out?" Noell straightened to see.

Rat got out of the truck and held the door open for her.

"The state wants it out. It's old, and many of the boards need replacing. It's too old to support new ones, but we'll finish taking it down and then a crew comes in to build another."

She stretched and walked to the bridge. One board was completely gone. That would hurt if someone didn't know it was gone! A tire would get caught.

Another board looked loose.

Ken and Bill picked it up, each carrying an end and loaded it onto the trailer.

The rest of the crew swarmed over the bridge, each knowing their task, except for Noell.

Steve handed her the flag and a roll of yellow tape. "Wind this around the whole bridge, but keep a sharp eye out. The people who live out here are used to using this bridge even though it's bad. They don't want to go the long way around the section, so they drive right over it. Make sure no one passes. Okay?"

She grabbed the tape and flag. "Okay." She looked both ways. Clear. For now.

She leaned the flag against the bridge railing and picked at the end of the roll of yellow tape as she surveyed where to even walk so she could string the tape. Attaching the end to a post one of the guys had driven beside the road she jumped down into the creek.

There wasn't any flow of water so she could step around rocks and clumps of grass to the other side. A snake skittered from between the rocks and slithered away, giving her a start. Thank God she didn't scream.

No one had seen her jump, right?

Dang. Rat was grinning.

Her cheeks grew hot.

Dang, he was cute.

She pulled her hard hat lower on her face and continued to traipse through the creek bed. Those pink boots were the best. They fit great and were super comfortable, but she especially liked how protected her feet were.

She almost laughed. She'd always worn sandals or joggers. She might have turned into a hiking boot fan.

Another snake. Ugh. She let it slither away before proceeding and checked behind and around where she needed to step for any more. With each step, she disturbed more.

Snake nest.

Only a few more feet to the other side of the creek bed. She could do this.

Just as she reached the other side, a rock gave way and she began to slide under the bridge pilings where the bridge met the road.

This time she did scream, and it was probably good she did, because she fell into a hole.

Coughing, she brushed away the dirt. Rocks tumbled down with her, opening up a bigger hole.

It was a small cave. Gah. What was it with caves these days? Dr.

Steven's research she had uncovered in the camper. The map. The pool. And now this … this little—

She stomped at the rocks to find a foothold and discovered that the seemingly small cave wasn't so small. It continued on down under the road.

Something surfaced in her thoughts from the other day—Clarence asking about caves.

Wow. If people only knew what they drove their cars over. They could be driving along and all of a sudden fall right through a hole in the road and be lost forever. She'd seen pictures on the internet.

Rocks and dirt underneath her shifted as she tried to stand, making her slide farther down the cave.

Something slithered.

She screamed.

"Noell? Noell?" Rat yelled from the surface. "You down there?"

"Yes! Yes! Get a line or rope. Anything." She froze and slid down even more. "I'm sliding down into a cave."

Three snakes skidded over her boots.

"Help!"

Gramps had told her if she saw a snake to hold still. Not move a muscle.

"Right away." He disappeared and yelled. "Get a rope. She is sliding down into a cave."

Rustling above her gave her hope.

Until vibrations from above shook her even farther down. And startled more snakes.

She shrieked again. Who was more scared—them or her?

Silence.

"Guys?" Where was the confidence now? "Anybody?"

Steve's head popped through the opening. "Hang tight, girl. We'll get you out." His eyes traveled past her and widened. "We'll get you out."

A rope appeared beside him and Rat looked in. "Here, catch this."

She reached for the end of the rope, but the movement only made her slide further down.

Splash! Rocks slid and plunked into water somewhere below. Oh God. A pool?

Waves of nausea hit her. One after another.

Layers of pictures opened on top of the dust and billowing dirt. Water rushed over her from below. No! Not now! The water poured in with the dust.

These dreams had to stop!

Sanitizer wouldn't help her now, even if she could find it.

Water rushed and overpowered her. She was drowning. Again. Yellow eyes mocked her. Gnarly hands reached out to her—pulled her down. A mouth opened in a scream that was amplified by the water.

Did *she* scream?

"Guys. I'm sliding." She shrieked. "Help!"

Vibrations from above turned into rumbles.

"What is that sound?"

Rat looked up from the hole. He hollered. "It's a pickup. Ken! Stop them!"

Footsteps pounded above.

The rumbling grew louder and louder.

Noell slid into the hole.

"Get me the rope!" She screamed again. "I'm sliding!"

The rope fell right in front of her and she grabbed it. "I've got it. Pull!"

"Wrap it around your hands."

She wrapped it around and around. "Okay. Pull!"

The vibrations and rumblings had to be right above her. She could hear the guys yelling.

"Stop! Stop!"

"Pull over!"

Just as she began to slide down again, the rope caught and pulled her up and away. Airborne. Her head emerged through the hole. Dirt and dust and rocks tumbled around her and on down to the pool, splashing as they hit water. A snake hung from the toe of her boot. She landed in the creek bed, scattering snakes again.

She kicked and tried to scoot away.

Steve and Rat kicked them away and carried her to the road like she was a feather.

A truck had barely come to a stop at the edge of the bridge, spewing dust and gravel. Air brakes released with a loud whoosh.

The cloud of dust cleared revealing a full sized semi-truck with a trailer-load of cattle, accompanied by loud mooing and jostling in the trailer. They were just as scared as Noell.

PU.

The driver jumped out.

Noell's legs went limp, and she collapsed where she had been standing. She felt like the wind had been knocked out of her. Like something stood on her chest.

"You okay Noell?"

"That was close."

Miguel and Ken and Bill were all corralling the truck driver, who looked to be a young kid, barely fourteen.

"I didn't do anything wrong. I was just … " He appeared to, at that moment, see the bridge out signs, the yellow tape, and missing boards, and his tanned face went white. Then he saw Noell sitting beside Rat and he pointed at her. "Was she? Was she under there?"

Rat nodded.

"I could have … I could have driven over her. Crashed through the bridge?" He looked behind him at the cattle and visibly shook.

He dropped in the dirt on the road.

Noell stirred.

Rat helped her get her balance. "You okay?"

She nodded. "Yeah." She looked up at him. "Thanks." And at the others. "Thanks. I thought I was going to end up in that hole down there."

Steve leaned down to look. "It seems to go forever." He walked to Noell and put his arm around her shoulders. "You okay Noell? We need to take you to the ER. Get you checked out to be sure."

"No." She kicked a foot and shook her arms. "I'm okay. Really. Nothing broken." She checked again. "And nothing bleeding."

"Just to be safe. We need to get you to the hospital just in case later something starts hurting and then we're too late." Steve thumped his chest, sending dust up in billows. "Your Gamma would never forgive me if something happened to you on the job. She'd come back to haunt me." He pointed. "Rat, take her into town to the ER and tell them it's on the Roads Department, City account."

"Sure." He hooked his arm around hers. "You okay to go?"

"I guess if I have to." She wiped at her face. Gritty and wet. She wiped again. Wet? Tears?

She glanced to the hole as they picked their way to the truck. That could have been her tomb. She could have been buried there.

Under all that dirt.

Drowning in the pool.

Just like Mommy.

Walking out from the ER, Noell shook her head. "I knew I was okay. We just spent city money for nothing."

Rat opened the truck door for her. "I'm sure Steve just wants to be careful. What's the saying? Better safe than sorry? It's worth it to have things checked out."

He shut the door, came around to the driver's side and picked up his phone. "Hey, Steve. This is Rat."

"Good. How did things go? She okay?"

"Yup. She's good. They took blood and did x-rays and everything. She is a little sore but nothing broken."

"Good news." Steve coughed. "Just take her home, okay? You wouldn't mind doing that?"

"Glad to."

Steve cleared his throat. "Okay. We have everything all buttoned down out here too, so we'll be heading into town. See ya soon."

"Right on."

Truck clock didn't work, she forgot. "What time is it? Doesn't feel like it's time to get off work yet."

Rat checked his phone. "It's 3:37."

"But I can't go home. It's not quitting time yet."

"Steve said to take you home." He looked over at her and brushed debris out of her hair.

She leaned away from him and sighed. "Feels really stupid. The guys will hate me."

"By the look on everybody's face when you fell into that hole, I think they'll be okay with it. I mean … " He stopped at a stop sign and looked over at her. "I can't believe you're okay. That had to be terrifying."

Tears stung her eyes, but she wasn't going to let him see. She looked out the side window. "Yeah. Maybe." Deep breath. "Yeah. Scary. But so quick that I couldn't really think about it. I just reacted. I … every time I moved, I slid farther into the hole. Hearing the rocks splash into water I couldn't really see was … scary." She gulped. "And the snakes."

She felt his hand on her shoulder.

Stay strong. Don't let him see. Don't let him know how crazy—

"I'll walk you up." He pulled the truck into the driveway and stopped.

Visions of the front porch terrified her even more.

She jumped out and lost her footing, stumbled to the ground. He mustn't see that porch.

"Whoa. Seriously. I think you need to slow down." He pulled her up and held her steady.

"I can make it from here. It's okay. I can—"

He grasped her hand and put his other arm around her shoulders.

Even through the work dust and tar, his aftershave provided another layer, taking her to a place she'd never gone before. Usually smells and touches plummeted her into visuals and knowledge she didn't want to know.

But right now, she only saw a morning sunrise and birds rising in flight along clouds. Crisp, sweet air jarred her senses—just about as nice as his aftershave. All very fresh and—

Fletch! He was peeking out through the diamond-shaped window of the outer door.

How had he gotten into the porch? What was he doing in there?

Rat stopped and pointed at the door. "Wait. Is that your brother?"

"No. He's a neighbor." She tensed. What was going on?

Rat turned to her. "You okay? Is he okay?"

She stared at the front door, frowning. "H-he's okay. I just don't know what he is doing in my house."

Rat stopped and turned to her, grasping her arms with his hands. "Want me to do something? Call the police?"

"No. I'm sure it's okay. I just didn't expect it."

The door opened just as Rat's touch activated powerful visions, knocking her back. A lake. Fishing. Rocks being thrown into water. Vicious laughter. Faces too close. Fists pummeling. Cries of terror.

The door swung open.

Fletch's wide eyes. Out of breath. Red face. "Noell." He looked from her face to Rat's. "Who's this?"

"Fletch. What are you doing here?" She stepped inside the house.

Rat stepped in behind her, his hand on her back.

She shuddered at his touch, stepping away.

Fletch backed to the doorway leading into the living room. "I'm getting those boxes out that we talked about."

Noell paused. Boxes? Whew. She must have hit her head falling down in that cave. "I … I forgot."

Fletch eyed Rat. He drew up taller and Noell could see the man he was becoming: strong, tall, honorable. All around him, the floor had been cleared. Half of the room, in fact, had been cleared.

Rat stared at Fletch. His black eyes seeming to pierce Fletch's. He pressed his hand into her back, drawing her closer.

Reminded her of a movie—sparing between two gladiators—right in her porch.

"Um, Rat, this is Fletch." She pointed to Fletch, then to Rat. "Fletch, this is Rat, a guy from work." Deep breath. Maybe she had hit her head harder than she thought. She put her hand out on a nearby box, but it slipped. She lost her balance.

Both guys reached for her.

Rat touched her first, and she gasped as Rat's face morphed into a shriveled old man with yellow eyes. Immediately, she pushed away.

When Fletch's hand came in contact with hers, a blanket-like-thing stretched from him and covered her.

So strange.

"I'm okay." She looked at Fletch. "Just kind of had a mishap at work. I went to the ER and checked out fine." She glanced at Rat. "I must have hit my head or something."

"Here. Let's sit you down." Fletch looked behind him into the living room. The only seat available was Gamma's place on the sofa.

Fletch reached for her hand.

Rat's hand still touched her back.

An explosion of emotion crossed her mind's eye. Tension and competition. Torn first one direction, then the other. First Fletch's face —kindness and honor in his eyes—but lacking self-confidence. Then Rat's—excitement, arrogance. Unfamiliar smells pushed into her brain. Even the pornographic mind-pictures from Mr. Grimes down the street hadn't had the hormonal power of this moment.

She heard their voices, saw their faces, but they sounded like they were far away and faces blurred.

Fletch held out his hands, almost bowing. "You need to sit down. You look like you feel terrible."

"I'm okay. I'm fine."

Rat gave her a push. "He's right. Sit down for a minute. I can help him get the boxes out." He stepped toward Fletch.

Fletch held out a hand, pushing him away. "I got it."

Noell looked from one to the other. "It's okay, guys. I'm fine." Not daring to say more, she nodded toward Rat. Seeing him stand against the backdrop of piles of boxes almost made her want to throw up. "Thanks for taking me to ER and home. See you tomorrow. Tell Steve thanks."

"Okay. If you're sure you're okay." Rat looked behind her at Fletch. "If it's really okay." He touched her arm. There was that awful, raucous laughter again. Why was she seeing Rat as so evil? He'd always been nice and polite. They were going fishing together, weren't they?

She glanced behind her at Fletch, who had his hands on his hips. He looked ready to spring. Back to Rat. "I'm fine. Really."

Fletch was staring at Rat. Hard to discern his thinking. Blank face. But his eyes never wavered.

Huh.

Never had she been caught between two men.

TWENTY-ONE

Clarence waved as Mrs. Hatly walked on down the hall.

"Have a good nap, Mrs. Hatly. See you at supper."

"God willing, if I'm still here."

She always said that. Her frail voice always pulled on his heart. Her eyes twinkled, and her laugh sounded like a sweet melody—that Jenny Wren in the spring.

"Silly," he said. "You'll be here. Where would you go?" And yet … what if something did happen to her? He didn't like to think about it, but since he'd been at Hillcrest Homes—six weeks—two residents had died. "Good night, Mrs. Hatly."

"Good night, Clarence."

He watched her walker-dance down the hall. She turned into her room farther down, stopped at her door and waved. Blew him a kiss.

Clarence jumped. First time for everything. He blew her one back just as Harold showed up in his wheelchair.

"Such a love duck."

"Love duck? You weren't supposed to see that." Clarence shook his head. "Is nothing private in this place?"

"Nope." Lisha walked between them. "There ain't nothing private here: your room ain't private, your birthday ain't private, your poop schedule ain't private and your birthday suit ain't private!" Those hips sang her attitude. "Got it?"

Harold chuckled. "So true. Even our sordid past isn't private."

"Hey. Got that right. Mr. Clarence here, rode with Jesse James and his gang. Thas how he got put in prison."

Silence.

Clarence burst out laughing.

Harold wiped his eyes.

Lisha kept on walking past, her huge hips declaring her victory. Up. Down. Up. Down.

Clarence could almost see her sarcastic grin. "Oh, that woman." He snapped his fingers. "Hey, you would be the man for the job." He righted Harold's American flag pin on his lapel.

Harold looked up. "What job?"

"I just got some boxes dumped on me from Pete Malovitch's … uh secretary." He paused. "You know I'm trying to be nice."

"Good job. New territory for you, Buddy." Harold grinned. "Go on."

"Well, one of the top papers from the box has my dad's name on it. I just had time to glance at some of the others farther down, when Carol came in."

"And?"

A couple visuals crossed Clarence's mind—Pete's blood spattered on Clarence's cheek and Pete's angry secretary. "Yeah, well, I was wondering. Since there is a legal case going on right now involving ole dead Pete, who was after me, and that Phil guy who was after Katty, I might need someone with me as I go through this stuff." He leaned against the railing along the wall. "Kind of like protection. You know, where two or more?"

"You spouting Bible at me? You? Preaching?"

Where did that come from? That was what preachers were for, and he didn't want any part of that kind of preaching. He only wanted the preachers that told jokes, or the one that came on Wednesdays and served them hot chocolate. That one he could stomach.

The preachers that used to come to the prison? Now those guys were all business. They didn't take any … crap off the inmates. They were about that Alleluia stuff and getting people into heaven. Whew. At least now at the nursing home, Clarence could walk away. At prison, he had to take it. Listen or …

Clarence shook his head. "Naw. Just sounded right. You up for it?"

"Sure. As long as there's nothing that you want kept private. You know, like family stuff?"

Clarence shrugged. "I can't see that there would be." He spied Lisha sauntering toward them. "Maybe Lisha, here, would bring us some tea and crumpets to ease our work."

She gave them the look—the look that warned of either flying objects or words.

Clarence chuckled and braced himself.

"Me?" She glanced over her shoulder, swinging loose dreads, a brown thumb pointing to her chest. "You talkin' to me?" She posed—one hip up, her pinky finger up, and one eyebrow up. "I'm thinkin' we all outa crum-pets. We might have some, let me see," she posed again, a finger beside her mouth, "vitamins or some laxatives. Somethin' like tha-t."

The t sound sent a spray, sprinkling Clarence and Harold.

Clarence wiped his face. Had to make it look like he was soaked. What a woman. Why did she remind him of the woman the last day at prison who gave him his beautiful wool scarf? She was nicer than Lisha. She had been precious.

He pushed his hands at her. "No, no. Thas okay."

Her other eyebrow shot up.

Oh-oh. "We'll just drink water, won't we Harold."

"Yup. Water'll be fine for me. Yup." Harold drove his wheel chair behind her, peeked around and motioned for Clarence to come with.

She planted in the middle of the hall. Not much room on either side.

Clarence sidled along the railing, keeping an eye on her. She could move fast, no matter how big she was or how much space she took up in the hallway.

Almost around.

Until she bumped out a hip.

Damn!

She was just a little too close. And she was closing in fast. He could smell her breath—must have had garlic for lunch. He could see her freckles—freckles on brown skin. There was a scar just to the side of her eye. Ouch. He'd never been close enough to see it before.

He pointed. "How'd you … how'd you get that scar?"

She flinched, and her fingers flew to the place. "What scar?" Her eyes went soft. No, they turned fearful. "I don't have no scar."

Lisha?

He cupped his hands around each of her massive elbows.

They stood like that. Connected. Connected skin-on-skin. Connected eyeball to eyeball.

And soul to soul.

She went almost trance-like. Sucked in a deep breath, trembling. Then she came back to reality. In her eyes, there was still fear, but a new thing. An intimacy? I'll keep your secrets if you'll keep mine? Friendship?

And just as quickly, it was over. Attitude was back. Hip bumped up. But something was different.

"You two have a good afternoon, okay?" She started to walk away. "I'll see what I can scare ya up in the kitchen, though." Bump, bump. She turned back. "Maybe some … soap pads. They're good in a biscuit."

She winked.

Clarence closed his eyes and shook his head. Chuckled to himself.

He popped Harold on the shoulder. "Ready to snoop through those boxes?"

"Yup. Ready."

Clarence flipped on the overhead light in his office. "Here they are." He patted the boxes on his desk. "Amazing Pete had all this stuff."

Harold wheeled into the room. "You said your dad's name is on some of it?"

Lisha popped in with a tray and placed it on Clarence's desk. It was covered with a plastic doily, and on it were two cups of coffee and a Mountain Dew. A pink plate served up raisin oatmeal cookies.

She bowed with attitude. "Now. Don't you two get yoselves all used to this." She wagged her finger in Clarence's face. "But jus know I appreciate you."

She bowed again, grabbed her Dew and a fistful of cookies and turned to go.

"Hey!"

She turned into the room. "What?"

Clarence stood and gave her a hug. With both hands full, she couldn't deck him.

Her eyes filled with tears. "Jes want you to know. Don't you ever do that agin." She shook her Dew in his face and smiled a very sincere smile. "Ever."

"I won't Lisha." He took a cookie. Only two left? "Ever. And thanks."

Harold mumbled between bites. "I believe. I believe. Now where were we?"

"What are you believing about?"

Harold snickered. "You hugged Lisha and she let you live?"

"Ha! I know. I should lock my door at night! Watch my back. She's scary!" Clarence bit into the cookie and held it up. "Mmm. Never had these in prison."

Harold parked his wheelchair next to the desk. "Tough in prison, I bet."

He shoved the rest of the cookie in his mouth and brushed crumbs off his hands. Swallowed. "In all reality? Worst thing was losing Annie —she was my angel, my connection to all things good. Prison was," he glanced at the empty plate, "easy, after losing her. It became my home."

Harold stared at Clarence. Nodded. He looked away then stared again. Cleared his throat. "Your home?"

"Yeah. Only two places I called home." He hesitated and counted on his fingers. "Well, three, counting Hillcrest. One with Dad as a kid. Two, Prison. And three, here." He opened the box flaps and reached inside. The top papers showed Dad's signatures on a … looked like a purchase agreement.

"Whoa." Clarence blinked.

"What'd you find?"

Clarence handed it to Harold.

He scanned it. "Looks like your dad owned property here." He handed it back. "Right?"

Clarence slowly sat. He scanned the document and blew out a breath. "Says here that Dad bought that bastard Judge Green's place of residence when he died."

"The judge that—"

"The judge that sent me to prison for sixty years and then set it up for me to be sent here."

Harold let out a long whistle. "The judge's house? Your dad bought it?"

Clarence drifted back. His memory of Judge's house layered over the view of the parking lot outside his window. It had been a beautiful home. Walking up the bricked sidewalk when courting Annie, he had noted every porch and railing, every gable. Upper balconies. The roofline had a dangerous pitch; a turret alone would have been terrifying to roof. Flaunted four bedrooms and two full bathrooms.

Dad always said that was excessive. Some people in town didn't even have one bathroom.

Clarence had always paused just before the bottom porch step to admire the carvings on the portico above the front door. As his eyes lowered, Annie always magically appeared at the front door, the sweetest smile on her face.

It still stirred him after all these years.

Amazing workmanship.

Amazing Annie. After sixty years, he could still see her precious face.

And Dad owned Judge's house? Or had at one time?

"Why would Dad have bought Judge's house, unless … revenge? Dad got revenge for Judge slamming me in prison?" Clarence whistled out a breath. "Dad, what did you do?"

TWENTY-TWO

Noell looked at the clock after Fletch left with the boxes. Still only four o'clock. Plenty of day left.

She wiggled her toes. Shook her body. She felt okay, just a little wired.

Visions of sliding into that hole passed through her mind. Dust choked her. The minute she had moved her foot or tried to find a stable footing, she slid farther down. And another snake slithered out.

Part of her had been terrified, especially when she heard the plunk, plunk, plunk of rocks bouncing off walls below. But when she heard splashes, her stomach had flip-flopped.

She hit the panic button then, but at the same time, curiosity bit her hard. Maybe not curiosity, but more like destiny bit her in the behind.

Could have been so much worse. She hadn't really been scared then … well …

But now, it shook her.

She had been totally at someone or something else's mercy.

She scanned the dining room where she and Gamma had set up the computer. God, she missed Gamma. She needed her right now.

They had laughed so hard when the computer arrived and neither knew what the heck they were doing. Gamma had figured out how to plug it in. Thank God for the telephone guy, who set it all up and gave them an Internet 101 class. Gamma had tried, but this was her first time ever, using a computer.

She got so she could email a very special friend who lived in New York City. When an email came in from the friend, she would laugh and cry. Such a special relationship.

Noell leaned back into the chair and bit her lips between her teeth. She'd had a rough day, so maybe the emotion rising in her right now was just from falling down a hole.

But … she didn't have a friend like that. She didn't even have the prospect of a friend who would send her funny emails when she was a hundred years old.

Moments passed as she stared out the window.

Gamma had been her only friend and had always been there. Never a day had gone by that Gam hadn't fed her, held her, taught her. Prayed with her.

The reflection of her own face looked back at her in the computer screen. It was all scrunched up. Eyebrows rumpled together. Tears sparkled in the reflection.

How could she go on alone?

Light from the windows illuminated a tear running down the cheek on the face in the monitor.

After the day she'd had, she could sense that if she let herself really cry, she might never surface in life again.

Pictures of Rat and Fletch stirred emotion, too. Mr. Grimes had been scary, but this seemed worse. Rat and Fletch were each so different—made of different stuff, that was for sure. Somedays she wasn't sure which one was the good guy and which was the bad.

She punched the on button and after a few minutes, the computer came to life.

She wiped her face and typed in "caves in Osceola, Nebraska."

What was going on with Rat, being so pushy? Gamma would have known.

The webpage turned out to be a site for things to do for kids and had pictures of a kid in a cave, but … not what she wanted.

And was Fletch getting too close? He had been in her house.

"Caves in Nebraska" turned up more. Great photos. Wow. One reminded her of … her cave.

Her cave?

Well, it might as well be hers. She'd almost been buried in it.

Robber's Cave. Cool history. Mostly by Lincoln, Nebraska.

Wow. A depth of sixty feet?

She looked up. How long … or deep was that?

She gauged the room as ten feet across. Take that times six.

She stood and crawled over junk to get to the window. Turning back into the room, she eyeballed the length, then looked outside the window and tried to measure that distance outside. Then again and again.

Sixty feet ought to be from that outside wall out to Mr. Grimes' house—the imaginary measuring line running right through the neighbor's house and yard.

As she climbed back over the boxes and clutter again, she shuddered. Was that how deep the hole had been today? And water below that?

She shivered again.

The article said that caves meandered through parts of Nebraska around Lincoln.

She wanted to explore every cave. She wanted to study Dr. Stevens' journals. She wanted to read every website Google found.

All at the same time.

Dr. Stevens' journals first. He had the most direct exploration research of anybody. She was sure other caves … Indian Caves especially … had been thoroughly studied and explored, but what if Dr. Stevens' research had never been studied? What if no one had ever followed up on his findings?

What if she was the first and only person to read his journal?

Something stirred in her.

She had to do this.

This was why she … wait.

If people had died even trying to dip water out for their plants, or retrieve a ball, how did she think she would be able to study them? She'd almost drowned so far—twice—once with Mommy and then today.

She skimmed the articles on the computer, not really reading, fussing with a strand of hair dangling over her ear. Twisting it. Winding it around her finger. "A string of pools … " "Depths to … " "Spiritual and magical."

She held her breath. Then let it blow out when she realized she wasn't breathing.

Licking her lips over and over was making them chapped. She dug out her lip gloss and popped the lid off. She applied some and smacked her lips.

Yuck. Full of dirt.

She grabbed a Kleenex and wiped it all off. Gritty.

Noell stretched. She'd been perspiring and wasn't even aware of it. It wasn't hot in the house. It had been shut up all day, so still retained the cool night temperatures.

Good articles.

She wanted to know more.

She was drawn … no, she had been set up to find the caves and pools in Dr. Stevens' journals. She knew in her gut—gut was Gamma's word—that she was supposed to explore. She knew she needed to follow his research. No matter what.

Just having been in that hole today made her even more sure, fear or no fear.

This was what she was supposed to do in life. Maybe not as a scientist.

Wait.

Why not as a scientist?

Dr. Stevens had studied many areas, many paths.

She needed to follow her heart. God's heart for her. That's what Gamma always said.

God's heart for her.

Katty wanted to kill. She had driven to Clarence's before she did something stupid, like booze, drugs or … hurt Bea. He could always talk her down. His place was better than being at that crappy trailer. Sometimes, with the new deck out front, it didn't seem so bad. But today … she wanted to kill.

She slammed the laptop closed. She had failed another one. Another test. Why did she ever let Clarence talk her into going to school? Her dad had always told her she was stupid—

"Katty?" Clarence looked up from the file he was reading. "What's wrong?"

Her face burned. She wanted a fix. A drink. Whatever made her think she was smart enough to be a paralegal for him?

"Katty." He put the paper down and leaned in. "Tell me."

Her eyes burned now, too. "I failed another test. I can't do this. I—"

"You *can* do this, Katty." Clarence stood, shuffled around the desk and sat on the chair next to her. "What was the test on?"

"Words." She glanced up at his face. "Just vocabulary." She opened the laptop again. "Affidavit. Adult. Ad—"

"I can teach you those." He looked at Bea watching educational

TV. "How do they teach the little ones?" He pulled a yellow legal pad close and clicked open a pen. "Let's start with … five words. Adult. Adultery. Adopt. Affidavit. And … apple." He tried not to smile, but his right eye twitched.

Goofy man.

He pushed the list to her. "And next week, we'll have five more." He nodded and held her gaze. "You can do this."

Bea crawled up on his lap. "I want a list."

He chuckled. "Okay." He tore off a corner piece from the yellow pad and began to write. "Red. Rose. Bea." He handed it to her. "And just like Mommy, learn everything you can about those words—what they mean, how you use them in a sentence."

"But one is me." Bea pointed to her name.

"Well, that's the most important one. Then find out everything you can," he tapped her chest, "about you."

Katty watched, mesmerized, then added her own name to the list he had shoved at *her*.

She stapled a couple sheets of paper together and skimmed the contents. Then glanced at the boxes in front of her. "Clarence, what am I looking for? These look like some kind of legal document … " She shook her head. Those boxes were stuffed with papers. This could take forever.

Clarence leaned closer, picked up Bea and sat her on his lap. "Hmm. Court proceedings." He motioned for her to flip over the page. "Signed by my dad." He scanned further down the page. "Clynder. Ted Clynder. That's the name of the lawyer we always went to for legal needs." He wiped Bea's nose.

He sat her down. "Set those aside with Clynder on them. Just put them in the same pile."

"Here's more." She flipped the page to read the signatures. "Signed by your dad." She put the papers down. "What was he like, anyway?"

"Who? Dad?" Clarence leaned back in his chair. "He was a great man. An artist. Creative. Great businessman." He sighed. "Mainly a master of wood working—a master at his craft. And known for it. People would come a long ways. One family wanted him to go to

Chicago to build their home. Wish I would have had more time with him." Clarence looked out the window. "Robbed of the best years of my life with him because of that bastard, Judge Green."

Bea looked up from the TV. "What's a bastard?"

Katty looked at Clarence.

Clarence looked at Katty, then Bea.

"It means … well, that he was not a nice man."

"Was your Dad a nice man?" Bea rolled on the floor and kicked the TV.

"Bea, stop kicking." Katty moved Bea away from the furniture.

"Uh, yes." Clarence grimaced. "Do you want to get some ice cream, Bea?"

Katty chuckled. "Skirting the issue. Good lawyer tactic, Clarence."

Clarence wiped his eyes.

First time she had seen him blush.

He pulled Bea to her feet, took her hand and closed the door behind them.

Huh. Shouldn't have said that. She might have hurt his feelings.

She was so messed up. Even now. Especially now.

She used to be messed up because of the drugs and booze—really messed up. But since she had met Clarence, he'd helped her get cleaned up and given her this chance. Being his legal assistant would be hard—he was tough—but it had already been so rewarding. Helping Carol with hard issues with her husband Joe. Even the Sheriff had enlisted Clarence in on some very interesting cases.

Just because a lawyer was fresh out of school didn't give him or her the experience Clarence had—what with his years in prison.

She looked at the closed door and sighed. She sat in Clarence's chair that he hardly ever sat in.

She was still messed up. Even though she wanted a drink in a bad way, she also wanted truth. She'd have to be careful where to use it. Like just now with Clarence. Several times with Bea, she'd caught herself demanding truth. Being perfectionistic. Bea was only four.

She wanted so badly to be a good mom. But who did she have to learn from? Her own mom had been …. Visuals of being slammed against the kitchen table. Of being pushed down the steps. Never outside. Always hidden from the outside world. The sting of a hand against her tender cheek. A reflection in the mirror of red welts that couldn't be disguised or hidden. There was no make-up that ever hid the scars deep inside.

Katty wiped her eyes.

She glanced at the closed door. Bea deserved a good mom.

Eyes closed. Elbows on her knees. Face in her hands.

"Help me Jesus. I can't … do this." She opened her eyes. "I want to be like Carol. Mrs. Hatly." Deep ragged sigh. "God I want to be … help."

She leaned her head back against the cushioned headrest of Clarence's chair and watched the door.

Maybe they'd bring her an ice cream cone too.

Someone knocked on the door and pushed it open.

"Clarence in here?"

Carol. Her beautiful green eyes had more in them than just color. She radiated love. How, with all she had … work, Joe.

Katty wiped her face. "Uh, no. He—"

"Ice cream, right? He took Bea for some ice cream?" Carol turned to the hallway. "I'll find him." She looked back at Katty. "You okay? You seem … "

Katty nodded. "I'm fine."

"You sure?" Carol's eyes softened somehow. Glistened.

Something passed between them. She had just prayed to be more like Carol and here … she was.

She shivered. That didn't just happen.

"Well, if you ever need to talk, Katty, I'm here." Carol raised her eyebrows and smiled.

The door closed softly behind her.

Had stuff like this happened before and she was just too drunk to see?

Papers became visible again. Stacks and boxes of papers.

She wanted to stay and wanted to run.

Help.

Huh. More documents with Dawes Timmelsen's name on them. "553 Hawkeye Street." Another piece of property purchased by Dawes Timmelsen. She picked up another sheet. Dawson Retrieval: Reclaim Systems. Who was Dawson? Or what? Clarence's dad's name was Dawes. This was on a legal document, and this was taken to Polk County Court, so it couldn't be his dad. His name was—

High sing-song voice and a bass voice burst into the room as the door pushed open.

Katty laughed. "What on earth are you two singing?"

Clarence handed her a styrofoam cup of ice cream covered in rainbow sprinkles, spoon claiming rights to the mountain. "Ice cream courtesy of me. Sprinkles are all Bea's."

"Aren't they pretty, Mommy?" Bea licked her cone. Her cone was covered with about as many sprinkles as Katty's dish.

She shook her head. "They are pretty. But do they taste good?" She took a bite and shivered. "Yum! Yummy!"

"I knew you'd like them Mommy. Clarence didn't think so, but I know you."

Katty blinked. "Who is this little girl who sounds so much like me?"

Bea stood up straight. "I'm me!" She pointed to her own chest. "I'm Bea! That's who!"

"Are you finding anything of importance?" Clarence sat and swiveled to face Katty. "Maybe we should just stack those boxes over there on top of the other boxes from prison." He stuck his spoon back in the ice cream and shrugged his shoulders. "That way we'll know where they are."

"Don't you want to know what's in these? Why Pete had them?" She wiped a sprinkle from Bea's cheek and fed it to her, licking her fingers. "What were they doing in that old building of his, anyway?"

Clarence shrugged and licked his spoon. "I don't know. And I do want to know what all this is, but I probably should get at Noell's Gamma's stuff. Get that settled for her." He shook his head. He stood and closed the door. "She doesn't realize it yet, but she is a wealthy young woman."

"With all that stuff in the house, you mean? The hoarding?"

"Well, there may be some good stuff in there." He shook his head. "I'd hate to go through it all. That was one good thing about being in prison—you couldn't keep much stuff. There just isn't room in a cell."

Katty glanced at the boxes of books. "Where did you keep all those, then?" She leaned back in her chair and scooped a bite.

He chuckled. "Since I was a lawyer, I had a small office." He looked from one wall to the opposite wall, waving his spoon as he eyed the room. "I guess it was a fourth of this room, but it provided privacy for any clients. Prison has big ears."

She shrugged. "Then what else did her grandma have? I know she worked a lot of years, right? At the telephone office?" She pointed to a drip on Bea's cone. "Lick that up, Bea."

"She did work and leave a nice pension, but she had also purchased land." He opened a file folder. "Her husband started before he died to buy up a section or half a section at a time. She just kept it up."

"Here in Polk County? Or where?"

"All over." He pointed to another drip running down Bea's cone. "Lick that. There." He shrugged. "Even in other states."

"Wow. Does Noell know?" Katty grinned as Bea licked around the outside of the cone and took a bite of the crunchy wafer.

Then her grin faded. What did she have to leave Bea?

Not. One. Thing.

She sucked in a deep breath and closed her eyes. She could do this … this life.

What was Mrs. Hatly always saying? Everything always works out.

Each day, Clarence taught her a little more. Every day, she learned from Harold, Mrs. Hatly and from Carol. Even Lisha.

If she started now … well, after she got through school, she could start then.

She opened her eyes. No. Now. She'd start now.

She tossed her empty cup in the trash and picked up a pile of documents. Some were stuck together and when she peeled them apart, a candy wrapper was in between. 3 Musketeers. Nasty. She threw it away. Names seemed highlighted on the papers: Judge Green, Dawes Timmelsen, Clarence Timmelsen.

She compared several documents and they all had those names on them. "Where's the legal pad you just had, Clarence?"

He slid it to her. "What'd you find?" He scraped at the inside of his cup. One last bite.

She began to copy addresses down and soon had a list of twenty or so. She took out her phone and tapped on the screen.

She looked up to see him watching her. "Who's Henry Green?" She flipped a page. "I get Judge Green and I know what your dad's name is. But who is Henry Green?"

He shook his head. "I-I don't—" He threw his cup away.

She spread out several papers in front of them. "Do you know you own maybe," she counted on her finger, "most of downtown—plus?" She pushed the papers to him.

He choked. "I own what? Do we have a map of Osceola?"

Katty tapped on her phone and passed it to Clarence.

He checked back and forth between the papers and the map on the phone. He looked dazed. "Damn. I own three-fourths of the whole town!" He stood and spread the papers out, moved the boxes to the floor to make more room. "Even Judge Green's house?" He plopped down hard on his office chair, rolling backward.

What do you say to a millionaire? Maybe even a billionaire?

He rolled forward again, pushing off with his good leg, both elbows on the desk. "What did you do, Dad? And I thought you were just a carpenter."

Katty scanned the papers in order by date. "He bought the town, piece-by-piece." She pointed to each sheet. "Day-by-day. Block-by-block."

He wiped his face. "And Judge Green's house was the crowning glory, I'll bet." He closed his eyes and leaned his head back against the chair. "Revenge. I bet he did it all to get Judge back." He opened his eyes. "And for me. He did it for me."

Bea climbed on his lap. "Do you own the swimming pool?"

Clarence laughed, then stopped and looked at Katty. "Do I?"

"Well, if you do, you own the park, too."

Bea chimed in. "And the swings?"

Katty laughed. "Oh you are too funny."

Clarence started digging through his pockets. "Where is that article?" He patted his shirt.

"What article?"

He stood Bea on the floor, and pulled it out of his jeans pocket. He opened it and read out loud. "It seems his assistant Henry Green, fell into a pool in a cave they were studying near the Old Ridge Road."

Katty had never seen Clarence's eyes so serious, except when she had first met him in the park and he had protected Bea from her. "What? Who is—"

"Henry Green?" He finished her question. "Could Henry Green be … Judge Green's brother?" He checked the documents, his fingers tapping the desk. "I think they were brothers. Judge Green's brother drowned in a pool?"

He looked down at his leg. "In *that* pool? What else was that Judge guilty of?"

Bill and Rat pulled up saplings growing around the camper, and Noell tried the door.

"Locked. I forgot to ask Steve for a key."

A saw buzzed behind the camper. Small trees flew into the air.

Bill walked up beside her. "I bet it's not. Bet it's froze shut—just stuck real good." He yanked on it, but it held tight. "Well, maybe not. Maybe it is locked." He looked down at her. "So, no key?"

"I forgot to ask." She scratched her head under her hard hat and settled it on her head again.

"Here. Let me." Rat threw a tree onto the pile and shoved his way between them. He planted his feet in front of the camper door, took one hard yank on the door knob and the door broke free. The door knob came off in his hand. "Oh-oh." He dropped it in her hand.

"Now, what do I do with this?" she asked.

Bill picked it out of her hand and examined it, holding it up to the door. "Aww, we can get this fixed in no time." He ushered her inside. "Take a look at your new abode, Little Princess."

Noell stood there a minute absorbing what Bill had just called her. Somehow it fit. She was living in a fairy tale and this was her kingdom. This was her coronation day. Well, it was just an old camper, but she knew big things were happening. This was the day.

She shivered as she stepped inside. Dark. Kinda creepy, but not bad. A veil of cobwebs barred her entry until she swiped them away. They added another layer to her already dirty orange shirt. Stuck like contact paper. Where they draped over her arm, her skin tingled. Strange stuff—spider webs.

The camper smelled, but not as bad as she expected. Musty, but not dirty. Except for stale air from being closed up for … a hundred years, it wasn't too bad.

Kind of warm, too, but it wasn't anything like it would be come August.

A little kitchenette: oven, cook top, tiny aqua sink, ice box—really a cooler. In all its glory. It was beautiful. Dirty yellow curtains were the reason she hadn't been able to see through the window. A long bench across from the kitchenette was upholstered in some kind of flowered vinyl. A built-in eating area.

She clapped her hands. "So cute!" Rich wood lined every surface that was not a bed or kitchen. "Sweet. Sweet. Sweet." Even after this long, the wood still looked fantastic. A good wiping down would restore it.

A calendar dated 1937, advertising Thelma's Eatery and Diner, hung on the side of a … she opened the door … bathroom! This thing had a bathroom? Cute little sink and potty. Checkerboard tiles on the floor. Oops. Some were loose.

She opened a cupboard door beside the oven, and a pan fell out.

Bill stuck his head in. "It comes stocked? Awesome."

Rat stepped in, and the trailer leaned with his weight on one side. "This is cool." He laughed. "Pint sized for a pint size girl." He opened the bathroom door. "You got your own restroom." He looked down at her. "How you gonna do that? How you gonna dump that shit?" He covered his mouth. "Oh, sorry. But really. How you gonna take care of that?"

Leaning against the doorframe, Bill nodded his head. "We'll find a way. It'll be fine."

Noell popped her head up. "You'll help me?"

"Of course, Little Princess. This is a piece of cake. Or pie—like in apple."

"I could do that. I could bake you a pie—with Gamma's recipe. She was a great pie baker." She started to jump up and down but stopped, knees bent, her hands spread out like she had just landed square off a balance beam in gymnastics. "Will we break through this floor?"

"Bet not. These things were pretty sturdy." Rat checked with Bill. "Unless there's a rotting issue." He jiggled and danced. "Feels okay."

"Once we move it out, we can check for rotting. It happens in the best of houses."

Hah, Bill. She was beginning to love him almost as much as Steve. Rat, though, seemed to be another kind of guy entirely.

"Thanks you guys for helping."

Bill scrunched his face like Grandpa used to, and nodded. "Sure thing. But should I put my order for apple pie in now—just to be sure, ya know?"

She laughed. "You better. Once I … we … get this home and moved in … I mean this settled … I might just be too busy to bake." She opened an overhead cabinet, and a book fell out on her head. "Ouch."

Rat picked it up and handed it to her.

She flitted through it and exclaimed, "Wow. Comes with my own personal library." The leather on it was embossed with a cross on the front. If only she wasn't at work—she'd sit down and study it. She stuffed it back in the cabinet and slammed the door quickly. "Should I clean it out first, before we move it, or wait?"

"I'd wait," Bill said. "Then you will have all the time in the world to go through things. You might find some treasures. If that calendar isn't a replica, that's even antique." He adjusted his hard hat. "Plus, moving it to your place would stir up dirt, I'd think. Might be junk in here you don't want and then you'll have the time to decide."

"When do you think we could move it?"

"Rat, you free after work today?"

Rat grinned and nodded. "Yup. But I don't think she can bake a pie that fast."

"I'll owe you both." She clapped her hands again. "I am so excited! I have always wanted my own little place. Tiny place," she corrected.

"Well, now you have one." Bill knocked on the outside wall. "Now that you have a camper, you'll need a fishing pole."

She stole a glance at Rat, but he didn't seem to pick up on it what Bill said. Good. She had reconsidered their fishing date.

Lots of work in store for her. Not as bad as Gam's house, but still work. But, this was going to be fun, no doubt about it.

Bill clapped his hands. "Back to work, guys. Steve won't be happy if we don't get this lot cleaned up."

The afternoon lagged, but they finished cleaning the back lot. It wasn't nearly as boring as running paper through a copy machine.

The sun was warm. Swallows dive bombed Bill's hard hat. The guys bantered back and forth, even picked on Noell, with laughter in between. Except for Ken. He just sulked, raked a little, then sulked some more. At the end of the day, Noell realized she hadn't thought of germs or hoarding once. Amazing. Must be good for her to get outside and experience real dirt, instead of people's germs.

When Steve let them all go for the day, they headed out back to get the camper hooked up and ready to travel. Anything that could fly around on the inside was shoved into a cupboard. Not many were empty.

Bill backed up his pickup to the camper hitch. It wasn't even the right size, it was so old. He rummaged around in the compartment behind his seat and held up several. "One of these'll work."

Rat laughed. "Wow, Bill, you have everything back there. You are the handiest guy to have around."

"Wife says I need to clean it all out. Now I have witnesses. I really need all that … junk." He grinned as he knelt at the hitch. "Even if we have to pull it with a rope tied onto my truck, it'll work. It isn't that heavy, like campers are nowadays."

"You think? It has a lot of wood in there." Steve tapped on the siding. "Even this siding is heavier than the plastic stuff they put on now." He looked back at Noell. "Pretty neat find, girl. This is cool. If this doesn't work out for you, I'll take it off your hands."

"Wait a minute." Ken stepped in front of the camper. "How long has she been working here? A week? If that?" He threw off his hard hat and crossed his arms. "I could have been using it last season for fishing." He pointed at Noell. "How come she gets it when I've been here for six months?"

"*Four* months." Steve corrected him. "Because she asked. You didn't. Simple as that."

"Ask and you get," said Miguel.

Steve nodded. "Right, Miguel. Something like that." He looked at Bill ready to pull away in his pickup and waved his arm. "All righty. Let's see what this truck of yours will do."

The screeches and groans of the camper would have made great sound clips for a spooky movie as the truck strained to pull it out. Steve motioned for all to get behind the camper and push. Tires had sunk in so deep she couldn't tell if they still held air. Eventually it released, standing pretty as you please, the late afternoon sun reflecting off the chrome. White—or dirty cream colored top half. Gold colored bottom half. Nice.

Ken stood aside, a frown on his face.

Only problem was four flat tires.

"It's not going anywhere like that."

"Oh no. I don't have money for tires." Noell shook her head. "You couldn't even tell they were flat when they were still buried in weeds and dirt." She hung her head.

Steve sidled up to Noell. "I think I can find some old tires somewhere. Maybe even the right size." He elbowed her arm and pointed to the old boundary fence. "Lookie there. There's a few spare ones, to boot."

"But—"

"I told you to clean this place. Cleaning out this camper *and* those tires." He held his hand up for a high-five.

She barely tapped his hand with hers and wiped her eyes. How could she ever repay this man?

Miguel and Rat pushed and shoved each other as they ran to the pile of tires. Were they still in high school? Ken lagged behind.

Rat pulled a tire from the weeds and rolled it to Miguel. Miguel lobbed it to Ken, only it knocked him over. They dove and wrestled for the tire. Rat ended up with it around his shoulders.

Noell lost it. Belly laugh. All the way from her toes. Laughing had never, ever felt this good.

Steve caught her as she misstepped, still laughing. What a blast! She caught her breath.

She had friends.

And six tires. Wow.

They rolled a couple to the back of Bill's truck and bounced them in, one by one.

"You get bonus tires."

"Hey, I need some for my car." Ken finally acted interested when it came to something for him.

"There's two left over." Steve took a vote. "Anybody have a problem with that?"

"Yeah." Rat spoke up. "Ken just bought new tires. Miguel needs them more than him."

Miguel grinned. "Really? I can have the tires?"

Noell pipped up. "He can have them all … Miguel, if you need them."

Miguel shook his head. "No. No."

"Okay." Steve clicked off each man. "Everybody okay with the two extras going to … Miguel?"

"Aye."

"Yup."

"Where do you want the rest?"

Steve pointed to the camper.

"Cool." Rat grabbed one and rolled it toward the camper.

Bill kept it going to Steve and waited for the next one.

"Hey Bill."

His head popped up from behind the ever-faithful backseat storage compartment. "Found my jack." He walked to the camper, carrying it over his shoulder. "I had no idea this would be so much fun."

With four guys changing tires and Bill's endless supply of tools, it took no time to get the new tires on. Wheel covers were kind of rusty and lug nuts were tight, but they had what they needed for the job.

Bill honked at them. "Come on. Let's get this done!" He waved them to the back bed of his truck. Rat held the passenger door open for Noell. She tossed her backpack in and jumped onto the seat. Rat got in and slammed the door, pounding on the outside with his hand. "We're off!"

Steve followed in his truck with Miguel and the others, except for Ken, who walked behind, still frowning. He wasn't cute anymore.

Noell was squished between Bill and Rat, and she had never felt more a part of something than now. Like a family. Everybody pitching in just to help her was overwhelming. No one except Gam had ever taken it upon themselves to do something so nice for her and to help her.

Well, except Fletch.

They pulled around a corner and the camper dragged to the left, right at the corner of the park where the old highway crossed the rail road tracks. Ahhh no.

Bill hopped out. "Flat tire."

Rat hopped out.

Noell kind of slid out, not wanting to see the damage.

Steve knelt to check. "Good thing you stopped. These rims are really strong, harder metal than they make nowadays, but better to stop and check instead of ruining them." He looked up at Noell. "Sorry the tires weren't the best of deals."

"It's okay." She shrugged. "Getting a camper for free, some … tires, and the help to get it all home is amazing."

Rat inspected the little area of the park. "Hey. What if you left it here? It's really not on park property, I don't think. You'd have bathrooms down there at the park if you needed them—showers too, I think —and a very nice little piece of ground to live on. Lots of trees and shade." He stopped and looked at Noell. "Or do you need it to be on your gramma's lot?"

Noell raised her eyebrows and stuttered. "Well, I … Gam maybe wouldn't like me to sleep here. She might need help in the night or something."

Silence.

Oh God. Gamma's gone. She wiped at her eyes.

Steve stepped to her, his hand on her shoulder.

She blew out a deep breath. Oh, to run away right now.

"You okay with it here for a while and see how it goes? Otherwise, we can throw on a new tire and keep on going to your … your place. It's up to you."

Noell thought a minute. "Seems okay here. For now." She spied Ken, lurking on the other side of the road.

Steve saw him, too. "Maybe we'd better get it over to your place. You never know who might want to pay you a visit when you're least expecting it."

Bill entered in. "Yup." He let down the gate to the bed of his truck. "Let's get another tire down and switch them."

They again made quick work of the tire change and were on their way to Gamma's. The place would never be Noell's. Forever Gamma's.

As they drew near, Bill pointed. "Okay if we back it over there? Kinda between the two houses. Your door would open facing your house. And it's kind of secluded from the road and the neighbors."

"Sure. Looks okay." Hard to know.

Bill was great at backing in, and pretty soon the little camper was in place. They all got out and unhitched it. "We can come over and jimmy it around for you if this doesn't feel right."

Noell shivered as she looked at the little camper, her new little home. Settled with a row of trees behind it, a backdrop of the old trellis framing an entrance to the garden that Gams hadn't used in many years.

Her own secret garden.

Goosebumps traveled up her arms and she rubbed them. It all seemed perfectly planned and ready for her to thrive here.

"Anything else we can do for you, Madam?" Rat bowed low, faking a plumed hat and sword.

She laughed in delight and curtsied. "No, my lords, all is well." She clapped her hands until she saw Ken following their trail. "Thank you all so much. I am so excited. I'll have to learn to cook so I can repay you somehow."

"Pie. Apple."

"You may repay at any time, M'Lady."

"I could buy you pizza," she offered.

The guys all perked up at that.

Bill held up his hand. "Wait a minute. Let's let her get this thing settled first. Let Noell get things put together and then we'll talk pizza. Okay guys?"

"Deal. Thanks again all."

Bill stepped away from the door. "I think that'll do it." He rattled the doorknob. "It is good as new."

"Uh … well, … uh, we'd better be going, right guys?" Steve stepped up to her and jingled a set of keys in front of her face. "I found 'em. Here you go, and may you have fun with this new adventure."

"Thanks Steve." She took them in her hands and flipped them over, reading the numbers and the inscription on them. There were markings—

Bill honked as he drove away.

Noell waved at them, even at Ken as they pulled away from the house. She shoved the keys into her pants pocket.

Gamma would have loved this.

She would have limped out with cookies in her walker basket, a delighted grin on her face.

Oh, Gamma.

TWENTY-FIVE

Mr. Zee stood by his window, scanning his new office space. It was not the best in the world, but it was better than it had been. The nursing home board, people from the community, hadn't agreed to all renovations, but he had found ways to expand his budget. And of course it was at the expense of every resident and staff in Hillcrest Homes.

The board had proposed a new resident and staff dining room and he had convinced them that the leadership of the nursing home was at risk if they didn't approve *his* new addition instead. Well. It was a little more dramatic than that—he had dropped the hint that their precious stipend would end if they didn't approve his plans. Wherever did they get the idea that the board was in charge?

Staff, unfortunately, had to sacrifice raises indefinitely. There weren't enough funds to do both, which didn't go well for the staff's team spirit. But there was always back-biting among the nurses and aides, so he enjoyed stirring that up as an added sidelight.

Loretta, the receptionist, had been promoted to his personal secretary, so she had no problem with his decisions. She loved her new space. New designer carpet with rich golds and browns—very plush. New equipment and computers, office furniture. Beautiful paintings of families engaged in … family things—like Thanksgiving meals, reunions. That sort of thing. Something he had no experience with. Nice facade.

Even the words on his coffee mug fed into his mounting ago—The Boss—and it was due for a refill. Ahh. Coffee aroma was always good, but this imported stuff was over-the-top.

He stepped to the window and sipped. He had a perfect view of who was coming and going at the front door. He had purposely designed the addition so he could enjoy the new landscaping—roses, bushes, trees, garden sculptures.

Deep sigh. Mmm. Delicious coffee. Beautiful day.

Who was that limping down the sidewalk? Splint on his leg. Cane. Longer gray hair.

Mr. Zee leaned into the glass.

Clarence.

Clarence was getting into a red truck. Couldn't see the driver. He didn't have any relatives. There was that younger woman … what was her name? She had a kid. Unless she had purchased a newer pick-up, that wasn't her.

Back to his desk. He keyed in Clarence's name on his computer. "T-i-m-e-l." Back-space. "Two m's." When the file opened, he scanned the records and nurses notes.

Nope. No known relatives. Even that young woman wasn't related.

One note was dated when Clarence was first admitted—"Repeatedly escapes to explore the town. Seems harmless. He grew up here in Osceola."

He keyed in a different date. "Came back with rusty pipes today. What the heck?"

Pipes?

Later date. "Always talking about a Michael guy." Huh. Mr. Zee glanced toward the window. He knew they worked together on a building in town.

Another date. "Angry old man." Ha. Lisha's notes.

Back to the window. The red truck drove off

Clarence was escaping again.

TWENTY-SIX

Clarence tucked the yellow legal pad Katty had written addresses on under one arm and lifted the cane with the other hand. This cane stuff took co-ordination. Made sense though. Cane on his right side to protect his right leg.

He limped his way from the front door of the old people's home to the street. Felt good to be outside, even with the damn cane. Air smelled better outside. Of course, *he* might be part of the stink indoors. Maybe.

Cane down. Right leg down. He had practiced in the hallway inside, but it still felt strange and unbalanced. Cane down. Left foot step. There should be a video teaching this because it didn't come naturally.

There was Michael in his new red truck. An automatic. Clarence chuckled even now about the many grinding rides he'd taken with Michael. He was going to miss those.

He paused to view the scenery before him. It had been awhile since he had escaped to explore the town. He'd get back to it once this leg healed. The park to his left, where the pool was, looked mowed up and beautiful. In front of him in the distance, the court house rose majestically above every other building downtown. He shook his head. Wished he owned the court house. That was one fine building.

He jingled change as he remembered addresses, mentally pointing out the buildings. "That's mine. That one's mine. The old Town hall is mine." He whistled. "Never saw it coming. Dad. Dad." According to Katty's map on her phone, he even owned many of the houses surrounding the town square. Many of the lots.

Ha. Including Judge Green's old lot. Would have been nice if the house hadn't been torn down, but he could identify with his dad for ripping the damned thing apart, no matter how beautiful it had been.

Clarence gulped when the enormity of what his father had done, hit him. He blinked. Blew out a deep breath and blinked again. How Dad must have suffered. His only son being dragged off to prison—never seeing him again. Clarence could forgive him for not coming to visit.

One of the hardest days, next to Mom's death, was when they had hauled him off to prison. He'd never, ever forget Dad's face. The pain in his eyes. Horrible even now. Horrible.

The hardest day of all—the day Annie died. A lump rose in his throat, even now. Had to swallow it down like always. Sixty years.

Michael drove up and parked in the handicapped spot. He climbed out and hurried around the truck to help Clarence in, opening the door. "Michael, hi. You don't need to help me. I can get in myself." He proceeded to trip over the cane and Michael caught him just as he fell into the door. He leaned into Michael until he got the cane out of the way and his feet straightened. "Well, maybe I do need help."

"I'll say you do. You just about crashed." Michael eased him into the truck and closed the door. He walked around the front of the truck and got in, shifted into reverse. "So the courthouse today? That where you want to start?"

Clarence nodded. "Yes. I can't remember if you were in my rooms then or not. But Katty started digging out one deed after another yesterday. All from that bastard, Pete's boxes." He paused. "Thank God his secretary dumped them on me." He glanced at Michael. "Might have never known what Dad did back then." He fumbled with the legal pad. "Did you know, Michael?"

Michael started to shake his head no but stopped. "I knew, but I have no right to interfere without Father's command … or yours."

Clarence pointed to his chest. "Mine?" He turned in his seat to face Michael as much as a bench seat would let him. "Like in, I could command you to do something?"

Michael stopped at the stop sign and looked directly at Clarence. "Yes, Clarence. But only if it's Father's will."

Clarence stared back. "Why didn't I know this sooner? I would have commanded you to release me from prison. To fly me home on your wings. Take me back in time before Annie died."

"I'm not an airplane, Clarence."

Clarence chuckled. "But you could have, right?" Why didn't he know? He'd gone to church all his childhood, well, after Mom died, it became sporadic, but they had gone every Sunday before she got sick. "What *can* I tell you to do, Michael?"

Michael glanced at him out of the corner of his eye. Back to the street as they stopped at the Railroad tracks. Glanced at him again.

"What. Did Father command you not to tell?" Clarence grinned. "You're afraid I'll tell you to do something …" He searched the sky and their surroundings. A train blasted its horn. "Something like jump in front of that train."

The train chugged in front of them.

No comment from Michael.

They bumped over the tracks after the train passed.

"Or, rob the bank for me. Clean 'em out." Clarence laughed again as they pulled into a parking space in front of the new bank.

Michael shook his head. "I couldn't break into that bank."

"Against your religion?"

"No. It's fortified with steel girders and the vault is impenetrable." Michael pointed to the front windows. "Says so in their brochures."

"Michael. Y-you read their brochures?"

"Well, what else am I supposed to do while I wait for you? It's a new bank and I wanted to find out more about it." Michael looked in the rear view mirror to behind him. "Looks as good as the courthouse does. Or, vise versa."

Clarence struggled to see behind him. "It does, doesn't it? I should get in there before they close."

Michael pointed to the bank. "There?"

Clarence pointed behind him. "No, the courthouse." He tapped his list. "Need to find out if my name is actually on the deeds registered in there." He opened his door. "Let's go."

They got out and jaywalked across the street—Clarence cane tapped and Michael followed.

"This is a great building, huh, Michael," Clarence said. "Do they even build them like this anymore?" He pointed at the level above them. "The windows still look great. The brick is solid. Everything looks well done."

A woman met them, coming out of the building.

Pete's secretary.

She didn't smile. In fact, she did the opposite, like in a soft growl. Her eyes could have penetrated the bank vault that Michael had been talking about. She'd be prettier if she smiled.

Clarence watched her stomp down the sidewalk and into Pete's old insurance agency. "Guess they're closing the place up, huh." He looked again. "How does she walk in those spike heels? I'd break my … well, it's …"

Back to the courthouse. Huge pillars. How had they done that back then?

A man pushed open the door from inside and held it for them.

Clarence nodded. "Thanks." He stepped into the entrance. "Wow. The marble. It shines. Stunning." The steps curved up forever. "Look at these steps." He looked up at Michael. "Is this one of those times I can command you to fly me upstairs?"

Michael grinned and hooked Clarence's arm with his. He took a step at a time, with Clarence by his side.

"Woah. We *are* flying. Kind of." Clarence moved each foot, but he didn't need the cane anymore. Felt like he was floating. "Michael."

"What?"

"Michael, are *you* doing this?" They made it to the first landing and Clarence got distracted by the marble. He paused to run his hand along the step above. "Look at the curve on this one. How did they cut this? Whoever built this was a fine craftsman."

Michael glanced above him, seemingly lost in the beauty, his face peaceful, beautiful.

"What are you thinking? It's beautiful isn't it?"

Michael flinched. "Uh, yes, but that's not what I was thinking of. It is beautiful, though."

They reached the top step. Clarence wasn't even out of breath or tired. He turned to enjoy Michael's expression again. "What were you thinking, then?"

Michael helped Clarence move out of the way of a person heading downstairs.

"What, Michael?"

Michael glanced at Clarence and then quickly tipped his head toward the Clerk's office. Back to Clarence. "I was with your dad when he registered the deeds to the plots he purchased back then."

Clarence swallowed. "How?" He slid down onto a nearby bench.

"I was assigned to you from before you were born to this earth." Michael sat beside him. "And I have been with you ever since." He watched a man in overalls walk out of the Treasurer's office and down the steps.

The tap, tap of the man's boots echoed throughout the building. The door downstairs clicked shut.

Michael spoke again softly. "But when your dad purchased all of the lots, Father sent me to him. He was grieving badly for you and your mom. But for you."

A tear slid down Clarence's cheek. A ragged breath escaped.

"That day, the day he walked into that office there," Michael pointed, "and registered each deed in his name, he didn't rejoice. He didn't party." Michael dropped his arm in his lap and bowed his head. "He wept." Shaking his head. "And wept."

Clarence finally found his voice, cleared his throat. "Revenge didn't help."

Michael shook his head, still bowed. "He loved you so much."

Clarence leaned forward, his face in his hands. The cane clattered to the floor.

He wasn't sure how long he had sat like that—probably seconds, maybe minutes—but as he straightened, his eyes landed on a portrait of some guy from the early days of Osceola. Clarence didn't know who the guy was, but he must have done something good, been someone so upstanding, that he had gotten his portrait on a wall in the court house.

Was there a wall of fame at the prison? Kind of. Either bad or good, it probably was in a guard's heart, or the dietary woman's memories of how she had been mocked, ridiculed, insulted. Or how an inmate made that life-changing, split-second decision to not go over the wall, or not throw that first punch.

He must have done something right. Dietary lady had made him a scarf—he still had it.

He knew he had made bad decisions. Hence the memory the day he left prison, of William Austin pacing along the cell bars, flipping him off. But the finger was nothing compared to the evil and hatred William had fired at Clarence. The scar on Clarence's cheek, mostly obscured by his beard, tingled. He rubbed it, remembering the brutal and bloody battle.

He glanced at the portrait again. Eighty years of living and the only acknowledgement for a life well lived was a wool scarf. It was beautiful, but the only thing he'd ever done right for that dietary woman was to tell the ring-leaders in prison to leave her the hell alone.

The man in the portrait passed judgement on Clarence. He swung the gavel down in conviction.

A Pearly Gates moment.

Who had he become?

It wasn't about the acknowledgement—the scarf and the time it had taken her to make it—it was about the heart.

And that arrow pierced the deepest.

As he sat next to Michael on this now very hard bench, the question was asked—the hand writing was on the wall—who had he become?

Michael picked up the cane and patted Clarence's back. "And now, you get to go in there and receive what you rightly own. Fair and square. All legal. Because your dad loved you. He couldn't get you out of prison and believe me, he tried."

Clarence looked up at Michael. "He tried to get me out?"

Michael nodded. "For years. He hated Judge Green—that hatred and grief are what killed him. When he couldn't get you released, he decided an undercover sort of thing might do just as much damage."

"Sounds like revenge." Clarence tapped his cane on his foot. "Sounds like *me*."

Michael nodded again. "Like father like son."

Clarence slammed his cane onto the marble floor. "But it didn't help. It didn't get me out of prison. I was in that damn place sixty years." He shook his head. "Revenge doesn't work." He searched Michael's face. "Does it."

Michael shook his head, paused, then shook it again. "Never has. Never will."

"What works then? We just get to live here on earth mad at each other? Bitter?" He swallowed. "Angry?"

"Read the instruction manual and find out." Michael stood. "Let's go in and get your inheritance."

Clarence struggled to stand. "The instruction manual?" He followed Michael through the door. "The Good Book? The Bible?"

A woman stepped to the counter. "Hi. Can I help you?"

Clarence, still in that moment, pulled out the yellow legal pad, placed it on the counter and spun it around for her to read. "Yes Ma'am. Evidently I own most of Osceola, Nebraska."

TWENTY-SEVEN

Growl.

Noell had been so caught up in exploring her camper, she had forgotten it was suppertime. One last peek inside and she locked it up. She faced the camper, walking backward on her way to the house. It was so cute, she couldn't quit looking at it! And it was hers!

In the kitchen. Cereal for supper. Today felt like she'd been living a fairy tale. She poured the milk and mindlessly ate. She could just barely see the back end of the camper if she moved her chair a little to the right.

Ahh.

A knock sounded at the back kitchen door. Fletch let himself in. His curly blondish-brown hair was even curlier—Nebraska humidity was beginning to rise. His shirt hugged his body. Why hadn't she noticed that before? How old *was* he?

He pointed. "What's that in back? It's really cool." He nodded at Noell. "Is it yours?"

She nodded, a lump in her throat. It still felt unreal. "Yes. It's mine."

"Where'd you find it? It's a little jewel."

"It needs a lot of work. It was behind the office at the Roads

Department in the trees along the fence. We were cleaning out since we were between jobs. Steve told us except for certain pieces of equipment, we could have whatever we found and I found … that."

Fletch raised his eyebrows. "So it's … yours?"

Noell nodded, holding her breath.

He stepped to the window in the kitchen and looked outside a long time, nodding. "Pretty cool."

"Thanks. This has been my dream for a long time."

"It's been your dream to have a camper?" Fletch turned around and half-grinned, his eyes crossed.

Noell laughed. "No, silly. It's been a dream to get out on my own, or at least out from under … this." She waved at the house. "But I can't afford it yet. So that," she motioned in the direction of the camper, "is a way I can make it happen without any … or much cost." She turned back to him. "The Roads guys helped me pull it out, and Steve gave me some old junk tires. All free." She bowed her head slightly. "I know it's kind of an eyesore right now. I'll clean it up so it doesn't look so bad. I hope you aren't mad at how it looks." She fidgeted with her hair. "Do you want to see it?"

"I thought you'd never ask." Fletch opened the door and held it.

Noell ran ahead and unlocked the door. "And I present … my new tiny home!"

Fletch stepped inside. "Oh cool!"

"I know. It needs a lot of work and cleaning, but—"

"Look at all this wood." He smoothed his hand against the trim. "They don't make 'em like this anymore. They're all plastic. Or vinyl." He tapped the stove. "And look at these vintage appliances."

"Yeah. Well." She eyed them. "I still have to find out how everything works."

"Propane. If you cook with electricity, we could find a hot plate somewhere. That would be better. Make it so you can use either one." Fletch was already inspecting the plug-ins, then he ran outside. He must have been checking the connections and exhaust on the outside.

She brushed the counter and checked her hand. "Pretty dirty. I can't believe I just did that."

She sat on the flowered bench seat. "I just swept my hand over that dirty counter." Deep ragged sigh. "Oh Gam. I wish you were here. I wish I could show it to you, too." She studied everything. "The wood just glows—even dirty like it is now. Think what it will look like when it's clean."

She tried to imagine what Gamma would have said had she been here still. Gam was almost visible. Almost.

Noell could almost hear Gamma's voice.

"You brushed the dirty counter with your hand." Gamma patted the bed for Noell to sit beside her. "I've seen you when you come home from work, from school. How you place the paper towel down, then your book bag down and change your boots into slippers."

Noell stared—she could see her now.

Her face burned, and a tear slid down her cheek. She wiped it away. "Gam I'm sorry. I didn't mean to make you think I don't like it here. I—"

"Little one, I know why you do all that—why you are afraid of germs and other people's dirt. It's because you were abandoned."

"I wasn't abandoned. I have you. I've always had you. You ... " She started to sob.

Fletch stuck his head in. "I found ... " He went back outside.

"Oh, Gam. And now you're gone."

She had almost been able to touch Gamma's hand, her face.

Almost.

She could pretend Gam's fingers were caressing hers.

"Honey, when a momma leaves her baby, something happens, no matter how good the caregiver is, something breaks. Does that make sense?" Gamma dried Noell's eyes and touched her cheek, pulling her close.

Almost.

Noell cupped her hand around Gamma's. "It does make sense. But how do I stop being afraid?"

"It's not something you can do on your own."

"So do I have to go to a doctor?"

Gam shook her head.

"Take some medicine?"

"No, Little One. He is the Way."

Noell leaned her head onto Gamma's shoulder.

Only, she was gone. Gam was gone.

That fragrance.

"Hey, uh, … sorry, but there is someone out here that wants to buy your camper." Fletch stuck his head in the door and pointed behind him.

"What? I just got it here." She wiped her face, stood slowly and looked behind her where Gamma had sat. Had that really—

"Sorry, Fletch. Can you tell them I'm not interested? I'm not selling it."

He looked behind him and shook his head. "Not for sale. Thanks." Stepping inside the doorframe, he smiled. "This is really the sweetest little camper I've ever seen. It's really old too, but in such great shape. What a find for you."

Noell slid her hand along the wood door to the little bathroom. "I know. I can't believe it. It has everything I would ever need." She swirled around taking it all in. "Not big, but I don't need big, just … mine."

"Well, I'll let you get on with exploring your new digs. I have some things Mom wants me to do, but if you ever need help, I'd love working on this with you. I mean—I don't want to intrude, but this would be fun to … well, you know what I mean." He waved as he jumped out onto the ground.

"Thanks, Fletch. I will ask. I'm sure I'll need it." She stuttered. Words wouldn't come out right when he was around. Her face got hot just thinking about him. She knew him, but she didn't know him. She knew he was always willing to help. She knew where he lived. But she didn't know his mom, his family. Him.

She opened a cupboard, and a pan fell out. A can fell out too, almost hitting her on the head. "List to make. I need a step stool, cleaning stuff, trash bags. I'll probably just need to toss everything."

She ran into the house and found trash bags and supplies. It would be so cool to sleep out there tonight, but she needed time to really clean. She'd need fresh sheets and blankets.

Hmm. She remembered a box inside Gamma's house somewhere … the dining room … where there were boxes full of sheets and blankets and comforters. Maybe hoarding wasn't so bad after all. She might have everything she needed. All she had to do was go in and find it.

And wash it.

When she returned to the camper, she started digging through all the cupboards, doors, and all the little nooks and crannies.

Books. Notebooks, newspapers, photos.

She took them to the dinette table and sorted through them. She wouldn't throw anything away until she'd had a chance to really figure out what this all meant. Kind of felt like hoarding, but something might be valuable.

Huh. Osceola Record. From … when? 1937. Pictures of a man who wore a shabby straw hat in every picture. A Dr. Walter Stevens.

Huh? A scientist. Researcher? Like in geography or what?

A newspaper article had a picture of him and another man.

She scanned the caption.

His assistant. They were standing beside a small pool of water. He had presented new information about the pool and the water. The assistant looked creepy, standing almost behind the doctor, but to the side, fully visible to the camera.

Something about his eyes.

Reminded her of … someone. Weird.

There was a map too. She wasn't sure, but it looked like Osceola. Couldn't be. There wasn't anything to discover here.

Was there?

She wasn't getting any cleaning done, but she couldn't stop looking at the journals and notebooks. Intrigued. This was an amazing find.

Did this guy—she looked for the right name, Dr. Walter Stevens— had he lived here in this little camper while studying whatever it was that he studied?

Wow. Maybe he was famous.

She grinned. Or not.

She opened the door to another cupboard, and something fell out and hit her on the head. Again.

A book.

She slowly sat.

Bound with soft brown leather. A ribbon had been tied around it to keep it closed, but the ribbon was shredded, falling off in her hands. The knot was still there, though.

She opened the book carefully. It was maybe four inches by six inches—just a small leather-bound notebook. Real leather. Not what they advertised today. It was soft, old.

An old style cross was burned into the cover. A regular cross—not skinny—not chunky, with a round coin-like piece covering the center. The coin had what looked like a thumb print pressed in, but a daisy-like flower was inside that.

She glanced through the pictures and articles scattered on the table, hoping for a reference.

What a unique cross.

Stains added to the beauty of the old leather. Probably coffee or tea stains.

Or was it … blood?

Oh, her imagination could run away sometimes.

As she opened the book, she held her breath hoping dust wouldn't make her sneeze or her allergies flare up. But she promptly forgot about any germs as she read the first page.

"I can't believe what is here. Henry wants to go in but I can't let him. There are reports of a young boy of eight years old falling in as he tried to retrieve his brother's ball from the back of the cave. He never returned. He couldn't be found. As searchers were called in, they dredged the pool as far as they could, but nothing touched bottom. Heartbreaking. His brother had sobbed and sobbed until their mother arrived and found him. Then there were two broken hearts. An older woman had tried to dip water out for her garden and plants. She believed the water contained some sort of magic minerals or potion to make her vegetables grow big. She fell in as she tried to fill pots with water. Again, rescuers tried to find her body. It never turned up. Where had these people gone? The human body floats because it is seventy percent water. They should have floated to the surface. They were never found."

Noell gasped. This was in Osceola?

Wait. Bill at work the other day. He remembered caves and drownings. This might be what he was talking about.

She flipped through the book even more slowly, wanting to read every word. Maps and directions, sketches of the pool and of the surrounding areas, must have been part of Dr. Steven's research. He even had sketches of people he had interviewed and places he had visited. A Mr. Bowman. Someone named Mrs. Bertrand—wasn't that the antique store lady's last name? Maybe her mom.

Bill. Bill at work had been talking about a cave. He remembered drownings … back …

She glanced up at her new little home in the camper. She had to go through the whole thing very carefully and slowly—every nook and cupboard. She couldn't miss a thing.

And who was Henry? Somewhere. She'd heard that name. Lately. Henry. She tapped the table.

She needed to visit the library to research every newspaper from back then to now, check every fact, every date. What a mystery presented by these journals and notes. She had to follow the trail.

"Henry. Where?" She tapped her forehead. "Somewhere." Her head bounced up. "Clarence's wall of frames! The newspaper article!" She shook her head. "He was studying it. I should—"

But a pool would have germs, bacteria. And water. Water was what took her mom away. Water was her nightmare.

She stopped at another page and read. "The water in the pool is the strangest I've ever seen or tested. Seems to be able to radiate light, to make a person turn inside out—I don't know any other way to describe it. I've seen things, too. Things that should not be in that pool—things from my past, my parents, a brother that died when he was seven and I was eight. How is that possible?"

How could she ever explore along the same path of this … this … Dr. Stevens, when she was terrified? She'd almost been on the threshold of digging out of her fears. Now she could feel them return, almost touch them.

At the opening gate was that stupid terror. It was almost … real. Like a person. Standing there in front of her. Guarding against any freedom she might experience.

As she entertained thoughts of exploring and following this path, her mind tingled. Her flesh got goosebumps.

But at the same time, thoughts of the unknown crippled her.

The germs. Disease. Death. What had killed his assistant … this Henry guy?

There was a distinct pulling inside her. First one way, then the other.

The battle.

Which would win out? Determination and adventure? Or fear and torment?

She gathered the articles and journals into a pile, putting the newspaper photograph on top. Dr. Stevens stood in front of a pool, in Osceola, Nebraska, what, seventy-some years ago.

Where was that pool?

TWENTY-EIGHT

Mr. Zee locked up his office and turned toward his secretary. "Loretta, I'm going downtown. Gonna find out a little more about this town, the history and such. Might be able to drum up more benefactors for Hillcrest."

"Sure, Boss." Loretta tapped on her computer keyboard, her eyes scanning one monitor to the next as she worked. Up to the minute technology.

He had been surprised at her abilities—especially with computing. Never put a blond down.

The wiring for this addition had been a nightmare, but he hadn't backed down when the installation guy had complained. There was no way he would give up his bank of monitors. He needed to stay on top of things in Hillcrest.

So far, it had been a frustrating morning. After he'd seen Clarence leave, there had been two staff disputes, a decision on where to have the family carnival in July—since he had taken the customary space for his addition, and a resident complaint. The woman's daughter had insisted her mother be given dining room privileges, a better view from her table. Why wouldn't she want to be seated next to the kitchen? She got her food faster than anyone else. Picky-picky.

He walked to his car and unlocked it but noticed a spot on the paint, beside the door. Oh-oh. Dirty. He licked his finger and wiped at the spot. Stepping back he scanned the whole car—a Porsche—he had always dreamed he would own one. Beautiful black. People said black was hard to keep up, but he didn't think so. Carl, the maintenance guy, hand washed it. He'd have him do it when he got back.

Truth be known, today he wanted to find the perfect spot for his new home. He had decided he liked Osceola and needed his own presence, other than the small temporary apartment he lived in that was connected to the facility. He needed to put down roots. What was the saying? Rule where you're planted—something like that.

He backed out of his personal parking space. There were a few lots in town he had spied that might be the perfect place for him to settle in. One, on the top of a hill, would need a house taken out. The other was perfectly flat—the house had already been torn down, and a line of trees provided privacy he required.

His car almost drove to the flat lot by itself. He was always drawn to this one. Hmm. Maybe today was the day to find out. He pulled over and got out. The trees cast shadows that played across the grass. Bricks were imbedded in the grass and seemed to line a path. He followed them to almost the center of the lot and rotated full circle. Oh the house he could build here. And right behind the nursing home. Convenient.

He pulled out his phone and snapped pictures. He had an architect in mind to design it.

Time to go to the court house to see who owned the land and to make it worth their while to sell.

As he drove downtown, he came to a realization that if he was to capitalize on his time in Osceola, he'd better get on the ruling boards and commissions. It'd be easy to get voted in, since he was administrator of Hillcrest. It was a natural progression in his career.

Hillcrest and Osceola were only the beginning.

The courthouse was an amazing building. Columns on either side of the entry were massive. When was this built? Amazing feat to put those in place when? There. The cornerstone read 1922. He'd have to do some research to find out how they accomplished that back then. Inside, marble lined every wall. Steps, too. He was smitten.

He needed marble for his offices.

He straightened and blinked. For his house.

The clerk's office should have information on who owned his lot.

A bell jingled as he opened the door, evidently startling the woman at the front desk. "May I help you?" She walked to the counter, a file in her hand.

"Yes." He loved name tags. "Shirley, I need to find out who owns some property here in Osceola."

She dropped the file onto her desk. "Do you have the address?"

"Well, there's no house on the lot, but it's on Ridge Street." He pulled out his phone and showed her the photos. "It's right next to the big Victorian." He pointed out the trees. "Nice weather break already there."

She checked the map. "Here. Hmm." She tapped the document. "No. Here. 530 Ridge Street."

"Could you please find out who the current owner is?" He tapped the address into his phone.

"Sure." She took the map with her into the backroom where two other ladies worked. Laughter and whispers echoed from the small room. One woman peeked out at him, then backed out of sight. More whispers.

Shirley walked in, a smirky expression on her face. Map and notes in her hand.

"What did you say your name was?"

Shoulders back. "Mr. Zee." Cleared his throat. "Otto Zee." He couldn't resist—his chest pushed out. "Administrator at Hillcrest Homes."

She tilted her head. "Well, Mr. Zee, we have had several inquiries on that property recently. In fact someone was just … Sorry, I'm not supposed to say." She put the map on the counter in front of him. "Just to make sure I have the correct property … is this it?"

He scanned the area on the map under her painted fingernail. He tapped on the same area. "Yup. That's it."

Shirley slid a post-it note in front of him. "The current owner is a Mr. Timmelsen. Mr. Clarence Timmelsen."

Goosebumps skittered up his arms and down his legs. "C-Clarence Timmelsen?" His chest was on fire. "Mr. Clarence Timmelsen?"

Shirley nodded and checked the address. "I believe his address is at the nursing home. You are new there, but I bet you might know him."

He shuddered. "I bet I do." Heh. Clarence was so close, he could almost smell the rat.

He wasn't done yet. "Um … curious. Who owns the lot next to it?" He shrugged. "Maybe he wouldn't mind being neighbors."

Shirley walked to the back room again. She returned, carrying the log book. "Probably not supposed to bring this out, but I had a feeling. I've been doing this a lot lately." She turned it so he could see and pointed. "Here. He owns that lot, also."

He began to fume. "And the next one?"

She leaned over the book. "Appears that Mr. Timmelsen does owns that, too."

Later as Mr. Zee walked down the outside front steps, he did what he was good at—he put on a mask of contentment, and not what he felt inside—rage.

Clarence Timmelsen had to die!

TWENTY-NINE

Clarence sat at his desk.

After Noell left, Katty and Bea had gone to the store.

He had talked the county clerk out of a blown-up map of Osceola and taped it to his wall on top of the framed documents. A little obvious, but he had to see what he owned.

Shirley was the clerk assistant's name. She had run back and forth between him at the front counter and the logbook in the back room, when finally she brought it all out front so they could work together. She'd cleared a desk off and pulled up a chair for him. "Maybe this isn't legal, but it's more convenient than me running back and forth."

Three hours. During that time, he'd heard all about her kids, her grandkids, her dogs and cat. Why her husband never fixed the toilet—he had been traumatized as a child when his older brother flushed their pet mouse down the toilet. Important things like that.

Before he left, he had been invited to her family reunion August 5th.

When he had asked her for a map, she printed it off in sections, and he and Katty had taped it together. No questions asked.

Well, there had been plenty of questions—how did your dad buy all these lots? What had he done for a living? Did he have a girlfriend?

Her elderly mom needed a man—or a bank account. Did *Clarence* have a girlfriend?

Some questions of his own had now been answered. But many more continued to gnaw at him.

Even though he had proof of his ownership of the properties. Even though Dad had destroyed Judge Green's credibility.

What had happened to Henry Green?

Why had he gone into the pool?

And where had Judge Green gotten the power back then to send Clarence to prison?

Now that he thought about it, hadn't there been *anyone* other than his dad, with the clout or authority to find out the truth, so Clarence wouldn't have had to spend the last sixty years in prison?

He slammed his hand down on the yellow legal pad.

That was the real question.

"Michael." Clarence squirmed in his chair. "Michael, please help." Didn't seem to be around right now. "Where are you?"

He'd dropped Clarence off at the front door not too long ago and Clarence had been so busy taping the map together, he had lost track of where Michael went.

Back to the question. Where had all Dad's clients, who had seemed so loyal, gone? People Clarence himself had built furniture for. He had pounded nails into their homes. He had helped put a roof over their families. Had anyone shown up at the court proceedings in support of Clarence?

He tried to go back in time. He'd relived the court scene every minute of everyday when he'd first been incarcerated. He'd mentally scanned every row in the jury box, examined every face. Was there no one who would stand up to Judge Green on his behalf?

He'd thought about this all of every sixty years and why now did it seem so important? After all these years.

Why did the name of Henry Green stir up so many questions now?

Clarence found himself staring at the boxes from Pete's as he tapped on the desk with his pen.

Had Pete's secretary gone through those boxes herself and decided which papers to give him and which ones she didn't? Did she know she had brought Clarence his inheritance?

Probably not.

He limped over to one, dragged it back to the desk and opened the flaps. On top was one of the warranty deeds with his dad's name on it —one of the first ones that had started Katty digging for more.

Something surged in him, pushed at him and he stood, cleared off the desk and began to methodically dig through the box.

Lisha knocked on the door some time later. "Supper, Mr. Clarence. Dinner bell." She shook her head. "What a mess."

He glanced up. "No time tonight for dinner, Lisha."

"You are chasin' those bunny trails, I can tell." She crossed her arms, stood beside the desk and watched him for a minute. "I kin bring you a plate."

He looked up. "A sandwich maybe?"

"Sure, Mr. C." She walked to the door. "Milk and some cookies?"

He nodded but didn't look up. He'd go through each and every paper—not miss a thing. The newspaper clipping. Why had that popped in his mind, now? He looked at the wall. There it was, tucked into a frame. He shuffled over and slipped it out, placing it in his shirt pocket. Not losing that.

An hour later, halfway through the box, he found it. He stacked the empty plates and chugged the rest of the milk.

Someone knocked. He groaned until he saw who it was.

Katty and Bea.

Bea walked in, holding up a bandaged finger. Her eyes were red.

"What?" He threw up his hands. "What happened to my girl?"

She had on a pout and was ready for a good cry if he'd give her just a minute of sympathy.

He could do that. He held out his arms.

She ran to him, letting the waterworks dam open. He held her on his good knee and let her cry it out.

When he looked up, Katty just stood there, still in the doorway.

Oh-oh.

He scanned the desk. Not one thing on this desk was more important than these two.

He caught Katty's eye and tilted his head, motioning for her to come in.

She just stood there.

"Katty."

Her waterworks opened too, as she stumbled into the room.

He pulled the client chair close to his and she sat, her head on his shoulder.

Just as Lisha came in the door.

All she did was put her hands on her hips and raise her eyebrows. She didn't say a thing. Just stepped into the room, picked up the plates and glass, and walked out the door. But not before giving him the biggest smile he'd ever seen on that beautiful brown face. Big teeth and all.

Bea hiccuped. She had stopped crying and now sat up and wiped her face. She jumped down and picked up the box of tissue. First to her mommy, then to Clarence who took one to blot his wet shirt. Then she helped herself and blew her nose but really blew out from her mouth.

He chuckled and Katty looked up.

One corner of her mouth lifted up.

Clarence had learned a few things since having girls. One—to never ask what was wrong, before it was the right time. And two—to remember that girls were different from boys. Period.

He wiped Katty's eyes and hugged her. "Well?" He looked from Katty to Bea.

Katty looked at Bea. "I had a melt-down." Tears trickled again. "I shut her finger in the car door." Her chin quivered. "I didn't mean to, I was just … I wanted a beer."

Silence.

Katty's face crumpled. "Bad." She started crying again. "I wanted it bad. I was trying to hurry her into the car. Just one beer." She shook her head. "And I slammed her finger in the door." She covered her eyes with her fists. "And she wouldn't quit screaming."

Bea's face crumpled too.

Clarence gathered Bea on his lap again, his cheek on her forehead.

He pulled Katty close.

She straightened and looked into his eyes. "I didn't hit her though. I promise." She bit her lips.

"I believe you, Sweetheart." Oh, these girls, how he loved them like they were his own. In a way, they were. He found himself staring at Pete's boxes again, containing his own inheritance. Maybe he should make it official.

Katty leaned against him again. She started to relax there and soon she began reading out loud. "Today sealed the deal. Judge and I made sure, since Timmelsen was knocked out in the accident, he would never know the truth—that he was supposed to die, and not Annie." She straightened and looked up at him.

He had followed along with her as she read. His chin twitched, eyes filled with tears. Not crying now. He hadn't cried then and wasn't starting—

Bea crawled onto her lap.

"Clarence?" Katty tapped the journal. "What is this?"

He swallowed. He read the next sentence.

She peeked around Bea's head and continued reading. "But she was thrown from the car." Her voice softened as she read those last words. "The evidence against him stuck, plus the testimony of well paid witnesses. Judge set it all up. Timmelsen will go to prison for life."

Clarence choked. His body shuddered. Head bent as he wept.

Bea hugged into him.

"Even if he goes before a parole board for good behavior, he'll never be free. Judge also passed down a decision that Clarence will be sent to Osceola nursing home when he turns eighty years old. Serves him right. Timmelsen was supposed to die and I was to marry Annie."

Someone gasped.

Carol had her hands over her mouth. Her eyes popped, as she moved closer. "Clarence." She pointed with both hands. "What is that?"

He shook his head. Never in his wildest dreams. His chest wanted to burst. He was sure his head would.

Carol slowly sat.

Katty read on. "Judge is brutal. I've seen evidence from years ago, that he screwed his own brother out of his inheritance and we know how Henry ended up. I need to watch my step. Judge paid people to keep their mouths shut in Timmelsen's trial, too. He paid them all off. Even the preacher got a new Sunday School addition for his church."

No one had come forward except the neighbor with her cookies.

He buried his head in Bea's hair. Little girl sweetness filtered into his heart.

The newspaper article. He reached into his pocket and unfolded it. "Henry Green," he muttered, "fell into a pool … "

Henry had been robbed, too. Just like Clarence. Robbed of a whole life of living.

Judge had caused his own brother's death. He'd literally murdered his own daughter, Annie. And he had sent the wrong man to prison. Three lives robbed. Four lives—there'd been a child—Judge Green had murdered his own grandchild.

He breathed in the presence of Katty and Bea, so close he could smell their fragrance—their essence. He might have missed this … these precious—

"I have to get to the pool."

Katty jerked her head away. "Get to the pool? Clarence that doesn't make any sense."

"We're swimming?" Bea jumped down.

Carol jumped up. "Clarence, you already hurt your leg there." She shook her head. "What if something else happens?"

Katty stood and picked up the journal. "They wanted you dead back then. What if … "

He took the journal from her. "What if … what if those demons come back to haunt me?"

He blinked. But they had.

He whistled at the realization. They had.

"I have to. There's something I have to find out there." He owed it to Henry.

He folded the article and stuffed it into his pocket.

"I have to go back to that pool."

THIRTY

His walking stick. Dr. Steven's walking stick. Score. That was a prime find.

What else was in the closet? Old straw hat.

Lots of straps. Ropes. One still appeared muddy.

Noell's imagination went wild with that. Fear prickled down her back. Had he been tying himself to something—a tree or rock beside the pool so he wouldn't drown?

She shivered. Goosebumps again.

She stepped away from the closet, still holding onto one strap. She shook her hand free and brushed her hands together. Something in her wanted to slam the closet door shut and run out of the camper, never to enter it again.

Sanitizer. Sanitizer.

Too late.

A kaleidoscope of colors and scenes rotated in her mind. Memories overlaid water movement.

Unfamiliar settings and faces. Exotic buildings. Spicy smells and snippets of music—either Egyptian or Israeli singing.

A flash of Mommy's face as she offered Noell a baby spoon of applesauce, layered on top of the exotic dancers, created an unholy mix of brain flashes.

"Here you go." Mommy's voice.

Noell slid to the floor. Oh Mommy.

Sunshine glinted off a rear-view mirror. Mommy's laughter tinkled like bells in a breeze.

"Noell?"

Water flowed in a river. Bubbled over rocks. Gurgles from the river matched her own baby sounds.

"Noell? You out there in the camper?"

Her head popped up and she blinked. Fletch's voice.

Back to present day. She was in the camper again. Still on the floor. The closet door still stood open, luring her into more incredible discoveries. Drawing her into the river of this research, this flow of what happened long ago.

And something else.

This camper, the books and journals—all dared her to break free. Dared her to break out of this bondage of fear.

She could sit here stagnant and helpless, or run back to her room, clean and sterile and live out her life, hiding.

At that word hiding, she hugged herself.

That was what she was doing. Hiding from her life, her destiny.

Knock, knock.

She jumped, coming back to the present again with a gasp.

Fletch peeked in the door. "You in there?" Blond curly hair. New T-shirt. Cute.

"Oh. Yes. Sorry." She struggled to stand. "I guess I was somewhere else."

"You hungry? We got pizza and I … saw you in here so I figured you might be hungry." Still standing just outside the door, he offered a paper plate piled with Supreme. Her fav.

The pizza aroma pulled at her.

"Yeah. You were on the next planet." He grinned.

"Uh." Noell was still partly trapped in her thoughts of a moment ago. Mommy. Water. Terrified to break out and really live. "Maybe. Maybe … I was on the moon?" Hiding. Oh yes, hiding.

"Yeah. That'll work. You were on the moon and couldn't hear me calling!"

Noell relaxed a bit and smiled. She really looked at him for a change, instead of quickly glancing away when he spoke.

He had a mole on his left cheek by his nose. Didn't only women have those? His blondish brown hair tumbled in thick waves to almost his shoulders. Deep-set blue eyes framed with dark lashes.

Those eyes sparkled and as Noell looked deeper, they became Mommy's blue eyes. Laughing. Gentle. Loving.

Then terrified.

Noell blinked.

"You okay?" Fletch stepped into the camper and slid the paper plate onto the table. "You seem far away today."

"Um, yes. Yes, I'm fine." She glanced up at the closet yawning wide at her. "The stuff I'm finding here is awesome." She reached in and pulled out the cane. "This must have been Dr. Steven's cane or walking stick. Pretty cool to think about where this has been."

He surveyed the camper. "He had a great little house here. Seems like it has everything a person needs."

Noell circled. Kitchen. Dining, living, sleeping space. Bathroom. "It's really sweet isn't it?"

"Have you dug through everything? Any rich discoveries? The pot of gold? Fountain of youth?" His eyes twinkled again.

Noell chuckled, nudged out of her fog. Corners and edges returned to their usually clear details. She wiped her hand along the wood of the nearest cupboard. "Yeah. Some great finds. Can you sit down awhile?" She pointed to the plate. "Have some pizza with me." Her stomach rumbled. When had she eaten?

He grinned. "Sure. I was kinda hoping … "

Noell laid the cane on the bench and sat at the table. "I want to show you what I've been finding in here."

Fletch eased onto the seat and examined the table, the seat, the cabinets, the floor. "This is so amazing." He caressed the tabletop. "What happened over this table back then, you know? Who sat here? I mean, what history happened?" He knocked on the table. "Right here?"

Noell sighed. "I know. It's pretty cool." She opened the leather journal and held it up. "Now this. This is amazing." She took a slice of pizza.

"What is it?" He cocked his head. "Looks like someone's drawings or notes." He looked up at Noell, as he took a bite. "What is this? *Whose* is it?"

"Dr. Walter Stevens." She waved around the camper. "He was some kind of professor or researcher. And this is ... or was ... his camper." She licked her finger, spun the book around and found a certain page. "Look at this."

A beautiful drawing of a small pool.

"That's awesome. The guy was an artist." Fletch took another bite.

Noell turned a few pages back.

"A map." He turned the book around so he could read it. "What"s it of? Where?" He grinned. "A treasure map?"

Noell tapped on the upper corner.

"Osceola, Nebraska!" He looked into Noell's eyes. "You don't mean ... did he explore here? Osceola?" He scratched his head. "Why?"

"I guess ... there were caves here. And pools in them." She shuddered at the thought. Pools. "He was hired to investigate some drownings that had no basis, no reason." Another shudder. "These are his findings." Noell flipped farther in the book. "I don't know why all this stuff and this old camper were just sitting in the back lot of the Roads Department, but I'm determined to find out his story."

He tapped on the book. His blue eyes met hers. "Maybe this is your calling. Stuff like this just doesn't happen."

"I know. I just *happen* to find a camper where I work. And I just *happen* to get it for free. And all of his journals and research just *happen* to still be in it." She checked her phone. "Time to go to Clarence's." She sighed. "Find out ... what ... from Gamma." Whatever could it be other than the house, this lot? She'd rather have Gamma anyway. "Sorry."

Fletch slid out of the booth. "You okay, Noell?" He hesitated. "I mean, anything I can do?"

She shook her head. "No. I'll be okay. Thanks for the pizza."

"Then I'll see you later." He stepped outside, only to come back in and give her a quick hug.

"Fletch. Thanks."

He nodded and closed the door. And he was gone again.

She wiped her eyes. Fletch was so nice. Huh. Always seemed to be around when she needed someone to talk to.

She scanned the camper, opened a cupboard door. Opened another. Still so much to explore. Her own little treasure hunt.

Another cupboard. An old mug. Another way in the back.

She checked it in the light—"Thelma's Eatery & Diner." Cute. Might have to start drinking coffee.

She gathered the treasures together and slid them into the oven. The only place right now that was uncluttered. She shook her head. How fast had her life changed? From Gamma dying, getting this trailer and now an inheritance? And Fletch? What next?

Gamma. How she wished for one more day with that precious woman.

She stepped outside. Beautiful day to walk. She locked up the camper and stood still. A bird sang from somewhere close by—Gamma had always called it a Jenny Wren. The sun warmed her skin.

It wasn't an all-is-right-with-the-world moment though. The pain in her heart was more than she'd ever experienced. Gamma had been her world. Even though there had been differences—hoarding, germophobia—what were those, but the same fear?

She stopped.

The same fear.

Just expressed in a different way.

The camper seemed God-sent, or Gamma-sent, to help her through this time … but to jog her fear of germs loose.

It had gotten warmer since she had been inside the camper. She surveyed her yard—*her* yard, and shook her head.

Help me do this right, Gamma. God.

This was a perfect place to park her camper—very convenient to the house and a bathroom. Her idea of a place by the creek could wait.

Onward to Clarence's to see what he had found.

Katty loved helping at Clarence's on a regular basis. She loved time with him. She might never feel like she was smart enough to help him, but he always made her feel like she would make a great paralegal. She had already learned so much from him—almost more than in her online class.

She glanced at the line of boxes on the floor. Still a lot to dig through, but they were making progress.

Knock, knock.

She jumped up, but Clarence beat her to it. How could he do that with a hurt leg?

Clarence opened the door. "Hello Noell."

She peeked inside. "Is … is this a good time? I thought I'd check to see what you found out … if you're not busy."

Clarence shook his head. "Found out?"

"Yes." She adjusted her backpack. "A-about Gamma's will?"

"Oh. I'm sorry."

"I can come back. I just thought—"

He opened the door all the way. "No. No. Come on in. We were just doing research. I just told Katty here … sit down." He closed the door.

Katty jumped up and cleared a space on the desk. "Hi Noell." Noell was so pretty, even in her orange T-shirt and ball hat. No make-up. "I forget. Where do you work?"

Noell sat and hung her backpack from the chair." At the Roads Department. I'm a flag girl. Among other things."

Huh. She was pretty even after working in tar and dirt all day.

"Nice to be outside on a day like today." Time to practice being Clarence's assistant. "Want some ice cream … or something to drink?"

Noell shook her head. "No thanks. I'm okay."

Bea climbed on Clarence's lap. "I want some ice cream."

Katty laughed. "You stinker. You just had some."

"Hi Bea." Noell smiled at her.

Bea snuggled into Clarence and hid her face.

Clarence patted Bea's back and shifted her to his other knee. "Noell, your Gamma and I'm sure Grampa were very smart people."

Katty passed him the file folder.

He opened it and showed Noell. "They had put everything in a trust with you as the sole beneficiary."

"What does that mean, exactly?" She leaned over to look.

"Katty?"

Uh-oh. A test. "Beneficiary." She could almost envision the word on the page. "It means you receive everything your Gamma owned."

He nodded. "Right, Katty."

Whew.

"Since it's a trust, it means no court dates, no probate." He pointed to the information in the file. "Everything passes to you as their named heir." He pulled out one sheet. "Here is a list of what you inherited."

Poor girl was gonna need tissues.

Noell was quiet as she read the list. Her eyes slowly moved up, first to Clarence's face, then to Katty's. "They … I own land? A-and," she counted with her finger, "five bank accounts?"

Katty nodded and pushed the tissue closer. "Seems you and Clarence own the town." Oops. What did her online class say about being discreet? She stole a look at Clarence.

He appeared overwhelmed, too. "I just learned that not only did my dad buy the judge's house—the guy that put me in prison all those years—but he proceeded to buy whatever your grandma and grandpa didn't own." He wiped his face.

Noell seemed to be absorbing the news that she was a wealthy young woman.

Clarence shook his head. "I spent time at the court house earlier. Finding out what I own, but also what *you* own, Noell."

Katty fiddled with the box of tissue. Clarence was a wealthy man. Noell, according to the documents, was rich, too. No worries. When bills arrived in their mailboxes, they could pay them.

She slumped. She couldn't even pay for Bea's new shoes.

THIRTY-ONE

Mr. Zee stood, scanned the room and faced the staff. "Yes, I've called this meeting to address certain problems that have come to my attention." If he had his way, they would build a whole administration wing with private offices and upscale conference rooms. Chandeliers. Real wood—oak or mahogany—desks and tables. Plush chairs. The best.

For now? This. The crowded room was pathetic compared to the dining room that the residents got to eat meals in. This would have to do until—

"Sorry I'm late." Lisha burst into the room and barely squeezed between chairs and the wall, her body bulging over the chair backs. "I was givin' a bath and couldn't just leave her." She found a chair at the end of the room.

That aide had to go. One of the first things he needed to do was clean house. People had to go. If there was any staff that might block his plans, boom! Gone.

Carol, sitting to his right, opened her files, making notes here and there.

She might be the first to go. He could find a good director of nursing anywhere. More than anyone else, she might be the main person hindering him. And no one must stop his work, his plan.

One last nurse scooted in, lidded coffee container in her hand. The only place left to side was on Mr. Zee's left. She skirted behind him and slowly lowered herself to her chair, as if any motion might set him off. Today anything might.

He cleared his throat. "Thank you all for coming." He cleared his throat again.

"It's not like we had a choice or anything." Lisha sat with her arms crossed as far as she could across that massive chest. No, maybe she was the first to be kicked out.

Mr. Zee looked down his black-rimmed glasses at each person there. A couple men, but mostly women. The men were part of his entourage—planted to befriend, to infiltrate and spy.

When he had them all squirming, except maybe Lisha, he began. "I have completed my inspection of this entire facility. The building is old. It has had several updates and remodels. The grounds have become overgrown, although Carl has done an exemplary job of maintaining and pruning things back."

Carl bowed his head and nodded.

"Oh, you want us to clap for him?" Lisha broke out in wild applause.

Tandy joined her until she realized no one else was clapping. She slowly stopped and clasped her hands together, glaring at Lisha.

"If we are to get through this meeting without having to stay here all day, there will be no more outbursts. Clear?"

Lisha rolled her eyes.

"Am I clear?" His blood was beginning to boil. These people would have to learn some respect and he was the one to teach them.

"Residents' rooms are fairly clean. I don't have much problem with the grounds, the condition of the buildings. That can always be updated," he paused. "I do have a problem, though, with resident safety." Pace. He wanted to pace, but even *he* couldn't squeeze between the walls and chairs. "As I have read through the files and reports given to me by each department head, it has come to my attention that there have been many accidental falls, inside our building and outside."

Carol began tapping her pen on the file, every-so-gently. He was getting to her.

He pushed on. "I have consulted with my board, and we have come up with a solution that we really don't like to implement, but for the safety and peace of all, we feel it is necessary."

Lisha started rocking forward and back, again and again. Her dreads flopped with each movement. She squinted, nostrils flared.

He could almost smell smoke. After Carol was gone, Lisha was next.

"For now, there are just a couple residents that this would affect, but we will be diligent to watch others, to make sure they are safe and their families are assured of that." Good sob line.

Carol had her eyes closed. He didn't think she was sleeping.

Not good.

"So." Louder than usual. She still didn't open her eyes. "The first resident that is badly in need of medication and activity changes is Mr. Timmelsen."

"Oh, he ain't gonna like that," Lisha said. "He—"

"He has no say in the matter. He has no blood relatives." Calm down. Deep breath. Lower the voice. "Since he has been escaping regularly, and especially since he has hurt his leg, it is imperative that he be restrained."

Carol stared at him. She blinked, frowning.

Restrain was maybe too harsh a word. "I propose he be confined to his room and medicated so he cannot harm himself again."

Many staff were now at full attention. Some with glee, like Tandy and Carl. Others appeared horrified.

"We're only doing this so he won't fall again and harm himself even more. We all know the woes of the elderly as they are injured— one thing after another until ... they go on to heaven." He almost choked on the word. He must be catching some virus—all this choking and coughing.

He handed the nurse on his left a printout. "Please, would you be so kind as to pass these out?"

She stood slowly, reading as she backed her chair into the wall, bumped her coffee but righted it before it made a mess. She continued to read as she passed them out. By the time she got to Carol, she was shaking her head. She sat again, slowly, her eyes never leaving Mr. Zee's face.

"Now as you read through this, we will need to be extra careful with charting so we can adjust these amounts if necessary."

"These amounts are enough to kill a cow." The woman who said it, ducked behind someone else.

He'd find out who she was. She didn't have a chance to remain anonymous, sitting between his two goons.

"This is the reference sheet that you will use for Mr. Timmelsen, Mrs. Hatly, and Harold Dexter."

Lisha rose in indignation, her chair hitting the back wall. "Thas murder! You can't do that!"

"Lisha, one more outburst and you will be cast out from this room." He locked eyes with the goons and they stood in unison. They pushed the women beside her to their own chairs and proceeded to sit in their chairs.

"Lisha, dear. Mr Timmelsen has to be protected from himself. He is falling. He is sneaking out of Hillcrest. He needs to be restrained and medicating him is the safest way to do it."

Heads began to nod.

"He has a violent temper sometimes."

"That's how he got into trouble before—he kept sneaking out."

That's the way. Light a match and the fire burns.

THIRTY-TWO

"Michael?"

No answer.

Clarence searched the cave. "Where'd you go?" He hobbled around to see the whole cave.

No Michael.

Sure. Dump me off and then leave.

Clarence peered into the water.

It had seemed the right thing to do back in his room. But now … well, the pool had lost its appeal.

But he had to know its secrets, its mysteries. Even if … if he didn't return to Hillcrest.

Flashes of dear Mrs. Hatly played through his mind. Her twinkly eyes.

Katty.

And Bea.

Something touched his back and he turned in time to see Michael.

"Michael, no! Help me. Don't let me … " Clarence fell into the pool with a splash. Had Michael pushed him?

He gulped, swallowed. Gagged. The water tasted like sewer.

He thrashed his arms and legs. His head broke the surface and he roared for help. He couldn't have been above water for more than a split second, but the sound of his roar reverberated against the walls of the cave.

Michael!

Father. I trust Your plan.

Michael watched as Clarence went under, bubbles breaking on the surface. It crushed him to have shoved him into the pool.

Father why'd you make him so stubborn?

Michael bowed his head. Some people never realized they even had an angel.

Being Clarence's guardian angel had not been boring.

Before Clarence went under water, a visual imprinted in his mind.

Michael started to glow in his angel costume—his wings spread wide, golden belt around his middle, wielding a huge sword left and right, stabbing into the air in front of him.

He didn't appear in costume unless something big was happening.

Michael had been there when no one else had.

And now …

Was it all a lie?

A sob burst from his chest. His eyes scrunched. Pain inside exploded in another roar that amplified in the pool, sound bouncing off the rock walls. The water circled about him in waves—a monster closing in for the kill.

Michael was still visible—his glow shimmered through the moving water. He seemed to be flying; his wings fluttered with the ripples of the waves.

Clarence kicked and dog-paddled, holding his breath, feeling every minute of his eighty years. He had always held his breath so as not to smell prison odors—and then nursing home smells. This slimy water was no different.

He broke the surface again, gasping for air.

"Michael?"

His skin crawled, and goosebumps made him shiver.

He'd only been under a few seconds.

This wasn't the same cave.

Making a conscious effort to slow his breathing, he groped for a handhold along the side.

This cave was darker. And the air had turned frigid. So had the water. The other pool had felt like a bathtub.

Two connected pools? Two different atmospheres and temperatures?

Got to get back to Michael.

He primed his breathing, taking several deep breaths, then dove.

He dove deeper, eyes open. Cold. Amazed by the amount of light under the surface.

In spite of the muck, his eyes wouldn't stay closed. His fingers followed the rock walls. There had to be another opening.

Was this what Henry Green had seen?

Carvings and writings extended along the underwater passage. Some glowed. Tiny gold speckles glistened from the rock walls, lit up his fingers as they traveled the walls. It had to be gold—real gold.

Memories flooded: Annie—he hadn't killed her, prison—evil men had intended to harm him in ways his young and mostly innocent mind could not have fathomed, and his life—becoming the rough-edged, angry, stubborn ex-con because of it all.

And now the nursing home—realizing he was a good man.

He shivered. The deep cold hurt his bones.

Colder. Colder.

Which way was up? Or down?

The water pressed against his chest. It felt like a giant had one hand on his chest and one on his back, pressing it's hands together. Tighter and tighter.

Something … two eyes glowed from the side of the wall. Couldn't be. Just something in the rocks flashing a reflection.

They blinked.

He jumped, kicking away.

Still he held his breath, but began flailing, treading, panicking. The eyes watched him and glowed ever stronger.

Something grabbed his hands. It pulled him down, down.

He couldn't find anything to hold onto. No tree roots or hand holds. Just cold stone.

A face—nose-to-nose with his. He screamed and he was sure that it could be heard at the nursing home and the grocery store. He pushed away. That face. Dark wrinkled skin. White hair.

Screamed again. Bubbles stormed around him, from his mouth, his nose.

If only this was a dream.

He sucked in water, gasped, then sucked in more. His eyes bugged out. Arms and legs cramped. He was sure his body was turning inside out.

The pool was winning.

He was losing.

Bubbles escaped his mouth and floated upward in a magical dance, making their own music. The colors of the pool appeared more vibrant, more beautiful than before: greens, purples, blues.

The waving and rippling of the water mesmerized him. No better lullaby. "Sleep my baby, sleep." Deep sigh. His mother's voice drifted in and out.

The water temperature turned warm.

He drifted, slowly, calmly.

Fear was gone.

He hiccuped and sucked in more water.

Deep breath in. Breathed in the water. Reason said it was impossible. He breathed in again.

He coughed and choked, but soon it wouldn't matter.

There was no question as to how this was going to end. A person had to die somehow—sometime. He'd wanted to die ever since he'd come to Hillcrest.

He sank farther down—deeper. His arms floated out from his body, his legs limp in the water. Fabric in his clothes rippled around him.

He didn't struggle.

Light beams diminished. Not only did the water grow colder, but his body shuddered as temperatures plummeted.

Sounds were still amplified through the water, but they seemed more distant.

A melody gently rose and fell with the water. His mother's pure voice seeped into his heart, his soul. Her hands caressed him, combing through his hair, massaged his wounds.

Or was it the water as it followed his movements? The activity of the ever-present demons in his soul?

Drowning wasn't that bad.

He was ready. He wasn't afraid. He'd see Annie and his mom and dad. Doubtful he'd see prison inmates he knew. They were too mean to get into heaven.

What happened after death?

Heaven? Probably just a myth.

So many lies.

His thoughts drifted.

Voices. Melodies.

A small boy, eyes of concern.

A hand.

A face like nothing he'd ever seen before.

Liquid eyes, and not from being in water. Kind eyes. Eyes so full of love that Clarence choked. He gasped and sucked in more water, but it didn't matter. His body was now so waterlogged his lungs and skin couldn't hold anymore.

Just as his toes touched bottom, the hand drew him closer.

I've missed you, my son.

Clarence half smiled. Had to be hallucinating. Even in his relaxed state, there was no one else underwater with him. All part of … dying.

I thought you'd never come.

Clarence's eyes drooped.

Almost gone.

A burst of electricity shot through him, jolting his arms and legs straight out. His eyes popped wide. His fingers shot out, vibrating and trembling. Even his inner organs shuddered. Every part of him throbbed.

What he saw shouldn't have shocked him.

Michael?

Not Michael.

A powerful energy penetrated, radiated. Waves of peace and love.

Son ...

Son?

Clarence stirred.

Dad?

Waves rippled, drew him, pulled at him.

A power traveled through him.

Enveloped him.

One.

THIRTY-THREE

Noell left Gamma's house after work. Today she would find that pool. With each step, she traced an imaginary path on Dr. Stevens' map. Her backpack bounced against her hip as she walked.

She wound her long blond hair into a bun on top of her head—it felt good to be free of that hardhat. She still had her orange T-shirt and overalls on. She figured if she ruined them, she had another twenty shirts back at Gamma's—and a couple more pairs of overalls.

She stopped and studied the map for the thousandth time—Dr. Stevens had even drawn the warning signs in: Keep Out and Witch Hole. The signs had probably fallen apart long ago, but the meaning still held—this was not a place to play.

She nodded. Three people had drowned in that pool.

Her steps slowed. So why was *she* looking for it?

He had drawn signposts on the map too: a tree that since then had probably been cut down, the Boy Scout cabin, and the railroad tracks.

She skimmed a journal entry: "A man … keeps repeating that the pool was of the devil … over and over … someone shushes him … city needs to fill in that pool." Dr. Stevens added: "I'm not sure dirt will keep demons in."

The day was warm, but chills traveled up and down her arms.

Dr. Stevens had parked his trailer—*her* trailer now—under a cottonwood tree. She knew what kind of tree that was. Grandpa had taught her that they had big shiny, almost heart shaped leaves that clapped together in a breeze.

The signposts today? Boy Scout Cabin—still intact. Railroad tracks —how timely that a train was chugging through right now. The horn blast made her jump. The engineer even waved. And a huge old cottonwood tree stood guard—still. The rough bark ran in deep channels up and down the trunk. The leaves applauded Noell.

This had to be it. Noell studied the map in Dr. Steven's journal, closed it and shoved it into her backpack.

She might have found the pool.

Others had been there. Footprints of different sizes and shoe-types trampled the dirt.

She climbed inside the cave and her stomach did flip-flops. There really was a pool.

An argument rose in her: one side really wanted to go in the water, but the sensible side wanted to go home and hide in her bed. She'd done that plenty in her lifetime—always taken the easy way.

Even as she climbed into the cave today, thoughts tried to dissuade her from ever dipping her big toe in the water.

But here she was.

She dangled her necklace in the water. It didn't seem to change the metal or anything, or dissolve any part of the chain. The cave had a smell about it that caves normally had—dank, moldy, damp. As she dipped her hand into the water and let her fingers swirl around in it, something zapped her, like an electric current or shock from an electric fence when it's grounded. She jumped and jerked her hand out.

What was that?

Part of her was still terrified, but that jolt felt like when she had flipped a light switch and had gotten shocked. The electrician had said there was a faulty ground wire.

Huh. Whatever was in the pool felt like real electricity—a sort of buzzing. And there appeared to be a layer of something on the surface, like oil on water.

She dipped her necklace in again and the cross began swirling in a slow circle, stirring the water, making concentric circles flow on the surface from the necklace to the perimeters of the pool.

She tried to hold her hand still, to hold the necklace still.

She couldn't. That swirling wasn't anything she was doing.

A jolt buzzed her hand again. It seemed to follow up the necklace from the water, stronger and stronger, until she dropped it.

She shrieked. Her fingers hugged her neck. She had worn it ever since Grampa had given it to her, when she started high school. "My cross. No!"

She stuck her hand in the water, trying to hook it.

She searched the edges of the cave. Spotted an old branch. Grabbed it and fished where the necklace had dropped.

Nothing.

Again.

No necklace.

Gah. She couldn't lose it!

The branch hadn't touched the bottom. She swished it again. Why wouldn't the chain catch on the twig?

She fished again, sticking the branch in as deep as she dared reach.

Nothing came up but a few strands of hair.

Her eyebrows went up.

Hair?

When she searched around the side of the pool, the walls of the cave caught her attention.

Writings. It didn't look like English. Old American Indian? But they used mostly pictures didn't they?

A big tree root poked up from under the surface. Maybe her necklace had caught on it.

She stretched down into the water trying to reach it. It was only a couple inches away.

"I want my necklace!" Splashing the water, she willed her necklace to appear in her hand.

Nothing happened, of course. Her hand automatically found its way to her neck again. No necklace.

Hugging her knees, she scanned the cave. The interior seemed the same as any cave. Partly dirt, mostly rock. It seemed to be sparklier than usual cave walls, glowing and sparkling. Kind of like gold.

She should go in and find her necklace. A slight shiver and butter-flies in her stomach told her no, don't go in.

She stuck her hand in. Not too cold. Almost like the sun had been warming it for her.

What was she thinking?

This would never work. An old lady and a kid had already drowned. And Henry, the assistant.

She stretched to touch the tree root—almost there—almost touched it.

And in she went! Splash!

Terrified, she kicked hard. Her lungs wanted to burst. She needed to open her mouth and breathe.

She swam with all the strength she could muster, but couldn't find the surface. There! Her necklace hung from a rocky finger at the edge. One gasp and she sucked water. Another push and she … but it wasn't her necklace, it was a tree root.

She paddled frantically, trying to find a place to climb out. Her hands slipped on the wet, slimy rocks. Her feet couldn't find a foot hold under the water. She couldn't get to the edge fast enough to push herself up and out before—

It started. Her mind played frames of visuals over and over, like a cinema. A boy floated. Balls bounced. Children splashed, then were chased away. A woman fell in, but didn't fight the pool. An angry man swam deeper.

Noell screamed in her heart.

Sanitizer! Sanitizer!

Something grabbed her and pulled at her. She was just conscious enough to feel the hand and arm around her throat, pulling her out of the pool.

The instant she opened her eyes, she sat up, and looked around. "Fletch?" He *had* suddenly appeared when Gam died.

Her voice merely echoed off the walls of an empty cave. She wiped her eyes and tried to look around.

Someone or something had just saved her life.

Her breathing returned to normal.

Shivering, she eyed the water. She sat on the edge of the pool and wiped her eyes again.

She looked to the cave opening. Felt like the same time of day she had fallen into the pool. She remembered her necklace and looked up. There it was, hanging from the root, the dim light from the cave opening reflected off the metal cross, causing rays of light to burst on the walls of the cave. A slight breeze must have blown through, for the necklace began to twirl and swing as if a fan had blown on it. Beautiful.

Noell got lost in the beauty as the rays spun around the cave, highlighting the carvings and writings on the walls. Things became clearer. A cross carved into the rock drew her attention. She edged closer. It was the same cross as the one on the front of Dr. Stevens' leather journal! Another sign. He had to have carved it here.

Dots were being connected.

Something had changed.

She had never felt more powerful in all her life. Fear had always crippled her, caused her to give up before a victory.

Gam had always said it was because her mom had drowned. Strong ties were supposed to glue the bonds between a mother and child. Growing up the way she had—no dad around for sure and seeing her mom drown when she was two—no wonder she had fears.

But today.

This minute.

She could change the world.

She studied the water. This pool brought back the terror she still remembered when her mother drowned.

But it also stirred a feeling of power, but more of ... a sense of Destiny. Of being who she was meant to be, following God's plan for her life. Gam had always prayed, "Be all God wants you to be."

What was her prayer? Jesus help. That was it. Two little words.

She sat up and pulled her necklace from the branch and dangled it in the remaining rays of sunlight that were peeking through a crevice in the wall. The necklace sparkled. She strung it around her neck and clasped it. The cold metal cross sucked to the skin of her chest—almost burned into her as the dampness helped it seal to her skin.

Sealed to her heart.

THIRTY-FOUR

Something moved at the far end of the water. Shadows snaked back and forth, leaving a bubble trail. A powerful tail slapped against the water with each twist and turn, pushing the water against Clarence, sending him tumbling against the wall behind him. Voices, like a radio blaring from across the hall at Hillcrest muffled through a head cold, reached his ears. Only he couldn't distinguish any words.

Even in the water, chills ran up and down his body.

The shadow swam closer. It wasn't a snake or water creature. It was a woman.

Someone else was in the pool.

The blue and purple and green water highlighted her red-brown hair. It flowed and billowed, swirled about her face. Pale clothes fluttered around her body as she swam back and forth. The water cast a bluish tint on the translucent skin of her hands as she treaded water.

Beautiful.

She swam closer, until she was right before him, her brown eyes wide open.

Annie! He reached to touch her face.

She cupped her hands around his, smiled and kissed them, turning them palm side up to kiss the scars.

A spark of light zinged from both hands and a deep shudder vibrated throughout his body.

But this wasn't Annie.

Mom?

Had she come for him at last?

His chest no longer burned. Breathing water worked as well as air. Songs played in the background from his memories.

It was time to go wherever it was that dead people went.

She caressed his cheeks and spoke to him from her eyes.

Clarence! We don't have much time. Father has sent me.

Dad sent you?

She smiled and shook her head. *No. Father.*

God sent you?

She nodded. Her hair billowed out. *I never got to tell you, and Dad didn't know how.*

Is Dad here now?

She held her hand against his mouth. *Hush. There is one thing you need to do before you leave this earth.*

Anything.

But instead of explaining she blurred. The water around them became violent, surging up and down, like the inside of a washing machine. Waves crashed into him, pushing him away from her. He couldn't lose her. Not now. It had been so long …

He struggled to hold onto her.

He would not let her get away. Her hair was still tangled in his fingers. Not letting go. He'd follow her to the next world wherever that was and back again.

She seemed to float away, but he sensed her coming back for him. She slipped her arm under his chin and towed him up, up. He was weightless. He couldn't feel his arms and legs.

His lungs no longer wanted to burst. He didn't need air to breathe. His thoughts were clear. His mind refreshed and revived.

As they reached the surface of the pool, he saw Michael through the water. He had never felt such vigor.

His head burst above the water and he gasped. Choked. Air in his lungs didn't feel right. His lungs were filled with water.

Somehow she pushed him to the rocks at the edge. Gasping and sputtering and choking, he gripped the hard rock. He threw up and threw up, coughing. Couldn't be any water left in the pool.

Mom!

He turned.

Blue eyes. Blond hair stuck to her face, plastered to her shirt, still tangled in his fingers.

Noell!

Wings pounded in front of him, as Michael flew across the water, commanding the host. Powerful, beautiful wings. There were many. A host of many.

And there was One.

Him.

Face to face. Inches apart.

Those eyes.

He was real.

Clarence gasped.

Such love.

Sobbing, he breathed Him in, into his lungs, his heart, his bloodstream.

Every cell.

"Father … "

Then He was gone.

Noell caught Clarence just as he blacked out, hooked her arm around his body and struggled to pull him out.

Dead weight, water-logged body.

She cried out. *Help me! God! Help!*

The water in the pool billowed and surged, bubbles swarmed. Images floated.

The pool seemed to vomit them onto the bank.

She rolled him over. He wasn't breathing. Water-wrinkled skin emphasized burn scars on his palms as she checked his pulse.

No pulse.

Long-forgotten skills kicked back in.

Check his throat. Tilt his head back.

CPR classes became automatic. Clarence was only the dummy from class. Glassy eyes open. Pasty gray skin.

God help!

She went through the motions of CPR, counting, her hair dripping onto his face. "One-two-three-four … "

"Come on. Breathe!" Drips from her hair became tears pooling around his closed eyes, his mouth. Each count became a cry—a prayer.

As vision blurred, his gray hair blended with her mother's wet blond hair, splayed around her head.

Noell's two year old voice replayed the awful truth. "Mommy! Mommy! Beathe!"

Hands held her away as a fireman leaned over Mommy, pushed on her chest, breathed in her mouth.

The fire chief leaned in and pulled the man away from Mommy. "Ted, there's nothing more we can do. She's gone."

Both men had looked at Noell—even a two-year-old could discern pity on their faces.

She wrenched herself free and pushed on Clarence's chest. Counting. "Breathe Clarence! Come on! Breathe!" Push, push, push. "One two three." Push, push, push. "One two three."

She glanced up. Back in the cave.

Michael. With wings on.

"Michael! Help me!" Sobbing now, she pushed again and again, counting. "Michael, do your stuff!"

Michael glowed as he knelt beside Clarence, his face crumpled. He beat his chest with one hand. Tears coursed down his cheeks. "Father. Father." His head lifted, eyes closed, voice louder. "Father, if it is Thy will." He focused on Clarence and Noell. "If it's Thy will."

Noell sat back and screamed. "Father!" She shook her fist at the sky. "You took my mom. You can't take Clarence too!"

She looked to the heavens, fist outstretched.

Motion and sound became one; her scream matched the force of her fist as it slammed down on Clarence's chest. Like a mallet meeting a railroad spike, it drove the Power into Clarence.

He gasped and rose partway off the ground, as if a medic had attached paddles to his chest and shouted, "Clear!"

His eyes opened wide.

A roar burst from his mouth.

It took a long time to come back to full awareness. Was this heaven? No, there was mold on the rock wall. Clarence didn't figure there were spider webs in heaven either. Angels would keep it cleaner than that.

There was his wallet, where he'd hidden it before he fell into the pool. He started to reach for it.

Michael peeked into the cave.

"Michael. Michael." Clarence puked up more water and mucus, spitting and foaming. "God, that water is terrible. It's burning my throat."

Noell! Where had she gone?

There. She sat panting in a corner, watching him. Her long blond hair hung wet in her eyes. An orange T-shirt with a big X printed on the front clung to her young form, mascara smudged under her eyes. He pointed at her. "You. That was you." He choked again. "Not my Annie. Not my mom." He slumped against the rock wall. "I was sure it was Mom … "

Noell crawled to him and pushed his hair out of his eyes. "I'm sorry. I'm so, so sorry. About your Annie. Your mom." She cupped her hand around his jaw and stared into his eyes.

Locked eyes with him until he wept.

Something had changed. There weren't many people he let look into his eyes—his heart.

"You." He swallowed and gagged. "You saved my life."

Then he remembered more. He fell back on the cold rocks, sobbing.

He struggled to speak. Sobs broke in. "Angels." He searched the cave for Michael, finding him sitting against the cave wall near the opening, face crumpling as he looked at Clarence.

Clarence crawled to him. "Michael. There were angels all around you." Clarence reached him and grabbed his leg. "You were ... you were in command."

"No, my friend." Michael pointed up. "*He* is in charge. I'm only a servant."

"But, you were ... He was here." He sobbed again. "He was here."

His face dropped into Michael's hand, and Michael's fingers curled around his jaw. His sobs echoed in the cave. Waves in the pool crashed against the sides. Every sob seemed to speak to the water, making it rush to and fro in response.

Clarence lifted his head. "He looked at me. He ... looked into me." Hiccuped and tried to talk. "He touched me ... everywhere." Pointed to his chest. "Here and ... here." Hiccup. "Everywhere. He showed me who I w-was. He showed me everything I ever did."

He sobbed again. "I saw my mom." He turned to look at Noell. "I saw my mom."

He collapsed, unconscious.

Noell started to cry.

I saw my mom, too.

I saw her die—again.

THIRTY-FIVE

Mr. Zee held his arms out, pushing people in wheelchairs and walkers back against the wall. "Give him some space." He had to make way for Clarence to be transported to his room on a gurney. "Let him through, poor man."

Mr. Zee was so close to ruling in this region. Not only was the receptionist his now, Hillcrest would be—soon. After that, the town of Osceola. The people, the businesses, churches, the farms? All would be his.

"Sir, this man needs to be transported to the *hospital*." The EMT checked straps on the gurney and patted Clarence's shoulder, checking his pulse. "He has been in and out of consciousness and his color is terrible. Considering his age, I think he should be admitted to the hospital. I don't understand why you redirected us here."

Mr. Zee stepped in front of her, toe-to-toe, looking down his black-rimmed glasses at her. When he spoke, it was an icy whisper. "Because I said to bring him here."

She blinked and stumbled back, trembling. She held her hands up in a kind of surrender. "You're the administrator."

Atta girl. All according to plan.

Mr. Zee raised his voice, like a preacher getting ready to deliver the final point of a sermon. "We have competent staff here—nurses and aides—who are very capable in caring for his needs." He beckoned them to follow, then hesitated. "I appreciate your concern though." Nosy little biddy. He'd better make sure she wasn't around for what came next.

They proceeded around the corner and were stopped again, by several people crowding the hallway.

"Oh, it's Clarence!" Harold leaned over his walker. "Clarence! Hey Buddy!" When Clarence didn't respond, he searched Mr. Zee's face and reached for the EMT. "Is he going to be okay?"

"Mr. Harold, maybe back up a little." Lisha stepped in front of him. "Give 'em some room. When he's settled in, I'm sure he'll need your comp'ny." She smiled, her eyes never leaving Mr. Zee's face. "Okay?"

Goosebumps on her brown arms. Mr. Zee was sure now, that even Lisha was understanding his power and authority.

Harold did the walker dance backwards—shuffle, lift, shuffle, lift.

Mr. Zee nodded. "Good job, Lisha. We don't want our residents to become agitated." Or suspicious. He escorted Clarence's gurney and the EMTs down the hall to Clarence's room. He glanced at the EMT's name tag and hovered an arm above her shoulders. "Just between you and me, Sally, and all HIPAA aside, he has a do-not-resuscitate order on his chart. So," he paused, "we believe it's important for our residents to be able to … direct their own passage into the next life."

"Of course." She nodded to her partner, who was pushing the stretcher. "You were right, Aldo. *I* thought we should go right to the hospital."

Good. She was now under his power.

Mr. Zee locked eyes with Aldo briefly, and an energy zing snapped between them. Aldo had complied with all the instructions of the plan precisely. Mr. Zee motioned for them to follow.

Glad Aldo was on the same side. A good plan needed a good team.

When they reached Clarence's room, Tandy and Carl were already waiting. Loyal subjects.

Carol had raised the bed and turned down the covers, so they could slide Clarence across the gurney to his bed.

He groaned when he landed.

They'd have to work fast if they were to complete the plan before Clarence became fully awake. If he became fully recognizant, their window of action would be closed.

Mr. Zee needed to get Carol out before she suspected anything. Lisha, too.

He helped push the stretcher into the hall. "Carol. Lisha. Would you please take Sally to the office so she can sign our release forms? Thank you."

Carol glanced at Lisha. "I need to be here, taking his vitals." She tapped a chart. "I've documented his return, but," she stood taller, "by law, we need to take his vitals and record them."

He firmly pushed her and Sally out of the room. "We've already recorded them on the Master Chart."

Carol balked. "What Master Chart?" She faced him. "I have never, in all my time here, heard of a Master Chart." Hands on her hips.

That woman was trouble.

Lisha stood behind Carol, hands on *her* hips.

She was even more trouble.

Mr. Zee alerted Aldo and Tandy with a blink. "Well there *is* a Master Chart, and it is in my office. But I don't have time to argue." This was going to be tough, but he was not quitting, Carol and Lisha, or not. He motioned to Tandy.

The town must be his.

Tandy glided across the hall and met Mr. Zee, pulling out the syringe—ready. He had trained her well on oranges and other residents. Just a couple people had actually died. She was quick, too.

Only Carol wouldn't cooperate. Lisha either. They seemed to be glued to the old man.

Aldo bumped into Lisha and began to flirt with her. Should have warned him about her—that kind of thing would not work. Bet she could deck a man faster than a cat on a grasshopper. And she did. She disengaged her hips and swung at Aldo, sending him flying against the opposite wall.

Not a problem. Tandy slipped Mr. Zee the syringe and she distracted Carol by shoving old Harold to the floor.

In the midst of a Lisha-brawl and Carol's cries alerting other staff, Mr. Zee had his moment of opportunity.

He turned to Clarence's bed, syringe poised, just as Noell skidded into the room and tackled him. She knocked him to the floor then shielded Clarence with her body.

"You're not going to kill Clarence." Noell kicked at Mr Zee. "You'll have to get through me first!"

Mr. Zee pushed off the floor. "I can accommodate you." He turned, syringe in Noell's face, just as three cops rounded the doorway into Clarence's room.

Mr. Zee tried to hide the syringe up his sleeve, but the cops lunged at him and the syringe bounced up, spinning in the air. Hands grabbed for it as it flew, end-over-end.

Noell sucked in a breath.

Mr. Zee's eyes grew wide. He dodged left and right—the cops tried to contain him—until the needle finally landed in *his* arm. Handcuffs clicked over his wrists.

Michael removed his fingers from the syringe. The demon had shuddered when the needle pierced Mr. Zee's skin.

With wings unfurled, Michael stretched up and out.

The demon screamed.

It appeared to have been so involved in Mr. Zee's plan to kill Clarence, it had forgotten all about Michael—something no demon should do.

It hissed and snarled, kicking as Michael drew his sword and plunged it into the demon's body.

Clarence's bed was bouncing.

Muffled voices.

He squinted his eyes open.

Noell was sitting on his bed close beside him and Mr. Zee was in handcuffs beside the bed, surrounded and restrained by three cops.

Wings billowed. Michael, in full dress angel costume, glowed—his sword extended to Mr. Zee's chest. His stature was twice the size as normal, his skin glistened, a golden belt gathered his white robe.

Bea and Katty stood outside in the hallway. Bea pointed. "Clarence *was* too swimming, Mommy. He's all wet."

Clarence tried to sit up, but Noell patted him down on his bed.

The cops ushered Mr. Zee out, his right leg giving out every other step. He growled as he passed Michael, his eyes fluttering almost closed.

"Whatever was in that syringe was meant for you, Clarence." Noell pulled Bea up on the bed. "And look what it's doing to *him*."

Clarence shook his head. Images confused him—memories of the pool and now this chaos.

Carol helped Harold onto Clarence's sofa, a pillow to prop up his leg.

Lisha held both Aldo and Tandy in a death grip on either side of her. They struggled to get free as she marched them away.

Carol turned to the bed. "Clarence. You're awake." She checked his pulse.

Michael pushed his sword in its sheath, metal ringing against metal.

Clarence blinked. "I ... " He cleared his throat. "What happened here?"

Noell scooted to the end of the bed to give Clarence more room.

Carol pressed her hand onto Noell's leg. "Noell, how did you know?" She fluffed up the pillows under Clarence's head as he pulled himself up. "You ran in here like a lion was chasing you. What happened?"

Noell met eyes with Clarence and wept.

Bea crawled onto her lap. She reached for the tissues on the side table, almost falling off the bed.

Katty sat beside Harold, holding his hand.

Noell blew her nose. In front of everybody. First time ever.

She looked at Carol, then the others. "I … have this curse. But maybe, now it's a gift." She hesitated. "When I touch doorknobs, or handles, or cups … I see stuff."

"Like you can see this tissue?" Bea swung her legs back and forth, handing Noell more, one-by-one. "Like when I saw you and Clarence in the pool?"

Gasp. Bea had said that days ago.

Clarence's eyes were as big as she guessed hers had to be.

It was now or never. Noell swallowed. "No. Like when I touch, say a handle—whoever touched it before me, leaves their handprint or molecules … or germs … and when I come into contact with it, I see their face, things they've done, where they've been."

Clarence cleared his throat. "Like when you touched my hand when we first met." He tapped Bea's shoulder. "You saw Bea."

Noell nodded and wiped her face. "Yes."

Carol pushed Noell's wet hair out of her face. "What did you see this time?"

"When I touched the entrance door, I saw Mr. Zee giving people here in Hillcrest shots, and those people died." Tears dripped.

Bea handed her one more tissue. "You have to stop crying now. We're all out." She held up the empty tissue box.

Noell smiled. "I knew he was after you, Clarence." She turned to him and touched his fingers.

Oh-oh. Where was her backpack?

Sanitizer. Sanitizer.

What had she been thinking? How could she have forgotten to protect herself?

Only, what she saw when she touched *him*, was the pool.

And an angel.

Clarence leaned forward. "Noell."

Tears dripped from her eyes before he could say anything else. "I was so afraid he was going to kill you."

Bea dropped the tissue box. "We need more tissue."

Noell laughed. "I'll stop crying."

"Noell." Clarence reached for her hand. "Dear Noell." His blue eyes were wet, too. "You saved me—twice. Once, at the pool. And again, just now."

Bea held up her hands. "Now Clarence is crying."

He laughed, then stopped and wiped his face. "How can I ever repay you, Noell? You gave your life for me."

She nodded. "Maybe it's not a curse."

He nodded, too. "Oh it's a gift." He kissed her cheek. "You used it well."

Lisha pushed Mrs. Hatly into the room.

Mrs. Hatly unloaded a big plate of cookies from off her lap. Then held up a box of tissue. "Somebody in here need this?"

Bea bounced on the bed. "We do!"

Clarence leaned back onto the bed.

Bea laid on his chest. "Where's Michael?"

He lifted his head and looked around the room. "He's here somewhere. But if *you* can't see him, I guess he had to do something or to maybe help with that bad guy, Mr. Zee."

She combed through his hair. "Your hair is still wet. Did you really go swimming? In a pool? Do you own the swimming pool?"

"Yes, I went swimming. Yes, in a pool. And no I don't own the swimming pool." He hugged her. "So many questions."

"I wish the swimming pool was yours." She lifted her head and patted his cheek. "Can you buy it? What did you do in that pool? Did you have water fights? Were there diving boards?"

He chuckled. "Well no, not exactly." He stroked her hair. He couldn't answer right away. What would make sense to her? "I … " Title deeds from properties he now owned flashed in his memory.

His head popped up. "I have to go do something, Bea. I know what my mom was talking about."

"Your Mom? She was in the pool with you?" Bea sat up. "Is she wet, too? Does she own the swim—"

Katty stepped to the bed and lifted Bea down. "Baby Bea, not so many questions. Maybe Clarence is tired."

"No he's not." Bea pointed. "He's getting up."

Noell jumped off the bed. "What's the matter, Clarence? Where are you going?"

He swung his legs over the side and stood. A little wobbly at first, but Bea and Noell helped balance him. "Katty, would you drive me?"

Carol stepped in front of him. "I don't know Clarence. You've just been—"

He cupped her face with his hands and spoke softly, just loud enough for her to hear. "Remember when we were talking about Joe and … well, you remember. You said something about forgiving him?"

She nodded.

He swallowed. "I need to forgive that bastard … uh, Judge Green." His throat began to burn and tighten. Tears rolled down his cheeks. "If there is one good thing," he glanced at Noell, "no, there are many good things from my time in that pool. But one is … God … He showed me I need to forgive." His face crumpled. He leaned his head down and kissed the top of Carol's head. "Like you forgave Joe."

Clarence sat in the front passenger seat in Katty's car, looking out at the green, tree-lined lot.

Bea had just been shushed for the fifth time and Noell, who was sitting in the back seat with her, was trying to distract her.

In his memories, he could envision the huge mansion from when Annie was alive. It had been massive. Window glass sparkled. The porch furniture beckoned. The bricked walkway led him to the front door, where Annie had always waited.

He opened the car door and stepped onto the asphalt street.

"Can I come, too?" Bea kicked the back of the seat in front of her.

"No!" Katty's voice grew louder. "And quit kicking my seat!"

Clarence closed his door and limped around the front of the car, holding onto it for balance. Using the cane in his left hand still didn't come naturally, but at least now, he knew how to use it.

Katty rolled her window down. "Want some help? You okay?"

"I'm okay." He glanced back at her. "But thanks."

Some bricks were still imbedded in the grass, still drawing him. Where they stopped was probably where the porch had started.

The weight of what he was about to do, almost crippled him. He'd always carried hatred and unforgiveness like a badge, a shield. Don't come too close. For sixty years. Maybe ... he turned around and motioned for them to join him. If he fell, they'd come running anyway.

Car doors slammed and Bea skipped toward him, her hair flowed with each step, her brown eyes sparkled. Too much ice cream? She was so cute. How he loved her and Katty.

He looked beyond.

And Noell. He could tell she was concerned about what he was about to do. With all she had been through why wasn't *she* angry?

And why not have them all here? Why not let them hear? He had no secrets ... well—

"Clarence!" Bea hugged his leg. She always managed to hug his injured one, but he didn't mind. She just forgot.

Katty caught up with her. Noell was right behind her.

He wiped at his eyes. "I have something I must do."

"Build a swim—" Bea started.

"Bea. Enough. Quiet." Katty picked her up and hugged her. "Clarence has something he wants to say and you need to be quiet."

Bea hid her face in Katty's neck. "Okay." She peeked at Clarence. "Sorry, Clarence."

He smiled and nodded. "I forgive you, Little One." He stepped away, then turned to face them. "Years ago ... " He swallowed. "I'll make it short." He searched the grass as if he'd find the words there. "I'm here today to forgive Judge Green. For … doesn't matter what. For everything." He licked his lips. "And so Judge Green, wherever you are … I forgive you."

Bea began to squirm again. She whispered something to Katty.

Katty shook her head.

Clarence cocked his head. "What does she want, Katty?"

"Michael is here!" Bea burst with the news and wiggled out of Katty's arms. "He's got his wings on!" She hopped and skipped toward Michael.

Clarence turned just as Michael raised his sword straight up. His wings glistened in the sunlight, each feather iridescent. "Michael. Where have you been?"

Michael's sword transformed into a beam of light as he aimed it at Clarence's chest, cutting into his flesh.

A roar of pain broke out from Clarence, echoing across the mowed lawns.

Bea was in mid-stride and fell to the ground. "Oh, no. Clarence." She screamed, "No!"

Clarence gasped. A jolt of power went through his heart, his whole body.

A thick, black shadow swirled out of Clarence's chest and floated to where two angels waited, ready to bind it with long golden threads.

Bea crawled to Clarence's shoes, sobbing. "Clarence. Don't die."

Clarence opened his eyes, staring into Michael's—eyes he had looked into for months now—as a friend, a confidant, and a protector. And right now Michael's eyes were filled with pain.

A warmth began to fill Clarence's chest. He looked down where the sword had pierced and blood seeped there. He stared at it, hands covered it, wanting to bandage the wound, to stop the flow. "Help me, Michael. I'm bleeding." He lifted his eyes to Michael's, not for a moment blaming him.

But the being in front of him was no longer Michael.

It was Jesus, His arms open wide.

Clarence dropped to his knees. "Lord." His cane was forgotten.

Bea crawled to his lap.

Katty and Noell on either side, arms around him.

Clarence began to weep. He wiped his face with his sleeve and picked up Bea, drawing her onto his lap.

She touched his chest. "Where's the blood?"

He looked. Patted his chest all around. No blood.

He looked up and now instead of Jesus, it was Michael. No wings. No golden belt. Just the usual jeans and T-shirt on his overgrown body. He walked toward them and knelt on one knee.

Again he and Clarence locked eyes.

Clarence spoke first. "Forgiveness is messy."

Michael smiled his half-smile. "Yes. It is."

Clarence looked out across the grass and shook his head. "Why didn't I see? It was eating me alive. It was … " He patted his chest. "I feel so free, now. I'm … so clean."

He looked down at Katty and Noell. "Help me up, can you?"

Katty helped lift at one arm and Noell the other side.

One foot on the ground, then the other, until he stood upright. "That's harder than it used to be." He patted his leg. "Feels better though." He hugged them. "Let's go eat Mrs. Hatly's cookies, shall we?"

Bea stood and hugged Michael's leg.

He picked her up and threw her onto his shoulders and carried her to the car.

"Can we have ice cream, too?"

Katty shushed her. "I think you've had enough."

"Aww."

Clarence felt a big hand on his shoulder and he turned. Michael was beside him.

The huge angel knelt on one knee, his arm across his chest, head bowed.

Katty and Bea were arguing about who had dumped the water bottle again. Noell was tickling Bea while she strapped her into the car seat. Bea was telling her she didn't need to be strapped in—she was a big girl. Katty told her she could walk, then.

Clarence chuckled and dropped his hand onto Michael's shoulder. "This is us, Michael. We're family." He looked out at the empty lot. "Thanks Dad. We'll build something here just to piss that Bast … uh, Judge Green off. Wherever he is."

They clasped hands, Michael's huge one and Clarence's old one.

Warrior Brothers.

THIRTY-SIX

July 11, 1937 ~ Journal of Dr. Walter Stevens, Professor of Agriculture ~ Osceola, Nebraska.

Just one month to the day.

What began as the worst assignment of my career just one short month ago, turned out to be the most enlightening.

I sit here in Thelma's Diner, where it all began.

The pain.

The people who had lost loved ones.

Henry.

Fear.

Depression.

Did I find answers?

Not really.

I was able to do the Professor of Agriculture things, like analyzing the water and soil. I helped the farmers find ways to push back the threat of losing their farms and livelihoods, due to drought. Makes it all worthwhile.

I was able to help people find closure.

These people will forever be in my heart.

I could say I'll be back. But deep down we all know that I'll go wherever the adventure leads.

The last month has been anything but fun. Oh, there have been laughs. But living life with the people of Osceola, Nebraska has been raw at its worst, and precious at its best.

Last night I gassed up the truck. Battened down my little camper at Paul's place—leaving it here since I have to drive to Lincoln to take care of some business. Even tucked this little journal in the camper. I put the final touches on the leather cover—a cross and a flower over God's thumb print. I'll be back. I figure leaving it here will insure my return.

The town came out to say good-bye. Literally, the town did come out, all except Mrs. Martin. She had the flu and is hereby excused.

One-by-one, starting with Frank Linder and Tommy Porten, people stepped forward from the crowd surrounding my little homestead in the park and gave their Testimony of the Pool.

Most had experienced a drowning of sorts. A reversal of life into death. I know that's opposite of most messages from the pulpit. But unless we die, we can't truly live. Something happens when we give Him our very breath. Life becomes precious.

I'm ready to go back to University. Back to my students.

But this experience will forever be imprinted on my mind and heart. These people let me dig into their memories and pain—only to find my own transfiguration and renewal.

RESTORED

THE GREAT ESCAPEE SERIES

ONE

"He's *mine*!" Phil Daynton slammed down his whiskey glass. The golden liquid erupted, splattered over his hand and soaked into the plush carpet in the warden's office at the Chicago prison. "Clarence Timmelsen thinks he can keep my little girl, Bea, from me." He stood, holding his hand away from his clothes. "Well, I'll cut him in half! And you can't stop me."

Warden William Ralston smirked as he sipped his drink, then quietly rested the crystal glass on his knee. Leather stretched and moaned as he leaned back in his chair.

"Don't look at me like that!" Phil stabbed his finger onto Warden's desk. "I get first crack at him!" Booze dripped onto the fine woodwork. His tongue flickered inside his mouth. Ohh. What a waste. He started to lick the back of his hand, but instead, wiped it on his jeans, then used his sleeve to mop the desk surface dry, bumping a family photo into another one right next to it. He caught them before they crashed to the floor. *Damn.*

Warden sat as calm as the calm just before dawn on every day. The calm before Phil knew his dad would be rising out of his drunken stupor soon. Just before the fear and chaos began. Just before the firing squad … fired.

Phil stomped toward the windows. Things had changed since Ralston had taken over the warden job.

For one thing, a new mahogany desk with leather bumpers had replaced grey metal government issue furniture from the last warden. Phil tapped the leather bumper, as he passed the desk. Should have been a pool table—it would have been a better use of beautiful wood and leather. The ceiling fan quietly sliced the heated air; the brass blades reflected the green desk lamp below.

He scanned the grounds outside, as he leaned against the rich wood framing the window, sipping what was left of his drink. Inmates lounged in the fenced-in commons area. *Must be break time.* Most sat at picnic tables or on the sidewalk, leaning against the brick building. Only a couple seemed to be running laps along the fence.

The fence wasn't your everyday-white-washed picket fence. Razor wire topped off the chain-link mesh in endless circles.

Phil shook his head. *Who would try to escape over that?*

What a kingdom.

The office wing formed its own three-story lookout tower, and crowning it was the warden's office on the third floor—with a view of the prison yard, parking lot and entrances in three directions.

Maybe after Clarence was dead and he had Bea all for himself, Phil could get his own warden position and they'd be set for the rest of their lives. He'd show this pansy-faced warden how to take control. Kill or torture off the weaklings and create his own powerful legion of cold soldiers. He straightened, chin jutted. Then he'd rule. Then he'd be the kind of leader this place was worthy of.

Warden stirred the ice in his glass with his finger, his gold rings glinting on his brown skin. "You'll have to get through me, first." He sucked the liquid from his finger and licked his lips.

Something was ... was Warden mocking him? "You think you're so damn smart." Phil faced him and folded his arms across his chest. "I used to be dead drunk, but I ran circles around you—got the girl *and* the drug money. And *still* stayed ahead of the cops."

Warden slowly lifted his head, his eyes locked on Phil.

Something tickled at the back of Phil's neck, like a fly had landed there. Or a feather drawn across his skin. He tried to lift his hand to brush it away, but he just trembled.

He couldn't move his hand.

He turned.

Someone had snuck up behind him.

But no one was there.

Cold chills traced up his back and shoulders, like the caress of a lover, only this was no lover. It was a sinister presence he had only encountered once before. Memories cut through his mind. Hot hands from his past raked over his arms and squeezed at his neck, teasing and taunting him into submission.

Warden was still staring at him—eyes piercing.

Phil tried shaking it off—residual twinges skittered in places he couldn't scratch in public. His face burned as he turned away too late.

"Reliving your past?" A deep voice spoke, but it wasn't the warden's. The voice vibrated every cell of Phil's body with an evil frequency.

Phil shivered and faced the warden. He couldn't help himself. The past pressed into … now. He was that little boy who had been harshly disciplined—picked up physically and planted in front of his dad—knowing what came next.

All the Warden had said were three words, but Phil knew the voice. Same one from every time he'd been hurt, taunted, or abused. Those deep gravelly words accused him, pulled a tarp over the truth, and buried the trail of pain.

Phil shuddered, shaking himself out of the sensations and sounds. "Get outta my head." He kicked the desk.

Warden snarled.

Phil dropped onto the chair across the desk from the warden and tossed the name plaque to the side. "That man. Clarence Timmelsen." He swung his arm wide. "You have hundreds of men to torture. Why do you need *him*?"

Warden's eyes narrowed. A glint of raw emotion, Phil guessed pure hatred, poured from those dark pools. They turned from black holes to blood red.

Phil's eyes locked on him. The walls, the ceiling fan, desk, even the carpet blurred, until all Phil could see in the room was Warden Ralston.

With each breath Warden blew out, the air grew thick, like 4th of July firecracker smoke. His whole appearance seemed to change. Were those faint outlines of scales and horns materializing through the smoke?

Phil shuddered and rubbed his eyes. His empty glass found its way to his lips, like a baby's thumb finds its way to her mouth.

A sick grin twisted Warden's lips. He sucked in a deep breath and the smoke disappeared. "I want Timmelsen, because he killed my brother. It doesn't matter how it happened." He shuddered, shaking off whatever had enveloped him, like a dog shakes off water. "He killed my brother, Lewis, and I want Clarence Timmelsen dead."

The door burst open and a skinny weasel of a guard entered. His filthy grin turned to horror as he realized his blunder. He quickly backed out, closed the door and knocked. "Um, Warden?" He cleared his squeaky voice. This time a deeper voice came out, only it wasn't the effect he had obviously hoped for.

"What a dork." Warden shook his head and shifted his shoulders, adjusting his tie. "Enter, Blockhead."

"I've told you and told you. Don't call me that." The guard glared at Phil. "It only undermines my authority."

"Okay, Tay. Baby Tay. Baby Brudder." Warden grinned, his teeth sparkling. "That better, Tay? Tay?"

Warden's brother, huh.

Tay's brown face turned red. His eyes clouded over. "All I want to tell you is," he straightened, "we are ready to go get that … that Clarence guy." His chin jutted out when he glanced in Phil's direction. "Van's all gassed up and Randy is getting the paperwork fixed."

Warden snorted. "You have any brothers, Phil?"

"Nope." He might have had a brother, but the kid wouldn't have survived his father. How had he, himself lived? How had Bea slipped through?

Tay's chest caved in like a popped balloon. His naturally dark skin took on a gray hue, his eyes appeared wet, but he gulped in a deep breath and his eyes turned hard. "You are a b-bastard!"

He turned and tripped on the expensive oriental rug, falling into the desk. His hands bumped the whiskey carafe. He desperately tried to keep it upright and he almost saved it, but a last grab sent it flying, soaking the paperwork on the desk and sloshing onto Warden's expensive suit.

Phil jumped away to avoid the flood, but Warden's anger activated more scales, this time visible to all. No smoke or mist to hide behind. They shimmered green and gray and gold. Flickered and reflected light. Warden's whole face changed. His eyes bugged out, cheeks stretched flat and his nose grew to a snout.

But those teeth.

Quickly, it all morphed back into Warden's handsome but cruel dark features.

Phil lifted the empty glass to his mouth again, fingers trembling. The booze must be affecting his imagination.

From the look on Tay's face, he guessed he'd seen those scales, too. Growing up with the Warden must have been quite interesting.

Warden smirked. "I'd fill that glass for you, Phil, but as you can see, I'm all out." He calmly tapped his ear and spoke. "Carmile, please bring the necessary equipment."

Interesting. No earpiece. No wires. Must be some sort of implant.

Someone knocked on the door and Warden nodded.

A striking person entered. Almost air-brushed light brown skin. Smoky dark eyes perfectly outlined—resembled an Egyptian goddess. The suit was tailored to fit her ... his body. Hair dangled long around a woman's chest. But lower there was—

"Thank you, Carmile. We had a little mishap." Warden stepped away from the desk, brushing at his pants.

Phil couldn't take his eyes off the secretary.

Tay couldn't either.

She moved with the grace of a woman, but with a man's stride. Lifting one end of the solid wood desk, she sopped the whiskey from the carpet.

What was … he? She?

Warden cleared his throat. "Time to roll. Gather in the Timmelsen man. Bring him to me." He glanced out the window. "Tay. Load up the van. If you leave now, you can drive all night and get there in the morning."

"Yeah." Tay turned to the door. "Whatcha say we don't drive all night, Bro, and get a motel halfway there?"

Tay's hand seemed to freeze on the doorknob.

"You will do as I say, Baby Brother." Warden's voice grew softer, with a growl, his eyes still on something outside. "You will leave now and drive all night. Gather Mr. Timmelsen and bring him to me by morning."

"Yeah. Okay, Bro." He stood, hand still frozen on the knob "You can let me go now. We ain't no kids in the backyard anymore." He squealed. "Let me go!" The door opened and he leaned into the opening but appeared to be suspended mid air—as if held by some unseen force—like a rubber band stretched tight, ready to shoot its missile. Suddenly, the force holding him seemed to release and he shot into the hallway. He picked himself up and ran.

Phil snorted a laugh but restrained himself. He stood and followed where Warden stared. One inmate was out of line, weaving back and forth. A guard abruptly turned toward the window where Warden stood and stared back. He then signaled for the other guards to handcuff the inmate. They took him out of Phil's line of vision. A sharp pop made the others in line jump, but none looked away from the guard in charge. All stayed obediently in line, eyes straight ahead. Intent on staying at attention. The other man never came back.

Phil disengaged himself from the scene outside to find Warden smiling at him. Eyebrows raised.

And a plan dropped into his mind. Why not let Warden *have* Timmelsen? Why fight over him?

If Warden arrested Clarence … then Bea and Katty, but especially pretty little Bea, would be unguarded.

And vulnerable.

TWO

Noell Carpenter sighed. Day off. Weekends were so long.

She stretched. Nice not to go to the Roads Department, but she missed the guys. She missed the camaraderie and the joking. The family atmosphere. Even Rat.

The family.

She supposed everybody had questionable members in their family. One might be nice, another maybe from a different culture. And everybody had a Rat. Her work family had one; he had tried more than once to interest her in his idea of love.

Ick. Hence the name.

Her room upstairs was pristine, as always, but today it seemed empty. She liked the clean feel—just a couple things on the bedside table—her Bible from Gamma, the "Osceola Times" cup from the porch and her baby bracelet. She rolled over and picked up the bracelet. So tiny. The smallest pearls she'd ever seen and little pink beads mixed in. A small round locket out of what looked like silver, created a center showpiece.

When she opened the locket, a photo of herself as a baby was on one side and Mommy's picture was on the other.

Noell hovered her finger over both photos, letting the emotion flow until she snapped the locket shut. Even though she had touched the bracelet many times, still she could discern other voices—Gamma's most of all. "My baby girl. You are so precious."

She blew out a breath and blinked back tears.

Before Gamma died, when grief and fear pulled her down, she could run downstairs and snuggle with Gamma and everything would be all right.

But not anymore.

Gamma was gone and so was Grampa.

And so was Mommy.

Loneliness.

Noell had never known Mommy by any other name than … Mommy. She couldn't remember her face, except from photographs like the one in the locket.

And the nightmares.

Gotta get up and focus on something.

Anything, other than loneliness.

Anything, other than nightmares.

As soon as she got dressed and went downstairs, more emotion flooded her. The stairway descended into the living room and Gamma's beautiful red leather sofa sat front and center. Her empty spot still … empty. Even though one end was piled with magazines and old mail, and boxes surrounded the sofa, Gamma's spot was always open. Waiting.

A sob rose in Noell's throat and she swallowed it. She didn't need to go down that road now, with no one to pull her back from the edge of pain and nightmares.

Get busy.

Do something.

Breathe.

The room was stuffed. Barely space to walk from the bottom of the steps to the dining room in front of her. Or from Gamma's sofa to the enclosed front porch or to Gamma's bedroom at the back of the house. At least from the bottom of the steps, it was just a right turn into the kitchen. She had used that well when freshly baked chocolate chip cookies still cooled on the counter. Just nab four or five, whip around the corner and zoom up the steps. Gamma never saw. But she knew.

She leaned around the corner now.

No cookies.

Books piled to the ceiling against the back kitchen wall, framing the back door. Gamma had always said they were good insulation.

Noell shrugged. Maybe.

She loved to read and was forever checking books out from the library or buying softly used books from Mrs. Bertrand's thrift store. Seemed like Mrs. Bertrand always found some that spoke to Noell. She loved that store.

Maybe she could give back. Her eyes skimmed the walls. Give back stacks and stacks of books to Mrs. Bertrand.

When Gamma was still alive, Noell had tried to get rid of some of the clutter by sneaking items out. She had donated them to the thrift store. Mrs. Bertrand and the other ladies working there promised to never tell. Anything to try and clear the house out.

She shook her head. Hadn't helped. She couldn't tell if it had made any difference or not.

She blinked. Really emotional today. She wiped her face with her sleeve.

Breathe.

She could go to the Roads yard and rake, whether they were open or not. She knew how to get in. Anything but stay here. It felt like every box and stack in every room had tumbled down on top of her.

Maybe Fletch could come over later after he got off work and they could … go for a walk or watch a movie at his house. There was no room here to do anything.

What if she cleared away clutter around the TV? They could watch a movie together.

If she picked up the magazine piles on the sofa and moved them to the kitchen, that would help clear room for one more person on the sofa. Cozy.

She hauled the magazines to the kitchen but when she got to the back door, she realized there were two more piles she'd put there yesterday. One pile was already sliding into the narrow path to the backdoor. She slid them as best she could with her foot, but the other stack started sliding until there was a mess of magazines covering her feet.

She needed a recycling bin. No, she needed one like at the dump for newspapers, magazines, cans, everything.

Good idea. Note to self. Call Monday and see if they could pull one here.

Noell had been working for an hour before her stomach growled. Breakfast. Taking the steps two at a time, she went up to her room for a book to read while she ate.

Two more doors opened off the landing hallway and Noell became distracted by them. It had been a long time since she had explored.

This house was all hers now, so she ought to find out what she owned.

She jiggled the doorknob to the first room, but it was locked.

What?

She dug around the boxes on the floor, felt along the doorjamb, the baseboards and finally produced a key stuck in a crack between the doorjamb and the wall. What on earth? What would Gamma have had that needed to be locked up?

She examined the key—a little bread wrapper twisty looped through the hole. Gamma used those for everything—from hangers for keys, to tighten an old screw. The twisty had been barely sticking out from where the key was hidden—just enough to be able to slide the key out. What if it had fallen further behind the wood?

Flipping the key one way and then the other, Noell inserted it in the door lock. Wrong way. She flipped it again, wiggled it back and forth and the lock clicked.

The door opened a crack—purple rug. Noell had to give the door a kick to get it open all the way. Cobwebs hung as if protecting the entrance, until she swung her arms, breaking through.

A bedroom. The bed was still made up with a pretty quilt, splashes of yellow sunflowers and green leaves outlined in purple and lavender.

Oh. No.

Just leave. Just close the door and pretend she'd never found that key. Go downstairs and cook. Go outside to the camper and forget this house was here. Some people actually did that.

But she couldn't. Her feet were stapled to the floor. She glanced at her feet. No. To purple carpet.

Deep breath.

Stay here.

Don't run.

Her hand still grasped the doorknob.

She knew where she was.

A movie of people played in her mind—a much younger Gamma, Grampa, others she didn't know or recognize. All moved together through time—through this house. The same house, the same rooms—only no clutter.

No boxes or stacks of books.

Anywhere.

The steps were beautiful, all cleared off and newer supple wood, instead of tired and dried out. And dirty.

She blinked.

Time dropped her back into the current day.

This room—she knew instantly whose room it had been, and that knowledge dropped her to her knees.

The quilt pattern blurred. The photos on the bedside table swam before her brimming eyes.

Mommy's room.

Breathe.

She couldn't move.

The movie played again.

Someone was crying. Dishes clattered. Telephones rang. A deep voice, "I'm sorry. We can't talk right now. We've … our daughter … " A little voice, "Where's Mommy? Gamma? Where's my mommy?"

Oh God.

Why had she never explored? Had Gamma told her not to—to protect her—to keep her out of Mommy's room?

A stronger will pushed her to her feet. Gave her strength to inch slowly to the bed. The old quilt was soft under her fingers. She traced the pattern of leaves and stitching. Gamma must have made this.

Or Mommy?

Noell held her breath as she sat on the bed. No springs squeaked. No sounds.

Just soft.

And comforting.

She willed herself to lie down, then curled on her side, hugging the pillows. Pulling the quilt around her shoulders, she breathed it in. A little musty but somehow so fresh.

Mommy had slept here.

As the quilt warmed her shoulders and back, the love she had longed for from her mother's arms surrounded her. Tears held back for so long spilled out.

This was not how she had expected this day to start.

"Mom. Gamma. Grampa too. I feel you all here somehow. Something here is so warm and comforting." She wiped her face and sat up. "Why Gamma? Why didn't you … "

Noell realized for the first time why Gamma had left this room intact. The pain had been too real. And as the years crawled on, grief grew into a formidable monster that Gamma couldn't fight by herself.

As she began to explore the room, she realized something else. Maybe this room had been preserved … for her.

For now.

She picked up a small framed photo and plunked herself back down on the bed.

Mommy.

Her nightmares were still there, slithering into her sleep, flooding her tormented nights. Mommy's face still screamed out at her, her hand still reached for her.

But this photo …

Mommy had been pretty.

Noell combed through her own hair as she noticed Mommy's long blond hair.

Her eyes. Kind. Loving. Same clear blue as her own.

Mommy's eyes in the dreams were terrified.

Mom, what did you go through that day?

She lifted her head to study the room.

Gamma … and Grampa, what did you go through that day?

Noell still had the nightmares, but her grandparents had lived with the cruel daily reality of that pain. Their daughter had drowned.

She pressed the photo to her chest as she wandered about the room, touched curtains, sniffed a bottle of perfume.

She reached the closet and paused, her hand on the doorknob.

No voices. No visuals.

Deep breath as she opened the door, not knowing if she wished it would be full or empty.

Creak.

Full.

So many revelations hit her as she explored—Gamma, to keep her own sanity, had held onto everything, so she wouldn't have to part with her memories.

Oh Gamma.

Noell gently touched each garment, releasing the fragrance of her mother. She closed her eyes, waiting for the onslaught of powerful visions and voices.

What she heard instead was laughter so melodic. Bubbles of it.

Dancing and laughter.

"You're so pretty little one."

"Look at your curls dance!"

"I love you."

Oh God.

Blinking back more tears, she slowly closed the door.

Turned into the room again. No clutter. No hoarding. Almost as simple as her own room.

She was beginning to understand Gamma even more.

While Noell had struggled with her own problems—germaphobia, nightmares—Gamma had been in such pain.

She treasured seeing this intact room and felt it was meant to be.

She needed to experience her mother's things and let the voices speak to her heart.

Someday she would need to take all this down.

Just that thought was enough to make her heart hammer in her chest.

Pictures flooded her mind of the rest of the house and she gasped. Struggled to breathe. She closed her eyes.

In that moment she knew she had to face what Gamma wouldn't. Couldn't.

She had to clean out this house and get rid of it all. Sell it.

She couldn't let it be a noose around her neck. She couldn't let it trap her and paralyze her whole life, like Gamma had.

She knew now that Gamma had been trapped by her grief, but Noell realized she couldn't let herself do that.

She had to find release and get free.

She had to sell this house. Clean it out and sell so she didn't end up the same way.

She walked to the door spurred on by those thoughts, the photo of Mommy cupped at her chest.

She could do this.

Until she saw the steps. Each step had stacks on it. Books. Magazines. Boxes.

How on earth … ?

Katty yawned. Good to sleep in today. She checked her phone. Wow.

Bea slept in too? It was seven o'clock and she wasn't begging for cereal and juice. Maybe she was growing up. Oh, for when Bea was sixteen and slept till noon.

Katty slipped out from under the sheet and stretched. So much she should do today.

Laundry. Always laundry.

What she really should do was work with Bea—let her practice writing her name. While she did that, Katty loved to draw. Bea always wanted to draw too—cute trees and sunshine, but Katty made her write her name several times before she turned her loose.

She glanced at all the drawings Bea had taped up in the living room, as she zipped up her hoodie.

Everywhere. Above the doorjamb. Down the legs of the kitchen table.

Well, she had taped the ones above the door. Bea had done all the rest. Tape was cheap.

She opened the refrigerator door. There was even a picture in there. Oh, so cute. A belly laugh rose up from her toes. A drawing of a cow was taped to the milk jug.

That Bea!

Katty took the milk and juice out. When had Bea done that? She left the drawing taped to the milk. Wouldn't be long till the tape got too wet, but for now—

"Mommy! Look!" Bea raced to Katty. "Look! I drew a Mommy cow and her baby! Can we go to a farm and see them?"

About a dozen paintings were scattered on the dining room table, the floor and on each chair. "How long have you been up, Bea?" She placed the milk and juice on the table.

"I just got up!"

"Right."

Katty picked up one picture and put it on the stove to dry. "Reminder. Don't turn on the burner without moving the picture." She pulled out bowls and spoons, muttering to herself. "I remember a day, not so long ago, when I started a fire doing just that and the fire department—"

"What, Mommy? Fire?"

"No Baby Bea. Just talking to myself." She poured cereal in both bowls and then the milk. "I also remember the days when we were always out of milk and cereal and you, my beautiful child had to fend for yourself."

She cupped her hands around Bea's full cheeks. "I would wake from my drunken stupor to find you eating peanut butter on stale, moldy bread." She wiped her eyes.

Bea stood up on her chair. "Mommy. You're crying. Can we have peanut butter?"

Katty hugged Bea. "So thankful, Baby. So thankful." She checked the cupboard.

"Yeah. Thankful." Bea nodded. "To Jesus. To Clarence. To the birds. To God—"

Katty burst out laughing. "Oh, I love you!" She moved some cans around and mumbled. "I don't see any peanut butter."

"I love you too, Mommy." Bea slurped her cereal. "I love peanut butter too."

"We'll have to get some, okay? Sit down and eat and I'll go out and get the mail. I forgot to get it yesterday. Be right back."

Katty peeked outside to make sure no one was outside. There had been a day also, when she wouldn't have cared, or even realized that she was outside in her pjs. She used to go to the store in these same shorties. Just roll out, grab Bea and go. She cringed, hoping people had either forgotten, or they had forgiven her.

She opened the door and stepped outside on her beautiful new wooden deck. Clarence was so generous. He had said they needed to be safe and to be honest, the old deck had been falling apart. New pots of lavender drew her, and she pinched a leaf, sniffed it as she went down the steps to the mailbox. She opened it and pulled out more than a days worth of mail, when she noticed a little red bike with a huge bow the size of a dinner plate tied around the handlebars.

She gasped. So shiny. She walked around it and patted the seat. "It's beautiful, but—"

Bea screamed from the door and ran down the steps. "Mommy! Is this for me? Did it come in the mail? How did they fit it in the mailbox? Mommy, it's beautiful!"

Katty shushed her. "It's seven o'clock in the morning." She glanced at the neighbors across the road and next door. Ugh. *He* was up. The guy next door had never done anything to them, but he still gave Katty the willies. He waved from the window. Shirtless. Ick.

"Did *he* give me this bike?" Bea pointed.

"No!" Katty shushed her again and gripped Bea's pointer finger in her hand. She lowered her voice. "No. I'm sure he would like you to think he did." She pulled at the bow, revealing an envelope.

She handed the envelope to Bea, shoved up the kickstand with her bare foot and pushed the bike to the deck. Bumping up each step, she steered it to the door.

"Mommy! *My* bike?" Bea followed her. "In the house?" She grinned. "Cool!"

Katty slammed the door. "Open the envelope Bea. See who it's from."

Bea tore it open and squealed as a ten-dollar bill floated to the floor. She held up the card for Katty to read.

"To Bea—"

"Bea! That's me! That's my bike!"

"Wait! There's more." Katty grabbed the card. "I can't read it while you're jumping up and down." She squinted. "To Bea. From your Secret Admirer." She flipped the card over and over. "Who on earth would do this?"

Bea stopped bouncing. "Clarence! He would. It's from him!" She started dancing around the bike. "Clarence would do it! Can I take it out and ride it? I rode Alexander's bike … one day."

"You rode his bike?" Katty leaned over and looked into Bea's eyes. "After I told you not to go over there anymore?"

"Well … only once." She brightened. "But I could ride it!" She hopped on the seat. "Can I?"

"No! We have to call Clarence first and make sure it's from him. Otherwise we don't know who did this. And if we don't know who gave it to you, then you can't ride it. Or keep it."

"What?" Bea's lower lip trembled. "The card. It said to me." She pointed to her chest. Her face crumpled and she stomped her feet.

"Bea!" Katty's hand swung but she drew it back. "Bea! Stop that right now!" She realized she had left the front door open and just her luck, a cop drove by.

God!

She slammed the door and scrambled for her phone. "I'll call Clarence and find out." She checked the time. "Almost eight o'clock. He'll be up."

Bea hopped on the bike, almost knocking it over.

Katty steadied the bike. "Hello Clarence?"

FOUR

Clarence Timmelsen tilted the coffee carafe toward Harold. "More?"

Harold shook his head and covered his cup. "Naw. Takes me too long to get to the bathroom. Sure is good, though. Better than down at the dining room. Theirs is like pee water."

"The very reason I make my own." Clarence filled his cup. "Coffee at prison was sludge. You didn't need a spoon to stir sugar in, you needed a concrete mixer."

Harold laughed and tipped his cup way up to get that last drop.

Old geezer. Wore his upside down American flag pin everyday. Did he have one for every shirt or did he take it out every night? Bet the nurse did it.

Clarence reached over and righted the flag.

"Bothers you, huh." Harold tucked his chin down to try and see the flag. "I do that every morning."

"What? What do you do every morning?" Clarence picked up his cup.

"I turn it upside down just to piss you off." Harold chuckled. "I know it bothers you, so I make sure, before I leave my room, that I turn it upside down."

Clarence slammed his cup down. "Isn't there something about that in the Bible? You'll go to hell for doing that." He bounced his head up and down.

Harold choked.

"Whoa!" Clarence patted him on the back. "Don't die on me." He looked toward the hallway. "Nurse!"

Harold waved him back, laughing. "I'm fine." He blew out a breath. Chuckled again. "Thanks for telling me that."

"Telling you what?" Clarence cupped his hand around one ear.

"I don't want to go to hell." Harold laughed again. "Damn. We're like a couple old ladies. Can't hear. Can't breathe."

Clarence chuckled, too. Good to laugh these days. Good to have a friend to laugh with. Sigh.

They settled back and watched the morning traffic pass Clarence's open door in Hillcrest nursing home.

"Do you really turn it upside down every morning?" Clarence peeked at Harold.

Harold broke out laughing, slamming his hand on the desk.

Clarence wiped his eyes. Belly laughs. He coughed to clear his throat.

"Everyday we can have one more laugh is a good day." Harold nodded and glanced out at the hallway.

People in wheelchairs, either being pushed or self-mobilated, headed to the dining room for breakfast. Nurses rushed past the door with med cups or charts or bedding.

Busy. Busy.

Clarence turned to gaze out the window. The maintenance man crouched in the corner, digging in the brightly colored chrysanthemum bed. Weeding? The guy was always quietly digging somewhere. In fact, he'd been there before—digging. Clarence leaned forward and pointed. "Wha—"

"Hey!" Harold waved at someone passing by in the hall. "We should start an agency together."

Clarence swiveled in his office chair. "A what? A government agency, insurance agency? We could run one better than that bastard Pete … Pete—"

"Pete Malovitch."

"That bastard Malovitch." Clarence shook his head. "One bad dude. Almost killed me." He leaned his head back against the headrest. "Thank God for Sheriff. That man saved my life."

"No. An agency. What if—what if we started with who we are? You're a lawyer and I'm a detective—still have my certification."

Clarence lifted his head. "You do? That's … awesome." He leaned forward and peered at his framed law certificates. He pointed. "Those haven't expired. I renewed that just before I was kicked out of prison." He shook his head again. "You think we could really do that?"

Harold shrugged. "Why not? We ain't dead yet. People hide from life and the law in small towns. Why not in a nursing home?"

"Yeah." Clarence jutted his chin and nodded. "Why not?"

"Think of the damsels in distress we could save." Harold flicked his eyebrows up and down.

The door pushed open.

"Clarence!" Carol rushed in. Her eyes appeared red; black smudged her cheeks. She was a beautiful woman normally, but right now, something had either scared her or hurt her, and it gripped his heart.

Clarence jumped up and grabbed her shoulders. "Is Joe okay? Carol, what happened?" He searched her face. "What happened to Joe?"

"Joe's like always … he's worse … but it's not him." She gulped. Tears spilled from clear green eyes onto fair cheeks. "It's you, Clarence —" She pushed past him to the TV and turned it on. The screen flashed. She flipped channels and Phil Daynton and Lex Forte's faces filled the screen, with a byline below looping their names.

Clarence pointed. "What are they doing on TV?" He leaned closer, reading. "And when did they become prison consultants?" He fumbled with the remote and volume blared. He punched it down.

The camera panned to the announcer interviewing Phil. "And Mr. Daynton, when did Mr. Timmelsen escape from Chicago prison?"

Clarence growled. "I didn't escape. Judge Green had it set up way back … he had me kicked out."

Carol shushed him.

A photo of Clarence flashed on the screen.

Every cell in Clarence's body went rigid. His jaw dropped and he grabbed at his coffee, only to knock it over.

Carol rushed to pull paper towels, but stopped and stared at the TV.

Harold pointed. "Look! They have a picture of you, Clarence!"

Phil looked full into the camera. "He was kicked out—"

Clarence nodded. "There you see? Damn right I—"

"—by mistake. He killed a man while incarcerated."

Clarence slowly lowered himself onto his chair, his fingers massaged the scar on his cheek. "I killed … it was self defense." He pointed at the TV. "He was going to kill me and … and—"

The announcer had asked Phil another question.

"Oh, he'll pay all right." Phil looked straight into the camera. "A posse was sent out overnight to the nursing home to bring him in."

A small crowd had gathered behind Phil and Lex on screen and they began murmuring. "A posse?"

"Where?"

A woman right behind Lex gasped, her hand over her mouth. "He's in the nursing home? A murderer loose in a nursing home?"

Loud voices could be heard from the hall.

Clarence's phone rang and he picked it up. "Hello?" He listened for a minute. "Katty. Hi. It's crazy here right now." He pointed to the TV. "What?" He listened again. "No, Hon, I didn't give her a bike. Why?"

The voices from the hall grew closer.

"Turn on your TV. That bastard Phil Daynton and Lex Whathis-name are on." He nodded. "The same. They are saying they sent a posse out for me and they're gonna take me back to prison." He leaned forward. "What? It's awfully noisy right now."

Sheriff Dennison pushed through the door, talking to someone behind him. "He's innocent. I've read his files." He stepped in front of Clarence. "You have to have papers. Authorization."

Harold set his chin. "Sheriff's here. He'll straighten things out."

A puny, dark-skinned prison guard followed through the door. Full prison uniform. Hand at his gun. Face stern. Another followed close behind, double the size. Same evil.

Clarence stiffened and backed his chair up, pulling Carol with him. Six months since he had seen a guard. Six months!

Randy Gerald followed, a brown envelope in his hand. Same guard uniform stretched over an expanding belly. His brown eyes determined.

"Randy!" Clarence dropped his phone and started toward him. Something else lurked in Randy's eyes. Frustration? Embarrassment? Yes, but something more. Randy almost growled.

"Clarence—" Randy handed the envelope to Sheriff.

Miss Oster, Administrator, flew into the room and butted in front of Randy and the guards. "I knew it! I knew it was a bad idea to let you live here, much less open your law office here." She planted her feet in front of Clarence and Carol.

"Clarence?" The phone spoke.

Clarence tightened his grip on Carol's arm. "Randy, what is all this?" He stepped in front of Carol and pushed Miss Oster aside.

The skinny guard flinched and drew his gun. The other guard followed suit.

Sheriff dropped the paperwork and drew his.

Everyone in the room immediately raised their hands in surrender, except Clarence and Randy.

The door pushed open to the tallest guy in Osceola, Nebraska and probably this side of heaven.

"Michael!" Clarence breathed a sigh of relief. Good timing, Buddy.

"Clarence. How's it going?" Michael ducked through the doorway and scanned the room. "This a party?" He slid around the guards to Clarence. "A costume party." He patted the guard's hat and tapped his gun. "Realistic. Guns look real."

The guard jumped. "Who's Michael?"

"Stand down." Randy stepped between the guards and Clarence and Sheriff.

The phone again. "Guns? Clarence, what is going on?"

Clarence bent to retrieve the phone, but the guard kicked it away.

Someone knocked, pushing the door open.

"You boys need any … " Lisha Hall stuck her head in, surrounded by three more aides. "prune juice?"

"Eek!" An aide pointed. "They have guns!"

Randy hefted his large chest and planted his feet, pointing at his guard. "Stand down! This is a nursing home. Old people live here!"

The guards backed down and holstered their guns.

Sheriff holstered his and gathered the papers.

Clarence pointed his crooked finger at Randy. "Randy, what gives?"

"I'll take some prune juice." Michael piped up.

Harold started to stand. "I'm a detective and I'll—"

Tay pulled him up by the collar and shoved him out the door. "Detective. My eye. Shut-up old man."

"Excuse me ladies." Randy escorted Lisha and the aides out the door. He bumped into Miss Oster as he turned into the room. "Ma'am, excuse me. This is private business." He shoved her out the door.

She stomped her foot. "I am Administrator of this nursing home and I have a right—"

Randy stood firm. "I have jurisdiction here. Clarence is my prisoner."

Clarence froze. Every vein turned to ice. "P-prisoner?"

FIVE

Katty switched the phone to her other ear. "Phil? And Lex? Posse? What is going on?"

"It's awfully noisy right now." Clarence's voice sounded tense.

Someone—sounded like Harold—said, "Sheriff's here."

Katty held onto the bike. "Sheriff?"

Clarence had obviously forgotten all about her and their conversation. "Randy!" Then clunk.

Katty jerked her head up and stared at the phone. "Sounded like he dropped the phone." She put it to her ear again. "Clarence? Clarence? What is going on?"

Bea climbed off the bike. "Mommy? Clarence dropped the phone? Is he—"

"Shh, Baby." Katty checked her phone. Still connected. She slowly sat on the sofa. "Clarence?"

Voices she had never heard before. A deep voice—Michael?

"… guns …."

Katty froze. "Guns? Clarence what is going on?"

Bea climbed onto her lap and leaned toward the phone. "Clarence? You there? He's playing with guns? I want to!"

"Shh. Bea, stop!" Katty listened again. Sounds of sliding, scraping along a surface and a bump into something.

She kept listening in spite of Bea pestering her.

"Did you ask him about the bike?" Bea slipped off her lap, almost knocking the bike over.

Katty steadied the bike, phone still at her ear. "More guns?" She stared at the phone. "At the nursing home? Oh my God!"

Bea, back on the bike, feet on the pedals, set the bike in motion, rode around the kitchen table and down the hall toward the bedrooms.

Crash!

Katty jumped up. Prune juice? "Bea? You okay?" She ran to see the damage.

She got to Bea in time to see her in the bathroom, crawling out of the toilet, splashing water onto the floor. "Bea! Are you alright?"

Bea was grinning. "I rode the bike, Mommy." She pointed. "Into the potty."

Katty put the phone to her ear. "Clarence?" She wiped her cheeks and hugged Bea. Then pulled away. Clarence's voice was shaking. Prisoner? "What? Prisoner?"

"What's a prisoner, Mommy?"

Katty tried to suck in a breath but couldn't. She blew out through her mouth.

Breathe!

"We've got to go!"

SIX

Click!

Clarence stumbled. The room blurred. Breakfast oatmeal fought its way up. Cold metal encased his wrists. Handcuffs.

"Michael! Help!"

Michael just stood there beside the door, head bowed.

The guards backed away a step but kept a tight grip on his arms. "Who's Michael?"

Clarence swallowed and cleared his throat. "Randy. What the hell?" He coughed. "Randy. Why are you doing this? What did I do?"

All three—Randy and the two guards—blended together. They wore the exact same uniform: drab brown with patches on the sleeves, ball hat. Same old uniforms Clarence had stared at for the past sixty years in prison.

One guard's eyes flitted to everything in the room but Clarence. The skinny one glared, eyes boring into Clarence as if he had a personal vendetta against him. An evil amusement. Name tag: Tay Ralston.

And Randy. His voice was firm, almost sharp, but his eyes betrayed him. Wouldn't look Clarence in the eye. He pulled out papers and unfolded them, reading, making it official, "I have been sent to retrieve one Clarence Timmelsen—"

"One Clarence Timmelsen! Randy, it's me, Clarence!" He struggled with the handcuffs. "What do you have against me?"

" … to be brought before the Chicago State Prison Board on the matter of the death of inmate Lewis Ralston."

Something in Clarence shifted. His right cheek prickled where Lewis's knife had sliced his skin. That had been almost twenty years ago.

Clarence read the guard name tags again.

Ralston's glistening eyes glared pure evil. Something else. He had a vendetta, all right.

Clarence struggled against the guards. "He was your … your—"

"He was my brother." Ralston grew taller. A mist enveloped him, like steam off a boiling kettle. An unmistakable sour stench filled the room.

Randy stepped between them, paper at his side, facing Ralston. "I told you if you became a problem today, no matter your relationship with Warden Ralston, I would report you." Face to face. Randy's barrel chest touched Ralston's belt. "You understand?"

Ralston didn't nod. He didn't relax. "I understand." His eyes still pierced with evil intent, voice mocking. "Sir."

Randy turned to face Clarence, still scanning the document. "The case went before the board and they determined—"

"They determined that you killed him in cold blood." Ralston finished with a squeak.

Ralston hadn't moved, but Clarence's skin crawled.

"It was self-defense. His brother was there. He saw it all." Clarence's voice rose in pitch. "They attacked *me*." He tried to point to his right cheek, but the handcuffs held. "D-Dirk was there. He saw."

"Dirk is dead."

Clarence stumbled back. The atmosphere took on an icy chill. "He's dead? Can't be!" He searched each face.

Ralston confirmed it, nodding his head, chin jutting out.

"This can't be happening." Clarence glanced at his rooms, one for the office—desk and all—and one for a bedroom.

How had this become home?

"Let's get going. It's a long way back to Chicago." Randy doffed his ball hat.

"But I'll need my stuff, my—"

"You'll get all prison issue again, just like before." The evil guard laughed. "Only this time, you ain't gettin' out."

"Enough." Randy pocketed the papers. "We don't know that. We have just been ordered to bring him in."

"But why didn't this come up when I was sent here? The warden didn't have a problem with it."

"There's a new warden in charge."

"In the last few months?" Anger began to boil. Clarence's old friend, rage, punched him in the gut. "He just figured this all out in the last few months?" His voice broke.

Ralston hooked Clarence's arm and towed him along. "Like the man said—let's get going."

Randy stood firm. "I have been delegated to bring you in Clarence. But be assured, you are under my care. Nothing's going to happen to you. This will be over soon."

"Oh it'll be over. I'll be back here tomorrow night."

A deep chuckle sliced through the silence. "I wouldn't count on it. If you have any hot dates, you'd better cancel them for the rest of your life because you're not go—"

"That's enough, Ralston. He'll be back here. I guarantee it." Randy opened the door. "Now let's get going. Lots of miles to drive."

Michael stepped aside.

"Michael." Clarence choked and leaned toward him.

"Who's Michael?"

Michael bowed his head. He seemed to diminish in size.

Clarence tugged at the handcuffs, looking up into Michael's face. "Michael. Why can't you help me?"

No answer.

No movement. Curly brown head still bowed.

Clarence waited.

Ralston pulled at his arm.

Randy pushed from behind.

Oatmeal threatened.

Michael looked away.

Clarence shuddered.

As they dragged him out the door, his eyes never left Michael's bowed head until the door silently swung shut.

Down the hall.

Carol hovered. "Clarence. You'll be back. You'll see." Her chin quivered.

A light touch on his back. Her touch tingled, sending a vibration through him, ending at his soul. Hit its mark.

Residents had gathered in the long hall, in the living room, on their way back to their rooms after breakfast.

"There he is." One pointed. "I knew he was no good."

"This mean our pool game is off?" No one laughed.

"Clarence … "

No.

Mrs. Hatly. She was openly weeping, standing next to Harold. Her glasses were off, in Harold's hand. Her skinny arm reached to Clarence.

He choked and gasped a sob. And another. "Harold … please … "

Harold nodded. "I'll watch over her." He cleared his throat. "Until you get back."

The guards pushed him toward the door.

Katty plunged her hand into her bag, digging, throwing tissues onto the floorboards of her car. "Where are my keys?"

"Mommy?"

Out flew her make-up bag and a half-empty pack of cigarettes. "I didn't know I still had those." Out went a brush.

Bea kicked the back of Katty's seat. "Mommy?"

"Bea! Not now!"

"But—"

Katty turned in her seat, her hand swung wide to strike.

Bea, wide-eyed, opened her mouth, but no words came out. Her pointer finger slowly lifted off her leg, arm rising. Eyes still wide open. She continued to raise her arm, finger pointing above Katty's head.

Katty sputtered. "What?"

"You told me you were going to keep them in the sun shade thing, so you wouldn't loose them." Her arm straightened, finger trembling.

Katty faced the windshield and looked up. There were her keys dangling from the visor—right where she had put them.

She wiped her eyes, started the car and hesitated. She turned to Bea. "Bea. Baby. I'm sorry." She could barely reach Bea's cheek to caress it.

Bea leaned into Katty's hand and kissed it. "It's okay Mommy. You didn't hit me. You haven't in a long time. I'm proud of you."

Katty wiped her eyes again. "You. Are so good. You. My Bea." She blinked. "Now we have to go to Clarence. Guns. Prisoner."

She backed out slowly. A cop was always patrolling their little trailer court. Must live close or have a girlfriend nearby.

At the highway, they waited for three semi-trucks and five cars, one pickup. "Good grief. Hurry!"

She crossed the highway and drove into Hillcrest parking lot. A huge white van was parked out front.

She got out, released Bea's carseat straps and lifted her.

"What's that van for Mommy?" Bea pointed. "What's it say?"

"It says, 'Chicago Pri … .'" That would break Bea's heart.

"What, Mommy?"

"Umm."

Michael still stood in Clarence's room behind the open door. He and the angels around him were the only beings there.

Awful visuals of what had just happened swarmed his mind.

"P-prisoner?" Clarence had blinked.

The guards had each grabbed Clarence's arms and stretched them behind his back.

"Agh!" Clarence grimaced and almost fell to his knees.

"Sheriff! Do something!" Carol pointed to Clarence. "They're hurting him!"

"Guys. He's eighty years old." Sheriff shook his head. Papers dropped at his side.

"Stop them!" Carol pulled at Sheriff's sleeve.

"I can't." Sheriff held up the envelope. "It's all here. I'll have to go to the office and get this cleared up." He shook his head. "But for now—"

Clarence shook his head. Arms behind his back. Eyes wild. Jaw jutting.

Michael wiped at his eyes. That moment had been the worst. Clarence's eyes.

"No! No!" Clarence had wrenched one hand free and slammed his fist into the guard's jaw. "You can't do this!" He screamed. "Michael!"

Michael flinched. His warrior buddies tightened their grip around his huge arms.

One guard popped Clarence on the head with his beat stick and wrestled his hand behind him.

Clarence had pulled loose and punched him in the chin, pushing him into the wall, knocking a couple framed pictures and law documents to the floor. Glass shattered and the balloon frame with Bea's photo in it flew apart as it hit the floor.

Michael flinched and tore at the other angels.

The three muscular angels, bigger than he, circled him, pinned him to the wall, smothered him with their fragrance. Fresh from Father.

Electric jolts zapped his body, electrifying the human skin, the whole body, until he shuddered.

Restoration. Crucial for the ever-present evil on this earth.

One angel, Zahab, blond and full of Golden Light, spoke in his ear. "My brother Michael. Listen to the voice of the Father. Go not against Him. He has a divine plan and you are a part of it. If. If you will obey and not interfere. We know not the future but can minister with the humans to bring in Father's plan. Help Clarence now by walking alongside, bringing messages to him, flowing strength from above. If he receives, all well and good. If he does not, that is not your concern."

Noises filtered in from the hallway. Gasps as people must have seen Clarence in handcuffs.

A shriek.

Mrs. Hatly. Poor precious woman. Michael didn't need supernatural powers to discern her love for Clarence.

Michael ached inside. "Father. Let me … " He shook his head. "I will not disobey. Please, Father." He wrestled his own will. Wanted to rush down the hall and throw the guards to the floor, freeing Clarence —but desperate to obey Father.

Zahab and the other angels released him. Sounds of an army preparing for battle—clattering swords and shields, horses stomping— layered over sobbing from the hallway.

The battle was on.

His sword slowly extended out of his right hand, as his human body deferred to the angelic. A shield appeared from his left. Powerful wings unfurled from his shoulders and back.

Head still bowed, he commanded the center of the room.

As he kept his head bowed, he grew even taller, through the ceiling. Feet apart, sword and shield above his head.

His face to the heavens, he cried out, his sword pointed heavenward. A tear tracked down his rugged cheek. He bowed on one knee and pounded his right arm across his chest. "Not my will, Father."

As soon as he said it, he appeared beside Clarence.

"Gonna go with me after all?" Clarence glanced sideways at Michael. "God, I need you."

"I'm with you for the long haul, Buddy. Only this time, it's not repairing old buildings." Michael's hand hovered just above Clarence's shoulder. His brother angels surrounded them as they walked.

All except for the guard, Ralston. He had his own entourage— demons, hissing and spitting at Michael and the other angels.

Clarence shifted his shoulders. "I can't believe I'm going back." He choked.

Residents gathered in the dining room. Wheelchairs glutted the entrance. Some stood by the beverage counter, dispensing their cup of watered-down coffee.

Every manner of supernatural creature hovered, each claiming rights to its assigned human.

Gnarled demons hissed and spit as Mrs. Hatly and Harold entered the room, their angels brandishing swords on both sides.

The demons covered the eyes and ears of their charge.

Michael shook his head. If movie goers could see *this*. Made Star Wars look like a church pot luck supper.

As Clarence and his guards marched by, one woman dropped her coffee cup. It shattered, pieces scattering across the floor.

Voices buzzed. One old woman chattered loudly into her phone and pointed. "Yes, he is. And there he goes. Back to prison where he belongs."

Michael braced for the explosion from Clarence. Clarence stared straight ahead until he saw Mrs. Hatly. His chin quivered—just barely holding it together.

A demon jumped loose from its human, wielding a jagged dagger that clanged against Michael's sword. It rotated in the air, swung its weapon, landing on one leg, the edge of otherworldly steel tight against Michael's right cheek.

Michael's angel brothers closed in, ready to restrain him if necessary.

The demon hissed and howled. He pranced about Michael, flicking his sharp talons at Michael's arms, his sword trailing about Michael's neck.

Michael didn't counter, his sword held in check.

"Ha! This angel's bound." The demon turned to the horde and roared, raising his sword. "This one's bound!" Its raucous laughter bounced off the chasms of hell, ending with a squeal.

The floor opened up revealing hideous yellow eyes in the underground flickering in excitement. All on Michael. The monsters sniffed the air, lust aroused.

The prison guards opened the way for Clarence and Randy into the reception area, unaware of the taunting and tension in the invisible realm.

"Strike him! Strike him down!" the hordes screamed.

Mrs. Hatly leaned into Harold, crying and reaching out to Clarence.

Michael edged closer to Clarence.

Connecting to Father, Michael sent a prayer. He could still help Clarence, only not interfere. One of the hardest assignments ever in eternity. His heart wanted to stuff all the guards back into their van. He'd even drive them back to Chicago—in a fiery chariot.

Clarence slowed as he neared Mrs. Hatly. His feet moved in slow-motion. He stopped between each step, dragging the guards to a slow gait.

Ralston flicked Clarence on the ear.

His demons roared, raising their weapons in celebration. "Finish him! Now!" they roared.

Clarence flinched.

Michael flinched with him, his own ear stinging.

He turned to see a demon lowering a bow and arrow aimed for the kill. Grinning, growling, its yellow eyes poured hatred Michael's way. Brownish scales covered muscular arms and legs. The creature rose to its full height in defiance, roaring, its thick tail pounded the ground. "My master is pleased. Your human is defeated! His destiny is decided!"

Michael held his weapons in check. He trembled with righteous anger, ready if only the Father released him.

Mrs. Hatly grasped hold of Clarence's sleeve and pulled him closer. "You don't need to go. You have been freed." Tears flowed freely. "Please Mr. Michael. Please help him. Don't let them take him."

Zahab leaned in. "How does she see you?"

"I don't know. She always has." Michael nodded. "She has a pure spirit. I bet she can see Father too, she just doesn't realize it."

Ralston perused the room. "Who's this Michael? She keeps talking about Michael. I don't see anyone who can help you, Clarence." He guffawed. "Unless it's this guy with a walker."

Harold stiffened and stood taller, one arm around Mrs. Hatly, totally unaware of the invisible forces in battle. Tears ran unchecked down his wrinkled cheeks.

Michael nodded at the angels surrounding Harold and Mrs. Hatly. Shields up, they blocked darts meant for Mrs. Hatly from the enemy.

Michael leaned down to Clarence. "You'll be all right. You'll be back."

"I'll be all right Mrs. Hatly. I'll be back." Clarence struggled to break his hands free of the handcuffs.

Ralston pointed to Mrs. Hatly. "Is this your girlfriend?" He squealed and pursed his lips. His voice cracked in glee. "How touching. I'm so moved." His face was inches from Mrs. Hatly's. "He won't be back. He—"

"Enough, Ralston." Randy reached for his beat stick. "I never would have brought you if the warden hadn't insisted." He glared at Ralston. "I'm in charge here and I'm telling you to back down."

Ralston rolled his eyes and withdrew from her.

She bopped him on the head with her cane.

Ralston lunged at her, his demons rushing in, but Clarence knocked Ralston off balance, and he stumbled to the floor.

Michael started to grab Clarence's shoulders but was pushed away by a demon flying full-force at him. The demon hissed in his face and screamed, "You are bound! You can't cover him. Obey the Father!" Other demons dropped in, pinning Michael's arms.

Residents close by screamed and ducked.

One man hit Ralston with a cane. The man's angel spread his wings, covering him. Gutsy humans.

The dietary aide pushed the residents back, his arms outstretched. "Get back, or you'll get hurt." He took the cane from the old man. "Get back." The angels surrounded him and the residents.

"That's enough!" Randy pushed past, his beat stick just above Ralston's head. "Get outside! Now!"

Ralston shoved off the floor and kicked at Mrs. Hatly, narrowly missing her.

Demons laughed, darting in to stab at her.

Michael struggled to get free.

Zahab and his brothers swooped in, swords raised, searing the demons that were restraining Michael. The stench of their rotten, burning flesh choked them, their eyes watering.

The other guard pushed Ralston toward the door. "Stop! She's an old lady. Treat her with respect." He saluted Mrs. Hatly. "No offense, Ma'am."

Randy stepped in. "Enough, people!" He escorted Ralston out the door and pushed back in for Clarence and the other guard. "I never thought we'd have to use tasers in a nursing home. And on my own men. Let's go before we cause a riot!"

Michael scanned the heavens. "I think you already did." The clash of swords and shields was deafening.

Zahab and his brothers were spread thin: one taking on monsters twice their size, another rushing into the battle both arms spinning swords, severing heads and limbs.

Zahab held back, hovering over Michael and Clarence, ready to enter in as needed.

"Go!" Zahab glanced behind him. "Now is the time! Go!"

Michael pushed Clarence out the door.

Helpless.

Michael hated helpless.

Father, Your will.

Sunlight blinded Clarence as they stepped onto the sidewalk. He blinked tears away, struggled to wipe his eyes but the handcuffs held … along with a guard gripping each arm.

"Clarence!" No mistaking that tiny voice.

Little arms hugged his leg.

No!

Bea, followed by Katty.

He blinked again and there was her precious face upturned next to his knee.

What was this? Just like sixty years ago when he said good-bye to his dad. And Annie. The town. His whole life.

Clarence tugged at the handcuffs. "Don't let them see me like this!" His voice came ragged. Hot tears blurred his vision again.

"Clarence!" Katty's eyes darted from the guards to Randy to Michael, who had stepped out the door. Back to Ralston. Then to Clarence.

Bea bounced next to him. She didn't miss a thing either. "Why do you have handcuffs? Who are they? Where are you going? Is this a movie?"

Naked.

"Clarence. What's going on?" Katty stomped right up in front of him. Planted her feet on either side of his, blocking his way. Her wide eyes dug deep into his. "Where are you going? Who are these people?"

Ralston edged toward her, hand on his gun. "Who wants to know, baby?"

Her look could have killed thousands. Hadn't taken her long to go back to who she had been—druggie, hard woman.

Clarence growled. "Leave her alone. Leave them alone!" He struggled with the handcuffs, managed to rip one hand free and slug Ralston in the jaw.

A gun went off and Bea fell to the sidewalk.

"Bea!" Katty screamed and covered her with her own body. "Bea!"

Clarence roared. "You shot my Bea!" His other hand went for Ralston's neck, handcuff dangling, both hands squeezing.

Another gunshot.

Pain. Deep. No.

Randy dragged Clarence off Ralston. He rolled Clarence onto the concrete and pulled up his T-shirt. "Good God, no."

Clarence gasped. He lifted his head. Blood on his belly.

No.

Six months ago, yeah.

But not now.

Six months ago, he'd wanted to go to the hills and die. Six months ago, he would have done the deed himself.

"Get Ralston's gun, Anderson. Get him restrained!" Randy yelled.

A nurse ran out the door.

Clarence's eyes blurred. He reached his hand to her, handcuff bouncing off her shoulder. "Carol. Ambulance." His head dropped to the sidewalk. "Bea."

SEVEN

"She won't come over." Lex smirked into his whiskey, pushing down the ice cubes with his finger. "She's one of the elite—stalks the bars for rich old guys, hoping for a hit and a marriage." He lifted the glass and slurped his drink. "High-dollar, believe me."

Phil squinted and picked up his pen, not looking at Lex. Hardly looking at the note he'd just signed. He didn't need to. Fold it and slip it in the envelope. He'd already addressed it and stamped it. Didn't even need to look up the address. He stashed it into his pocket to be mailed later.

He wished he could be there to see Katty's face when she figured out who had sent the note. He could just imagine. She'd go all crazy with fear just like she probably had when she found the bike. He knew that face of hers. He'd caused much of that panic in her, himself. Visions of … he almost shuddered when he thought of what he'd done to her.

This note would keep Katty in check, especially since the old man was probably on his way to prison by now. She was vulnerable, just like a naked baby bird falling out of a tree into a pack of cats. Almost made him shiver.

Now on to the business at hand.

Every part of that woman's body was delicious—from her glossy reddish-brown hair, pale shoulders to red-enameled toe-nails flashing from open toed heels. "She knows. She senses us." He gulped down his drink. "It's the frequencies I give off that turn her on."

Lex rolled his eyes, but Phil ignored him. He rose from the table and walked to the bar, signaling the bartender for another whiskey and whatever she was drinking.

As he walked to her, she shifted onto her other foot, her hip swaying, making her already short red dress ride up even more. She didn't tug it down.

My kinda girl. No need to prime the pump.

He stopped behind her. No panty line. He moaned a little too loud and she turned.

Her hair brushed his cheek as she swung around. Blue eyes questioned his and she half-smiled.

Tease.

He reigned in and held his eyes to hers, but worked his peripheral vision hard. Natural young curves. Mountain climbing was his best sport. Red was definitely her color.

She glanced at the drink in his hand and raised her eyebrows. She followed to his whiskey in his other hand. "Heavy drinker? Or are you meeting a date?"

"I just met her." He pushed the extra drink toward her, still keeping his eyes on hers. Women loved it when he took them seriously.

She raised up on her toes and hovered close enough for him to be able to sniff her perfume. Her chest brushed against his arm, sending tingles to his nether regions, his breathing quickening. "Really? Where is she?"

Oh, playful, huh? Something else lurked in those blue eyes and they flickered to the right just a second, almost imperceptible.

Before he could turn to check it out, she leaned in again and accepted the drink. Her long red fingernails clinked against the glass, just as an arm circled his neck from behind.

He dropped his glass and it bounced against the carpet, splashing whiskey up onto her pale legs.

She never flinched, but licked her lips and sipped the drink he had just handed her. "What's your name?"

"Phil." The arm tightened, and his voice gurgled. His eyes never left hers, even as his body was dragged backwards. He sputtered when the grip on his neck grew tighter, choking out air.

"Nice to meet you, Phil." She held the glass up in a toast. "We don't want to waste the booze now, right?" She tipped her beautiful head back and slugged the drink down.

He felt and heard a deep chuckle from whoever dragged him, until he was swung around and punched in the gut. He doubled over and bounced back against a table, then face-planted onto the floor. Drinks and popcorn slid off, sprinkling him.

When he opened his eyes, Lex's face was an inch away. Phil could almost count every whisker and pore.

"Told you she wasn't in your league." Lex tossed his head in the direction of raucous laughter.

Phil twisted and rolled to his stomach.

Lex snickered. "Rich old men, huh?" He shook his head. "That guy has got to be a prize-fighter. Look at him. Gray hair, wrinkles. He has to be eighty. But, that body. Good example of a head transplant. Wonder where the guy's real body is."

Phil rubbed his throat, coughed and sat up. Opened his mouth to comment when his phone notification went off. He struggled to get to his feet, then to a nearby chair. "It's Facebook. I have it set to alert me when Bea's mom posts anything." He snorted. "She got the bike." He laughed. "Look at this picture. My Baby Bea is sitting on the bike." He showed Lex. "She looks like a little doll on it."

Lex read the post. "How'd you do that? She'll know who you are."

Phil rubbed his neck. "I faked my picture and name. She'll never catch on."

Lex raised his eyebrows and nodded. "Yeah." His eyes lingered on the photo. "You should leave them alone. They don't deserve what you want to do." He signaled the bartender for two more drinks.

"Her momma done me wrong. She escaped and I didn't even know about the baby—Baby Bea. She hid her from me until you heard through that dealer—Harsden." He scrolled through the posts. "I might never have known I had a daughter." He stopped at a message. "Aww. Katty says here, 'What will we do without Clarence?'" Phil mimicked in a high falsetto. "What will we do without Clarence?" He tapped his phone. "Oh baby, I'll show you what to do."

Lex shook his head and laughed, handing a drink to Phil.

The beauty and her fake boyfriend slipped past them. The old man shoved his arm behind his back, a certain finger waving at them.

Phil stood up and adjusted his jeans. The door closed behind the couple and he clinked glasses with Lex. "Clarence is getting tucked away in prison just in time."

EIGHT

August skies were so beautiful. The clouds were huge, white fluffy blobs floating against that startling blue—the most beautiful blue Clarence had ever seen.

Tears slid down the sides of his face as he was carried, or rather jostled, to the van.

"Get the first-aide kit." Randy clicked the key fob and unlocked the vehicle. "Warden will kill me if Clarence dies now."

Clarence almost laughed at that. Someone else's life depended on him living.

Another guard pushed open the doors from inside and stepped to the ground. The guy with the goatee looked familiar. But the other guy —that awful red patch would be unforgettable. Angry red thing sucked into the whole left side of the guy's face. Clarence remembered his own clenched hands. Same red ropey scars—now with a little fresh blood. Maybe it wasn't a birthmark.

"Here. Get him in the van and lay him down." They lifted him onto the seat and strapped him in.

God it hurt. Clarence had been knifed, beaten, gored with a screwdriver, and penetrated in every other way, but seeing Bea fall, knowing she had been shot, hurt just as much as losing Annie. Tears brimmed, but he would not let them see how badly he hurt and feared for her life.

"Really?" Randy unhooked the straps. "You think he's gonna escape with a gunshot wound?"

"We were warned." Goatee Man climbed in and sat on the bench seat across from Clarence. "They say he's as strong as an ox."

How Clarence wanted to lash out. The nursing home had relaxed him, softened him. But self-preservation kicked in. Not crying. Not opening his mouth. Rage boiled. Either he would break out and escape —get back to Bea and Katty, Mrs. Hatly—or he'd die trying.

Goatee Man, the name on his shirt read Ralph—but Goatee Man fit him better, clicked Clarence's handcuffs to an armrest bar. "Seems he can fight his way out of any handhold." He turned to Randy. "Killed one of the baddest guys on the cellblock." He sat beside Scar Man.

The back door opened behind Clarence and a struggle ensued. Grunts and scuffles.

"You, my man, are in deep trouble." Randy growled. "If Warden wasn't your brother, you'd be fired." Seemed Randy had changed. The real Randy was hopefully still there, layered under this gruff, growling man. "Gimme that!"

"Not my gun. My brother gave—"

The back door slammed on Ralston's words.

Randy opened the side door, checked Ralston's gun and stowed it in the waistband of his own pants. "Baby Tay won't ever be fired. He's got a job for life."

Tay Ralston kicked the back of the seat Clarence was on. His foot dug into Clarence's back—must have just fit between the back of the seat and the bench. Figured. His whiny voice sounded like a string of prayer words Mrs. Hartsen prayed at the nursing home, only Tay's words weren't prayers.

Randy crawled in beside Clarence. His belly was even bigger than Clarence remembered.

Clarence tried to reach toward him, but the handcuffs stopped him. "Randy. Get help for Bea." His voice sounded gravelly and strained. His hand fluttered like Mrs. Hatly's.

Oh, Mrs. Hatly.

A sob tried to burst from his throat but he swallowed it back down.

"That nurse called 911. I heard her." Randy pulled up Clarence's shirt. "Damn." He opened the first aide kit and stirred the contents. "Poor excuse for a first aide kit. Not much left." He dug until he found tape and bandages. "Clarence, it wasn't supposed to go this way. We were told to bring you back. That's all."

Funny, the wound didn't hurt that bad now. When he was shot it had, but not now. Must be a flesh wound.

How was Bea?

Then pain hit inside his belly, like a punch to the gut. Groaning, Clarence doubled over. Didn't help that Randy was pressing tape onto the bandage to his skin.

"Blood inside your gut hurts bad." Goatee Man talked like he knew. "It's meant to be inside your veins. That's the point of all our blood vessels." He rubbed the back of his hand and sat back in his seat. "It'll get better once it dissipates."

Clarence gasped. The pain was sharp and almost made him nauseous. He looked around on the floor. *Breathe.* Felt like he could fill somebody's boot.

The van rocked as Randy stepped out.

Heavy van.

Heavy man. Randy slammed the side door shut and climbed into the drivers seat.

"Timmelsen. You look green." Goatee Man scooted his feet out of the way, against the van door.

"Oh no." Scar Face glanced under the seat. "No bucket." Behind the seat. "Nothing."

Ralston kicked the back of Clarence's seat, giggling.

Breathe! He would not puke here. Suck it down. He swallowed. Belched. Tasted the vile stuff that wanted to come up. Swallowed again. His face burned, mouth watered. The guards eyes bored into him —Randy's too through the rearview mirror.

"We'll get you to the infirmary just as soon as we get back to prison." Randy inserted the key and started the van, put it in gear. "Keep a lid on it."

And it all came up. All over the guards—Scar Face and Goatee Man.

The van lurched as Randy stomped on the brake.

"Ha ha!" Ralston kicked the seat. "Good shot."

Goatee Man opened the van door, hands spread wide, away from his dripping clothes and ran into Hillcrest. Back in the van with towels and wipes—staples in a nursing home—he and Scar Man mopped themselves and the seat, the floor. "Dude! This stinks!"

Clarence's eyes stung. His throat burned. He tried to wipe his mouth only the handcuffs wouldn't let him reach. He looked down at his T-shirt. He had missed his own clothes and hit everyone else. Good thing. His shirt seeped blood again.

Randy pulled out of Hillcrest Homes parking lot and turned onto the street.

Clarence strained to see Bea, Katty. Carol.

Anybody.

God help them.

It had only been a couple months or so since being transported *to* Hillcrest Homes. Kids waited in line for the school bus—backpacks loaded, bright new shoes—as the van drove past. The swimming pool was closed after a hot summer.

He squirmed in his seat—every time he moved, blood seeped. He might bleed out before they reached Des Moines.

Different van—not the old musty, cigarette smell. New car smell … and now … he'd baptized it well.

Randy was the same guard that had driven him from the Chicago prison to Osceola, Nebraska. The other guards were a new addition. Did the new warden think he'd bulked up at Hillcrest Homes? All that ice cream.

Goatee Man leaned forward. Click!

Scar Man snapped the others. Click!

Shackles.

Clarence sighed. Tears threatened again.

Randy glanced over his shoulder and he caught Clarence's eyes.

"Warden ordered shackles." Randy turned onto the highway. "Not my doing."

Ralston tapped Clarence on the shoulder from behind and snickered. "Cozy, huh, Clarence?" He dragged cold hard metal around Clarence's shoulders. Click!

Clarence jumped.

Ralston must have cocked the gun. "Real cozy." Ralston's whiney voice.

Cold sweat ran down Clarence's back. He shivered.

So much had changed.

He'd changed.

He did not want to die. He didn't want to go back to prison.

Goatee Man braced himself against the seat. "Knock it off, Ralston. Holster the gun!"

Randy swerved. "He has *another* gun?" He pulled over at Terry's Dive Inn and hoisted his bulk around in the seat. "Ralston!"

His booming voice hit Clarence like a sledge hammer.

"I'll put *you* in shackles next!" Randy shook his finger. "You are on detention. Holster the gun!"

Ralston slid the gun from around Clarence's shoulders, down his arm, and into his side. Lingered there.

It had been a long time since the hard muzzle of a gun was aimed at Clarence, much less stuck in his side. His thin T-shirt was no protection from the cold metal. He held his breath. In a short second, it'd all be over. Wouldn't even matter that the first gun wound was bleeding around the bandage.

When Randy had transported him to Osceola, he'd just wanted to find a hill and die. But now, faces flooded his mind: Bea, Katty, Mrs. Hatly, Harold, Carol—

"HOLSTER!" Randy roared.

Ralston slid his gun into his holster. Snapped it in and whispered, "I'm keeping my hand right where I can reach it, Clarence."

"I see your lips moving, Ralston!" Randy didn't miss a thing.

After spending time with little Bea, that precious four-year-old girl,

Clarence had realized what purity was. Yeah, she got ornery. What kid didn't? But her heart. Clarence could almost smell her sweetness.

Here, Ralston oozed evil.

Clarence blinked.

It had a distinct stench … like sweaty, oily, filthy socks. Or worse.

Blatant difference between Bea and Ralston. Never had Clarence seen good and evil so clearly. So glaring.

Thinking back on his sixty years in prison, he realized he had accepted the gray between good and evil. Prison lived by its own standards, and those standards sat just this side of evil.

A powerful silence hovered between Ralston's last threat and Clarence's next breath.

Clarence cleared his throat. "Why am I being taken back to prison?" He leaned forward, stopped by the seatbelt and Goatee Man's hand on his shoulder. "Randy!"

Randy swerved back onto the highway and took a deep breath. He adjusted the rear-view mirror and looked Clarence in the eye. "We were told to come get you, not why. They will fill you in when we get back to Chicago."

"But—"

"Sit back or I'll stick my gun in your side again." Cold metal against his neck gave him goosebumps.

"Ralston!" Randy swerved off the highway again, came to a stop on a side street. "Get his gun and shackle him. Now!"

Goatee Man and Scar Face jumped up and opened the side doors.

Rear doors burst open.

"Gotta be handcuffs. This back seat doesn't have shackles."

Clarence guessed by the scuffle behind him that Ralston wasn't giving in easily until metal clicked on metal.

Doors slammed.

They jumped back in and Randy pulled away, leaving Scar Face to pull the doors shut.

"I am a lawyer and I know my rights!" Clarence cleared his throat. "This is pure harassment and I don't have to take this! Sending me to Hillcrest Homes was set up by the judge back then. You know that!

That's by a court of law!" They didn't need to know he hated Judge Green who had set it all up.

Randy gunned the engine, head and eyes forward. "All I know, is that we were directed to bring you back."

Emphasis on the word directed. Like he didn't have a choice.

Clarence shook his head. Like *he* had a choice. He looked down at the shackles. The guards in front of him vibrated—ready to pounce at the first chance. Maybe Clarence should give them cause.

"I don't want to go back!"

Randy slumped. "I have no choice. It was go get you, or my job. I have three kids in college now."

"What is the just cause?"

Ralston snickered. "We don't need just cause." He lowered his voice so just Clarence could hear—maybe Scar Face could hear too. "Warden has the prison all wrapped up. The last warden was a loser. This guy's sharp. You'll like him. He don't put up with no crap." He hissed in Clarence's ear. "He pays real good, too."

"You mean, he's bought and paid for." Clarence shivered.

Ralston laughed. "Oh he's paid for all right. And so are the rest of us … or most of us." He snickered. "Remember Will? My other brother? Not the one you killed."

Clarence froze. He stopped breathing. His chest felt as if Will was still standing on it like he had … what thirty years ago? That had been the fight of his life. Or one of them. His right cheek prickled where Will had sliced him.

No! When he had walked out of prison back then, Will had still been incarcerated, still angry, even flipped him off, but he had been locked up.

"He's like family to me, the warden." Ralston giggled like an excited girl just about to dance her first dance. "Oh, wait!" He leaned forward. "He *is* my family. He *is* the warden."

Randy yelled from the front, "Ralston, I swear, knock it off!"

Ralston released his seatbelt and leaned into Clarence, his face just within Clarence's peripheral line of sight, his gun out of Randy's line of sight. "See, when you beat Will up back then, it kinda ticked him off. So he got word to the outside—to Daddy—and well, it's all history. Daddy is a big-time lawyer ... even bigger than you, Clarence. And he got Will the warden's job." Ralston's black eyes got big. "I only hope that the old warden is okay." He grinned. "He was never heard from again."

Goatee Man laughed. "He was heard from, but not like in a letter or email."

Ralston snorted. "Well, right. He was heard from ... like in a humble apology ... from a hospital." He clucked. "He'll never walk again. Too bad. He had a nice wife and some grandkids, I think." He tapped Clarence's shoulder with the gun. "Oh, and you are gonna get reunited with some old friends of yours, too. What were their names? Yeah. Phil was one. I think Lex was the other. They kinda have a bone to pick with you, too. Seems you made some enemies along the way."

Clarence met eyes with Randy in the mirror. For a spit second, was there a grimace? Remorse?

Clarence's fingers went cold and numb. Hard to breathe. The smell of his own blood, compounded with Ralston's stench, sickened him.

Where was Michael? Why wasn't he doing some angel thing—like taking this guard that shot Bea down or helping Clarence escape before they reached the prison?

Goatee Man grinned.

Ralston popped him on the head with the gun. "Oh, you're gonna like the changes they've made."

NINE

Noell shivered. The walk to Hillcrest Nursing Home wasn't far—just a couple blocks—and it was still summer, technically, even though school buses had been dropping off kids at the corner for a few weeks now. The kids always looked so tired as they walked home. Book bags. Homework. One kid always carried his trumpet case too.

She knew trumpet cases. She had begged to play, knowing Grampa would never deny her anything that was legal. But her band teacher only had a seat available for a flute. He had a whole row of trumpet students and only one flute player. Even saxophone would have been good but there were five—in a middle school band of thirty. Flute would have been just okay, except for the fact that the one and only flutist was Mary Jane Brixton, their papergirl, who one day when the newspaper had gotten lost, glimpsed a peek into Noell's world and home. Never would she sit next to someone for a whole period who knew some of Gamma's hoarding secrets.

She had loved school at first. People must have been nice to her right after Mommy drowned, because she remembered moments when the kindness of people overruled the bullies. Her kindergarten teacher, Mrs. Townsend, always had a hug for her and a "you can do this" when she helped Noell with her coat. She must have lost her mom young, too.

But once Noell entered middle school, things changed. She was different from the other small town kids. She didn't have a mom, or dad. Gamma tried to be the mom who baked treats for the class or invited little friends over after school, but once their mom picked them up at the door and saw the ceiling-high clutter, they didn't let their child come back. The one-and-only mom that did let her daughter come back made it clear that the girls would play outside or just in Noell's room where clutter was against Noell's rules.

In high school, students treated her just like every other classmate, except when it came to social time. They never invited her anywhere. No mother pushed her child to include her in anything.

The Peters and Pauls at churches must have thought she needed saving because they were all over her—inviting her to youth conferences and hayrack rides. She had gone on one hayrack ride. Never again. Those sweet Christian kids were vulgar and crude.

Startled, she realized she was almost at Hillcrest. Why had she gone back to those awful memories?

Clarence would be able to help her sell the house. He was almost becoming that Grampa she missed so much—someone she could talk to, confide in. When he hugged her, she felt like she had been snuggled in a warm blanket on his lap. Just like Grampa.

Sigh.

Strange though, that she was so shivery today. She rubbed her shoulders and arms. Should have worn a hoodie. The sun was out and there was no breeze. But goosebumps popped up on her arms. No time to get sick.

Mrs. Carton stood outside the dining room door at the nursing home, smoking a cigarette. Ick. She looked to be more than a hundred years old, instead of eighty or however old she was. Amazing she was still alive after smoking all her life. She said it calmed her, when her neighbors drove her crazy. The woman half smiled as she blew smoke and gave a wave with the fingers not holding the cigarette, then flicked the ash into the bushes.

Ick.

Noell stepped up on the curb, just as a deputy and the sheriff pushed open the front door from inside. They barely nodded to her, then stooped to examine something on the sidewalk in front of the entrance.

As she walked past, they wiped up something with a rag. When they lifted the cloth, it was dark red. They quickly hid it.

Too late.

Someone must have fallen on the sidewalk and the home had to report it according to policy. It broke her heart to see the elderly age and go through trials. Disease, handicaps, injuries robbed them of these sweet years. Hope it wasn't Mrs. Hatly.

As she opened the entrance door, sounds of people sobbing and screaming pierced her like a bolt of lightning. Her mind exploded with visuals of guards overlaid with pictures of evil mist, like a trailer of the newest horror movie.

Noell hadn't done that in a long time. She had been so distracted with whatever the Sheriff and Deputy had been wiping off the sidewalk, that when her skin had come in contact with the metal door handle, she had forgotten to protect herself.

Pictures popped in and out of her mind. Faces. Homes. Restaurants. Animals. Layer on top of layer. Chaos of people and their lives, the horror, the good times and bad. The noise was deafening.

Goosebumps tracked down her right leg. Involuntary shivers.

From just one door handle. Multiply that one handle times millions of people—day-after-day, over many years.

She quickly slid between the door jam and the door, as it closed.

Inside Hillcrest, the noise and chaos continued, only it wasn't her visions. This was real. Curiosity overcame her need to run back home.

What was going on?

Nurses flurried in and out of the office. People stood with their walkers or sitting in wheelchairs down both sides of the hallways, as if a parade had just gone by—the most heartwarming parade, even to the point of affecting them to tears. One woman in a wheelchair blew her nose.

Harold. He'd fill her in. Where was Mrs. Hatly? Mrs. Monson was sobbing and mumbling something about a little girl dying.

What?

Noell tried to catch someone's eye as she passed them, but they seemed deep in conversation, so she hurried to the nurses' station.

Carol was charting, writing almost frantically. She glanced up at Noell, grimaced in recognition. Her chin quivered and she wiped her swollen eyes. Other nurses busied themselves with meds. Lisha leaned in a corner, sobbing.

What the?

Noell walked on down the hall to Clarence's room.

Residents in the neighboring rooms either hid with their backs to anyone passing their doorway, or one or two babbled, pointing, shaking.

Confusion.

As she passed Mr. Harold's room, all he did was look up at her and nod. His eyes appeared to be watering. He wiped them with one hand, eyeglasses hanging from the fingers of his free hand. He raised his eyebrows and shook his head.

What?

He cleared his throat and attempted to speak, then shook his head again. He motioned and pointed toward Clarence's room.

She walked to 204 and knocked on the door jam.

No one hollered, "Come on in!"

As she stepped inside his room, something crunched under her shoe. Shattered glass. All over the floor. Pictures had fallen, or been knocked off the wall and frames were broken apart on the floor. She picked two up—one was his law certificate and the other was the photo of Bea. The decorative frame had broken—red, blue and green balloons scattered on the floor.

Oh my God. Tears filled her own eyes.

On the desk, Clarence's cup was tipped on its side. Coffee stained the newspaper and other papers underneath.

She pulled a string of paper towels out of the dispenser above the sink and mopped up the coffee.

A visual of the deputies out front, wiping what seemed to be blood from the sidewalk popped into her mind, as she soaked up the coffee on Clarence's desk. She lifted the paper towels, and the coffee stains merged with her memory of the blood on the cloth in the Sheriff's hand. "Oh my goodness."

"C-Carol?" Noell glanced down at the broken glass again. "Carol? Lisha?" She felt gut-punched. Her heart pounded in her chest as she ran out the doorway and down the hall to the nurses station.

Carol bumped into her at the entrance. Lisha was still crying, only now she was standing and wiping her face with her brown hands.

Carol took one look at Noell's face and the paper towels in her hands and drew her into the station. She sat her down at the desk and pulled up a side chair, wiping her own face. Then took Noell's hands in her own. "I know you have become good friends with Clarence, so … there's something I need to tell you."

Lisha's sobs erupted again from behind Noell. She squeezed between the back of Noell's chair and the counter and started to leave the nurses station but stopped and cleared her throat.

Noell swiveled toward her in the chair, Carol's hands still on hers.

"I know I had my problems with dat man." She blew her nose and wiped it. "But I love him. See, he and I are alike. Stubborn." She swallowed, pointing her finger at her chest. "Angry. I gits him." She turned into the hall, but rotated back to face them. "That man'll die in prison. He is strong, I know. But he is old and they will kill him." She walked away, another aide's arm around her shoulder, side-by-side.

"A-hem!" The administrator stepped into their line of vision, hands on her hips.

"Screw privacy regulations right now!" Carol stood her ground.

Noell blinked. "P-Prison?" She turned back to Carol and checked her eyes, then glanced back at the administrator. "Lisha … said prison." One-by-one, the med nurses scooted out and left Carol and Noell alone. Even the hovering administrator left. "What did she mean?"

Carol bit her lip, her wide eyes brimming.

Noell's own eyes filled. "And there's blood out front. When I walked up the sidewalk, two deputies were wiping up what looked like blood. And at the door handle … " She caught herself before saying too much.

Carol sucked in a breath and blew it out. "This morning Sheriff called me and said the prison where Clarence used to live had put out a warrant for his arrest, to bring him back."

"But—"

Carol shook her head. "I know. He doesn't belong in prison." She blinked. "Guards—they must have driven all night—almost immediately came in and handcuffed him and dragged him out. One guard was awful—ranting about Clarence killing his brother—waving his gun."

"Gun?" Noell's mouth dropped open. "Here?" She pointed down the hall. "With all these people?"

Carol nodded and swallowed. "They got him outside and Clarence was fighting them all the way. He hit that guard in the mouth and knocked him against the wall in his room. His pictures are all broken."

Noell nodded. Her hands shook, still holding the paper towels.

"Anyway, when they got outside, Katty and Bea had just driven up and … there was a scuffle and the guard shot Bea."

Noell shrieked. "Bea!" She pulled her hands away.

Carol caught them, threw the paper towels away and gripped Noell's hands tighter. "Clarence went crazy. Slugged the guard." She broke down. A sob escaped, but she got control. "And the guard shot Clarence!"

"Oh God!" Noell slipped her hands from Carol's, her fists covering her mouth. "Clarence." Noell jumped up. "We have to … " She sat back down. "Where's Bea? We have to get Clarence back. Is he ok?" Her hands gripped the armrests. "Oh God!"

Carol placed her hands on Noell's shoulders, her face inches from Noell's. Her beautiful green eyes swollen and red. "We have to pray— that somehow this is all a mistake and he'll come right back to us. That Clarence and Bea will heal and be ok." She shrugged. "We have to pray."

Noell nodded, coming to her senses. "God … help."

The phone rang and she jumped.

Carol picked it up. "Hillcrest. This is Carol." She listened then curved into the phone. "Okay." She nodded and reached for Noell's hands again, her face toward Noell's. "Bea is going into surgery right now."

Noell's face crinkled. "Oh, God."

Carol pushed a finger at her. "Hang on." Into the phone, "What? Okay. I know. We're fine here."

Lisha sobbed behind them. "We're *not* fine. We need a posse, or sumpthin. Is that Sheriff?" She reached for the phone. "Gimme that. We need to go get Clarence!"

Carol pushed her away and spoke into the phone. "No. She won't. But that's what we all want to do." She straightened. "Call the governor?" She glanced at Noell, then Lisha. "It's a start. But there's got to be something more. I know." She closed her eyes while listening, nodded, tears streaming down her cheeks. "I … Thanks. Bye." She turned her face away and blew out a breath, wiping her eyes.

Noell stood. Hesitated.

Carol came to and stood with her. "I don't know how." She reached for her hands, feet on either side of Noell's, her body almost curving into Noell's. "And I don't know when. But I know he'll be back." She reached one hand to Lisha, gripping hers, too. "He might have to go through some things. That guard was evil." Her eyes darted from Noell to Lisha and back. "But the other one—Randy, I think—is good." She tried to smile, but it only brought more tears to her eyes. "Clarence has been through a lot, and he is strong. He will be okay."

An aide rushed up. "I'm sorry, Carol, but it's Mrs. Hatly. She's in distress. I … I've never seen her like this."

Carol nodded, dropped Noell and Lisha's hands and pulled her stethoscope from around her neck.

To Noell, "Go to Katty." She paused. "She needs you now."

TEN

Katty watched as two nurses in scrubs guided the gurney through the double doors marked surgery. A white sheet covered Bea's tiny body.

Katty hugged the teddy bear to her chest, wishing she was hugging Bea.

When a volunteer had tucked a soft, pink teddy beside Bea, the woman looked up at Katty and had slipped her one too. Katty's was exactly the same as Bea's only a smaller version.

"Look Mommy. They're the same." Bea had compared them. "Same eyes. Same color."

Then she had been hit with a spasm of pain and blacked out.

Katty wiped her face. So many thoughts raced through her mind. Thankful she was off drugs, so she could really be here for Bea.

A random thought—where was Clarence?

Back to Bea. Horrible to see her in pain. Would she be ok? Would she live? Where was Clarence? He was always with her, ready with advice or hugs or … love.

Tears started again. She blew out a breath and ducked away from a Housekeeping lady. Must be strong. Must keep the stiff upper lip.

"God, she looks tiny." Katty unconsciously followed the gurney, step by step, even after reading the painted sign on the doors. "No Admittance Beyond This Point."

A nurse spotted her and met her at the double doors. "Honey, is there anybody with you? To keep you company?" She gently shook her head, her wide brown eyes concerned. "Because you can't come in here." She glanced behind her at Bea. "I'll take good care of her—just like she was my own."

Katty could only nod and watch the nurse walk away.

The doors began to close when the nurse did an about-face. She quickly slid between them and grabbed Katty in a bear hug. "She's gonna be all right. We pray for healing in Jesus' name." The woman let out a sob but staunched it.

Katty gasped and held on like the two had become one. "Oh, God. Help." She burrowed her face into the woman's neck and shoulder.

The double doors opened again. "Beth?" The nurse hesitated. Her eyebrows slowly pinched together. Eyes filled and she took two steps toward them, her arms open wide and enveloped them both. "Baby. She's gonna be okay."

Nurse hug—Oreo style. The nurses were the strong, outside cookies and Katty was the sweet, soft center. She could hardly breathe, but didn't want them to let her go.

She swallowed when they finally did. "Th-thanks." She held in the emotion so hard, her head and throat hurt.

They slowly let her go and without a word, stepped to the doors, pushed the open button and walked through.

Katty could still feel them against her skin, pressing into her back, her arms. Fragrance of sweet woman and antibacterial soap lingered on her skin, swirled around her. Almost tangible.

She blinked.

Had she really seen … ? For a split second, a ring of creatures? beings? surrounded her.

She blinked again. Must have been the soap smell, the stress.

The doors closed, but Katty didn't move. She scratched the teddy bear ears. Her feet were planted till they wheeled Bea out again.

Until someone gently touched her back.

Katty didn't turn, but Noell peeked from around her back. Her blue eyes were wide, eyebrows raised slightly, mouth parted. Not smiling, but face open. She continued to touch Katty's back.

Katty blinked. As Noell continued to caress her back, gentle tingles raced across her skin. She shivered.

Oh God. Can't break down.

Noell tipped her head toward the hall behind them. "You want to go sit down? I think they have coffee."

Katty hesitated and shook her head. If she didn't move, then maybe Bea would come back through those swinging doors. If she—

"Or we can stay right here." Noell nodded, glancing up and down the hallway.

Katty sighed. Turning her back on the double doors felt so wrong, like she was turning her back on Bea.

"I'm sure they'll keep you informed about her."

A receptionist close by nodded. "We sure will." She patted the phone beside her and smiled. "We have a direct line, but usually someone comes out. In person."

Deep sigh. "Sure. Let's sit."

A loud group of four commanded the small waiting room. They were laughing and eating, playing cards. One was chasing a small bouncy ball. He retrieved it and bounced it so high, it hit the ceiling and they all laughed again. They stopped and looked straight at Noell and Katty.

"Uh … " Noell smiled. "Hello."

One woman smiled. The others sat down on a row of chairs against the wall.

Noell stuck her head in another room and motioned for Katty to follow.

This smaller room was unoccupied. The sun was warm and welcoming through long windows. Four chairs circled a small table. Two more chairs filled a corner.

Noell shrugged. "Here okay?"

The other people could still be heard, but the receptionist desk and hallway created a buffer.

Katty sat. "Thanks Noell." She rubbed Teddy's ears again.

"The hospital give you that?" Noell pointed to Teddy.

Katty held it out and nodded. She retied the flowery bow and swallowed. "Bea has one too, only bigger." She fiddled with one ear, then hugged it. "What if this is all I have to—"

"She'll be fine, Katty." Noell reached for her hand. "Such tiny fingers."

Katty watched as Noell caressed each finger, outlining each one with her own, like her finger was a pencil and she was going to make a Thanksgiving turkey picture.

A thought blinked in—a neighbor had faithfully taken her, as a child, to Sunday School and they had made the turkeys in class. That had been the first time Katty could remember that someone's touch could be sweet and comforting, rather than painful and bruising.

"You had a grandma, didn't you? Did she do this with your fingers?" said Katty. Oh, she hoped so. With everything she had been through, she hoped some little girl had experienced this soft touch.

Noell nodded, her eyes misty. She glanced down at their fingers, clasped together.

"I'm sorry. She just died, didn't she?"

Noell flinched. But nodded.

"I'm sorry." Katty gripped Noell's fingers. "I didn't mean that to sound so … I'm not used to being … and talking … I'm not sweet like you."

Noell stared, wide-eyed. "Who raised you? Did you have a mom? A dad?"

Katty nodded. "Yeah … yeah." What could she say to this beautiful, sweet person?

"You know, I have to use the restroom." She stood and faced Noell. "I'll be fine and I'm sure you have stuff to do." She shrugged. "They say she'll be fine, so you don't have to wait."

"Oh. Okay." Noell glanced at the exit door. "Are you sure?"

Poor Noell wanted out anyway. She would never be back. Even though she was a friend of Clarence's. They were too far apart—too different to even be kind-of friends.

"Yeah. I'm sure. I'll … just go to the bathroom and then I'm sure they'll be done." She started down the hall, toward the nurses station and looked behind her at Noell and waved.

Poor girl. She probably wasn't used to being snubbed or lonely.

Katty spied a housekeeper. "Can you tell me where the restrooms are?"

The woman dumped the contents from a trash can into her cart dumpster and pointed down the hall. "Last door on your left."

"Thanks." Katty let her peripheral tell her if Noell had left. The chair was empty. She knew she might have hurt Noell's feelings but Katty never had a friend that stuck. She'd always hidden her family and life away from the world. Anytime kids or neighbors had tried to pry or get close, she closed—no slammed—the door on them. Same thing now.

If you didn't allow people in, you didn't get hurt.

But somehow, she had let that jerk Phil in. She had thought he was rescuing her from her abusive home life, but instead, he had opened up a whole new dimension of abuse. Visuals flashed before she could stop them. She found the bathroom and closed the door softly and locked it. She leaned against the door, shaking her head. Would not cry.

She had trained herself well. No crying. Her mom could punch her hard in the ear, right before they entered the principal's office, and Noell would enter the room like a queen waltzing to her throne. Mama knew where to throw a punch so it never showed, unless you had x-ray vision. One little old neighbor lady could always tell when Katty was having a bad day. She'd invite her for cookies on her porch. Katty would go, but learned to hide so her mom wouldn't see her when she drove past on her way home from work.

She stared at herself in the mirror. Truth. It was a miracle she was alive. Another truth. It was a miracle Bea was still alive.

Oh-oh. The face in the mirror was soundlessly sobbing. Katty watched as if the face was someone in a movie and not … her. The face was red, wet. Eyes swollen. Mouth scrunched up. Snot everywhere. Ugly. Ugly.

She rushed to use the toilet but threw up instead.

Oh God.

She leaned over the sink.

Breathe.

She washed her hands and face, then slipped into the hallway.

Surely they would be out from surgery by now. She'd better get back.

The noisy bunch were now playing cards. Still noisy.

She peeked around the receptionist desk. Noell's chair was still empty.

Funny. She'd sent Noell away, but … reality. She wished she'd stayed. Katty wished Noell had been rude back to her and told her to take a hike—that she'd never leave. That she'd be there through thick or thin, through every bad word, every hurt, every joy. Who'd tell her to shut up when she was being stupid.

Katty needed a friend like that.

Nurses smiled at her. She knew what they were thinking. *Poor girl. What a bad mom. Your daughter got shot. She needs a new mom.*

She tapped her phone. Maybe Clarence had called or texted. Where was he? In all the scuffle, she hadn't seen where they had taken him. Sheriff had scooped Bea up and they all jumped in his squad car and rushed to the hospital.

No texts.

God. Don't cry. Keep it in. Don't look up when someone walks by.

Like now.

Oh no. The person sat down. Right beside her. And pushed a steaming cup-to-go under her nose.

Katty peeked up.

Noell.

ELEVEN

Clarence moaned. Something was wrong. Something was off. Lisha must have given him the wrong meds.

Wait.

He never took any pills. He tried to roll over in his bed but something literally punched him in the gut. He must have gotten out of bed in the middle of the night and run into a chair or stumbled into—

"I think he's comin' round."

Something cold and hard touched his ear.

This wasn't the nursing home.

He opened his eyes.

A van. Not just any van—a prison van. Randy was driving. Goat Man was snoozing on the bench seat facing him, and Scar Face sat beside Goat Man, eyes on Clarence.

Clarence floated somewhere between knowing he was in some sort of horrible nightmare and the reality he saw before him.

It all rushed back. He must have been dreaming. He looked at where his hands had been resting. Dried blood.

A cold, hard object slammed into his left ear. Again.

"Ralston!" Randy yelled from the drivers seat. "I told you to holster your gun. Now!"

Ralston tapped him again from behind.

Cold hard steel against his temple. He held his breath. There had been many moments like this in prison: another inmate had him in a vise grip—an arm choked around his neck from behind, or three inmates closed in on him in a shower, each one wielding some sort of homemade weapon. Every time, Clarence had remembered that life was precious and could end in a second.

"Ralston!" Randy yelled, making Goat Man jump awake. "Guys! I don't care if he is a guard and that he's Warden's baby brother. Keep Ralston in check! Got it?"

Goat Man and Scar Face nodded and leaned forward, seeming to invite combat with Ralston. Welcoming it. "How the hell did you get out of cuffs?'

Ralston snickered. "Always hated begin skinny as a kid. Not anymore."

Goat Man shook his head. "You are a dork."

"Got it?" Ralston chuckled and tapped Clarence on the ear again. "Just so we're clear."

Clarence clamped his mouth shut. *This* should have been the bad dream, the nightmare.

And Lisha giving him meds should have been reality. He never thought he'd want to go back to the nursing home. When he was kicked out of prison more than a couple months ago, he'd wanted to go back to prison, but now that he was, he was terrified. Terrified of prison, when it had been his home for sixty years. Didn't make sense, except that he'd learned a whole new life at Hillcrest, in just a few months.

And right now, this very moment, he wasn't sure he'd ever make it back to Hillcrest alive. This moment felt like his last; no more Bea or Katty or Noell. No more Mrs. Hatly.

His heart lurched. He hadn't realized how much—

"Stopping for gas and pee break." Randy flipped the blinker on and turned into a truck stop. Neon lights flashed even in daylight. "Open, Fresh Coffee, Sandwiches To Go, Clean Restrooms, Showers."

Each guard on the facing seat unbuckled their seat belts, then leaned forward, unsure of what to do with Clarence.

Scar Man cocked his head toward Randy. "What do we do with the prisoner?"

Clarence froze. He had become so used to freedom in Osceola that the very word chilled him. The shackles on his arms and legs told the story. Prisoner Timmelsen. He had to get used to that sound once again. Interesting how short a time it had taken for him to be used to freedom and never being referred to as an inmate.

He blew out a breath. He hadn't realized how well he had adapted to freedom and thinking of himself as a man, a man with a future— however short that might have been. Now, he guessed by the constant tap of Ralston's gun against his head, he had no future, except a few bitter, painful days.

Randy opened the side door and handed Goatee Man a credit card. "You get the fuel while I check Clarence."

Goatee Man and Scar Man stepped out onto the concrete and proceeded to get the gas pump started.

"Let's see how you're doing Clarence." Randy stepped one foot into the van and reached several places before he found a strong hand-hold and pulled his bulky body into the van. Two men had stepped out, but one big man replaced them. His bulk filled the bench seat. The brown uniform was stretched to its limit across his wide belly. After-shave wafted from him.

What had happened to this man in just a few months, other than a huge weight gain? If Clarence remembered right, he himself had been mean and abusive when Randy drove him to Hillcrest, and Randy had done everything he could to smooth things over for the nurses and residents. When Clarence would cuss, Randy had gently touched his arm, warning him to settle down.

Now, here they were, going back to prison. And Clarence wondered if he'd even be alive when they arrived.

"The pain bad?" Randy lifted Clarence's shirt and grimaced.

"Just let me die, Randy." Clarence shook his head. "We both know if I'm going back to prison, I won't live long." Clarence swallowed.

"It's not that bad."

"No, Randy. You know it won't be this that gets me."

Randy stared at Clarence for a long moment, then lifted the bandage and peeked. "You'll be okay. We just have to get the bullet out." He looked behind Clarence at Ralston. "You should have your gun confiscated— shooting a little girl and a prisoner without cause. I don't care if the warden is your big brother, I'm still writing you up."

Ralston growled from the back seat. "He won't do anything. He's scared of me. He's scared of Mama. If he hurts me, she'll come after him."

Clarence's eyes widened but he didn't say what he was thinking. He was tired of being pounded on the back of his head for so many miles.

But Randy wasn't afraid. "Mama's boy, huh?"

Ralston hovered over the back of Clarence's bench seat. "Be careful. My bro—"

"Yeah. I know. Your brother's the warden." Randy pulled Clarence's shirt over the wound. "I've heard it over and over, by now." He raised his eyes to stare down Ralston, "And I'm sick of it. I don't care if he is your brother, I'm reporting you."

Ralston snickered into Clarence's ear, "Yeah, well I think this time he'll see it my way." The gun tapped Clarence's head harder with each tap. "My brother hates this man so much, that he will applaud anything I do to him, in honor of our brother, Lewis." He faked a sob he obviously didn't feel.

Randy swallowed down any words or anger he wanted to spew. "Clarence, I'm taking you into the truck stop for a bathroom break. Think you can move around a bit?"

Clarence glanced at this shirt and then the shackles. He nodded as he looked toward the store. A visual flooded his mind of the last trip he'd made with Randy and how mean he'd been, kicking him in the shins when Randy had unshackled him. "I'll be fine." It wouldn't be fun to be seen in this condition but for Randy, he'd make the effort to be civil. "Let's go."

Randy unhooked Clarence as Scar Man stepped to the back of the van, his hand on his holster.

"You are all gun-happy." Randy moved out of the van with one motion and held out his hand to Clarence. "What did Warden tell you that he didn't tell me? Huh?" He glanced at Scar Man. "Help Ralston out."

Clarence reached his hands to Randy and tried to scoot forward in the seat, expecting major pain, but it wasn't bad. Surprised, he edged his foot out the door and onto the ground. When he brought his other foot out and onto the concrete and straightened, the pain hit his abdomen and he doubled over, groaning.

Randy caught him before he went all the way down and steadied him. "You okay? You've been sitting there for hours and the wound kind of cramped you. You'll be better off the more you move around—just as long as the bleeding doesn't start all over again." He put his arm behind Clarence's back and braced him to take a step.

Clarence sucked in a deep breath as Ralston stepped out behind him and came around to his side. He moved first one foot and then the other. Everything hurt—his back, his shoulders from the way he'd been snoozing. Odd that the wound didn't hurt that much right now. It had been terrible right when he'd been shot but now it wasn't too bad.

He'd been knifed, abused, violated, but never shot—until today. It still didn't even come close to how bad he hurt for Mrs. Hatly, Bea and Katty. And Noell. Carol. Even Lisha.

Lisha had been his enemy for the first month at Hillcrest, but not now. Oh, they spat a lot and argued everyday, but something had changed.

Randy and Ralston urged him toward the entrance to the truck stop just as a young woman about Katty's age was leaving with one, two, three kids following behind her like baby chicks. She took one look at him and gasped.

He glanced down. His Led Zeppelin T-shirt was bloody and had a hole in it now. On down to the shackles. He had slept in the van so he imagined his hair was a mess, too. He guessed he looked frightful from the look on her face, plus each little kid looked terrified.

"I'm sorry." He tried to smooth it over even with the guards on either side of him. "I'm sorry for what they see." All he could imagine was Bea and how frightened she would be, seeing him or anyone in his condition.

The mother gathered the children behind her, but made room for Clarence, Randy and Ralston to pass in front of her. Her dark eyes scanned everything, from blood to shackles, then straight to his eyes. Clarence read fear there, but something else. Fear. And sympathy.

As they stepped past her, she bowed her head, her eyes still on Clarence's face. "We're praying for you, Sir."

Sir?

His knees crumpled under him and Randy had to heft him up again. "Praying for—?"

Randy interrupted. "Please, Ma'am, we can't allow any contact between him and you." He looked into Clarence's face and stopped.

She spoke even stronger, still keeping the children behind her.

Little hands gripped the seams of her jeans and wisps of black hair flowed from behind her knees.

He took another step as the guards pushed him forward into the store.

A hand touched his arm and stopped him. She stepped in front of him, her little brood bouncing in line behind her. Now one small, dark eye peeked.

She hesitated. "I saw you."

He stopped. "You saw me? I—"

"Yes. I saw you in a dream." She gathered his whole body in her glance. "Just like this."

He looked down again.

"You were surrounded."

He guessed he was. A guard on either side.

"No. Not them." She hesitated. "Oh they were there, but … there were others."

"Others?"

Randy interjected. "Excuse me Ma'am, but we need to keep going."

She became more determined, and focused even more on Clarence. "You were, *are* surrounded by … " she seemed to be looking behind him and around him, "by hundreds of angels."

His skin tingled and he barely breathed. He would not cry.

Ralston started to laugh but she shushed him. He blinked, like he'd never been shushed with such respect, but total authority.

"Angels?" Clarence looked around. *Michael?* He wasn't there. Or maybe he was and Clarence just couldn't see him. No way when he was being transported from prison to Hillcrest had he ever thought there had been angels, but this trip? Already was different.

"Yes. Hundreds. With *you*." She pointed at his chest. "And you will survive this … uh, trip." She hesitated. "More than survive. You will go … back to," she looked directly at him, her face questioning. "Back to a nursing home? Your home."

A child quickly burst out from behind her. A small girl with black eyes and hair. "And you have a girlfriend!" She giggled.

"Hush." The woman pushed her behind. "Yes. There is a woman, a tiny gray-haired woman with a pink ribbon in her hair."

Clarence blinked and his legs buckled again.

Mrs. Hatly?

Oh God. What was this?

Randy and Ralston lifted him away, into the store, but Clarence stared behind him at the woman and children, who were now stepping from behind her. One. Two. Three.

"Wait." Clarence put on the brakes and looked at the kids. All bright and shiny. They almost sparkled, they were so pure. He pointed, even though his hands were in cuffs. "There is a fourth kid." He'd never done this before. "You left one in the store?" What was he saying. How did he know that?

But he did.

Her chin quivered but she regained her composure. "Yes. There is a fourth—in heaven with Jesus."

The little ones all nodded. "She is playing with Jesus!"

Were these people crazy? Or was *he* crazy? As he walked away, he couldn't help but stare behind him until he couldn't see them anymore and he almost tripped over a huge man's boots who was waiting in line at the cashier. The man growled as they stepped around him.

Randy smoothed it over. "Excuse us. We're a little bulky here. Excuse us."

Clarence shuffled forward as best he could in the shackles, but his heart was still with the woman and her children. He had never felt so disjointed. He was one place in the natural, but another place in his heart. But when he thought of it, he'd lived his whole life that way— his body was in prison but his heart was with Annie, wherever she was.

Restrooms. Women's. Men's.

Randy sent Ralston in to clear the area so they could take Clarence in.

A young man in a suit rushed out, still zipping up, a wild look in his eyes. When he spied Clarence in all his bloody, shackled glory, he edged around them.

Ralston held the door open.

"What?" Randy pointed at the young man. "What did you do? What did you say to him?"

Ralston chuckled. "I just told him that a murderer was needing to use the premises and that he needed to cut it short and zip it and git out." He smirked, his hands on his hips.

Randy shook his head, but pushed Clarence into the restroom. "Let's get this done before Ralston gives anyone else a heart attack."

Humiliating. His own hands in handcuffs. He couldn't even pee by himself. Old anger climbed from his gut to his throat as Randy zipped him up. Steam had to be misting off his face, it was so hot. This was way more invasive than Lisha in the nursing home when she was being ornery. She would knock on the shower door, wait one second, then yell "Get done or I'm comin' in!" Then she'd rattle the keys. There was never a long hot shower there and he remembered it would be the same in prison. Get wet. Get soaped. Rinse. Get out. Hopefully with everything intact.

Back in the van he was both exhausted and exhilarated. The young woman and kids were gone when they walked out, but Clarence still felt the impact of what she had said. He looked around him. Maybe Michael had shown up.

"There ain't no angels around you." Ralston squeaked. "There's jus demons, and a whole lot of 'em." He sniggered.

Clarence was determined to not lose the feeling, the rising up of something he'd felt only a few times in his life. An undeniable knowing that something, someone, was on his side. That someone had his back.

Maybe he wouldn't die in prison after all.

TWELVE

Noell handed Katty the cup, but her expression was puzzling. "I couldn't remember if you drank coffee, so I got hot chocolate instead. Hope that's okay." Maybe she shouldn't have—

"I ... " Katty's chin quivered and her eyes brimmed. A ragged breath escaped her lips. "I love hot chocolate." Another breath. "Thanks."

What do you say to a mommy who has just seen her child shot down? Noell fiddled with her hair braid. Did Katty like being touched? Did she hate it? And what had she seen? Her daughter had been shot. Had she been bloody? Was she awake? Crying in pain?

What had Gamma seen when Noell's own Mommy died? Mommy had drowned, so was she ... bloated? *Oh God.* Had she closed her eyes? All Noell could see in her nightmare was Mommy's eyes wide open in terror. Had they ever closed in peace?

Oh Gamma. What you must have gone through—losing your own daughter. Grampa too.

Noell hadn't been born with a bank account attached to her name, although because of Gamma's investments, she was now a wealthy young woman. But she had grown up with constant nightmares of her mother drowning. Plus Gamma's own pain of hoarding. Losing

Grampa. All they had was each other—Gamma and Noell. A hard life. Never having friends over because of Gamma's hoarding.

And now Noell was alone. No Mommy. No Gamma. No Grampa.

No one to share her life with. No one to care whether she came home or not. Not one person to have dinner with.

Noell stopped.

But Katty's most precious possession in the whole world was across the hall in surgery. And her best friend in the world, Clarence, had been literally kidnapped back to prison.

Noell shook her head. She swallowed and reached for Katty's hand.

Katty jumped, her eyes on their hands, as Noell slowly wove her fingers with Katty's. She slowly looked up at Noell and nodded, her hands clasping Noell's even more firmly. She continued to nod, until a tear dropped on Noell's hand.

Noell gently rubbed her thumb against Katty's knuckle. She blinked a tear away and swallowed. She didn't care how long they had to sit like this, she would never take her hand away.

Katty blew out a ragged breath just as the door to the surgical wing swung open. A youngish doctor walked toward them, untying the mask from the back of his head, letting it flop loose at his chest. He seemed confidant and pleased.

Oh please, God. Please let Bea not only survive, but thrive.

He nodded at Noell, then pulled a chair directly across from Katty and sat. "She's going to be fine. She will recover without any complications." He held up a bullet. "This is what we took out of her. We were able to repair the site closed and I am confidant she will heal completely and never miss a four-year-old beat."

Katty placed her cup on a table, but she didn't reach for the bullet, so Noell did. She started to put it on the side table, almost tucked it into her jeans pocket but instead held it in her other hand.

"Can I see her?"

"They are taking her into recovery and it will take them a few minutes to hook her all up, but then someone will come out and get you." He nodded at Noell, "You can come, too."

Noell nodded.

She looked up as Carol pushed the open button from outside and squeezed through the automatic doors before they were open all the way, followed by Lisha.

Reinforcements.

Carol winked at Noell and nodded.

Upon seeing the doctor, Carol stopped and stepped away to a respectful distance.

The doctor glanced up and smiled. "Carol. Lisha." He stood to shake hands.

Carol took his hand in both of hers, her eyes never leaving Katty's face. "How is she? How is our Bea?"

The doctor nodded and backed away. "I'll let you all visit while I go check on our tiny patient." Directly to Katty, "I'll keep you informed, especially the next twenty-four hours or so."

Katty stood to thank him and after he left Carol and Lisha embraced her. Lisha peeked over and pulled Noell into the group hug as Carol murmured, "She's going to be okay. She will be alright. She's a strong little girl."

Katty collapsed just then.

Lisha held her and kept her from falling.

There was no way Katty would fall as she was held up by two strong women who were used to lifting residents in the nursing home. Their training kicked in and they gently sat Katty back down, finding chairs for themselves.

No one spoke for a few seconds until Lisha broke the ice, a grimace on her face. "Nobody in my family ever been shot." She shook her head.

Noell leaned forward. "This is all too crazy to believe."

Carol checked Lisha's face, then Katty's. "I know. In our little town of Osceola. Everyone was so upset—the residents most of all. But those guards—pushing and shoving Clarence and—"

"Yes. They was brutal. They had him handcuffed." Lisha shook her head. "I had problems with that man from the beginning, but ... " She didn't finish her sentence.

Carol glanced at Lisha's face again and continued, nodded to Katty.

"When you and Bea ran up—she was asking questions as only little ones would." Carol sighed. "She doesn't miss a thing—the handcuffs, the guards." But when the guard said something to you, Katty—"

Katty shook her head, her eyes wide. "He came on to me. Said something like 'Who wants to know, baby?'" She imitated his slimy voice. "I had stepped in front of Clarence," she added, "and asked what was going on. I think I asked him where he was going." She stared at the wall. "Bea was right in there, asking him stuff. That's when that skinny weasel of a guard said what he did." Her forehead wrinkled and tears began to flow. "And that's when Clarence broke loose and slugged the guard." Her other hand flew to her mouth as she realized the truth. "Clarence was protecting me—us. He slugged that guard in defense of me, of Bea and me." She choked. "Never has anyone done that before. My dad, my mom, my brothers. None of them ever stood up for me." She made it a point to look into Noell's, Carol's, and Lisha's eyes. "Ever. Until Clarence today."

Noell glanced away. Grampa had always stood up for her. He had always been the one to rush into her room when she cried out in her nightmares. He had always come to school to take the principal to task over someone bullying Noell in the lunch line or at the lockers when the teachers weren't looking.

Until he had died, Grampa always had Noell's back, except for one time when he had let her stand up to a bully herself, and he supported her. She had come home crying one last time. He must have been fed up. He marched her back to school and stood behind her as she punched the bully in the jaw. He had grinned all the way home. She never knew she could hit that hard. And the kid had become a friend all through school until graduation. Where was *he* now?

Noell realized she had been gripping Katty's hand hard and relaxed her hold. She also realized something she really down deep knew—her growing up years had been sweet—despite the hoarding, despite loosing Mommy at a young age and despite the nightmares.

The doors to the surgery wing opened and a perky nurse walked through. "Katty? Katty Randolph?"

Katty rose. "Can I see my Bea?"

"You sure can." The nurse gauged the others around Katty. "Family? Friends?" She realized who Carol and Lisha were and grinned. "Nurses."

Carol looked at Lisha. "Oh, we have to get back. We just wanted to come and check on Bea and you, Katty."

"Yeah. I gots to give a bath and … " Lisha trailed off.

Neither seemed ready to leave, torn by duty to job and wanting to stay.

"We'll try to come back after work." Carol tried to smile. "We knew the residents would want an update on Bea. Even the Hate Clarence Club wanted to find out how she is." She popped her hand over her mouth. "Said too much. Wipe that from your memories, girls."

Lisha stood. "If those biddies start in on Clarence, I might have to drown one of them today." She grinned.

Carol stood too. "Well so much for the privacy act!" She leaned over and hugged Katty, then Noell. "Bye, Katty. Let us know how we can help." She raised her eyebrows. "Okay?"

Katty nodded. "Sure. Thanks." She stood and reached for Noell's hand. "Ready to go in?"

Felt like family. Noell nodded and slipped her hand into Katty's. Almost felt like sisters. Almost. Cousins maybe.

Carol and Lisha waved as they pushed the open button to the automatic doors.

Noell waited for Katty to take the first step. When she did, she seemed conflicted. She had to be eager to see Bea, but—

"W-what will she look like?" Katty took a deep breath. "I-I guess we'll have to go find out. She might still be asleep."

Noell nodded and pushed the open button.

Katty linked her arm in Noell's and stepped through the doors as they opened. Odd. It felt so right.

The nurse waited for them near an open door and ushered them inside.

THIRTEEN

"I can't believe this." Randy flipped on the blinker and made a slight right turn into a truck stop. He glared into the rear view mirror. "We are literally," he pointed at the windshield, "less than fifty miles from the prison. You can't wait?"

Ralston growled from behind Clarence. Growled again. "No, I cannot." He kicked the back of Clarence's seat like a child. "I gotta go."

"Grrr." This time growling came from Randy up front. He pulled into a parking spot and opened his door.

Goatee Man stroked his goatee. "This is stupid. This is when things happen."

Clarence had been thinking the same thing only with a different twist. If only he wasn't shackled. He could push out the back door while it was open and make—

Scar Man leaned forward. "You were thinking the same thing, weren't you Timmelsen?" He grinned. "Weren't you."

Was he that transparent? He hadn't even turned his head. But the wheels had been turning. He cleared his throat. "Since we're stopped, I have to go, too."

Both Scar Man and Goatee Man groaned.

"Told ya."

Goatee Man tapped on the window at Randy and pointed at Clarence.

Randy opened the side door. "What?"

"He's got to go, too."

Randy dropped his head to his chest. "Alright. Let's get going. We are almost there and I want to be done with this whole ordeal." He twirled his finger in a vortex. "Get him out. Make it snappy."

Clarence scooted to the edge of his seat as Goatee Man and Scar Man unbuckled the shackles. He had a sharp memory drop in of when Randy had taken him to Osceola. Randy had hoped to trust him and had unshackled him, but Clarence had kicked Randy in the shin. Clarence had deserved to be completely shackled. He had settled down and they came to an understanding. The last half of the trip, Clarence rode in front.

He had tensed at the thought without realizing it. Settle. Relax. Because it isn't happening this trip. Goatee Man and Scar Man *and* Ralston and Randy. It had just been Randy from prison to Osceola.

Not happening.

"Easy Cowboy." Goatee Man positioned a hand on his holster and unsnapped it.

Clarence grimaced. "I'm just an old man who has to pee. Give me some slack." Somehow, they'd slip up—somehow. Just one guard might turn his back and Clarence maybe could slip into the trucker area and catch a ride with one of them. He looked down. Blood on his shirt might be suspicious, but it was worth a try.

Prison this time would kill him.

Scar Man stepped out and turned to help Clarence down.

Clarence slid over to the door.

Goatee Man held out his hand to steady him and Clarence stepped down.

"Damn! Hurts … to stand." Clarence slowly straightened, breathing in shallow breaths through his mouth. "Wow. Wow." He grabbed at the air and finally his hand found the door handle. Yeah, he'd be able to run and escape. He was a damn pansy.

People parked next to the van gave him sideways looks. Everyone of them gasped at the blood on his T-shirt. Then to the handcuffs on his hands. Then the leg irons.

As they walked inside, people seemed to part on either side to let them pass, like magic. Must have been impressive. A guard on either side of him. Humiliating. In spite of the pain, Clarence stood as tall as possible, head held high, eyes kind.

As he passed people, they'd first glimpse the blood, handcuffs, then quickly look away. They were horrified.

Him too. Embarrassed by the attention, by the guards seriousness … and it was serious. Embarrassed by the curiosity of the children. They poked their heads from behind a parent or pointed.

He must have looked like a common criminal.

God.

Clarence couldn't even smile. He tried to seem pleasant, but after awhile, it grew tiring and he assumed a cold hard stare which he guessed was more fitting for the occasion.

Surely he'd been exonerated and released. They were making this long trip for nothing—a waste of time and gas and manpower.

Goatee Man stepped into the restroom and cleared it out. Clarence almost laughed at the expressions of the men and boys racing from the room. What had Goatee Man told them?

Play the part of the con man. Put on the terrible face. Cold, hard eyes. Act out the part that people believed without knowing the facts.

The fact—these guards had literally kidnapped him, taking him against his will to prison for defending himself against a thug years ago.

His cheek *still* tingled as he remembered the scene when Lewis Ralston came at him with a knife and four more, equally vicious inmates surrounded him.

He still couldn't figure out how he'd gotten a knife in time to defend himself against Lewis. When two guards had busted into the shower room with beat sticks and guns, the others thugs had dispersed, leaving Lewis and him to duke it out with knives. Lewis had sliced Clarence's cheek and Clarence hadn't even hesitated. He knew he had to strike, seeing the guards were on Lewis's side. Roaring, Clarence plunged into him and the knife flew. Before he knew how, the knife was in his hand and it hit its mark in Lewis's neck, slicing open the artery. Lewis still lunged into him, but a second later, collapsed. The guards yelled for help and backup. None came and Lewis died on the spot, blood everywhere. His body—legs and arms—splayed at odd angles. How could Clarence be held responsible when five men came at him with knives?

Clarence used the toilet, with the help of the guards.

Humiliating.

They turned to leave the restroom when a man with a trimmed, long pointed beard, wearing a strange cowboy hat, entered the restroom.

The guards, on either side of Clarence, stiffened. Their hands gripped his arms even tighter, ready to reach for weapons if needed.

The man seemed to absorb everything in one glance—from Clarence's bloody shirt, handcuffs, guards ready to beat him away if he appeared to be threatening in any way.

Strange. The man seemed to know Clarence. He looked him straight in the eyes in a friendly way—kind of like Michael did.

Where on earth was Michael, anyway?

This guy made Clarence feel like Michael had.

Michael always made Clarence feel like he had a purpose, like he was strong and could do anything. This guy knew something. Or was someone important without looking like it. Who was he and what did he want? Was he one of God's creatures or an angel?

Hard to even walk by the unlimited displays of candy, snacks, chips and drinks. He had gotten so used to freedom. Walk to the grocery store any day of the week and spend money. Buy candy bars from Mindy or John who worked there. Be harassed by John—a far cry from what he was going through right now with the guards. Oh, to have John threaten him right now.

They made it to the cashiers and the man was there—face-to-face. He smiled. His plaid shirt was odd too. Odd hat. Odd beard. Odd shirt. Odd smile, or odd that he smiled at Clarence and the guards.

The guy had to be an angel.

There was no way even six months ago, Clarence would have thought that. He'd have shooed the man away, insulted him. Thinking he was a pest, or a scammer. Or gay.

Back in the van. Back in shackles. The longest day of his life.

Again.

The last thing Clarence wanted to see was the entrance to the prison—Maximum Security Prison in Chicago. The front gate security guard waved them on. As they drove through the gates, chills ran up and down Clarence's spine, so much that he hardly felt Ralston's gun tapping his ear. He shuddered repeatedly.

Ralston whispered, "You're gonna love the changes here. He's waiting for you."

Didn't even faze Clarence. Those whispers were only background noise to the louder voices shouting in his own mind. "You'll never get out of here. You'll die a horrible death in here."

"Ralston!" Randy's eyes glared from the rear view mirror. "How many guns do you have? Holster your gun!"

Ralston continued to tap Clarence's ear. Cold, hard metal slid across his throat, then rested at his temple.

Ralston knew they were in home territory and he was Warden's baby brother.

Clarence held his breath and squeezed his eyes shut. Not crying. No tears.

A garage door opened and Clarence blinked in the bright overhead lights. Every cell sweated. Every cell vibrated with fear. Radios squawked with the news—"Timmelsen is on the property. Timmelsen has arrived."

Ralston leaned in. "See? You're famous. Timmelsen is in the building. Timmelsen is here." He chuckled. "Kinda like Elvis." He laughed even harder.

Clarence shuddered at the sound of his laugh. This move was going to be the toughest of his whole life. Losing Annie, his dad, seeing the townspeople at the train station for literally the last time and entering prison at nineteen years old—everyday since.

This would undoubtedly be the worst day he had ever lived through. If, he indeed lived.

His heart wanted to cry out to God but even Michael had abandoned him. What god would ever help him again?

His dad always used to remind Clarence that God never turned his back on a person and that was from a man who had never entered a church since his wife's funeral.

But God had turned His back today.

FOURTEEN

Bea's hospital room was right across from the nurses station. Katty guessed they put the serious cases there and she guessed that Bea's case was pretty serious. She prepared herself for the worst. Seeing Bea from surgery, tubes all over, white as the sheets.

"Ready?" Noell's hand hovered over the door handle, waiting.

Katty nodded. "Yes."

Noell slowly slid her sleeve over her hand and pulled the door open.

Odd. Noell's expression was odd, too. Like expectant fright. Katty studied the door. She couldn't see what might be so terrifying.

They stepped into the room. Bea faced the wall, away from them. She must still be out from the anesthesia. Baby Bea.

Katty's eyes filled with tears at the sight of her, pale against the pillow. She swallowed back a sob. All she wanted to do was pick her up and snuggle her. To keep her safe. Awful how she used to be drunk all the time and leave Bea all night and a good part of the day, alone. She had cared more about partying and drugs than her own daughter.

Awful, awful.

She tip-toed toward the bed and Bea turned her head, a grin on her face. "You're awake."

"Look Mommy. Can you see them?" Bea pointed at what seemed just the air. "They're sparkly. They have eyes and wings." She sighed and leaned back against the pillow. "I think they're angels. I think they saved me, Mommy."

Katty raised her eyebrows and hugged Bea. "Where do you hurt? Is it okay that I hug you? Are you okay?" Now she sounded just like Bea did. Asking every question in the book, five times each.

Bea sighed.

"Are you tired? Do you hurt?"

Bea shrugged. "Kinda. But the nurse said I'd be okay and better in no time. She was nice. She said that the lights would go away when I woke up more." Bea searched the room. "They're all still here, so is it okay that I can still see them? I don't want them to go away."

Katty glanced at Noell. She was searching the room, following where Bea pointed. Damn. How could she ever talk to Noell with a straight face again? "Baby, maybe the nurse was just trying to make you feel better."

"Don't you see them Mommy?" Bea pointed. "You did before in the car. Remember?"

Katty blinked and leaned her head toward Noell. "She's just sleepy, I think." The lights were beautiful. Maybe it hadn't been a good idea to bring Noell in with her. Because she really wanted to talk to Bea about them. She could almost see a face. Wings for sure. So beautiful that Katty could feel her knees buckling. No. She had to stay standing and strong. Light reflected from somewhere. She didn't see any except for the light fixture over the bed. They seemed to have light from within somehow.

Beautiful.

Noell was silent.

Katty peeked at her and blinked. The expression on her face mirrored Bea's. Rapt. Awe. Tears. There were tears in Noell's eyes. She was definitely seeing something.

A nurse pushed the door all the way open, carrying a tray. "Hi, Little One. Just a light lunch. You are so tiny, you need to eat fairly often." She placed the tray on the table and pushed it closer to the bed and leaned to Katty. "My name is Candy and I'll be your nurse today and maybe tomorrow. Is she still talking about seeing things?"

Katty raised her eyebrows. "Uh—"

"She seems determined that there are angels in this room. Or at least lights." Candy lifted the cover revealing broth and jello. Apple juice sat beside it, with utensils and a napkin. A tiny stuffed pig decorated the tray. "Just so you know, she could be hallucinating from the anesthesia and other meds they gave her in surgery. It happens."

A light swooped around the nurse's head and landed on her shoulder. She fussed with the bedding and the tray, checked tubes and the IV drip, totally unaware of anything going on around her.

"You have a great room here, too." She nodded out the door. "Right close to the nurses. And it's so peaceful." Deep sigh. "It's ... peaceful."

Bea giggled.

The light flickered from Candy's shoulder, almost waving at them. If the nurse felt peaceful with it there, Katty figured maybe that's what these lights were for, what they were supposed to do—bring peace.

Bea reached for the tiny pig. "What's this?"

Katty stepped in. "It's a tiny pig. Maybe a toy. Cute." She moved the juice closer. "Maybe take a sip—just a sip—to make sure your tummy is settled."

More lights flew in and circled the nurse's head and shoulders. They seemed to hover around her. Almost putting on a show.

Bea pointed. "See, Mommy? Look at all of them around her head." She giggled and blinked. Still sleepy.

"We'll watch her and chart it and if she doesn't come out of it, we'll alert the doctor and see what he wants to do. He has kids so he gets them." She smiled and tucked in the sheet around Bea's feet. "Are you still cold, Honey?" She pushed the table right up to Bea's chest. "Want to be careful for where the wound is in her tummy, around her belly button."

"Do I still have a belly button?"

The nurse stopped and stared at Bea. "Why ... of course you do, Sweetie! You just ... well there is kind of a bandage over—"

"Is it a pretty one?"

"Uh … what?" The nurse evidently didn't have kids.

"Is it Star Wars? Or a—"

"I think it's white." The nurse shook her head. "Or maybe blue."

"That's okay." Bea leaned up a little to the tray and tapped the jello. "What's this? It's green."

Katty came to Candy's rescue. "It's jello." She shook the bowl. "See? It wiggles." She moved her shoulders and hips in a dance. "It's dancing! Shake it baby!" Things were definitely more fun when the lights were around.

Bea tapped it again. "Fun!" She reached for her spoon. "Can I eat it?"

Noell laughed. "Sure." She took the spoon from Bea and tapped it. "Fun!" She scooped up a tiny spoonful and aimed it at Bea's mouth. "Taste it?"

Bea stared at it, then up at Noell, then Mommy. Then Candy. "Okay." She opened her mouth.

Noell fed her and put down the spoon. "Good?"

Bea's eyes opened wide. "It's good! Tastes … green. Or like … green." She hesitated. "Grass is green. Broccoli is green, but it doesn't taste like that." She picked up the spoon and took another bite. "Tastes like—"

"Lime?" Noell took the spoon.

"What's lime?"

Katty perked up. 'It's what you put in … uh. Maybe it's apple flavored."

Bea nodded. "I think it *is* apple. How do they do that? Put apples in there and make it all jumpy?"

Noell laughed. "Well, they put a bunch of apples in a bowl and tell them to dance. When they dance, the skins all fall off and juice runs out. And they put that juice with other stuff to make the jello dance."

Candy rolled her eyes.

Katty chuckled. Noell got kids. She should be Bea's nurse.

Noell shoveled another bite into Bea's mouth.

"Well … I think you have this covered. I'll go make rounds." Candy seemed to come to and took a deep breath. "She is coming out of it, so I'm not too worried about what she was seeing anymore."

Katty bit her lips. A grin slipped out and she bit her lips again.

The angels were swirling again—almost making a joke—only Candy didn't know about it. Candy could chart what she wanted, but the lights and angels were more than ever. More flew in from … where? They appeared at the walls, in the doorway.

Candy checked her watch, evidently wanting to get away from the crazies. "Let me know if you need anything." She pointed to the tray. "Try to eat something else. Try the broth. It's great." She waved as she left the room.

Katty nodded. "Yeah." Broth to a peanut butter and jelly girl. Right.

Noell was still seeing them too, because her face was joyful. She covered her mouth, trying to be deadpan.

Katty's face wanted to burst. She was grinning from ear to ear! Bea had just been shot and had to have surgery and Clarence was … gone. But her heart was full and bursting with … joy? Never. Never had she felt this way. When the lights had appeared in the car a few weeks ago, she had felt peace, but something more. She had known that in spite of what was going on, everything would be all right. She just knew, somehow.

This was kind of the same, but even more so.

Out at the nurses station, Candy could be heard talking to someone. "I don't know what Bea's background is, but her mom stares at the air too. We maybe should chart that something runs in their family. Like they're all seeing things." She seemed to pause. "Still, it's so quiet in there—peaceful somehow."

Noell snorted.

Katty shut the door and giggled, covering her mouth.

"Mommy! They're dancing around your head, like the jello!" Bea grinned an all-teeth grin.

Katty looked at Noell, her heart bursting.

Noell looked up and laughed a delightful laugh, wiping tears from her eyes.

Poor Candy.

FIFTEEN

Harold tapped the cell phone and shook his head. Rubbed his eyes.

A list of phone numbers was written neatly on a pad of scratch paper beside him on the table—neatly for him anyway. The pad was a freebie from the hospital. He had a stack of them to use just for moments like this.

He shook his head again and combed fingers through his hair.

He used to be good at contacting people when he'd had the detective agency. Never hesitated—just dialed the number. Talked to many kinds of people: women and men who were influential or poverty-stricken, all cultures. Suspicious wives. Criminals. People hiding from life. Even people who had been given asylum. Interesting business.

He missed it. And yes, he had worked long hours. Lucille, his wife, had complained once-in-a-while, but for the most part, she was very patient—knowing his love of the job and how much he helped people.

That was it—the whole reason for doing what he did—he helped people in tough seasons.

Seemed so long ago. Hell, he probably should have quit sooner than he did.

He stared out the window. The trash dumpster was his mountain view. He didn't care. Clarence teased him about it because the view out of Clarence's window was the rose garden.

Harold gulped. They'd had many laughs over that.

Damn, he missed that man. He glanced at the dumpster again, the lines blurred.

Who would help Clarence if he didn't?

Lisha poked her head in. "You okay?" She checked his water carafe. "I'll get you more. Be right back."

He wiped his eyes. Now he had an excuse to delay the call. Lisha said she'd be right back.

And she was, carrying his water carafe and a cup of coffee. Good girl. She was worth gold to the residents.

"Thanks Lisha." He sipped the coffee. Wasn't like Clarence's but it'd do. Damn, he missed that man.

They'd started out kind of rocky, but he'd not had a friend like Clarence since Lucille had passed away.

Lisha smoothed the bedcovers and re-arranged his toothbrush and toothpaste on his sink. She pulled the blinds down then released them back up.

"Say it, Lisha."

She turned to him. "Who me?" She shook her head, long dreadlock ponytail bouncing. "Just cleanin' up a bit."

"Right."

She sat on the bed. "I was just thinking. Since you were a detective and all—"

"Go on."

"And since you have your phone out and all." She folded her arms across her chest. "Can you call somebody about Clarence? Didn't you used to know somebody, who knew somebody else, who could git him out? Somebody that could help him?"

Harold dropped his chin to his chest, his eyes closed. Lord, you send 'em when I need 'em. This woman.

He tapped the pad of paper, underlining one phone number with his gnarled finger. "This one is the governor. I knew his dad real well— good man. This one is Sheriff Dennison." He had racked his brain to come up with names, but other than the governor and Sheriff, he couldn't think of anyone. "I'm trying to think of people I used to know or work with." He picked up the pen. "Help me?"

Lisha nodded and blinked. "Okay. Well, let's see." She stood and paced. "Clarence wasn't in the military. The governor is a good one. Maybe just call him and he could give you names." She snapped her fingers. "What about our senator or representative? I don't know their names, but … "

Harold clapped his hands and pointed his pen at Lisha. "Good one. I used to know someone from back in my day." He stared out the window. "A couple of them. Good men, too."

"Can you get hold of them? Would they remember you?" She caught up a stray braid into her ponytail.

"One would remember me. We worked together on a murder case for years. Didn't crack it, but we tracked down every lead. He had a brother too, that had a high-profile business. He'd come on board and help. Now what were their names?" He snapped his fingers. "Somebody else. I don't know if this one is still alive, but there was a woman, Eva Trumble, who was a senator back then." He chuckled. "My Lucille was jealous until they met. They became good friends."

He wrote her name down. "The other one was Stan … Stan Martinson? I don't know how to find these people now." Felt good to be doing something. This detective thing was still in his blood.

Lisha held up her phone. "I know how we can start."

SIXTEEN

These guards were going all out. Were they really that afraid of him, locking everything on him from his hands and feet to his head? Every shackle, every handcuff, every bit of armor—locked.

Clarence blew a breath out. He pulled against the handcuffs, without letting on—not moving a muscle. Tight. Everything was tight. His hands had begun to tingle.

But as Clarence scanned the people gathering, maybe the extra protection was for *him*. Men gathered in every allowable place that inmates could gather. It had only been a couple months since Clarence had been shipped off to Hillcrest Nursing Home, but these people seemed more evil than he remembered. He knew he hadn't changed that much in such a short time.

Their eyes were more evil—squinting, but more than that. The eyeballs were black. As Clarence passed each man, they almost growled, teeth showing in a snarl. A low growling.

Was this a pack of wolves? Smelled as bad.

Clarence's skin prickled. The sounds and faces and eyes gave off some sort of frequency that bombarded every cell of his body, making him shudder and shiver.

In just a couple months the whole atmosphere had changed. Oh, it had been bad before—very evil, prisoners always fighting, threatening. But right here and now, it felt like the prisoners were in charge, not the guards.

The more Clarence studied the people as he was pushed through, the more tense he became.

"Bring him here." A huge man standing at a counter, wearing the typical brown uniform, pointed at Clarence. His fat finger flipped over and beckoned. "He has to sign here." He tapped on a paper. "He doesn't go anywhere else, until he signs in."

They unlocked one handcuff so he could sign the paper. He put the pen to it, but caught sight of the words, "for life," and quickly withdrew his hand and protested. "I'm not signing that." His law degree kicked in.

Four guards pressed him into the counter. He gasped. Right on the wound. Someone popped him on the head. Two held him planted there, while one slipped a cable around his neck and kept him tethered. The other grabbed his right hand, cupping his own hand around Clarence's, making him sign his name. "How you spell it? C? T-i-m?"

Clarence watched as his scrawled name appeared on the page, the words flowing out of the pen that he himself grasped but had no real control of. He was able to read part of the document, since he didn't have to think about what was being written.

"What is this?" he yelled. "That says—"

The big man, his name tag read Teddy, growled at him. "None of your damn business. Warden wants you to sign it, that's all."

"None of my business! It says I signed over to Warden my whole life. My savings. My family. My future."

The guards all laughed.

Clarence blinked. Bea would be Warden's. A vision of her, dressed up in gold, a huge gold bow in her hair, flowed through his mind. Katty. What would happen to them? The whole town of Osceola that Dad had spent years quietly buying. This couldn't be happening.

Warden walked to the railing from upstairs, grinning. He waved. "Howya doin' down there, Clarence?" He spread his arms wide. "Welcome back!"

Clarence froze. He couldn't take a breath. Felt like Warden was standing on his chest, *plus* the huge man in front of him.

The guards around him laughed even harder. All in on the little joke. Joke's on Clarence. Funny. Funny.

The cable around his neck pulled tighter. The shackles on his ankles burned through his jeans.

Clarence grimaced. He would not let on … the pain.

The guard dropped the pen and the others replaced the handcuff, only this time his hands were in front. Strange. They had enjoyed tearing his arms out of the sockets to pull his hands behind his back.

Pain in his hands. His wrists were burning red. The handcuffs were cutting into his skin. How on earth? They hadn't cut into his wrists until now. Felt like little blades were on the inside of each one. He looked. There were … little … how?

This was all his imagination. Had to be. But how could it hurt so bad if he was in a dream?

Nothing in the nursing home had compared to this. God, this was not going to be good. He was in good shape but no time in working out or running could have prepared him for this.

It was almost … .

Michael. Where was Michael?

He looked where he had seen Warden standing. This had to be a … nightmare.

Warden was standing there, grinning, but behind him or morphed over him was … something moving. Outlines of … something … .

Every cell in Clarence's body screamed, "Run!"

The mist rose above Warden at least ten feet. Seemed to be a part of him, but had scales, horns.

Satan?

Clarence blinked. He started to bring his fingers to his eyes, but a guard grabbed the handcuffs and yanked his hands down.

Warden had almost become one with the … creature. His body and face grew and glowed. He still grinned until he stretched and then he stood alone.

The guy was nuts.

Something still flickered in Warden's eyes. Clarence stood in awe and fear as he watched. Had they slipped him drugs?

He shivered. Whatever it was that moved in Warden's eyes was worse than that devil. It could see into his very soul. Clarence tried to back away. It knew things. He could almost feel it inside him.

Even the guards cringed and backed away. So they saw it too.

Randy stomped. "This is rubbish." He might have been the only sane person there.

Two men standing to the side of the Warden looked familiar.

God.

Phil and Lex.

Clarence had known they were evil but never guessed they were connected to Warden.

He tried to move. Tried to move his feet and run away, but the shackles were glued to the floor.

Even the huge man looked like he wanted to run, but he just stood there.

Randy turned, took one apologetic look at Clarence and ran.

Chicken.

Clarence was doomed. This must be hell. He never figured he would die in the pit of hell. Why had Michael been his friend from day one at the nursing home? He had never been a great person, but never figured he'd go here. How could a prison turn into the very picture of hell?

The reality of where he probably was, hurt more than any burning shackles or handcuffs.

Clarence's eyes blurred. The whole place was on fire. He squinted through the smoke. This couldn't be real.

Inmates seemed free to roam and revel in the pain of one man— Clarence. They danced around him along with the guards. They played on the same team.

This was worse than dying.

Where was Michael?

"Michael, please. Help."

Warden must have heard him for he tossed back his head and

roared. "Michael won't save you! Your Bea, can't save you! She's dead. Poor baby. Tay shot her and now she's dead." He turned it all the way up. "You weren't there to save her, to protect her. You're a cheat and a liar and a loser."

With each accusation, Clarence bent lower and lower until he was on the floor. Each person pounded him on the head or worse, where he was burning, as they danced around him.

SEVENTEEN

Phil stared at Clarence.

The man was formidable. Even though he was old—eighty some-thing—when he came in, he stood almost a foot taller than the guards and even though he was fully shackled, he still walked upright and strong.

Hadn't the report said he'd been shot?

But here he was. His white hair was long and he had a full beard. He looked better than when he'd been in prison before.

Phil had an inside track even before that. Working as a dietary assistant in the prison kitchen gave him access to the needs of staff but also the inmates. He'd been around food and grocery stores all his life. When he'd been hired at the prison, he realized he would fit in with the community of inmates, although he'd never served time. And just because he'd never served time didn't mean he didn't deserve to.

He grinned. He just hadn't gotten caught, like all these other yayhoos.

The atmosphere in the rotunda exploded when they dragged Clarence in. Every cell, except the maximum security cells, lined the space, so every man could see them. Something changed in the inmates. A definite beat could be heard as they pounded on any surface near them—bars, doors, walls, floors. It was thunderous. It was darkly powerful.

The beat grew stronger and louder and all united in a chant.

Faces grew more vicious.

Eyes turned yellow and black.

Someone shouted, "Bea is dead."

Phil started. "W-What?" He leaned closer to Warden, but even he had changed. Something, a mist or film, a transparent layer of a creature, demon or dragon rose around him. Warden's eyes … shadows or tiny sparks flitted inside, like firecrackers. Something behind him pounded the floor in time with the beat.

Phil backed away. A tail?

Warden had something going on, alright. Just like his own dad.

Phil looked around for the stairway. Where was the whiskey?

Again, the crowd yelled, "Bea is dead."

His heart lurched. "Warden! What is that?" Phil tried to talk to the man. "Bea is dead?"

Warden grinned. The mist cleared but he didn't look any better. Sweaty. Flushed. Eyes hard. "Oh, she isn't dead. She's just wounded."

He raised his arm toward Clarence, who was kneeling under the attack and roared a sick laugh, shaking his fist. "Break him! Break him!"

EIGHTEEN

Michael was allowed in the prison but only at a distance. Demons were posted on every corner, every hallway, keeping any creature from the Kingdom of Heaven out.

The demons always thought they were in control, but Michael knew differently. Father was always in control and he had a plan—even here.

He followed the guards, who escorted Clarence, as close as they would let him. His army followed close behind him, weapons raised.

He could see Clarence. They were going to kill him if they kept up that torture. He was in great shape for anyone, but if they kept it up, he'd be gone from this earth.

Michael didn't think that was Father's plan for Clarence, yet. There seemed to be much for Clarence to do back in Osceola. So many lives to touch, especially Katty and Bea.

Making Clarence sign his life away, literally, was a big mistake. Maybe Clarence didn't remember, but Michael had been with him since his birth and he couldn't sign his life away. He was Blood-Bought. A member of the Blood Family. Not that one couldn't resist and turn away. Michael knew every decision Clarence had ever made. He had them in a book.

The demons and Warden, his guards were liars. All of them.

Humans needed to learn the Truth.

Michael cringed when the shackles became red with fire and the handcuff blades cut Clarence's hands.. He had lived in a human body, himself. He knew pain. He had pounded nails into his hand, not to emulate Lord's death at the cross, but because he was terrible with a hammer.

He checked his army—all kinds of angels, from different cultures, different colors, different ranks—all willing to follow Father and to guard Clarence. All willing to go into battle alongside Michael. All hard-core, seasoned warriors from eternity.

Jarrel leaned into Michael. "Randy is splitting. He is no longer with them. How do you want us to handle him?"

"However Yeshua would. Gather round him and minister according to Father's plan." He held his sword up. "Let Randy dictate. He will learn to direct you. Some are learning even now to be kings and sons. Let him grow into who he is to be." He glanced at where Clarence stood. "Just as Clarence is learning and growing right now. Learning that this is real."

Jarrel bowed low and backed away toward Randy.

On other days, Michael might have tripped Jarrel or maybe started a tussle—an angel wrestling match—but not today. So much hinged on this one battle here at the prison. The future for Clarence, but also for Katty and Bea, Noell, many residents and staff at the nursing home, community people who would possibly be affected by whether Clarence lived or died here. This battle could end now—this moment. Or last for months, even years. There were no time restrictions in the Kingdom.

This battle was Clarence's personal Armageddon. What he did here at the prison held the destiny of many future generations. Father was in control, but Clarence had the opportunity to change history.

They couldn't afford to lose focus. The battle was on and they were in enemy's territory. They had to stand no matter what the humans did.

Michael cringed when Warden stepped out onto the bridge. The man was crazy. Infested with every demon. He was sold out. He had progressed to a very high level in the enemy's camp. Only Michael outranked him, even though the Father was in control.

Warden had held such promise for the Kingdom when he was a boy. His mama worked hard to provide, his daddy, too. They had struggled with three little boys to raise and provide for. But one night's decision gone wrong had changed everything. Daddy had taken a job in another state for more money than what he was currently making. Mommy had decided to stay put, keeping the boys in school, not wanting to leave her friends. She had just started back to school to become a nurse. Commitment in the marriage had fallen apart and one thing after another, that old word divorce became more and more part of conversations until the papers were signed.

Michael could never figure out if since the demons all knew, every one of them, that Father was in control and the plan set forth in the Book was still the plan, why they even put forth such effort to try to win. Why didn't they all go on vacation to the Bahamas or the mountains? They knew how the Book ended.

Satan knew he had to work every moment to try and draw each and every human away from the Light. To fill his hell, he had to use every tactic to win souls to his side.

But it wasn't hard work. Plant a seed here and there and the humans ran with it. Discontentment. Rejection. Materialism. Consumerism. They deserved it. More. More. More.

And then they wondered how all this had happened. If they'd just go back to the roots, they'd figure it out. And some did.

If the humans only knew. If they only read the Book, they would know that the devil is a liar. That the enemy had no hold over them. The Destroyer had no power unless the humans gave it to him.

The humans gave their power that Jesus had died for them to have, to the Enemy.

Michael shook his head when Warden rose up and displayed his real self. Amazing that they were taking a chance in opening up their realm so the humans could see everything.

Even the angels.

But the humans were now so deceived and intoxicated with the

Flow and Magic that they couldn't even see the angels. Or they could but they didn't think they had any power. They didn't care. Again, if they had read the Book.

Or believed.

Wait.

What?

Clarence was crying out. "Bea! My Bea!"

Again. Lies flowed from Warden. Warden was raising his fist, yelling with the throng.

Oh, how Michael wished he could take Clarence and just show him Bea. That she was engaging with angels, even now at the hospital.

Show him that simple faith in Jesus …

The stage was set, though. The plan was set forth in the Book.

They couldn't interfere unless the Father directed.

So Michael stood steadfast as Clarence crumpled to the floor.

NINETEEN

Clarence snored himself awake, but slowly drifted back into dreamland.

The bed seemed hard. He rolled to his side, but couldn't quite make it all the way over. Maybe the other side would be more comfortable, but something stopped him, restricted him.

Lisha must have played a joke on him and put up his side rails. She could be very sneaky when she wanted to be.

He chuckled. Lisha was never quiet except when she wanted to play a trick on him.

He blinked his eyes open, knowing she was standing over him, that toothy grin wide and an ornery quip to start his day right. He'd follow with his own and the banter would take off from there. Carol usually rolled the med cart by in the hall and would come in to join them. She always just laughed with them, because no one bantered like Lisha.

He opened his eyes again, a thought coming to him, ready with his smart remark.

His vision of her massive body, dark-skin, black eyes, hair swooped up in rope-like dreads layered over a man, and by the looks of him, a doctor. He had a white doctor coat on and a stethoscope looped around his neck. White hair, green eyes and skinny as a rail.

The vision of Lisha evaporated and reality hit hard.

He must have had an accident and was in the hospital emergency unit or some physician's office. The walls were lined with cabinets, a sink area and a desk workspace. Fluorescent lighting make him blink.

He raised his head, intending to sit up and get out of bed, but something restricted him. Shackles. But more like a straight jacket/shackles combination. Some sort of macabre kind of torture suit. His arms were in a sleeve crossed over his chest, hands each handcuffed to the opposite side of the bed. No bed—but a table. His legs were treated the same as his arms in pants of sorts, but all attached to the table. Little zippers opened everywhere.

"What is this? Where am I?" The suit began to close in on him. He lifted his head. "Get me out of this!"

The doctor smirked. "Oh you'll get out soon enough but not to where you'd like to go." He pointed to the floor emphatically. "*This* is your home now. You'll end your life here, one way or another."

The doctor had something going on in his eyes that made Clarence think of doctors in Nazi Germany at the death camps. He'd read where they invented all kinds of morbid and gruesome experiments.

"Let me show you around a bit." The man took hold of the gurney and gave it a shove, sending Clarence and the table in circles. "We have everything a regular hospital has and more." He walked to a cabinet and opened it, revealing strange looking equipment with all kinds of dials and knobs. "We offer a complete range of treatments, aimed at benefitting every need."

And in an instant, Clarence was in a different realm. Same doctor. The same cabinets. Not the same torture suit. Only handcuffs locked to the table, ankle cuffs too.

The man was examining his hands when he noticed Clarence looking at him. "You're awake." He smiled. Nothing macabre about him. Same white hair. Same green eyes. He lifted his narrow reading glasses off his nose, letting them drop to his chest from a cord and took Clarence's pulse.

"Where did the torture suit go?" Clarence tried to point. "There was a different feel to this room and you." He lifted his head. "You twirled the table around."

The doctor smiled. "You have been unconscious for quite a while and to wake up in the infirmary has to be confusing."

"Infirmary?" Clarence lifted his head again. "Where am I?"

"Don't you remember the van trip here from … " he read the chart lying beside Clarence's leg, "Osceola? You don't remember the trip here?"

It all came crashing back. But more than that.

"Where are the fires? Where is the Warden and that beast he changes into?"

The doctor shook his head. "You have been hallucinating in your sleep about demons and angels and fire and burning shackles." He smiled.

"But I—"

"When a person has been through a distinct life change—change of location, loss of relationships—it becomes hard to grasp what reality is." The man put down the chart. "Reality. You are now residing at Chicago's own MSP. Maximum Security Prison. You will be here the rest of your life. You most likely will always be in some sort of restraints—hand cuffs, shackles, leg cuffs. You are never going back to … Osceola, Nebraska."

Clarence heard the words. He comprehended each one. But grasping the full meaning eluded him.

Never going back to Hillcrest. Never seeing Katty or Bea. Or Mrs. Hatly. Carol. Lisha.

He had wanted to die here before the warden had taken over. The old warden was nice enough. He'd never turned into some sort of dragon, that's for sure.

"What about when I came in here? There was fire. There were creatures—"

"You were dreaming like I said. Sometimes dreams or hallucinations appear so real, we can't discern between reality and the dream world." The doctor smiled, opened his mouth to speak again, but didn't.

Something felt off. The dreams were so real. He could almost feel the pain from the burning shackles. The blades piercing his skin from the handcuffs.

He raised his head and tried to hold up his hands, tried to turn them in the handcuffs. Before the doctor could stop him, he pushed his arm farther into the cuff and twisted so he could see his wrist.

His wrist was circled with pierce marks. Black dried blood at each point. "See? See there?" Clarence raised up, his shoulders off the table. "What are those?"

TWENTY

"I can't believe how fast she is recovering." Katty walked alongside Bea as Candy, the nurse pushed her in the small wheelchair.

"Little ones seem to heal fast and get over sickness and injuries much faster than adults." Candy patted Bea's shoulder. "I think it's because they move around so much more. They are always fidgeting or playing, bouncing."

Katty rushed ahead to the car. "I know. She is always bouncing to some kind of music in her head." She opened the car door. "Especially when music comes on the car radio or the TV at home." She laughed and wiped her eyes. She couldn't believe how emotional she was. Bea was okay, and would be fine, but—

Candy touched her arm. "You've been through a lot, too. Seeing your own child shot. Then surgery. It has to be scary."

Katty straightened.

Candy's blue eyes were so intense and concerned.

Katty couldn't stop the tears when Candy hugged her.

"Mommy, look! I left my candy in my car seat!"

Katty looked down. Bea wasn't in the wheelchair. She was already in her car seat. "What? Bea! How did you … " She wiped her face.

Bea was kicking her feet, happily munching something, her mouth already smeared with brown chocolate.

It felt so good to laugh. "Well, Candy, I guess you're right. She can move around better than I could." She found a wipe and began to clean Bea's mouth.

Candy grinned. "We're gonna miss you, Bea!" She leaned in the car and waved to her. And to Katty, "Call us anytime if you have any questions. Don't hesitate and really, let me know how you're doing, too. I have tomorrow off and I could come over and check on her."

Katty immediately got a visual of the trailer court and her trailer—falling apart, tacky trash—wait! Clarence had helped her replace that crumbling deck and the warped fake paneling inside. She tossed the dirty wipe onto the front seat of her car and nodded slightly. Her humble little trailer actually looked cute. "Uh, sure." Deep breath. She truly didn't know how to do this friend thing, if that's what this was. "That'd be fine. If you want to."

"Sure! I'll call before I come over to see if you need anything." Candy hugged her again. "Gotta get back to work." She spun the wheelchair around to face the hospital. "And you obviously don't need this thing anymore!"

Her laugh sounded like bells tinkling.

Katty buckled Bea in. "Does that hurt your ow-y?" She loosened the straps. "We won't make it as tight as those people told us to. Just for a couple days. Then it's back to making it so tight you can't breathe!" She tickled Bea then thought better of it. "Does that hurt?"

Bea kicked and finished the candy. "No Mommy." She giggled. "I love you Mommy." She pointed. "And the angels are laughing too, just like if you tickled them."

Deep sigh. "I wish I could—" A sensation of pure joy and peace overwhelmed her. "Never mind. I think something … I think … " She shut the car door and hugged her chest, walked around the car to the driver's door. "I think … I just … they're here." She looked into the air, not sure what to look at, or what she'd see. In the hospital, she had seen something more than the beautiful lights.

She sat in her seat and looked at the hospital door. Candy waved.

She waved back. She'd never had a friend. A friend that would come over and … what? Have a drink? She wrinkled her nose. Not going there, ever again. A cup of coffee? She could learn to like coffee if that's what friends did together.

A friend that would care enough to check on her and Bea?

The people who she used to do drugs with were not friends. They were people in the same trap and prison, same pain that Katty had been in. Users, abusers, willing to do whatever it took to get whatever they wanted, from whoever they wanted. And what they had wanted most was to numb out and forget their own past and pain.

But a friend, a real friend who would give as much as they took? Or give as much as Katty gave? A give and take relationship.

Doing healthy things together. What would that be?

Uh. She tapped her finger on the steering wheel.

Coffee.

Katty grinned and started the car, waving once again at Candy. Candy had already moved to her next task on her job.

Shopping. Maybe friends shopped together.

The only time she'd ever shopped for anything other than groceries, had been when Phil took her shopping to fussy her up— show her off to his friends when they had first lived together. After that, it had been all downhill.

The times when she'd meet Clarence in the park. They'd watched Bea play or they pushed her on the swings.

Together.

She sighed as she turned into the grocery store.

Friendships were going to be a new experience and it would take time to learn how to do it right. And to trust anyone with seeing her home and her life—who she was.

Bea kicked the back of Katty's seat. "Mommy! Can I have some Bubbly Pebbles cereal? And … and—"

"Sure Bea. I think we can do that." Interesting. Clarence had just paid her the day before yesterday. She actually had money in her account to buy groceries and sugary cereals. Something kicked in at the same time. She'd never lived extravagantly—never had much of her own, and if she had any money, she'd spent it on booze and drugs —groceries always came later.

But now. She had money. Some anyway. Clarence had been so good to her.

"Oh, Clarence." She put the car into park. Even this car wasn't new, but it was all in one piece and ran like a top. Clarence had made sure of that. He'd had it all gone over at the auto shop. They'd washed it and detailed it. She ran her hand along the steering wheel. "Beautiful." She leaned her head into the steering wheel. "Clarence. Where are you? Are you okay?"

"Mommy. Can we go see him after this? I want to show him my cereal."

She didn't know. *God*. There had been such craziness at the nursing home when Bea had been shot, that Bea hadn't seen Clarence get shot. Thank God she hadn't seen that. But what now? How could she tell Bea?

Katty turned in her seat and opened her mouth and immediately shut it. What could she say? Deep breath. "Honey, I think he's busy. Maybe we can go ask Carol if he's there. He might have a client."

Bea knew what that meant, since Katty had become his paralegal. Bea knew that meant go get the coloring books and color or draw. And be quiet.

"Okay. We can get some ice cream then." Bea clapped her hands. "Can we go in now?" She yawned. "I want my cereal."

"Time to get our shopping done and go home for a nap before anything else." Katty unbuckled her. "You just got out of the hospital! So we need to get home and get some rest!"

She helped Bea out of the car and onto her feet. All those times when Katty had been drunk and had just left Bea home alone. Once, Katty had actually been partly sober by the time she'd gotten home around noon. She had looked everywhere for Bea and become terrified. Finally, when Katty was about to give up and call the police—which would have been bad—she saw Bea's foot sticking out from under the old rocking chair. She had rushed to it and found her, all wrapped in a little tent of her own making under the seat of the chair. Still shuddering and sobbing, but asleep, sucking her thumb. Bea never sucked her thumb, but she had then.

Katty got her purse and ran after Bea to the store entrance where a man who was coming out, loaded down with bags of groceries, held the door open for them.

"Hey little one." He looked up at Katty. "Is she the little girl that got shot? How is she doing?" He didn't stop talking long enough for Katty to answer. "That old man—shooting innocent kids. Awful. I'm glad he is getting locked up. What did he need a gun at the nursing home for anyway?"

Wait. What?

"Clarence didn't shoot her!" Katty ran after him to his car. "He didn't shoot her!" She caught hold of one of his bags and stopped him. "The guard shot her and him!" She was yelling. "Clarence got shot too!"

He yanked the bag out of her hand and opened his car door. "Not what I heard. He shot her and then shot himself."

Katty stomped her foot and snapped at him. "He did not! Clarence is our friend. He is like a grandfather to me—to us!" Emotions boiled over. Frustration at this man and the gossipmongers of the community. Lies. Pain of seeing her own daughter shot. Terror—would she die? The pain and horror of Phil's abuse, her own parents abuse. Fear of being alone with those voices. Everything rose up at once as she pounded the hood of his pickup. "The *guard* shot Bea and Clarence."

"Mommy?" Bea sang out from the open door of the grocery store, Mandy Ashton standing behind her, holding the door open. "Are you coming?" She held up a box of cereal from behind her back. "I found my cereal."

Mandy grinned. "She's ready to eat it and that's okay. I just wanted to make sure it was okay that you buy it before I let her open it."

Small town grocery store.

Katty watched as the man backed out of the parking space. She stepped off the curb following the truck out of the parking place. She flipped him off, then caught herself. Some habits took longer to break.

"Mommy!" Bea was persistent and Katty didn't want to tire her.

She wished she could follow that man to wherever the other gossipers were and set them straight. Where was Clarence right now? Maybe Sheriff would know how he was.

She walked to the store. Bea was so cute, waving the cereal box at her.

"Can we buy this Mommy?" Bea shoved the box in Katty's face.

Every bright color, especially red, exploded in front of her eyes. Crazy figures and characters ran across the picture and a graphic of the cereal came close to jumping off the box.

Katty laughed. "Are you sure this is the one, Bea? I mean you seem a little unsure!" She scooped her up into her arms and squeezed her tenderly. "I love you!"

"Let's get a cart. We might need one."

"No doubt." Katty broke a cart free and sat her in the cart. "I think you should ride today, okay?"

"Okay, Mommy." Bea grinned. "That way I can see everything."

"Thanks Mandy for corralling her." Katty pointed outside. "That man out there was saying that *Clarence* shot Bea and I had to set him straight."

Mandy nodded. "That's what everybody is saying. I don't know what they all have against him except he was in prison before. He's a good man." She hugged Bea. "Is she okay? We all heard she was dead."

Bea patted her chest. "I'm not dead. I'm alive!" She stretched her arms up for emphasis.

Mandy hugged her again. "You sure are alive! And we're glad you are."

John Potter sauntered to the check stands. "She *is* alive!" He bopped her nose. "We heard that those cereal balls," he tapped on the box, "kidnapped you and carried you off to … Cereal Land and made you queen of their clan. You get to eat their cereal all the time and live happily ever after." He bowed low. "Queen Bea." He chuckled.

Bea's eyes popped. She looked at Katty and Mandy, then back at John. "Really? I dreamed that I think."

Katty wiped her eyes. "Oh you guys. You make me laugh when I need it."

"That's what the sign outside says. Didn't you see it?" John spread his arm wide, as he said the words. "Blank blank blank—the place where the employees make you laugh." He pointed outside. "It's up there … or it was yesterday."

Bea looked outside wide-eyed as Katty wheeled her away.

"Let's buy our stuff and get home, Bea." Soup. Crackers. She'd only been gone from home twenty-four hours, but couldn't remember what they needed.

"'Roni." Bea pointed. "Shells." She started to stand but one word from Katty and she sat down. "Cookies, Mommy."

Oh no. The toy section.

Bea stood up in the cart without any struggle or pain and began to inspect every toy.

Mandy was stocking gum in the same aisle. "She's doing good, isn't she?" She stood and adjusted her apron and retied it. Her round belly filled it out. "She moved easy enough. Is she going to be okay?'

"Yeah. They did surgery and took out the bullet. It was right next to her liver, but didn't do any real damage, other than to make a hole in her."

Bea didn't miss a thing. "There's a hole in me?"

"Yes. It's so we can feed you cereal right there instead of wasting time feeding you through your mouth," Katty laughed. "We'll just pop it in that hole and … " Bea's face was so funny—her mouth dropped open and eyes perked up bright and happy.

"Really?"

"No. I'm just teasing. They fixed it all up when you were in the hospital. No holes!"

Bea wasn't listening. She was reaching for a doll, then a stuffed kitten. And a … oh how to say no to her today. With what she'd just been through. It had broken both their hearts when Katty had said no to the beautiful red bike. Seemed like a million years ago.

If it wasn't from Clarence, then who?

"Mommy. This? And this? Can I have this one too?"

Bea was so cute. So pretty. Flashback to when she came out of surgery, all hooked up to machines and pale as the white lights.

"Sure. Put them in the cart. We need milk and bread."

Bea broke in. "And peanut butter. Remember we were out."

Katty tapped her on the nose. "We were. Good job remembering."

They picked up a few more things and hit the check stand.

"Look at all this fun stuff, Bea." Mandy handed the toys to John. "Can I come over to play, too?"

John bagged the groceries and toys and held one up. "What's this? They didn't have this when I was a boy."

Mandy chuckled. "You *are* a boy!"

Bea grabbed it from him. "It's a cubic rube. A round one." She flipped it to the backside, all encased in a clear plastic cover. "See all the pretty colors?"

She didn't have a clue how to twist it to make the game work. Katty bet she'd figure it out fast though. Bea was so smart.

"Okay Bea. We have to get you home to rest." Katty picked her up out of the cart and let her walk. "Thanks Mandy. See you."

"Yeah, Katty." Mandy followed her to the door. "And don't let those people in the gossip factory get to you. You know the truth." She nodded. "We know the truth about Clarence. He's our friend."

"Yup. He's a good guy."

Katty drove into her driveway and helped Bea to the house.

By the time she had unloaded the groceries, Bea had the packages opened and the toys all around her on the floor, playing. Cereal boxes surrounded her too.

Katty'd given into every whim. She'd made Bea give up that red bike from nowhere so she guessed some cheap little toys and cereal would be okay.

"Look Mommy. This doll's eyes open if you sit her up and close when you lay her down. She's so pretty."

"So are you!" Katty picked up the trash. "Bea, I'm going out to get the mail and I'll be right back."

Bea hadn't even heard her, she was so immersed in her playing.

Now that Katty was assured that Bea was all right, all she could think about was Clarence. She'd forgotten to go to the Sheriff's. Maybe she could call.

Not much mail—a newsletter from the hospital, she must be on their mailing list now. A flyer from the grocery store—she should start reading those and shopping by them. Two credit card applications.

And a note. To Bea. Weird.

She flipped it to the back and then the front again, as she walked into the house. Dropping the rest of the mail on the counter, she examined the envelope.

That handwriting.

The way the sender had written the capitol R in Randolph. It curled to a tail at the bottom of the R, then swooped it around under the rest of her last name.

Her heard pounded. She swallowed.

Only one person made his Rs that way.

TWENTY-ONE

Phil had raised his hand in the air, chanting with the inmates. "Bea is dead. Bea is dead." Even though he was as much in the flow of evil as anyone there, he'd had trouble saying those words.

When he had tried to say the words, he couldn't, even though Warden had assured him Bea wasn't dead.

He must really be her father and not some slime-ball Katty had gone to bed with. Otherwise, saying those words wouldn't get to him.

It was startling the way everyone had been engaged with the beat and the words. Lex, right next to him, backed away to the wall behind them. He'd done his share of battles and stupid, but even Lex seemed shocked.

Phil had watched as every face in every cell had become his own dad.

Ew.

The face and time was imprinted in Phil's memory. He'd been just a kid, like maybe ten.

His dad had been such a fake. Meat cutter at the local grocery store by day and priest of the local cult by night. His day job served him well—he was the everyday neighbor and friend. People confided in him and women flirted with him, which helped fill an already long list for his harem. He was King Pin in his own life and mind.

But the deeper he got into his night life, the harder and more abusive he became. A man at the store called him High Priest, which earned the man a fierce look from Dad. Phil hadn't known what that meant until later.

The expressions Phil had witnessed on all the faces at the prison as they frolicked, was the same as he'd see on Dad, when he'd come to the store after school. Dad was supposed to pick him up and he'd waited thirty minutes before he started walking.

At the store, he'd pulled the heavy door into the meat room open and greeted his dad, but his dad appeared to be zoned out—in some sort of ecstatic state. Chunks of meat were all around him on the counter, on the floor. Blood dripped off the cutting table. His eyes were just staring, and he was licking blood from around his lips.

Phil had hated the stench of the meat room anyway, but the acrid smell that day had made his eyes burn.

He'd tried to wake his dad. Called his name several times. Phil hadn't wanted to go near him. Only when the store owner tapped Phil's dad on the arm did he start awake again, lost in the horrible dreams he must have been in. He had been holding the meat knife in one hand and when he woke, startled, he just about stabbed the owner in the chest. Phil was mortified at what the owner had seen of his dad, but at the same time he was titillated and entranced, drawn into the ecstasy.

His father's blood ran through his own.

That had been the expression on every face at the prison.

He'd tried to join in the revelry and wanted to, especially when one of the women danced near the stairway downstairs. He'd found himself drawn down there, but when he glanced back at Lex, the expression of fright on his face stopped him.

Lex had been scared? What a baby.

If Phil had admitted it, he had been too. But he'd also been excited.

From Dad's face to the real faces, from Warden's face to Dad's face.

A woman had slipped upstairs and run straight to Warden, only he'd rebuffed her, taken her hand and placed it in Phil's.

"For you, Brother."

The video that played in his head at that moment was the same one as when his own dad had done exactly the same thing at a cult meeting.

Dad had led a young woman to Phil, placed her hand in his and said, "For you, Son."

The only time he'd called Phil anything but Bastard.

TWENTY-TWO

Noell walked home from the hospital. What a strange day, outside and inside. Her heart was full after all she'd seen in that hospital room with Katty and little Bea.

What was that? What were they? They looked like little Christmas lights, only they moved! By themselves!

Had to be real because Bea and Katty kept talking like they saw them too. Like they'd seen them before.

Noell thought at first they were reflections from outside, like a car driving past and the sun beaming off the car and then it flashed inside, along the walls. Only the sun wasn't out much. The cloud cover was complete. Odd for a late August day.

Or if the sun had been shining through the windows, they could have been dust specks floating through a sun beam. Gamma used to call them angel dust.

But the sun hadn't been shining in.

What would science call them? She opened the browser on her phone. But what should she google? Sun beams? Angels?

She stared into the distance and stumbled over a curb. The sparks of light seemed real, seemed to be something or someone.

Someone?

Yes. Because they interacted with Bea. They moved around her and Katty. Not Katty as much as Bea. They had landed on Bea's hands and head. Even on her nose, which Bea said tickled. She had held out her hand and three landed there.

Noell smiled. They were real. A real *something*. Noell saw the lights flitting here and there. Katty saw them too.

Her newly awakened science mind wanted to find answers. But the rest of her wanted it to be real, not something that could be explained away. Spiritual. Real, but God. No matter if they were angels or God. Whatever else He had up His sleeve, she wanted it to be Him. Real.

She was automatically heading home but as she crossed the highway from the convenience store, and looked both ways at the railroad tracks, her heart fluttered.

The pool.

She didn't want to go home. Nobody was there. It had become a lonely place. She hadn't seen her neighbor, Fletch, for a long time because he had a full-time job now. Were they becoming adults? He had a full-time job and she was a home owner.

Before she had gone to the nursing home and found all the chaos and then to the hospital, she had made the decision to sell that old house and all its contents and live in the camper.

Maybe that would have to get put off—at least until Clarence came back.

She shook her head and found herself stepping over the embankment. Since all that had gone on at the pool, the park board had deemed it necessary to build a short wall around it to prevent kids from wandering in. But she still knew how to get in.

Looking behind her, she checked to see if anyone was watching. Houses lined the park border on the west and north. Railroad tracks lined the south and a road on the east.

But that was stupid. There was no one about and how could she expect to see if someone was watching from a house? Always so afraid of what people would see. Always concerned with what would people think.

Nobody cared. Nobody.

Except for the gossipers. They seemed to have a radar for seeing and hearing about people, to have something to gossip about. She knew all about that. She'd been the butt of jokes and gossip all her life.

"What happened to your mom, little girl?"

"Why do you live with your grandma?"

"Why doesn't she ever have company?"

"The mailman says that when he hand delivers mail, he sees all the junk in her house."

The junk. The clutter.

And no Mommy.

Made the junk even more visible when there wasn't a person to see or talk to.

That might be the real reason she wanted to put off going home.

She stepped down into the cave where the pool was. She hadn't been in there since she rescued Clarence that day. She had told herself she would come back often to research it. To study it. But what did she know about doing that?

All she knew right now was that this place made her feel peaceful. She could breathe here. She could think and dream in here, no matter that the place made some people creep out. She should have felt that way too, what with her nightmares and all.

She sat on the rock next to the pool. She'd study that too. Nightmares and dreams.

Next time she'd bring her notebook. Maybe Dr. Steven's journal from the camper. Let him help her research this cave and pool.

She dangled her necklace—the same necklace she had dropped into the pool. Only this time she didn't fear jumping in after it.

She loved how the simple but limited light caught on the necklace as it twirled, casting reflections onto the rock walls of the cave. They resembled letters, maybe a different language. There was stuff carved into the walls in places and the reflections seemed to highlight them.

The water felt just like she remembered it—silky and oily at the same time. She hooked her necklace around her neck and trailed her fingers in the water again. It almost felt like baby oil, only thinner. And cleaner feeling. It had more substance than the water out of her tap at home.

She wanted to go in, and she would again, before it got cold. Reminder: bring extra clothes and a towel. That journal and her notebook.

She stuck her fingers in again and it felt like it went through something. Like when she combed her fingers through her hair and they scratched her head. Through the hair strands.

She glanced at her phone beside her. What if when she tapped the glass screen, her finger went through? That it went through the glass but to another realm or another place?

She picked it up and tapped it. An app opened. That was it.

But what if it could go through and enter somewhere else?

Like in a sci-fi novel. Or movie, when a portal opened up and the character ran through it to another dimension.

What if she stuck her fingers into glue? Stupid. They'd just get glue all over, not go through to anywhere. To the glue dimension. Duh.

When she was little, she had been entranced by TV, the scenes, the characters in the program. Gamma and even Grandpa had to pop her on her fingers because she'd always go to the TV and try to touch the trees or people she saw there.

What if she could have gone in there and touched them?

Or better yet, what if she could have gone into the TV, her whole body, through that glass and lived in the story?

It was the same feeling she had felt when she laid down on the carpet in the living room and imagined herself walking on the ceiling —a whole new world. Her bed could have been over there. Her chair in the corner above Gamma's red leather couch.

She forgot about her phone in her hand and almost let it slip into the water. It hadn't but what if she could have gone in after it and the whole pool was the open door to a different realm?

She was getting excited.

Back to the lights in Bea's room at the hospital. What if they were real and part of another realm that humans could access.

She dangled her finger into the pool and wondered.

The water was just molecules, right?

That stopped her.

Right?

She was just a bunch of molecules zooming around each other. Some were for skin. Some for inside organs. Maybe?

Science class seemed ever so much more fun right now than it had in high school.

She knew she had been led here. Definitely to the camper to find the journals and then to explore this place. Maybe this pool, this cave was a place where people had felt close to God. She certainly did. It made her think of Him and think of the eternal, but wonder what He had in store for her, her life.

She tapped on the rock that she sat on.

That was made up of molecules, right?

She stabbed her finger there again. "Ow!"

She sucked on her finger. What if there was another realm through there? If she was made of molecules and the rock was too, why couldn't she stick her finger through the rock?

That stopped her.

What if she couldn't get it back out?

TWENTY-THREE

Michael watched as Noell unhooked her necklace. He nodded at her angel, Jasper.

There was freedom from the Father for Noell. Freedom to explore this part of her life. Freedom for her in this time of her life.

"Father is pleased she is here and we are to support her in this journey of exploration." Michael nodded at the pool. "This pool has been one of pain and loss. Of people being robbed of their destiny, but no more." He pointed at Noell. "She will take it back for what Father really intended."

Jasper nodded. As Noell's angel, he had the mandate to protect and guard her. He had been assigned to her from her entrance into the Earth realm at her birth. He stood by her, ministering to her from the Father's heart.

Jasper smiled as Noell tapped on the rock. "She's gonna try it sometime and when she does the whole world will open up to her. She has the Einstein heart and spirit, doesn't she?"

Michael chuckled. "Yes she does. And more." He shook his head. "They all have so much more to explore, but they just tap on their phones."

They watched as Noell stood and stretched. "Note to self—bring notebooks and Dr. Stevens journal next time." She wandered next to the cave walls and shone her phone flashlight onto the rock. "Things are written here." She tapped her phone to the camera and snapped a few photos. "I should find Gamma's old camera and take pictures of each drawing or words. I love that old camera." She traced the lines with her finger. "Something else is here. Before I felt evil at times, but now it's different. I wonder why."

Jasper started to open his mouth but shut it. He motioned to Michael. Pointed to his own chest, then his mouth, then to Noell.

Michael slowly shook his head. "We're not opening up that portal, brother. It's not our call. She has to initiate it. Plus, Father's plan is in place. He is opening up the humans to this realm, but they have to learn to storm heaven."

Jasper nodded. "I want that interaction."

"We all do. But it can't happen until time. Time when all is in place. Time when the sons of God are ready, and some are more than ready. Doing everything that Yeshua did on earth and more."

"But some?" Jasper raised his eyebrows.

"Some are not even realizing they are sons of God. They are still … well, let's just say they're not ready." Michael smiled at Noell. "She hasn't had any training along those lines—wondering if she can push her hand through rock—but she is just about there." He squinted. "She would never say that though."

Noell broke in, still unaware of their presence. "Gamma always used to say she felt close to God on her red leather sofa." She grinned and wiped a tear. "I would too. It's beautiful."

She gazed at every crevice, every chunk of rock. "I feel close to Him … " She paused and tried again, looking up. "I feel close to … You God, here. Right here in a cave." She grinned. "Why a cave and not that church where Gamma's service was?"

Jasper nodded at Michael. Precious moments only an angel could witness. And the Lord.

Noell spoke the answer to her own question. "That church belongs to something or someone else. You God, don't live there."

She touched the rock wall, rotated and scanned the cave again, her fingers connecting with the rough, damp surface. "When I think about it, I think some people would have a problem with me saying You live in a cave when ages and years have been spent building massive and gaudy churches for ... not You." She sighed. "For them."

Michael pointed at Noell. "She is closer to Him right now than most humans."

Jasper nodded and grinned. "In a cave."

Noell lifted her hands, eyes closed. "I want to know *You.*" Her eyes blinked open. "Who You really are."

A cloud drifted into the cave, filling every crevasse, every crack.

Michael blinked as Noell knelt onto the cold, hard floor, her arms still extended high.

Jasper swallowed and closed his eyes, his wings unfurled.

Michael bowed his head, hands open. His body and wings expanded along with Jasper's.

"Lord, I love You." Noell whispered.

Michael nodded as another angel dropped in, his hand across his chest. The angel nodded in acknowledgment.

Another flew in.

And another.

Soon, there were many and the cave was crowded.

All surrounded precious Noell, as she worshipped, totally unaware of anyone but the Lord.

TWENTY-FOUR

Clarence waited while Ralston unlocked the cell door. Two other guards stood behind them, ready to beat him down if he tried anything.

Clarence could have found his way there himself. For some reason they put him in his old cell—the one he had been in when they had kicked him out, months ago. Up the steps and half-way down the corridor.

As he stood there, it felt like he had never left. Only, a chill swept around his shoulders, a ghostly presence engulfed him, a faint howl echoed through the corridors.

He shivered when the door slid open and Ralston pushed him inside the cell.

The noise must have triggered the neighbors, because inmates on both sides rattled the bars on their doors and began to heckle him.

"Hey baby. Welcome home."

One man close by must have remembered Clarence. "Clarence, we killed Dirko for you! He didn't like it without you anyway."

Another man piped up. "Yeah baby. And we helped staff make your new bedroom very comfy. We painted over your love notes to that bitch, Annie."

Clarence held his breath.

Ralston laughed. "Oh, you big meanies. That's not nice." He pushed Clarence onto the pull-down bed. "Here you go. Home at last." He rapped Clarence on the head with his beat stick. "Now don't go redecorating the walls or nuthin. You won't last very long in here, so don't make no more drawings. Otherwise we have to repaint and we don't want to. Got it?"

Clarence literally remembered every drawing, every word he'd written or carved into the walls. He could close his eyes right now and visualize them all. He could read the walls from inside his imagination —Annie and hearts, Dad, every important person in his life, words of encouragement, a calendar of days, months, and when time had stretched—years. He could read it all.

Ralston slammed the cell door with extra vigor and inserted the keys with a flourish.

Damn guard loved putting him back into prison.

Damn him!

Clarence stood too fast. The wound and bandage stretched and pulled. He stumbled to the bars and pushed against the door before Ralston had it locked. "You are a bastard! I don't belong here!"

The door knocked Ralston off balance and back into the cell block railings. The guards pushed him upright and tried to scramble around him to get to Clarence.

Clarence had already pushed his way down the walkway to the end of the cellblock. First one inmate yelled, then another, until the whole cellblock was in an uproar. Most were on Clarence's side for the first time since he'd been back. They wanted to be the one to be running free, even though there were three guards running up the steps, ready to capture Clarence as soon as he ran down the steps. One minute they taunted him, the next minute they cheered him on.

The bandage had torn off when he broke through the two guards upstairs and he could feel the T-shirt fabric rubbing against the wound as he ran. He was going to pay for running. He was going to pay for breaking through the other guards. He'd pay for pushing Ralston against the bars. He'd pay big.

But he couldn't let them think he'd gotten soft and wimpy. He had to be tough.

Or die.

"Cla-rence! Cla-rence! Cla-rence!" The inmates chanted just as they had when they chanted "Bea is dead. Bea is dead." Two-faced bastards. Hypocrites.

The guards just stood and waited for him to get downstairs. They weren't even focused. Lazy bums.

Just as he got halfway down the steps, a dietary staff pushed a fully loaded cart out of the hallway to Clarence's right. It was loaded with cases of soda, blocking the guards from Clarence. Blocking Clarence's escape.

He thought.

He turned right into the same hallway and pulled the heavy cart in behind him. He had no idea how to get outside or if he even could.

He'd die trying.

But he wasn't going to be a pawn or sissy or lily-livered. They'd have to work to keep him in check and locked up. Or kill him.

He almost ran into another kitchen staff. He remembered her. She was the one who gave him the hand knitted scarf!

"In there!" She pointed to a door. "In through there, Mr. Clarence!"

He slammed into the door, right into the kitchen—right into supper prep—pans and loaded carts everywhere.

He couldn't stop his momentum and overturned several carts, meatballs flying everywhere. Seemed like the kitchen staff was all on his side, because carts and equipment parted, clearing a path through the chaos. A door opened at the far end of the kitchen and Clarence ran toward it.

A semi truck was parked right outside the door, the delivery man was checking his clipboard just as Clarence jumped from the building. His eyes popped, seeing Clarence running toward him. He stepped aside.

How had he gotten this far?

But three guards ran from the back of the truck to the loading dock and two more ran from the front end, surrounding Clarence.

The kitchen noise behind him was deafening, the inmates working in there cheered him on. But when they saw he might get caught, they threw pans and utensils—anything they could get their hands on.

The guards drew their guns.

A tall inmate from the kitchen pulled Clarence back inside and slammed the door. "Dude. You're gonna get killed. You can't get outa here. You don't have a gun and you're bleeding."

Clarence glanced down at his shirt. Yup.

Three guards skidded in behind Clarence and grabbed him just as a pot of hot spaghetti sauce flew through the air and landed on one of the guards. "Gaaa!" He screamed, trying to wipe it from him. "I'm burning!"

Clarence jumped back, just in time to land into the arms of a guard who was prepared with handcuffs. The guy was quick. He had them over his wrists and clicked before the other guard had quit screaming.

Clarence shuddered.

He was dead. His heart pounded.

Whatever made him think he could escape?

The guards shoved him back through the kitchen. The kitchen staff cheered him on, but they weren't the ones that would be beaten, he was sure of it. They wouldn't feel the brunt of breaking away. They were thrilled right now, but he would pay for their thrill soon enough.

The guards marched him through the kitchen and past the scarf woman—"Dorothy" her name tag read. She wiped her eyes. "I be praying for you, Mr. Clarence."

He nodded. "Pray for my little Bea. She got shot too."

Dorothy's eyes widened. "They shot you?"

He nodded and lifted his shirt.

She covered her mouth with her hands. "You-you need a doctor."

The guards dragged him away, but he turned them all back toward Dorothy. "Thank you for my scarf. I still have it in my room at the nursing home. Maybe I'll even get to wear it … I hope."

She nodded as they marched him away, her hands together at her mouth.

The closer the guards got to his cell, the fiercer and unrestrained they became, giving him a punch here and there.

When they reached his cell, the noise was thunderous. Inmates stomped on the floor which made the whole floor shudder and creak.

Ralston squealed. "We gonna break the prison!" He gripped the walls. "In here. Git 'em in here now!"

In that single second before they shoved Clarence into the cell, he glimpsed Warden at the end of the cellblock, surrounded by several men, hit men Clarence guessed. Warden had a smirk on his face, like Clarence was playing directly into his hands. Doing exactly what he had foreseen and getting exactly what Warden had wanted all along.

The breath went out of Clarence's chest, like a beast had just butted him. What had he been thinking? What had made him think he could outrun guards who were half his age? That he wouldn't suffer any consequences— like beatings and maximum lockdown?

Stupid. Stupid.

This was probably what had happened to Dirk. Huge, dark-skinned, friendly Dirk. Prison had been his only family and that was his only crime.

As the guards pushed him into the cell, they descended on him, like gnats on dying fruit. Pummeled him. They punched him over and over in the wound, till he didn't feel anything anymore.

He would not die. He had to make it back to Bea and to Katty. Mrs. Hatly.

His last thought before he lost consciousness—he loved his little family in Osceola, and he might never see them again.

TWENTY-FIVE

Katty shuddered as she let go of the notecard and watched it flutter onto the counter beside the cereal box.

Bea sat before the TV, watching her favorite show—The Gummy Family. Why that was her favorite, could only be explained by her love of the candy. Otherwise the show had no merit at all.

Back to the note. Katty had thought Phil was dead after he had left Bea to burn on the slide in the park. *She'd* almost burned to death because of him. Surely Phil had been locked up somewhere. Sheriff hadn't told her he was loose. Maybe she had just … hoped he was dead.

Well, she'd march over to the sheriff's department and make sure he knew Phil was still stalking them.

She tapped her fingernails against the cereal box. Bet the bike had been him too. So like him. Make others believe he was a saint.

Bea loved that bike and thought whoever dropped it off, tied with a big red bow, was the best person in the world.

And Katty looked like a bitch—a crabby old bitch—because she had made Bea give up the bike.

Grrr!

She was glad they hadn't kept it and hoped that whoever had it now was happy, but she wavered back and forth. Should she have let Bea keep it or given it away?

Gravel crunched. A vehicle had driven in her driveway.

She peeked out and froze.

A cop.

Her old mentality kicked in, until she realized she didn't have anything to hide. She hadn't done anything bad.

Whew.

Maybe it was from the shooting and they needed more information. Or maybe Sheriff wanted to make sure Bea was okay.

Ha. Ha. Like that'd ever happen. He was a nice guy and all, but why would he worry about her and Bea.

The deputy replaced his radio and opened the car door, stepped out and walked to the deck.

Glad the deck was fixed. It looked so much better.

Still, her breathing was coming in gasps. Her face felt hot and she was sweating.

She opened the door just as he reached up to knock.

He stood there poised, eyes wide, mouth open. "Uh, hello."

"Hi." She looked behind him at his patrol car. "Nice car. All nice and shiny."

He glanced behind him and let his arm drop. "Thanks."

No distractions. Back to her. "Are you Katty Randolph?"

"Yes." She cleared her throat. "Yes I am." She tapped her fingers against her leg. Evidently he wasn't going to start the conversation. "I just re-upped my car registration—last week—as a matter of fact." She kept on tapping. "And my bills are paid." Thanks Clarence.

He brushed his hand at her. "Oh, no. That's all good. Um. I'm Officer Scott and that's not why I'm here." He checked inside. "Mind if I come in?" He slowly fished his identification out of his back pocket and showed it to her.

"Uh-okay." Officer Scott. She stepped aside to let him in.

He smiled as he entered the house and removed his ball hat. "I see you have a little girl."

Katty glanced at Bea and swallowed. "I probably shouldn't let her watch so much TV, but we just got home, and I was putting groceries away." Truth. Well kinda. She had really been wanting to kill Phil Daynton, so maybe her murderous vibes had reached the police department.

"Oh no. She's fine." He cased the kitchen area. "Is there someplace where we can talk?" He tipped his head toward Bea. "Someplace more private?"

Katty frowned. Didn't sound like a true cop request to her. "Private?" Was this a come-on?

He shook his head. "Someplace away from your daughter."

"Oh." She shrugged. "Outside?" She pointed to the door. "On the deck?"

"She'll be okay?" He pointed over his shoulder at Bea.

"Yeah. We won't be long, right?" She opened the door. "Bea, this kind man wants to talk to me a minute. I'll be right outside."

Bea didn't move or turn her head.

"She'll be okay."

He chuckled. "Must be a great show. I should find out what it is and watch it myself."

She stepped to the deck.

He closed the door partway, checking to make sure Bea was still watching TV and that they could still see her from there.

He cleared his throat and glanced at the neighboring trailers.

Katty began to lose patience. "What is this about? And why all the secrecy?"

He reached into his pocket again and pulled out a paper.

She'd seen those before. "A summons for my arrest?"

"No. Just a complaint filed against you."

She fumbled with her thumb, her fingers circling it. "A-Against me?" That old presence of fear sat on her chest.

"Yes." He took a deep breath and watched her face. "Someone reported that they felt you were abusing your daughter."

Katty stopped. "Uh … when was this filed? Because she just got out of the hospital. Today. There was stuff going on just these last few days."

He checked the paper. "This was from three days ago."

Katty blinked. She wanted to cry. "Did they say what I did?" She fell back into the defensive druggy misfit character. The lines she used to feed the cops then, wanted to flow out of her mouth.

"Look. This is just a complaint." Officer Eddington waved her to the small table and chairs. "Can we sit?"

Katty nodded. She motioned for him to take a chair and she sat in the other one, taking time to glance inside. Bea hadn't moved. She had to be so exhausted.

"Is she okay?"

"Yeah. She just got out of the hospital and we needed to get some food, so she is really tired."

"I won't make this long." He folded the paper. "I just need to make sure you two are okay and see if there is anything we can do."

One of the neighbor kids rode by, younger siblings running along, their laughter barely broke through Katty's fog.

Who had turned her in?

Something clicked on though as she continued to squint. The sun glared off of … a red bike. A brand new, red bike. A spanking shiny new red bike!

She stood up and waved at the kids. They were so happy. Laughing and yelling. "My turn." If Bea couldn't have it, those kids deserved it.

Bet Mrs. Crabbyface had seen her with Bea when she'd discovered the bike. Katty had walked the bike to the huge trailer court dumpster with Bea following behind her, crying all the way. "Mommy, I'll be good. If you let me keep it, I'll pick up my room everyday … and and—"

Katty remembered her response and she had yelled the words, "Bea, you are in no way keeping this bike, if it's not from Clarence. I don't care what you do, you aren't keeping this bike."

Bet Mrs. Crabbyface had heard every word. She probably even pushed her window open just a little bit more so she could hear every word they had yelled.

But what Katty remembered next made her skin crawl. Cold shivers ran up her back.

She had spanked Bea.

And that must have set off the do-not-abuse-your-kids siren in the trailer court. Mrs. Crabbyface had seen her spank Bea and for her accusing heart, that was enough for her to call the cops on Katty.

Whew.

Katty sat down hard. "It was Mrs. Crabbyface, wasn't it? She is always spying on us." Katty turned to Officer Eddington and really saw him for the first time since he had knocked on her … door. Blue eyes. Short, sort of military cut blond hair. Kind of skinny, but not super tall. Freckles? Kind of cute.

"Mrs. Crabbyface?" He brushed his hand against his mouth. "We don't ever report who filed the complaint. We just follow up on it." He seemed to get uncomfortable. Blushing. He was blushing.

Katty realized she had been staring at him. She averted her eyes, but not before she caught him checking her out. Or was he assessing her like a good cop should? Checking her eyes for any sign of drugs or booze. Were her eyes bloodshot? Or did her breath reek of booze? Did her hands shake when she brushed back her hair?

Sigh. "You know Mrs. Crabbyface used to be nice."

"Nice?" He tilted his head toward that trailer.

That's who filed the complaint for sure. "Yeah. She really tried to help us back then. She was really sweet—bringing us sweet rolls, cookies. Tried to be friends or at least neighborly." She shook her head. "I was okay with it at first. Thought she'd make a good babysitter for Bea when I … when I went out." Katty looked away from him. Dang. Why had she gone there?

"Out?" He shifted on the chair.

She always managed to make guys uncomfortable, especially since she had quit using. "Yeah. I used to … I did … a lot." Courage girl. If she could ever have a relationship with a guy again, she'd have to start with truth. "Yeah. I did drugs. Booze. Everything."

He nodded and swallowed. "Me too."

She built up steam. "I did every party drug. Every hard drug. Booze."

"Me too."

"I … wait. What?" She stared into his face. Open as her Bible had been lately. "You too?"

He nodded.

"I started abusing her." Katty pointed toward the trailer. "I'd leave her all night alone. And part of the morning. Out all night." She wiped her eyes. "My parents did the same thing to me. No, I haven't been as bad as they were. They were …" She wiped her nose.

He just stared.

Why was she telling him all this? "But that's when Clarence came around pulled me out of that stuff."

"Clarence?" He pointed at her. "You mean the guy who got shot when your daughter did? That Clarence?"

Her nose began dripping. She grabbed a leaf of the lamb's ears in a pot nearby. Soft. She wiped her nose. Then blew it. On a leaf! "Yes, that Clarence. He happened to be sneaking back into the nursing home through the park. I was … and I almost … Bea." She choked. "Thank God he … got there when he did." She unconsciously waved as the kids rode by again. "I'll never forget the feel of his rough old hand in mine, as I took a swing at Bea—and I don't mean a park swing." She covered her face with her hands and sobbed. "You must think I'm awful."

"No." He shook his head and started to cover her hand with his, but removed it. "I don't think you're awful. We all have stuff. Junk." One nod. "Only most aren't as honest as you are." He adjusted his ball hat. "But Clarence. Is he a relative? Grandfather?"

Bea slipped out the door, carrying the box of cereal, shaking it. "Mommy, you should taste this! It's so good." She stopped. "You're crying." She glanced at the deputy, then climbed onto Katty's lap, placing the cereal on the table. She peeked at Officer Eddington from under Katty's arm. "Mommy? Why is he here? Are we in trouble?"

Katty peeked at him. "Well—"

He smiled at her. "No, you aren't in trouble. Some nice person told us you might need some help is all."

"Yeah. I got shot."

"I know you did. But you're better now, right?" He held out his hand to her.

Bea hesitated a minute. She walked over to him and crawled onto his lap. "I'm better. It still hurts. Some." She lifted her shirt. "That's where I got shot." She looked at Katty. "Mommy, we forgot to go see Clarence."

Officer Eddington straightened and glanced at Katty.

"I … I know we forgot Bea. But. Well. Clarence isn't at the nursing home right now."

"Did he go get groceries, too?" She shook the box again. "I should let him taste these. He'd like them."

Officer Eddington continued. "So Clarence is your relative?"

Katty shook her head. "No. He's a friend." Stress took its toll and she forgot about Bea. "And can you believe that a guy at the grocery store was saying that Clarence shot Bea?" Her jaw jutted out. "The guard shot Bea, then he shot Clarence."

"Who shot Clarence, Mommy?" Bea's eyes were wide. "Who shot him, Mommy? Did he get shot like me?" She stared at Katty then at Officer Eddington. "Is that why he's here?" She pointed at the officer and her chin began to quiver and her voice broke. "Mommy, where is Clarence?" She winced as she walked to Katty. "Mommy, why is he here?"

God.

The look on her face. It must have looked the same back when Katty was still using and trying to talk her way out of a jail sentence. She'd sweet talk the officer and when that didn't work, she'd throw a fit. Katty couldn't remember what Bea's face must have looked like back then, but it must have been exactly like it was now—terrified eyes wide, mouth open, tears running down her cheeks.

Katty gathered her in her arms. "Sweetie. We haven't done anything wrong. It's not like it used to be." Katty plunged in further. "And Clarence was shot trying to save you. And me."

TWENTY-SIX

Clarence couldn't remember where he'd been. He'd been somewhere, like a dream or existence. Another realm maybe. Another dimension. Felt like he'd been asleep for years instead of overnight. Lisha must have turned on the overheads. She must have drugged him.

He blinked and his eyes started watering. He reached to wipe them, but his hands wouldn't move. Couldn't move.

Man, whatever Lisha had given him had him slammed. His couldn't even make his body move, his hands move.

The more he tried to shift positions, the more he realized he was in pain. And deep pain—so deep that he couldn't feel until he moved. The pain as he tried to move woke up another pain and another and another until his whole body screamed.

Someone moaned.

Voices. Voices heard in the distance. Sounded like his head was in a can. When he was growing up, he had a friend who would always walk the distance to his house from town, just two miles or so. But Clarence could always hear him coming. He'd sing and throw rocks into the water in the ditch. Or he'd holler for Clarence when he was at about a mile from his place.

Voices from a distance. Another room. Another mile. Another time.

"He can't possibly live through all that."

"I told you to beat him, not kill him. I had future plans for him." A sick laugh followed.

"And you may kiss the bride." He shivered. She was so beautiful—had that glow about her.

"That kid'll turn out just like his dad. They both have sawdust for brains."

"Dawes Timmelsen has had his hands on every building in this town."

Voices.

"It'll kill him."

Clarence jolted. Nobody from Osceola, Nebraska had ever been sent to prison before him.

Tears wanted to break free.

No.

Judge Green had found him guilty and had shipped him off to prison without a thought for his future, his welfare. He just wanted revenge. Revenge for Clarence marrying Annie instead of what Judge Green had set up.

Well, he got it.

Maybe nobody from Osceola had ever been incarcerated before, but no one had ever lived to tell about it either. And he would. He was still young. He could rise above. It would take everything he had in him, plus what his dad and mom had put there, to survive. But he would do it.

Lights felt brighter.

Clarence blinked. Tried to open his eyes, only the light was blinding. Like a dentist light aimed directly into his eyes. Or piercing sunlight in winter.

His eyes watered. He tried to wipe the tears away but he still couldn't move.

Something, a cloth or tissue wiped his face. "There you go, Clarence."

He opened his eyes. Closed them.

Opened them to see a woman with the tissues in her hand. "That better, Clarence?"

A man stepped forward. "Don't baby him. He needs to get used to prison life."

Clarence moved his legs. Tried to sit up. To get up.

Nothing worked.

He looked down.

No.

Memories shifted with memories and they all collided. He wasn't that young man first convicted and sent to prison.

He was old Clarence back in prison. "What happened to me? I know I got shot, but—"

"You, sir, had the worst beating I have ever seen. I'm surprised you're not dead." The nurse shook her head and she tended to his IV. "Makes no sense to beat a guy to death, then give him medical attention to do it all over again."

Someone back against a wall cleared his throat. "That's enough. You take care of his needs and nothing more."

"Where am I?" Clarence looked around the room, then down at his body. "And what hap—" Then he remembered. All too clearly. They had taken him back to his cell after he escaped and beaten him. He must have blacked out at a certain point.

A black man in an expensive suit and tie stepped alongside his bed. Warden. "We're going to let you experience what you did to my brother, Lewis. No mercy. You killed him without giving him a chance to live." He half laughed and half growled. "We're just going to let you experience that over and over and over ... until you can't heal or get back up. Just like Lewis."

Chills skittered through Clarence, making every injured cell scream. This was it.

He'd never get back to Mrs. Hatly. Katty or Bea. That old saying was true. Distance made the heart grow fonder. Or something like that. Because just the thought of never seeing any of them again, made him hurt more than any beating. He'd started to let himself dream of the day he could walk one down the aisle—especially Katty—maybe even Bea if he lived long enough.

That probably wouldn't happen now.

Another man stepped from a darkened corner. Deep chuckle. "And while you are being well taken care of here, I'll be heading back to dear Osceola, Nebraska, to take care of two ladies for you."

Phil.

Lex stepped up beside him.

No.

Clarence's whole body went cold, from his feet to his head. He didn't even feel the old gunshot wound. Not even the new wounds, whatever they were.

Katty and Bea.

God.

Rage began to boil within, making his stomach tighten.

"You can't." He choked. "You-You … " He tried to move. Every part of his body that could be mobile, was shackled down to the table. Something had to come loose, even a finger to point into that evil man's chest. "You'll never get away with it. Too many people know them now and care about them. I'll kill you first."

Laughter erupted. Deep guttural laughter echoed off the walls. It was only a hospital size room, but it sounded like a huge cavern. The laughter expanded and filled the space, like thousands of people laughing together. The laughter turned taunting, then raucous.

Phil leaned close to Clarence's ear and growled. "Even if you do manage to get out of here—and I don't know how that would be humanly possible—your girls—Katty, and especially little Bea—will be different when you get back to them. I'll make sure of that." He tapped Clarence on his forehead. "Oh, I'll take good care of them for you, Clarence."

Clarence's insides wanted to explode. Every cell, every emotion, his whole gut wanted to chop Phil up in pieces and never put him back together—just like a horror version of Humpty Dumpty. Chop Phil up, so no one could put him back together. So he could never hurt his girls again.

He'd kill Phil Daynton. He'll rip his arms and legs off if he so much as touched Bea or Katty. He'd take his insides and … feed them to the hawk. Where had that hawk gone? Was he still at the park? Oh, that park—he missed it too.

If he ever got back to Osceola, he'd have to try to find that bird. It had been around when he'd first gone to Hillcrest—always.

What if that hawk had been an angel, too?

When Clarence had first been shipped off to the nursing home, all he dreamed of was to come back here—to prison—the only home he'd lived in that long—sixty years.

But now.

"How are you doing, Clarence?" That doctor with the googly eyes. He must be infested with about thirty demons to make his eyes dance like that. Must have played dominoes too much when he was younger. Dad always said that the game of dominoes was demonic, hence the name—demonoes. That was how Dad said it.

"We are moving you today, Clarence, so pack your bags."

He didn't have a thing of his own here with him. They'd ripped him out of his room and shot him and bussed him here. No bags. No toothbrush. Guess the prison would have to pay for one.

"Where are they moving me?" Clarence guessed after all the trouble he'd caused, he'd get to live out his life in death row. He'd at least caused supper to be late.

"Back to your cell. You cost the prison too much money to keep in Maximum Security. Besides there are friends there who would like to get reacquainted with you."

Clarence could only guess that reacquainted meant beat up again.

He had almost never prayed during his eighty years. He had no idea why he should start now. Did God ever listen? He knew God had never answered one way or another the last sixty years. He'd spend sixty years in prison with the love of his life dead.

That's the way God answered.

But at this moment in time, Clarence had no one else.

Where had Michael gone? Weren't angels allowed in prison? He guessed not, because even Michael had deserted him.

He wanted to wipe his eyes.

But there was something about God today.

Here.

Now.

The doctor had left the room so now was his chance.

Gulp. He literally had no one else. Carol always said she could feel people praying for her. Right now, Clarence could only feel his body waking up from the beating.

Tears threatened.

"God?"

It almost felt as if the Man upstairs was pulling on him. "God? You there? Where is Michael?" Did he really expect an answer?

He was beginning to hurt.

A lot.

"God, I don't know how to do this but … please take care of Katty and Bea. And Mrs. Hatly. And Carol. And Harold." He paused. "And Lisha." A sob surfaced but he swallowed it down. "And me, God. Help me."

"Aww. How sweet." That squeaky, voice.

Damn.

Tay Ralston looked over his shoulder at the guards following him through the door. "He's praying." He laughed. "That God of yours must not be listening to you because you are still here!"

Nasty laughter. Loud laughter.

Served him right. He should have known better. Never talk to God. Why would God have anything good for him? He'd lived eighty years and nothing good had ever happened in his life. Except Annie. And God had taken her away too.

He had given Clarence Katty and Bea and others. He was taking them all away.

God didn't care.

TWENTY-SEVEN

Noell woke, the sun streaming in through her window. She stretched and yawned. So good to have a day off from the Roads Department. She loved her job and pretty much liked, even loved the guys working with her. But today to sleep in and have the whole day to … wait. She had informed herself last night that she was cleaning the porch today.

Shoot!

Well. She would do it. No matter what.

She stretched again. Felt good. Slept well, except for the usual every-night-nightmare. If only she could have one night without it—one night!

You'd think for as many times as she'd experienced it, she would be used to it by now—that it wouldn't affect her.

Until she thought about it.

Everyone had dreams.

Everybody had nightmares, too.

But did everybody have the same nightmare over and over for … fifteen or so years?

Every night?

Every damn night?

She sat up. Maybe she should go to a doctor. A therapist.

She lay back down across the bed. For some reason this time, this morning, she didn't want to run away from the dream.

She only wanted to be rid of it forever.

And the more she thought about it, the madder she got.

Why couldn't she have some peace? If she couldn't have any family, why couldn't she have one night when that stupid dream didn't show up.

How does a dream happen anyway? What started it?

Who started it?

Did some demon sit there with a movie reel and hit start? Play the nightmare over and over? Must be how it happened.

Only this morning, she was getting angrier and angrier.

Somehow this had to stop because she didn't want to go to bed anymore, knowing she would have to face the dream again and again.

That first drip of water followed by a deluge, pouring over her.

Terror.

She couldn't breathe. She gasped, but she sucked water in. She was drowning.

That was bad enough, but then Mommy … Mommy appeared, her eyes wide, her mouth open in a scream that sounded like it came from every direction, wrapping Noell in more terror.

Even stranger—there were times during the day that the dream attacked and when it was over, water dripped, from her nose, her hair, her clothes. Real water. Really dripped. More than once, she had lied to Gamma about water dripping as she leaned to kiss her. Gamma had enough to worry about.

It was just a dream.

Probably nothing she could do, but what if there was?

Time at the cave yesterday had made her question everything. Even to where she tried sticking her hand through a rock!

So what if she could go back? Go back into that nightmare.

Wait. Why not go into Mommy's room. Would that take her closer? Would being near Mommy's clothes, her bedding and smells and keep-sakes … would that make it easier for her to go back in?

She sat up.

She wasn't sure if that was a good idea. Would she find herself trapped in some sort of time warp? Another dimension?

That'd be better than getting trapped in some rock.

Maybe in another dimension, she'd wouldn't have bad dreams.

She hesitated. then hopped out of bed, grabbing her flannel shirt and almost ran to Mommy's room. She'd never locked it back up and enjoyed seeing the door open when she came upstairs to go to her own room.

She turned on the light.

Flipped it off again and opened the shades and curtains, letting in natural light. Somehow she was sure that Mommy had loved sunlight when she had been alive. She even opened a window to freshen the air.

Then she turned into the room.

Beautiful. The sunlight zapped the yellow in the bedspread and it reflected into every corner of the room. Maybe she should move into this room.

No. She loved her room.

She sat on the bed and then slid onto the rug. She had no idea how to do this, but she knew for sure that somehow she was mad enough at the dreams that no matter what she had to do, she was going to take her life back and never let those dreams terrify her again.

She closed her eyes and prayed. "God?" She tried again. "God? If this is okay to do, please help me. Let me go back into that dream and make it stop!"

Quiet. She didn't move. She pictured the beginning of the dream when the water burst in on her. She had no trouble doing that. Visuals were clear. Every day when she closed her eyes, she could see that. When she wiped her eyes, when she put on mascara, when she blinked.

Here it came. The torrent of water.

Only this time, it was different.

This time she was in her mom's car in the back seat. The two of them were jabbering away about something. Making up and singing goofy songs about dinosaurs. She even remembered some of the words, "big fat tail, bang, bang." And, "tiny pea brain." She wasn't sure if she'd just made that up or if that was the way they sang it.

She just remembered a jovial time. It had been raining all day, but they still went shopping. At first it was cold and uncomfortable, but she remembered Mommy making it fun. They jumped over puddles that were getting bigger by the hour. Mommy had to help her over one by the curb. When they decided to stop for supper and watched it continue to rain while they dipped french fries into a shared ketchup container, Mommy called Gamma and told her they were on their way home—that it'd be half an hour or so.

Noell remembered the sound of Gamma's voice as she told them to be safe. They piled into the car, Mommy buckled her into her car seat and off they went, never realizing how much rain had fallen by that time.

Grampa once said since then that if he'd realized how much rain they had gotten, he'd have driven his pickup to get them. Or told them to find a motel room—a little hideaway retreat for the two of them.

They still sang songs, but Mommy seemed distracted. After awhile she just drove and Noell almost fell asleep until Mommy cussed. Mommy never cussed—at least not around Noell.

And that's when Noell noticed water over the road. Mommy tried to make up a song about driving through water but the words weren't as much fun as the dinosaur songs. Mommy leaned closer to the steering wheel maybe to see better. Noell had a clear view of water on the road.

Then Mommy's voice shook. Was she crying? "I can't see where the road is." The real words Noell would never forget and she still heard them in Mommy's voice. They were not anything she might have made up, "Oh no! I think we're in the river. I think the bridge is out!" Then a whole tree floated right for the car. It slammed into Mommy's door and shattered the glass.

Next thing Noell knew Mommy was floating and not talking. She must have gotten knocked out but when the cold water rushed in, she probably came to and realized the extreme danger they were in.

That's when Mommy swam over the seat like the car was in the bottom of the swimming pool, not just on a road covered with water.

Mommy's face would haunt Noell forever. Her eyes were huge and her mouth open, "Noell! Noell!" Her arms reached toward her, fingers fluttered like she was already unbuckling her. That's when the car must have slammed into the bridge and Mommy disappeared.

Even though Noell was a little girl of four years old, she would never know how she got out. Somehow her seat belt unbuckled and as she let herself go back into the memory, she remembered some hands lifting her out of the seat, then the car, then the river and she woke up higher on the river bank, lights blinding her and Grampa screaming their names.

Then she was safe in his arms. He trembled and shook.

When Noell looked up into his face, he was crying. Sobbing.

He had saved Noel.

But Mommy was lost.

Her last memory of Mommy was her terrified face.

How could Noell go back and change that? How could she do that? If she could, she'd go back and save Mommy. Someone had saved Noell, so why couldn't they have saved Mommy?

But what if … Noell tried to breathe, only the air stuck in her throat. What would make that nightmare just a dream and not something terrifying? What if she could change it and see Mommy smile? Feel her touch of love.

God.

Her throat tightened.

Noell laid back and stretched out on the rug, with Mommy's pillow under her head. All she wanted was peace. She didn't want to make God mad or stir up any demons. She just wanted to live in peace somehow.

She closed her eyes again and prayed. "God, if you are really who Gamma used to say you are, could you please help me see Mommy smile?

A photo of Mommy and Noell popped into her mind. She sat up. Mommy had been smiling and so had Noell in that picture. She even remembered where it had been taken. Just out in the back yard after they had picked strawberries from the garden and Noell had her mouth full. Red strawberry juice on her lips made it look like she had lipstick on.

Noell jumped up and ran down the stairs, jumping the last three just like she had as a kid. The photo was on the mantle across from Gamma's famous red leather sofa.

There!

Exactly as she had remembered. Right after Mommy drowned, Noell had practically slept with the framed photo. She had even taken it to school a time or two until the teacher sent it home with a note, "Please have Noell keep this photo at home. It is lovely though."

And right now, Noell could almost go back to the day it was taken, hearing the laughter, tasting the strawberries, the color so rich, the day so warm.

When Noell looked at the picture now, Mommy's expression was terrified just like in the nightmare. Eyes wide. Mouth open in a scream muffled by all that water.

"No!" She shoved it aside. "It's not like that! How did it change? She was smiling! I've looked at it all my life and she was smiling!" Noell almost screamed.

Just that fast, the vision started like it had everyday when she came through the front porch door. She'd open it and the clutter seemed to slide toward her off the piles. Then it would turn into water in the vision. The water was always real—again she'd lie to Gamma and tell her that somebody had their sprinklers on and she'd gotten hit.

This time the water crashed toward her in the vision, more violently than it ever had, almost knocking her over physically. These visions were too real. She hung onto the railing as she waded up the stairs that she'd just run down. The water rushed down the steps like a waterfall might over huge boulders. It took all her strength to hang on and pull herself up the steps.

She would not let this beat her. She had to stand firm.

When she reached the landing, the railing was bending under the weight of the water. Thunder! She heard thunder—like a storm had hit in her house—flashes of light startled her. She looked toward the windows and the bright day had turned into a dark sky.

Impossible!

Whoever had taken over her dream had now raised the bar. The terror ramped up a notch or two. Not only was the water even more violent but there was wind.

She grabbed the doorknob to Mommy's door. As she passed her own door which was open, her own room seemed undamaged, unaffected. No rain. No wind. That was tempting, but she plunged on into Mommy's room and crawled the rest of the way to the bed.

She dove for the middle of the bed, clutching the photograph to her chest. She could feel the sides of the car around her and her car seat under her bottom.

Mommy was in the front seat.

If the dream had been a nightmare, then this reality was a horror movie.

The car lurched just as it had when it hit the bridge. Mommy seemed unconscious, but then slowly turned to Noell.

Noell covered her face. She didn't want to see this. It would be some sort of ghoulish face, a Halloween horror mask.

Noell screamed.

She peeked through her fingers. It wasn't an awful mask. It was Mommy, beautiful Mommy, reaching out to Noell, a sweet expression on her face, eyes full of love and her mouth open but in a kiss. Noell could almost hear Mommy crooning to her, to be a good girl, to help Grampa and Gamma.

Had Noell pictured Mommy wrong all along? Had the sweet smile from the photo switched with reality in her nightmares?

She lifted the frame from her chest.

Ohhh.

The smile was back in the photo.

Noell closed her eyes and focused on Mommy's face—the last visual of Mommy—sweetness, full of love.

No terror.

No fear.

Just love.

TWENTY-EIGHT

Clarence could barely move, but pushed himself to flop his feet over the side of his bed and sit upright. He began to sweat with the exertion, his vision blurred. The bars swam in front of him.

Didn't matter when he'd eaten last. Whatever was still in his stomach was working its way up.

"Take deep a breath, real slow." A voice from his past? A voice inside his head. That made sense. He had to be crazy to still be alive.

Clarence looked up and realized the voice had come from a man standing at the bars. "Yeah. Real easy considering they probably broke my ribs." He tried it though. Helped with the blurring. His stomach contents went back down where they belonged.

"I'm new here and I just realized that you are new, too." The man reached his hand through the bars. "I'm the Chaplain here—been here three weeks."

"Three weeks. That would explain why you think I'm new here." Clarence didn't want to sound rough or rude. He just hurt.

Chaplain looked at his clipboard. "Says here you just arrived."

"Well if you look deeper, you'll find that I've been here for sixty years. Then one day they decide to kick me out—according to the decision of my judge back then, who was a bastard. Sorry, Chaplain. Sent me to a nursing home. But … I don't even know what day it is … they sent out four guards to bring me back because—"

"Because you killed my brother in cold blood. Knifed him, cut him, then inflicted several wounds on me and you think you should get away with it."

That voice.

Strange scratching noises at the window. Was that—?

Warden stepped up to the bars, edging the chaplain aside. Right behind him stood Phil and Lex.

Clarence stared at each one, then at the chaplain. "See, the people in charge here have their facts wrong. It was self-defense. Five men surrounded me, each with a knife—and let me tell you they were not kitchen knives. They pushed in closer. Me, I didn't even have a kitchen knife. They start swinging when what's his name … Lester, a guard, stepped in, his own life in danger. He pounded one with his beat stick and I got one guy's knife, when Mr. Warden, here—only he wasn't the warden then—closes in. Nice for their Mama that both her sweet boys were here in prison, so she knew where they were at night, right?"

Warden growled.

"Well, then, Mr. Warden's brother rushes me and slices me on my cheek." It still stung, even though it had been—

"That's enough Timmelsen." Warden put his arm around the chaplain and escorted him to three guards standing behind him. "Sir, we are thankful for your service, but right now, Mr. Timmelsen needs to get his facts right."

"Oh. I forgot. You're right. He sliced my cheek open and in self-defense, I aimed my knife at anything I could and it happened to be his neck. Kinda stopped the attack." Clarence shook his head and stood. Shaky knees. Sweat running down his back. But he stood and faced the men. The chaplain was still there. "If I remember right, you, with all respect Mr. Warden, ran. Like a dog with its tail between its legs. Left your brother to die alone on a cold concrete—"

"Enough!" Warden's eyes bugged out and his voice echoed off the walls of the cell block canyon and slammed back into them. His face, even though he was dark-skinned, was bright red. He stepped forward to the bars, just like the last warden had when he had kicked Clarence *out* of prison to the nursing home. He gripped the bars in the same way.

Clarence couldn't quite pass up the opportunity. He was gonna die anyway. "Feel good to be holding onto those bars again, huh? It's where you belong."

Warden vibrated, the bars rattled as he pounded his fists into them.

Silence.

Even the neighbors were quiet.

The scratching started up again. It was a bird … a huge bird, right outside his window.

Warden pulled out his phone. "What is that?" He tapped his phone. "Tower, shoot that bird."

Voices echoed. "What bird? Where?"

Warden pointed. "Outside Timmelsen's window. Shoot it down."

Clarence realized too late. "No! No."

The chaplain broke in again. "This should go before the board."

Warden glanced over. "None of your business, Chap." He signaled the guards. "Get him out of here."

"Y-you can't do that." The chaplain protested all the way down the steps.

Shots.

The bird flapped its wings against the building, clawed at the window.

More shots and it fell away.

Warden shook his head at Clarence. "Back to the bars—at least I'm on this side and not that side." He was back in control. "Oh, and here are some friends you need to say good-bye to."

Phil and Lex stepped forward, one on each side of the warden.

Phil smiled a sick smile. "So we're on our way." He trailed his fingers across the bars. "Back to Osceola. Since you're here in prison, Katty, and especially little Bea, are all alone. No one to protect them."

Clarence stepped close to the bars and grabbed them. He shook the cell door, making the warden and all step back. He roared. "You wouldn't dare!" The noise he made shook the entire cell block—every inmate was listening. The atmosphere was electric—lightning could strike at any moment and blow them all up.

As Clarence gripped the bars, he envisioned first Judge Green. Phil's face morphed with Judge's—both evil men. God, he hated the man who had first sent him here.

At that moment, Clarence knew he was a father, a grandfather, a protector.

But at the same time, he knew he was trapped and might never get out of this prison. He might never get back to protect them, to embrace them and who he had become.

Trapped where he didn't want to be.

And terrified for Katty and Bea.

He had to find a way out of prison.

TWENTY-NINE

Michael knew the surge was coming. He could feel a rising, a shift in focus, in intensity.

In power.

He had to remain steady and firm for just a short time and then all hell would be cast out of this evil prison.

After all hell broke loose.

Even though he was in human form, he could still access the heavens as needed. He could still float back and forth from dimension to dimension, realm to realm.

And when he accessed the heavens, he literally felt every weapon loaded and revealed. Every angel and creature banded together for one purpose—to engage with the evil there in the prison and release the captives.

The comrades were getting excited and as they readied their weapons and armor, sparing broke out. They loved a good fight and this was no exception.

Battle cries rang out. Sword clanged into sword and shield.

Horses stomped as they were brushed and saddled. They snorted and danced, hardly letting their rider capture and harness them.

Chariots lined up, each one equipped and polished, wheel spokes woven and lined with victory streamers.

Excitement pervaded all and as Michael walked among them, he was saluted and hailed from every side.

The hubbub echoed throughout the heavens and mountains.

The Master, at his throne, watched and laughed, enjoying the Kingdom preparations, following His words and decrees.

Michael grinned.

Father's laughter.

Ahh.

Melodic. Deep. Stirring.

Powerful.

And soon, Michael knew … soon would come the moment when all would stand in readiness. All would be accomplished and each warrior and steed would stand at attention. Every creature, every chariot ready.

A deep quiet settled in, every eye of every angel, horse, and creature locked onto The One Who had made them.

Locked on for when He gave the command to ride.

THIRTY

Katty wandered into Hillcrest, feeling like a lost lamb. Her own little lamb followed her a few feet behind.

Bea had gone back to dragging her blanket along everywhere. And while it was extremely annoying—shutting it in the car door every time they got in the car and a corner trailing into the toilet—Katty realized why Bea needed it. Her only source of wellbeing and stability was gone.

Katty hadn't realized how much they both had grown to depend on Clarence.

And to love him.

She turned to see how far Bea was behind her. Five resident doors. And she was dragging the blanket. Ah. She could wash it.

Katty sighed. Her own heart ached. Maybe she could find a blanket of her own.

Harold. He was saying something to Bea from his doorway and she stopped in the middle of the hallway. Head down. Blanket at her feet. He tried to reach for her and he couldn't. His head bowed and he kept bouncing it up and down, until Katty realized he was crying.

She turned to go back when Lisha showed up. She gave Harold a long hug, her lips moving. She wiped her eyes and stood.

Bea hadn't moved, except to bend over even more.

Lisha glanced up at Katty, then scooped little Bea up in her arms, like a newborn baby. She gently covered her with the blanket and hid her face with it, standing just like that. Just swaying. Just hugging.

As Katty stepped closer, she could hear a deep, soft humming and tears filled her eyes. Lisha reached out an arm to Katty and drew her into that hug.

"My babies." Lisha cried too. "We miss that old, ornery Clarence." Her massive chest rose and fell with each ragged sigh. "Oh Lord, you gotta bring him back to us." She started walking. "You heading to his room?"

Katty nodded. "There's probably some work I could do." She broke again. Wiped her face. "I just want to be here." She took Bea. "And so does she." She swallowed. "When I used to do drugs and was gone all night, she used to hide under my old rocker." She hesitated. "She's doing that again. So I thought maybe it would do her good to come here and see the people she loves—you, Carol, Harold." She turned toward Harold's door and took a step in that direction.

"It's okay. I'll git him." Lisha nodded. "He's takin' it hard too. They had become buds. Gonna start a detective business with him a detective, and Clarence a lawyer and all." She handed Bea and blanket to Katty and waved them on. "You go on and I'll git him."

Katty nodded. Her heart broke to see Harold sob like that. Lisha too. She hugged Bea harder.

She passed the nurses station and heard someone blowing her nose. Carol looked up, wiping her face and threw a wadded tissue into the trash.

Carol walked to Katty and Bea and enveloped them. "It's rough." She turned and blew her nose again. "Blow your nose. Wash your hands. Then do it all over again."

Katty nodded. "Have you heard anything? Is he … is he okay?"

"Sheriff is doing all he can to intervene, but the prison is kind of closed to inquiries right now. Really odd." Carol rubbed her arms. "We have to pray."

Katty nodded. "Sometime, could we … pray?"

Carol hugged her. "You bet." She turned back to her desk. "I'll be down later."

Katty sucked all the air out of Clarence's room as she and Bea opened the door. Someone had evidently cleaned things up because she'd been told that frames on the walls were broken and the desk messed up. She walked in and sat her bag down on the floor. The desk was always a mess so that wasn't new.

If she could just keep things going here for when he was released, that might help. And it would give her something to do, instead of sitting at home thinking too much. She began to make piles and organize a little and came across a picture Bea had colored for him. "Bea, we should tape this one up. We forgot." She turned. Bea was still at the door. "Come on Bea. We have to be strong. I'll help you and you help me. Okay?"

Bea looked up with the most forlorn look on her face. Her eyes were swollen and red and her chin quivered.

Katty walked to her and picked her up again, careful of her tummy. "What do you say we get some ice cream."

Bea shook her head. "I just want to stay here."

Katty blinked. "Y-You don't want ice cream?" She sat down on Clarence's office chair, Bea on her lap.

Bea settled in and leaned against Katty's chest.

They sat that way for a long time, just looking at the room, the pictures, out the window.

Bea took a breath. "It smells like him here."

Katty blinked. "It does." She continued to breathe him in. What if he could feel them, right now? All of them—Harold, Lisha, Carol, Katty and Bea. What if he could hear them, feel them all crying for him to be safe and come back to them?

"Bea, we need to pray."

Bea immediately folded her hands, still resting against Katty. "God help Clarence come home." She leaned carefully forward. "And help his shot place."

"What? His shot place?"

Bea held up her shirt and pointed to the bandage. "His shot place. This."

"Oh. Yeah. His shot place." Katty nodded.

"Amen."

"Amen."

Another amen came from the doorway. Carol walked in with cookies and juice. She set the tray down and hugged Bea. "Good praying, Bea. That's exactly what I wanted to pray for him."

Bea climbed down and sampled a cookie. "Yum." She wandered to the TV. "Can I watch?"

"Sure." Katty nodded. "Funny. Since he isn't here, she is being so respectful. She would have just turned it on like at home if he had been here." She stood and picked up a box. Set it on the desk and opened it. "Clarence doesn't belong in prison and I'm thinking there might be something in one of these boxes from when he was there before that might help get him out."

"Might be. Good thinking." Carol walked out munching a cookie.

"Better than sitting around." Boxes and boxes from Pete's Insurance Agency. Clarence had never wanted to go through any of them. And she couldn't blame him but while she was here she might as well do it.

She opened the flaps and fished through the papers. A new yellow envelope was on the top. Might as well start there.

"Huh."

"What Mommy?" Bea was more tuned in than usual. She always zoned out to the TV; Katty usually had to set off a bomb to get her attention.

"Nothing, Baby." Adoption papers. She glanced at Bea again. For her? She read more. Several names were listed. Bea Randolph. Katty Randolph.

Oh God!

She slowly sat and began digging into every word. "Adoption process."

Bea climbed onto her lap. "What's 'doption, Mommy?"

These were adoption papers for her and Bea to be adopted by Clarence!

Bea tapped on her arm. "Mommy, what is that 'doption stuff?"

"Oh baby, it's when a person takes on the care of another kid when it's not really their kid. Like when they love a kid so much they want to have them as their own."

"Is Clarence 'dopting us?" She pointed first at Katty, then herself. "Me and you?"

Katty hugged her. "I'm not sure yet, Bea. The papers say so, but I have to check first." It was like Clarence had left these here for her to find, but maybe not with him gone to prison. Maybe he'd planned a party to announce it.

Was this even possible? How was it possible if she had a mom and dad? Or kind of? She didn't even know where they were and better yet, didn't care.

Wait!

And somebody named Noell Randolph Carpenter.

Who was that?

"Noell?" Katty sucked in a sharp breath. "Noell."

Bea climbed on her lap again. "Noell too?"

But Noell Randolph Carpenter?

Randolph?

That was Katty's name.

Katty jumped up and began to flit from box to box, then back to the desk. She dug into the box there, into the papers under the manila envelope.

Whispered the names she had discovered—Dawes Timmelsen, Dawes Retrieval Systems, Judge Green.

What if she could help Clarence from here? What if she could find information in these boxes that could help get him home?

She cleared the desk of anything that didn't have something to do with getting him out of prison. Old stained newspapers. Daily devotion and activity sheets from Hillcrest Homes—he had quite a backlog of those. Used napkins.

The trash can was going to overflow today.

Every paper she picked out of the box, she placed on a pile, sorting them according to dates and themes.

Bea was asleep on Clarence's bed. Good. She needed the rest.

Katty walked to the bed and watched her daughter sleep. Her thoughts went back to before all this when they'd discovered the red bike and how naughty Bea had been—demanding to keep it, stomping her feet to get her way. But here she was curled up on Clarence's bed, recovering from a gunshot wound.

Today.

Katty realized that her day could have been so very different than right now—just watching Bea sleep and working at the desk. She wouldn't let herself go to what might have been, but.

She pushed Bea's hair away from her face. So sweet. So pretty.

She walked to the window and drew a deep breath, hugging herself. What if those papers were real? What if Clarence had really adopted them all—even Noell?

A tear trickled down her cheek and she wiped it away with the back of her hand.

Please God, bring him back so they could actually live like he was their relative. She had never realized how much she depended on him but … loved him.

Back at the desk, she picked up the envelope again and flipped through the adoption papers. No one but her and Clarence knew about this.

Wait.

The court house had to know. He was a lawyer, but he had to have filed something at the court house.

When Bea woke, they'd take a little drive and see what they could find out.

Time to get into all these boxes and find out the mystery. She felt like she was snooping and in fact she was, but she knew in her gut that Clarence would totally approve.

She dared not hope or dream about what all this could actually mean for her and Bea.

Noell too.

So many things: someone would have their back first of all, Clarence had already helped them immensely, but might there be more, financially. Maybe they could move out of that crappy trailer court where Mrs. Crabbyface always reported them for child abuse.

Stop!

She had no right to even be thinking that.

Clarence was in prison. He had a gunshot wound himself. And He might never get to come back to Osceola.

Don't think that either. She wiped away another tear.

Back at the desk, she picked up one pile of papers. The Dawes Retrieval System agreements. Clarence's dad had been a very smart man. His son gets ripped out of his life because of lies and he goes in and gets back at the judge by secretly buying up all of the available land and real estate.

And leaves it all to Clarence.

Brilliant.

THIRTY-ONE

"Sure." Noell nodded at Fletch. "Let's just go for a bike ride." She checked the windows in the camper. "It's really nice out."

"I'm sorry I can't afford much right now." Fletch hung his head. "I didn't think my car would take so much money to fix."

"That's why you should ride a bike and not drive cars." Noell smiled and winked. "They are really cheap annnnd … uh, good exercise. Double plus!"

He continued to hang his head, only this time his dimples showed.

Noell jutted her chin. "That's why I'm selling this old house and living in the camper forever. It's cheap and mobile and—"

"Good exercise for when you don't have a car to pull it. You just pull it yourself, right?" Fletch scratched his thick dark hair. "Do you have straps for it? How do you h-hook on for when you want to move it to the park?" He grinned.

"Pretty proud of yourself, huh?" She popped him on the shoulder. "Smart aleck. Really. Let's go for a ride." She walked to the old garage and pulled the slider door open. It was like a small barn.

Barn. That would be fun. Get some animals and … she had no idea how to do that.

She mounted her bike and headed toward Fletch's house, two doors down.

He jogged along beside her and tried to talk. "So … what have you been doing lately?" He started to pant. Must be out of shape, now that he wasn't a high school jock anymore.

Oh, that small talk. Should she tell him about the cave and how she wanted to stick her hand through a rock? Or maybe about how she was going back in time to change her nightmares? Yeah. Or—

"Hey, did you know that guy that got thrown back in prison? What was his name?" Fletch slowed to catch his breath.

"Yes. Clarence Timmelsen." It was the first time anyone other than the nursing home had asked her. No one cared about her like Clarence had. She peeked at Fletch and slowed to a stop. They were in front of his house.

Fletch's house was a cute white bungalow style with black shutters and a black trimmed front door. Simple but cute.

"Yeah. Sounds like he's in a lot of trouble for shooting that little girl." Fletch unlocked the detached garage and rolled out his own bike. "Pretty awful. I hope she's okay." He steered it toward the park. "And to think he was a lawyer and all."

Noell just stood there and shook her head. However could people get the facts straight if they hadn't been there? If she hadn't walked to Hillcrest right after it happened and talked to Carol—who had been there, she'd think the same thing.

Only this time she did know the truth. "Clarence didn't shoot her." She followed him down the sidewalk, walking her bike. "Carol was there." They waited for a car to pass. "They had Clarence in cuffs and outside—they were taking him back to prison—when Katty and Bea got there. Katty isn't shy and demanded to know what was going on. A smart mouthed guard got in her face, flirted with her, calling her baby and Clarence came unglued. He got one hand out of the cuffs and slugged him and the guard or one of the guards shot his gun and it hit Bea."

"God. He shot her." Fletch stopped his bike on the other side of the street. He turned to her, his eyes wide. He loved kids.

"Yeah." She caught up to him. "Clarence went crazy and slugged him again and the guard shot Clarence, too."

"Wow. Was Sheriff there? How's Bea?"

"She's going to be fine. They did surgery and removed the bullet. They already dismissed her from the hospital." She wiped her cheek. "But nobody knows how Clarence is."

"Wow. You okay?"

His concern touched her. He was cute, too. He really reminded her of someone but she didn't know who.

She nodded. "It was hard to see Katty so scared. Her little girl shot down." She circled around the playground equipment. A little boy waved, and he zoomed down the slide. She smiled. "And she is really close to Clarence. She says Clarence saved Bea's life when Katty was on drugs."

They followed the path down to the cave under the bridge.

She opened her mouth to tell him about the cave and pool, but closed it again. Wait for a better day. She still wasn't sure of what had really happened down there. But, she *was* sure she wanted to go back.

He stopped riding and walked his bike to the big bright blue sign. "This is really a show stopper. I love the way you can read 'Osceola' from the highway."

She pulled her bike beside his and leaned it against the huge cottonwood by the creek. "I should have brought a blanket but I guess the grass is its own blanket." She sat facing the creek. Crossed her legs and patted the ground next to her. "Come and sit. The grass is soft and … like green pastures." She cocked her head back. "Where did I hear that? Green Pastures."

"'You make me to lie down in green pastures.'" Fletch recited as he sat beside her. There were those dimples again. "Um … Mom says that one all the time. It's in Psalms, but I'm not sure where." He dropped his chin to his chest. "She would so have my head if she was here now!" He mimicked her, "What do you mean, you can't remember where that's at? I speak those verses to you all the time!"

Noell laughed but then retreated into her own memories. So that's what a mom would do, if she'd had a mom. Her thoughts went to

Katty. Maybe not every mom had that in her upbringing to give to her own children. Fletch had a mom who spoke Bible verses. Katty was a mom that had abused, but was now trying to be that Bible verse mom.

But Noell had had Gamma, a Bible verse grandma. And Grampa.

Fletch waved in front of her face. "You still there?"

Woo. Her cheeks puffed. She rubbed her forehead and tried to hide behind her hand. "Yeah. I just was thinking about what it was like to have your mom speaking Bible verses to you."

"Must seem kind of dorky, huh."

She stared at him. "No." She shook her head. "Not dorky." She picked up a twig and began to skin it, peeling the outer bark. "I just never knew or thought about what that would be like. My mom … " She trailed off.

"I'm sorry." Fletch swallowed. He started again. "Your mom." Hesitated. "She drowned, right?" He faced her. "How old were you?"

"Four." The twig was just a naked toothpick by now.

"Do you remember much about when she drowned?"

Oh man. Did she remember? Should she tell him about when it happened? The nightmares? Her mom's face as she drowned? Her life since then and when she touched a handle on a door, she heard and saw something of every person who had touched it before her?

Did she dare tell him that?

He'd think she was crazy. And right now as she was hesitating, he probably was thinking he had intruded, when in reality she wanted— she *needed* someone to talk to about it.

About it all.

She maybe could tell him some of it, but he would think she was crazy if she told him about the creepy vibrations she had when she touched stuff.

No, better left unsaid.

THIRTY-TWO

Clarence tried to find a comfortable position. He didn't know if the wound in his side was better or if he was just getting used to it, but it hurt when he rolled to his side—either side.

Sleeping on his stomach was totally out.

His back was the best, although it still hurt. What if he had some sort of infection and no one was aware of it. The doctor seemed incompetent, like he was half crazy with those rolling eyes. Maybe the guy just had a twitch.

Or maybe he was evil like everyone else here in prison.

But if there was infection, they weren't doing anything about and Clarence knew from experience he could die.

Fear stole every bit of breath he had left in him.

He couldn't die in here. That would not happen. Even if he became sick, he had to get out of here somehow. Even if infection was inside of him, he would somehow get out and go home to Osceola.

He had planned for so much. Those documents still were legal no matter what. He had dropped them into the box where his dad's papers had been. There were a lot of boxes still in his rooms at Hillcrest, waiting to be unpacked or burned. But that one box held his very inheritance—his proof of ownership, other than what they now had proof of at the court house. His dad had been so smart in buying up most of the town.

Clarence knew that what his father had done was all for revenge. Revenge against Judge Green who had sentenced Clarence to life in prison for killing his daughter.

Interesting how life happened and the seasons rolled away and then back again. Back when Clarence was young, he had been in love, married the love of his life, only to have her ripped out of his life in an accident that he had been framed in. After all this time—sixty years of blaming himself for her death—he had just learned in the last few months that he himself was supposed to die in that accident and Annie would have been free for Pete's dad to marry, making *him* the son-in-law of Judge Green—not Clarence.

Spending sixty years in prison was pretty much dying in Clarence's way of thinking.

Something tapped against the bars on his cell.

Phil Daynton.

Evil man.

Probably the devil himself for how he had abused Katty. Thank God he had never gotten his hands on Bea.

Yet.

"Mr. Timmelsen. I just stopped by to let you know that I am taking a long road trip. And I suspect that you have an idea of how far it is."

"I don't give a damn about where you go or what you do. Just stay away from my girls."

"Your girls?" Phil smirked. "How do *you* get to claim them?"

Clarence almost burst out about his last visit to the court house but clamped his lips shut. That bastard would never find out about the adoption until they switched places and Phil was on this side of the bars instead of Clarence.

Clarence turned toward the wall. It hurt to move, but he didn't want to look at that damn devil's face. Evil seemed to ooze from him. Hard to tell, but Clarence was sure there was something like another being that hovered over Phil. Something that licked at every part of Phil. Almost like flames or a massive tongue of fire.

Unfortunately, he might have turned away too late, because the visual was stuck in his brain.

"Clarence." That voice laced with syrup. Reminded Clarence of when Dad had tried to give him medicine from old Doc. He had told him it was juice with honey in it. That it was a treat. But as soon as the liquid hit his tongue he knew he had been deceived. There was no juice in it. Honey maybe.

"See Clarence, I'm going back to Osceola. You just came from there, so's you remember the road. Or parts of it." Phil trailed his fingers along the bars. He made a sort of choking sound.

Clarence flinched.

"I'm going back to bury my daughter, Baby Bea."

Clarence froze. He had known Bea was Katty and Phil's, but—

Phil suppressed a sob. "You shot her. And I have to go back to take care of my family. To bury my own blood daughter."

Clarence winced as he rolled onto his back. "You are a liar. She isn't dead. I know it." He tried to sit up and pushed through the pain. He swung his legs over the side of the cot and stood. "She isn't dead." He roared. "I know it in my veins." He stomped to the bars. "She is more my blood than yours. She'll run from you!"

"Well, I guess we'll never find that out will we." Phil squinted. "You are here." He tapped on the bars. "Locked in. And probably going to die here, with the way you are bleeding."

Clarence glanced at his shirt.

Damn!

"And Bea is at a funeral home as we speak, lying in state. Her little limp body waiting for Daddy to pay his respects and then get tossed into the ground."

Clarence froze; the visual was too clear in his mind. He could feel his face wanting to fold in on itself. A picture popped into his mind— Bea's sweet body lying in a casket lined with pale pink satin, a rose tucked into her clasped hands.

Nooooo!

He backed to his cot before his legs gave out and landed hard.

No. No, no. Don't let that be true.

Phil walked away tapping against the bars, but stopped while he could still see Clarence. "So tell me, Mr. Timmelsen. How does it feel to have everything ripped away from you … again?"

In the past, Clarence would have rushed the bars, hoping to somehow mangle the man. Reach through those bars and choke out his life.

But today.

The life had been ripped out of Clarence. The rug of truth was pulled out from under him. He wanted to cry or throw up.

His shirt was becoming wet with sweat, either from infection or fear for himself and his girls.

His Bea might indeed be in a coffin.

THIRTY-THREE

Michael leaned against the cell wall, watching the transformation of Clarence as the man lay on the cot. The dark stain on his T-shirt grew and spread as his chest rose and fell with each gulp of breath. Tears tracked down into his hair, his ears. He wiped his face then cupped his hands over it.

Michael tried to remain distant, to not let emotion get in his way, but experiencing this metamorphosis was the best thing he'd seen in all eternity. Well, besides when Father revealed his creation of mankind, or when Yeshua was born into this Earth realm.

And the worst thing he'd seen lately—he bowed his head—was Clarence locked in the cell.

Okay.

Michael breathed in deeply, connecting with Father for strength.

What was happening with Clarence was good, but nothing surpassed when Yeshua burst through sin and death, crashed into the Earthly realm, baffling every demon in hell by his resurrection to life and took his rightful place at the right hand of the Father.

Nothing.

THIRTY-FOUR

After Fletch left, Noell puttered around the house. She picked through a box; there were so many and she was always overwhelmed. Would anyone want this pretty little jewelry box? She didn't.

Another box. What about that box of notecards? Again, pretty, but she didn't want them. She never wrote notes to people. She didn't have anyone to write notes to.

Where was the trash bag she'd had out yesterday?

She kicked away a half-full box, picked up the box that had been underneath and parted a stack. No trash bag. Even if there was one started it was definitely easier to just go get a new one.

In the kitchen she got distracted by all the cookbooks lining the walls. One stack was from the floor to literally the ceiling. She shook her head. How on earth had Gamma done that? Must have been when Grampa was still alive, but she doubted he would have allowed that.

Gramps and Gamma had gone to auctions together and bought treasures at each one. But they had kept it to a low roar when he was still alive. When Grampa died, Gamma had gone into another level of buying and hoarding.

And this mess was the result.

It was hard not to be mad at her, when Noell was left with it all.

She couldn't live like this anymore. Either sell the house and everything in it—even the red leather sofa—or clean it out.

Neither option satisfied her longing to just be herself. That was her dilemma. She just wanted to find what she wanted to do in this life.

Most people her age were going to college. No, most kids her age partied and drank and had a good old time. For just a split second, she let herself imagine what that would be like.

Carefree.

No worries.

She'd seen girls from her graduating class at another town, when Gamma had needed to go to a different doctor. The town was big enough to have a shopping mall with some of the popular stores. Each girl swung several bulging bags, chattering and laughing. Two had looked her way but pretended they didn't see her, but the third one kept glancing at Noell, then staring down at her purchases.

Would that be fun?

Maybe.

Just someone to have a coffee with or go to a movie with. Maybe.

There. Dang. She'd been past that kitchen counter three times and hadn't seen the trash bags sitting there. She pulled one out then knocked over the pile of books stacked there from yesterday and had to start over with those.

She had never thought of herself as an angry person, but the frustrations of today were turning into a lit fuse that would explode if she didn't squelch it.

She had to get organized.

Somehow.

The counters all had stacks of books and bowls, There was not one vacant space.

The kitchen table just had junk piled on it. Instead of putting an object in a box or the trash bag, she'd get frustrated and dump it there.

She didn't use the table for eating. She ate in the living room on Gamma's red sofa, sitting in Gamma's spot, watching TV.

She swept everything off to the floor.

Wow.

A clean surface.

Everything went on pause as she snapped a mental photo of that cleared table. A clean surface. A blank spacc. No clutter. No piles right there on that one spot. Nothing on that piece of furniture.

Something inside released and she found she could relax as she captured that image of the table cleared off. Even if everything that had been on top was now in a heap on the floor or on top of the piles on the floor.

Just that one image was enough to give her hope.

She kicked aside the clutter on the floor, clearing space to stand at the table and either pack or go through a box. She'd start where she was, which was in the kitchen and not go onto another room, another space until the kitchen was cleared of junk.

Her eyes scanned the kitchen. Whew. This was just one room. The cookbooks lining the walls. Every surface was loaded. You could no longer see the granite countertops Grampa had installed years ago; the space was all covered with boxes, spices, canned goods, and junk.

If all that was on the counter, what was in the cupboards.

Her breathing started to come in short gasps as she allowed herself to take the whole kitchen in.

Never.

Never do that again.

Just take care of what was in front of her.

She cleared a path between the table and the back door, pushing everything to the sides, making it wider so she could use the back door. She vowed to take whatever she had gone through—whether it be trash or give-away—she vowed to dispose of it that same day.

To the dump each day if they were open. Note to self: find out when they are open.

Or to the thrift shop or Mrs. Bertrand's shop. Or to another town if they didn't have room for all this stuff. Somewhere someone had to need some of this stuff.

Or she'd host the biggest marshmallow and hot dog roast in the history of this town … or nation. Force each person to take a box home. A sort of grab-box event.

She sat on one of the clear kitchen chairs. That was a good idea. Wonder if it was legal.

Note to self: go to the court house and check when and where she could have a fire. She could invite her neighbors … except Mr. Grimes. No way would she invite him to anything but his own funeral.

She grinned at that thought. That would make a great story.

But there was that young family across the street and down at the end of the block. And Fletch's family. Fletch. Maybe some of the road guys. That would be fun. She actually did know someone she could invite, especially with the guys from work.

She cleared space off next to the box of trash bags and arranged the tape, scissors, box cutters and markers there.

Which box? Didn't matter. Just pick one.

Just the next box.

Then the next room.

Then … no.

The box in front of her was all she would allow herself to see. No more scanning the whole room and getting overwhelmed. Just one box at a time. And the next box. Or the next pile.

And carry it all outside to the … where from here?

She walked to the back door and spied Grampa's old truck. Did it run? Wait. He used to have a pickup box trailer to haul stuff to the dump … tree branches and trash. Where was that?

She ran outside and there it was—behind the old garage—an old pickup box, white chipped paint and a few dents, but very usable. Now she just needed to make sure the pickup started and hook it up.

She knew where the keys were. Grampa always told her and reminded her again and again, "Now where did I tell you I put my extra keys in case your Gamma loses hers?"

She'd giggle and run for the old radio on the stand beside the back door and lift off the cover and there they were—always safe.

She ran back inside and did just that.

There they were!

Back outside to the old truck.

Please start. Please.

A visual of Grampa's foot pumping the gas pedal up and down reminded her do the same thing. Then she turned the key, foot down on the gas and boom!

It started.

Grampa had always said that it was the most dependable vehicle he had ever owned. Before now, Noell had planned to sell it, but not now. Not if she could start it after this many years.

Gamma had started it right after Gramps died because she too had trash and give-away stuff to get rid of, but that was what five years ago? Didn't cars or trucks get all gummed up after a while of not being driven?

But here was this fantastic truck and it started right away! Well, fantastic old truck with a few dents as well, the red paint was now kind of a rust color and not very shiny anymore, but it ran! She slid her hand over the glovebox. It was a Chevrolet. Spelled out.

And it started!

It felt like Noell had won a marathon! Or the lottery.

She ran around the truck. Funny colors. Each part, from the hood, the doors, even the tailgate, were all different colors—brown, green, black, red—all unified by the rust and worn patina. Gramps used to drag parts home from junkyards or farm sales. This must be where he put them.

Gramps.

A lump formed in her throat. He had been such a good man. Literally raised his granddaughter, along with Gamma.

She shook her head..

Onward.

She inspected the hitch and whatever that thing was called. Just like on her camper. She had helped hook that up.

She could do this.

Once inside the truck, she backed until she heard a bam.

Oops.

Shouldn't have given it that much gas. Now there was another small dent, but the hitch was right over the ball.

Now what?

Maybe Fletch could help her the rest of the way with it.

She had done it! She was in business. She could throw the bags into the old trailer and get them out of the house at least.

She ran inside and grabbed a box. Into the trailer.

And another box.

She cleared space around the table floor. The trailer already was a fourth full.

Just having a plan and a system was enough to fuel Noell's day.

Back in the house, she stood over the sink, drinking a glass of water. Katty and Bea kept popping into her mind. Maybe now would be a good time to walk to Hillcrest and check on them. See how things were at the nursing home too.

The walk did her good and as she pushed the automatic door button and watched the door open, she thought of Gamma. She'd never had to live here. She would have been fine with it, only her red leather sofa had to fit in a room.

Noell grinned as she walked down the hall toward Clarence's room, envisioning the sofa jammed in one of the rooms. Wouldn't fit in that one. That one either.

Then Clarence's room. Maybe Clarence's room would work.

She knocked.

Katty looked up from the desk and Bea on the bed.

Oh-oh.

Katty's expression literally changed when she saw Noell.

Before, she had almost been smiling—pleasant expression at least.

When Katty realized Noell was knocking on the door, her face changed to … fear?

THIRTY-FIVE

"Hi guys." Noell swallowed and waved. Still stood in the doorway.

Bea popped up. "Hi." She rubbed her eyes.

"Shoot. Did I wake her up?" Noell pointed at Bea.

Katty glanced over at the bed. "No. I think she was awake before you knocked." She kept busy with the box on the desk. Her hair hid her face.

Noell glanced down the hall. Both ways. Shoulda stayed home. This was awkward.

Katty glanced up. "You can come in." She smiled, then glanced around the room. "Doesn't seem the same without Clarence, does it."

Okay. Maybe Noell had misread Katty just now.

Noell stepped in.

Bea smiled at her.

"How are you feeling?" Bea was so pretty. Brown eyes were huge, framed with dark lashes.

"I'm good." She patted the bed beside her. "Want to watch Daryl and Dumpty with me?"

"Uh, sure. What is Daryl and Dumpty?" Noell smoothed the covers and sat beside Bea.

"It's that."

The TV showed hundreds of colorful fish swimming around a little girl, who was wearing a rainbow stripe swim suit.

"Her name's Daryl. And she swims with the fish in the pond. The fish are learning their numbers, so Daryl counts the fish." Bea took a breath, like she was diving underwater. "One. Two. Three."

Katty smiled, looking at Bea. "She'll go on and on. She goes past five hundred, so if you get bored, you can take a nap." She pointed at the bed.

Noell chuckled. "I can count to four hundred."

Bea sat up. "You can?" She clapped her hands. "Good girl!"

Noell laughed. What a cutie.

Katty cocked her head and pulled Noell away from the bed. "Hey Bea. I'm going to talk to Noell for a little bit. Just stay here and watch TV."

"Okay Mommy." Bea watched them as they slid out to the hallway.

"Ha." Katty smirked. "She knows something is up. If Daryl is on, she never hears me. I could tell her that I'm going for ice cream, and she wouldn't even move or look my way." She shook her head. "Today, she is on high alert."

"Mommy, don't forget about the book fair. Okay?"

Katty shook her head. "And there's that."

"Book fair?" Noell raised her eyebrows.

"Yeah. They're having a book fair here this afternoon. With all the ruckus going on around here, everybody forgot about it. I guess the people sponsoring it walked in this morning, loaded with boxes and boxes of books. Surprise!" Katty shrugged. "Hey, do you think you'd be able to stay with Bea for a little bit." Katty pointed behind her toward the desk. "I need to check on something I found on Clarence's desk. At the court house."

Babysit?

It'd been awhile. Noell glanced at Bea. "Sure I can. I was tired of … doing what I was doing at home."

Katty grabbed her purse and some envelopes and waved good-bye.

Bea hardly waved back.

"Can we go to the book fair? They brought us face paints. Can I paint your face? Can I paint you a lion?" Bea hardly stopped for a breath. She had a plan.

Noell sat in front of the mirror as Bea painted her face. Why had she agreed to be the lion? Cool idea to bring books alive at the nursing home. Not so cool to let a four-year-old apply orange paint.

They had barely just met, but Katty had needed a babysitter so she could go to the court house, so here they were.

This was for sure going to strain her germaphobe habits. The sink was her savior.

THIRTY-SIX

Katty parked the car and walked to the building. This court house was amazing. A new one could never match the beauty of it. Why didn't they build new buildings like this one? She turned. Well, the new bank was close. Really close. But it had to be hard to mimic the architecture of these old buildings. She should look up its history and find out how old … oh yeah, the year was right there. 1922.

The minute she walked through the doors, she gasped. "This is huge."

The walls were smooth and cold to the touch. She traced the pattern in the stone with her fingers. "Beautiful." The railing was made out of marble. Steps were too.

At the landing, Katty read all the signs.

County Treasurer. County Clerk. Assessor. Where to go?

County Court. She vaguely remembered having to go there with Phil over something he'd done and he'd dragged her with. She'd stumbled into the court room and lost her balance, knocking over a couple chairs in her drunken state. But she wasn't too drunk to be unaware of the shame and humiliation, especially when Phil didn't even try to help her. He made it seem like she was the one at fault—which she was, but before she knew him, she'd never had a drop of booze or done drugs. She hadn't been pure, but …

She didn't think the Treasurer was the place. Or Assessor. Maybe the Clerk. She'd had to come here about something before, only she couldn't remember what it was.

A little bell dinged as she pushed the huge door open.

Katty opened the manila envelope and drew out the papers. "I don't know if I'm at the right place or not." She bit her lip. "I'm not even sure I should be doing this."

"Why not start at the beginning?"

"Okay. I'm Katty Randolph." How much should she tell this woman? She didn't know her. Would she tell the whole town? Dive in. "I am friends with Clarence Timmelsen and well, I am his paralegal."

The lady wasn't going to help her at all. Katty plunged in. "He was shot and taken back to prison and I have been going through some of his papers in his room—trying to find something to help get him back home and I found this. I just wondered if it's real and legal."

"Well, first, do you have a valid driver's license?"

Katty nodded and dug it out of her purse, setting the purse down on the floor. She held it up for her to see. Thank God she had kept hers up to date through all the drugging and boozing. At least there was one thing good out of that time.

"Okay. Thanks." The woman took a look at the documents and smiled. "I remember when he came in to do these. It wasn't that long ago." She checked the date on it. "Yes, just about two weeks ago." She scanned it, looked at the second page. "Yup. It's all here." The woman's name tag read Shirley. "I take it he didn't get a chance to tell you about it."

Katty shook her head. What on Earth was she doing? What made her think she had the right to snoop?

What made her think this was real? Had Clarence really adopted them? She swallowed.

"No. I was just trying to find something … something that could maybe be used to get him out of prison and back home and this was on the top of the box I was going through."

Shirley nodded.

"Well, is it real? Is he really—"

"Adopting you?" She nodded. "Yes he did."

THIRTY-SEVEN

Thanks to a friend he still had contact with, he had been able to secure a car—a four-door Grand Marquis—a late 80's model. Phil didn't need to know much about cars, only that they ran good enough to get away in, but also to become part of his disguise.

Some people might remember him from when he was in Osceola before. And they might not like him back here after almost killing little Bea on the slide. Someone, especially the sheriff or maybe the deputies, might have a problem with him driving around the town, scouting things out. No, spying.

He had a plan and part of that plan was being seen in many different towns and places so that when he did land in Osceola, he would have some alibis. They didn't need to be hard core, like in exact timing but he needed to be seen several places other than Osceola.

So. First stop was Wahoo. He could have skimmed around the town on the by-pass but he made a point of driving through.

Coffee shop first. It was more high-class so had a different clientele. Those rich old women who were lonely.

"Hey there, Sweetheart."

The woman finished pouring water into the coffee brewer and looked up at him. "Can I help you?"

"I would love a real man's cup of joe. None of that foo-foo stuff. No flavorings. Just raw courage." He flashed his I'll-get-you-in-bed-before-you-realize-you've-been-had smile and pulled out his bundle of cash.

Her eyes widened as he pulled several bills from the clip and she blushed. Her skin took on a radiance—partly from embarrassment—but a light sheen covered her skin maybe from sweat.

Priming the pump.

Maybe he could create a vacuum when he left Wahoo, so that when he drove back through here with Bea, this little coffee barista would be drawn in and ready to roll. Fun times in the old Wahoo tonight.

"Look at those muffins." He licked his lips, tilting his head so the old ladies at the neighboring table could get an eye full. "I probably don't need any, but how much for the stud muffins?"

One of the old ladies tittered. Another gasped.

"Stud muffin." The youngest of the group who looked to be about eighty, laughed. "I know what that is." She had something going on what with her red lipstick perfectly applied.

"Stud muffin? Raspberry and blueberry are all we have left." She tapped on the counter with her fingernail. "And they are two dollars apiece."

Another lady snorted. "A piece."

Phil burst on the inside at what he had started. Dirty old ladies. But this young thing in front of him. Hmm. She was as fresh as the muffins and needed some—

A gnarled old hand reached in front of him for a blueberry muffin and flaunted it right past his nose. She chuckled. "Sonny. Seems you think you are God's gift to woman." She tilted her head toward the table of her friends. "We could teach *you* a thing or two."

A cackle from that direction almost made his skin crawl. Those ladies were terrifying—even to him.

"Where do you live?" The muffin floated in front of his nose again and he couldn't help but smell it mixed with her perfume. His stomach rumbled.

She laughed.

He'd never been one-upped by a bunch of old ladies. If the old ladies were this horny, what about the younger set?

He glanced at the barista around the muffin. Her face was as red as the "I Love Coffee" poster with red hearts all over it on the wall behind her.

He cleared his throat. "I'm just driving through ladies and had the unexpected pleasure of meeting you all."

They giggled again. Two high-fived each other. These ladies didn't miss a thing. His own grandma was younger, he thought, and didn't know what stud muffin meant. Of course, he'd never had this kind of discussion with her so … maybe she did.

The barista slid the muffins and his coffee across the counter. "That'll be six dollars and seventy five cents." She wouldn't look at him. Or at the old ladies either. They'd totally embarrassed her to the point of wanting to die where she stood.

He counted out the money and made it clear he was leaving a substantial tip. One pile was payment. The other was the tip. Maybe that would relax her so she'd—

She scooped the payment pile across the counter and put it in the cash register. The other pile, she left on the counter and turned, walking into the back room.

Huh. Guess he'd gone too far with her. Win some, lose some.

He picked up the pile of money and scattered it on the table where the old ladies all sat. At least they appreciated him, screaming and laughing. He pushed the door open with his arm, coffee and muffin in his hand, and could still hear their lewd comments. "Wonder what he'd give us if we—"

The door closed before he could hear the end of that sentence. He never got embarrassed but he almost was now.

Next stop—get gas. The windshield washer fluid in the container was out, so he had to go in. "Hey there, Sweetheart. How's it going today? You're looking beautiful."

She looked up at him from what she was doing. She was squinting, a hard look in her startling blue eyes and her right eyebrow twitched.

Her skin was over-tanned and wrinkled before its time. Her beer themed T-shirt hung off her shoulders.

"My name's not Sweetheart." She pointed to her name tag. Audrey. "And I know I'm not beautiful, so cut the shit."

He swallowed. Women in Wahoo were hard to read. "Well. My mistake." He held up the windshield squeegee. "Just was wondering. If you have time and all. I don't want to trouble you—"

She slammed the cash drawer. "I said, cut out the shit."

A couple men at a near by table grinned. "You better treat old Audrey good. Otherwise, she'll haul out her bazooka and blast you with it."

"Got more windshield cleaner out there? You're all out."

"That's better." She cocked her head toward the pumps. "Get your ass back out there and use one of the others."

Phil stood there, the squeegee up in the air and so was his proposition. Had he lost his touch? Never had he met such a diverse pack of female products to shop from. Wahoo would definitely be on his hit list.

"Okay." He dared not look at the men's table. They were already chuckling, obviously knowing her better than he did. Tail between the legs time as he walked out to the car and cleaned his windshield. Even that was humbling, but he knew if he drove into Osceola with a car like he wanted, a Mustang maybe, that the cops would be alerted to watch him.

He started the car and drove away.

Next stop.

Osceola.

He'd have his daughter soon enough.

THIRTY-EIGHT

Noell glanced down at her T-shirt when Bea dipped the brush for more paint. Not cool to apply paint to her favorite shirt. The Escher design would never be the same. Hopefully it washed out. At least there wasn't paint on her boots—yet—her thrift store treasures.

"Sit still." Bea sighed, her rosebud face flushed. "It's really hard for you to sit still, isn't it?" Her husky voice had the ring of a mom's exasperation. She had learned well.

"Uh, yes. Yes, it is hard to sit still."

Bea closed in, her sweet breath on Noell's face. The brush tickled. Goosebumps zinged up Noell's spine as Bea lightly touched her, bracing her hand against her cheek.

"You smell good."

"It's the paint."

Detective Bea sniffed closer, then smelled the brush. "No. It's you. Did you just have ice cream?"

Noell burst out laughing. "No-o." Her face itched already.

"Cimmamon rolls?" Bea got really close and squinted her eyes. "They make them right here."

Clearly, Bea had been around. Tough little girl. She had to be, with her mom's drug habit.

At least she had a mom.

Whoah. Where'd that come from?

Maybe she's been neglected but she's only four—she has a chance at life with a mommy.

"Are you crying?" Bea lifted her hand from Noell's cheek.

No. I just see my mom drown—every night in my nightmares.

"I must have something in my eye." Noell leaned in to check the mirror. "Yeah. See?" She wiped a speck away. "There. Better." She opened her eyes wider so Bea could paint around them.

"You need to practice your roar." Bea dipped the brush and roared a baby roar. "Like that. Can you do it?"

Noell tried it.

She hadn't signed up for this.

"No, louder. Your voice is too soft. Don't roar like you talk. Roar like you … roar!"

Noell stared at Bea, then at her lion self in the mirror and roared so loud the paint shimmered in the jar. Something dropped in the hallway, clattered to the floor.

Bea laughed and laughed. She grabbed at Noell's arm to keep from falling off the stool. Amazingly, she kept the paint brush from making anything orange.

A nurse stuck her head in the room. "You okay in there? I heard some jungle sounds."

Noell caught Bea this time before she fell.

She stared into the mirror. Her thick blond hair roped back in a ponytail. The orange paint on her forehead and cheeks made her blue eyes pop. Blue like the sky.

Roar!

Something … something changed in those blue eyes. Snapped. Sparked. Her flesh trembled. Chest wanted to burst.

This was a foreign emotion. Power. Strength. Like the lion in the book.

Roar. Roar like a lion.

She'd never realized how prominent her cheekbones were or how her jaw jutted out. Or maybe it was the red circles Bea had painted on each cheek.

The paint flowed freely on her smooth skin. She needed to wash this off. Now. How long would she have to walk around in the lion costume someone had donated? She swiveled to see it on the other chair.

"Hold still." Bea groaned. "I painted orange where the red was 'posed to go."

Oh-oh. This would take forever if Bea had to start over.

Picky little girl.

Lucky little girl.

Katty walked into the room just in time to save Noell from further embarrassment. Her eyes popped wide, like she was in shock, but her chin quivered.

Noell was sure Katty didn't want to break into tears on seeing what Bea was doing to Noell, but maybe she did. Noell and Bea had to look pretty funny—good for a belly laugh.

Nurses walking past the room either looked shocked or burst out laughing, then walked away, their hands over their mouths.

Katty slowly laid the envelopes she had been carrying on Clarence's desk. She was still staring at them, shaking her head.

"Um. Uh." Katty couldn't seem to speak.

Noell had been ready to scream before Katty walked in, but now a belly laugh was working its way up in her too.

"Hold still. I'm just about done." Bea waved the paint brush in front of Noell's face.

Carol knocked at the door, a big smile on her face. She was barely under control. "Can I take a picture of you two? Since it's for the book fair, we will need a few pictures for the bulletin board and the newsletter."

"Uh, no. We don't need our pictures in there, do we Bea?" Noell hopped up and checked the over the sink mirror by the door. "Holy moly!" she needed to watch her words. Bea was so excited that Noell had let her do this. "That's a lot of paint, Bea."

Bea jumped down. "Please? Please can we get our picture taken together? You and me?"

Noell turned toward them. Katty and Carol both had tears in their eyes and were having trouble not laughing.

She shook her head. "I guess." This wasn't what an introvert ever wanted to be doing. She just wanted to actually go home and get back to work cleaning and pitching stuff out.

She let Bea drag her back to the sink. "Okay if we stand here where we painted?"

Carol was biting her fist and she turned her back on them, her shoulders were bouncing up and down.

Katty was having the same problem, but she was used to Bea's antics and she had a huge grin on her face—not at her daughter but at Noell's face. "Noell, I can't thank you enough for watching Bea for me. It was something I had to check on for Clarence and—"

"Yeah." Bea butted in. "Clarence is 'dopting us."

Noell bounced on the chair. She could barely talk with all the paint on her face. She checked Katty's face again, then Bea's. "He's adopting you?"

Had to be true because Katty got tears in her eyes right away. She slowly nodded, glancing at Carol too.

Carol nodded back. "He's been talking about doing it for awhile now. I know he hasn't been here all that long, but he is so attached to you girls." She snapped a picture of Noell and Bea, then scooted Katty beside Noell and took another one.

"You too, Noell. Clarence 'dopted you too." Bea grinned up at her, wiping paint from her fingers.

Noell jumped. "Me?"

Katty looked at her with a sweet smile on her face. "If you are one Noell Randolph Carpenter." She raised her eyebrows.

That needed to soak in. "I am. I mean that's my name." Why would Clarence be adopting her? "Wait. What is your last name?"

Katty, standing right beside her, turned and looked at her. Eye to lion eye. "My and Bea's last name is Randolph." She raised her eyebrows. "Same as yours." She smiled a tender smile. "I did some checking while I was over at the court house." The orange paint covering Noell's face must have gotten to her because she grinned, then let out a laugh. She tried to be serious but wasn't successful. She laughed again. "Your grandmother was my grandmother's sister. Your grandma was my great-aunt or something like that. Shirley at the Clerks' office tried to explain it, but all I know is your name is my last name and that makes us cousins somehow."

Noell blinked. "How come we didn't know each other till now?"

Katty reached for a paper towel and wet it. She gently proceeded to wipe the paint around Noell's eyes as she talked. "Because my grandma got into trouble. She chose a different life and that's one that my mom and then I chose, too." She wiped her eyes with the backside of her hand. "I know your grandma tried to figure things out and get the family back together, but my grandma wouldn't hear of it. She called your grandma a goody-two-shoes. Which wasn't true." She dropped her hands to her chest. "I remember your grandma. She would bring sweet rolls for us or a casserole. My grandma would throw it all away." She wrinkled her nose. "I climbed into the dumpster to get the sweet rolls once and ate one behind it until Grandma caught me and made me throw it out. It was so good."

Noell smiled. "She was a good cook. Her rolls and cookies were so good." Her eyes started to sting, and not from the paint.

"Well, I should leave you girls to get acquainted." Carol patted their shoulders. "Clarence always wanted a family. And now he created one of his own."

Katty leaned in. "We have to get him out of prison."

"But is this really true?" Noell checked her face in the mirror.

Katty nodded. "I asked the same thing at the court house and what's her name … Shirley I think, said yes. We are actually adopted." She folded her arms across her chest. "It's true."

THIRTY-NINE

Bang!

Clarence jumped!

Powerful dreams wouldn't let him wake.

Bang!

He blinked.

A guard stood directly above him.

Where?

His eyes were open, but he couldn't completely tear himself out of the dreamworld of mountains and green pastures. Beauty. Light. Creatures.

"Git up!" The guard raised his beat stick for another whack, only this time instead of hitting the cot Clarence was sleeping on, he threatened to pound Clarence.

He'd been lying there all night and when he tried to move quickly, like he used to, he couldn't. He was stiff. Everything hurt. No surprise there. He'd been beaten on every part of his body.

The guard had his beat stick ready. "Get your lazy ass up and get dressed. Day's a wasting."

He shuddered as he pushed up from the cot and lifted one foot at a time to get to the facilities. The guard gave him some time to clean up:

wash his face and brush his teeth, but when he started to comb his hair, the guard had had enough.

"Come on. Get moving. We have work to do."

Clarence followed him out to the walkway and down the steps. Each step down felt like his bones were breaking apart. Like they were moving in ways never intended. Must be how football players felt after a game. It would help if he could have breakfast, but he guessed that wasn't on the schedule for today. Grin and bear it.

The guard led him to a closet that held housekeeping carts and cleaning supplies. He showed Clarence what he needed and pulled a cart out into the hall. "You'll need this and this."

Toilet cleaning supplies.

"And this."

Shower sprays and sponges.

Great. He'd done this detail many times when he was first incarcerated back sixty years. It had been dangerous back then and he was sure it would be just as bad now, or worse.

At least the prison building itself hadn't changed all that much. He could still remember the layout.

"Come on. Let's roll. I have lots to do before my shift is done." The guard pushed him into the cart and it hit his gunshot wound. He winced but wouldn't let himself cry out. No sense calling down more trouble than it was worth.

He glanced down at his shirt.

Bleeding.

Again.

He remembered this shower and bathroom. It was *the shower*. The one where he had been attacked. Where he had killed Warden's brother, Lewis, in self defense. Loud voices echoed from inside. Evil laughter. Someone screamed just like Tay did—high pitched girl scream—from a guy.

He parked the cart right outside the door and picked up the cleanser spray and mop. He knew the drill. Evidently the guard was staying with him—showing him the ropes, or making sure no one killed him on the first day. He'd wasted several days in the infirmary so he hadn't had a chance to set up a day count in his cell. Hash marks worked well. Tonight he'd try.

As he stepped into the shower, several huge men stood around another puny young kid. They were poking him and yelling at him. The kid was stripped naked and his towel was in the hand of one of the larger men.

But when Clarence entered the room, all eyes turned to him. They forgot all about the kid, which he took to his advantage, grabbed his towel and ran past Clarence and the guard.

Clarence had been in the same situation when he'd first been incarcerated. He hoped the kid appreciated it because Clarence was obviously going to take his place in the grand scheme of things. Didn't really matter who, just that they had someone to taunt and beat.

Or worse.

The guard looked the other way and backed out of the room.

Clarence had been set up.

He skirted around them and kept his distance. At least he had some weapons—just a mop and cleanser spray but that might not feel too good in the eyes or mouth. He hoped.

"Oh, Mr. Cleaning Man. Sorry. We left a little mess for you to clean up." One of the men glanced over his shoulder and nodded. "You might want to bring in a shovel." He grinned a greasy, evil grin. "And some sweet smelling spray because it really stinks in there."

Clarence held his breath as he walked to the toilet area.

The smell brought tears to his eyes. He put his arm over his mouth just when someone pushed him from behind and he landed right in the middle of the most shit he'd ever seen in one place, except for a feedlot back home. Smeared all over the floor and the fixtures, the mirrors.

They shoved his face in the muck just as someone ripped his pants and underwear down from behind. Lewd comments. He was in for the prison initiation. He'd been a lot younger the first time. Didn't matter. If he lived, he'd kill every one of them.

As soon as Clarence had that thought, he found himself on a rocky cliff.

No more men.

And no more shit.

Just him high above a drop-off. He tried to step back, only to find he was at the very top of a knife-edge precipice, with only enough room to stand.

Gasping, he stumbled. A chasm dropped below on all sides. It extended farther down the longer he looked. Soon he couldn't see the bottom—only rock walls of the canyon, ever stretching away.

No river. Just dry rock.

"God! What?"

Sweat broke out on his forehead, his neck.

His chest constricted. Each breath became more difficult to draw.

Tears broke from the corners of each eye.

"Oh. God!"

A quiet enveloped him.

"This is it." He lifted his eyes, his head rigid. "God. This is it, huh? I thought we just flew into heaven. Maybe Michael … "

As he blinked, a cloud appeared in front of him.

No.

Not a cloud.

It flowed closer.

Took shape.

A head. Shoulders. The body. Legs.

A man?

He floated close.

"God? 'S'at you?"

The man smiled and held out a hand. "Come."

Clarence glanced down then barely moved his hand at his side, pointing to the drop-off. "Y-you see this? Am I the only one seeing this here? Like … I die, Jesus."

The man smiled.

"Damn. This is getting annoying. I'm freaking out and you're smiling? Saying come?"

Jesus held out his hand again.

Those eyes.

Clarence had seen those eyes before.

At prison—Lester.

Carol.

Bea.

"Come."

Clarence searched the edge right below. No ledge. No place to …

"Come."

Tears burned.

Clarence swallowed. Slowly nodded. "Then this is it, Lord?" His heart pounded in his chest. "No more Lisha."

Jesus smiled and beckoned with his fingers.

Clarence lifted his hand.

Tried to reach.

A rock broke loose and tumbled, bouncing off ledges. He lost sight of it as it crashed outside his peripheral vision.

Where it landed didn't matter. Not looking down.

A tear escaped and ran down his cheek.

Sob.

Deep in those eyes.

"Come."

No worse than drowning, right?

No worse than …

He sucked in a breath and stepped off.

FORTY

The road, as Phil drove into Osceola, was decidedly very pretty. It curved into town from the veterinary clinic, past that Dollar Store. You could see the cemetery from the road. Grave robbing would be an interesting and profitable job. Bet some of those graves had valuable stuff buried with the bones.

He'd spent time there, hiding out with Lex. Too bad Lex hadn't come along, but they'd decided that both of them would draw too much attention. He might have to fly in later. Buses ran through these small towns.

He shook his head. But right now, all he had time for was kidnapping his daughter and doing whatever he had to do, to make that happen. Just the thought of her sweet tender skin, made him itch.

The implement business had added some little tractors in front. Bet Bea would like riding on one of those. Wonder if the guy Lex had bribed with a beer, was still working there. They'd have to reconnect.

And there was Phil's favorite place to hide behind, next to the implement dealer—the drive in. The guy there was always nice, even though Phil had caught him staring as he had jogged up the hill to his stake out car. Suspicious. Some people couldn't let things alone. They thought they had to be the look out, ready to report any suspicious goings on.

If that guy could see him now. He'd have to stop in for some ice cream while he was here. Better yet, he'd bring Bea in too, on their way out of town. Unless, of course, she was tied up.

He turned off the highway into town and headed to the trailer court. Better be careful not to get noticed by Katty, but even the neighbors might know who he was. He dug in his bag for a ball hat and sunglasses. Bet if those little old ladies from Wahoo lived here he could get them to watch out and spy for him. Wouldn't take much to buy them off.

Phil choked. Gross.

Not much had changed here. Same tumble down trailers. Oh, some were nice, but Katty's was … nice. Fixed up. The deck was new. Potted plants. A new skirt had been added around the base of the trailer and it looked like it had been painted. Bet old man Timmelsen had sprung for all that. Katty had a good thing going.

Her car was gone so he slowed. Windows were the same—so good possibilities for entry some night.

Oh-oh. Old lady alert.

A woman about the same age as the elderly ladies at the coffee shop hobbled from around the end of her trailer and waved at him.

If he didn't wave, she'd get all mad and remember it later, probably talk to her phone buddies, ripping him. So she'd remember him.

But if he waved, she'd remember him for being a nice guy, friendly, willing to engage.

He was cooked both ways.

He waved a normal wave. Not too friendly or over done, but not too sissified either.

And he shouldn't look too interested in Katty's trailer or anything else here. Being a criminal was hard work.

Especially kidnapping.

He didn't see the red bike he'd sent Bea, so he guessed it caused the right amount of stress and arguing to cause a rift between Katty and Bea.

He drove to the park next. Touring the town. Typical family playing on the equipment. Mom sliding down the slide. Dad pushing a kid on the swings. Nothing out of the ordinary.

Hillcrest seemed the same. He'd have to find a way to scope that place out without causing any suspicion.

He checked Facebook on his phone. What was Katty posting lately? Huh. And who was this Noell that commented on her posts? Noell Carpenter. Huh. Must be just a friend, but they seemed to know each other pretty well from the feed.

He'd have to check her out. He logged her name into memory. Maybe she would be a way into Katty's life. Maybe he could use Noell to set Katty up and steal Bea away.

He parked on the square across from the bank. It was new and very well done. He nodded in case anyone was looking his way, as he slowly slid the gun from under his leg to behind him and into the waistband of his pants.

The streets surrounding the court house were bordered by pickups and cars. Mostly county 41 which was Polk County Nebraska. One or two other counties.

Amazing building. Those pillars could support the Empire State building or at least the prison. Marble. Whoever had built this place was rich. It was well done, and the builder and city builders had spared nothing with materials.

Sign on the entrance door—no guns allowed. Right.

Country Treasurer. Assessor. He guessed the County Clerk would know. Now what angle?

"Hello. What can I help you with?" The woman in front of him had a name tag but it was on edge so he couldn't read it. But he could see that she was the clerk. He had the boss lady.

"Hi. I am looking for some property." He still wore his hat and glasses so he hoped his identity was secure. "Only I'm not sure of the address." He took out his phone and did a quick search. You had to love internet. There was Noell *and* her address. "Ridge Street." It also had that her grandmother had just passed away. How convenient. "531 Ridge Street."

The woman wrote it down on a scrap of paper and walked to a back room. If only he could think of a good reason to go back there with her and snoop through all those old journals. He'd have to think about that. He knew they were part of public access, but he guessed they would frown on him if he just asked to snoop around a bit.

She returned with her paper and a huge book. She dropped it onto the counter and flopped it open where her finger had been holding a place. She pointed to the line. "It's right here. What did you need to know?"

"Well, for one thing, is it for sale? And who owns it?"

She shook her head. "Not at this time. It is owned by Gwendolyn Randolph Carpenter. She passed away a short time ago, so I'm guessing it was inherited by her granddaughter, Noell." She handed him the scrap of paper with her scribbling on it. "Anything else?"

"No. No. That looks like everything I need." He tapped the paper. "Just to make sure I got this right—Gwendolyn—that's quite a name. Then Randolph Carpenter?"

"That's what the book said. I think they called her Gwen."

"Oh. Right. Gwen." Randolph? That was Katty's name. He tipped his hat. "Thank you for your time and trouble."

"Oh, no trouble." She smiled. "Just like to help out. Are you moving to the area? Because there are other properties that are available. The property on Ridge Street might not be available."

"I'm thinking about it. Yes." Not on your life. It'd be a cold day in—

"Well, if there is anything else I can help with let me know."

He opened the door. "Thanks. I'll do that. Have a good day." He saluted and left.

Ridge Street. He remembered driving past here not long ago as he looked for hiding places. He hadn't remembered the house though. It was nice enough. A front porch that had been built in. Camper in the side yard. He slowed.

If this kid, Noell, was living there, she'd likely have a car. Should have found a way to check that at the court house too.

Randolph, huh.

Seemed pretty dead right now. He might not have much time. He drove around the block and found an alley that bordered the property. Who did the camper belong to?

Back on the street, he found a place to park his car in the parking lot at Hillcrest. There were always lots of cars and people coming and going at shift ends and during the day with visitors and such. He guessed no one would get suspicious for a few days.

Yup. 531 Ridge Street. He needed to sneak around back and break in.

First he'd try the legal way.

He knocked.

No one came after waiting several minutes. He knocked again and tried the doorknob.

Unlocked.

Don't open it. Find another way.

He walked around to the back of the house. No one seemed to be around.

A little shed sat between the old camper and a garden—or what used to be a garden. An old pickup and a trailer. Trailer had some trash and boxes in it.

The camper was locked, although if he really wanted to, he could jiggle the knob enough to break in. If he wanted to. Or if he really thought there might be something in there. He kicked the step. It was just an old junky camper.

The shed might be different. It was pretty well kept, like maybe there was something going on in there. Phil could almost feel the next scam on its way to his mind. He just had to open up to it.

He checked the doorknob. Locked tight. Even with more jiggles, he couldn't open it. What was in there?

He was getting so engrossed in the mystery, he forgot to be scrupulous and act like a neighbor.

Which of course was happening.

An old man limped with a walker a few doors down, to his back shed. He stopped and waved to Phil.

Caught.

He waved back.

He'd have to scope the neighborhood at night.

This Noell probably didn't matter in the scheme of things anyway.

He walked around the house acting like an inspector. That might fit since the old lady had just died. That window had been fixed. A shutter was needing to be repaired.

Back at the front door.

Don't look behind. Don't see if anyone is about. He'd go on in like he was a relative or friend.

"Hello?" What would he say if her knew her? "Noell? You home?" He pushed the door open but something was keeping it from opening all the way.

Whoah. Holy shit. Did the kid even live here? The something that was against the door … was a whole household of crap.

He tripped over a pile of magazines, into a stack of boxes.

It was still light out so he could see relatively well without turning on lights, but this was a maze that no one could navigate, unless you knew the map.

Wow. Every room was piled high with boxes and junk. He'd seen this on TV once. A hoarder show, where they tried to intervene. But this was even worse than on TV.

He opened the refrigerator. Pretty skimpy. A container of leftovers. He opened the lid. Spaghetti.

His stomach rumbled. He hadn't eaten all day.

Smelled good but he put it back. Just the minute he stuck a fork in, she'd come back and interrupt his dinner.

He pushed the door shut and scanned the kitchen. He picked up a butter dish and slid his finger along the top of the butter stick and licked it. Tasted okay. Seemed like she'd been here recently. So maybe she lived here.

The old lady's bedroom probably looked as she had left it when she died. Tons of junk. Only one side of the bed could be slept in. Bibles piled up on the other side of the bed. Religious old lady. Probably the same as the little old lady who kept inviting Phil to Sunday School when Dad was in the cult. Never in a million years.

He opened a door revealing a stairway going up. Might be where the kid slept. He'd find out more there. If she came home while he was upstairs, he'd have to jump her or jump out an upstairs window.

He clomped up the wooden steps. No carpet. Noisy. He tucked his shirt behind the gun at his back, as he peeked in one room first. It was very simple and clean. Austere. Like a hospital or library. He pushed the door all the way open, just to make sure she wasn't hiding behind the door.

Noell opened the back door. She congratulated herself as she glanced back at the old pickup box trailer. Good girl, Noell. It was already a fourth loaded with trash and boxes. She had gotten a great start on decluttering and it invigorated her to keep on going.

After being somewhere like the nursing home, though, it was hard to come back here. The nursing home was so clean.

In her own home, she never knew what might be lurking under or behind all those boxes.

A little Bible, a cup and a tiny bracelet were all that sat on the bedside table. Phil picked up the bracelet. It was he guessed, a baby bracelet, with tiny beads and pearls that spelled out Noell.

He had never had one himself, he was sure. His bloodthirsty father would never have saved such an heirloom. When Phil had been kicked out to the orphanage, they had even taken his stuffed turtle away.

An angry growl surfaced from somewhere inside Phil. His past wanted to surface. The things he had seen and done. Abuse. Atrocities.

Noell shook her head. Don't look at the rest. Just focus on the next box or the next pile.

Maybe she should call Mrs. Bertrand and ask her if she'd take all those cookbooks. Surely someone would want to collect some. A new bride might want them for her kitchen.

She had no idea of what could be in all these boxes here in the kitchen—spices? Canned goods?

Sigh.

She had some idea of what might be on the porch. She'd dug in those boxes searching for work clothes for the Roads Department. Actually saved her a lot of money.

Maybe she should have a sale. Sell it all. Hire an auctioneer and maybe they'd help set it all up. She had no idea how much money it would take, but at least she wouldn't be left with all of it.

The growl and pain in Phil's gut grew larger and louder. He stretched the bracelet until the old and weakened elastic broke, releasing the tiny pearls and beads.

They seemed to be suspended in the air, all across the room like tiny soap bubbles floating.

Voices were released with the beads. Words of kindness and love. "My sweet baby. Oh, you are so cute."

Words he had never heard directed at him in all his life.

Then words of pain and horror. "God, help! Save my baby!"

Pictures too. He cringed as he saw a woman caressing a baby. The same woman screaming underwater.

Who was this Noell?

Who was the woman?

He knelt at the bed. What was happening? How could an object speak? Or store pictures?

He'd never had anything like this happen. Why now?

He had to get to Bea.

Something was happening to him—trying to take him over. Something he'd never experienced before. He'd always known demons and spirits but this was different. This was … pure and holy.

Noell slid a box over to the table and started to lift it onto the work surface.

This would never do. Phil needed strength to counter these voices.

He roared.

Boom!

She dropped it back onto the floor. Super heavy. She opened the flaps.

Books! More cookbooks.

The box was gonna stay there. Cleaning this house out didn't mean she needed to hurt herself. Maybe Fletch would help with that one.

All the pearls and beads immediately fell to the floor and bed.

Felt good.

At least felt like himself again. Which wasn't saying much. It had taken him a long time to embrace his dad's level of evil, but now he'd never go back to that wimpy little boy he'd been before.

Kitchen stuff was heavy.

She lifted the next box the way the guys at the Roads Department taught her. Butt in, feet apart, back straight. Lift with the legs.

This box was even heavier.

She dropped it on the table. Boom!

He roared again.

He needed to be strong. He needed to keep with the plan.

Get Clarence killed. Get his Bea.

Soon.

Before he gave into these … these—

Soon he'd have help.

Lex would be here soon.

The table swayed.

Noell sidestepped.

Oh-oh!

Crash!

Phil froze.

Someone was downstairs.

He drew his gun and stood still, barely breathing.

Noell opened the box flaps. No wonder. Cast iron pots and pans.

"I broke Gamma's table." Noell still had trouble calling things hers. "I broke *my* table."

Time to quit. Time to call it.

She stopped. If she had quit every time she had felt like it, she might not have made it past third grade.

The kitchen walls wanted to push in at her.

Well, she could push back. Maybe she couldn't fix the table or lift every box, but she could keep on going.

She stooped to open another box.

Just someone's old household goods. Smashed boxes of plastic zip style storage bags. Aluminum foil. Every one of the boxes was smashed.

She gathered the box and stomped out the door. She had to be strong. She had to get rid of all this stuff. Enough, already.

She gave it a heave into the trailer.

Felt good.

<hr>

Phil inched to the window.

Must be her. Must be Noell. Long blond hair, pulled back in a ponytail.

Down, boy. You came for Bea.

He stood and watched her as she pushed some boxes together.

Now was his chance.

He stumbled down the steps, two at a time, almost turning into the kitchen.

Front door. Dumpy porch.

Out the door.

Slow down. He turned back into the doorway before shutting the door. "Okay. Everything looks okay." Lady at the court house said the grandma had just died. "Sorry about your grandma passing."

Perfect.

He quietly closed the door and walked down the sidewalk in the opposite direction of his car. Hell, from here, he could walk to anywhere in this town, it was so dinky. And walk back later for his car.

FORTY-ONE

Back in the house, Noell checked the cupboards and sure enough there were two rolls of foil and several boxes of bags. This was stuff that people bought in the store, though. Her too. She should probably keep stuff like that. It would save her money.

She opened another box. Spices. When she checked in the cupboards, there was more of everything. She didn't have a clue how to use them. Did a person use sage in tacos? But it would save her money to keep them.

Noell went through several more boxes.

She glanced up, knowing how good it felt to see things cleared, but there wasn't anymore space than before. Boxes were stacked on the keep pile and where she always dumped them to go out to the trash trailer was clear.

What?

"Oh man. I … "

She wasn't getting rid of anything. She had just done the same thing that Gamma had always done. What if she needed this or that? She'd have to buy it and keeping it would save money.

She looked at the pile she'd already done. It was bigger than before. She was doing the same thing. She was following in Gamma's footsteps all right.

She sat on the chair hard. She needed help.

What if Katty could use some of this? Katty was a single mom and had endured, from what Noell had heard Clarence say, a rough life. She'd seen the trailer they lived in and it wasn't much.

A picture of Mommy's room upstairs hit front and center. It would be so cool to let Katty or Bea have that room. This was way too much house for Noell alone. She could share it.

She had family.

Katty and Bea were her family.

She wasn't alone.

What if she had them come over and go through stuff—find things they might need? It would help both.

She glanced around the room. What would they need?

Her chest wanted to burst. She had family. It hadn't been that long since Gamma died but the pain and loneliness that was left behind made it seem like years.

She had family!

She should call Katty and have her over and …

She looked around at the stacks of boxes, books, junk. What would she think? Katty didn't have a lot, but Noell was sure that she was not living in a mess like this.

Noell could show Katty her own room and she would know it wasn't Noell's fault.

Silence.

No.

Katty and Bea would never set foot in this house.

FORTY-TWO

Katty wasn't sure Noell was so thrilled to have them as family. With all that orange paint on Noell's face, it was hard to read her.

Katty checked Bea. She was on Clarence's bed watching TV, so Katty stepped to the window. The leaves were beginning to change color. Even the rose bushes out front had a different hue.

It couldn't be fall already. School had just started..

Clarence had a great room. He had a view of the park, the parking lot, the rose garden. He could watch people come and go if he wanted. She'd never seen him just stare out the window like some people here, though. He was just too busy. And she loved the idea of him and Harold cooking up a detective-lawyer business. Maybe that would keep those two out of trouble.

How was Clarence?

She was so scared for him. He had told her stories of his time in prison, especially at first, before he became a lawyer. He'd been just a kid.

People were leaving, waving to their loved one as they walked down the sidewalk. They must be able to see into the resident's room. She'd never checked to see if Clarence was waving when she and Bea left. She'd have to do that.

Sigh.

When he got back.

Tears threatened. Not going there. Bea would ask.

A car drove into the parking lot but parked clear on the edge of the other side of the parking lot.

She was so worried. Carol said to pray and they had.

Would God hear?

Bea stretched on the bed. "Mommy can we have ice cream?"

Katty smiled. "Sure. You have't had any yet." She held out her hand, "Let's walk down together and get some. Maybe even take Harold some. Or Mrs. Hatly."

Mrs. Hatly. She and Harold both were suffering so badly with Clarence gone. They had both sent Bea a get well card with money in it. Sweet.

Katty looked down as Bea slipped her little hand in hers. So soft. Tiny. She hoped she could keep this closeness they had right now. Stupid that it took a tragedy to kick her in the butt, to be a better mom —to care more.

At least Bea was better. Funny how little kids healed faster than adults.

She looked up as Harold raced toward her, walker or not.

Bea ran to him. "Harod!" She hugged his leg, but stopped. She had learned not to trip anyone in the nursing home. They were so unbalanced sometimes. Katty and Carol, even Lisha, had worked hard with Bea so she didn't knock anyone over.

"Katty!" Harold shook as he walked to her. "Katty!" He started stuttering. "You-you-you."

She caught up to him and he was trembling.

"Harold?" She grinned. "Are you okay?"

He didn't laugh. His face was serious. "N-no. Don't … ice cream. Don't." He gripped Katty's shoulders. "No!"

His eyes bored into her. She held his arms. "Harold? What are you trying to say?"

He began stuttering again, like he did sometimes when he was tired.

"Harold, we'll be okay. We'll bring you back some, okay?" She grinned. "Unless we eat it all. Then we'll have to bring you some tomorrow."

Katty released his arms, but he wouldn't let her go. Lisha came down the hall and helped walk him to his room.

"Poor Harold. I don't know what got into him." She looked behind her as Lisha steered him into his room. He was still reaching for her. And stuttering.

"Mr. Harold. What's the problem?" They could hear Lisha's loud voice well and still even hear Harold—he was so upset.

"I-I-I bad men. I-i-ice. No ice. No-no ice. Bad men."

Lisha leaned out the door. "You know what he's talking about?"

Katty shook her head. "He just came at us and grabbed us."

Lisha nodded and looked past them down the hall. Then back in the room. They could hear her page Carol. "Carol. I'm on a hunch but Harold has gots something up his ... no. No. Not that. He is—"

They rounded the corner. "Huh. The machine looks like it always does—inviting, right Bea? We want ice cream!"

They could still hear Lisha. "Carol call—"

Bea laughed. She could almost reach the ice cream cone holder. One more month and she'd be tall enough.

Katty pulled a cone out and handed it to Bea. She'd gotten pretty good at serving up this stuff. A perfect curl at the top every time. She pulled the handle down and the soft creamy ice cream slowly filled the cone.

A voice behind her. "Mmm. That looks good. You've gotten really good at that. You need to be a soda jerk."

Katty looked behind her and smiled. Mrs. Hatly was up and around. Since Clarence had been gone, she had taken to her bed but especially her room. Katty hadn't seen her since. "You want one, Mrs. Hatly?" She turned, holding the perfect cone out to her.

"Give that one to little Bea. Then I'll take a tiny, tiny one." She sat on the loveseat across from the ice cream machine and leaned her cane against her legs. Her twinkle was not as twinkly, but her smile was still sweet. She had definitely suffered with Clarence gone. There seemed to be something special between them—love maybe? So cute.

Wait. Why was it cute when little kids had a love thing going on and when old people did, but when just adults had it, it wasn't cute anymore. It was serious.

This might be serious for Clarence and Mrs. Hatly. They only had maybe a few more years to live. This was serious for them.

Bea sat down beside Mrs. Hatly and Katty handed her the ice cream cone.

"Be careful."

"I know." Bea heard this warning every time someone handed her anything to eat. And she always was careful. Just things happened that were out of her control. She licked it and smacked her lips. "Yum."

Katty smiled. "How come it always tastes so good? You have it several times a week. Or more! Why is it always so good?"

Bea's face took on wisdom. "How come the booze always tasted so good when you had it every night and got sick from it every morning?"

Katty held her breath. She didn't get angry. Just blew out a breath. She stared at Bea, then looked at Mrs. Hatly, who was happily licking her cone.

Mrs. Hatly glanced up and licked her lips. "Me too."

Katty filled her cone and sat on the chair nearby. "You too?"

Mrs. Hatly nodded just as Sheriff Dennison and two deputies rushed in through the entrance. They were red-faced and breathing hard. Guns were drawn.

Katty dropped her ice cream cone and it landed ice cream down. She jumped up and stood in front of Bea and Mrs. Hatly. "What is going on? Why are you waving guns?"

A deputy checked the door they had just come through. "Sheriff. There they go. They must have gone out another door."

"There are too many entrances in this place. Needs to be secured."

They all three slammed out the door, shaking the walls as they pushed it open.

"There who goes?" Katty followed them to the door and checked outside. Sure enough there were two men racing toward … that car …

she had seen earlier through Clarence's window. As one turned around to get into the drivers seat, she got a glimpse of his face.

Phil!

"Oh God!" She backed away, stepping on the ice cream. She slipped and started to lose her balance but before she could land on the floor, a strong hand gripped her arm and caught her.

The cute cop. "You okay? You look like you saw a ghost!"

Carol gathered paper towels and wiped up the ice cream cone and Katty's shoe. "You okay?"

Katty glanced from her face to the cop's. "What just happened?" She pointed outside, oblivious of the mess she'd made. "That was Phil! And probably Lex his crappy partner!" She pushed her fist to her mouth. "Oh man! They're back!"

She started to collapse, but he caught her again and settled her on the chair. "I should have seen it coming."

He leaned closer to her. "Seen what coming?"

"I should have known." She straightened. "I bet the bike was from him, too."

"What? A bike?" He knelt on the floor and retrieved his phone. He tapped a couple times and looked up, phone at his ear. "Tell me. Tell me all."

FORTY-THREE

"Jerk!" Phil pounded on the steering wheel. "I told you to bring beer. Remember?"

Lex smirked. "Is it for you, or for our implement buddy?"

"Me, of course!" Phil slipped his gun out of his back belt to under his leg. He wasn't about to tell Lex about losing his cool in that a girl's room. Beads scattered all over. Just floating in the air, suspended there. Weirdest thing. "Go down to the bar and get us some. And get some for our buddy. This gig is almost over and we need to keep him happy until we're gone."

"If I'm driving, you have to get out." Lex opened the car door.

"I'll drive. Dammit man. You don't know what I've been through. This has got to get done before something happens with Timmelsen."

Lex slammed his car door. "What could happen? He's locked up tight."

"I don't know. I just have the willies, like I used to before … " Like he used to get before Dad went on one of his rampages and things went flying, including Phil. Something about the air. What were those things? Frequencies? Wavelengths? He sure as hell didn't want to ever be on the same wavelength as Dad. Ever. Again.

He started the engine. There had to be a way to wipe memories.

Like an app. Wave the app on his phone over his brain and wooop! Any memory of Dad? Gone.

Heh. Maybe that was Phil's million dollar idea.

Maybe not.

They drove downtown and parked in front of the bar. "Busy. Hey. Get two six-packs."

Lex opened his door. "What are *you* gonna drink?"

"Ha. Ha." Phil tapped his gun as he scanned who was in the bar. Man he had to get out of this town soon. The people here were starting to look familiar. And good.

Lex opened the door, the beer under his arm. A woman held it for him, chatting. He nodded and smiled. Those dimples pulled the girls in every time.

"What'd she say to you?" Phil watched her walk away through the glass door. "She want to meet you later? Cause I'm sleeping in this car, too."

Lex chuckled. "So what if she does?" He shoved a beer at Phil.

"All's I'm saying is this gig better work." He popped it open and chugged. "I need to get out of this town. Get Bea. And out." He drank again. "I don't care what happens with Clarence. Not even Warden." His jaw jutted. "Screw them."

FORTY-FOUR

Clarence came to when something flopped over his body. He tried to move but could only turn his face sideways. Somebody had dropped a dirty towel over him.

He tried to roll over, but he slipped in … shit. He was face down in the muck. Every time he tried to move to get up, he slipped. Every movement churned up the smell. He was sure his nose would never smell anything so rank, ever again.

Hands seemed to grip him from every point: his legs, his arms, shoulders. He was barely standing when hands tucked the towel around him and secured it around his waist.

He must have been beaten badly because he wasn't really seeing anyone, just feeling hands trying to move him, someone helping him.

Then he saw boots by his mucky feet. "Geeez, Clarence. You really got yourself in it this time." A deep chuckle. "Shit and all."

Seemed like about thirty people surrounded him, supporting him and wiping him off, but all he really saw were boots. One pair of boots. Dirty boots.

Clarence ventured a look up and what he saw startled him so much, he began sliding and falling.

Again, hands caught him and steadied him, keeping him upright and covered.

"Whoah there, Clarence." The voice choked. "You've been … you've been beaten pretty badly. Let's just take it easy and not fall. You don't need that."

Clarence found the voice with his eyes. Found the face belonging to the voice.

Lester.

For once, Clarence let the tears flow. The pain and humiliation, but the relief of seeing a true friend.

Lester.

He wasn't sure he was sane. Might be delusional because about fifty angels stood surrounding him and right in the middle of them was Michael.

"Michael." His voice was husky. He could barely get the name out. "Michael." He broke and slumped to the floor again, not caring what he was landing in or how he'd get back up.

When he came to, he was on his cot. His hair was damp and plastered against his head just like he'd had a shower. He was covered in several blankets. He had clothes on.

Cozy.

Must be how a newborn baby felt after its first bath and then was swaddled in warm blankets.

The whole morning came back to him and tears as well. The mess must have gotten up his nose because he could still smell it. He tried to rub his nose, but all he could feel were bandages.

He must have broken his nose when he was pushed onto the floor.

He wasn't sure he wanted to know what else was broken.

Then it all came rushing back. The threats. The guard stepping away. Brutalized.

Through the years, he'd gained a sort of respect among the ranks of inmates and had appreciated somewhat of a protection. He helped them with their legal issues and they helped him stay safe.

The visual of the boots. "Lester?"

A voice out of recent past. "Lester isn't here right now, Clarence."

Clarence burst into tears.

Michael.

He reached out his hand, tried to make contact, but wasn't sure he'd ever had contact with Michael. They'd spent a lot of time together, but had they ever touched?

Clarence wiped his face. Ow. He tried to see, but his eyes were swollen.

There.

Michael.

The huge angel was in full-dress angel costume instead of work clothes and a plaid shirt jacket.

Clarence blinked.

Michael glowed. His wings reached up through the ceiling. Michael's head touched it. He guessed that if Michael stood up straight, he'd be taller than this building.

But those eyes.

He reached for his hand. "Michael."

Michael reached for his.

At that moment, he remembered another hand reaching for him.

Jesus.

Everything from that moment on the cliff rushed back at once. Crashed in. He remembered taking that step of faith off the cliff into Jesus. He didn't understand it all, he just knew.

"Michael. Jesus said come."

Michael leaned down on one knee, completely filling the cell. His glow softened but light still emanated from his face, his eyes. The angel nodded, his eyes watered.

"Michael, are you crying?" Clarence tried to lift his head but couldn't. "Michael."

"Clarence." The angel's hand clasped Clarence's. It was so huge that it covered his whole arm and hand.

Clarence wanted to ask him where he'd been, but something held him back. He didn't need to know. Just the fact that Michael was here now.

"Who were … those other people in the bathroom? I saw thirty or more there. And whose boots were those?" Clarence closed his eyes. "They were right in front of my own feet."

Keys jangled in the cell door.

Clarence braced himself.

Lester.

"Hey buddy. You're awake." Lester approached with a tray. "Just a little something to build you up. You've had quite a … a … day." He wiped his face with the back of his hand. "Sorry to see you here again." Lester put down the tray at the foot of the cot. "Your old cell." He swept his arm around like he was showing off a new car. "Sorry this is all … " He lowered his voice to a whisper. "And sorry these people are out to get you."

Clarence nodded, not sure how to respond. "It was your boots I saw in the bathroom. You helped me get up." He felt his hair. "You cleaned me up. I don't know how you did it but … thank you."

Lester shook his head. "Oh believe me. I had help. Maybe not the kind of help most people would expect, but I had help." He held up a sandwich. "You need to eat—get your strength back. There's a glass of milk too." He held up a piece of paper too. "And a note from Sara in the kitchen."

"She helped me try to get away yesterday." He took a bite of the sandwich. "Was that yesterday?"

Lester chuckled and glanced at the walls. "You're going to have to start your calendar again aren't you."

"I tried but I didn't even know the day. I have no reference. I can't even start it."

"Well, this ought to get you started." Lester held out a pencil. "Hide it well. I'd probably get fired for just giving you that." He chuckled. "But I'm sure it hasn't been all that long, that you'll remember your hiding places and secret routines. Right?"

Clarence searched the walls. "The only thing I could remember was where I carved Annie's name—up there." He tried to point but let his arm flop back down on the cot. "What all is wrong with me? Is my nose broken?"

"Yes. I'm sure of it. Probably some ribs as well, your backside is really bruised up. You should be okay, but you are going to have to work hard and move like you used to—get back in shape." He held up his hand, teaching. "You need to get back on your feet as fast as possible. Even faster. You can't let them see you as weak." He shook his head. "That, I'm sure, is part of their plan. To weaken you until you give in." Lester stood straight, arms like they were holding weapons.

Maybe they were in some realm.

Had he really seen Jesus?

He checked to where Michael had been standing and he was still there, listening, but beckoning to—

Clarence gasped. There were about twenty angels, all lined up around the cell walls—side-by-side—not a gap between them. Angel insulation.

He could see them clearly, but also see the walls, the bars. Annie's name was still visible.

Amazing.

Since Clarence had stepped into Jesus, things seemed different. It was like he had needed to embrace Jesus so he could change. So things could change. He remembered the embrace. It was like hugging little Bea, her head on his shoulder, his on hers. But somehow he'd gone into Him. In Him. Inside of Him.

Become one.

He didn't understand. He only knew.

"Michael?"

The angel knelt again. "Yes, Comrade?"

"Comrade?"

Michael shushed him. "Rest, Comrade. We have to rest in order to …"

Clarence must have passed out. When he came to, his eyes wandered over the walls. The bars. The ceiling and the facilities. Everything held memories. He had stared at each thing for sixty years.

He hadn't appreciated the nursing home for what it was. Freedom. Friendship. People who cared. Love.

And there was Annie's name carved forever into the concrete walls. He was surprised he could still read it, even with paint covering it.

When he had carved her name, there had been no one else in his life that he loved so much, that he had wanted as badly as her.

She had been his life. His world.

He had lived this long without her. In pain because she was gone. Because she had been taken from him.

But now.

He could still feel her. He still loved her. All these years and he would still embrace her and if they still had the chance, to spend whatever time he had left with her.

But she was gone.

He didn't understand it, but he could feel her pulling away from him. Not in anger, but in reality.

In love even.

Well, he guessed it was time—it had only been sixty years. He guessed no one could blame him for moving on after being faithful for that many years.

"Annie." He swallowed. "My Annie. Please forgive me."

And there she was.

Their daughter stood beside her.

Both beauties.

Both smiling sweet smiles.

"Clarence, my love." Annie touched his cheek. "It *is* time for you to move on and there is one who loves you like I love you. She is a faithful servant and is waiting for you. You are free to love another."

"But Annie—"

She shook her head and put her finger to his lips.

He looked from her beautiful face to their daughter.

She nodded.

And they were gone.

He shook his head. Since he'd met Jesus, he couldn't stop the tears. Wouldn't go well here in prison. But what could be worse than what he'd already been through?

Well. Dying.

Today that would be worse.

Because for the first time, he finally had something to live for.

Some*one* to live for.

The envelope with the adoption papers was back in his room at Hillcrest, but it was all done except the screaming and crying when he told the girls. He had done it without telling them, yes, but he knew it would make them happy. And he needed someone like them—young women and Bea—who would use the funds well and who would deserve it.

Katty and Bea had been through so much. He sighed. And right now Phil and Lex needed to die. He didn't believe Jesus would mind that. They were evil men and intended to do evil to Katty and Bea— maybe others.

Right now, someone needed to slam both Phil and Lex into a cell or better yet into a grave.

"Michael?"

No answer.

"Michael!"

He wasn't in the cell. Where had he gone now? He'd just come back into Clarence's life.

Where had he gone?

FORTY-FIVE

Back home, Katty unpacked the groceries. She hadn't bought much, just milk and bread and the constant peanut butter. A cookie or two.

And … she peeked at Bea. Already engrossed in the program on TV.

Katty pulled a small paper bag from the groceries, fingers trembling. Bea had been so excited over new peanut butter, she'd never noticed the small bottle of whiskey being checked out.

Mandy and John weren't working, so Katty didn't care what the checker thought.

She hesitated.

Not true. She did care.

She shoved the bottle, still in the paper bag, behind the sugar canister.

Click.

Katty held her breath.

The TV was noisy but she was sure she had heard a noise from in back.

She checked the window.

Nothing moved. She guessed she was getting jumpy what with seeing Phil and Lex at Hillcrest.

And probably because she had bought booze.

Just knowing they had been there and were in town made her uneasy and fearful. At least she'd talked to the cop—the cute one. He knew everything. He knew about Phil and their past, her past, but he also knew from Sheriff's point of view what Phil had done in Osceola.

The booze called to her. What if the cop came by?

There it was again. A sort of squeak. She checked out back again, then out the front windows.

Her imagination was going crazy, and who could blame her?

Phil was here. He was coming after them. He had a gun.

Stop it!

She opened the bread and made a couple peanut butter and jelly sandwiches.

That was healthy, right? Bea loved them and so did she, if she let herself admit it.

There it was again.

A bug crawled across the screen. So that sound was made by a bug?

Man, she needed a drink. Fear piled on top of fear: Phil coming back to town, Clarence gone, Bea getting shot.

She pushed the flour canister in front of the bottle.

Must be a demon. After all that had been going on, she could believe it was more than a bug.

When she heard the sound again, she handed Bea's sandwich to her and walked outside, her own sandwich in her hand, nibbling as she walked. She stopped and just listened and watched. Pretty soon a cat crept out from under a bush and scared her silly.

She laughed but then stopped. What if Phil was sneaking around. Not only trying to scare her but trying to get her and Bea? What if he did get them?

She had begun to feel safe before Clarence had been hijacked to prison. She had even left her windows open at night for fresh air.

But now.

Would she ever feel safe again?

She went back into the trailer.

Bea stood by the sink … holding the bottle of whiskey.

Katty blinked. "Bea! What are you doing?" She grabbed the bottle from her.

Bea's chin quivered. "I know what that is, Mommy."

For as long as Katty lived, she would not forget the expression on Bea's face. Betrayal. Fear. "I'm … " Katty opened the bottle, her eyes never leaving Bea's face.

They stood there like that for at least an eternity, before Katty came to.

Bea's eyes told a million stories of a million nights spent hiding under the rocking chair while Katty caroused all night.

Shaking her head, tears threatening, Katty turned and poured the yellow liquid down the drain. She turned on the faucet and flushed it. She looked back at Bea.

Bea wiped her cheeks with trembling hands. Her chin jutted out as she nodded. "Good job, Mommy."

Katty rinsed the bottle over and over, then plunked it on the windowsill. She pulled a sprig of lavender from another bottle and dropped it into the whiskey bottle. "There. What was in it was evil, but now it's good." She leaned down and slowly picked up Bea. "I'm sorry, Baby Bea. I'm so sorry. I'm just scared right now. Scared of—"

"We'll be okay, Mommy."

Who was this wise child she'd been blessed with?

Another scratching sound. "Bea, we are going to have a party at the nursing home. Wanna come?"

Bea's eyes grew wide. "Yeah! Can I watch my shows?"

"Sure! We'll bring our jammies and toothbrushes and watch your shows."

Bea jumped up and down. "Yes!"

"So come on. We have to go." She dropped Bea's sandwich and what was left of hers into a baggie, and shoved some clothes into a bag. Grabbed her purse and dragged Bea out into the car.

Katty buckled Bea in and backed out of the driveway, knowing someone was watching. She tried not to panic. Didn't want to scare Bea.

She hadn't been this scared since Phil had left her. He had used her up, gotten tired of her and left. But she had hidden the fact that she was pregnant again—with Bea. He wasn't going to kill this baby.

She'd hidden out, delivered Bea by herself.

Tried to make a life—just Katty and the baby.

How Phil had found out she'd had a kid … didn't matter now.

He knew.

He was back.

And he was going to do all the evil crap he could to get her, but to get Bea.

She pulled up at Hillcrest Homes. She didn't even try to find a parking place farther away. She parked in the Visitors Only spaces. Her eyes on the door.

Just get inside. Get Bea inside.

"What are we going to do here Mommy?" Bea kicked the back of Katty's seat but for some reason it calmed her. It used to make her so mad.

"We are going to see if they will let us stay here. Maybe they have a spare bed and you and I can have a slumber party together." She unbuckled Bea and grabbed her, bag and all.

No way she would let Bea even run loose. She wouldn't take any chances here tonight or ever again.

With every car they passed, she expected someone to jump out at them.

Her fingers trembled just like when she had been using drugs and needed a fix. When she needed a fix, every cell in her body screamed and shook until she could get more drugs or booze.

Whatever was going to happen, at least she would be among friends and people who cared about them.

She pressed the auto open button and stepped in. The receptionist had gone home, so Katty walked on down to the nurses station. Lisha was still on duty.

"Girl. You look like you seen a ghost." Lisha held out her arms and Katty ran into them. Bea got squished between them.

Katty fought to hold back the tears. She didn't want to scare Bea more than she already had. But those big beautiful arms around her made it feel like no one could ever hurt them again.

Lisha released them. "What's this about? Is it about those bastards that showed up earlier? What's their names?"

Katty nodded. "Phil and Lex."

"Did they come out to your house?"

"No. Well I don't think so. I kept hearing noises." Katty shifted Bea to her other hip. "I just didn't want to stay there. He knows where we live." She shivered.

"Well, I know just where you can stay for as long as you want." She winked. "And I don't have to ask permission. If the board has a problem with it, well they can just eat it!"

Katty smiled. Something about Lisha made her happy. Somehow she knew they'd be all right. It was comforting here.

As they followed Lisha to Clarence's room, dragging a pillow pet and bag, she felt so at home. They belonged there.

How was that for crazy? She belonged in a nursing home?

Lisha flipped the lights on and pulled down the shades in both windows, both rooms. "You both have your own bathroom. You have your own bed. But I reckon you'll end up together. You know which one Clarence sleeps in all the time, so I guess you can have this one." She checked for sheets. "Still made up, so have at it." She checked the closet in the office. "Full up with boxes but there's room on top for your bags. Need a toothbrush?"

Katty shook her head. "Could we call the sheriff and let them know where we're at? I told one deputy that I might do this and he said to call if I did."

Lisha pulled her phone from her pocket and dialed. "Who you want to talk to?"

"Um. Deputy Scott."

Lisha grinned. "Oh, the cute one. He's kinda short, but he'd be great for you. You're short too."

"Hello? Sheriff's Department. Deputy Scott speaking."

Lisha laughed and handed Katty the phone. "Handy."

Katty cleared her throat. "This is Katty Randolph. We talked at the nursing ho—"

"Hello. I remember you. Are you doing okay?"

She nodded. "Yes. I just wanted to let you know … uh, let the department know that I decided to stay in Clarence's rooms at Hillcrest."

"Good idea. Glad you called. Need to make some rounds later anyway, so I'll stop by and check in on you. And your daughter. What's her name?"

"Bea. Her name is Bea."

"Like the buzz bugs, right?" Katty turned away from Lisha, who was doubled over laughing. "Well kinda. It's B. E. A. It sounds like bee though."

He laughed. "Okay. My bad. I'll be up in a little while. Got some paperwork here to catch up on and then … I'll be … there."

"Okay. Sounds fine. Thanks." Katty handed the phone back to Lisha.

"Well, that went fine, I think." She winked. "You have your own personal deputy. I'd say that's fine."

Katty shook her head. "Where can we get some washcloths?"

"Comin' right up."

Bea had already turned the TV on and was getting caught up on her shows.

Katty flitted through the papers on the desk, stacked them and sighed.

No work tonight.

She picked up Bea and sat, pulling Bea onto her lap.

Lisha returned with towels and washcloths and soap. She wrapped them both in a blanket—burrito style—and patted Bea's head. "Not used to having people so young here. Kinda nice to hear cartoons."

Katty smiled. "Oh, you'll get tired of it. Hey. How's Harold doing? He was pretty upset earlier."

"He's back to his self. Still upset about Clarence gone, but we finally got him settled down so he could rest. I think he was so intent on taking care of you two, that he just couldn't get the words out."

She headed for the door and closed it part way. "Do whatever makes you comfy and I'll be back in after meds to check on you." She peeked back in. "Doors auto lock at eight o'clock so we're locked in tight here. No one can get in."

Katty hung her head. "It feels so stupid to be scared."

Lisha came back in the room and reached for Katty's hand. "Now don't beat yourself up, Little One. My man used to beat me till my ears rang and blood dripped. I was terrified all the time." She blinked. "Never told anybody that."

"Oh, Lisha." Lisha too. She squeezed Lisha's fingers. "I hope Clarence is okay."

"He's okay. He's a stubborn old man. He'll be back." She waved and left.

Bea was already asleep on her lap.

Katty was glad for that because she felt that the emotional floor was dropping out. She tried to keep it quiet, but she couldn't stop weeping.

She stood and carried Bea to the bed. Wouldn't be the first time she had gone to bed in her clothes.

She brushed Bea's hair from her face and shook her head. She closed the door and sighed.

Would she ever be free of the memories?

She guessed not, but someday they might be safe.

Dreams of a simple man, a kind man made her feel better.

FORTY-SIX

Noell wandered into the living room. She'd been in this room all her life. Maybe she was restless, knowing what she now knew about Katty and Bea being related to her.

It was the oddest thing. Almost as if something or someone—Clarence maybe—had drawn them all together.

She had some cousins!

There were so many stacks of junk, boxes, books that she'd never know if something here was valuable or not. Did Gamma have photos that were family heirlooms? Treasures?

She knew now what was in her mother's room and what those things meant. She hadn't come to a decision as to what to do with all that upstairs, but she knew whose it was and what it meant.

The rest of this she had no idea.

Where would Gamma had kept things that meant something to her? Her bedroom?

She was restless right now.

The date with Fletch had stirred up emotion about her future.

The news that Katty and Bea were related to her had begun questions.

Some were the same old questions: like what should she do with the house—sell or keep it, if she kept it did she want to live here all by herself? She had fun with Fletch but was he the one? Was he a person that she would or could spend her whole life with?

How had Grampa or Gamma figured that out? She didn't have that time with her own mother to ask questions about life and love. Who could she ask? Who could she trust?

With Clarence in prison, she didn't feel she had anyone she could trust. She trusted Fletch, but right now he was part of the problem.

Gamma's bedroom had stayed the same as when she died just like Mommy's. The only thing Noell had done was change the sheets. She didn't even know why she had done that, but it seemed the right thing to do. Tough job to put everything back on the other side of the bed. Again. Seemed like the right thing to do.

Otherwise the room had stayed the same. There was a small private bath off to the left but that wasn't too cluttered. Gamma's bedroom had stacks and stacks of books—again was it her way to insulate the house? Wouldn't it have been better to have called a business to do that instead?

When she got the house all decluttered, it would seem huge.

Bathroom first.

Gamma'd had so many pretty perfume and lotion bottles on display but when Noell sniffed some, they smelled stale and rancid. She grabbed the trash can and dumped them all. Would they sell at the consignment shop? What would anyone do with these anyway? Maybe she should just pack it all up, except for real trash and take it down there. Let Mrs. Bertrand decide if it's worth anything. She'd know.

This was hard.

She was snooping.

She had to.

But she was snooping.

The closet made her want to scream.

Maybe the bedside table. Cute little piece of furniture. Three drawers in each one. Couldn't be too bad.

But the first one she pulled open was packed with little oil bottles. She knew Gamma had been into them but not like this. She didn't know a thing about them so she grabbed a box and started pulling them out. She sniffed one or two, wrinkled her nose at most of the others.

Done. She pushed the bottom drawer closed. She pulled it open again. It was actually empty!

Okay. Next drawer up.

Gah. Full again. Smelled the same. Looked the same. Full of little bottles of oils.

Same drill. She packed them all into the same box. If everything was this tiny, it'd take forever to go through.

Empty.

She braced herself for the top drawer. She just knew it would be full of tiny bottles again.

She pulled on the knob and got knocked back. Odd visuals of a man doing awful things to someone else flitted through her brain. Awful.

She pressed her fists into her eyes. What was that? Voices yelling obscene words. Who was that man and what was he doing in Gamma's bedroom?

Calm down.

She had been so engrossed in all that had happened to Clarence and hearing the news about Katty and Bea being related, she had forgotten to be afraid to touch handles and doors. And drawers.

But this. This was in Gamma's private stuff. She finally relaxed telling herself that it was just a fluke, that no one had been here. That man, whoever he was, had left Osceola and was long gone.

She also told herself that the top drawer would be either full of little bottles again or empty.

But it wasn't. It wasn't full of little bottles *or* empty.

It smelled like the other two drawers. The smell probably seeped from one drawer to the next.

Two book size notebooks were on top and a stack of letters underneath. The cover of the top notebook was covered in little drawings. They hadn't been printed on but ... drawn. Had Gamma been a doodler? They didn't feel raised or printed on by anything. She opened the journal and inside there were more. Really cute. Some were ... amazing.

Most pages had been dated. She checked the calendar on her phone. The most recent had been dated two weeks before she died. The handwriting was kind of messy but Noell guessed she had just scribbled down her thoughts as they came to her. These entries weren't probably for anyone to read but Gamma.

And here she was reading them.

The last entry was short. "Slept in till 6:30!"

That was sleeping in?

She had heard Gamma rustling around some nights but she figured she had needed the rest room or a drink.

"Every time I fell back to sleep, I slept hard. Felt like I worked hard in the night season. 'You did. You did all kinds of things.'"

Quotes. Odd.

It was like a conversation between Gamma and ... someone else. Who was it?

Huh.

She set the journals aside to read later. They would stop her momentum. She peeked at the empty drawers. Gotta keep going.

Letters. All tied in ribbons. She flipped them over and back again.

Were these love letters?

Naw. She'd never heard Gamma or Grampa talk about such things.

She untied the ribbon—a blue lace-edged satin ribbon—and opened the top letter. It was dated since Grampa had died so it couldn't be from him. Who would have sent her love letters? And why would she have tied them all up fancy like this if they weren't from him?

Did Gamma have a secret admirer? Or a secret boyfriend? Oh my. That would be awesome.

"Dear Father."

Her dad had to have died a long time ago. They had talked about when he died, in fact.

"Today I had to teach Noell about forgiveness."

What?

Noell slowly sat on the bed. She skimmed the page. "I remember this. It wasn't all that long ago."

Mr. Grimes.

She had long ago told Gamma about him being so creepy, but ever since then she had not talked about him very nice. Well, he wasn't very nice. But Gamma had been right—Noell had needed to get rid of unforgiveness.

She hated him. That was more than unforgiveness. Still working on that one.

The second page she skimmed again until the bottom.

"Noell doesn't seem to have the curse that I have lived with all my life."

Curse?

"Today I was at the store and checked out after an old man who had always flirted with me."

Aw. Cute. Gamma *did* have a secret admirer.

"I tried to avoid everywhere he touched but I missed the obvious— the credit card machine. I don't often use it but I didn't have enough cash for the groceries. So I checked out with that and could barely keep it together. Right away I heard heavy breathing and saw awful pictures from what looked like a magazine."

Noell dropped the pile of letters and backed against the wall.

Gamma.

Gamma could see things too?

She grabbed the letters again and found her place. "When I went out to my car, Mr. Tate was standing by his car talking to another man. I avoided his stares, but when I got to my car, he scared the daylights out of me. Stood right next to my car and I didn't even hear him walk up. I still ignored him until he put his hand on mine to open the car door for me. Nice move, but I wasn't having any of him. When he touched my hand, I started trembling and I couldn't control it. He thought it was from his sexual aura. I told him to go away. That I wasn't interested in his filth."

Go Gamma!

"He went away, but not before touching my arm. Gonna go home and take a shower!"

Noell shook her head. Same things had happened to her, but she'd never told Gamma about it. "Oh, Gamma. Why didn't we talk about this?"

What if they had? They might have been able to help each other somehow. Maybe they could have grown even closer than they had been.

And did Grampa know? He had always been super protective of her. Super gentlemanly, too. They always held hands so she guessed Grampa was okay in the filth department. Gamma probably wouldn't have let him live here if he had been different.

Mommy. Had she had the gift?

She'd have to search her room better sometime.

Another pile of letters was tucked into the side of the drawer.

"My dear Gwendolyn." This one was definitely from Grampa. She read the whole thing, then two more. "Wow. Grampa, you were the best … lover. Such neat words." He had adored Gamma.

She sat staring out the window. Blinked a couple of times.

That's who she wanted to spend the rest of her life with. Someone like Grampa. She hadn't known her dad, but it didn't matter. She wanted someone just like Grampa.

Fletch came into view out the window. He must have just gotten home from work and was chatting with his mom outside the back door. As Noell watched, he hugged her and patted her back.

Sweet.

She sat for a long time watching them, enjoying their obvious banter and love.

She realized something as she watched them. He reminded her of Grampa. She had always known he was like someone she had known or knew, but she had never realized it was Grampa.

FORTY-SEVEN

Within fifteen minutes, Sheriff and his deputy knocked on Clarence's door.

Katty had been thinking about getting ready for bed. Glad she hadn't gotten that far.

Sheriff removed his cap. "This okay for time?"

Bea stirred on the bed.

"Oh, I'm sorry." He whispered and held his finger at his lips. "I woke her up. Will she go back—"

"Hi Mr. Sheriff." Bea rubbed her eyes and slid off the bed.

"Guess not. I'm sorry."

Katty shook her head. "It's okay. We'll have a slumber party after you leave."

They all sat down around Clarence's desk. Bea climbed on her lap.

"How are you doing, little Bea?" Sheriff leaned over the desk. "We didn't get to talk much the other day."

Bea looked up at him from under Katty's arm. She looked from his face to the deputy's face. She smiled, then tucked herself under Katty's arm.

"Just a little shy." Deputy Scott walked his fingers toward her on the desk.

She giggled and pushed his fingers away.

Katty knew Bea still wasn't sure of any man's touch other than Clarence's. She was all over *him*. He could tickle her, kiss her, hug her and paddle her little bottom. He'd only done it once, but Katty guessed that was the only time he'd have to ever spank her. She'd remember it for life. All he'd have to do now would be to remind her of it and she'd behave.

"Is it okay if she is here for this?" Sheriff pointed at Bea. "I don't want to upset her if—"

"No. She's okay. She knows it all anyway." Katty glanced down at Bea. "At least I think."

"Well, if she does get upset, maybe I can take her for a walk or something." Deputy Scott made it known that the something meant ice cream as he pretended to hold an ice cream cone and then lick it.

Katty grinned. "That would be fine." She rubbed Bea's back. "It'd only take her seconds to warm up to you."

Sheriff opened his notebook and clicked his pen. "Well, I'm glad Lisha called us. This whole thing has gone on far too long. About what time did you hear noises at your trailer?"

Katty checked the clock on the wall. "Maybe about six o'clock? Something like that. We'd just gotten home from the store. And before that, we were here when people saw Phil and Lex hanging around. Or rather hiding around."

"Okay." He scribbled in his notebook. "So you saw them here, then left for the store and got home. What noises did you hear at home?"

"Just … noises. Like something hitting against the trailer. Or something slamming. Or scraping. I ran out and saw a cat, and it could have been that. But after seeing Phil and Lex here earlier, I was scared already, so maybe it was just a cat. But I thought of Phil right away."

"Was there any contact when you saw them here before?" Sheriff glanced around the room. "They didn't come down here?"

Katty shook her head. "No. We didn't talk to them and they didn't come down here."

Bea peeked out from Katty's arm. "They wanted ice cream 'cause that's where Mr. Harold saw them."

"Right." Sheriff got busy with his notebook. "Let me write that down." He dictated as he wrote. "They. Wanted. Ice cream." He tapped the pen on the notebook. "I got it down."

Bea grinned. "But they didn't get any. You were too fast for them."

He diligently wrote that down. "Well I'm glad you called. We need to know every time you see them or hear from them."

Katty nuzzled Bea's head, pursing her lips. "Well, when you say it like that, there have been a couple other times."

Sheriff straightened. "Really. When?"

Deputy Scott tapped the desk in front of Bea. Probably trying to distract her. He walked his fingers over to her and tried to tickle her.

"Well, we got a bike left at our place."

Bea sat upright on Katty's lap. "Yeah. It was red and bright and shiny. It had handlebars and a basket. And pedals. And a great big bow on it."

"How big was the bow?" Sheriff was ready to write it down.

"This big!" Bea held her arms wide. "And Mommy wouldn't let me keep it."

Katty shrugged. "I figured it was from Clarence. He's been like a grandpa to us—to her. So I called here and that's when they were picking him up to go prison. I heard the whole conversation and we rushed down here. But Clarence hadn't left the bike. He told me so over the phone, before they got him."

"That was just before he and Bea were shot, right?" Deputy Scott folded his hands on the desk in front of him. "Why did you think Clarence had left it?"

"Because he was always doing something like that. Nothing so expensive as the bike, except for when he pays me and he helped with our new deck."

"He bought me a new car seat so I wouldn't fall out of the car." Bea nodded, her face serious.

Sheriff and Deputy Scott glanced at each other.

Sheriff bit his lip.

Deputy Scott wiped his eyes.

"So you don't have any proof that it was Phil who left the bike for her, then."

"No. Except." Katty hesitated. "Yesterday, I got the mail and there was a note in there for Bea."

"There was?" Bea jumped down, holding her side. "Where is it? I didn't see it!"

"You didn't see it, because I didn't show it to you." Katty reached for her purse and pulled the note out. She held it for a second, but when she looked at it again, she was afraid she would get so mad that they would arrest *her*. She handed it to Sheriff.

He took time to look it over and to read it before passing it to Deputy Scott.

He read it and gave it back to Sheriff. "What makes you think this is from him?"

Katty was almost jumping out of her chair, she was so sure of herself. She showed them the envelope. "I'd know this handwriting anywhere. It's his."

Bea craned to see.

Sheriff and the deputy exchanged looks. "If you can give us some sort of example of his handwriting that is his name for instance, or has something written and signed by him, we could compare them and send them in for analysis."

Katty shook her head. "I hated him so bad, that I burned—" She tapped her finger against the notepaper. "I have … " She got her purse and opened her wallet. She pulled out a piece of paper. "I don't even know why I kept this." She opened the note and pushed it to Sheriff.

He skimmed it and glanced up at her. "Why? Why did you keep this?" He pushed it over to the deputy.

She fumbled with the latch on her purse and shook her head. "I thought … I thought he loved me. When he sent me this, I wanted to leave my parents so bad. They … ," she glanced at Bea, "they weren't very nice people."

Bea crawled on Katty's lap. She looked at the note, then searched Katty's face.

"When he sent me this, it was a way out." She shook her head. "I didn't know what he was really like." She bit her lip. "It started the minute we got to his place. I didn't have a chance."

Awkward.

She'd never told anyone that. Never showed the note to anyone.

Deputy Scott handed the note to Sheriff and he compared the signatures. "Looks the same to me. Okay if I keep these? I can send them in and get an official assessment."

Katty nodded. She had loved him once. "I don't ever want it back, Sheriff." Good to break ties to her past.

Sheriff stood and pushed the chair up to the desk. "Okay. I guess until we get the samples back, we're done. And, like I think Lisha might have told you, they automatically lock up here at eight. No one comes in. No one goes out." He checked the clock. "Except us. In an hour."

"Okay." Kathy looked at Bea. "Maybe we'll go down for ice cream before we go to bed, huh Bea?"

Bea hopped down. "Let's go, Mommy!" She dragged Katty out to the hallway and gestured to the men. "Come with us."

The men laughed.

"Feel free, Deputy. I want to get these in." Sheriff tipped his hat. "Another time." He bowed to Bea. "Thank you, Ma'am." He straightened. "And Katty, I assure you, we will do everything we can to keep you two safe. I wish I could say the same thing for Clarence."

FORTY-EIGHT

Phil parked the car at the implement company and walked across the highway to the park. He guessed the employee would be okay with him parking there since he'd left a six-pack for him in his vehicle a couple times. This evening produced the grand prize of a bottle of whiskey in a paper bag on the drivers seat.

No traffic on the highway. He didn't even look both ways. Bad boy. These small towns were such a joke. People just lived in them to hide from life.

He raised his eyebrows. Maybe that's what he should do—hide. He guessed that just like ole Jessie James though, his past would catch up with him at some point.

As he stepped across the railroad tracks and into the park, he spied Katty and Bea outside the nursing home eating ice cream with a deputy. He dipped down behind a tree. What a coincidence. He definitely planned to kidnap Bea and whatever he had to do with Katty, he'd do. But not in a public place.

He had found their crappy trailer park. Katty was such a loser, but he'd always known that. Why they had hooked up years ago, he couldn't remember. Probably because he was just his usual horny self.

He smiled. Yeah. He lived life through testosterone.

He ducked. Had she seen him? She didn't grab Bea and run inside, so maybe not.

He shifted behind a closer tree for a better look.

Closer to that old slide.

Still there. He got a rush just looking at it. He'd had Bea back then. He should have kept on driving with her in tow and not given them a chance at her. He never once figured old Timmelsen would be able to rescue her especially when he lit it on fire.

If he himself couldn't have Bea, then he didn't want Katty or Timmelsen to have her either. Something in him rose up that day. He had not forgotten that moment when he knew he'd kill Bea by duct taping her to the slide and then setting it on fire.

He didn't understand what that something was—that moment—but he knew it well. It was the same as when he'd gotten rid of a few babies for Katty. And when he'd beaten Timmelsen. And when he touched Bea's cheek—so tender and pure. And when he'd almost killed Katty.

As he watched Katty wipe Bea's face, that something rose up in him again. Powerful. Terrifying. Growling.

Damn, he knew what it was and still, after all these years, he wasn't ready to admit what it really was.

A demon.

And not just one.

He remembered moments when he'd watched his dad drink blood. Dad had been a meat cutter and had plenty of access to the stuff.

When he drank it, his face changed. Phil hadn't understood it then. It had been terrifying yet fascinating at the same time. There was something in that blood—some power—that could actually change a person's skin and structure.

Crazy.

Even crazier was one time when his dad had set down the paper cup, his eyes were almost delirious—the guy used knives to cut meat for Pete's sake—he looked at Phil and filled the cup back up and shoved it to Phil.

Like he would drink blood.

But sweet dad, when Phil said no way, picked up a knife and grabbed his hand, ready to inflict pain if he didn't drink.

He drank.

That day something changed in him. Something was different. He almost felt that someone had taken up residence in his body. Back then, he didn't understand that stuff and he wasn't all that sure he really understood now, but every time he inflicted pain or drew blood, power grew and surged into something even he couldn't control.

Katty laughed and smiled. That deputy was chasing Bea around Katty's legs. Did they have a thing?

Phil was shocked at the jealousy growling inside him.

Bea didn't seem to have as much energy as she had months ago when he was trying to tape her down. She held her belly.

Oh, right. She'd been shot.

Something Phil didn't understand flickered inside. When he had taped Bea to the slide, he hadn't cared that she might die, but now he gets all soppy because someone else shot her?

She was cute.

Katty picked Bea up and snuggled her.

Even seemed like *Katty* had changed.

She nuzzled her nose into Bea's neck and hair.

Sweetness.

He peeked around the other side of the tree.

Katty *had* changed. She seemed … more tender. Nice.

Too bad she hadn't been that way back … why was he wanting to kill them or even kidnap Bea when they could be a family?

Holy shit! Where had that thought come from?

A slow growl rose from his very toes and surfaced in a snarl.

Look what he could have had back then but … even now. He could have had a family: a wife and kid. They could all be playing together, instead of that deputy. Damn, he had been robbed.

Katty laughed as Bea tickled her neck.

Why should Katty get all the love? Why should she get all the snuggles from that sweet pure little girl?

At the thought of how perfect Bea was, more rose up within him. He could feel it where you couldn't scratch in public.

It was a demon and it began its stinky progression up his torso to his chest. Every part of him wanted what Katty had.

That little girl had to be his.

Oh-oh. He ducked behind the bigger tree and peeked around it. The deputy patted Bea's head and walked to his squad car.

What was this? Phil wanted to growl. Did they have an admirer? A boyfriend? Or more. A lover.

The thought pushed Phil over the edge.

This had to stop.

He had to get his little girl.

FORTY-NINE

Clarence tried to lean up off the bed, to check the cell door but could hardly move. All he could do was roll to his side and let his head lift.

The lights were dim, but he couldn't see anything or anyone.

He needed to move around. Who had told him that recently?

Lester.

Was Lester real? Was he an angel?

Lester had given him good advice to just get moving.

He gripped the sides of the cot and tried to sit up. Oh God, he couldn't do it.

He rolled to his left side and grabbed the metal bed frame.

He was able to slide his legs to the edge and barely get them over and toward the floor. He pushed up with his right hand and set his feet onto the floor at the same time.

Luckily, the bed wasn't far off the floor so his feet touched.

Man, he hurt. He had been beaten to the very end of his life before. But before, he had been a hundred years younger.

He leaned, his arm supporting him and almost sat up. He pushed harder and sat up right. Felt like he'd run a marathon, instead of just sitting up in bed.

"I see you're back to your old self, Mr. Timmelsen."

Clarence jumped. He almost fell back against the wall. Still on the cot, but he would have hit his head which had taken enough hits.

Warden stood on the other side of the bars with five fully armed guards. "Glad to see our welcome committee didn't keep you down."

Clarence could only growl. Welcome committee my—

"You better get used to that kind of treatment." He smirked. "I'm sure you know you'll be here till you die, so get used to it."

One of the guards looked familiar now that his eyes had adjusted a little to the dark.

Randy.

How could one man change so quickly? On the trip to Osceola, Randy had been almost a friend. Said he'd wished he could buy Clarence a steak supper instead of the fast food they had eaten.

What would have changed a man so quickly?

He seemed to avoid Clarence's stare.

"Randy." Clarence's voice was almost gone. He coughed. "What are you doing following this man?"

Randy flinched.

Warden roared. "You shut up. He doesn't need to listen to you. He reports to me now."

"Maybe so. But Randy is a good man. And you have changed him. You have lured him into the devil's snare and now he is one of you."

Where had that come from? The devil's snare?

Something had changed in Clarence and he suspected it had something to do with when he'd stepped off that precipice last night into Jesus' arms.

"Randy, there is another way. You have another chance to be free of this man. You can be free of this evil."

Wow. Those words were not from him! Out of his mouth maybe, but not his.

The warden stepped closer to the bars. "No, you shut up, Timmelsen. He is just fine doing what he's doing. He has served me well." The warden roared. "Shut up!"

Clarence had never been so aware of evil and good. Of the difference in people. He could hear it in Warden's voice. In Tay Ralston's voice. He could see it in Randy's eyes.

"You know I didn't kill your brother in cold blood. He drew a knife on me and it was all in self defense. You know that. You know that's the truth." Clarence stretched to full stature. "Randy, you know that's the truth. It was self defense. Get the old files. See for yourself. This man who calls himself the warden is a liar. He's willing to cheat, lie and steal from people like you and me. Just to make himself look bigger."

Randy wouldn't look at Clarence. He just kept his eyes downcast, his hands at his sides.

"Go to bed, Timmelsen. We'll deal with you tomorrow. We have some surprises for you then. Maybe some reunions between old friends. We're bringing guys in who were there when you killed Lewis. They have a few things to say to you, too. They'll set things straight."

Clarence shuddered.

Randy stared at him from between the warden and another guard. His eyes had changed from just minutes before. He shook his head and prepared to leave with the others.

They started to march off down the walkway, when Warden turned and stared at Clarence. "I just want to thank you. Because you signed all your property over to me, I can afford to take a little trip." He squinted. "It seems the government doesn't like my little family dealings, so we will be leaving soon. Phil left to take care of your girls—all of them—and tomorrow, you'll get repaid for killing my brother—firing squad style." He glanced at Randy. "I don't think anyone does that anymore, so it should be," he leaned closer, "spectacular."

He turned and walked on down the hall.

Clarence was left alone.

He shook and shuddered at the thought of what tomorrow might bring. Warden must be bringing in the very guys who had fought him that fateful day and lost.

Clarence had never been a fighter, but he figured he had enough anger in him at losing Annie and being robbed of his life, that it must have given him power. Fueled the fight so he could defend himself against those monsters.

He moved around the cell as good as he could. Shuffled back and forth. From bars to the facilities. From his cot to the other wall.

It was painful but the more he moved and walked back and forth, the easier it got so he could almost walk right. He made himself stand up straight—head up—shoulders back. He willed himself to walk up straight instead of leaning over and bent like an old man.

He would fight. He had no idea how he would get out of here, but he would.

Even though the guards and Warden had left, the evil was still there. Clarence looked in every corner. Under his cot. Behind the toilet. He could see nothing.

But he would bet his life's savings and holdings—he actually had some now—that there was evil present. It made his skin crawl. He needed to find a way out. Out that tiny barred window. To get away from this evil, this madness.

He didn't understand what it was, but he felt it with every cell of his body.

He made himself walk more. Stretch more.

Even as he tried ignoring the presence, it didn't go away.

He bent over at the waist. Tried to do squats. That hurt too much.

He knew he'd lost a lot of blood because he was so weak.

Another circle around the cell.

Another.

And another.

More stretches.

Leg lifts.

Arm lifts.

He moved every way he could think of without crying out.

The evil persisted.

Dammit. Enough.

"In heaven's name go away." He tried some words he'd heard Mrs. Hatly say at Hillcrest.

"In Jesus' name."

Some song he'd heard—didn't even have to be Christian.

"How Great Thou Art."

Where had he heard that from? They'd hardly gone to church after his mother died. Must have heard it on the radio or TV. Or Lisha had been singing it.

"Help me, Jesus."

The evil would not go away and Clarence wouldn't have admitted to anyone but he was afraid to try to lie down and sleep for fear it would overtake him and kill him as he slept.

"And the roll is called up yonder."

That was stretching it.

He lowered himself onto his cot. At least he could move. Somewhat.

"That's it, whatever you are." He spoke to the evil and then thought a minute. "You are a someone. Aren't you. You are real."

Something rose up in Clarence. A righteous indignation. Anger so powerful. A knowing that he was on the right track, he just didn't know the right words to say.

"You know what, devil?" Clarence gathered force. "I'm not giving up."

Another breath.

"And I'm not giving in."

"For nothin' or nobody."

FIFTY

Noell opened the back door. Somedays—like today—she just wanted to come home from work and not face the mess. It had been a good day; everybody bantered and joked as they filled potholes—a never-ending task. Steve Ivertson, her boss, had brought a case of soda for them all to share. Just made the warm day go a little better. Maybe he was also feeling a little sheepish over the fact he had been gone all morning, taking care of his grandma at the nursing home. It worked. The soda had invigorated them all.

Stacked boxes had the usual effect as she dropped her lunch cooler on the floor. She shook her head. There was much to do.

The keys to Grampa's shed dangled in the sun, hanging from the crazy key closet on the wall beside the back door.

Thank God they had been diligent in keeping track of keys. There were still things that Noell couldn't find. She guessed that there were legal papers Clarence might need to sell this house, but maybe she'd still find them. And she could go to the court house and check there too.

The keys beckoned. Unpack more stuff or go outside and explore Grampa's shed?

No contest.

She grabbed them and stepped out the door. Beautiful fall day. The rains lately had turned the grass a lovely green. Leaves falling on the lawn were golden yellow and rust against the green. A bush by Grampa's old shed was a beautiful rose red.

She checked the camper. Still locked, but weird vibrations ran up her arm from the knob. She shook her hand. That was crazy. No one came back here. Not even her until now. Gamma hadn't even been able to get here for years she guessed.

The shed wasn't a falling down shed. It had been kept up through the years by Grampa. She used to love being out here when he was working. He had always been tinkering on some little thing. She would play at his feet with her … what? Noell couldn't remember any dolls out here. He had given her tools, all her own. She remembered them but what had she done with them? Were they still in here?

Now that became the most important thing in this world to find: her tools and what she had made with them. More than anything in the house, this became the piece of gold that she needed to dig up.

She grasped the doorknob and the jolt she got from it knocked her flat. A grumbling, growling voice ran through her mind, her being. She could almost hear this voice audibly.

The pictures that scrolling through her mind were terrible. She closed her eyes, but they only became worse—even more graphic. Awful bloody pictures. Babies. A woman.

Katty?

Awful things with her. Awful.

Noell covered her face with her hands and wanted to scream but she was sitting in her backyard, exposed to the world of her neighbors.

This wasn't Mr. Grimes or his stuff.

This was someone else.

Something totally different.

She couldn't do this. If she was to get into Grampa's shed, she'd have to get some kind of bulldozer or little skid loader. Maybe even back the old pickup into it so she didn't have to touch the doorknob again.

Ever again.

She turned away and walked toward the house, wiping her cheeks. When had she cried? That jolt had been so powerful it must have jarred tears lose.

She looked behind her at the shed. Who had been here? Who had been back here and when?

More steps toward the house.

Each step slowed until she stopped mid yard. Right next to the clothes line she never used.

Wait. This was her property and just like the nightmares and the pool, she would not let it scare her away. She would rise up and claim what was hers.

Tears ran down her cheeks and her neck.

This must be another one of those moments when she had to face her fears.

And face them she would.

She turned back to the old shed.

One step.

Another.

And another until she was standing at the door.

She swallowed, aware now of someone farther down the block in their back yard.

Kids. Kids were swinging and singing.

She braced herself.

Hand on the knob.

She would not let go.

She made herself keep holding onto it.

The voices and visuals swam around in her mind, mixing with others there. Screaming. There was blood.

But somehow there was Grampa.

And a sweet child's voice.

Hers!

Her voice.

Her whole body vibrated. Trembled with the frequencies of the voices and all, but she forced her hand there on the knob and inserted the key into the keyhole.

At first she couldn't hit it right. She turned it upside down and it fit in.

One turn and the lock inside clicked and it opened.

Even in the darkness, she sensed Grampa. Even after all the voices and such, his presence was so much stronger in here.

She found the light cord and pulled, expecting it to break or not even work, but the light came on.

Not just one light bulb but a series of shop lights that illuminated every corner.

Her whole being wanted to burst.

Everywhere she looked she sensed him. She walked farther inside and she could smell him.

Trailing her fingers along the tools still on his workbench, she remembered. Things had been left as if he had just walked into the house to eat. He loved his food.

She remembered where she had dropped one of his prize roses.

She clapped her hands.

He had been the gardener, not Gamma! All this time she had thought it had been Gamma who had kept up the gardens until she couldn't anymore. She probably had done it for him—to keep up his memories. Just like she had kept up going to auctions, only at some point it had turned into an obsession that neither had foreseen.

She touched the router and waited for any voice or picture. Several popped up. Grampa had been making cabinets for inside. She could see the lines he made with the machine, the beautiful carvings he had done. Carvings of flowers.

Of course since he had been the gardener.

Interesting.

If she didn't shy away from touching tools or door handles, she could maybe learn something, see things that could help her. Help other people.

She picked up a hammer and immediately she sensed many men and women using it. Heard familiar voices. Grampa's distinctive voice —his voice had always soothed her with its melodic, deep smoothness.

Some older men had raspy harsh voices but his was like a river or like caramel or smooth wood that he so beautifully finished.

But there was another voice that was familiar from this hammer.

She rubbed the wooden handle. Almost lovingly. After the blast from the doorknob outside, this was soothing and peaceful. Calming.

Who was the other voice?

Sounded like Clarence but couldn't be. He wouldn't have been around … unless.

She froze. Skitters of inspiration and even joy ran up her spine.

Grampa always bought a lot of tools at auctions.

What if he had bought some tools of Clarence's dad's and Clarence had used it before he went to prison? When he was still at home as a boy and helped his dad.

She began to touch everything in the shop.

She didn't hear anything from some tools or items she picked up, but some almost yelled at her.

Rat?

The guy from work at the Roads Department?

When had *he* been out here?

She'd have to see if her gift helped her find a timing to the visuals.

Like had he used a tool that Grampa had purchased at an auction or had Rat somehow stolen them or broken in here? And when?

She had discovered things in here. Things that had scared her as a child and possibly would scare her now, but she knew she had to go back there and remember.

Had this guy who knocked her back at the doorknob wanted to cause her pain?

Rat had. He was a creep. If she hadn't have stopped him, he would have taken all she was. In one night. In one action that would have closed her to ever being or finding herself.

She found herself getting excited and drawn to this shop—to discovering everything here and how it spoke to her.

Just like in the camper. Some things just pulled at her and she knew she was to follow.

She hated to go back inside, but now she knew there was nothing she wanted to get rid of out here in the shop.

With a deep sigh she opened the door, at first careful to avoid the doorknob, but she touched it almost without thinking, knowing she needed to.

And braced herself once again as she locked it.

The voices were as clear as before, but this time she saw a man driving past Gamma's house in an older model car. She'd seen this before. When Gamma was still alive.

Was the man in the car, the same man who had touched the doorknob?

As she walked to the house, she felt someone watching her.

Sure enough, Mr. Grimes waved at her through his window.

Gross.

She wouldn't wave at him if he was going to get run over by a truck.

She continued inside the house and randomly touched things to test her gift. Most things she didn't sense anything from—voices or otherwise.

She walked upstairs, taking the steps two at a time.

The railing didn't give off anything.

Oh, don't let him have touched anything from Mommy's room. The doorknob didn't give off any vibes.

She turned to the doorway to her room.

Don't let him have gone in there.

She touched the doorknob and got knocked back almost as violently as she had outside the shed.

God. He had been up here.

She should report this to the police, but how would she ever say it? They would never buy the fact that she could *feel* and *hear* the people.

In her own room. How that was any different than all over the rest of the house she didn't know. Thank God he hadn't gotten inside the shed. She had locked it up right so no one could ever get in there except her.

The doorknob to her bathroom was quiet. Just her.

Whew.

Her bed frame was fine. Nothing.

When she touched her Bible, she felt something but not him. She chuckled. Could her Bible speak to her? Could she discover or hear voices from it? See visuals? She'd have to test it sometime.

The little cup from Gamma was sweet. There were voices that she'd never detected before. Little kids laughing and playing.

Deep breath. Such peace from the Bible and cup. So thankful Gamma had given that to her before she died. It gave her peace.

Another deep sigh.

She knew Gamma had kept and hung onto too many things. She stared out the window. She could forgive that as she was learning so much more about her Gamma since she had died.

But her baby bracelet was gone—wait! The tiny beads and pearls were scattered all over the floor! They hardly showed up against the old painted wooden floor.

She screamed and fell to her knees.

As she picked up each one, she screamed again and again with the visuals that hit with each bead.

Awful pictures of a little boy and a man who hit the boy repeatedly. The boy hiding in a closet with creatures all around him as he cried and raged. Babies. Babies mutilated.

That man!

God, help!

Noell couldn't help herself. She was compelled to pick up every bead, each pearl, but with each one came horrible and gruesome pictures and sounds.

She finally sat with her hands cupping the remains of her baby bracelet, sobbing.

Who was this man?

Murderer.

Violator.

Defiler.

Destroyer.

He had broken one of the only direct connections to Mommy that she had left. Maybe Mommy had been the first to touch it. Maybe she had even put it on Noell's own wrist.

That man had desecrated that purity, that sweetness.

Noell had always reached for it anticipating Mommy in a sweet moment before the drowning. It had comforted her.

Now as Noell held every bead cupped in her hand, the culmination of evil now on each one threw her back against the closet door.

The same voice from her bracelet was the same voice and visuals at Grampa's shed doorknob.

That man had been on her property.

He had been inside her house.

In her room.

He had touched—and destroyed—her bracelet.

FIFTY-ONE

Harold pushed his walker to the sink and grabbed his toothbrush, squeezed some green toothpaste out and paused.

What was Clarence doing about now?

He glanced behind him at his alarm clock. Nine a.m.. He could see it from clear across the room—nice big numbers. He'd had breakfast and a sweet conversation with Mrs. Hatly. They had lingered over coffee, both worried about Clarence.

Harold was just as worried about her. She seemed even more frail than before. Her hands shook a little and the twinkle in her eyes wasn't as … twinkly.

He started brushing and spit. Mrs. Hatly and Clarence had something so sweet and deserved—

Ring!

Dang. Where was that phone?

He grabbed his towel and took a step. Forgot his walker. Dilemma. He needed his walker.

Ring!

"I got it, Harold!" Lisha burst into the room and stumbled. "Wait. Where is it?"

"Oh … I … there!" He pointed to the pocket attached to the arm of his wheelchair. "I left it there."

She fished it out and tapped it on. "Hello?" She turned and faced him. "Harold's phone."

Harold wiped his mouth and reached for it, only she didn't give it to him. Her eyebrows twitched and her brown eyes opened wider.

"Um." She straightened. "Yes, Sir. He is." She nodded and pointed at Harold. "He's right here, Sir." She leaned into Harold. "It's the governor's office."

He cleared his throat and took the phone. Glad he'd brushed his teeth. "Hello?" The professional detective kicked in. "This is Harold Dexter."

Lisha clapped her hands together against her lips.

"Yes." He slid into the wheelchair and searched for his notepad. Where was his pen?

Lisha patted the newspaper and papers on the table. No pen.

Damn. What had he done with it? "Yes. I do have time." He tapped Lisha's shoulder and pointed to her pocket.

She whipped her pen out and handed it to him then tapped his phone speaker on.

Harold hovered his hand over the phone and accidentally hit the "end" button.

"Oh! Harold!" She picked the phone up. "You cut him off!"

"Damn it! I'm … he was just getting to the phone. He'd had his secretary or somebody dial and he was just—"

Lisha hit redial and handed it back to Harold.

He carefully placed it on the table and picked up her pen, poised over the notepad.

Ring!

An aide waved from the open door. "Want juice, Harold?"

Lisha shushed her. "He's talking to the governor."

Hand at her mouth, eyebrows arched, the aide backed away and swung her noisy juice cart to the other side of the hallway.

Good. He needed quiet. He used to be smooth and together—even with distractions when he talked to people, but now he couldn't concentrate.

"Hello? Governor's office."

Cleared his throat. "Hello? This is Harold Dexter, again. I apologize for hanging up on … er, tapping off, er, the decline button on you."

A deep voice came on, laughing. "That's okay, Harold. I've done that too."

Harold, hand half covering his mouth, whispered, "It's the governor." Back to the phone. "What can I do for you, Sir?"

"First of all, where do you live, Harold? What town and all?"

Lots of noise on the governor's end. "I live at Hillcrest Homes in Osceola, Nebraska. The nursing home."

"Okay. So, you knew my dad? Did I get that right?" Phones ringing. Voices. Busy office.

Harold nodded. "Yes. Yes I did. We worked together on several cases, but I lost touch with him after I retired."

"That's what he said." Governor chuckled. "I talked to him last night about you. He had great things to say about your work and how you used to go out of your way to help people out. Sounds like you are the same man today, with the way you want to help … uh, Clarence Timmelsen? Is that his name?"

"Yes. He is one of my best buddies here and has been dished a hard road. All his life." Harold blinked. "All his life. And now they took him back to—" Harold choked.

Lisha rubbed his shoulder. Her eyes filled, too.

"Hmm. I've had a friend like that. They don't come along very often, do they?"

Harold swallowed. "No, they don't."

"Well, I just wanted to thank you for calling the office. You have no idea the ruckus you have caused here." He chuckled again. "I can't tell you all the details right yet, but because of your call, you have given us the missing link of a huge … well, I can tell you and know you are a professional. Just keep it under your hat, okay?"

"Yes, Sir."

Gasps came from the doorway. Four aides stood there, hands over their mouths. One was noiselessly jumping up and down.

"You have helped open up one of the nation's largest drug ring and sex traffic dynasties. It seems to be based in Chicago—at that prison. If you're a praying man, teams are organizing. The timing has to be just right, so prayers are needed. There is unusual resistance right now, but when we are able to put this last piece of the puzzle in, we will be able to free many people, including Clarence."

Lisha walked to the door, her arms wide, pushing the women back and shushing them.

"Yes, Sir, Mr. Governor." Harold blinked. He couldn't believe what he had just heard. First of all to get Clarence out, but to break up something that big! He'd just told them what he knew, in order to get Clarence home. He wanted to salute, just like back in—

"Well Harold, I'll let you go. I need to get to work. Okay if I call back, if we need more information?"

Someone must be talking to him. Lots of noises: more phones ringing, voices. Something dropped.

"Yes. Yes. Anytime." Harold held up his finger. "Say. Would you greet your dad for me? Tell him hello?"

Governor paused and shushed someone near him. "Harold, I would love to do that. It has been a pleasure talking to you. And I'm not joking. This is a huge deal. We even traced something going on out there in Durant, a non town out there by you." He stopped. "There. I've said too much. I'll keep in touch, Harold."

"Thank you, Sir." Harold blinked. "Get Clarence home!"

FIFTY-TWO

There he went. Clarence counted five times Warden had circled around the cell block.

Didn't he have security to make rounds?

Pacing. Up the steps. Past all the cells on that level, across to the other wall and down the other side.

Again and again.

After the fifth time when Warden passed Clarence's cell, Michael appeared.

Ever since Clarence had stepped off the cliff with Jesus, Michael had been around.

Clarence guessed one had something to do with the other. Him stepping into Jesus and Michael being released to help Clarence or even appear to him. He didn't understand, he just kind of knew.

Michael leaned out the cell, watching Warden.

Dear Father, he loved this guy—this big angel. All the moments they had shared. Grinding gears in that old pickup. Times in that pool.

God. Osceola.

Clarence watched the warden march across the commons area on the opposite cell block, exactly across from him.

Stomp, stomp, stomp.

"Michael." Clarence reached out a hand to him. "Michael. Are my girls okay?" He shook his head. "You know I can call them that now, right?"

Michael didn't turn his head. He didn't even flinch.

Louder this time. "Michael. Can't you hear me?"

He wasn't paying a bit of attention to Clarence. Like he was deaf. Like he didn't even want to talk to him. Or was a statue.

Michael stomped his foot once. The whole cell block shook.

Clarence's cell door swung open and when he looked down the block, all the other doors flew open too. On both sides.

Warden had just gotten to the left of Clarence's door. He started yelling for the guards to come and trap the prisoners who had started to run out.

Michael grabbed the warden by the neck and held onto him while Clarence ran out of his cell.

He flung the warden inside the cell and slammed the door.

Warden rushed to push his way out, but he smashed his head into the bars.

Locked!

For a moment, Clarence was just as shocked as Warden appeared to be.

The bars had always separated them. But Warden was always on the outside and Clarence was always on the inside.

Clarence grinned and ran his fingers against the bars as he walked past, tapping each one for effect. "How do you like it from the inside, Warden? Feels just like home, right?"

Warden roared. "You can't do this!" He saw the other inmates running down the steps—yelling and jumping and thundering. "How did you do that? You are a bastard! I'll get you back."

Clarence calmly walked to the bars again. "You—"

Michael hooked Clarence's arm with his huge hands. Full on angel costume. Wings spread up and out as Clarence watched.

Breathtaking. So much so that Clarence couldn't breathe. Couldn't finish insulting Warden.

A door slammed downstairs and gunshots echoed across the block. Security entered and ran upstairs both sides and trapped some of the inmates. Several were caught and cuffed.

Randy led two more guards up the steps to Clarence's side. He stumbled when he got upstairs and saw the Warden inside a cell.

Clarence's cell.

"Get me out! Get me out!" Warden yelled and rattled the door.

"You scream like a girl, Warden." Clarence loved it.

Randy just stopped where he landed and stared at Clarence. "How'd you do that?"

Clarence shook his head. "Randy."

They stared at each other for what seemed like hours.

Michael leaned down then. He was ten times taller than normal. "You want to stay and taunt the warden or do you want to go home to your girls?"

Clarence blinked. "Home. Michael, home!"

As soon as he closed his mouth, he landed outside the prison.

Clarence turned in circles. How on Earth?

Cars and TV trucks whizzed past him. Some other inmates ran down into a gully, guards chasing them.

A siren blared but no one followed Clarence. He had the prisoner uniform on and everything, but no one even looked at him.

It was like … he was invisible.

Michael and several angels walked right in front of him, some surrounding him. He could see them now. Were they hiding him? Why not the other prisoners?

Wait. He looked over beyond the gully and one other prisoner was surrounded just like he was. He waved.

"Michael! Who is that? What is he?"

Michael looked up. He was concentrating so hard. "Where?"

Clarence waved back at the man. "There."

"Oh. You might get to meet someday." He grinned. "It'll be a surprise. Sort of."

Someone was on the intercom from inside and it blasted all over the grounds.

Screaming, "Find him! Now!"
Warden.

FIFTY-THREE

Katty brushed her teeth. She tried not to invade Clarence's space, so she just kept her private stuff like toothbrush and female things in their bag. She had packed so fast. She had her jammies and her robe and right now that was all she cared about.

Bea was already crashed. She'd let her watch a TV show, but she'd fallen asleep right away. Carol and Lisha said she would be that way for awhile. She was still healing.

Katty shuffled in her nursing home issue slippers to the window.

Clarence.

He was in great shape, but it couldn't be good. She had never spent time in prison, just a few nights in the local jail but prison was way different. When she had spent time in jail, women there had talked about the brutality—even in women's prisons.

Katty cringed thinking of what Clarence might be going through.

Nursing homes didn't seem so bad. If a person had a car. She had no idea how much it cost, but bet it was expensive.

Well she was going to enjoy it while she could. She had all kinds of service. Meals. Housekeeping. Nurses at her disposal. She loved the place because of the people but never would she be able to give a stranger a bath or do those other things they had to do.

She'd heard Lisha make a comment or two she wished she'd never overheard.

"There you are!"

Katty turned to see the administrator standing in the doorway, her hands on her hips. Frizzy, dyed hair framed her full face. Eyes seemed stern. Couldn't this nursing home ever find nice administrators?

Maybe the free ride wasn't so free.

"Uh, hello." Katty glanced over at her sleeping Bea. Dang. Where would she go now? "I'm sorry. I forgot your—"

The woman tapped her name tag. "Miss Oster. And you need to clear out. This is totally unorthodox."

"Isn't it paid for?" Katty shuffled some papers around on Clarence's desk. Where were his bills? "I mean, he already paid, right?"

"Hey girl. You okay?" Lisha framed the administrator by a foot, above and both sides.

Lisha. Thank God.

She pushed around the smaller woman, bumping her aside, and stood between them. "Ain't this awesome, Mizz Oster? Clarence isn't using his rooms right now, so Katty and her baby girl might as well, since they going through some stuff." She held out her arms wide. "Ain't it great?"

Miss Oster squinted and shook her head. "I suppose. As long as—"

"They don't drink as much coffee as Clarence or won't eat here," she glanced at Katty, "so the home saves money, actually. We won't even wash their clothes."

The administrator threw up her hands. "I suppose." She glanced at Bea sleeping on the bed. "Nice to have little ones here." Back at Katty. "I suppose." She turned. "Have a good night."

Lisha bit her lips.

Katty raised her eyebrows.

Silence, except for the sound of heels clomping away, down the hall.

Lisha covered Bea up and brushed her hair off her face. "How you really doing?"

Katty stacked the papers. "I'm okay." She hugged her arms. "Just thinking about Clarence and wondering how he is. I've heard awful stories of prison and—"

Lisha held out her arms and Katty walked into her. This woman's heart was as big as her body. And Katty loved every cell of her. "I know, baby. Carol and I pray all the time for him. We … " She shook her head and blinked. "God keep him safe and bring him back home."

Katty nodded

"Look." Lisha pointed outside. "Ain't that the deputy man?" She tapped on Katty's nose. "Bet he's coming to check up on you."

"Me?" Katty backed away and shook her head. "No way." She pointed at the car. "He's coming to check to see if those—"

"He's checking up on you." Lisha grinned.

"So what if he is? I can't stop him, right?" Katty smirked. So what if he was?

Lisha left and laughed all the way down the hall.

There had only been one man in her life that she would have cherished and that was Tommy Sand. When they were both twelve, he used to ride his bike by her house everyday on his way to school. He'd ride past even though it was blocks out of his way. And then back home from school. Summer was the worst. She almost got tired of it until her mom figured it out.

Reliving that day was awful.

Katty had been hanging out on the porch, reading, waiting for him actually. He always waved and smiled. With what she had going on inside her house, he was a breath of the air that had been sucked out of the house.

That day—here he came, pedaling for all he was worth—up a small hill. You'd think he would have been used to it. Built up his muscles.

When he was even with one corner of the house, Mom stepped out from behind a bush and threw a log at him.

A log.

Not a twig.

A log that you would burn in your fireplace.

It knocked him over. Mom was a strong woman. She had built herself up beating her kids.

Blew him over like he'd been hit with a battering ram like on the movies.

He didn't get up right away and Mom had started laughing.

Katty had screamed and started to go help him, but Mom caught her by the arm. All she could see as she was dragged away was Tommy stumbling, trying to pick up his bike. Terrified. Horrified.

He had been a sweet kid.

Wonder where he was now. Could be living in the same town as her, but he'd never again acknowledge her.

Knock, knock.

Katty turned and there was Deputy Scott.

He waved. "Hi. How're you doing?"

She smiled and nodded. "Better."

He glanced at Bea all snuggled in one of Clarence's beds. "How is she?"

Katty nodded. "She's better. She gets really tired though."

"A gunshot wound takes a while to heal."

Lisha rumbled in with her cart. "Anybody for coffee and cookies?" She glanced at Bea then shushed her mouth. "Oh, sorry. I forgot. Most people here are deaf so—"

"She's fine. Sleeps like a little log." She looked at the Deputy. "I'd like coffee … if you have time."

Nursing homes had great dating services also.

Catering too.

He checked his phone. "I have a few minutes. It's okay. Thanks."

Lisha served them and snuck a cookie for herself. "Yum. I love it when they make macadamia nut." She winked and pushed her cart away and partly closed the door.

A set up.

He smiled. "This is a nice break. Usually I just roll up to the corner convenience store and grab a slice of pizza." He patted his stomach. "And it shows."

She laughed. "I know. I used to be a beanpole but now I have a donut roll." She didn't say that she used to be a beanpole because Phil would never spring for food. It was always booze and drugs. Maybe a pizza thrown in once in a while.

They'd barely gotten to speak five words and taken one bite of the cookies when he got a call.

He shook his head. "It never fails." He checked the read out. "I better go."

"Aww. You can take the coffee and cookies with you for later if you want."

He helped himself and stuck two in his pocket. "This'll make the rest of the night go better." He reached to shake her hand, but then hugged her.

Oh my. The old Katty rose up and embraced him hard and kissed him hard.

He pulled away and looked her in the eye. "Uh. I better go." Then he pushed her away.

"I'm—" She didn't know what to say. "I'm—"

"It's okay. I better get back." His face was different. "Duty calls. Hope you both have a good night."

And he was gone.

It had all happened so quickly.

She was so stupid. He must hate her. She should have known better. But she didn't. That was how she'd always been with guys because that was what they wanted.

Every one of them.

FIFTY-FOUR

Clarence walked on, angels on every side—some as tall as the three stories of the prison, many with weapons he'd never seen before and had no idea how they would be used. How long this could go on he didn't know. He just knew that Michael had set him free.

"Michael."

The huge angel slowed down and turned toward Clarence. They were well hidden by the huge beings surrounding them. Some were even bigger than Michael. Although since Clarence had known him, he had seen Michael grow through a three level building before, so he was sure that Michael was shorter right now just for him.

"Michael. Thanks."

Michael clapped him on the back. "All part of the plan. Buddy." He grinned. "You used to put up with me grinding the gears in that red pickup."

Clarence chuckled. "Buddy? You've never called me that. Yup. If you can't find 'em, grind 'em." He must be dreaming. How did an angel stomp on the floor and all the cell doors fly open?

Whatever.

He was happy to go along with it, just as long as he didn't wake from this dream and find out he was still in his prison cell. Or worse.

The sirens went off again and didn't stop this time.

"Do you figure Warden is out of my cell by now? That was pretty slick, shoving him in there." Clarence slowed. He'd never forget looking into his prison cell—*his* cell—and seeing the warden looking out at *him*. "I'll never forget that as long as I live."

Michael smiled. "It just seemed to be a fair swap. Him for you. Or you for him." He grinned. "I wish we could have gone further with him."

"Further?" Clarence stumbled and tried to catch up with the angel's huge strides.

Michael shook his head. "I shouldn't even admit this, but several of us wanted to torture him the way he tortured you."

Each warrior surrounding him nodded in agreement. They lifted their weapons above their heads and roared. "Onward for the King!"

Clarence shuddered and stumbled again. These beings were ... they would have ... paid Warden back for the pain he'd caused Clarence?

Michael gripped Clarence's elbow and another angel on the other side did the same. Even lifted him off the ground a little as they crossed railroad tracks at the edge of the prison grounds.

Whew.

He blinked and turned to look at the prison. He wiped his wet cheeks and crumpled onto the grass in the ditch.

Immediately angels moved in tight around him, backs to him, facing any outside danger.

Clarence could still see the natural dimension through them clearly. Overwhelmed.

Michael rustled behind him and lifted him up. "We must go, Clarence."

Warden must have been rescued and sent out word—sent out the troops. A prison break wasn't good on a warden's resume. Judging by the numbers of prisoners that had already escaped, the warden would be in deep trouble with his backers. That possible loss of revenue would close the prison for good.

Clarence seemed to cover the steps, then miles quickly. The angels were still surrounding him, but not as close as before. He had no idea of where to head, just west. Then southwest.

Osceola, Nebraska.

Truck stop. He didn't remember how he got here, but it was a place to start.

He wasn't even tired. He glanced down at his shirt as he opened the entrance door—no blood. He still had the inmate uniform but people who held the door for him and others he met, didn't even look at his clothes. They just smiled at him and said hello.

"Michael? Do they even see me?"

Michael smiled and pushed him forward, his hand on Clarence's back.

Clarence passed behind the people standing in line to pay and his stomach growled. He patted his empty pockets. He had no idea how to get something to eat or what time it was. But his stomach said it was time to eat.

The last man in line, a huge mountain of a fellow wearing a crunched straw cowboy hat looked down at him. The man was almost a big as the angels. "Hey, Buddy."

Clarence glanced to make sure Michael was still beside him. "Uh, yes?"

"Need something to eat?"

Clarence nodded. "Yeah. I guess." He didn't have any money. He didn't have his wallet. No identification. Where was his wallet? Probably back at Hillcrest. Hopefully Katty found it and put it away. Better yet, she took it with her. They had grown to trust each other in the short time they had come to know each other.

The trucker didn't even have to get out of line to grab a banana and some packaged muffins. And he was next in line.

"Is this all for you?" The cashier began to ring up his purchases. "Er. Did you find everything you need?"

The man chuckled. "Well, to answer your first question, it takes a lot to keep a man of my size going." He patted his chest then handed off the banana and muffins to Clarence as she rang them up. "Here you go, Buddy."

"Th-thank you." Now he was taking handouts. "Really. Thank you for your kindness."

Michael was bowing his head to honor the angels with the trucker. They did the same to him.

When Clarence saw him do that, he bowed his head to the man. "You are an honorable man to help out a stranger."

The man laughed out loud, and his big belly shook. He held out his hand for the change and stuffed his purchases into his pockets. "Hey you need a ride somewhere? Can I give you a lift?"

Clarence couldn't even think. Why was this man being so kind? "Uh. Well, if you are going my way."

"Where are you headed, Old Man?"

Clarence had been called many things in life and old man was one. But this man said it with respect and kindness. Were his ears and eyes open more now or had others spoken in the same way, but his heart had been so hard, he couldn't sense it?

"Nebraska?"

"The man nodded. "Where in Nebraska?"

"Osceola."

The man next in line turned. "I had family that used to live in Osceola, Nebraska. Nice little town."

Clarence couldn't believe what was happening. First an angel breaks him out of prison and a whole raft of angels hide him from the guards. Then somehow they get him to this truck stop in record time. And these truckers treat him like he was their long lost uncle and fed him!

Never, ever—

"I'm going that way. Or rather near there. I could drop you off anywhere near there."

"Why are you being so nice to me?" Clarence bit into the banana. "You don't know me." He threw the peel in the trash, cupping the muffins in his other hand against his chest.

"Well, if you don't want to ride with me that's okay." The man turned the key in the door lock of his big rig. He faced Clarence and waved his hand toward his own chest. His face was kind, eyes were soft. "Come."

Clarence was transported immediately to the top of the precipice with Jesus. He had beckoned to Clarence in the same way, used the same word.

He wiped his eyes. Guess he could trust this guy too.

He nodded. "Thanks man. I could use a ride if it works for you." Locks clicked on the passenger side door and the man started to walk around to help Clarence up and in, only Clarence was already climbing into the cab.

The man smiled. "Guess you don't need my help to get in." He climbed onto his drivers seat and held out his hand. "Names Bender. Robert Bender."

Clarence shook hands. "Clarence Timmelsen." He checked around him for the angels or Michael. They were nowhere to be … wait. Was that a wing sticking out from behind the cab?

Michael leaned out and grinned. Three others did the same.

Clarence never realized what a comfort those guys or angels had become. When they were around—

"Glad to meetcha, Old Man." The huge truck roared as Robert pulled out of the parking spot. "Ever ride in one of these?"

Clarence shook his head. "I don't think I have." He checked behind the truck for wings. Still there.

"It's okay, Old Man." The driver cleared his throat. "They're still there."

Clarence blinked.

FIFTY-FIVE

Noell began packing her bags. That madman might come back when she was here. She had to move. Had to get away before …

She sat on her bed and spied her baby bracelet, now all together in a small bowl. So tiny.

She picked up the bowl and braced herself for the voices and visuals to come back.

She made herself sit and listen and not throw them down. She willed herself to focus on the voices, the words, the pictures, no matter how awful. Maybe she could learn something about the man that would help her find him.

She sat upright. What would she do if she found him?

Maybe she should go to the police.

They'd never believe her. They'd think she was crazy.

And she sometimes wondered if she was.

Just one bead at a time.

She grabbed a notebook and pen, then carefully picked out one pearl.

Once she got past the painful parts, she waited for pictures of the man as an adult. What did he look like? What did he sound like? Were there any pictures of a place she might recognize?

She shook her head. She'd have to work on that. It was too hard to try to get past the bad stuff to find anything helpful.

What if Katty had these same gifts?

Did Bea?

She stood and tried to envision them all living here.

If she could get it all cleaned out.

Katty could even have Gamma's bedroom downstairs. Or Mommy's room. It didn't matter that it had been her mom's room.

What if they could all live here—one big, well, small, happy family.

Her heart started to soar.

Remembering that man made her even more determined to offer Katty and Bea a home with her.

Wait! One of the pictures the first time she had touched the bracelet … had it been of Katty? A younger Katty?

What if this was the man who had been after them?

What if this was the same man?

She stood abruptly and grabbed a trash bag, ran out into the upstairs hall and pulled open the closet door. All she saw were toys and games and dolls. No. She couldn't throw all that away. Bea might want some of it.

She slammed the door and ran down to the door at the end of the hall.

She had never ventured anywhere but where she had to be: her room, the kitchen, porch, living room. Not even Gamma's room much. Just like Mommy's room, she had never opened this door—always afraid of the clutter and stacks of stuff.

Opening the door, she ventured a look as she held her breath.

Grampa's stuff?

It was all placed just so. Books and books, but all on bookshelves. A lamp glowed on a square oak table that warmed the room. She had never realized the light was on. She'd never seen it from outside through the window or under the door.

Wait. How long had that light been on? How long did light bulbs last anyway?

She bent and examined the door. A small rubber strip like weather-stripping followed the bottom edge.

Huh.

Once again she felt like an intruder—like that evil man that had been in her room.

But this was Grampa's. There were framed pictures of old buildings. Was that … was that the old drug store? People posed in front of it. Interesting. She followed the pictures along one wall and onto the next. Then backed up. The whole room was a museum. Shelves across from the bookshelves had old guns, old helmets.

She picked up a tool of some sort. She had no idea what it was. She needed someone to come in here to show her around and tell her what everything was.

She pulled at a metal knob on an old oak cabinet. Locked. Through the glass she could see little drawers. Some little shelves with parts. Metal. Old. Not really rusty but really old. Some type of collection but she had no idea what it all was.

She looked around for a key.

That was a mystery. Maybe whatever was in there was dangerous and he had kept it locked up so she, as a little girl, wouldn't get into it.

An old patterned rug covered the wood floor. She picked up one corner. Maybe the key was under there. Interesting floorboards, too.

No key.

Noell slipped out and quietly closed the door. Something in her wanted to respect the privacy and memories until another day.

On downstairs.

She still had the trash bag in her hand and while on the front porch, she pushed everything within grasp into the bag. No matter what it was. She couldn't stop herself. It was almost as if her hands were disconnected from her head.

As she worked, all she could think of was, there were two museums upstairs—Mommy's room and now Grampa's. She didn't want to mess with them, to tear things out of there, but then she would be acting just like Gamma.

She needed to find someone who could appreciate what Gamma had hung onto. What she had not wanted to part with for so long.

Doorbell.

Noell jumped. No one ever rang that!

Fletch just opened the door and yelled. And no one ever came to visit.

She dropped the now full bag and ran in time to see Katty turn away to her car.

Noell rushed to open the door. "Katty!"

Katty turned. She'd been crying. Her eyes were puffy and red.

"What's wrong?" Noell looked behind Katty at the car. Bea waved from her car seat. "Is she okay?"

Katty nodded. "I don't even know why I'm bothering you. I just wanted to know where you lived and—"

Noell waved to Bea. "Go get her and come in. Please."

There were some cookies left in the freezer if Fletch hadn't gotten to them all. And she could make tea. Maybe even peanut butter sandwiches. Wait. Did she have any bread?

Katty had Bea in tow.

No time like the present for them to see it all. Like, in all.

"Come on in." She opened the porch door farther and by the look on Katty's face, she saw it all. "Well, this is where I live."

"Uh, it's nice. Nice. Isn't it Bea?" Katty's eyes bounced around on every pile and stack.

"No it's not. But *you're* being nice." Noell dropped the trash bag. "It's awful but I just started again to clean out." She pointed the way. "Come into the kitchen. I'm not sure what I have, but we'll find something."

Bea jumped up and down. "Mommy! Look at the red couch. Mommy she has a TV too."

In the kitchen.

Even Bea's face was surprised at all the stacked cookbooks lining each and every wall.

Noell laughed. "I know! Lots and lots of junk, right?" She picked up Bea, then remembered the surgery and gently lowered her to a chair.

"Let's see what I have." She opened the cupboards. "Looks the same inside and outside." She swung her arms around the room. "I am sorry for the way this looks. Still freaks me out."

Katty had wandered into the room. Her face was appalled, but when she met Noell's eyes, she smiled. "Is this all yours?"

Noell started to shake her head no. "Well, when Gamma was alive, it was hers." She shrugged. "It's mine now." She glanced around the room. "Every cookbook. Every box. Every … you get the idea." She pointed to a chair beside Bea. "Sit. Please."

Katty nodded and sat.

Bea couldn't keep her hands off the little sugar bowls and salt and pepper shakers on the table.

"No, Bea." Katty shoved them away from little fingers.

"Oh, she's okay. She can look at them." Noell pulled two glasses and a cup from a shelf and filled them with water. "I don't keep much here. Just lunch stuff for work."

Bea dropped a salt shaker onto the floor, scattering salt all over.

Noell had an awful visual of the beads on the floor upstairs in her room and her face must have showed it.

Katty jumped and slapped Bea's hand.

"Oh, no! It's okay. She didn't mean to. It was an accident." Noell sucked in a deep breath. Katty had been in the visuals.

Oh, dear Lord.

She picked up sobbing Bea carefully and hugged her. They just swayed back and forth. She reached her hand to Katty and Katty burst into tears.

Slowly she sat down, still holding Bea and still holding Katty's fingers. "What is going on?"

Katty opened her mouth, but Bea beat her to it. "There's a bad man after us. He keeps sending me bikes and notes and scaring us." She hiccuped. "He's a bad man."

Noell glanced at Katty.

Katty met her eyes and nodded. "That's pretty much it."

"And Clarence is shot. He's gone." Bea burst into tears again.

"Wow. We all need each other, don't we." Noell sighed, her cheek against Bea's head. "Bea, do you like peanut butter? Cause that's all I have. We could have some on crackers."

Bea sat up, wiping her face. She could put on an especially sad face, but this one was real. She nodded.

"Gamma used to keep some bottled juice around here someplace. Cranberry I think for when she got a bladder infection." Noell sat Bea down and checked the pantry.

Bea immediately followed her, pointing at the donkey salt and pepper shakers along one shelf. "Are those toys?"

Noell laughed. "Nope. But they're cute, huh." She found the juice and checked the date. "All good. You want some Katty?"

Katty straightened. "Yeah. Sounds good. Peanut butter and cranberry juice." She smiled. "Sorry but you'd have a hard time beating coffee, cookies, juice, a full meal where we are staying right now."

"What? Well we better go there."

"We get to live in Clarence's room!" Bea took a sip of the cranberry juice. "I don't like it." She wiped her mouth with the back of her hand.

Noell laughed. "I don't either. My Gamma used to make me drink it so I didn't get sick."

"Do you have any toys?" Bea leaned over into Noell's face.

"I do! But you have to follow me up some steps to get them."

They started up the steps, Katty following behind. Bea crawled up one at a time.

"Where? Are there dolls? Do you have a stuffed monkey?" Bea badgered her with questions until they got upstairs and Noell opened the hall closet door.

Bea stopped. "Ohhh. Y-you have lots of toys, Noell."

Noell giggled. "Yes, I do! What would you like to play with first?"

Bea looked up at Noell, eyebrows raised, a half smile on her lips. "Really?" She got down to business. "Can I play with that?" She pointed to an old doll, one eye was open and one eye shut.

"She's kind of broken. I think she's winking at you, right?" Noell handed it to Bea along with a little truck. She hadn't even thought about voices or visuals. They were all … hers, from the past.

"Is this your house now?" Katty pointed at the doors.

"Yes. And I was just thinking that I need to sell it."

"You'd get rid of this? This is a great house." Katty peered at the pictures on the walls.

"Well … really … what I was just thinking before you came over was, since we are related now and all … you and Bea should move in with me." Noell stopped and bit her lip. "After I get it all cleaned out anyway."

Katty burst into tears. "Oh, you wouldn't want us here."

"Katty." Noell hugged her. Maybe they didn't want to move. Maybe this wasn't the right thing to ask. Maybe they didn't like her.

Katty held on, still sobbing.

Bea carefully put the doll on the shelf and hugged their legs. Then she looked up at Noell. "Mommy's scared. The bad man who tried to kill me on the old slide is back." She was so grown up right then.

"Bad man?"

Katty lifted her head and looked into Noell's eyes. She nodded. "If we moved in here, he'd just follow us and hurt you, too. We can't."

"Mommy."

"Shush, Bea." Katty swallowed. "That would be so cool, but this is your house."

"I'll clean it up. It's not too bad up here, but downstairs." Noell winced, thinking of her baby bracelet and all she'd learned about the bad man.

Something felt so right about this.

Bea jumped up and down. "We'd help, right Mom?"

Noell slowly looked around the upstairs, and visualized the rest of the house, the lot and came back to Katty and Bea. "Gamma was your family, too."

FIFTY-SIX

The trucker shifted gears. One gear after another. Clarence guessed he had been in prison so long that he'd never learned about semi truck driving. The engines and how they needed to be shifted. "That must take a lot of practice."

Robert looked over at him. "What?" He continued to shift almost without thinking. "You mean shifting?"

Clarence nodded. "Yeah. That looks complicated."

"It's not. You just have to know how." He shifted again. "See, there are different levels to it." He checked his rear view mirror and shifted again. He chuckled. "Lots of levels. I'll teach you sometime if you want. You could do it."

Clarence had no clue when that would be. He was interested in how it worked, but he was more interested in getting back home.

The engine droned on.

Clarence must have dozed because the brakes were loud. They were pulling off interstate. "Gotta get gas?"

"Gotta take my half hour off, so I figures we could stop here and get a bite to eat. Okay by you?"

Clarence once again patted his pockets. "I don't have any money with me."

"S'kay, Old Man. My treat." Robert eased his truck into a space and stopped. He filled his trucker log out and checked with Clarence. "You ready?"

"Sure. Thanks Robert. This means a lot."

"No problem. I believe in paying it forward or whatever that saying is." He opened his door and hopped out. "You need h—"

Clarence was already on the ground. How was that possible, since this morning … just this morning … he couldn't move off his bed?

"Guess not." He locked the truck and met Clarence in front. "Lots of troopers out today."

A state trooper pulled into the parking lot.

Clarence had almost forgotten he was an escapee. They had to be looking for him. He held back behind Robert. Good thing the man was big. Did Clarence imagine that Robert stepped in front of him at the same time?

The trooper drove on by and waved.

Robert waved back.

Clarence blew out a breath. Somehow the truth had to come out about how evil the warden was and his illegal dealings, so Clarence could be free and not constantly looking over his shoulder.

But probably not today.

"Nice guy. Lots of them around—must be because of the prison break. They said on the radio earlier, that thirty guys or so had escaped. A couple even were killed." He smirked. "The ones that got away must be really bad guys to send this many troopers out looking. If I heard right, they said that one had been in maximum security—the really bad ones."

Clarence peeked up at Robert. His side-long glance was with a smile.

What did that mean?

Clarence didn't let on but walked on beside him. He opened his mouth to say something.

Michael shook his head and kept on shaking it all the way to the entrance.

Guess that meant, "Do. Not. Talk."

Same as at the last truck stop. Everyone looked him in the eyes and smiled. Didn't even see his prison clothes.

He looked down. Still there. Just checking in case angels could make his clothes look different. He should ask for a Led Zeppelin shirt.

Clarence hit the restroom. He was hurting still from the beatings but made it inside. Doors were even heavy today.

Did his business. He didn't know how far he'd get to travel with Robert. He didn't know the next miles. He didn't even know if Robert would be waiting for him in his truck to take him farther down the road.

His stomach growled. He did know he was hungry, but even that could wait for a long time to get back to Osceola.

He pulled the door open and came face to face with Randy.

Randy slowly drew his gun, keeping his eye on Clarence.

"Randy." Clarence slowly raised his hands. "Randy."

Michael stepped between them.

Clarence took a step to the side so he was clear of Michael. "We have to do the right thing, Michael."

"Michael. Who's Michael?" Randy shook his head and lowered the gun.

A state trooper came along beside him. "Is this your man?"

A man from inside gasped and slid alongside Clarence and then Randy. He practically ran. So easy to escape when you weren't wanted.

Randy stared at Clarence for a long time. He didn't speak right away. "No. No it's not. Looks like him, but I'd know the guilty man anywhere." He holstered his gun. "This man is innocent."

Randy.

Clarence had always said no crying. And he'd kept to that rule for a lot of years. But right now when he was on the receiving end of grace, he wanted to bawl like a baby.

"Okay. You know your man." The trooper saluted both Randy and Clarence. He picked up a package of chocolate morsels and went to wait in line.

Clarence stepped forward and held out his hand.

Randy didn't hesitate. He shook Clarence's with vigor.

"Clarence. I … I can't apologize enough." He checked around him and pushed Clarence into an empty aisle. "Warden had us all snowballed into believing his lies." He shook his head. "Only Lester kept the faith that you were a good man. And thank God he did. Otherwise—"

"Otherwise I'd be dead." Clarence wiped his face. He almost asked about Warden but didn't. He had to keep moving forward. To his girls. "And thanks, Randy."

"How about I try and make it up to you and give you a ride home." Randy looked dead serious.

Robert stepped up beside Clarence.

Clarence searched Robert's face then looked at Michael.

Both nodded yes.

Who was this Robert?

Michael knew he wanted to ask. Maybe later when this was all over.

"Hey, I think I'm out of a job at the prison." Randy shook his head and looked like he wanted to cry. Then he chuckled. "My wife would love for me to get out of that line of work. Maybe they need a maintenance man at Hillcrest." He cleared his throat. "Anyway. Let me take you the rest of the way."

Clarence slowly nodded. "Thanks, Randy. I'd be honored."

Randy bowed his head. "No. I'm the one that would be honored."

Clarence turned to Robert and shook his outstretched hand. "I can't thank you enough, Robert. You took a chance on a man. Thank you!"

"S'okay, Old Man." Robert faced him, his massive body blocking out most of the convenience store. He still held onto Clarence's hand and bent his head down. "You go back home and make one tiny lady happy."

Clarence raised his eyebrows. He hadn't talked about the girls to Robert. How—

"No. I mean Mrs. Hatly."

Clarence froze. Especially Mrs. Hatly. "How—"

"You don't miss this, all right? So many don't take the chance for love. So many let love slip through their fingers." Robert withdrew his hand from Clarence's and held his Get This finger in Clarence's face. "Don't let your testosterone get in your way—even you as an old man know what I mean. Go home and marry her."

Clarence cried out.

Marry Mrs. Hatly?

Robert nodded.

Clarence nodded along with him. He had barely been married long enough to make a child with Annie and then she was dead and he was off to prison. He guessed he wouldn't be making babies this marriage, but … marry Mrs. Hatly.

Robert stepped away. "Well, I have to get going to my next gig, so good to meet you and I know you'll be just fine in this man's care." He pointed to Randy and turned to go.

"You ready to go, Clarence?" Randy brushed off his round tummy. "We can grab something to go, if you're hungry. I'll get gas and we could get you home in four hours. If we're lucky."

Clarence nodded and started to look around.

Randy tapped him on the shoulder and slipped him a twenty. "I'm sure you didn't get back your property before you left." He smiled.

Clarence nodded. He hadn't taken anything with him. They'd just ripped him out of his room and shot him and he was gone. No wallet. No pictures. Nothing. Just like the first time. Except for getting shot.

Randy walked away. Clarence sighed. This moment. Something was going on. He could feel it. Right here, but back at home, too.

He didn't understand how, but something real moved inside of him. It was like how it had felt when he'd had a soda with Annie and they would sit back in his old car and watch the world. Together. Not saying anything. Just … sigh.

He grabbed some candy bars—made him think of home—the grocery store and Mandy and Stupid John. He needed to be a nicer person to them.

Robert had stopped by the exit and was … talking … to Michael? Was Robert … ?

Clarence slipped closer. They were face to face, opposite arm locked between them. Heads bowed. Quiet.

Were they—?

He could still see people coming and going around and … through them?

Robert grinned. "And brother, somewhere in our training, we need to learn to drive those stick-shifting trucks."

Michael laughed. "If you can't find 'em, grind 'em, right?"

High five.

Did he really hear Michael and Robert tease each other about grinding gears?

Then Robert stepped away and … first his head disappeared, then his chest and upper body, then … he was gone. Like he walked into a waterfall and disappeared.

Clarence gasped.

Michael met eyes with Clarence and smiled.

FIFTY-SEVEN

What was that sound? Things banging. Metal on metal.

Katty rubbed her eyes.

The nursing home.

Oh.

Bea was snuggled into her side just like a kitty would. Still sleeping. So sweet.

Katty just watched her. This moment. She had never done this. Never woke up and just watched Bea sleep.

Pain. Regret. Hot tears. Her chest burned with grief over what they both had lost.

She swallowed.

Lisha peeked in and smiled. She tip toed in and set a steaming cup of coffee on the bedside table and stroked Katty's hair. "You good?"

Katty nodded and stretched.

Lisha leaned close to Katty's ear. "Mrs. Hatly is sick. Think about her while you can."

Katty started to lift her head, but Lisha pressed her back down.

"Nothing you can do, but she needs prayer." Lisha's chin quivered. "I think she's just heartbroken over Clarence being gone." She hovered her hand over Bea's head. "So sweet." And she started for the door.

Katty lifted her head and whispered, "Thanks for the coffee."

Lisha nodded, threw a kiss and left.

Bea blinked and rubbed her eyes. She smiled a sleepy smile and rolled to her side, spooning with Katty.

Katty put her head down next to Bea's. Tonight they'd have to try the showers here. Bea hadn't had a bath since the hospital. Hospitals had to be clean so she guessed Bea was cleaner now than if she'd just had a bath at home.

Bea stirred again. When she turned her face toward Katty, she had the sweetest smile on her face.

"You doing good, little Bea?" Katty traced Bea's face, around her eyes, over her nose and circled her mouth.

Bea giggled. "That tickles, Mommy."

Deep sigh.

"Do it again."

Katty smiled, laid her head back down and traced Bea's ears.

Belly laugh.

Giggles filled Katty too.

"I have to go potty." Bea pushed the sheets off and jumped out of bed. "Mom. My shot place is better." She held up her jammie top. The tape had come loose and the bandage was hanging off to one side. Sure enough the incision was very smooth.

"It is!" Katty gave her a love pat on her behind. "Now go potty!"

Bea giggled and ran.

Katty knew there were some days she'd get busy and forget, but she was determined to forever appreciate and cherish this little girl she'd been blessed with.

It felt like they were in a motel—a motel with extremely great service. She sipped her coffee. This wasn't the usual resident coffee. They must have a pot just for the staff. She rotated.

Clarence had his own coffeemaker right here. But it hadn't been brewing.

She sipped again. This was good stuff!

She set the cup down and pulled their clothes out of the bag. Hers would do another day. Bea's not at all. There was dinner, all over the front of her shirt. Dang.

It wasn't really Bea's fault, because Mr. Harold had tickled her from behind, making her drop her spoonful of spaghetti. It slid all the way down her shirt to her jeans and onto the floor. Thank God it was that polished wood or vinyl flooring. Easy to wipe up. Not so easy to wipe off Bea's shirt.

She needed to go home for more clothes. And to wash this.

Knocking at the door.

"Yes?"

The door pushed open and a coffee carafe appeared. "You proper?"

Bea pushed out of the bathroom just at the same time and gasped. "What is that Mommy?"

Harold peeked in.

"Mr. Harod!" Bea jumped toward him.

"Bea! It's hot! Be careful!" Katty jumped just in time to rescue Bea and the coffee and Harold.

She sat it on the desk. "Can you stay for some?"

"No. I have baking right now." He smirked and wheeled his chair to face the door. "Like I need cookies to feed this pot belly." He hugged Bea and started to leave. "You two doing okay?"

Katty nodded. "Yeah. We just need to go back to the trailer for some more clothes for Bea."

He grinned. "I made her make a mess, didn't I."

"Yup. You did."

"Are you sure you should go back there?" He shrugged. "Maybe alert Sheriff you are going and one of the deputies can meet you there." He winked.

Did everybody know something she didn't? "Good idea. I'll give him a call as soon as we get changed." She poured more coffee. "And thanks for the coffee."

He hesitated. "You hear anything about Mrs. Hatly this morning?"

She shook her head. "Just what Lisha said. That she's sick and probably missing Clarence. Right?"

He nodded. "She's really sick. He has to get here. He has to."

She slowly sat on the bed. "She's that sick, like in … " She glanced at Bea who was trying to pull her jammie shirt off. "Wait Bea. Man in the room, remember?"

"Oh. Sorry." She pulled it down over her wound. "Wanna see my surgery?"

Harold laughed. "You two can live here for a thousand years if you ask me!" He nodded at Katty. "Just letting you know, Katty." He headed for the door. "Maybe go see her. That might cheer her up."

"We will Harold. Thanks." She jumped. "Thanks for the coffee."

As soon as the door closed, Katty pulled Bea's top off and pulled the dirty one back on.

"Ick Mommy. It's all smelly."

"We'll get some clean clothes for both of us when we go home."

"I don't want to go, Mommy." Bea looked up at her. "Will it be okay? I mean will the bad guys be there?"

Katty shook her head. "Thanks for reminding me. I'll call Sheriff right now and check in with them. Maybe the bad guys are locked away in jail and we don't need to worry where they are, right?"

"Right, Mom."

"Where is this Mom stuff coming from? Aren't I Mommy to you?"

Bea sighed and zipped her jeans. "I guess I'm just growing up, Mom." She grinned. "Big girls can call their mommy's Mommy, right, Mommy?" She laughed. "Mommy?"

"You!" Katty swatted her behind with her clothes as she opened the door to the bathroom. "I'm getting dressed. Oh. First call the Sheriff." She tapped her phone.

"Hello? Sheriff's Department."

She tapped speaker. "Hello. This is Katty Randolph. Is Sheriff there? Or—"

"Deputy Scott?"

Katty held the phone away from her. Did everyone think—

"Hello this is Deputy Scott. How may I help you?"

"Hi. Hello." She swallowed. "This is Katty."

Bea jumped and knocked the phone out of her hand. "Hi Scott. Hi!"

"Bea!"

He laughed. "Sounds like everybody's awake."

"Yes." Katty tapped the speaker to off and held the phone to her ear. "Yes. We are." Pictures of her foolishness from last night stopped her.

"You there?"

"Uh, yes." She cleared her throat. "Yes. Sorry to bother you, but Harold thinks I should let you know that I need to go home for more clothes and things. He said you should at least know I was going there."

"Good idea." Deputy Scott seemed to be smiling through the phone. "When were you thinking about going?"

"Well, right away. Or as soon as we can brush teeth and get shoes on."

"Okay. I'll meet you there. Will that work?"

Katty sighed. "Y-yes." Oh man. He wasn't mad. And she didn't want to be there alone. "If that's not too much trouble."

"No trouble. I'll leave right now. That way when you arrive, I'll already be there." He paused and lowered his voice. "Last night was okay, Katty. I'm not mad. It just took me by surprise."

"I'm glad. I'm so sorry. I won't do it again. Promise." How could he read her mind over the phone?

He laughed. "Well, we can figure that out."

Katty blinked. He wasn't mad. And … figure that out?

"So I'll meet you there so you don't have to worry about the bad guys showing up when you're there. Okay?" Someone must have walked past him.

"Thanks, Deputy."

When Katty put down the phone, Bea was singing. "Mommy likes Deputy. Mommy likes Deputy!"

A laugh burst from the phone

"Oh crap! I didn't hit end." Katty hit end and made a face at Bea.

Bea's eyes were wide, her hands covered her mouth. "Oops!"

Katty shook her head. "Get your teeth brushed and I'll get dressed. Quick! Quick!"

FIFTY-EIGHT

Clarence hesitated.

Same big white van they had dragged him into and shackled him to take him back to prison, bleeding and broken. Fearing for his own life, but even more for Bea and Katty's lives.

Hard not to go back there right now.

He tried to breathe but could only get out a short gasp. The memory of that day, the sounds, the voices, the pain, the fear, tried to wrap themselves around his windpipe and pour into his belly. They all needed to get pushed down. This day was a new day and he would see his girls and if he had to, he would fight for them.

Randy was watching him through the van, from outside the driver's door, his beefy hand on the door handle, three large candy bars sticking up out of his uniform shirt pocket.

He was reading Clarence's mind. He must have been thinking of the same thing—that awful trip from Osceola to prison.

Maybe. And here they were again, Randy driving him to Osceola— once again.

Clarence nodded at him across the van and opened the door.

Randy slid in at the same time, his hand on the candy bars in his pocket so they didn't fall out. Doors slammed at the same time.

"All gassed up and ready to go. One last tank on the prison's card." He started the van and tapped the steering wheel.

"What are you going to do now, Randy?" Clarence strapped himself in.

He immediately thought of Katty and Bea. Katty never used to buckle Bea in at all. She used to pretend to, but never did. Now she consistently buckled Bea in and was always nagging him to buckle his seat belt.

There was that feeling again.

He needed to get back.

Something didn't feel right.

Something was wrong.

There was a yearning or foreboding.

Something wasn't right back home.

He checked behind him. It was a huge van with three bench seats. All three were filled with angels, Michael right behind him. They seemed different this time. Dressed different.

He faced the front. Angels were different. He himself felt different.

He turned to look back at Michael and realized the difference. Each angel had battle gear on—armor and weapons.

Michael was watching him. They met eyes and he nodded.

Clarence blew out a breath and nodded back. This could get bad. Maybe it already was.

"What's the matter? Someone following us?" Randy checked his rear view mirror. "It could happen." He gripped the steering wheel. "It could happen. I'm sure the warden put out an APB on you, if he's still alive. Especially to your Sheriff—what's his name?"

"Sheriff Dennison." Clarence nodded. God, what was Sheriff thinking right now? The man had to do his job, but—

"Yeah, that's right." Randy was quiet for a minute. He shook his head and wiped an eye. "That must have been a rough day for him as well."

Clarence stared ahead.

That day. So many visuals and sounds.

Don't go there. Focus on what was ahead.

Focus.

He glanced behind him, knowing Michael was right there. But there was something different even in that. He searched the landscape around I-80 as they headed West from Des Moines. Trees. Fields. Farmland. Small towns. Signs.

A short movie played in his mind. "Come." Jesus holding out a hand to him. He had let it all go when he had jumped.

That.

He didn't know anything about Jesus except what he had learned when he had spent a year or two in Sunday School.

He searched the blue sky. Little songs—kids songs—about lights and bushels and love rainbows filled his hearing, his being. Little voices all rejoicing.

He shook his head.

Hearing things now.

He *was* crazy.

Randy looked over and held out a candy bar. "Want one? I shouldn't eat them all."

Clarence took it. "Thanks."

Baby Ruth. He tore open the wrapper and it made him think of Mandy and John again. He was going crazy with all these thoughts and sounds.

Candy might help.

FIFTY-NINE

"There. I think that's him." Phil pointed at Deputy Scott. "That's your man."

Lex gunned the engine. Then backed it off a bit.

They watched as the cop car drove a little closer. Didn't want to tip him off.

"Now!" Phil yelled.

Lex gunned the car forward, letting the tires catch on the pavement, then hit the gas. The car swerved, but he kept control.

"Good driving, Cowboy!" Phil slammed his hand down on the dash. "Get him!"

The deputy was gripping the steering wheel, giving it a hard yank to avoid hitting them.

Lex jerked his steering wheel again, putting them right in the car's path.

Deputy's eyes popped. He leaned into the steering wheel and swerved hard.

Lex turned just in time.

Bam!

The cop lurched forward in his seat just as Katty could be seen pulling into her driveway, behind him.

"Right on time!" Phil pounded Lex on the shoulder. "See you soon. Stay on him."

Lex pulled his gun out from under the seat.

The deputy ran to Lex's car door. "What the hell do you think you are doing?" His hand was on his weapon. He had unsnapped the leather strap. "You are under ar—"

Phil didn't hear any more. He pushed the car door open and ran for Katty's trailer. One look back. Lex had pushed the car door open into Deputy Scott and knocked him to the ground.

Dork Deputy! Damn Dork Deputy!

Phil poured it on to Katty's car. She had seen the crash so was already grabbing the doorknob to the trailer house. She had hold of Bea's wrist.

Bea was crying. "No! No!"

She remembered him.

Katty got inside and slammed the door in his face.

He kicked it open and pushed himself inside. Katty faced him. Bea peeked from behind Katty.

"Bea! To your room! Get under your bed. No! Run to your hiding place."

What? Phil tore at Katty and knocked her down. He grabbed Bea and started to the door with her in his arms.

Score! He hadn't thought it'd be this easy.

She screamed and cried. Didn't matter. She'd be his. He'd show her how a daddy could treat his daughter.

What was that? He looked down at his arm and shirt. "Did you pee?" He brushed at his shirt. "You did! You ungrateful little shit!" He threw her against the wall, knocking a lamp off a table. He wiped his arm against his chest and looked up.

Katty had a gun. Trained on his head.

"Now, Sweetheart." Phil slowly raised his hands.

"I was never your sweetheart. I was your punching bag. Your surgical experiment! Your bitch!"

He stepped toward her. "Now, now. You probably have never shot a gun in your life. Just put it down and no one gets hurt." He pointed to where Bea lay on the floor. "Especially our sweet daughter." He took another step. "Why didn't you tell me about her?"

Katty took a step back, bumped into the table and stumbled.

He rushed her, but she recovered sooner than he'd expected.

Blam!

Just missed his head! The bullet whizzed by his ear.

He took another step.

Blam!

God! "My leg!" He fell, clutching his thigh. "You shot me."

Gunshots from outside. Good. Lex must be cleaning up the deputy. He'd be here.

Blam!

"Don't shoot! Don't shoot again!" He collapsed to the floor.

Katty raced to Bea and gathered her in her arms. As she passed him, he grabbed at her foot.

Missed.

She kicked him in the thigh and ran out the door.

God! Right where the gunshot wound was.

Lex would get her.

He limped to the door.

She was already in the car, strapping Bea in the car seat in back. She was struggling to buckle her in.

He stepped out the door and almost collapsed to the deck. The railing saved him, but he still tripped. Where had she learned to shoot? He'd never allowed her to have a gun.

She slammed the driver side door and started the car.

He searched for Lex. The deputy sat on Lex's chest, straddling him. He clocked Lex on the head with his gun.

Ow.

Katty backed out of the driveway, tearing up grass and throwing gravel at him. She squealed onto the pavement and took off.

There. An old red Chevy pickup. He limped to it. Hope for the keys.

Score!

He hopped in, trailing blood over the seat. He slammed the door and turned it over. Please have gas. Please start.

He pumped the gas pedal and turned the key.

Vroom!

SIXTY

Katty could only hope Deputy Scott was okay and that she was far ahead of Phil or better yet, he couldn't move because she had shot him —because she was out of gas.

The blasted E on the gas gauge was bright red, screaming at her. "Why didn't you fill the tank?"

From now on, keep the gas tank full.

"Mommy. Mommy."

"You're awake!" Katty checked her rear view mirror. "Are you okay?" A huge bump was already on Bea's head. She pushed down on the gas pedal. It sputtered. "Car get us to the gas station."

It lurched.

"God, please!"

It caught. Somebody must have poured gas in because it was running like a race car.

She checked the gas gauge. Still empty.

She knew Phil's car had to be out of commission. He couldn't follow them right away. But her chest felt tight like an elephant was sitting there, when she thought of him.

Too many awful memories.

She turned a corner and a picture blinked into her mind. Slap! Phil's hand was powerful across her cheek.

"Mommy. Mommy! He's coming!"

Katty blinked. No!

She drove through the intersection by the old school. Another visual—a boot kicked her belly. "The baby! Phil! The baby!"

She almost doubled over now with the memory.

To the highway. Stop sign.

"Stop Phil! You're hurting me!" She could never get free from him. He was too strong.

Bea kicked her seat.

This baby was alive and kicking.

"It's gonna be okay, Bea. Hang on."

The traffic blurred. A truck zoomed by. A white van followed. Another car. She blinked again and wiped her eyes.

A nurse's face from the past was in hers. "Hang on, Katty Randolph. We gotta pump your stomach." She'd never forget those concerned brown eyes—that moment. The nurse knew everything—in that moment. Katty had been sure she would die.

She blinked. She could face dying again, but Bea … never!

She panicked and froze.

A picture in her mind layered over highway traffic.

She'd had flashes since she was a kid—some freaked her out and others she hardly acknowledged. They flew in and flew out.

This time the visual was a red truck cutting the turn and slamming into her car head on. Glass exploded everywhere. And that was it. End of vision.

What *was* that?

Red truck just like her neighbor's truck.

She skipped the highway and turned into the implement company drive and almost hit a sign that read, "This is not a driveway."

She wiped her face again and zoomed through the Dive-Inn's back employee parking lot, bouncing over the breaks in the concrete. They would be mad. Almost hit the owner's car.

She stopped beside an unoccupied pump at the gas station. They were busy. Cars and pickups parked everywhere, across the highway even, blocking the entrance. Old guys sat at the tables inside, drinking coffee, looking out of the windows, like fish in a fishbowl checking out the world.

The gas pump. She panicked. She never had any money. Phil aways kept it so she couldn't buy food.

No. Not back then.

Now. She reached into her purse and pulled out the debit card.

Just as she turned and faced the windshield to open her car door, an old red truck appeared out of nowhere, roaring down the hill, and turned into the gas station.

Phil!

For a split second, their eyes met and raw emotion traveled between them. Hatred both directions. A growl rose from inside Katty.

"Shit! He's not stopping!" Katty was still buckled in. "Bea. Hold on!"

Bea screamed the same time Katty did.

The truck slammed into the front of her car, shoving it way back into old gas tanks behind them.

Katty's head was thrown back hard against the headrest and the world went black.

She didn't know how long she'd been out, but when she came to, people were screaming and running. Pointing.

What could they see that she couldn't?

"Oh shit!" Gas sprayed into the car through the broken windshield. Katty's clothes were wet and she guessed Bea's must be too. Gas fumes leaked everywhere. Smoke and steam rolled from the front of the car and the old truck. Broken glass was everywhere.

The vision!

She could barely see Phil. His head and body had broken through the windshield and had landed on the hood, blood oozed from his face, his nose was smashed to the side. Unconscious.

An emergency truck screamed down the hill, into the gas station along with two fire trucks.

Fire trucks!

"Bea!" The rear view mirror was broken and on the seat beside her. Katty tried to turn her head but met with horrible pain. Her eyes blurred and the world started to spin. "Bea!" She tried to unbuckle her seat belt. Her right arm was fine, but her left arm was smashed against the car door.

Trapped!

She tried to raise her good arm over the back of the seat, when her door was jerked open. Hands reached in and pulled her out.

She screamed. Her left arm must be broken, the one they dragged her out with. A man—it was the deputy— tried to help her to stand, but her legs gave way beneath her. Intense pain spiked through her left leg. "Don't worry about me! Get Bea!"

Flames burst up from the old pickup and a fireman carried her back against the building. "We will. We'll get her."

She could barely see Bea through the smoke. Her head was slumped against the car seat.

"Bea!" Katty started sobbing and screaming. "Help my Baby! Get her out!"

SIXTY-ONE

Clarence always liked the curves coming into Osceola. He needed to get to Katty and Bea to make sure they are all right, but he was coming back.

His home town.

Just a few months ago, he had been so angry about being shipped off to Osceola. He swallowed. If he really took time to admit it, he had been an asshole. He shook his head. To everybody. Carol and everybody at Hillcrest. Mandy and John at the grocery store. Lisha. The Oust Clarence Brigade or whatever they called themselves. They probably had disbanded since he'd been gone.

He'd have to make things right somehow.

The vet clinic. Maybe he should get a dog. Or get Bea a dog.

Good to be back.

The old ball field. No body ever used that. Nice piece of grass. Close to the tracks though. The town should do something with it. Somebody had to mow it. They should just expand the park to here. Plant some trees. Or sell it. It'd make a great business opportunity. Maybe he and Harold should build a little office there for their detective business.

"Wait. Let's turn here." Clarence pointed to the street almost too late. "Go past the cemetery and down to the trailer park." He nodded when Randy made a sharp left. "We can start there and see if they're home."

"Ya coulda told me a little earlier." Randy chuckled. "This is a pretty little town, Clarence." He slowed. "That's a nice cemetery—got your plot?"

Clarence grinned. "As a matter of fact I do. Thanks to Dad. I have a couple plots there—besides where Dad is buried anyway." He'd never thought about that before. Guess that's where he'd go when he died. Funny with how old he was, he'd just never thought about it. Most geezers his age had it all planned out. He should go visit Dad's grave … sometime.

"One … two more blocks I think." He chuckled. "You'll find it. It's not too hard to find—" He pointed. "There. The first trailer on the right. Her car isn't there, but I'll jump out and knock on the door. Maybe she's having the car worked on."

The new deck looked so nice. Made the old place look better. They'd have to do something about the trailer itself when he got settled at the home again.

He knocked and the door pushed open. Unlocked.

Not like Katty.

He started to step inside when he noticed something on the floor. He pushed the door open farther. The room was a shambles. A chair was overturned and the sofa lamp was broken on the floor.

A trail of what looked like blood led him back to the deck.

Blood on the deck.

"Randy!" Clarence roared. "Something happened." He tripped down the deck steps. "Nobody's here and there's blood on the floor and the deck!"

Sirens went off.

Goose bumps skittered up his arms. He rubbed them, searching the sky, the trees, toward the town.

Smoke.

He met eyes with Randy and moved.

Randy shifted into reverse before Clarence opened the door.

Clarence barely got in, when Randy gunned the van back onto the street.

"Where to?" Randy swerved, just missing the mess on the street. "Holy cow! Want to stop?" He slowed to inspect the scene. "Cop car head on with that old Buick." He sped up. "No blood there anyway."

Clarence craned his neck as Randy drove past. "I don't see anybody. That might be Deputy Scott's squad car." He shifted to the front. "Where would the girls be?" He shook his head. "I guess try the nursing home. Remember how to get there?"

"Really? This ain't Chicago, where I'm from." He drove back the way they'd come. "Keep an eye out for anything. Smoke. Cops."

This might be about Katty and Bea. There were lots of reasons for sirens, but he knew in his gut that the siren was about his girls.

At the highway. "Turn left." Smoke and fire billowed at the gas station. "There!"

Randy poured it on and they pulled in.

"Katty's car is on fire!"

SIXTY-TWO

Every angel was in place.

But so were demons.

Michael rose above the chaos along with other angelic beings. The host was with him. He glanced on every side. Angels in heavenly armor glowed, each reflecting the Father's love. Swords reflected the light in their eyes, clanging against each other, as angels prepared for battle.

The scene below was normal from their point of view.

Humans being humans.

Hurting each other.

So much pain caused by so much pain.

Demons hovered with Phil and the truck, not willing to let go of the man's body. The man looked to be horribly mangled. Smashed through the glass in the windshield, his face was undistinguishable.

Angels were posted at every corner of the property and lined the rooftop. But demons badgered them from every direction—just like sparrows pestering an eagle, the demons picked and slapped and poked but that seemed all they were able to do.

They knew they were defeated in this battle.

Michael nodded to a huge angel—Mrs. Hatly's intercessory angel —and he flew off to stand with him.

The angels rose higher into the Light.

Another angel tipped his sword and hundreds flew off in response to stir others to pray. To houses, the school, businesses. Inspiring people who would hear and listen and bow their hearts.

All was ready. All were in position.

Michael nodded.

Only the Father knew the outcome, but they had done all they could. Now it was up to the humans to press in, to push forth and not give up the battle.

SIXTY-THREE

There! Before Randy had the van stopped, Clarence was out the door. He rounded a pair of old dump trucks parked beside the service station and stumbled to a stop.

His girls. He finally knew who he was meant to be. Once it had been for him to be Annie's husband, but now … Katty and Bea's family. Mrs. Hatly.

Katty's car was sandwiched between a pickup into the front end and gas tanks at the rear. The hood was crumpled and pushed up. Smoke poured from the engine compartment. Steam rolled and hissed from both the car and pick-up as they sat, hood to hood.

Fire trucks roared onto the lot, horns blasting, as Clarence skirted between them. Firemen leaped off the trucks and ran hoses from the tanks. Police roped off the area. Radios blared for additional help. An ambulance backed in beside a fire truck. People stumbled to get out of the way.

Clarence ran. No one noticed an old man darting about, in all the confusion. He skidded to a stop.

A man was draped over the hood of the pickup, bleeding and unconscious.

Phil! The bastard! "Die Phil!"

There. Katty was being detained against the building. She pointed to the car, screaming, crying. "My baby's in there! Get her out!"

A cop pushed her from the wreck, but she kept breaking away from him until another cop grabbed her.

The Deputy.

Where was Bea?

Clarence stopped beside the passenger door of the car but was knocked off his feet by a fireman, who pushed him away. "Not now old man." The fireman took a second glance at Clarence and growled. "Get away you ... filthy jailbird. How'd you get out? Go back to prison where you belong!"

Clarence struggled onto his feet and fought his way between the two firemen, only to be pushed back again. The fireman turned away to yell at a cop. "Get this bastard out of here."

Clarence saw his chance and dove under him, pushing himself into the back seat.

Bea. Unconscious. Bleeding.

He reached for the car seat. Buckled. He'd never buckled or unbuckled a car seat in his life.

Boom!

He looked behind him to the front of the car. Flames burst from the engine, rocking the car.

"She's gonna blow! Get out! Get away!"

Clarence fumbled at the straps. His eyes watered. Smoke filled his lungs.

If he had to die trying, he'd go with her.

But she had to live.

Moments collided and Clarence couldn't tell whether he was in his past with Annie and that accident or the present with Bea, but he screamed and wrenched the straps, breaking them, shredding them until Bea was free. He gathered her in his arms and backed out, tucking her into his chest.

As soon as he was free from the car, arms pried her from him.

Someone pulled him to fresh air. They pushed him onto a gurney and rushed him away from the burning car, bumping, jarring him.

"Bea. Bea." He reached his arm out. "Where is she?"

People hollered. "It's gonna blow!"

Engines gunned. Tires squealed.

Ka-boom!

The ground shook as someone laid on him, covering him. "It's okay, buddy. You—we're gonna be okay."

Debris and shrapnel bombarded them.

"Feels like a war zone."

Someone covered his eyes. An oxygen mask lowered over his mouth, but he ripped it away.

"Where's Bea?"

The mask was forcefully strapped on.

"Leave. It. On. Jailbird. You breathed in too much smoke back there. Don't you dare take it off." A female voice growled.

A blanket of sorts draped over him. He fell back onto the gurney. A strap tightened around his middle.

Someone forced his hands together in front of his stomach and handcuffs clicked.

SIXTY-FOUR

"No! No!" Katty fell again. God, help! "You've got to get her out!"

Ka-boom!

The car and truck exploded.

Everything slowed. Debris hung in the air. People moved their mouths talking or screaming.

Deputy Scott moved in front of her, shielding her.

She was caught in another realm. She watched people move. She could hear them scream. She could feel the heat even through the Deputy.

Her heart pounded. Beat. By. Beat. She could feel it in her chest—hear it in her ears.

She didn't even feel pain from her arm or her leg.

She was gripped by another pain much deeper than any broken bones or torn flesh.

Nobody had gotten Bea out.

She pushed at the Deputy only he wouldn't let her go.

She pounded on his back.

He was too strong.

Visuals took her back to Phil and she pounded on his back to get away. She had to save her baby. He always killed her babies.

"No. No. No!"

People seemed to hold their breath collectively. No one moved.

Until they saw a fireman grab a tiny girl from a bent old man and run to the emergency unit.

<h1 style="text-align:center">SIXTY-FIVE</h1>

Clarence jumped and tore the oxygen mask off. "Michael, tell them! I'm innocent. You broke me out of prison."

Sheriff grimaced. "I'm sorry Clarence. Whether Michael is real or if he's an angel—"

"Others see him, too. I'm not crazy. I'm innocent." No one in the room but Clarence and Sheriff … and angels—all lined up around the walls of his hospital room.

"Clarence. The law is the law. You broke out of prison." Sheriff blinked. "That's a federal offense. You will go back to prison and I can't do a thing about it." He flipped the papers in his hand. "I'm bound by the law. When they release you here, you're going to jail to await trial."

John burst into the room, followed by Mandy. "Sheriff. Governor. The governor!"

Michael slid behind them against the wall.

Mandy shoved John aside. "He's here."

Sheriff walked around Clarence's hospital bed. "Who's here? And this is a private conversation." He shoved the door, but stopped just before slamming it on the governor. "Whoah. Governor!" He glanced at John and Mandy, then backed away. "My apologies, Sir."

Governor chuckled and shook his hand. Then slapped John on the back. "Nice job, my man." Nodded at Mandy. "You too. Great work." He stepped closer to the bed, reaching his hand out to Clarence. "So is this the man?" He shook his head. "Where do I start?"

John leaned in. "Maybe we should turn up the TV." He pointed.

The TV was on, but no sound. The news.

"That's him!" Clarence pulled the mask clear off and handed it to Michael, who slid it to John. "Turn it up! That's Warden."

Mandy found the button.

The announcer looked directly into the camera. "This is the man behind several incidents in recent news." The camera showed Warden being escorted out of the prison, hands cuffed behind his back. He tried to hide, ducking into his sleeve.

Where was the cocky, evil warden now? Clarence closed his eyes, holding in emotion. Rage. Terror. Pain. Relief. All flooded him now.

Something touched his hand. He blinked his eyes open.

Mandy. She gently rubbed his fingers.

He blinked. He wanted to hide his face too, but for way different reasons than Warden just now. God he hated that man. What he had suffered because of that man. Others, too. If only he knew Warden would get what he deserved.

"Look!" Clarence pointed at the TV. "That's the guard that shot ... " Clarence swallowed. "That's the one that shot my Bea."

Right behind Warden shuffled Tay Ralston. His eyes glanced up at the camera, then quickly down at his feet.

Clarence blinked and wiped his eyes. His fists clenched, balled into fists.

Mandy kept on caressing his hands.

Breathe.

"You okay, Clarence?"Governor cleared his throat. "I have driven all this way to inform you—"

Mandy gasped. "No. He's a good man. He doesn't deserve jail." She patted Clarence's chest. "He doesn't deserve to die."

"Oh, Clarence. How blessed you are to have such great friends."

Governor swallowed. "No I'm here to inform you … that you are a free man. You have been exonerated."

Clarence pulled himself upright.

Mandy pushed the pillow under his shoulders.

"Did … did you just say exonerated?" A legal term Clarence understood. He'd helped a couple inmates achieve that status, but only through hard work and more evidence. He searched the governor's face.

The man appeared serious. "I did. I said exonerated. You, as a lawyer, know exactly what that term means."

Clarence slowly nodded and leaned back onto the pillow. "How?" He glanced at Sheriff. "We have tried and—"

The TV announcer. "Durant, Nebraska is being investigated as the local hub for this huge operation."

Governor pointed at the TV. "Mandy turn it down for me, please."

She raised the remote and punched the button.

Governor pointed at the screen. The picture showed run-down buildings formerly used for grain storage. As the camera panned inside, a high-tech world was revealed—rows of computers, lockers of guns, dorm rooms. "That. That was the … he said it … the hub for Warden's family business. Drug running and sex trafficking. The outside of the buildings never let on what was really going on inside. No one ever knew. Local people. Railroad—it's right on the tracks. Farmers? No one had a clue."

The screen picture shifted to a photo of Clarence.

Mandy punched the button.

Clarence froze. Felt like Michael was sitting on his chest. What now?

"This man." The announcer continued. "His name is Clarence Timmelsen. He had served time for a crime he didn't commit and released to a nursing home in Osceola, Nebraska.

"Knock." Bea peeked in. "Knock, knock." She looked behind her, pulling at her hospital gown covered in ducks. "Mommy. Clarence is home." She looked into the hospital room. "He's having a party."

Katty reached for Bea, just missing her. Her eyes bounced from one person to another. "I'm sorry. We'll come back."

"Hi Mandy." Bea crawled under John's legs to Mandy. "Hi Clarence." When Mandy lifted her onto the bed, she pointed at the TV. "Look, Clarence. You're on TV."

Clarence reached for her. "I know." Startling to look up and see his own grizzled face on the screen.

"Did you win?" Bea snuggled down next to him.

Clarence glanced at the governor and raised his eyebrows. "Did I?"

"You did win, Clarence." Governor nodded.

The announcer continued. "He was incarcerated again, for allegedly murdering Warden Ralston's brother during his first stint in prison. When two guards stepped forward to testify against the warden's family accusations, the truth came out. Clarence Timmelsen had acted in self-defense and will be freed of all charges, according to the governor of Nebraska."

Governor raised his eyebrows and nodded. "That's what I was trying to tell you, Clarence. The guards testified that you acted in self-defense."

Bea pointed. "Michael's here."

Katty stepped to the bedside and started to lift Bea.

Clarence closed his eyes and held onto her. He grabbed Katty's hand. Oh God. Savor this moment. "How?" He cleared his throat and opened his eyes. "How? Who? Who were the guards?"

Governor shook his head. "I don't … I don't remember names, but—"

John dropped the mask on the bed and pointed. "Was it them?"

The screen showed two men in drab brown guard uniforms.

Clarence leaned up. "That's Randy and Lester." He looked over at Governor. "Them?"

"Yup." Governor nodded. "When your friend called us, certain things seemed to fit together with other crimes that were unsolved. This man, William Ralston, was the missing piece to tie it all together."

A man in a suit stuck his head in. "Governor." He waved. "Sorry to interrupt, but we need to get back to Lincoln."

Governor nodded. "Yup. I"d love to stay and enjoy the news with you all, but I'm sure you don't need me to do that." He stepped close to the bed. "I assure you that all your property, finances, real estate is safe. Titles had not been changed over. Luckily, Ralston was kept pretty busy trying to track you down, Clarence." He reached his hand to Clarence. "You're a good man. Never forget that. In tracking down the details of the case, your name came up many times because you helped people—stuck your neck out for them."

Solid handshake. "Governor. You'll never know what—"

"Oh, I think I have an idea. These people are your friends."

"Family." Bea piped up. She tapped Clarence's chest. "He's my grandpa."

Katty shushed her.

Too late.

Clarence lifted his head to see Katty. "Did you … did you find it?"

All she could do was nod and bite her lip.

"Ha. I'll let you all enjoy the news." Governor bowed and headed for the door.

Sheriff followed him out. "I'll walk you out, Sir." He turned back to Clarence. "I'll be back."

Clarence jumped. "Say, Governor?"

Sheriff hooked the governor's arm. "He wants to ask you something, I think."

"Yes." Governor stepped in.

"You said a friend of mine called you?"

"Yes. In fact he knows my dad. Name is Harold … Harold Dexter." He nodded. "A good man. And a good friend to you."

"Thank you." Clarence sank back down in bed and blew out a breath. "Yeah. A good man." He nodded. "A good friend."

SIXTY-SIX

Clarence checked himself in the mirror. He'd really wanted to wear his Led Zeppelin T-shirt for this important day, but he knew she would look so pretty that he had to gussy up a little.

He brushed his teeth and spit into the sink. The morning's conversations at breakfast had been so funny. The threesome—Harold, Mrs. Hatly and Clarence had lingered over coffee. Harold had been teasing Mrs. Hatly about marrying a young stud.

Clarence inspected himself in the mirror now. Well, he was a stud, but an old one for sure. He'd earned every wrinkle, every scar, especially the latest ones.

Then Harold had wheeled away, chuckling.

Still sitting next to her, Clarence had held out his hand. "Mrs. Hatly."

She chuckled. "Not for long." She took his hand in hers and pressed it against her soft cheek.

He paused. "You sure? You've been Mrs. Hatly for a long time."

She smiled sweetly at him from her wheelchair. "I'll be Mrs. Timmelsen for eternity. Oh, and you can call me Violet."

Clarence blew out a breath. Tears stung. He was such a cry baby today.

Flashbacks to the prison beatings. Only one way he could have lived through that. He blinked. Swallowed. All for today. This day.

He stepped back against the bathroom door in order to see most of himself and smoothed back his hair. She liked it long so he'd just had it trimmed.

"Pretty slick, Buddy." Harold knocked at the door and wheeled into the bathroom. "Lookin' good."

Clarence adjusted the bowtie and turned to him. "You sure about this? I've never worn one of these in my whole life."

"You've never even worn a tie in your whole life." He chuckled. "You said yourself, she's a bowtie kinda girl." Harold nodded. "Looks good."

"I think I must have worn a tie to my mom's funeral back then. I think." Clarence nodded. "Yeah." He followed Harold into his office and picked up the jacket. "Never worn one of these either. Thanks for loaning it to me." He pulled it on. "Buttoned or not?"

Harold nodded. "Buttoned."

Clarence buttoned it and turned the American flag pin right side up. He stepped back.

Harold shook his head. "Not."

Clarence unbuttoned it and laughed. "Yeah, I've eaten too good here lately. Gained some weight back." He adjusted his bowtie again. "I think I'm ready. How's the time?"

Harold checked his watch. "Time to go. It's almost three o'clock. Everybody's had their naps and the dining room guy has set things up. Hillcrest even supplied the preacher—Pastor Anderson—from down the other hall." He grinned. "Everything looks … well, I'll let you find out."

They made their way to the dining room. Residents were too. Everyone had been invited—the perky and the bedridden and all in between.

"Excuse me, Harold." Staff wheeled beside them. "Oh the groom! Don't you look snappy!"

Sheriff Dennison looked smart in his uniform. He edged around the wheelchairs and walkers to follow Clarence and Harold.

"Hey Sheriff! Glad you could make it." Clarence patted his shoulder.

"Wouldn't miss it." Sheriff bent between the men, his mouth close to their ears, pulling them to the side. "Just relieved everything worked out."

Clarence locked on Sheriff's eyes. *Yeah.* "Yeah. Me too."

Harold held up his finger. "Well, hello Mrs. Brandon. You look nice today."

The woman took one look at Clarence and the sheriff and shook her head. "Clarence, I might have been wrong about you."

"It's okay, Mrs. Brandon. We all make mistakes." Clarence smiled.

"Well, Mrs. Hatly has been my roommate for a year and she … well, she is a good woman. She helped me see who you are." She fiddled with the brooch at her neck. "I'd better let you get to your wedding. You don't want to hold up the bride."

Pastor Anderson peeked around the corner.

"I need to let you go, Clarence." Sheriff patted his back. "Just wanted to update you. There will be TV coverage about the prison later. Warden is all locked up."

"Pretty convenient right there at the prison, right?" Clarence chuckled. "Hey, before they kidnapped me back to prison, Harold and I were talking about starting our own detective agency. I hope we can work together."

Pastor Anderson beckoned.

"Guess we'd better get, Harold." Clarence grinned. "I don't want anyone else marrying my bride."

"I'll let you go. We can talk later … or tomorrow—next week." Sheriff laughed. "I suppose you'll be pretty busy for awhile."

Clarence let his eyes close for just a second, relishing the thought, smiling. He had no idea what marriage was like. But he was excited to try it out. He ushered Harold to where Pastor Anderson had been standing just inside the dining room.

Clarence's breath caught. Tears threatened. He couldn't start now.

Streamers of gold and silver were strung from light fixtures and draped along the top of each wall. Every table had a small bouquet of white roses. Tables had been rearranged so there was an aisle down the middle, from the back to the front, where the minister stood with the guy running the sound system. Tech guy.

They both looked up when Clarence entered the room and waved. It was hard to believe this was all for Mrs. Hatly … Violet and him. He chewed on his lip to keep from crying again.

The preacher talked into a nursing home radio and nodded. He held his thumb up. The bride was ready.

Preacher Anderson motioned for them to walk down the center aisle.

Mindy and John! They waved. Would wonders never cease? John had a tie on. Mindy had pink hair, probably in honor of Mrs. Hatly, and a pretty black dress. Hid her tummy rolls well. Very pretty.

Clarence waved back and mouthed, "Who's running the store?"

They grinned. John shrugged. "We don't care."

Mrs. Margin piped up loudly. "Aren't we going to have our afternoon coffee?"

"Shush." The woman next to her shook her head. "We're having a wedding today. See all the decorations? We'll get coffee later." She licked her lips. "Maybe cake."

Randy.

Clarence nodded.

Randy closed his eyes, patted his big chest and almost bowed.

The preacher showed them where to stand. Harold had been stubborn about not using his wheelchair. He wanted to stand with his buddy on this important day.

The tech guy started the music. People turned toward the front, some snoozed. Even had beds rolled in and lined up in back. Mrs. Bernadine was wiggling all over, babbling.

Clarence held up his index finger to the preacher and rushed back to her. She calmed as soon as she saw him approach. "Hi, Mrs. Bernadine. I don't think I ever thanked you for hiding me from Pete back then. I interrupted your breakfast and everything." He bowed to her. "Thank you."

A tear slowly tracked down the wrinkles of her cheek.

He wiped it away and patted her hand. "Well, I better get back up there." He adjusted his bow tie. "I'm getting married today!"

She babbled back.

"I know. And thank you for being here." He turned and made his way back up front just as the music started.

Sounded like "Here Comes the Bride" but in piano. Nice. Harold stood like a soldier next to him. He glanced at the people in attendance.

Katty. Bandages and cast on her arm. Oh Katty. He couldn't lose it now. He hadn't even seen the bride yet. Noell sat next to her.

They were both beaming and beautiful. He hadn't gotten a chance to tell them about the adoption. He straightened. Had been the right thing to do. He especially knew it now.

Lisha was first to come out and down the aisle. She was beautiful in all her ... she was beautiful. Her dreadlocks were all caught up at the back of her head. Ribbons or something had been woven through. They matched her gold, sparkly dress. She walked proudly, looking straight at him. She caught his eye and stuck out her tongue.

He lowered his head, shaking it, biting his lips. Can't laugh. Not going to laugh.

Next was Carol.

Oh, he was gonna cry now.

She looked beautiful in her gold dress. Different from Lisha's. Her hair had sparkles in it, but her smile wobbled. She was already wiping her eyes and she nodded, her eyes on him too. Such a good friend. Probably his best friend in the world. Next to ... Violet. Next to Harold. Next to—

They both stood on the bride's side.

The music got a bit louder.

This was it.

Oh, Jesus.

Jingle. Jingle. Clarence's fingers had found the coins in his pants pocket.

Preacher Anderson tapped Clarence's arm and shook his head.

Oops. In trouble at his own wedding. He clasped his hands in front.

Bea walked out, knowing she was pretty. Oo's and ahh's—even

from this sleepy crowd. Clarence had never seen her act shy before, but she was now. She wore a gold dress too, her hair in skinny braids, gold ribbon woven in each one and swooped into loops to the back on her head. Almost like Lisha's. And a Band-Aid on her hand.

A hush fell as Violet appeared at the back. Her grandson, Steve Ivertson, was at her side, standing tall, a huge grin on his face, eyes shining.

Ohh.

They took the first steps toward him.

At first, when Clarence looked down the aisle, he only saw Anne. She had been beautiful back then, in her white dress, veil, her eyes sparkling with love. He could even erase Judge Green, walking her down the church aisle.

But today, he knew he needed to set Anne aside—he would always love her and honor her—remember her. But today his heart focused only on Violet.

Her eyes twinkled with love too.

Breathe.

Harold leaned in. "She's beautiful." He chuckled. "You okay, Buddy?"

Clarence had tried to be so strong—all those years in prison through everything—not gonna cry.

But now. His chin quivered.

And he let it.

Tears ran down.

And he didn't wipe them away.

This precious dear woman had watched him repeatedly sneak out and escape from the nursing home. He had kissed her, surprising especially himself and she had not bashed him with her walker. She had fought Pete off with her wheelchair, ramming him down.

She had never doubted him. Never joined the Oust Clarence Brigade.

She had *prayed* for him.

And now here she was before him, going to become his wife.

Those eyes twinkled underneath a short veil of soft rose netting attached to a pretty ivory wide brimmed hat. Her ivory suit was simple and perfect, although he was sure he wouldn't remember what she wore tomorrow.

Steve patted her arm. She was walking without her walker.

They all turned to the front and the preacher started the dearly beloveds, and the we are gathereds.

Thank God it wasn't the same preacher that buried Noell's Gamma. It was Preacher Anderson, who lived at Hillcrest. Nice guy, even when the Brigade ladies were being their worst. He had welcomed him home after prison this time.

The wedding was all a dream or felt like it. Clarence didn't come to until the I dos.

And the rings.

He wept all through it.

Openly.

Unashamedly.

And he kissed the bride—his bride—Mrs. Clarence Timmelsen. Sweetest moment in eternity.

Some country guy started singing the walk out song, only they didn't. They just stood, facing each other, eyes locked and holding hands.

Finally they broke free and started down the aisle as man and wife.

Mr. And Mrs. Clarence Timmelsen.

Even halfway there, they stopped and turned to each other. Just gazed into each other's eyes and listened to the last verse and chorus of "How Great Thou Art."

Had he ever imagined this would be how he could spend the last part of his life? After sixty years in prison and then being kidnapped and back to prison. Beaten. Cut.

Yet, here he was.

He'd dreamt of years with Annie. Children with her.

But that wasn't meant to be.

Here and now, his wife at his side, they had many children. Bea bounced toward them. Katty and Noell hugged them. Lisha. Steve.

Carol.

He hugged her. Never a truer friend.

A dark curly head towered above all.

Michael.

In a tux.

Stud.

Clarence drew his arm around Mrs. Timmelsen.

She searched Clarence's face and followed where his eyes gazed.

Michael bowed his head and wings grew out of his back. A gold belt held weapons and a sword.

Tux stayed.

He opened his eyes and looked at the newlyweds and smiled, nodding.

She hugged deeper into Clarence's side.

He rested his chin on the top of her head.

Michael lifted his arms, closed his eyes again and disappeared.

"Where'd your angel go, Clarence?" Bea tugged on Clarence's pant leg.

He picked her up and wrapped his arm around his wife again. "He'll be back. He has to report in to Father."

He didn't know why he said that, he just knew.

"We'll see him again."

THANK YOU READER!

Katty's evil ex-boyfriend tries to kidnap their daughter, Bea.

When druggies from her past want to reconnect—she's their next free lunch.

Voices haunt her. "Mommy, Mommy!" But they're not her daughter.

A cute cop seems interested in her, but she doesn't deserve that kind of love.

Katty reverts to the only comfort she knows—tiny bottles filled with burning, yellow liquid.

Book 4 in The Great Escapee Series. Book 2 in Katty's Story.

I greatly appreciate you taking time to read my work. If you enjoyed it: 1) Please leave a review wherever you buy books. 2) Or tell your friends about it! 3) Check the shelves of your local library. 4) Use hashtags #bonnielacy whenever you talk about my books online.

About Clarence and Harold's venture into detective work? Yes. They have their own trilogy! Michael is in it. Yes, I sprinkle Katty and Bea in. It will be fun to see what those two codgers are up to! ~~ What happened to Phil? I know. Ugly, evil man. But what if … ~~ Why is Noell in Rescued, book 2, drawn to the pool? What are her other gifts? She goes to strange places in her own trilogy!

Find out by going to www.bonnielacy.com

Sign up there on my website to receive my newsletters, just to keep you up on what, when, and why! There is a FREE short story or book for you when you leave your email address.

Be blessed. No. Really. I don't just say that. I'm praying that you are indeed blessed by the One Who gives freely as we learn to receive!

Keep in touch! No. Really. There is a contact page on my website. Or reply to my email newsletter! I'd love to hear from you!

AUTHOR NOTES

Where does a story come from—other than the awesome, but strange brain of an author? So many things and experiences draw an author to an idea.

You know how there are days when you repeatedly see a person, or hear a song, or think of a word? The common saying, "We are on the same frequency," intrigues me.

So, were we? Were we on the same frequency, when you called me, the other day? Or when we both ended up at the same store at the same time?

And what is a frequency, anyway? A wavelength?

The dictionary defines frequency as "the rate at which something occurs or is repeated over a particular period of time or in a given sample."

I don't pretend to understand this stuff. I love it. I just don't understand it … yet.

When I wrote book two in The Great Escapee Series, I saw sink holes everywhere! On the news. On vacation. Crazy. And caves. And underground pools.

You remember when you were wanting to have a baby, and everywhere you went—the grocery store, restaurants, church—there were prego ladies everywhere!

Or when you were looking a buying a new car? Yeah. You noticed every vehicle—every make and model.

What is that?

So, in my writing, I mean to explore those wavelengths that draw us together.

Are they God?

That'd be cool.

Anyway, enough of my wonderings and wanderings.

My editor, Kathy, called me out on letting Clarence just drift along, never being held accountable for the prison break, so I added three chapters and scenes elsewhere. Funny how my main beta reader, my sister Jan, has comments and recommendations very close to my editor!

Our nursing home. A great place to work, to live. I have to write this—there is no way our administrator, or staff or residents are anything like in this book. Anything from a flawed character's point of view (like Clarence—he's still stubborn—or Phil) might be one-sided, critical and snarky!

Our court house is a wonderful building and the people working there are even more wonderful—helpful, knowledgeable. Even though information held there is public knowledge, they still would protect it from an evil guy like Phil!

Again, the comment somewhere in this story, "Small town grocery store." We used to own that small town grocery store, here in Osceola. I loved the customers who blessed us with their trust and business and friendships. Again, I write a disclaimer that any current business or hospital or nursing home we enjoy in our small town, is appreciated and supported. Just because the character has a problem with some entity doesn't mean this writer does! Doesn't mean it's true!

Phil hates small towns. I love them. Especially Osceola. Quirks and all. Negativity and all. I love the old buildings—falling down and all. Phil is Phil—an evil man. What he loves and what I love are two different things.

So, if you are a resident of a small town or even Osceola, Nebraska, please don't take offense at his attitude. He. Is. Evil!

Oh, yeah. The Dive-Inn? Whose opinion do you suppose that is? Right! Phil and Lex's from Released, Book One. My opinion? We love Terry's Drive In. It's our favorite place to get ice cream, then take a drive through town. Or a burger. Or broasted chicken. Or …

So … just in case I didn't make this clear … any negative comments in the book about the town, any businesses, the nursing home and any staff or residents are purely from the bad guys. This town is a great town. The people are great!

But, I might want to keep Lisha and Carol. They are sweethearts.

I am taking a couple of courses to help me with marketing and website maintenance. One asks what my usual themes are in my books. Well yeah: sink holes, demons, angels, caves, prisons, sweet little girls, drug abuse. And more. But even more: faith, hope, surrender.

And as authors write, Someone takes us through the darkness to where we are free. Or freer.

Hence this book.

Clarence in taken back to prison.

Don't we go back into those dark places again and again? Heartbreaking, but true. When I do, I know God is leading me there for a reason; he wants to take me a little deeper, so I can get … a little freer.

Clarence went to the very end of himself (and the edge of the precipice).

Me, too.

When Jesus says, "Come," it's over. We are at the end of ourselves and if we step off that cliff, we will never be the same. Is life perfect then? Naw. But at that divine moment, we have been given the power to become the sons of God (John 1:12.). New family. New life. New mind. New faith.

ACKNOWLEDGMENTS

Thank you to my editor, Kathy Tyers Gillin, for putting up with my comma messes! I learn so much from her and appreciate her! WE KNOW!

Jane Dixon Smith is my cover designer. I give her a short synopsis and she gets it. I never stress over them. Ever. Forever lovely to work with. Thank you, Jane!

Thank you to my beta readers. You keep me sane by catching the mistakes. It is a huge deal to take the time to read my manuscripts in the middle of your busy lives. Thank you!

Jan. You have read my words. And reread them. And again. Either you are terrified of what your sister will put out there, or you care deeply that it's well done. Either way, you're my Boss and I love you. There are so many cliché ways to say that. They are almost meaningless. I love you says it all.

I kept hearing as I pondered this book: "Pull out all the stops. (A musical organ term meaning blast it out!) Go where you don't want to go. Take the story to the dark places, the hard places." God usually does that because he wants me to personally go to those places—to face my messes. To God, I give eternal thanks.

Speaking of messes, if there is any part of this book that is not quality writing, it's mine! My editor and beta readers made it shine!